Praise, then and now, for Thomas Hope's masterpiece, *Anastasius*

To have been the author of *Anastasius,* I would have given the two poems which brought me the most glory. **Lord Byron, author of *Don Juan,* 1820.**

Once again, the pioneering publishers of Classic Travel Books have uncovered a forgotten treasure. Thomas Hope's book, *Anastasius,* shook the literary world when it was first published by John Murray in 1819, and it influenced the great writers of the day, including Byron. Then, on his death when barely 60, it was discredited and banished from view. Now this stirring tale of early Oriental derring-do can be read again in its entirety and the readers eyes will be opened in unexpected ways. **Robin Hanbury-Tenison, author of *The Oxford Book of Exploration,* 2008.**

I am passing a few days with Thomas Hope, one of the most extraordinary men in England and the author of *Anastasius,* a work of great merit…It is a vast pity that he cannot be persuaded to publish more. **Washington Irving, author of *Rip van Winkle,* 1820.**

The Long Riders' Guild Press are to be congratulated on republishing Anastasius - at once a classic travel narrative and a work of picaresque fiction. Its author, Thomas Hope painted a vivid portrait of the Ottoman Empire based upon his personal experience. First published in 1819, this book, one of the most important novels of the nineteenth century, should be much more widely read. **Robert Irwin, author of *For lust of knowing: the Orientalists and their enemies*, 2008.**

Surely James Bond had his roots in the dashing Anastasius who swashbuckled his way across the Ottoman Empire in the 1780s? This book is a literary treasure, as fresh today as any modern novel. What gives it power is that it comes from first hand; the harems, dangerous streets, deserts, galleys and prisons found in the world of the Agas and Mamelukes. All intimately known: all experienced. Thomas Hope was a writer of outstanding talent - leaving one to wonder about the double life he must have led to know the world of the Porte so intimately." **Jeremy James, author of *The Byerley Turk,* 2008.**

I had forgotten that *Anastasius* was originally a John Murray book, so the Introduction to the new Long Riders' Guild Press edition was most enlightening. I think it is marvellous that The Guild is reissuing this classic. **John Murray, whose ancestor first published *Anastasius,* 2008.**

As a Trustee of the National Portrait Gallery, I was encouraged to learn that during the re-publication of Thomas Hope's *Anastasius* an intense academic investigation of Sir William Beechey's portrait revealed that the author was depicted wearing the regal robes of an Ottoman official. As a travel author myself, I welcome the long overdue re-issuance of this neglected classic. The donation by the publishers of the royalties to the National Portrait Gallery reflects the importance of this literary and artistic union. **Sir Christopher Ondaatje, author of *Woolf in Ceylon,* 2008.**

The author of *Anastasius* has described the manners and vices of the Eastern Nations with fidelity and humour. **Sir Walter Scott, author of *Ivanhoe,* 1820.**

There are few books in the English language which contain passages of greater power, feeling and eloquence than *Anastasius*….Thomas Hope's descriptions reveal a depth of sentiment and a vigour of imagination which Lord Byron could not excel. **Reverend Sydney Smith, Chairman of the Edinburgh Review, 1820.**

Early nineteenth-century bust of Thomas Hope by
the famous Danish sculptor Bertel Thorvaldsen.

ANASTASIUS

by

Thomas Hope

The Long Riders' Guild Press

www.classictravelbooks.com
www.horsetravelbooks.com

ISBN: 1-59048-282-4

First published by John Murray in 1819.

The cover image of Thomas Hope, dressed in the sumptuous clothing of a high-ranking Ottoman naval officer, was painted by Sir William Beechey, and appears here courtesy of the National Portrait Gallery. © National Portrait Gallery, London.
The royalties from this book are being donated to the National Portrait Gallery in London, where this portrait of Thomas Hope by Sir William Beechey forms part of the collection. A detailed history of the National Portrait Gallery can be found online at www.npg.org.uk/live/history.asp. The National Portrait Gallery is located at St. Martin's Place, London, WC2H 0HE. Further details at www.npg.org.uk.

For a ground-breaking analysis of Hope's Turkish clothing, please see Appendix I.

CONTENTS

Volume III

INTRODUCTION

Thomas Hope: Triumph, Tragedy, Obverse Worlds

Jerry Nolan

Thomas Hope was the eldest son of John Hope (1737-1781), a Dutch merchant of Scottish extraction and a member of a very wealthy and powerful family of merchants and bankers who had settled, four generations earlier, in Holland. Thomas was born on 30 August 1769 in Amsterdam. By the early 1780s the merchant bank of Hope & Co were in the business of raising large sums for kings and governments throughout Europe and in the United States of America, and were recognised as one of Europe's greatest banking dynasties. After the death of his father in 1784, Thomas shared his father's fortune with his two brothers but appears never to have been active in the management of the lucrative family business, which remained the source of his considerable wealth, and he began as a young man to devote intellect, fortune, time and energy to the arts, with the study of the architecture of ancient civilisations as the starting point. In a letter written in 1804 to Francis Annesley Esq. M.P 'Observations on the Plans and Elevations designed by James Wyatt, Architect, for Downing College, Cambridge', Hope closely linked his early interest in architecture with his travels:

> 'No sooner did I become master of my own actions, which unfortunately happened at the early age of eighteen, than disdaining any longer to ride my favourite hobby only in the confinement of the closet, I hastened in quest of food for it to almost all the different countries where any could be expected. Egyptian architecture I went to investigate on the banks of the Nile, Grecian on the shores of Ionia, Sicily and the Peloponneus. Four different times I visited Italy to render familiar to me all the shades of the infinitely varied styles of building peculiar to that interesting country, from the most rude attempts of the Etruscan to the last degraded ones of the Lombards. Moorish edifices I examined on the coast of Africa, and among the ruins of Granada, Seville, and Cordova. The principle of the Tartar and Persian construction I studied in Turkey and in Syria.'

From 1787 onwards, Hope spent most of the following eight years travelling as a student of cultures. During these travels, Hope stayed for about a year in Istanbul/Constantinople where his considerable skill in drawing was practised – some 350 drawings of the life style which he observed among the rich and powerful in the Ottoman Empire now form part of the collections held by the Benaki Museum, Athens.

After years of travel, Hope, at the age of twenty six, returned to acquire an Adam House in Duchess Street, Portland Place, London – a city where other members of his family had fled during 1794 in anticipation of the French invasion of Holland. Hope was to establish himself in London, for the rest of his life: as a scholarly collector of art, an interior designer and a patron of artists and craftsmen. Unfortunately very few of Hope personal papers have survived. Records show how Hope's considerable wealth enabled him to collect, especially on his oriental travels, many paintings, sculptures, antique objects and books, which were displayed at first in the Duchess Street mansion and later at the Deepdene, his country house in Surrey. Hope was joined in London by his brother Henry, another art collector and patron. Hope became influential in many London societies connected with the arts such as the Dilettanti, the Royal Society of Arts and the Society of Antiquaries. In 1804 Hope opened exhibition galleries, after having had the Duchess Street house extended by one of the foremost architects and designers of the period, Charles Heathcote Tatham, where visitors paid for admission by ticket. The popular view of Hope was as 'the Furniture Man'. The sobriquet was regarded as a compliment by enthusiastic supporters; but in the case of hostile critics, it was often used as a term of ridicule and an opportunity for caricature, most memorably in the portrait of Hope and his wife as *La Belle et La Bête* by the artist Antoine Dubost who had failed to be commissioned by La Bête! Hope's ambitions to influence taste pressed on regardless of criticism as he sketched designs for furniture, room interiors and costumes which he included in books for which he wrote accompanying scholarly texts. The main thrust of Hope's project in this area of interest was to advance historically based knowledge of design. Eventually the number of his books as designer were: *Household Furniture and Interior Decoration* (1807); *Costumes of the Ancients* (1809); *Designs of Modern Costumes* (1812); and posthumously *An Historical Essay on Architecture,* with the illustrations based on early Hope drawings (1835). Hope triumphantly adapted many of these designs for the interior decoration of his house in Duchess Street and for the house in Deepdene, Surrey which he bought after his marriage and commissioned the architect William Atkinson to alter according to Hope's own plans.

After some years of anxious searching among notable women for a wife and the future mother of his children, eventually Hope was introduced to the beautiful youngest daughter of William de la Poer Beresford, Archbishop of Tuam in Ireland and later first Baron Decies, who a little reluctantly accepted his proposal. Hope was so pleased by this triumph that when the Archbishop handed over three thousand pounds, Hope handed the dowry back to Louisa when they were married in 1806. Apart from his children, what Louisa quickly facilitated were Hope's plans to entertain and court in a grand manner the fashionable world of London. An old friend of the Irish family, the novelist Maria Edgeworth, recorded her impressions of the Hopes at home at both the Duchess Street mansion and Deepdene, in letters written to her own family in Ireland. In May 1813, Edgeworth wrote about a grand reception in Duchess Street: 'We have been to a grand night at Mrs. Hope's – furniture Hope – rooms really deserve the French epithet *superbe*! All of the beauty rank and fashion that London can assemble I believe I may say in the newspaper style was there and we observed that the beauties past fifty bore the belle. The Prince Regent stood holding converse with Lady Elizabeth Monck one third of the night… About 900 people were at this assembly… I asked him (Hope) who somebody was who was passing and he answered "I really don't know. I don't know half the people here nor do they know me or Mrs. Hope even by sight. Just now I was behind a lady who thought she was making her speech to Mrs. Hope but she was addressing her compliments to some stranger.'

In 1817 the Hope family (father, mother and three young sons) went on a tour of Italy. On the tour there was great joy when one of Hope's favourite protégés, the Danish sculptor Bertel Thorwaldsen, made marble busts of the family which included a bust of Hope showing him as a dignified and calm thinker; but there followed horror on the death of his beloved 7 year old son Charles in Rome; after which the boy's ashes were taken back home to Deepdene where a mausoleum was erected within the year for the casket with his ashes. When Edgeworth visited the Hopes at the Deepdene in April 1819, she noted a change in Hope and his wife: 'Mr. Hope himself has in his whole appearance marks of having suffered much. The contrast between their depression of spirits and the magnificence of everything about them is striking and speaks volumes of moral philosophy to the observer'. Perhaps it was after the unexpected death of his Charles that Hope experienced not only a sense of personal tragedy but a growing self-confidence which enabled him to express his wider human sympathies and well-informed views of the wider world than had so far appeared in his writings and his entertainments. About this time, Hope began work on the novel which was published by John Murray in 1819 as *Anastasius or Memoirs of a Greek, written at the close of the eighteenth century* in three volumes. Hope held back from revealing his authorship of *Anastasius* in the first edition, choosing to adopt the mask of an anonymous editor of a recently found ill-written manuscript which was being brought to public notice for readers with an interest in the regions 'once adorned by the Greeks, and now defaced by the Turks.' The erasures and imperfections of the journal were used as a justification of the editor's knowledgeable and enlightening notes at the back of each volume. In the light of the immediate success of the novel, Murray persuaded Hope to reveal his identity as author in the second edition of 1820 which would now include a map of the travels of Anastasius, some extensive pruning of the text which did not include any revision of the novel's narrative flow. The revelation that Hope was the author was greeted with widespread incredulity in the literary journals. In *Blackwood's Edinburgh Magazine* (September, 1821), there appeared a facetious article entitled 'On Anastasius. By – Lord Byron' by Christopher North who argued strongly that there was evidence on every page that Byron actually wrote the novel. This challenge to his authorship provoked Hope, in a strong echo of his previous summary of travels to back up his knowledge of world architecture, to proclaim in a letter to the editor of *Blackwood's Magazine* from Duchess Street dated Oct. 9, 1821 that not only had he written the novel but that it was all based on his travels in the Orient some twenty years earlier, a significant time before Lord Byron's work appeared:

> 'I beg to state, that in the course of long and various travels, I resided nearly a twelvemonth at Constantinople; visited the arsenal and bagnio frequently; witnessed the festival of Saint George, saw Rhodes, was in Egypt, in Syria, and in every other place which I attempted to describe minutely; collected my eastern vocabulary… on the spot, and whilst writing my work; … adopted a fictitious hero in order to embody my observations in the East in a form less trite than that of a journal; avoiding all antiquarian descriptions studiously, as inconsistent with the character assumed; for the same reason, omitted my name on the title-page.'

What most puzzled Hope's Regency contemporaries about his claim to authorship of *Anastasius* was the pressing psychological question as to why and how Hope, the self-professed neo-classical aesthete and the generous host at the magnificent houses of the Duchess Street mansion and Deepdene, could have ever written such a romantic novel which entered convincingly into the character of Anastasius, the young highly intelligent rebellious youngest son from a wealthy Greek Orthodox family on the island of Chios, who was imagined by Hope as an intrepid traveller, the Muslim convert Selim, and the ambitious mercenary soldier who achieved social and cultural mobility, political insights, and a blistering degree of self-knowledge once he had fearlessly vaulted well beyond the frontiers of parochial Chios to experience periods in prison and among the poor on the streets of Constantinople before fighting against Austrians, Russians and Arab factions during the twilight years of the Ottoman empire. What probably most attracted the admiration of contemporaries like Lord Byron and William Beckford was Hope's unexpected ability to express deep intensity of feeling in the story of Anastasius/Selim, careering across the whole Christian/Muslim divides within the Ottoman empire, embracing friends and lovers and killing assorted enemies and recounting utterly unexpected desert adventures like his encounters with the Wahhabee tribes (Chapters V-IX in Volume III). Nothing of this romantic resourcefulness surfaced during his grand receptions when his wife glittered and he often seemed cumbersome and shy. However acute observers of the 1798 portrait by Sir William Beechey of Hope as a rich Oriental traveller hanging in the Duchess Street mansion might not have been so surprised if they had spotted the depiction in the background of Abu Ayyub al-Ansari, a mosque for Muslim pilgrims at one the most revered Muslim sites in the whole of Turkey as a prophetic sign of Hope's stirring passion for Islam which then cascaded onto the pages of *Anastasius*.

The triumph of *Anastasius* among the reading public continued until 1849, the year of its last edition, after which the novel drifted into neglect and virtual oblivion. One suspects that from the very beginning, his family were not too keen on the novel. The family view was expressed in *The Book of the Beresford Hopes* by Henry William Law and Irene Law with an Introduction by Viscountess Ullswater, published in 1928. Irene Law was Thomas Hope's great-granddaughter and her aunt Viscountess Ullswater was his granddaughter. Both women were descended through the line of Hope's youngest son Alexander. According to the Laws, *Anastasius* can be best understood as one of Thomas Hope's 'recreations', a straying away from his neo-classical ideas – with some 'literary help' from the tutor to his sons, the Anglican clergyman. Rev. J. Hitchens. The Laws included an extract of a letter from Hitchens to Louisa which praises *Anastasius* along generalised lines: 'Whenever it makes its appearance, of the splendour with which it will shine, and the wonder and admiration and speculation which it will excite there can be no doubt. A new star will have appeared, and the learned will seize on it as a theme for their criticism, and the curious as an object for their speculation, and all as a matter of wonder and amazement'. Perhaps the purple passage was included by the Laws as an expression of gratitude to the memory of the flattering Hitchens for his devotion to Louisa who had nominated him as a trustee of the settlement made on her second marriage. However, other comments strongly suggest that probably the only section of *Anastasius* deemed wonderful and admirable by the Beresford Hopes would have been Hope's preface to the second edition in which the author referred to his wife Louisa as 'the sole partner of all my joys and sorrows whose fair form but enshrines a mind the fairer,' The financial success of the book prompted Hope to purchase the so-called 'Anastasius pearls' (two rows) for his wife 'from the profits'. The 'Anastasius pearls' were another example of the cult of Louisa as a supreme beauty which glowed forth from the picture and engraving of 1812 in which George Dawe painted a radiant Louisa posing on the bottom steps of staircase before an overawed and adoring dog. The striking difference between Dawe's lovely representation of Louisa and Hope's representation in the 1798 Beechey portrait was noted by the Laws with some relish: 'Thomas, himself a short and rather ugly man, was represented in Turkish costume by Sir William Beechey, who thus succeeded in hiding his physical defects, and giving him a more or less romantic appearance.' Here was the Beresford Hope family's own distinctive version of the theme of *La Belle and Le Bête*!

The Laws suggested that the initial reluctance of Louisa to accept Hope's marriage proposal was linked to her earlier affection for a childhood friend, William Carr Beresford, the illegitimate son of her uncle, the Earl of Tyrone and the first Marquis of Waterford. Carr, who was born in 1768. After a period of tough military training in Strasbourg, Beresford's tours of military service from 1785 onwards included such places as Nova Scotia, France, Corsica, the West Indies, India, Egypt, South America, India, Portugal and Brazil. The period of military service for which he became best known was his spell as Marshal in the Portuguese army, fighting alongside a fellow Irishman, the Duke of Wellington, in the Peninsular War (1809-1811). In 1811 Beresford began dabbling in Tory parliamentary politics in County Waterford in Ireland. In 1828 his old comrade-in-arms appointed him to the post of master-general of the ordnance in Wellington's first ministry. In his novel Thomas Hope imagined Anastasius/Selim as a soldier in the ranks of the Turkish armies in the latter days of the Ottoman Empire where the grim realities of the battlefields, the appalling political intrigues of the period, and reflections on the collapse of empire were not excluded from the records. The exposure of such gory goings on was far removed from the manners of the Duchess street mansion and the Deepdene, and somewhat closer to the London's Holland House set where Hope was more intellectually at one with certain Whig causes. Edgeworth's strongest sympathies always lay with Louisa and she was always frank about her dislike of the Egyptian influences in the interior decoration of the Deepdene which she described as 'hideous'; but in April 1822, she warmed a little to the storyteller in Hope: 'The Deepdene is beautiful at this time of year – The hawthorn hedges – the tender green of the larch and sycamore in full leaf. We had a delightful walk one morning – Mr. Hope all the time conversing very agreeably and telling me anecdotes – fresh from life'. Yet nowhere in Edgeworth's published correspondence is there any mention of *Anastasius*. Perhaps the very idea of reading it seemed beyond the reach of her imagination?

Louisa tried to secure an offer of a peerage to her husband by using the good services of Wellington; but even Hope's offer of ten thousand pounds for that honour was rebuffed by Wellington's short-lived Tory government in the late 1820s. Probably with a great masked sigh of relief, Hope turned to concentrate on writing a vast philosophical work, to be entitled *An Essay on the Origins and Prospects of Man* with the objective of exploring explicitly his unusual ideas about the nature of the universe, the origin of species and the diversity of human cultures which would amount to the fullest fruition of his world travelling in the external and internal worlds. Hope's death at the age of 62 prevented this very ambitious work being brought to full fruition. Apparently against the wishes of his family, the work was posthumously published in three volumes by Murray in the year of Hope's death which led to a very great deal of incomprehension among the reviewers. *An Essay* was cursorily, if courteously, dismissed by the Laws: 'The book seems worthy of mention, inasmuch as in the passages quoted there is certainly a suggestion of the idea of evolution, but as far as can be judged, it appearance made no impression at the time, and none reaped the reward or gained the applause that the author anticipated.' Edgeworth recorded her last encounter with Hope a few days before his death in February 1831 when that she 'followed Mrs. Hope through all the magnificent apartments and then up to their attics and through and through room after room till I got into his retreat and then a feeble voice from an armchair "Oh my dear Miss Edgeworth, my kind friend to the last". And I saw a figure sunk like La Harpe – in figured silk robe de chamber and night cap – death in his pallid sunk shrunk face. A gleam of affectionate pleasure lighted it for an instant and straight it sunk again'. Edgeworth's reference to La Harpe evoked the memorable costume of the controversial French literary critic whom she had met in Paris before he died. After Hope's death, Louisa received letters of sympathy from her friend at Court and frequent guest at recaptions, Queen Adelaide, wife of William IV.

In 1832 Marshal Lord Beresford married Hope's widow. Beresford joyously responded to the devotion of his stepson Alexander, then a schoolboy at Harrow. At this time Alexander's older brothers, Henry, Thomas and Adrian, became conscious of the need for financial independence and determined to curtail Marshal Beresford's involvement in their family, a position which was being much welcomed by their mother and brilliant young Harrovian brother. In 1836 Lord and Lady Beresford purchased Bedgebury Park, in Kent, the seat of Francis Law whose descendant Henry William would marry Irene Beresford Hope. His brother-in-law, Henry Philip Hope, helped to pay for extensions to Bedgebury Park. On Henry Philip's death in 1834, there was open warfare between the Marshal and his disobedient stepsons who battled in the courts for a greater share of the Hope inheritance, which included the family's collection of jewels. The retired Marshal had a battle on another front where he engaged in an acrimonious verbal battle with Sir William Napier in three angry, somewhat ponderous, long pamphlets about alleged mishandling of the Albuera campaign during the Peninsular War in 1811. The Laws recorded how Louisa changed as Lady Beresford: while she retained her old fondness for jewels and of wealth, largely as a result of the influence of Alexander – Cambridge University luminary, Tory M.P. and one of the most vocal leaders of the Anglican High church party – she began to devote some of her wealth to educational and pious objects and 'observed Church seasons and ordinances with far greater regularity than of old.' Lady Beresford died in 1851 and bequeathed the Anastasian pearls to her eldest son, Henry Thomas. Marshal Beresford died in 1854, whereupon his titles became extinct. Thereafter, Alexander decided to found a Beresford Hope dynasty by changing his family name to Beresford Hope, a change which had been the wish of his stepfather. Alexander married Mildred, daughter of J.B.W. Gascoyne-Cecil and niece of Robert, the third Marquess of Salisbury and future Tory prime minister. Alexander and Mildred had three sons and seven daughters. Their daughter Mary married James William Lowther, later the first Viscount Ullswater and speaker of the House of Commons. The male line of Beresford Hopes lasted two generations and ended when Alexander's grandson, Harold Thomas, died in 1917. As the most publicly honoured of Thomas Hope's sons – closely associated with Lord Salisbury's coterie of relatives and decorated with honorary doctorates on both sides of the Atlantic – Alexander felt in 1861 that he might deign for one reason only to pigeon hole his father as 'a man of genius' in *The English Cathedral of the 19th Century* as he looked back on his childhood in Duchess Street:

> I may be allowed to leave on record that impression of early but vivid recollections of the taste, the fancy, the eye for colour and form, which characterised the whole conception. The style was not suited for practical use, and so the experiment broke down; but it was the experiment of a man of genius, and not to be confused with the contemporary and parallel, but far more insipid, Empire epoch of French art. The great fact for which Thomas Hope deserves the gratitude of posterity… was that he, first of Englishmen, conceived and taught the idea of art – manufacture, of allaying the beauty of form to the wants and productions of common life.

In reality, Hope's legacy as the Furniture man was already in decline in A.J.B. Beresford-Hope's lifetime. Duchess Street house was sold off in 1850 by Henry Thomas Hope, great friend of Disraeli, Young England politician, promoter of the London and Westminster Joint Stock Bank, patron of the Great Exhibition, after which the Duchess Street house was demolished in 1851. The Deepdene was modified by Henry Thomas into a pioneering example of a Victorian High Renaissance *palazzo* and landscaping, and remained in the possession of the Hope family until 1917, when it was sold off and the collections appeared in Christie Sales Catalogues. Quite a few of the objects which had been illustrated by Hope in *Household Furniture* were bought by the great enthusiast for a Regency Revival in furniture, the playwright Edward Knoblock, who went on to trumpet his Hope collection. Subsequently the stripped-out Deepdene building was used as a hotel, and after having being reordered into British Rail offices, was finally sold off and demolished in 1969. In the grounds remains the mausoleum erected by Hope in 1818 over the buried ashes of Charles and consecrated as the family burial place by Louisa's cousin, Lord John Beresford, Bishop of Raphoe and afterwards Archbishop of Armagh. Of the 33 tomb-recesses, only 9 were filled over the years and the last internment was that of the 8th Duke of Newcastle in 1941 before the mausoleum was sealed up in 1957 and lurks in the countryside as an obscure monument to the tragedy of a forgotten Hope.

In retrospect, one of the roots of Hope's personal tragedy seems to have been that, for all of his anxious protestations of love of Louisa, and genuine gratitude for her acceptance of him as her husband, there was in their arranged marriage a disconnectedness of mind, a sense of separateness which was perpetuated among the Beresford Hopes and recorded by the Laws. Certainly Alexander seems to have had little respect or understanding for the diversity of his father's vision, possibly because in parts it included radical criticism of the conventional wisdom of the High Anglicanism which Alexander espoused. Alexander's political convictions included admiration for Stonewall Jackson's part in the American Civil war. Clearly Thomas Hope's youngest son felt closest to his stepfather and expressed that adoration by organising at the church in Kilndown school, on the first Sunday after the Marshal's funeral, a solemn *missa pro defunctis*, with the Beresford motto *Nil nisi cruce* displayed on large black wall hangings. There is a very sad irony in the fact that Alexander was determined to restrict his father's triumphs to the world of furniture design. When Alexander was in the womb, Hope was creating the character of Alexis as the son of Anastasius who became the solar star leading his father out of the desert and whose death as a child in Trieste was the blow from which Anastasius would never recover. The inspiration for Alexis was his deceased son Charles who in the Laws version of family history was, by intention or an oversight, omitted from the family tree included at the front of their book: neither was the Sir Thomas Lawrence portrait of Charles as an Infant Bacchus, commissioned by Hope in 1816, reproduced by the Laws. If Alexander ever yielded to the temptation to glance over his father's novel in later years, doubtless he would have grown ever more determined never to be mentioned in the same breath as poor Alexis! It was left to the daughter of Henry Thomas, Henrietta, who married Lord Lincoln, later the 6th Duke of Newcastle, to take care of the Lawrence portrait of Charles as a central part of the Hope legacy, a tradition which has been preserved by subsequent Dukes of Newcastle.

Hope had his contrasting triumphs: as the 'Furniture Man' and as the 'Anastasius/Selim man'. During his lifetime, few of Hope's guests, not even the attentive Edgeworth, seem to have understood, or even sensed, the sources of his great imaginative power when he first turned to write about the obverse of western cultures and civilisations as a direct consequence of his travels in the Orient shortly after the early death of a beloved son. In the tradition of the Beresford Hopes, Hope enthusiasts today still choose to value one side of the Hope coin and to devalue the other. The Hope Exhibition at the V & A in London and at the Bard in New York will provide a prominent showcase to appreciate one triumph; and this edition of Anastasius, the first in a single volume, ought to prompt the same people, and many others, to respond to the both. What a tragic loss of opportunity if the two sides of Hope are not at last pieced together in the wake of 2008, the year of the exhibition and the book.

Selected Bibliography

A.J.C. Hare, editor, *The Life and Letters of Maria Edgeworth*. 2 vols. (London; Arnold, 1894)

Henry William Law & Irene Law, *The Book of the Beresford Hopes* (London: Heath Cranton, 1925)

Sandor Baugarten, *Le Crepuscule Neo-Classique: Thomas Hope* (Paris: Didier, 1958)

David Watkin, *Thomas Hope and the Neo-Classical Idea* (London: Murray, 1968)

Christina Colvin, editor, *Maria Edgeworth: Letters from England 1813-1844* (Oxford: Clarendon, 1971)

Marilyn Butler, *Maria Edgeworth: A Literary Biography* (Oxford: Clarendon, 1972)

Dictionary of National Biography (Oxford University Press 2004-7): The entries for Hope Family (c.1700-1813) by John Orbell; Henry Thomas Hope (1808-1862) by Mary S. Millar; William Carr Beresford (1768-1854) by Gordon L. Teffeteller; Alexander James Beresford Beresford-Hope (1820-1887) by J. Mordaunt Crook.
Gordon W. Batchelor, *The Beresfords of Bedgebury Park* (Goudhurst: W.J.C. Musgrave, 1996)

Editor's note: Thanks to the foresight of the current John Murray, the immensely valuable family publishing archive, consisting of over 150,000 manuscript items, together with ledgers and letter books have been placed for safe-keeping within the National Library of Scotland with access for all. Those wishing to research Thomas Hope's literary connections to the fabled John Murray publishing company are urged to visit the Murray Archive.

The John Murray Archive
National Library of Scotland
George IV Bridge
Edinburgh
EH1 1EW

Telephone: +44 (0)131 623 3878

Or visit the John Murray Archive online: www.nls.uk/jma/index.html

*Jerry Nolan is a London-based freelance writer who has researched forms of Irish transcultural nationalism in writers who are marginalised in standard accounts of the Irish Literary Revival, including Edward Martyn, George Russell (AE), James Cousins and James Stephens. His ongoing research is concerned with the work of three writers who looked to the East for inspiration: William Beckford (*Vathek*), Tom Moore (*Lalla Rookh*) and Thomas Hope (*Anastasius*). His website is: www.jerrynolanwriter.com*

FOREWORD

Anastasius: Towards Background and Meaning

John Rodenbeck

In the summer of 1877 the editor-in-chief of *The Atlantic Monthly* drew his readers' attention to a forgotten novel: "A revered bibliophile," he wrote, "counseled me to read *Anastasius*. . . . Here, he said, is one of the great books of the world, more neglected even than *Clarissa Harlowe* or *Tom Jones*. Yes, and open to the same ethical criticism, but nonetheless a marvel of erudition, eloquence, and profound insight into human character."[1] The *Atlantic* editor was William Dean Howells (1837-1920), friend of Mark Twain (1835-1910) and Henry James (1843-1916) and no mean novelist himself; and his article on *Anastasius* remains, despite its brevity, one of the most informed, helpful, lucid, and suggestive statements yet made—let us say at once that we agree with the "revered bibliophile"—about Thomas Hope's great book.

Anastasius was a roaring international best-seller in its time: issued anonymously by John Murray, the most prestigious London publishing house of that era and of many long afterwards, it went through three editions within a matter of weeks. Its first readers universally ascribed it to Lord Byron (1788-1824), who had already used his own experience of the Ottoman Empire to write the first two cantos of *Childe Harold* (1812) and four verse romances, *The Giaour* (1813), *The Bride of Abydos* (1813), *The Corsair* (1814), and *Lara* ((1814).[2] Byron had presented *Childe Harold* to the public as a versified travelogue, complete with footnotes and a hero who was introduced, according

---

[1] William Dean Howells, "Contributor's Club," *The Atlantic Monthly*, XL, issue 237 (July 1877), 93.

[2] One early reader who was not fooled was the extremely level-headed John Cam Hobhouse, who probably knew Byron better than anyone. "Murray sent me *Anastasius* or *Memoirs of a Greek*," he wrote on 16 November 1819,

> —a delightful book, I think —it seems to me quite a new and yet a likely view of the manners of the East, and shows the Levanters living very much in the same way as we Westerns do—the same dissipation and intrigue, passions and everything, set off by that extraordinary contempt of life which is certain[ly] the most striking feature in the Oriental nations, at least that I have seen. The man himself is a real man—must have been a strange creature—very vicious and headstrong—but having courage and generosity.
>
> I was sure at first reading that our good folks would think of Lord Byron in reading it — and I have since found that the work has been attributed to him—neither he nor any Englishman could have written a page of it I think.

Hobhouse's Diary from: Peter Cochran, assembler, *Hobby-O: Lord Byron and John Cam Hobhouse* (http://www.hobby-o.com/newgate.php)

to the author, only "for the sake of giving some connexion to the piece."[3] The second edition of *Anastasius* was sold out in 24 hours; and it was in the brief preface that he added to the third edition that Hope at last revealed his authorship and disclosed his aims, observing that his hero was largely a structural device. Such remarks were so like Byron's about *Childe Harold* that many readers rejected Hope's authorship even after his open avowal. They also dismissed the modesty of his stated aims, believing it to be mere affectation. A French translation was published in Paris that same year.[4]

By 1851, 20 years after Hope's death, *Anastasius* had appeared in seven editions in England, two in America, four in France, four in Germany, and two in the Netherlands.[5] Murray kept the book in print until the 1850s and as late as World War I—in the famous eleventh edition of the *Encyclopaedia Britannica* (1913), for example, or the *Cambridge History of English Literature* (1907-1921)[6]—it was still reckoned as a significant cultural document, its author being identified not for his accomplishments as a scholar-popularizer, artist, designer, architectural historian, collector, or philosopher, but as "Anastasius" Hope, novelist and traveller. Ian Jack author of the relevant volume in the *Oxford History of English Literature* (1963), excuses himself from a discussion of the book only on grounds of available space.[7] A new edition of the French translation was published as recently as 1999.[8]

Howells identifies the reason why, however, after its early vogue, this book had by 1877 already lost ground with the Anglo-American public: like *Clarissa Harlowe* and *Tom Jones*, he says, it was "open to . . . ethical criticism." Howells' specific reference to these two eighteenth-century masterpieces tells us as plainly as possible that *Anastasius* was regarded as, like them, simply too sexy for an increasingly pious and Pharisaical readership, which in England included members of Hope's own family. Thomas Hope (1769-1831), on the other hand, belonged to an earlier, much less pious, and much more liberal-minded generation. By background cosmopolitan, by education a classicist-polyglot, and by temperament a freethinking man of the Enlightenment, he wrote *Anastasius* during a very different epoch from the one that succeeded it.

---

[3] Byron, "Preface to the First and Second Cantos," *Childe Harold's Pilgrimage: A Romaunt* (London: John Murray [February], 1812).

[4] For an excellent summary of the critical and popular reception of *Anastasius*, see Sandor Baumgarten, "Un Don Juan en prose," *Le crépuscule néo-classique: Thomas Hope* (Paris, Didier, 1958), pp. 164-206.

[5] Philippe G. Kerbellec, "Présentation" to the 1999 French edition of *Anastasius* (Lyon: La Fosse aux Ours, 1999).

[6] *The Cambridge History of English and American Literature: An Encyclopedia in Eighteen Volumes*, ed. by A. W. Ward, A. R. Waller, W. P. Trent, J. Erskine, S. P. Sherman, and C. Van Doren (New York: G. P. Putnam's Sons; Cambridge: Cambridge University Press, 1907-21), XIII. *The Growth of the Later Novel*, 38.

[7] Ian Jack, *English Literature 1815-1832: Scott, Byron, and Keats* (Oxford: Clarendon Press, 1963), p. 245.

[8] See n. 5.

The contrast in attitude and tone between the Regency and the Victorian era is most succinctly characterized, perhaps, in the well-known remark by Lord Melbourne (1779-1848). His first wife, Lady Caroline Lamb (1785–1828), who had been the most flamboyant of Byron's multitudinous mistresses, died during the reign of George IV, but Melbourne himself lingered on to become the most trusted advisor of the young Queen Victoria. Emerging from yet another confrontation with Prince Albert, who was no fool and saw significant political advantage in siding publicly with Evangelical virtue, Melbourne was heard to mutter, "This damned morality will ruin everything!"[9]

Even some readers during the Regency—Mary Berry, for example, and Crabb Robinson—found *Anastasius* too racy, too Epicurean.[10] They undoubtedly noticed the Circassian damsel, bound for an Egyptian harem, whom Anastasius encounters on the ship taking him to Alexandria (Volume I, Chapter XV). After she has told him her very brief history, she is set upon by her travelling companions, jealous Georgian girls, who strip her to the waist. What would a gently-reared middle-class mid-Victorian young lady have made not only of this act, but also of Anastasius' unchivalrous reaction to it?

---

9 Byron and Lady Caroline's mother-in-law, Lady Melbourne (1751-1818), remained great friends and were both among the crowds at Louisa Hope's tremendous receptions in Duchess Street, where apparently 900 guests could be accommodated. Melbourne's remark is recorded in many places, *e. g.*, David Cannadine, "The last Hanoverian sovereign?," in A. L. Beier, Lawrence Stone, David Cannadine, James M. Rosenheim, *The First Modern Society: Essays in English History in Honour of Lawrence Stone* (Cambridge: Cambridge University Press, 1989), p. 134.

10 Mary Berry (1763-1852), editor and biographer of Horace Walpole and Mme. du Deffand, was a friend of Hope's, but made these remarks in a letter posted to an unknown correspondent from Bagni di Lucca in August 1820:

> I have been reading after dinner, when it is too hot to write, 'Anastasius.' It is, as I had supposed, the substance of the MS travels in the East which he long ago gave me to read. But in this its new form so arranged! in such a pert style—such an evident copy of Lord Byron's prose, which hardly his verses can make one forgive. Such a tissue of ignoble crimes and villainies, described without any variety of motive, and commented on without any elevation of sentiment. Were it good as a story (in which it fails), I would not be the author of it for millions!—for altho' nobody in a fiction is answerable for the sentiments of their actors, there are fictions which certain minds never could feign.

Extracts of the Journals and Correspondence of Miss Berry from the Year 1783 to 1852, ed. by Lady Theresa Lewis, 3 vols. (London: Longmans, Green, and Co., 1865), III, 225–26.

A year or so later Crabb Robinson expressed his horror as follows:

> I was reading on the last days of this journey Hope's *Anastasius*, a book of perverted talent and abused strength, of which I retain a disagreeable impression though I have happily forgotten all the facts. Hope, my journal remarks, is after Maturin and Shelley a third imitator of Lord Byron's horrors. Shelley should not have been placed in such bad company. Mrs. Shelley might not improperly be placed there, and Godwin was in some sort a precursor.

Henry Crabb Robinson on Books and their Writers, ed. by Edith J. Morley (London: Dent, 1938), I, 274.

> They all fell upon poor Hamida, forcibly tore open her feridjee, and displayed her bosom. It might not answer the utmost amplitude of Asiatic ideas, but I confess, though I looked hard, I perceived no deficiency.

What would the same Victorian young lady have said about the particular pursuit of happiness after his return from the austerities of the Hajj as recorded in this introduction to Anastasius' only adventure in Damascus (Volume II, Chapter VI)?

> One Friday morning, after my devotions, just as I stepped out of the mosque, my eye happened to be caught by one of those celestial beings, found in large cities, who, anticipating the office of the Houris of Paradise, have no objection to cast a ray of bliss on the existence of mortal man. Unfortunately my eagerness to pursue this flitting form of brightness made me overlook some nearer but less attractive objects that stood in my way. Foremost among them happened to be a little man. . . .

And apart from his several marriages and amorous liaisons, what indeed would such a young lady have made of his penultimate adventures, his rambles northward through Italy, where, though worn down sorely by the burden of his ailing son and his own mortal injuries, he nevertheless emits one final flash of casual lust (Volume III, Chapter XIV)?

> After passing through several cities, which looked like the deserted habitations of Titans, in[to] which had crept a race of pigmies, we arrived at Loretto, where, pulled one way by the guardian of a holy house, anxious that I should wipe away my old sins, and the other by a fair vendor of crucifixes, desirous that I should commence a new score, I was only saved from leaving my cloak in the hands of the syren, by a pilgrim who had stolen it before.

Apart from the fact that the last two passages actually link religion with commercial sex, the mere irreverence, wit, length, and elegance of their sentences and many others in *Anastasius* make it extremely doubtful that they were written, as has actually been suggested, by a clergyman, of whatever persuasion.[11]

---

[11] This notion has nevertheless been deemed to be supported by the extraordinary position in Hope's household of the Rev. J. Hitchens, Hope's sons' tutor, who remained attached to the family well after Hope's death, and was made a trustee of Louisa's fortune. (Under common law, freshly enunciated in the eighteenth century, British married women had no legal control of their own earnings or wealth until the Married Women's Property Acts of 1870 and 1882.) Hitchens was additionally offered specific thanks by the family for some unspecified deed, which some people have presumed to be the composition of *Anastasius*. Given Hope's family's obvious aversion towards the book, such thanks for such a deed seems profoundly unlikely. My own guess is that Hitchens prepared a bowdlerized version of *Anastasius* that may have won the enthusiastic approval of Hope's pious widow and children, but could not attract the attention of any responsible publisher. That a rumour to this effect was current in 1820 is suggested by a letter from the Scotch writer Henry Mackenzie (1745-1831) to James Chalmer on 6 June 1820:

The book would probably have escaped penalties under the Obscene Publications Act, passed in 1857. But the trade in novels in Victorian Britain had already become controlled by large circulating libraries that adhered to the rising Idealist-Evangelical ethic—their eye was on the newly literate, newly leisured, and newly moneyed—and were determined that nothing in their stock should "bring a blush to a maiden's cheek." Thanks to the expanding penetration of their commerce in a rapidly growing mass market, these distributors were able to dictate terms to publishers and ultimately even to writers. Such a situation anticipated in many ways the substantive control over Hollywood that was exercised between 1934 and 1967 by the so-called Hays Office, which censored American films in accord with strictures laid down by the Legion of Decency in defence of what it perceived to be Catholic "family values." The cases of *Lolita* (1958) and *Lady Chatterley's Lover* (1928), finally decided in 1959 and 1960, eventually meant the end of censorship in American bookshops, but until 1966 many so-called public libraries in America were in fact governed by the Index Librorum Prohibitorum, which banned such authors as Defoe, Voltaire, Gibbon, Balzac, Sartre and Kazantzakis, as well as virtually all modern philosophy. Even now *Anastasius* is not a book for pietists, puritans or prudes—unless, of course, they'd like to learn something. Nor is it for the semi-literate.

It is his irrepressible energy, much of it expressed through sex, that makes Anastasius, the eponymous diarist of these three volumes, different from other vaguely similar heroes, far different from Byron's languid Childe Harold and even from his Don Juan, to whom Anastasius bears otherwise considerable resemblance. Compared with Anastasius, however, who is always game for another adventure, Juan is almost an accidental or passive lover, generally more pursued than pursuing, that fact being precisely what gives point to Byron's satire. There may be a great deal of resemblance between Donna Inez' letter in *Don Juan* I.cxcii-cxcvii and Helena's letter to Anastasius in Volume I, Chapter XIII of the novel, but Hope could not have read the first two cantos of *Don Juan* before writing all or most of *Anastasius*, simply because they were not published until mid-July of 1819. Byron's admiration for Hope's novel, on the other hand, is well known and Cantos III-V of *Don Juan* almost certainly owe a great deal to *Anastasius*, as do many of the later cantos.[12]

"Here is a Clergyman preparing a New Edition of *Anastasius* professing to rid it of all that has been deemed offensive & consequently to make it very mawkish—People seem not yet agreed as to the original Author." *Literature and Literati: The Literary Correspondence and Notebooks of Henry Mackenzie*. Volume I: *Letters 1766–1827,* edited by Horst W. Drescher (Frankfurt am Main: Peter Lang, 1989), p. 294.

12 The relationship between *Anastasius* and *Don Juan* is thoroughly explored in Anton Pfeiffer, *Thomas Hope's "Anastasius" und Lord Byron's "Don Juan,"* Inaugural-Dissertation, zur Erlangung der Doktorwürde der philosophischen Fakultät (1. Sektion) der K. Ludwig-Maximilians-Universität zum München (Munich: O. Schuh & Cie, 1913). Pfeiffer quotes (p. 29) P. B. Shelley (1792-1822), Byron's friend and fellow poet, writing to his wife Mary on 10 August 1821: "I am reading *Anastasius*. One would think that Lord Byron had taken his idea of the three last cantos of *Don Juan* from this book. . . . It is a very powerful and very entertaining novel, and a faithful picture, they say, of modern Greek manners." (Mary read the book in

The Picaresque

Hope's book has an instantly recognizable literary pedigree in the long tradition of the picaresque novel. This tradition had its beginnings in the cultural penumbra of Hellenistic Alexandria, where the ancestor of all Western novels, the Greek prose romance, was invented. Surviving records give us five more or less complete ancient Greek romances, with others known only from summaries. The archetypal plot involves a virginal young couple whose idyllic happiness is interrupted by a criminal incursion that quickly leads to many journeys and separations. After a great deal of danger, both physical and moral, the couple is rescued by divine agency and is eventually reunited to reaffirm or consummate their love. [13]

This basic plot continues to inspire countless Western works, especially films, down to our own time. The relationship of *Anastasius* to such a plot, however, is sidelong and ironic. The action of Hope's novel takes place in a world immune to Providence, in which boy meets girl, their love is quickly consummated, and then they part, never to meet again. The hero's ultimate passion is not for a heroine, but for his own child, the only tangible record of his passage through a universe from which the gods remain withdrawn, occasionally illuminated for him by such human attachments.

One quality, however, *Anastasius* indeed shares with the Greek romances: their central theme or motif and certainly their central structural device is in fact not love, but travel. Displacements followed by landings in exotic ports of call are their major feature. And as Hope's preface to the third (1820) edition makes clear, his chief aim was identical with that of the travel literature of his time: to display, with "minute and characteristic details," the "manners" of the Ottoman Empire, supplementing the mass of what he had personally observed with historical and statistical information from current written sources. The story he tells, the imaginative part of *Anastasius,* he describes as merely a "fictitious superstructure."

Designed chiefly as diversions, to suit the Alexandrian taste for charm and frivolity, the Greek romances are never set in nor ever seek to represent their own place and time. In the only two lengthy fictional prose narratives that have come down to us from ancient Rome, on the other hand——the fragmentary *Satyricon* of Petronius and the *Metamophoses* or *Golden Ass* of Apuleius——the motif of travel is combined with critical and often satirical analysis of contemporary society. This fact, which shows a deliberate closeness of reference to real life, is what entitles them to be considered as novels rather than as romances. In subject, settings, aim, and spirit, *Anastasius* obviously has a great deal in common with them.

September. In the Preface to *Hellas*, dated 1 November 1821, Shelley refers to *Anastasius* as an "admirable novel . . . a faithful picture" of Greek manners as they had been two decades earlier.) On p. 54 Pfeiffer describes *Don Juan* as an "epic of Epicurean Nihilism" (translation mine).

[13] See B. P. Reardon, "General Introduction," *Collected Ancient Greek Novels*, ed. B. P. Reardon (Berkeley, Los Angeles, London, 1989), p. 2; *The Search for the Ancient Novel*, ed. James Tatum (Baltimore and London: The Johns Hopkins University Press, 1994).

The English word *picaresque* derives, as is common knowledge, from the Spanish word *pícaro,* meaning "scoundrel" or "rascal." During the Spanish Golden Age, when classical literary forms were revived and made new, the term was applied to the roguish heroes of such works as the anonymous *Lazarillo de Tormes* (1553), the great Cervantes' *novela* "Rinconete y Cortadillo" (1613), Alemán's *Guzmán de Alfarache: Atalaya de la Vida* (1599-1604, Espinel's *Relaciones de la vida del escudero Marcos de Obregón* (1618), and Quevedo's *La vida de Buscón* (1626). These picaresque novels constitute the beginnings of a modern subgenre clearly descended from both the Greek romance and the Roman novel, which overlap in their mutual use of travel.

The picaresque mode was imported early into England by Thomas Nashe (1567-1601) in numerous works, especially *The Unfortunate Traveller* (1594), but did not re-emerge into English literature generally until a hundred or so years after Nashe's premature death. *La vraie histoire comique de Francion* by Charles Sorel (1599?-1674) meanwhile carried the subgenre triumphantly to France. Published in several editions (1623, 1626, 1633, 1645), *Francion* was almost certainly read in his youth by Hope, whose primary mother-tongue (of three) was undoubtedly French.

Nearly a century before *Anastasius,* Daniel Defoe (1616-1731) created a brilliant picaresque novel in English with a first-person female narrator in *Moll Flanders* (1722). The outstanding exemplar of the picaresque novel in that period, however, is Le Sage's *Gil Blas de Santillana* (1715/1724/1735), a French masterpiece that points directly to its own inspiration by being set in Spain. A vigorous English translation of *Gil Blas* was published under the name of Tobias Smollett (1721-1771), himself the author of three rollicking novels of travel deeply influenced by the Spanish picaresque: *Roderick Random* in 1748, *Peregrine Pickle* in 1751, and *Humphry Clinker* in 1771. Smollett had already been anticipated, however, by his arch-rival, Henry Fielding (1707-1754), whose *Jonathan Wild* (1743) and *Tom Jones* (1749) both belong to the picaresque mode. The latter has triumphantly escaped from Victorian oblivion, even winding up in two cinema adaptations, the first produced in 1917, the second, Tony Richardson's delightful romp with a distinguished cast, in 1963.

The Mysterious East

But there is another element that enters into both the reception and the formation of *Anastasius,* a literary fascination with the Near East that likewise began in Spain, where the dispossession and expulsion of the Moors was accompanied by widespread admiration for their doomed civilization, represented now by the great architectural monuments of Andalucía, scattered physical and literary remnants as far north as Switzerland, and much of the music of Spain: the very words *guitar* and *tambourine* both derive from Arabic. Representative of such an attitude are Ginés Pérez de Hita's famous and widely read *Historia de los vandas de los Zegries y Abencerrajes* (Part I) and *La guerra de los moriscos* (Part II) known in English together as "The Civil Wars of Granada." Part I in particular was wildly popular and went through at least eight editions in five Iberian cities between 1595 and 1605, propagating a romantic view of

Arab culture that lasted consciously for at least 300 years—"Recuerdos de la Alhambra," for example, Albéniz' guitar transcription of the Muslim call to prayer, dates from 1899—and unconsciously even longer: flamenco and Arab singers both still begin sessions with improvisations on the Arabic invocation, "Ya layl!"[14]

French interest in the Ottoman Empire, where the French ambassador outranked all others, had long been fostered by common strategic concerns, naval and military alliances, and consequent high-powered diplomacy, as well as by long-standing commercial connections. It received great impetus from the publication of such works as *L'Espion turc* (1684) by Giovanni Paolo Marana (1642-1693) and the *Bibliothèque orientale,* an entertaining compendium first assembled by the Orientalist Barthélemy d'Herbelot de Molainvillle (1625-1695). From 1697 onward the *Bibliothèque orientale* was published in constantly expanding successive editions and influenced two or three generations of French writers.

Between 1704 and 1710, finally, appeared the first European translation of the *Kitab Alf Layla wa Layla*, the *Book of a Thousand Nights and a Night*, otherwise known as the *Arabian Nights*, a work second only to the Bible among Oriental books in its impact on Western culture. The author of this version was Antoine Galland (1646-1715), an Orientalist who had sojourned three times in Constantinople between 1670 and 1679. His notion of translation involved not only the rendition of an Eastern original, but also its elaborate adaptation to current Western tastes, which had already become rococo. His ideal remained the norm throughout the following century, when a translator was expected to add connecting material, to insert "colour," descriptions, and explanations into the text, to invent speeches, to modify, add, or excise as he felt inclined.

Even more accomplished as an Orientalist than Galland and a diplomat of proven skill, François Pétis de la Croix (1653–1713) was the son of the Court translator of Arabic and ultimately became professor of Arabic at the Collège Royale de France. He saw the possibilities opened by Galland and published his own *Contes turcs* in 1707, but not before two of his tales had already been pirated by his own publisher for inclusion in Galland's collection. The entire book was published in English the following year. Two years later he began publication of five volumes of purportedly Persian tales called *Les Mille et un jours* (1710-1712), which were published in English in 1714. Pétis de la Croix's tale about a character called "Turandocte" supplied the plot for the Venetian playwright Carlo Gozzi's satirical *Principessa Turandot* (1762), which provided in turn the inspiration for Friedrich Schiller's romantic adaptation, *Die*

---

14 For a detailed treatment of the image of the noble Moor in Spanish literary culture, see Maria Soledad Carrasco-Urgoiti, *The Moorish Novel: "El Abencerraje" and Pérez de Hita* (Boston: G. H. Hall, 1978). See also Rhona Zaid, "*Las Guerras civiles de Granada:* The Idealization of the Assimilation," *Medieval Christian Perceptions of Islam.* ed. John Tolan (New York and London: Garland, 1995), pp. 313-330. See also my article, "Cervantes and Islam: Attitudes Towards Islam in *Don Quixote*" in *Images of the Other: Europe and the Muslim World Before 1700,* Cairo Papers in Social Science, XIX, no. 2, edited by David Blanks (Cairo: American University in Cairo Press, 1996, pp. 67-71.

Prinzessin Turandot (1802), which finally gave Puccini the basis for the libretto of *Turandot* (1926).[15]

During the same period several French travellers, well armed with the necessary languages, published authentic and serious first-hand accounts of travel in the Middle East. To name only a half dozen: Jean Baptiste Tavernier (1605-1689), François Bernier (1625–1688), Jean de Thévenot (1633-1667), Sir John Chardin (1643–1713, a Huguenot who received his English title after moving to London to escape persecution in France, and Paul Lucas (1664-1737), who had been responsible for bringing Yuhanna Diab, Galland's Syrian collaborator, to Paris from Aleppo in 1709. The memoirs of another traveler of the time, the adventurous Laurent, Chevalier d'Arvieux (1635-1702), a favorite of Louis XIV, also found publication, but more than 30 years after his death. Meanwhile between 1666 and 1670 Thévenot's uncle, Melchisédec Thévenot (1620-1692), librarian to Louis XIV, published an important collection of travel narratives in which descriptions of the Middle East figure largely.

In Britain such French works, unparalleled in English, were eagerly seized upon, as was an ensuing spate both of fresh translations and new non-translations, Orientalizing fiction and verse inspired by the success of Galland's *Arabian Nights* and François Pétis de la Croix's Turkish and Persian tales, but wholly themselves a fantastical invention. An early example of the latter is *Les Aventures d'Abdulla, fils d'Hanif, envoyé du Sultan des Indes à la découverte de l'Île de Boreco et de la fontaine merveilleuse dont l'eau fait rajeunir* (1713) by a distinguished member of the Académie Française, Jean-Paul Bignon (1662-1743), who became chief of the Royal library. The Parisian playwright Thomas-Simon Gueullette (1683-1766) produced *Les Mille et un quarts d'heure, contes tartares* (1715), then *Les Mille et une heures, contes péruviens, Les Sultanes de Gazarate, ou les Songes des Hommes éveillés,* (1732), and finally *Les Mille et une soirées, Contes mogols* (1749). Scores of similar titles followed, including the *Lettres persanes* of Montesqieu (1721), the "Oriental" inventions concocted by Voltaire (1694-1778), and operas like *Zamire et Azor* (1771) by André-Ernest-Modeste Grétry (1741-1813).

Between 1735 and 1786 the English likewise produced their own fanciful "Oriental tales" in abundance, by such authors as George Lyttelton (1709-1773), Eliza Haywood (1693-1756), Horace Walpole (1717-1797), Samuel Johnson (1709-1784), Oliver Goldsmith, (1730?-1774) John Hawkesworth (1715-1773) James Ridley ((1736–1765), Frances Sheridan (1724-1766), Alexander Dow (1730?-1779), who apparently knew Persian, and Clara Reeve (1729-1807).There was no one in Britain, however, who was both capable or daring enough to publish a direct translation from Arabic to English and Britain therefore remained dependent upon France for its *Arabian Nights*. Twenty English editions of Galland's *Nights* thus appeared before the end of the eighteenth century. In France there were meanwhile also several genuine additions to the *Nights,* translations of newly surfaced Arabic material. One, for example, is the work of the

[15] See Christelle Bahier-Porte, "Les notes dans les premiers contes orientaux," *Féeries*, no. 2 (2004-2005), 91-108.

extraordinary Anne-Claude-Philippe de Tubières-Grimoard de Pestels de Lévis, comte de Caylus, marquis d'Esternay, and baron de Bransac (1692-1765), soldier, artist, and man of letters. His *Contes orientaux, tirés de manuscrits de la Bibliothèque du roi de France* (1743) is an elaborated translation in Galland's style. He also published fairy-tales and a series of licentious novelettes, however, which points to the fact that an imagined Middle East was becoming the repository for a great deal of suppressed Western libido.

Anastasius and *Vathek*

One of the very few Englishmen equipped to translate from Arabic was a man whom Thomas Hope later came to know personally and quite well, the extraordinary William Beckford (1760-1844).[16] Beckford certainly owned copies of Melchisédec Thévenot's anthology, Thomas Guellette's *Contes moguls* (1732), Pétis de la Croix's *Mille et un jours* (1710-1712), Abbé François Blanchet's *Contes Orientaux* (1784), and probably dozens of similar books. More importantly, however, Beckford not only was able to read Arabic, but also had access between 1780 and 1786 to a complete Arabic version of the *Nights* that was then in the possession of the Duke of Bedford.

This version was a manuscript that had been purchased or commissioned in Egypt by Edward Wortley Montagu (1713-1776), who had lived in Egypt for the better part of the decade between 1763 and 1773 and had become a convert to Islam, forswearing neither the Muslim religion nor Turkish dress when he returned to Europe at the age of 60 to live out his few remaining years. In 1786, when the Wortley Montagu manuscript came on the market, an agent of Beckford's was able to purchase one of its several bundles. Beckford had already been at work much earlier, however, on the whole corpus—aided by a Muslim informant, an Arabic-speaking Turk from Mecca, and two aristocratic ladies—and had produced two sets of translations: a French one that was more or less literal and an English one that followed the elaborating model of Galland. As far as anyone knows, these translations of the *Nights* are the first to be made directly from Arabic into English. Unfortunately they were never published.[17]

In January 1782, still under the spell of a three-day Christmas party that he himself had just constructed around Turkish themes, Beckford began drafting—in French—a sensational Arabo-Gothic romance called *Vathek*, his wildly fictionalized version of the life of Al-Wâthiq ibn Mu'tasim, who acceded as Abbasid caliph in Baghdad on the day

---

16 David Watkin has observed that there was a family connection between the Hopes and the Beckfords: William's bastard brother John had been trained in a counting house of Hope and Company, the Hope family banking firm. See David Watkin, *Thomas Hope and the neo-Classical Idea* (London: John Murray, 1968), p. 15, citing Boyd Alexander, *England's Wealthiest Son: A Study of William Beckford* (London: Centaur Press, 1962), p. 33.

17 See Tania Collani, "La traduction/création du *Vathek* de William Beckford et la théorie de la traduction au XVIIIe siècle," tesina in traduttología (Bologna: Università degli Studi di Bologna, 2005), pp. 3-20; Laurent Châtel, "Les sources des contes orientaux de William Beckford (Vathek et la 'Suite des contes arabes'), *Études Epistémé*, no. 7 (Spring 2005), pp. 93-106.

after Christmas AD 842 (AH 227) and reigned for a mere five years. *Vathek* was finished by the end of May 1782. Beckford's current tutor, the Rev. John Lettice, was invited to translate the novel and attempted to do so more or less literally, frequently therefore making nonsense.

Dissatisfied, Beckford then passed the job on to a former tutor, the Rev. Samuel Henley, who eventually completed an English version. Beckford departed for Switzerland near the end of July, 1785 and sent instructions to Henley the following February prohibiting publication. In early June, however, a few days after Beckford's wife had died giving birth to a second daughter, leaving him prostrate with grief, Henley not only published *Vathek*, but did so under his own name, presenting it as his translation of an anonymous Arabic manuscript. To assert his authorship Beckford therefore published his original French text in Lausanne a few months later and in Paris, with some changes, the following year (1787).

Two decades or so after these events, Thomas Hope was to conduct an unsuccessful courtship of Beckford's second daughter, Susan Euphemia (1786-1859), who eventually married the Marquess of Douglas and Clydesdale, heir to the dukedom of Hamilton, and became Duchess of Hamilton in 1819, the year *Anastasius* appeared. Beckford's *Vathek* was therefore probably one of the influences on *Anastasius*—not in its setting, plot, or characters, certainly, but rather in its levity and occasional persiflage, as some contemporary readers observed. Gothic rather than picaresque, Beckford's book is one of the last important European literary works to look at the Middle East in almost purely fanciful terms. *Anastasius*, on the other hand, is one of the first—like the Waverley novels of Scott or the *Childe Harold* of Byron—to offer a fictional form that unites historical fact and real experience of alien societies with imagined elements that give them fictional life.

Richly adorned and dripping with proto-Wildean High Camp, *Vathek* is also problematic in tone: one frequently doubts whether the bizarre excesses commanded by the main character or the outrageous obtrusions of supernatural special effects are being treated by the omniscient narrator—a mask of Beckford himself—with approval or disapproval. Three examples:

> 1. "Bababalouk [the chief black eunuch] was parading to and fro, and issuing his mandates with great pomp to the eunuchs, who were snuffing the lights and painting the eyes of the Circassians."

The French original should have been correctly translated as "combing the beautiful hair of the Circassians." The amusing exaggeration here seems to be the result of mistranslation by Henley, who mistook the verb *peigner*, "to comb," for the verb *peindre*, "to paint" and changed *les beaux cheveux*, "the beautiful hair," into "the eyes," [*les yeux*], in order for his erroneous reading to make sense. In any case, Beckford was charmed with the absurd result, rather than offended, introduced a version of it into his second French edition, and let it stand in the English edition of 1816. [18]

2. As Vathek's enormous caravan prepares to depart,

> Nothing was visible but plumes nodding on pavilions, and aigrettes shining in the mild lustre of the moon. . . . For some time a general still prevailed, which nothing happened to disturb but the shrill screams of some eunuchs in the rear. These vigilant guards, having remarked certain cages of the ladies swagging somewhat awry, and discovered that a few adventurous gallants had contrived to get in, soon dislodged the enraptured culprits, and consigned them, with good commendations, to the surgeons of the serail.

The "cages" are howdahs, for which Beckford lacked the appropriate French and Henley the appropriate English word: it had entered the English language from Arabic [*haudaj*] by way of Urdu only a decade earlier. The fact that this horde of over-enthusiastic lovers are, "with good commendations," all forcibly castrated, willy-nilly, one hopes need hardly be spelled out.

> 3. The dark clouds that overcast the face of the sky deepened the horrors of this disastrous night, insomuch that nothing could be heard distinctly but the mewling of pages and the lamentations of sultanas."

This delicious sentence, much loved by many readers of Beckford, epitomizes his narrative technique, which depends upon casting the omniscient narrative voice as that of a gourmand whose idea of amusement is not far off the tastes of the Marquis (so-called) de Sade (1740-1814).

Set in an imaginary hedonist utopia like the Alexandria of Lawrence Durrell (1912-1990), *Vathek* is hardly intended to be satiric of Western society and only perfunctorily moralizing. It nevertheless also continues an international mode in which Orientalist fantasies, ignoring any geographic, ethnographic, or historic realities or particularities, serve either entertaining or didactic ends. In Hope's novel, on the other hand, which is narrated from Anastasius' own serious and jaded first-personal point of view, romantic and historical irony pertain throughout, history, geography, and observable social conditions are treated scrupulously, no action is incredible or unreal, and the supernatural is banned. It belongs to a new fictional mode in which interest has shifted from the author's critique of his own society through the device of a pseudo-Eastern setting to the facts themselves, whatever they may be, behind the alien setting, which has suddenly become real. [19]

---

18 See Collani, p. 16.

19 Beckford admired *Anastasius* enormously. He had his own copy "magnificently bound in russia extra, covered with gold tooling in the Grolier style, by C. Lewis." See Baumgarten, p. 200.

Oriental Romances

What Hope's earliest readers thought they were looking at in *Anastasius* was yet another Oriental romance, yet another production in a mode or subgenre with which they were thoroughly familiar, this one having been written—obviously—in the style of Byron, the most recent and most fashionable practitioner. Between the publication of *Vathek* and the publication of *Anastasius*, a whole series of such romances had appeared in both England and France.

Of the two most important French works from this period the first was *Suite des Mille et une Nuits*, published in 1788/89, based it seems on inept translation from extant Arabic manuscripts by a Syrian monk named Dom Denis Chavis, which were adapted or re-written by Jacques Cazotte (1719-1792). Cazotte was already the author of Orientalizing works such as *La Patte de chat* (1741) and *Les Mille et une Fadaises* (1742), but had become far better known as a mystic.

The second was *Gonzalve de Cordoue ou Grenade reconquise,* a novel published in 1792 by Jean-Pierre Claris de Florian (1755-1794), a grandnephew by marriage of Voltaire. This work harks back to Pérez de Hita, "The Civil Wars of Granada," and sixteenth-century Spain. It supplied the libretto for *Les Abencérages ou l'Étendard de Grenade,* an opera by Cherubini that premiered before the Emperor Napoleon in 1813. Florian's real immortality, though, rests on having written the haunting lyric "Plaisir d'amour," later set to music by Martini, orchestrated by no less than Berlioz, and sung by artists ranging from Yvonne Printemps, Tino Rossi, Nina Mouskouri, and Brigitte Bardot to Barbara Hendricks, Joan Baez, and Louise Witt.[20]

But times and tastes were changing in France: Cazotte was to be guillotined in the Place du Carrousel during the early evening of 25 September 1792, at the age of 73. Nor did Florian's relationship to Voltaire suffice to save him: he survived the Terror, but died at the age of 38 on 19 September 1794. a few weeks after being released from a Revolutionary prison, his health having been destroyed by the privations he had suffered there.

In English, meanwhile, Oriental romances in prose poured from the pens of such authors as the under-estimated Robert Bage (1728-1801), Ellis Cornelia Knight (1757—1837), Isaac Disraeli (1766-1848), father of the great Tory politician, whose *Mejnoun and Leila* (1800) retells an authentic Eastern tale, Mary Pilkington (1766-1839), Maria Edgeworth (1767-1849), Matthew 'Monk' Lewis (1775-1818), Mary Lamb (1762-1847), Henry Weber (1783–1818), and an American, Royall Tyler, (1757-1826), author not only of the first comedy written in the U.S., but also of a novel called *The Algerine Captive* (1797). An important travel narrative in English by William George Browne, (1768-1813), *Travels in Africa, Egypt, and Syria, from the year 1792*

---

20 Idealization of Moorish culture is also an important element in Chateaubriand's *Les Aventures du dernier Abencérage* (1828).

to 1797, was meanwhile published in 1799 and a French translation appeared the following year.

More popular than any prose works in English, however, were the four oriental romances in verse published by Byron in 1813 and 1814, which sought to impress readers with the authenticity of their Oriental background, and *Lalla Rookh* by Thomas Moore (1779-1852), published in 1817. In *Lalla Rookh*, Moore returned to the inspiration of the *Arabian Nights*, offering four verse narratives linked by an over-arching tale in prose. In a later poem, *The Loves of the Angels* (1822) he was actually to use the Qur'an as his source; and his novel *The Epicurean* (1827), set mainly in Egypt, shows evidence of a great deal of research not only in Western sources, usually French, but even in Arab authors. In April 1819, meanwhile, the same year Anastasius was published, London audiences were regaled by a revival of *Le Marchand d'esclaves*, a ballet created by Charles-Louis Didelot (1767-1837) to music by Grétry with the most delicious scene set in a pasha's harem.[21]

Anastasius and *Anacharsis*

To its earliest readers *Anastasius* thus seemed to bring together two well-known literary traditions, the picaresque novel and the Oriental romance, and to offer a new literary mode, which might be described as the Oriental picaresque. Hope's original aim, however, as his preface to the third edition makes clear, was far simpler: to give his readers an authoritative tour of the eastern reaches of the Ottoman Empire as it was when he travelled there in the 1790s and to do so in a palatable fictional form. He even had a model for such a project, as he undoubtedly expected his readers to recognize. His full title—*Anastasius, or, Memoirs of a Greek; written at the Close of the Eighteenth Century*—is clearly an allusion to a similarly-named book that had already gone through several editions and would go through many more: *Voyage du jeune Anacharsis en Grèce dans le milieu du IVe siècle avant l'ère vulgaire*, otherwise known as *Anacharsis*, published in 1788 by the abbé Jean-Jacques Barthélemy (1716-1795) after 30 years of classical research.

Barthélemy's fictional traveller is a young Scythian descended from one of the Seven Wise Men, the sixth-century philosopher Anacharsis. Like his famous namesake and forebear, he has gone to Greece for instruction; and after making a 27-year-long tour of city-states, colonies and islands, he has returned to his own native country to write his book. His fictional travels in Greece, lasting from April 363 BC to early July 336 BC, take us from the era of Plato, Aristotle, and Xenophon to the beginnings of the Macedonian invasion of Persia and the eve of Alexander's accession, after which everything will change. Through his hero, Barthélemy provides an extensive account of the manners, customs, government, and antiquities of the places Anacharsis is supposed to have visited. A copious introduction and abundant notes at the bottom of each page,

21 Theodore Fenner, "Ballet in Nineteenth-Century London as Seen by Leigh Hunt and Henry Robertson," *Dance Chronicle*, I no. 2 (1977), 85-86; Baumgarten, p. 164.

frequently pillaged by subsequent writers too lazy to do their own research, cite the classical sources for each historic detail.

Through Anacharsis, the abbé thus discusses virtually every feature of ancient Greek life: music, literature, laws, social structure, the economy, cuisine, religion, festivals, and entertainments. Barthélemy's aim was to construct a complete and authentic picture of ancient Greek civilization at a particular era in an apprehensible form. The book became a major document in the furthering of Neo-classicism, the conscientious attempt at reform in a cultural area that ranges from Russia to the American South by a return to what were believed to be the purest Hellenic origins in architecture, furniture, clothing, and eventually in styles of thought, institutions, and even political formations.

Hope probably remains best known today as a fervent Neo-classicist; and Barthélemy's intention in *Anacharsis* anticipated the aims of Hope's two most celebrated non-fictional works, *Household Furniture and Interior Decoration* (1807) and *Costume of the Ancients* (1809). Like *Anacharsis,* both these books were intended to be instructive about the ancient world and were based upon the same conviction, enunciated in the preface to *Costumes of the Ancients*:

> Those who to a fine natural feeling join a cultivated taste, can only receive unqualified pleasure from that scrupulous imitation of historical truth, carried into even the minutest accessory parts, which alone gives every person the peculiar physiognomy and every scene the individual locality that serve to distinguish them from all others; and that bring the place and the action at once home to the mind of the well informed observer. [22]

In *Anastasius* Thomas Hope merely turned his attention for the moment from the ancient Eastern Mediterranean to the modern, a region in which his own experiences, rather than the writings of other people, would serve as the major source. Like *Anacharsis*, however, which is still quite often described as a novel, *Anastasius* was seen from the first as primarily a work of fiction, an Oriental picaresque.

A major difference between *Anastasius* and *Anacharsis* is that Hope, once having committed himself to the only possible artistic method, actually understands and develops the personality of his narrator-hero and allows it to shape the core of the book. Thus, for example, antiquities are rigorously excluded, because they are of no interest to a modern Greek like Anastasius, who lives in Constantinople without looking at the great architecture of Sinan and visits Egypt without a glance at Luxor or even the Gizah pyramids. He never goes to the Greek mainland; and though he traverses the Aegean repeatedly, he never sees any of its great Hellenic sites, either in the Archipelago or on the Turkish mainland. His visit to the Vatican to see antique sculpture of the Hellenic divinities is not his idea, but an inspired whim of his friend Silva; and its

22 "Introduction On the Costume of the Ancients," *Costume of the Greeks and Romans* (New York: Dover, 1962), p. xvi. This book is a one-volume republication of the second edition of *Costume of the Ancients*, in two volumes (London: William Miller, 1812). The first edition had appeared in 1809; further editions were published in 1841 and 1871.

effect, thoroughly in character, is to make him "absolve all paganism" and see in the Christianity to which he has just formally returned a display of "the features of death and the forms of corruption" (Volume III, Chapter XIV).

The name "Anastasius," certainly inspired by "Anacharsis," is one of Hope's many brilliant touches. Apart from alluding to Barthélemy's book it offers a few other suggestions. In a post-classical, Christian Greek setting, for example, it means "Resurrected" or "Resurrection"[23] and is clearly a baptismal name. To an ancient and pagan Greek, however, it might have suggested meanings like "restless," "uprooted," "bold," or "combatant," which would be very much in character with the hero of Hope's novel. Hope was surely aware, as well, that "Selim," the Muslim name taken by Anastasius, is the Turkish form of an Arabic proper name meaning "safe and sound, secure" and comes from the same Arabic root as *Islam* ("surrender, reconciliation") and *salaam* ("peace, salvation").

Hope and the Character of Anastasius

It is important that Anastasius should belong to a family of dragomen. The word for this trade, somewhat disguised by Hope's bizarre spelling of its Turkish pronunciation, has actually existed in English since at least the fifteenth century. It derives from the Arabic *turguman*, meaning "an interpreter," and the plural ending *-men* in the English word is a traditional, but false, formation demanded by English euphony. Some idea of the status of a dragoman is suggested by a watercolor portrait of a dragoman painted in Constantinople in 1840 by David Wilkie (1785-1841), now in the Ashmolean Museum. Presumably by sheer coincidence, this dragoman bears the same name as Anastasius' family name: Sotiri. This particular Sotiri was the dragoman of Robert Colquhoun (1804-1870), a friend of Wilkie's, British Consul General in Bucharest and, a few years later, in Alexandria. (Colquhoun's memory deserves special respect: in 1859, after Samuel Baker (1821-1893) had abducted his future wife, the brilliant and beautiful Florence Stasz, from a Bulgarian pasha's harem, it was Colquhoun on his own initiative who supplied her with the safety of a British passport.) The Wilkie portrait was concocted to look like a family scene: with great patriarchal dignity, Sotiri occupies the centre and is being served a nargileh by the elegantly dressed son of Colquhoun's janissary, while Wilkie's Italian landlady, in a white veil, poses with a baby as Sotiri's wife in the background. In the distance is a view of Constantinople.

As a dragoman's son, the young Anastasius has considerable standing even outside his own island Greek community. His family has many connections. And he can obviously be expected to know the requisite languages for commerce, diplomacy, and social life in the Eastern Mediterranean, which include Arabic, Turkish, Persian (the three court languages), Romaic (Anastasius has also learned classical Greek), Italian, French, and the lingua franca. Anastasius knows some German, as well, as evidenced by his encounter with the little man in Damascus (see above). He fleeces German

[23] Or perhaps "born anew."

tourists in French, though, and that is the language he uses in Carinthia as he dictates his memoirs to Conrad.

In the Eastern Mediterranean such linguistic accoutrement for a single person remains by no means unusual, though English has long since been added to the list, as quite often has German. Hope himself, whose family owed much to the Prussian kings and who had spent crucial times in Braunschweig or Berlin, undoubtedly knew German in addition to ancient Greek, Latin, and his three mother tongues. He also knew Italian, as most cultivated men did in his time, and quite possibly had acquired some practical Spanish, Turkish and Arabic. Casanova records a dinner (we would call it a luncheon) in Constantinople in 1743 to which the Comte de Bonneval (1675-1747), military advisor to the Ottoman government for more than a decade and a convert to Islam, had invited several of his Turkish friends. All the conversation throughout the meal, including the personal exchanges between Turks, was conducted in Italian, simply as a courtesy to Casanova, the young Italian visitor.[24] In Cairo, Alexandria, or Beirut to this day at receptions in good society local guests will casually shift from language to language to suit the linguistic limitations of a visiting foreigner, even one who is not taking part in a conversation.

With his languages, intelligence, some financial support from time to time, a handsome face, and a robust physique, Anastasius Sotiri is well equipped for travelling. Hope's own travels, the basic source for the book, began at the age of 18 when he embarked on an incredibly grand Grand Tour (1787-1795), and continued intermittently for a least the next thirty years. Apart from Western Europe (England, Portugal, Spain, France, many of the various states of Germany and most of the states in Italy, including Sicily), he also travelled extensively in the Ottoman Empire, which even at that late date still included the territories occupied by our present-day Slovenia, Croatia, Serbia, Albania, Macedonia, Greece, Romania, Bulgaria, Turkey, Iraq, Syria, Lebanon, Jordan, Egypt, and the Arab peninsula, as well as most of North Africa. Hope spent nearly a year in Constantinople, the capital of the Empire. What enters into Anastasius' memoirs is in fact that portion of the Empire that Hope knew more or less from personal experience, which runs from Constantinople southward to Upper Egypt, eastward into what is now Iraq, northward to Wallachia in present-day Romania (did Hope actually

---

24 Another of Casanova's hosts, in Holland some four or five years later, was Thomas Hope's grandfather, also called Thomas (1704-1779), who was then a widower and thus kept the house where he chiefly lived unoccupied. Casanova nevertheless marvelled at the luxury of its marble walls, casements and floors, a different colour for each empty room, with Turkish carpets that had been made to measure. The family and its connections are mentioned in Casanova's memoirs, of which the only complete published version is *Histoire de Ma Vie* (Wiebaden: Brockhaus; Paris: Plon, 1960). In Willard Trask's English translation, *History of My Life* (New York: Harcourt, Brace; Baltimore and London; John Hopkins University Press, 1966), there are references to the Hopes scattered throughout most of Volumes V and VI, encompassing both business matters and his fascination with the young woman he calls "Esther." See also Baumgarten, pp. 13, 14, 17, 21, 239.

go there?), and westward to the Ottoman Empire's borders with the Habsburg Empire, with which it was almost constantly at war throughout several centuries.

In his preface Hope refers to the heart of this Empire as "the ever interesting region, once adorned by the Greeks and now defaced by the Turks," a judgment that seems so breathtakingly at variance with Hope's explicit statements and implicit attitudes elsewhere that it requires some analysis. Hope was no Philhellene.[25] By "Greeks" he clearly means "the ancient Greeks," not the modern ones, whom he exemplifies repeatedly in *Anastasius* and in Anastasius himself. For Anastasius the glories of the ancient world are not even a memory, but exist only as a kind of vague literary ideal immutably lodged in the distant past. Actual monuments of any kind have no value or attraction for him and his sole encounter with the art of his forebears, as we have seen, is in the Vatican a few months before his death.

Hope's Neo-Classicism excludes what Greece has become and concentrates instead on fusing the physical remains of an otherwise vanished past with what is expected to be a carefully man-made future. His words *adorned* and *defaced* are meant literally, not figuratively, and refer to actual substance, which to him was Truth. The trouble with the Turks, he seems to say, is that they have obscured whatever of material truth may have survived from ancient times.

It has been pointed out however, that Hope also saw the Ottoman world as the entryway into the past and the key to its reconstruction. The border of the title-page of *Household Furniture and Interior Decoration*, for example, is thus in fact an Ottoman picture frame, of which he offers a lengthy explanation. Its stalactite moulding is edged with five-pointed stars and at each corner is a Greek palmette. He points out that the same kind of moulding appears in Muslim buildings ranging from Spain to India, but supposes that it originated among post-classical Greek architects and has spread throughout Western Europe north of Spain. The frame thus symbolizes both the survival of a form from earlier times and its expansive influence over an enormous cultural catchment basin.[26]

Preoccupied with the products of arts, the objects made by mankind, Hope likewise seems to have seen humanity itself not as a metaphysical quality, but as primarily a physical one, and human beings not as a post-Homeric "souls," vehicles for ideas or ideals, theories, abstractions, but as bodies worthy of respect for their substantial reality alone. Thus he says in *Costume of the Ancients*:

> If the painter cannot draw correctly the naked figure, he cannot array it according to truth: since the very folds of the raiment must depend on the forms and motions of the body

---

[25] On this subject, see Reflat Kasaba, "The Enlightenment, Greek Civilization and the Ottoman Empire; Reflections in Thomas Hope's *Anastasius*," *Journal of Historical Sociology,* XVI, no. 1 (March 2003), 1-21.

[26] See Wolfgang Ernst, "Frames at Work; Museological Imagination and Historical Discourse in Neoclassical Britain," *The Art Bulletin,* LXXV, no. 3 (September 1993), 490; Watkin, p. 65.

and limbs underneath: above all, he cannot attire it with elegance: since, in order to render his figure pleasing to the eye, the general attitude and proportions of the frame itself should ever remain perceptible through the fullest drapery. Where the human figure, instead of only being covered, is concealed by the garment, it no longer offers beauties superior to what the various articles of apparel might have displayed, collected in a mere bundle.[27]

In *Designs of Modern Costumes* (1812) he advocates fervently what is now called the Empire style, which treated Hellenic nudity as a touchstone for both sexes, women being expected to display a great deal of skin, men the perfection of their physiques. Except for the opacity of the red velvet dress she wears, the style is epitomized in the sensational portrait of Louisa, his beautiful wife, painted by Henry Bone (1755-1834) the following year. [28]

The same theme reappears in *Anastasius* when, en route for Italy, Anastasius changes from Middle-Eastern to European dress.

It seemed to me a sort of degradation to exchange the rich and graceful garb of the East, which either shows the limbs as nature moulded them, or makes amends for their concealment by ample and majestic drapery, for a dress which confines without covering, disfigures without protecting, gives the gravest man the air of a mountebank, and, from the uncouth shape of the shreds sowed [sic] together to compose it, only looks like the invention of penury for the use of beggars.

Anastasius, it would appear, shares the views of his creator.

Anastasius comments on other differences between East and West:

Every day that new world presented itself to my imagination more as a gloomy desert, to me without interest, without friends, and without happiness. The peoples of Europe seemed heartless, the virtue of the Franks rigid, the very crimes of the West dull and prosaic; and I was like a plant which, reared in all the warmth of the hothouse, is going all at once to be launched into all the inclemency of an atmosphere, ripe with chilling blasts and nipping frosts. . . . "Glorious sun of the East!" cried I with faltering tongue, "balmy breath of the Levant! warm affections of my beloved Greece—adieu forever! The season of flowers is gone by; that of storms and whirlwinds howls before me. Among the frosts of the North I must seek my fortune."

Anyone who has ever lived in the Middle East will understand what he means and will sympathize.

---

27 "Introduction On the Costume of the Ancients," *Costume of the Greeks and Romans* (1962), p. xv.

28 See Marion P. Bolles, "Empire Costume: An Expression of the Classical Revival," *The Metropolitan Museum of Art Bulletin*, N. S. II, no. 6 (February 1944), pp. 190-195.

A little later Anastasius has a new and typically European experience:

> For the first time in my life I journeyed in a square box on wheels: the two masters sitting face to face with their two servants, while my little Alexis, the most delightful and amusing of the party, placed in the middle, looked like a gem surrounded by its inferior accompaniments.

No reader should be astonished. Anastasius has moved from a society like those in most of the world in his time, where the only wheels were either on artillery or children's toys, a society dependent upon saddle- and pack-animals, wind, and manpower for its locomotion, to one in which the wheel is already important, steam will come next, and the combination of wheels with consumption of fossil fuels will eventually become central and vital. When the French invaded Egypt in 1798, for example, a few months after Hope's last visit there, they found no provision whatever for wheeled traffic, because it did not exist. It is a brilliant touch on Hope's part thus to give us something of the sensations of someone encountering the most basic European technology for the first time. It is worth noting as well that Anastasius learns instantly and henceforth takes carriages for granted.

At the same time, through Anastasius and throughout the book, Hope explodes an unhappily recurrent Western delusion, to the effect that because it has from time to time not taken so rapidly to things like the wheel, the Middle East is somehow "eternal," "unchanging," "static." The mere political history of the places Anastasius visits shows the opposite, as indeed does his own story, in which his fortunes ride a constant roller-coaster between affluence and esteem and poverty and humiliation.

Anastasius' conversion to Islam is necessary, of course, to fulfill Hope's conception of the book. Unless he were a Muslim Anastasius would not be able to do most of what he does, as he himself thoroughly recognizes, and would therefore be unable to go to the places he goes or to experience what he sees, hears, and feels. His initial motives for conversion are thoroughly cynical, but as time wears on he behaves increasingly like a Muslim born, to the point where he finds among the Wahhabis, the most puritanically Muslim of Muslims, a place where "I could gladly have ended my days, where, only seeking refuge from an enemy, I had most unexpectedly found a friend, a family, and a home."

In Volume III, where Anastasius sojourns among the Wahhabis, Hope clears away an extraordinary amount of Western conceptual rubbish. In Volume III, Chapter V. we are told that the Turks considered the Wahhabis "new and heretical." This designation allowed them legally to conduct war against this fundamentalist sect, which has a relationship to Sunni or Shi'i Islam not wholly unlike that of various recently founded Christian fundamentalist sects to the traditional apostolic communions represented in Orthodox, Catholic, Anglican, Lutheran, or Calvinist Christianity. This portion of the novel is also Hope's only account of Arabs and Arab society, the other peoples he encounters all being among the multitudinous other kinds of Ottoman citizens.

The first revelation for Anastasius is the nature of the Syrian desert, which is by no means merely the forbidding waste of traditional accounts:

> The month of March was just opening, and the heat, save only at mid-day, still easily borne. The verdant carpet of the desert, bruised by the horses' hoof, emitted at night its most aromatic exhalations; and the plants and shrubs in full bloom sent forth invisible clouds of the most powerful perfumes.

To what published documents could Hope have turned to find testimony beyond his own experience to the truth of this description and of others in *Anastasius*? One real contemporary Western traveller, a convert to Islam who covered a similar portion of the Arab world, also wrote superbly about it: John Lewis Burckhardt (1784-1817), the great Anglo-Swiss explorer. But all Burckhardt's works were published posthumously, those of possible relevance to Hope appearing years after the appearance of *Anastasius*, his *Notes on the Bedouins and Wahabys* not until 1831.

Another cliché exploded in *Anastasius* is the idea that Muslim women are universally downtrodden, veiled, victimized, sequestered, sexually repressed and, above all, submissive.

> The wife of Mansoor had only suffered herself to be perceived: the consort of Nasser came forth, and met our gaze undaunted. Not only she permitted me to see her features unveiled, but she very minutely scrutinized my own. A native of the west I was, I suppose, a novel sight to the lady: for my person and my attire seemed equally to attract her attention. Indeed, her investigations became by degrees so close that, to my great relief, the husband thought fit at last to interfere. I must otherwise have been, by little and little, completely undressed. Even after she had been compelled reluctantly to retire, I heard the fair Farzané (or whatever was her name) loudly complain to her sympathising maids, of the shackles imposed upon her inquisitive spirit.

Anastasius is given several lessons in manners:

> [The audience] took place in the open air, at the gate of what I must needs call——more from the dignity of its tenant than its own——a palace; and the schaich received me squatted on a rush mat. . . . Through all the affected meanness of his dress shone a lofty and commanding air. I felt a sensation of awkwardness at the richness of my own apparel, so much exceeding that of the high personage whose favour I came to seek.

Where and how often did Hope see the following kind of meeting between Arabs, still visible daily millions of times throughout the Arab world?

> When both were dismounted, there commenced between them a conflict of civilities, partly in speech and partly in dumb show, which lasted several minutes. Each repeated

> the same inquires and the same protestations a dozen times, and each touched a dozen times the hand of the other.

In young Omar, Anastasius finds a friend like the Greek friends he has left behind: "So exalted were his sentiments and so pleasing his conversation, that when I shut my eyes, I sometimes could fancy I heard my friend Spiridion."

Time-Spans, Life-Spans

The time-span covered by the narrative is 35 years, the length of Anastasius' life, running from about 1762 to about 1798. The inaugural date of the fiction is obscure, but the terminal date is fixed by a few words in Volume III, Chapter XIV, where Silva speaks of seeing the statues of the ancient Greek gods collected in the Vatican "previous to their departure for the banks of the Seine," a reference to the Treaty of Tolentino, signed on 19 February 1797, when Napoleon imposed terms on the Pope that included the surrender of works of art. At the beginning of the following chapter, Anastasius is "basking in the April sun" as he sails towards Trieste. It is raining, however, when they disembark and Alexis dies on the jetty. Anastasius carries his body to the lazaretto, where he is to be held in quarantine, and there Alexis' body is buried. Anastasius remains in Trieste until late October 1797, a date fixed by a reference to the Treaty of Campoformio, signed on 17 October that year. After once again meeting his old friend Spiridion, he departs the following morning and travels four days before finding his last resting place. He dies a few weeks later, presumably in December 1797 or January 1798.

Anastasius' active life begins in about 1780, when he is roughly eighteen, in flight from parental supervision and unwanted fatherhood. He is taken up by Mavroyeni, a character based on a real historical personality, the Chief Dragoman to Gazi Hassan Pasha Cezayirli, who was Grand Admiral from 1774 to 1789 and (alternating with Koca Yusuf Pasha) Grand Vizier in 1789/1790. By birth Mavroyeni was a Greek named Nikolaos Mavrogenis (Hope uses the Turkish form of the name) who did indeed, with the support of both Hassan Pasha and Yusuf Pasha, become Hospodar of Wallachia in 1786. A surviving painting shows him enthroned among his Wallachian *boyars*, all of them dressed *à la turc* in robes of honor. The following year saw the beginnings of a joint invasion of Wallachia by the armies of Joseph II and Catherine the Great, against which Mavroyeni led an increasingly disastrous Ottoman defense. In 1790, thoroughly defeated, he fled to Bulgaria, where he was tracked down and executed by order of Selim III, as recorded in Volume II of the novel.

Hope describes in detail Mavroyeni's preparations for death, including his last-minute conversion to Islam, followed by ablutions and the ritual prayers. Though this scene could only have been imagined, Anastasius' adventures in Wallachia are based on historical fact and his description of Mavroyeni's character is so convincing that one historian has claimed that Hope knew him personally. If so, which seems very doubtful, he must either have met Mavroyeni in Constantinople before 1786, when he was still a mere boy, or somehow have visited him in Bucharest or Bulgaria during his Grand Tour, when Wallachia was in turmoil.

The beginning of the composition of *Anastasius* is also rather vague. A note on the name "Lorenzo" in Volume I, Chapter V, suggests, perhaps accidentally, that the novel may have been begun as early as the 1790s or thereabouts.

> *Lorenzo*; Nucciolo, a Ragusan, physician to the Seraglio, and only lately (as I find from Mr. Turner's account) beheaded, in his eightieth year, by order of his chief patient, Abd-ool-Hameed.

Abdulhamit I (1725-1789) ruled from 1774 to 1789, after which this sentence would not have been carried out. Which "Mr. Turner" is intended here, however, is unknown. The best candidate, William Turner, the diplomatist (1792-1867), author of the excellent travel narrative *Journal of a Tour in the Levant* (London: John Murray, 1820), was probably an acquaintance of Hope's, since they had the same publisher and indeed published books with John Murray at the same time. Not yet born when the execution of Nucciolo occurred, William Turner may nevertheless have learned about Lorenzo's fate some two and a half decades later, during the five years he spent at the British Embassy in Constantinople (1812-1816); and he could easily have made a report that was published earlier than his book. Thus Hope's use of the word "lately" as if it applied to the beheading itself rather than to the information about it received from Turner may be a slip of the pen. In the French translation this note is suppressed, though Lorenzo is identified as "Lorenzo-Nucciolo." In subsequent English versions it survives unchanged.

The date when *Anastasius* was completed is also unclear, though commentators are undoubtedly right in guessing that the chapters of the book where Anastasius describes his anguish over his son Alexis reflect the suffering of Hope and his beautiful Louisa throughout the extended illness of their second son, seven-year-old Charles, who fell ill in Pisa in December 1816 and died in Rome in early 1817, leaving them stunned with grief.

The setting and atmosphere of the final pages are quite different from anything earlier. The genius of their prevailing mood is Johann Wilhelm von Goethe (1749-1832) and they utilize many of the stylistic features of the German *Novelle*, another popular fictional subgenre. Though new characters are introduced, for example, no historical figures are among them, they are not developed, and are, with the exception of Conrad, the hero's amanuensis, not even named. They are identified only by their functions, all of which serve merely to move Anastasius closer to the death he now yearns for. Except for a vague "Carinthia," the settings are not identified with real or specific geographical names nor is the map that is included in most English editions any more forthcoming. Anastasius' death is prefigured in his foreknowledge, moreover, and, unlike any other event in the book, it is thoroughly inevitable, There is perhaps some reminiscence here of *Frankenstein* (1818) by Mary Shelley (1797-1851), which

Hope almost certainly read at about the time he was completing the book, and which also makes use of powerful effects learned from the *Novelle*.

Towards sunset on the third day after Anastasius has left Trieste, moving north, his calèche enters "an extended heath" where he has an extraordinary vision (Volume III, Chapter XVI).

> Every where a carpet of anemones, hyacinths, and narcissuses covered the undulating ground. The oleander, the cistus, and the rhododendron, blushing with crimson blossoms, marked the wide margins of the diminished torrents: glowing heaths, odoriferous genistas, thyme, lavender, and jesmine, started from every fissure of the marble-streaked rock. . . . Alternate tufts of arbutus, and mimosa, and bay, intermixed with the wild rose and myrtle, canopied the beetling brow of the precipice.

This pagan and paradisaical landscape, like that of southwestern Turkey or Syria in spring, but impossible for Carinthia in late autumn, seems to be a flashback to an experience he had near Akhisar many years earlier. This vision leads to Goethean philosophizing on the extravagance of nature, which leads in turn to comforting and anti-Idealistic conclusions as to the supremacy and indifference of Nature to human thoughts or control, a situation that may indeed leave room for things that are inapprehensible or unimaginable.

This vision also shows how henceforward Anastasius' past will intrude upon the present, an effect symptomatic of his diminishing will to live and thus heralding his death. The cottage where he finally settles is described as surrounded by fir-trees, which he also sees as symbols of death. Hope owes a great deal here to Goethe's *Werther* (1774). Like Werther's death, that of Anastasius is necessarily described by a new narrator, somewhat in the manner of a messenger in Greek tragedy, and is made more moving by his dry and anonymous reconstruction.

Aftermath

The creator of *Anastasius* had an immediate and successful imitator in James Morier (1780-1849), who was the son of the Consul General of the Levant Company, was born in Smyrna, and was employed as a diplomat for ten years (1807-1817), spending nearly six of them (1808-1809 and 1810-1814) in Persia. Two travel narratives published in 1812 and 1818 were not enthusiastically received, but his picaresque novel *The Adventures of Hajji Baba of Ispahan* (1824), inspired primarily by *Anastasius* and secondarily by *Gil Blas*, became popular, went through many editions, and is still in print. Unlike Hope's Anastasius, however, Morier's Hajji Baba is a greedy and ingenious rogue incapable of courage, friendship, or love. Of a piece with his venal hero is Morier's contemptuous depiction of Persian society, which coloured the narratives of many subsequent travellers. It provided a moral rationale that was explicitly used to bolster three or four generations of Western racism and to justify a great deal of imperialist meddling. In the U. S. Department of State—who knows?—*Hajji Baba* may well have remained required reading. Morier wrote six more oriental romances, none of which had a similar success.

Among later works in English influenced by *Anastasius*, the most obvious and significant is probably *Barry Lyndon* (1844) an early novel of Thackeray (1811-1863), which may have been saved from twentieth-century oblivion by Stanley Kubrick's stylish and generally faithful film adaptation of 1975: it has the same over-all plot as *Anastasius* and a hero who is as peripatetic, swashbuckling, and sentimental as Hope's Greek, if a great deal less intelligent. On 26 July of that same year, in fact, Thackeray himself departed on the tour that is wonderfully described in his own travel book, *Notes of a Journey from Cornhill to Grand Cairo; by Way of Lisbon, Athens, Constantinople, and Jerusalem,* published two years later. In Chapter 51 of his masterpiece, *Vanity Fair* (1848), Thackeray introduces an Orientalist charade and in *Our Street,* published the same year, he pillories the affectations of a character called Clarence Bulbul, "the Lion of Our Street," an Oriental traveler *par excellence*, suggesting that Eastern travel was no longer a novelty.

There are plentiful traces of *Anastasius* in the novels of Benjamin Disraeli (1804-1881) who diverted the peripatetic form to the uses of political propaganda, and Lord Lytton (1803-1873), who praised *Anastasius* in 1838 for the "sustained and noble interest" it maintained as the record of a "bold and insolent life" and observed that its composition required "on every page, deep knowledge of human life."[29] Towards the end of the century Anastasius-like characters reappear in the fiction of Robert Louis Stevenson (1850-1894), whose energetic and morally ambiguous Alan Breck Stewart and wicked Master of Ballantrae look forward to glamourous criminals such as A. J. Raffles and Fantômas, forerunners in their turn of certain amoral and charmless fictional heroes of our own debased era, whose governments, defining virtue for themselves *ad hoc*, give them official licence to kill.

In America, where the same tastes for Oriental romance had also prevailed, the subsequent history of the Oriental picaresque is somewhat different. Herman Melville (1819-1891) undoubtedly had read *Anastasius* in his youth and bought a copy in Paris in December 1849, only to have it confiscated on the other side of the Channel by English customs officers. His London publisher, however, Richard Bentley (1794-1871), who had also published Burckhardt, gave him copies of both *Vathek* and *Anastasius* a few days later and the latter has survived, showing heavy use and many of Melville's own markings.[30] His interest in the Middle East is well known and permeates all his work. He finally made a tour there between October 1856 and May 1857 and the direct result was works published only posthumously. *Anastasius* may well have contributed something, however, to the singularly gloomy and pessimistic version of the picaresque he offers in *The Confidence Man* (1857), published shortly

---

29 As quoted and paraphrased in Harold H. Watts, "Lytton's Theories of Prose Fiction," *PMLA*, L, no. 1 (March 1935), 283. *Anastasius* is also discussed by Lytton's characters in *Pelham* (1828). See Baumgarten, pp. 200-201.

30 Melville's heavily annotated copy of *Anastasius* is in the Houghton Library at Harvard.

after his return. With the Mississippi as its setting, it was his last major work of prose fiction before the posthumously published *Billy Budd.*[31] Mark Twain, who was actually becoming a pilot on the Mississippi at about the same time that *The Confidence Man* appeared, was almost certainly introduced to *Anastasius* some 20 years later by William Dean Howells, his closest literary friend. Twain's *Huckleberry Finn* (1884), America's great picaresque novel, is akin to *Anastasius* in that its hero has the same Homeric simplicity of aim and manner and the same pragmatic ethic as Anastasius and likewise tests each situation not only by the belly and the purse, but also by the heart. A difference is that Huck is an innocent, a half-grown pre-pubescent whose gentle naiveté Twain uses to make his moral points, and Anastasius is a polyglot cosmopolitan sophisticate.

A question that needs further exploration is the extent of Hope's influence on subsequent French literature. The anglophile Stendhal (1783-1842), for example, almost certainly read *Anastasius* and his Julien Sorel in *Le Rouge et le Noir* (1829) has more than a little in common with Hope's hero. That Stendhal's attitude toward religion was much like Hope's is evidenced in the two passages quoted above; and in Chapter XVII of *Le Rouge et le Noir* he slyly suggests that religious emotion, especially in the young, is quasi-sexual, an idea later taken up by Flaubert in *Madame Bovary.* A famous passage in Chapter XXIV, where Stendhal's shy young provincial enters a café for the first time in his life, is distinctly reminiscent of *Anastasius*:

"La demoiselle se pencha en dehors du comptoir, ce qui donna l'occasion de déployer une taille superbe. Julien la remarquer; toutes see idées changèrent."

"The young lady leaned out from behind the counter, which gave her occasion to deploy a superb figure. Julien took notice of it; all his ideas changed."

Clearly descended from *Anastasius*, in any case, are works such as *La Bédouine* (1835) by Jean-Joseph-François Poujoulat (1808-1880), which the author himself described as "not at all a novel, but a story; not at all, thank God!, a political book, but a book of morality and philosophy, of sentiment and intimacy."[32] Its hero is Augustin, a young European fed up with Western values who finds a more congenial home with a *badawi* tribe and falls in love with Iellé, the daughter of its *shaykh*. A similar dramatic situation is at the centre of many of the Middle-Eastern narratives of Julien Viaud (1850-1923), better known as Pierre Loti.

---

[31] For an excellent survey and discussion of Melville's fascination with Islam and the Middle East, see Dorothee Metlitsky Finkelstein, *Melville's Orienda,* Yale Publications in American Studies no. 5 (New Haven: Yale University Press, 1961). See particularly pp. 53-59.

[32] My translation of a sentence presumably taken from Poujoulat's introduction, as quoted in the Bernard Quaritch catalogue entry describing a presentation copy of the first edition. In 1836 *La Bédouine* was honored by the Académie Française with its third prize (a medal worth 1500 francs) the first prize that year going to Alexis de Tocqueville (1805-1859 for *De la démocratie en Amérique*. Understandably, however, Catholic authorities in France found themselves discomfited by the sentiments displayed in *La Bédouine* and had the book placed on the Index Librorum Prohibitorum a year later.

Curiously enough, there is a legend to the effect that Hope, like Beckford, first wrote his novel in French This notion was apparently first put forward in public print in 1838, seven years after Hope's death, by Henry Hart Milman (1791-1868), Dean of St. Paul's Cathedral, an outstanding Early Victorian editor, translator and historian, in a footnote to his 1838 edition of Gibbon's *Decline and Fall*, which was repeated in the editions of 1845 and 1863. Given that Hope grew up trilingually in English, Dutch, and French and undoubtedly relied most on French throughout the first half of his life, it is a plausible idea. And there are, in fact, occasional Gallicisms in the English text. A parallel allegation—not made, however, by Dean Milman—has it that the English version was somehow largely due to Thomas Hope's sons' tutor, the Rev. J. Hitchens.[33]

If the book was originally written by Hope in French, however, it is odd that the standard French version, which appeared first in 1820, when Hope's authorship was already acknowledged and well known, should have been presented to the public as the work of a well-known professional translator, Auguste-Jean-Baptiste Defauconpret (1767-1843), a French citizen resident in London throughout two and a half decades, the best known, most prolific, and certainly most important popularizer in French of English and American literary works (*e.g.*, Fielding, Scott, Dickens, Morier/Cooper, Irving) and chronicler of London life for the Parisian intelligentsia. If the two allegations about Hope's authorship are both true, either the published French version is really Hope's and someone therefore—for whatever obscure reasons—paid M. Defauconpret to put his name to a work in which he had actually had no hand at all; or someone hired Defauconpret to construct a new French version from the already-published English translation of Hope's French original, which Hope must have—for whatever obscure reasons—refused to surrender for translation or perhaps destroyed. Either option seems a bit absurd. The occasional Gallicisms would tend to confirm Hope's authorship rather than deny it; and Hope's "French original," unlike Beckford's, must therefore continue to float ectoplasmically in the intense inane of literary legend.

The novel in English should be good enough for anyone, though, and good for rereadings and repeated delvings. Hope was a profound and original thinker, a fact that is not always evident in his non-fiction. It is, however, one of the many things that make the career of his Anastasius worth following. Another is the richness of the book in terms of observation, especially of people and their enormous variety, such perhaps as only a kind of Epicurean could prize and understand.

John Rodenbeck is a founder-member of the Association for the Study of Travel in Egypt and the Near East (ASTENE) and writes frequently on Middle-Eastern travel. He is Professor Emeritus of English and Comparative Literature at the American University in Cairo, where he also was head of the university press from 1973 to 1982. After sojourning in Egypt for nearly 35 years, he retired with his wife to a mountain village in Languedoc, where they live in a 300-year-old presbytère. He has children in Cairo, New York, and Oxford and three grandchildren.

---

33 That man again. See n. 11.

Preface of the Editor to the 1819 first edition (the Author being anonymous)

Some apology may seem required for the publication of these Memoirs. The editor indeed trusts that no one will suspect him of proposing their hero as a model, his actions as examples, or his principles as praiseworthy: but he would not even willingly be supposed to present scenes – too frequently of vice – merely for the sake of affording an idle and unprofitable pastime. His aim is not wholly frivolous. In an age in which whatever relates to the regions, once adorned by the Greeks, and now defaced by the Turks, excites peculiar attention, he thought that this narrative might add to our information on so interesting a subject, not only by presenting a picture of national customs and manners, but by offering many historical and biographical notices, not to be met elsewhere, and yet, as far as their accuracy has been investigated, narrated with scrupulous regard for truth: – for though the author has probably brought forward under the mask of fictitious names, the persons and adventures of some private individuals, whom he might not have deemed himself warranted to drag before the public undisguised, he seems to have described public events and personages with all the fidelity of an historian. Unfortunately, the weeds in his work are so closely interwoven with its flowers, that only some of the rankest among the former could be plucked out, without detriment to the latter.

The MS. being ill written and full of erasures, some names of persons and places may have been mistaken; and in all of them it was extremely difficult to alter the original orthography to that which in English would produce the same sounds. As a great part of the language was moreover in a familiar tone, and full of idiomatic and proverbial expressions, a still greater difficulty occurred in the necessity of rendering these by such English equivalent, as might convey the sense, and render it intelligible to the English reader, without wholly destroying the Eastern turn of the style, and the French, and Greek, and Turkish peculiarities of phrase, in which the narrative abounds.

For the explanation of such Turkish words or allusions to Eastern customs as might be least generally understood, the editor has added a few notes, conveying what little information he has been able to collect, respecting the constantly shifting scene of action, to which we are conveyed by the restless writer of these unvarnished *confessions*.

Final Note by Editor (1819)

The editor acknowledges that the effect produced by the loss of his child on Anastasius, seemed to him – even allowing for the peculiarity of the adventurer's situation – somewhat improbable, until in Mariner's account of Finow, king of the Tonga islands, he found what power the feelings of nature will sometimes, among semi-barbarous nations, retain even over minds in other respects ferocious and pitiless.

Hope's Preface to the 1820 edition
(After he had revealed his identity)

To you, my Louisa; to you, the sole partner of all my joys and sorrows; to you whose fair form but enshrines a mind far fairer, I inscribe *not* these pages. Composed of materials collected ere I knew you, ere I was inspired by your virtues or could portray your perfections, they are not worthy of bearing your name: - they were not even intended to divulge that of the writer, had his secret been preserved as inviolate as he wished. Should they, thus avowed, continue to meet with an indulgent reception. I may then feel encouraged at some future period to publish, with the sanction of your beloved name, that which, suggested by the contemplation of your excellence, and written under the guidance of your unerring taste, is in truth your own work.

To the public at large I can only plead, for sending forth into the world this unpruned performance, the desire of imparting a few perhaps unimportant notices, - but the result of personal observation, - with respect to the ever interesting regions, once adorned by the Greeks and now defaced by the Turks. I shall therefore observe that the historical and statistical parts are (as far as my knowledge extends) strictly correct, and that the fictitious superstructure is as conformable as I could not make it to the manners of the nations whom it was my aim to describe; and as the form of biographical memoirs was adopted solely with the view of affording greater facility for the introduction of minute and characteristic details, I trust that I shall not be considered as identifying myself with all the opinions which the peculiar nature of the work has obliged me to bestow upon my hero.

THO^S HOPE
Duchess-Street,
April 25 (1820)

N.B. by Thomas Hope (1820)

It should be observed throughout this work, that, as scarcely two European nations pronounce the vowels alike in their own languages, and as in different parts of the East vowels are inserted between the consonants in the same words and names, their uncertain sounds seldom are the same in different writers. I have endeavoured as much as possible to adapt my spelling to the sound of the different letters in English.

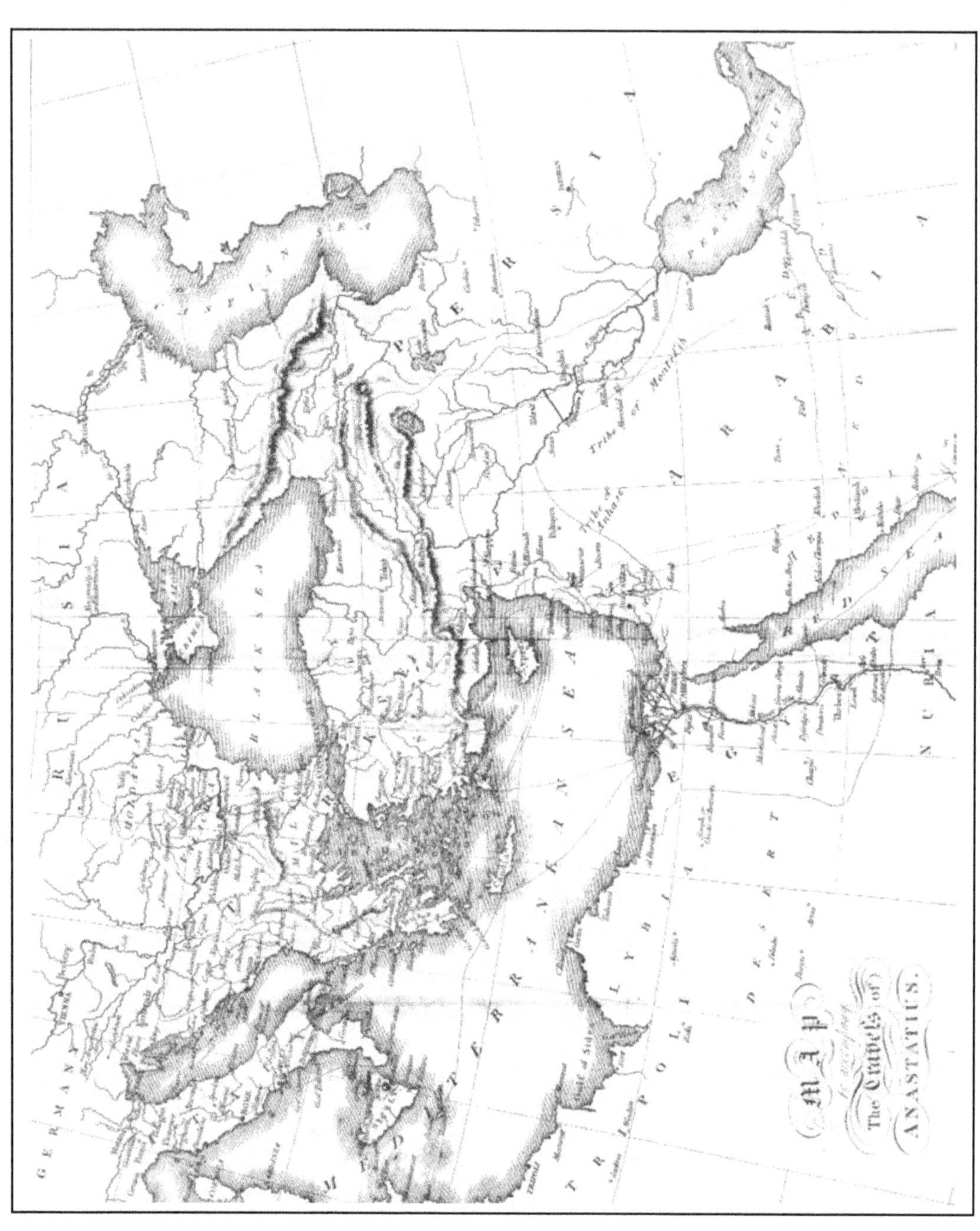

Map of Anastasius's travels

VOLUME I

CHAPTER I

My family came originally from Epirus: my father settled at Chios. His parentage was neither exalted nor yet low. In his own opinion he could boast of purer blood than any of the Palaeologi, the Cantacusenes, and the Comneni of the present day. "These mongrel descendants," he used to observe, "of Greeks, Venetians, and Genoese, had only picked up the fine names they flourished about in, when the real owners dropped off: he wore his own;" and signor Sotiri saw no reason why he should not, when he went forth into public, toss his head, swing his jubbee,[1] like a pendulum, from side to side, and shuffle along in his papooshes, with all the airs of quality.

This worthy man combined in his single person the various characters of diplomatist, husbandman, merchant, manufacturer, and the master of a privateer. To be more explicit, he was drogueman[2] to the French Consul at Chios; in town he kept a silver loom at work; in the country he had a plantation of *agrumi*;[3] he exported his stuffs and fruits to the principal sea ports in the Archipelago; and in the first Russian war he employed all his money in fitting out a small vessel to cruise against the enemy; – for so he chose to consider the Russians, in spite of all their amicable professions towards the Greeks. As a loyal subject of the Porte, and an old servant of the French government, he felt no sort of wish to be delivered from the yoke of the Turks; and he looked upon those barbarians of the North, who cared no more for the Patriarch of Constantinople than for the Pope of Rome, as little better than rank heretics, not worthy of being treated even like his silk worms, which every year he got carefully exorcised before their spinning time. I however remember, when a child, some buzz in the family, about my father's partner in the privateer – an Ispariote reïs[4] – having one day made a mistake in capturing under the rocks of Jura a rich Turkish vessel, which he went and sold to the Russians themselves, then stationed at Paros. Signor Soriri shook his head at this intelligence, as if he did not approve of the transaction, and observed, "the less that was said about it, the better." I suppose therefore it was out of sheer humanity, that he preferred receiving his share of the prize money, to the sterile and barbarous satisfaction of hanging an associate.

Much improved in his circumstances by this untoward accident, my father would have given up the interpretership. Besides rendering him more or less dependant, it was uncomfortable in as far as, being very deaf, he never heard what it was his business to translate. But my mother liked the title of droguemaness. She had never heard of the necessity of a drogueman reporting speeches as he received them; and she reminded her husband how essential the protection of the French mission might be to some of his Greek speculations.

My mother was a native of Naxos, and esteemed a great heiress in her country. She possessed an estate of three hundred piastres a year, clear, managed by a relation of her own, Marco Politi; very wealthy himself, primate of all the Greek villages of the island, and a very great rogue.

My brothers and sisters, – and there came, one by one, just three of each – all contrived to take precedence of me at their birth, and consequently throughout the whole of their subsequent lives. The punctilio of the thing I should not have minded; but, among my countryman, a foolish family pride exhausts people's fortunes during their lifetime in portioning their daughters: the elder sons ran away with what remained, and poor Anastasius brought up the rear with but an indifferent prospect. My kind parents, however, determined to make up for leaving me destitute at their death, by spoiling me as much as possible during their lives.

My eldest sister (I begin, as is proper, with the ladies) married a physician of the country, graduated at Padua. Robust as a hamal,[5] and never until her marriage having known a moment's illness, Epiphania seemed to bid defiance to her husband's utmost skill in medicine. But she was not proof against her own imaginations. Signor Sozimo expressed such constant anxiety about his "dear wife's" precious health, and gave her so much viper broth to keep up her strength, that she soon began to fancy herself in a bad way; and died at last of the mere apprehension of not living.

My sister Roxana who would have been a beauty, but for a scar, which she chose to call a dimple, at an early age fell desperately in love with a Turk; and spite of all the remonstrances of her friends, bestowed her hand upon this unbeliever. Nor was it until the very last of her offended relations had been prevailed upon to grant her an unlimited pardon, that she became conscious of the heinousness of her crime, and began to feel an unconquerable desire to re-enter the pale of our holy communion. This she at length effected, by never failing to bewail her apostacy, until her husband, in disgust, allowed her a divorce. Immediately she flew back at once into the arms of the church and into those of a young Greek, who, an effective instrument in her reformation, obliterated every trace of her first unhallowed wedlock, by a more canonical union. He truly laboured for the church; for he was by trade an agio-graphis, or painter of Saints; and connoisseurs esteemed him the Apelles of our district, in that line. His spouse sat for all his Virgins; and accordingly as she behaved well or ill, he used to paint them handsome or ugly: a practice which kept her very much upon her good behaviour. She was conceited about her looks, and wasted as much time upon her cheeks as her husband did upon her canvas; a circumstance, however, which produced a striking resemblance between the portraits and the original.

As to my youngest sister, she deemed a two years' obedience, well or ill performed, to a single lord and master, quite trial enough for a woman, in this world. Her husband dying, she took the habit of a caloyera,[6] in a nunnery near the delightful district of the Lentiscs. There, the interest of her portion, together with the produce of her handy-work, enabled her to set up, according to the practice of our religious communities, an independent establishment; and to entertain her friends of both sexes, in a manner at once comfortable and decorous.

What shall I say of my brothers? The eldest was a loose and dissipated youth. To cure him of his extravagance, my father had him nailed to the desk of the strictest merchant of Smyrna. The consequence was that, instead of the clerk staying at home, desk, contents and all, followed him out of doors; until, in a notorious tavern, the well tempered Brescia blade of a Zantiote captain put an end to his prowess, and saved him the mortification of being returned on our hands, as a hopeless profligate. Of all the family I felt the most grieved for his loss. He had a dark complexion, and a fine commanding figure. I looked upon Theodore with a certain veneration, as the prop of the house; and had proposed some day to take him for my model.

The dove is not more distinguished than the game-cock, than differed the noisy blustering Theodore the sly demure Eustathius, destined to succeed my father in his place of Drogueman. A sleek, smooth-spoken, sanctified lad, with a round face and a red and white complexion, Eustathius, beside that little treasure his own dear self, which he almost kept with the utmost care, valued but one other thing in this world – namely, money. Of this article his good fortune, or rather his unabating perseverance, enabled him at last to wed a prodigious heap; encumbered, however, with a wary widow its mistress, who, after four distinct refusals, finally condescended to accept my brother as her slave, under the name of husband. But the chains worn by this admirer of solid worth were of gold; and all he wanted was the pleasure of contemplating their reflungence.

Constantine, my third brother, managed the farm. This hopeful youth, only a few years older than myself, used to hate me with singular asperity. I never could understand the cause of this aversion. He was crooked indeed, and I unfortunately walked straight. If this however could be called an offence, so many others shared it with me, that he must have hated the whole human race: – perhaps he did. It is true I much aggravated my crime by one day observing, on his talking slightingly of the advantages of a handsome person, that "they were what no one affected to despise, who could not make good his claim to them;" – I thought he would have stabbed me.

After all the rest of the brood had taken wing, I remained alone at home to solace my parents. Too fond of their favourite to damp my youthful spirits by fitting me for a profession, they kindly put off from day to day every species of instruction – probably, till I should beg for it; which my discretion forbade. Unfortunately, nature chose not, in the mean time, to be equally dilatory with my parents; and from an angel of an infant, I by degrees became a great lubberly boy, without any other accomplishment but that of flogging my top with my left hand, while at the right I dispatched my sign of the cross – for in some things I understood the value of time. My parents, as may be supposed, were great sticklers for punctuality in every sort of devout practice; mass-going, confession, lent observance, &c. Of moral duties – less tangible in their nature – they had, poor souls, but a vague and confused notion; and the criminality of actions, in reference to one's neighbour, they taught me chiefly to estimate according to the greater or smaller risk connected with them of incurring the bastinado from the Turks. As to manual correction at the hands of my own father, it seemed so desirable a circumstance, from the ample amends my mother never failed to make her 'dear, ill-used poor boy', that my only regret on the subject arose from being able to obtain it so seldom.

These good people having contented themselves for a reasonable number of years with wistfully contemplating – the drogueman my active make and well set limbs, and the droguemaness my dark eyes, ruddy cheeks, and raven locks – they at last began to ponder how they might turn these gifts to the best advantage. Both agreed that something should be done, but neither knew exactly what; and the one never proposed a profession, which the other did not immediately object to, – till an old relation stepped in between, and recommended the church, as a never-failing resource to those who can think of no other. My cousin had set the example by making his own son a little caloyer at twelve. Prohibited by the Turks from the trade of soldier, and by my parents from that of a sailor, I myself saw nothing better, and agreed to the proposal. It now became necessary to give me a smattering of learning, and I was put under the tuition of a teacher of the Hellenic language, who assumed the title of logiotatos, and only averred himself inferior to Demosthenes, out of sheer modesty. My idleness got the better of my preceptor's learning and diligence. All the gold that flowed from the lips of his favourite St. Chrysostom could not, to my taste, gild the bitter pill of his own tiresome comments; and even Homer, much as I liked fighting out of doors, found but an indifferent welcome in the study. The truth is, I had a dislike to reading in the abstract: but when away from my books, I affected a great admiration of Achilles; called him, in reference to Epirus the land of my ancestors, my countrymen, and regretted that I was not born two thousand years ago, for no other reason but to be his Patroclus. In my fits of heroism, I swore to treat the Turks as he had done the Trojans, and for a time dreamt of nothing but putting to the sword the whole Seraglio – dwarfs, eunuchs, and all. These dreams my parents highly admired, but advised me not to divulge in common. "Just rancour," they said, "gathers strength by being repressed." – Upon this principle they cringed to the ground to every Moslemin[7] they met.

The inclinations of the little future papas[8] for the church militant began meantime to appear more prominently. I had collected a troop of ragamuffins of my own age, of whom I got myself dubbed captain; and, having purloined from my uncle, the painter, one of his most smirking Madonnas for a banner took the field under the auspicies of the Panagia,[9] and set about robbing orchards, and laying under contribution the villagers, with all the devotion imaginable. So great was the terror our crusades inspired, that the sufferers durst not even complain, except in a body. Whenever, as chief of the band, I became the marked object of animadversion, I kept out of the way, until my father had paid the damage, and had moreover sued my pardon for his backwardness in doing so. Once indeed when, tired of my pranks, he swore I should be his ruin, I suggested to him an effectual mode of quieting his fears, by granting me an unlimited leave of absence; and pledged myself not to return till doomsday. This was too much for a doting parent. Sooner than part with his Anastasius, Dimitri Sotiri would have bribed the peasants beforehand to suffer all my future depredations.

Thus early disposed and trained to the business of tithing, my father felt a little surprised when, on the eve of taking orders, I begged to be excused. For the first time in his life, Signor Sotiri insisted on implicit obedience; but that first time came too late. I made it the last, by swearing that if he forced me to take the mitre[10] I would hide it under a turban. He yielded, and contented himself with quietly asking what I finally meant to do. "Nothing,' was the answer of my heart: but the profession of doing nothing requires ample means. I therefore pretended a wish to learn a trade. My father assented, and forthwith wrote to a Smyrna merchant of his acquaintance to receive me into his counting house.

Meanwhile I found an employment for my leisure hours, which put an end to all childish pastimes. Signor Sotiri, though, as before mentioned, a little hard of hearing, wanted not fluency of speech. His oratory had chiefly been exerted to render his patron dumb. He constantly represented to him how absolutely the dignity of his station forbade having the least conversation with the natives; and how incumbent upon him it was, though born and bred in the Levant, to appear not to understand a single word of its idioms. By this device, he kept all the speechifying to himself; and in truth, with the Turks in office, at all times more prone than strict politeness permits to compliment the representatives of Christian powers with the titles of "infidel, yaoor,[11] and Christian dog"; and at this particular juncture, more than usually out of humour, in consequence of the Russian war,[12] this was the only way to save the consular pride from some little rubs, otherwise unavoidable in the necessary intercourse with the government. Hence Mr. de M— not only never stirred from home without his interpreter by his side, but had him constantly at his elbow within doors; and made him the sole channel of all his official transactions: a circumstance which my father perfectly knew how to turn to the best advantage.

I too, in my capacity as the Drogueman's chief assistant and messenger, was in daily attendance at the consular mansion; which proved useful to me in one respect, as it gave me an opportunity of learning the French language, and that with the greater fluency, from the circumstance of no one offering expressly to teach me. The old consul had, between his dignity with the Greeks and his punctilio with the Turks, but little society, and I therefore soon became, by the sprightliness of my repartees, a very great favourite. M. de M— not only encouraged me to take a part in conversation, but would even condescend to laugh mostly heartily both at my witticisms, and my practical jokes; whenever neither himself, nor his relations, nor his friends, nor his protégés, were made to smart from their keenness or involved in their consequences.

Mr. de M— had an only daughter, the blue eyed Helena, the child of his old age. Deprived of a mother's watchful care, this lovely girl was allowed in her father's house an unrestrained latitude, and availed herself of her privilege with all the freedom of unsuspecting innocence. The consul, without being fond of music, loved the sound of an instrument. Helena had been taught the harpsichord; but, full of life and spirits, she hated the mechanical drudgery of running over the cold clumsy keys of a huge cumbrous fixture, to which the performer, she thought, looked a mere appendage. Our light portable lyre, which the arms encircle so gracefully and the fingers seem scarcely to touch, she would learn to play upon most readily, – could she but find a proper master! "Who more so," thought I, "than the son of the father's interpreter?" and forthwith offered my services. Though but a moderate performer, I had the advantage of always being at hand, and without being either accepted or refused, was soon employed.

Parents! who do not particularly wish your daughters to fall in love with their teachers, be cautious of admitting under your roof any music masters except such as are antidotes to that passion. Where harmony alone is to rule the sense, can souls remain unattuned to each other? The boy's hand, in guiding the taper fingers of his pupil, will sometimes make them stray from her chords to his heart, and mistake for the vibrations of one the pulsations of the other. The very lips of the fair one accustomed to re-echo the sounds of her teacher's voice, will by degrees respond to his feelings; and he who has so many means of disclosing his passion, and of insinuating a reciprocal warmth, without any imputation of forwardness, or violation of respect, will be more anxious to interpret the sounds he utters, than to disavow their sense.

For my part, I almost immediately felt my heart on fire, and soon Helena, too, caught the consuming flame. Nothing could tear us away from each other. The duets, begun in the heat of the day within doors, were repeated in the cool of the evening on the stone seat before the house. Sighs interrupted the songs: and when the advancing night forced Helena to retire, her blue eyes looked like drooping violets steeped in dew.

The consul had destined his little favourite, as soon as arrived at a suitable age, to a rich young Smyrniote, nephew to his correspondent. He dreamt not of the possibility of her falling in love with a Greek boy, habited in the dress of the country, and the son of his interpreter. It was rather a gratification to him, on seeing us together, to think that in her solitude she should have found the harmless pastime of our concerts.

My father saw deeper into the business. Had he conceived it likely to end in a marriage, and that marriage likely to bring his family any accession of weight or of fortune, he would, I make no doubt, become as blind as he was deaf; but this he by no means thought probable. The old consul was a good deal distressed, his salary must cease with his life, and he had nothing to leave his daughter at his death but his consular pride; – "and with that portion," observed my father, "she might indeed become a gem of the first water in the hands of a rich Smyrna merchant, who would set her in gold, but round our bare necks she could only prove a millstone." He therefore warned me against carrying the intimacy too far.

His caution came too late. The less experience my pupil at first brought to her lessons, the more rapid was the progress she made under my tuition. Love's fullest harmony was struck, almost ere she suspected it whispered in our sighs. Indeed so much was she still in the first spring of her innocence, that she scarce seemed aware that in due time blossoms turned to fruit, till taught by experience. On this discovery the timid girl at first sobbed incessantly; but, by degrees, persuading herself that our attachment, when divulged, must end in our permanent union, she recovered a kind of composure, and resolved to let the disclosure take its course – neither hastening it, nor yet trying to avert it; and rather rejoicing than dismayed that the slim Perote[13] dress, which she wore for the sake of consular dignity, must betray the secret of her father's villa sooner than the ample involutions of silk and cotton, of which our more wary females so well know the advantages.

I by no means sympathised in this calmness, or agreed in these wishes. What the too confiding Helena looked upon as the harbour in which her ineptitudes must end, my father had taught me to consider as the quicksands on which all my hopes must perish. I therefore tried to impress Helena with my utter inability to support her as my wife; and with the expedience of such a timely confession, on her part, as should enable the consul to save her honour without my inadequate assistance.

To the fair one flushed with love, the least proffer of prudential considerations is an insult. Exasperated at my discreet suggestions, Helena treated me with haughtiness – with contempt. "When she could bring herself to stoop to my lowness, did I fear any sacrifice that raised me to her level?"

Feelings so proud as mine could ill brook this taunting speech. To be told I was to consider as an honour beyond my desserts, the penniless hand of one whose heart had attested too warmly my merits; – was this to be endured? All the blood of Achilles rose within me; I ran to the quay, and there let it rage in unison with the foaming breakers.

As long as the Smyrna scheme had remained in suspense, I saw an opening through which to escape; but my father had just received a flat refusal in that quarter. The merchant to whom he applied in my behalf, acquainted with my brother's adventures, felt little anxious for another scion of the same hopeful stock.

This disappointment had soured my father's temper, and disposed him to visit on me the sins of my brother. Having begun my education at the wrong end, by leaving me every species of latitude, when he might easily have curbed my licentious disposition, he now gave it the finishing touch equally injudiciously, by trying, after my unbridled habits had become confirmed, to restrain me even in what I considered as reasonable freedom. I now was thwarted in every wish, deprived of every indulgence; and all this, apparently, for no other fault, except that from a chubby prattling child, to be hushed with toys and sweetmeats, I had not prevented myself from growing into a slouching, thoughtful youth, who too often demanded a supply of solid cash.

My mother, too, was to be an altered woman. The moment I no longer submitted to be fondled like a baby, she transferred her affections – against all rule and precedent – from me to the one among us, who had neither the claims of the youngest, nor of the eldest; – to Constantine. His hump had evidently operated the revolution in his favour; but whether, by making my mother wish to console him for this defect, or by causing her to consider him as endowed with an additional perfection, I never could make out. Certain it is that she used to gaze on his back as she before had done on my face, until her admiration sometimes put his own modesty to the blush.

Not habituated early enough to filial submission, I no sooner felt the weight of parental authority, than I began to question its justice; and, able to derive its rights only from the voluntary concession of the child, while its feebleness forces it to barter obedience for food, I considered its continuance beyond that period as an usurpation. Long, therefore, had I been meditating to seize some opportunity of eluding the parental yoke, even before I got entangled in the snares of love. The wound which my mistress inflicted on my pride, added new incentives to this resolution, and, after her mortifying speech, the only wish my mind was capable of forming was, to abandon father, mother, mistress, friends, relations and home for ever. Indeed, no way in which I might sever myself from Helena seemed to me unfair, when I considered the stamp of humiliating selfishness she had chosen to imprint upon my constancy.

My brain thus in a ferment, I entered the first tavern I found open; and though by no means addicted to intemperance, drank off draught after draught of our strongest wine, till the houses in the street seemed familiarly to nod to the ships in the harbour.

Among these latter lay in the road a Venetian brig, ready for its departure. While I sat pondering over my grievances the evening breeze sprung up, and the song of the sailors on board marked the heaving of the anchor. I accepted it as the summons for putting my design into execution. Running out of the house I was soon rowed to the vessel; and reached it just as the sails were unfurling. I offered my services to the captain. He had lost half his crew in his last Egyptian caravan:[14] but still would only receive me as a simple cabin boy. The office seemed little suited to the son of a drogueman, whose garment alone, I thought, should sweep the deck; but it was not a time to bargain, and I submitted. I crept into the hold among the ballast, until we should be out of reach of pursuit, and, when informed of my safety, jumped upon the deck, and ran to the stern to see what way we had made.

The moon was just rising in all her splendour, and a bar of silvery light shot along the spangled waves. The gradually increasing breeze rapidly carried us out of the straits of Chios. The different objects on the shore – mountains, valleys, villages, and steeples – seemed in quick succession first advancing to meet us, then halting an instant alongside our vessel as if to greet us on our passage, and, lastly, again gliding off with equal speed – till launched into the open main, we saw the whole line of coast gradually dissolve into distant darkness.

Various and opposite were the feelings which, as I stood contemplating the luminous track we left in the rippling wave, agitated my bosom; but, whatever direction I tried to give to my thoughts, they always reverted to Helena. In vain I sought to banish from my guilt-struck fancy her upbraiding image. As if in mockery of my endeavours, it seemed to assume a tangible shape. I persuaded myself I actually beheld the pale form of my mistress, half rising from the boisterous billows, follow with piteous moans the fleeting vessel, and call back her Anastasius to her outstretched arms. I wished I could have stayed the mighty mass, – could have converted the swiftly moving keel which hurried away my person and my fate into a solid motionless rock, – in order to enable the dear phantom to join me; or at least, in order to have a few instants more to reflect on my conduct, and to retract my errors, ere the opportunity should pass by for ever. In vain! I felt as if an uncontrollable force kept impelling me on, – and at last: "it is useless," I exclaimed, "to contend! I feel it; I must yield to my destiny: I must perform the things set down for me be they good, or be they evil!"

As the dawn began to dispel the dark visions of the night; as the sun rose in all his glory to pervade the blue expanse of the heavens, and the returning day showed Chios like a faint cloud floating on the utmost verge of the waters, my thoughts assumed a brighter hue; my heart felt the weight upon it lightened; and the idea that I now was going to explore those distant realms which I so long had yearned after, filled me with expectation and delight.

Yet even this new joy was mixed with a terror of its own. At no period in my life had I yet outstepped the narrow pale of my native island, or obtained so much as a peep at the nearest objects beyond the streights by which it was bounded. Crossing over to the neighbouring islets seemed to me a long voyage. Smyrna had been, in my imagination, the utmost limit of the habitable globe; and as to Europe, I deemed it to lie somewhere not far from the antipodes. The unbounded prospect of the whole wide world bursting all at once upon me, struck my young heart with awe; and the sight of nothing around me but strangers, utterly unknown, and indifferent to my fate, was sad and appalling.

Soon, however, I was recalled from these vague and indistinct reflections, by feelings more definite, and more immediately connected with my present situation. I had scarce closed my eyes, when the captain, not wishing that I should have unpleasant dreams, or any dreams at all, with a familiar tap on the shoulder, reminded me that it was time to begin earning my passage; and handed me over to the crew, to instruct me in my task. Mine were no longer indulgent teachers; and from being the little tyrant of my father's domestics, I now found myself the slave of every common sailor. While my companions – my masters I should say – sat down to their meals, I had to fast; and when they slept, I must watch. Their scanty leavings were my food, and it was only now and then that I could snatch from my constant toil a few moments of hurried and broken rest. Whatever awkwardness I shewed was followed by immediate blows; nay, it became a standing joke to call me to different places at once, that I might incur the punishment of unavoidable delay. My appeals to the mercy or justice of my comrades were treated with equal derision.

As I found it useless to complain, I stifled my feelings, and only kept watching an opportunity for escape or revenge. This made me particularly observant of all the manoeuvres of the captain; some of which seemed sufficiently strange. At times, for instance, when not a cloud was to seen in the sky, he would pretend to expect foul weather, and run for shelter under some lonely cliff, where he seemed more intent upon looking out for something on the water than in the air; and though he affected vast displeasure at the unceasing drunkenness of the crew, one could almost have sworn that he put flasks of brandy purposely in their way.

One evening, in a profound calm, and while all the sailors, drunk as fishes, were capering round a tall pole crowned with myrtle, a boatful of Maynote[15] pirates, concealed behind the rocks of Antiparos, stole unperceived under our stern, and climbed up by the poop into the cabin. The master, who just before had gone below on some errand, and had been seized in the midst of his business with a most unaccountable fit of sleeping, was soon laid hold of, and gagged. All the stand of arms, neatly arranged round the room, were next secured; and the pirates, now rushing upstairs, easily mastered the few among the sailors who were still able to stand upon their legs; while they had nothing to do but to bind hands and feet, the remainder, lying about the deck in a state of perfect insensibility.

Amid the general intoxication, I had been kept sober by my grief, and happened to stand near the cabin door, just when, at the window opposite, appeared the ugly features of the Maynotes, who was preparing to slip in. My figure caught his vigilant eye, as he advanced his head; when, drawing it back, he put his finger on his mouth, and frowned most formidable threats, should I disobey the sign. To this I felt not in the least inclined. I might indeed, by giving the alarm immediately, have saved the crew from the captain's treachery; but all had used me ill alike. I therefore answered the command by a gesture of ready compliance, and let things take their course.

In the beginning of the fray, the pirates affected to treat the captain very outrageously; but this appearance of enmity soon subsided, and by degrees they sat down amicably together, like old friends who understand each other's ways. Having so handsomely performed my neutral part in the business, I now was thinking to approach and put in my claim, if not for poundage, at least for hush-money, – when a new incident most provokingly blew up the well-concerted scheme.

It happened that just at this juncture, the famous Hassan Capitan-pasha[16] was in the act of delivering the Morea from its Arnaoot[17] oppressors. One of his caravellas,[18] stationed before Nauplia, by chance espied our doings, and immediately gave us chase. She soon obliged us to bring to; but, instead of liberating the vessel, treated her as a lawful prize. It is true that, while the Turks tied the pirates back to back, they only handcuffed the real owners. The captain shared the fate of his crew. Thus was poetical justice dealt out to all, except myself; and thus was I, hapless Greek, compelled, in the space of four days, to bear the yoke of four different nations – French, Venetians, Maynotes and Turks. Whether I gained by the last change, or only fell from Charybdis upon Scylla, I can only relate after I have premised a short account of the celebrated expedition, which I was so unexpectedly made to witness.

CHAPTER II

In the first war between the Russians and the Turks, the most natural proceeding for Russia, would have been, to attack Turkey from its southern frontier, where the two countries joined: – the most surprising was to send an armament from its northern extremity, whence the whole circumstance of Europe must be sailed round ere the Turks and the Muscovites could meet. This latter, therefore, was the measure preferred; and the Russian fleet had passed, in its progress, a whole winter at Leghorn, ere its commanders were determined in what part of Turkey to strike the first blow. The Greeks themselves decided the question for the avengers they expected. A few turbulent Codgea-bashees[1] of the Morea, fearing the lash of the Turkish governor, sent to the Russian commanders a forged plan of insurrection, as one already organised; and on the return of the deputation, employed the promise of Russian assistance thus fraudulently obtained, to produce the commotion they had described as already on the point of breaking out. Their labour was assisted by the Turks themselves. Suspecting a plot against them, these pusillanimous oppressors acted like men who, from the very fear of falling from a precipice, plunge headlong down the steep. In their panic they massacred a whole troop of Zaccuniote peasants, peaceably returning from a fair at Patras, whom they mistook for an army of rebels marching to attack them. The cry of revenge now resounded from all quarters; and when, therefore, in the spring of 1770, the Russian fleet cast anchor in the bay of Vitulo, its commanders were received by the bishops of Lacedemon[2] and of Christianopolis, followed by Greeks of all descriptions, only begging as a favour to enlist under the Russian banners. Fair as seemed this beginning, the understanding between the two nations was short-lived. The Greeks expected the Russians alone to accomplish the whole task of their deliverance. The Russians had laid their account with a powerful co-operation on the part of the Greeks. Each, alike disappointed, threw on the other the whole blame of every failure. Their squabbles gave large troops of Arnaoots time to pour from every neighbouring point of Roumili into the peninsula; and the Russian commanders, seeing all chance of success vanish in that quarter, sailed higher up the Archipelago, – leaving the Moreotes to their fate, and carrying away no other fruits of the momentary contact of Greeks and Russians, but an increase of rancour between the two nations, – too nearly allied in faith, not to feel to each other the most cordial aversion.

The ferocious mountaineers of Albania, who, under the name of Arnaoots form a chief part of the forces of the Othoman empire, and of the bodyguard of its various Pashas, present in their rugged and yet colourless countenances the greatest possible contrast to the regular features and rich complexions of the Greeks. In the faith of the two nations the difference is less marked. Wavering for the most part between Christ and Mohammed, the worship of the Arnaoots is generally determined by the master they serve; and many a buskined hero[3] who came on the spur of pay and plunder to assist the Moreote Moslemen against the Christians, himself professed the Christian faith. The total number of these savages was computed at about twenty thousand; and when their work was achieved, they demanded their wages. The money was wanting, or at least the pay was withheld. This furnished them with plausible pretence for disbanding on the spot, and paying themselves, by pillaging the country. Some, after laying waste the villages, drove the inhabitants before them, like herds of cattle, through the derwens or defiles that guard the entrance of the peninsula, and thus regained, with their new slaves, their native mountains. Others remained stationary in the Morea: by installing themselves in the houses and lands of the Greek peasantry, they deprived the soil of its husbandmen, and the Turks of their subjects; and at last, finding no more rayahs[4] to oppress, turned their violence against the Moslemen themselves, and treated like the vanquished those whom they had come to defend.

Nine following years had seen eleven governors arrive, one after the other, with the most peremptory instructions to exterminate the banditti, and again depart without succeeding; some for want of sufficient force to repress their outrages; others, it is said, for want of sufficient resolution to resist their bribes. At last the Porte sent Hassan.

By birth a Persian, by the fate of war a Turkish slave, by choice among the recruits yearly raised at Smyrna for the Barbary powers, and by his own merits advanced to the rank of Port-admiral of Algiers, Hassan-bey became at variance with the Dey. Justice was so entirely on his side that prudence urged his immediate flight. After many wanderings, he found a patron at Constantinople in the famous Raghib, Grand Visier[5] under two successive Sultans, and who has been permitted to die in his bed. In the memorable battle which the Russians, after abandoning the Morea, gave the Turks in the straits of Chios, he commanded the admiral-ship of the Turks, which was attacked by that of the Russians, while the two commanders, Khassim and Orlow, both kept with equal prudence aloof from the fight. Prevented by his instructions from unmooring, Hassan towed his ship on its anchors, boarded the Russian vessel, and, only when both hulks blown up together mingled their wrecks in the sky, sought his safety in the sea, and swam ashore.. The Sultan, seeing his navy annihilated, and himself threatened with bombardment in his Seraglio by a fleet from the Baltic, now named Hassan his Captain-pasha, – and was saved.

At the peace, this commander exerted himself to form a new navy, and to introduce among the Turks as much of the European tactics as their prejudices could bear. He had not very soon an opportunity to try the effect of his improvements against a foreign enemy; but in an empire so extensive as that founded by Othman, when age had enfeebled its head, some distant extremity will always refuse obedience and call for compulsory measures. Hassan constantly found in some quarter disturbances to quell. In 1776, he made the Arab Daher – usurper of the sovereignty of Acre – atone with his life for the league he had formed with the Egyptian rebel Aly. The year following he punished Daher's sons for continuing their father's rebellion; and finally in 1779, he received the Sultan's orders to expel from the Morea the refractory Arnaoots. Already was his army encamped in the plains of Argos, when one of the caravellas of his fleet stationed in the Bay of Nauplia conveyed our mixed party of Venetians and Maynotes to that port, where, with my companions, I was – unceremoniously enough – stowed away for the night under a strong guard in a crazy barn; wondering what was to be our fate the next morning.

The place of our confinement had long been the undisturbed domain of swarms of mosquitoes, who, ignorant of our unwillingness to trespass on their premises, seemed determined to resist the encroachment to the utmost. The constant buzzing and stings of these troublesome insects would alone have sufficed to deprive us of all chance of repose; add to which that, paired as we were according to the fancy of our guardians, and each closely connected with his immediate companion by very strongest tie of twisted hemp, the blows which each intended for his winged enemies in general only fell upon his pinioned associate. Excuses indeed followed, but were of little use in composing us to sleep. My other, but not my better half, in this forced union, suffered as much as myself, but seemed to be the person most endowed with philosophic resignation of our whole party. On my throwing out a few hints respecting the inconvenience of our bed chamber, the patient personage assured me I was fastidious. He had often seen worse apartments, and without the comfort of so much good company. This excited my curiosity; and, observing that it was impossible to think of sleeping, I entreated him to favour me with the description of some of those habitations, compared to which our present abode was such a fairy palace.

"And so you want," he cried, "to know my adventures? – Well! and why not? You are young, and seem of a promising disposition. My example and my precepts cannot fail to benefit your inexperience, and I will therefore this once do violence to my natural modesty, in order to gratify your wish for instruction. What in fact is the use of great achievements, but to tell them? Only let me entreat that your feeling heart may not be too deeply touched by the distressing tale of my ill rewarded virtues."

"My early years," continued the person with whom I was any thing but in *tête-à-tête*, "offer nothing remarkable. They were spent in the inglorious occupation of cultivating my paternal soil. I thought it rather hard upon me that, whether I sowed my field or let it lie fallow, and whether it was I that reaped its produce or the locusts, the waywode[6] should equally exact the same enormous tithe, should look upon the destruction of my crops by hail or tempests, as the mere effects of my own malice, and should seize upon my instruments of husbandry, in order to make me more industrious. I thought it harder still that, on hearing how the conflagration of my hovel had had consumed all my haratsh tickets[7] for some ten years back, he should demand the whole sum, already paid, over again; and I thought it hard beyond all bearing when, after a temporary absence, in order to save my dearly taxed poll, I should, on coming back with some money, laboriously scraped together, for the purpose of redeeming my person and property, find all my little patrimony confiscated to the profit of my tyrant, as a punishment for abandoning what I returned to. In my rage, I flung myself on the ground; with my teeth gnawed the earth, that I might at least carry away some morsel of my paternal inheritance; and swore to make every Mohammedan I could lay hands on, however innocent, pay for the murderous waywode."

"This oath brought me good fortune. I succeeded in sacrificing several victims to my just resentment; and as I chose by preference such as, being in good circumstances, had most to lose, I always made a point of retaining what I found about them, lest any Mussulmen should profit by my performance."

"Steadfast attention to this particular gave my task a double interest. The only individual I admitted to share with me, was the magistrate of the district; except, of course, where he himself happened to be the person stopped. Justice was much the gainer by this proceeding. Instead of the usual process of hanging a single individual, the cadee[8] generally fined the whole community, for not being able to produce the offender."

"I had a distant cousin at Zante, – the flower of the family, and so much admired by all ranks for his bravery, that people used to contend for his assistance in settling their affairs of honour. The nobleness of his sentiments equalled his courage. He only killed, as it were, to oblige his friends; and so nice were his feelings, where his character was concerned, that, on being paid one day before hand by a certain nobleman, to chastise another sprig of nobility, and, on mature deliberation, thinking the reward too ample for the service, he dispatched his man outright, and so quieted his scruples, to the great delight and surprise of his employer. But these too disinterested sentiments at last obliging him to quit Zante, where merit exites envy, he came and joined me at Patras. From that period we only went out in search of adventures together, like Theseus and Pirithous, Orestes and Pylades, and all the other worthies of old, whom my cousin had at his fingers' ends; and astonishing was the number of monsters of which we rid the world, not only above ground but under: for one night, in a cellar, we killed half a dozen Arnaoots, lying dead drunk on the spoils of our country; and that, without any body the next day being the wiser, thinking but that the scoundrels had done the deed themselves, in a frolic. Never did we take a fellow's booty, whom we did not also rid of his life. To do otherwise would have been tempting Providence, and was against my oath. My conscience being thus kept clear of premeditated sin, and my mind regularly unburthened, by confession, of unintentional offences, I continued to prosper, until justice, entirely disregarding gratitude, chose maliciously to turn against me. In disgust, I joined some Dulcignotes, who, with the help of Algerine colours, avoided some awkwardness in taking Christian vessels. I myself had now begun to consider religious prejudices as unworthy of a liberal mind, and to view all men as equal before God. What right had I to indulge in partialities founded upon my own fallible judgement? – On this principle I no longer made a difference between Turks and Christians, and most conscientiously treated both alike. Still, such is the force of habit, that I own I always felt a particular zest in stripping an heretic. To this moment, my mouth waters at the thoughts of the broad-bottomed Hollander, full of the richest spice and dainties, which I once helped to unload. Its crew had not – the reprobate wretches! – a single image of a saint on board; and accordingly they only went, with the wind right astern, at the rate of two knots an hour; but the idols of their heart seemed to be their short black tobacco-pipes. Even when chucked into the sea, they kept puffing on, as long as their blubber-cheeks remained above water. Their cargo set me up for a while, until fresh misfortunes led back the way to my old trade. The greatest piece of ill luck I reckon to have been my partnership with our present captain. Had I foreseen the bungler he would prove, I should have carried my wits to a better market. But no matter! – The most laudable intentions are sometimes defeated; and a little rub disconcerts not Panayoti."

Highly edified with the incidents of this worthy man's history, and still more with his candid and unassuming manner of relating them, I almost regretted that the dawn should so soon, through the chinks of the wall, break in upon his artless and unvarnished tale, to announce a speedy change of scene. In fact, very soon after, the doors of our saloon were thrown open, and our party called out to be formed into marching order. The separate pairs, connected together by a thick rope into a single body, of small width but of handsome length, were thus made to add to the beauty of distinctness of parts, that of unity of whole; all set in motion by the simple mechanism of a kick bestowed on the rear of the foremost pair, immediately advanced, guided by a few spahees[9] before, while others followed behind. Argos was the place of our destination, and in less than four hours our column reached Hassan's camp, scattered over the whole plain. Not only all the troops of the province had flocked round the commander's standard, but several Greeks even had obtained permission to join the Turks against those very Arnaoots whom, some years before, the Turks had called in to save them from the Greeks.

I had never seen an encampment, and the novel and striking sight absorbed all my faculties in astonishment and awe. I thought I beheld forces sufficient to subdue the whole world; and I knew not which most to admire, the endless clusters of tents, the enormous piles of armour, and the rows of threatening cannon, which I met at every step, or the troops of well mounted spahees, who, like dazzling meteors, darted by us on every side, amid clouds of stifling dust. The very dirt with which they bespattered us seemed to me imposing; and every thing upon which I cast my eyes, gave me a feeling of nothingness, which made me shrink within myself like a snail in its shell. I envied not only those who were destined to share in all the glory and success of the expedition, but even the meanest follower of the camp, as a being of superior order to myself; and when suddenly there arose a loud flourish of trumpets, which, ending in a concert of cymbals and other war-like instruments, re-echoed in long peals from the surrounding mountains, the clang shook every nerve in my body, thrilled me to the very soul, and infused in all my veins a species of martial ardour so resistless, that it made me struggle with my fetters, and try to tear them asunder. Proud as I was by nature, I would have knelt to whoever had offered to liberate my limbs, and to arm my hands with sword or a battle-axe.

The tumult of my senses had not yet subsided, when, leaving the camp on our right, we were ushered into the court of a small habitation, in the town of Argos, there to undergo an interrogatory from Hassan's drogueman. Fixtures as we were under the azure canopy of the heavens, the sundials on our faces had time to shift their shadows from right to left before a gentleman came. At last he arrived.

How widely things often appear in reality, that bear the same names! In the drogueman of the Capitan-Pasha, I had figured to myself a personage nearly of the same stamp with the consular interpreter at Chios, who had the honour of being my father. I might as well have compared a wren to an eagle. The individual of the Tergiumanic genius, before whom I now stood, came with the state of a little prince, and seemed surrounded by a miniature court of his own. When he spoke his attendants only answered in a whisper: at his slightest commands they flew as if the fate of the whole empire were at stake; and when he smiled at a joke of his own, they all shook with laughter. As his movements were abrupt, and often eccentric, it was amusing to see them scamper after him, trying to keep close to his heels, and not to be thrown out of their ranks by his vagaries.

From what cause it so happened I know not, but the moment this great man addressed our captain, who stood first and foremost of our troop, his eye fell upon me, though one of the very last in the column; and from that time forward he never more changed the object of his attention. For the space of half a second or so, indeed, he might glance at the intervening individuals who he successively interrogated; but, uniformly, after addressing two or three words to them, his eyes again began to wander, to seek something further off, and when they found me, they fixed themselves with their former steadfastness upon my humble person. My business was to have looked away from so exalted a personage, or to have modestly dropped my eyelids on the ground, as if I durst not encounter his sublime aspect. But this I attempted at in vain. As if under a fascination, I scarce could keep myself from gazing on him with the same steadiness with which he perseveringly eyed me. I felt as if my future was to depend on his nod.

At last came my turn to speak. Questioned respecting my birth, parentage, country, cause of absence from home and other topics, I told my little tale with tolerable ease as well as veracity, and my candour particularly shone in my strictures on the captain, who had not perhaps yet had so impartial and so observant a biographer. My recital amused, and when finished: "You little Greek rascal," exclaimed the drogueman, "you will corrupt all these worthy Roman Catholics, if I leave you among them; so I'll keep you here, and let them go home, to swing on St. Mark's after their own fashion." With this compliment my companions were dismissed. They slunk away, muttering some curses, which, under the drogueman's mighty wing, I could afford to disregard.

Mavroyeni belonged to the most distinguished family in the island of Paros. He had from a child felt a spirit too expansive tamely to brook the restraint of his confined birth place. The restlessness of his temper was increased by the predictions of a priest of Sant-Irene, – one who foretold so much, that it was impossible but something, now and then, must fall out as he predicted. Fixing his eye on the little taooshan:[10] "Young man," cried he, as if inspired; "brilliant will be thy career; but may thy end be happy!" The first part of this two-fold oracle gave an additional stimulus to the youth's ambition, the latter a new motive to his parents for checking its sallies: but, like other predictions, the one in question at last worked its own accomplishment. When Hassan Capitan-Pasha made the harbour of Drio in the island of Paros the summer station of his squadron, in its yearly cruise through the Archipelago, young Mavroyeni threw himself so frequently in his way, so anxiously implored his accepting an entertainment from his father, and so successfully paid his court to the commander, as to obtain the promise of his protection at Constantinople. Upon this he immediately went forth, plunged headlong into all the intrigues of the Fanar,[11] and through his own dexterity, and the patronage of the High-

Admiral, in less than three years supplanted Argiropoli, the old and long respected drogueman of the navy. He soon contrived to give his new situation an importance which it never yet had known. Former droguemen were nothing more than interpreters and spokesmen, even to the most imbecile and stupid of commanders. To the most energetic and quicksighted of Pashas whom the Turkish navy yet had obeyed, Mavroyeni became an adviser and a friend. The lion at whose roar Moselmen trembled, showed with the subtle Greek the meekness of a lamb; and even when, informed of his interpreter's unlawful transactions, Hassan for a moment felt his anger rise, and swore that he would cut off the head that thus mocked his commands, Mavroyeni's appearance was sufficient to turn his wrath into complacency, and to draw down new favours on that head just devoted to destruction. Every outrage of Mavroyeni on the laws, and on the habits of the Turks, only seemed to increase his influence with his patron; and the Greeks, still as prone as of old to ascribe each strange effect to some supernatural cause, ceased wondering at the drogueman's sway, only to wonder at the drugs of which he composed his philtre.

CHAPTER III

Received among the suite of the important Tergiuman[1] aforesaid, I was soon made to exchange my miserable tarred jacket of a sailor, for the ample benish[2] of finest broadcloth, the first mark of my promotion; but I could not help regretting the loss of my "raven" locks, indifferently replaced, in the owner's opinion, by the short black lamb's wool of a clumsy calpack.[3] I swore I would some day, cost what might, doff my uncouth headdress for one of those smart turbans of gilt brocade, worn with such a saucy air over one ear by the Pasha's Tshawooshes,[4] – gentlemen who were seen every where, lounging about as if they had nothing to do but to display their handsome legs, their vests stiff with gold lace, and their impudent bullying faces.

I had confidently expected that my first apprenticeship in my new service would have been to the use of the carbine and the sabre. Great, therefore, was my mortification when instead of learning to shoot an enemy, or to cut down a rebel, I had to practise carrying a coffee-pot, or presenting a tobacco-pipe: and once, when a young fellow attendant displayed his wit in jokes on my awkwardness, my wrath waxed so high, that I thrust the lighted pipe head foremost into his grinning mouth, and made his pert tongue smart for its petulance. An oldish mild looking man, a privileged domestic, who, having served his time out, now earned his salary as a sort of pedagogue to the new comers, witnessed the act, and took me aside.

"Listen, young man," said he, "whether you like it or not. For my own part, I have always had too much indolence, not to make it my study throughout life rather to secure ease than to labour for distinction. It has therefore been my rule to avoid cherishing in my patron any outrageous admiration of my capacity, which would have increased my dependence while it lasted, and exposed me to persecution on wearing out: but you, I see, are of different mettle; I therefore may point to you the surest way to that more perilous height, short of which your ambition I doubt will not rest satisfied. When you have compassed it, you may remember old Demo, if you please.

"Know first that all masters, even the least lovable, like to be loved. All wish to be served from affection rather than duty. It flatters their pride, and it gratifies their selfishness. They expect from this personal motive a greater devotion to their interest, and a more unlimited obedience to their commands. A master looks upon mere fidelity in his servant as his due, – as a thing scarce worth his thanks: but attachment he considers as a compliment to his merit, and, if at all generous, he will reward it with liberality. Mavroyeni is more open than anybody to this species of flattery. If he speak to you kindly, let your face brighten up. If he talk to you of his own affairs, though it should only be to dispel the tedium of conveying all day long other men's thoughts, listen with the greatest eagerness. A single yawn, and you are undone! Yet let not curiosity appear your motive, but the delight only of being honoured with his confidence. The more you appear grateful for the least kindness, the oftener you will receive important favours. Our ostentatious drogueman will feel a pleasure in raising your astonishment. His vanity knows no bounds. Give it scope therefore. When he comes home choking with its supposed ebullitions, be their ready and patient receptacle: – do more; discreetly help him on in venting his conceit; provide him with a cue; hint what you have heard certain people, not knowing you to be so near, say of his capacity, his merit, and his influence. He wishes to persuade the world that he completely rules the Pasha. Tell him not flatly he does, but assume it as a thing of general notoriety. Be neither too candid in your remarks, nor too fulsome in your flattery. Too palpable deviations from fact might appear a satire on your master's understanding. Should some disappointment evidently ruffle his temper, appear not to conceive the possibility of his vanity having received a mortification. Preserve the exact medium between too cold a respect, and too presumptuous a forwardness. However much Mavroyeni may caress you in private, never seem quite at ease with him in public. A master still likes to remain master, or at least, to appear so to others. Should you get into some scrape, wait not to confess your imprudence, until concealment becomes impossible; nor try to excuse the offence. Rather than you should, by so doing, appear to make light of your guilt, exaggerate your self-upbraidings, and throw yourself entirely upon the drogueman's mercy. On all occasions take care how you appear cleverer than your lord, even in the splitting of a pen: or if you cannot avoid excelling him in some trifle, give his tuition all the credit of your proficiency. Many things he will dislike, only because they come not from himself. Vindicate not your innocence when unjustly rebuked: rather submit for the moment; and trust that, though Mavroyeni never will expressly acknowledge his error, he will in due time pay you for your forbearance."

As it was not "a single yawn" with which I answered this long speech, good old Demo vouchsafed to spare me its sequel; but, though I thanked not my adviser, I took care in due time to profit from his advice.

Mavroyeni's situation subjected him to a species of persecution which almost unbalanced the pleasure – great as it was – of beholding the proudest Agas of the country daily cringe at his levee, perhaps more lowly than at that of the Pasha himself. It was the annoyance of being visited by all his relations and kindred, from every island in the Archipelago, far and near, large and small. He had not, in the remotest corner of the Levant, a cousin in the fiftieth degree, known or unknown, whom the fame of his favour drew not out of his den to Argos, for the purpose of sharing in the good things which it was supposed the drogueman had nothing to do but to give for the asking; and relationships, before dormant or wholly obliterated, were now brought to light, and supported by oral and written proof, so as sometimes absolutely to confound even his not easily shaken sturdiness. Nor could these anxious kinsfolks and friends be made to comprehend why the particular time when Mavroyeni went forth into public, or was surrounded by his whole court, should not be the very best for bustling up to their cousin, and roaring out their claims, or reminding him of their former intimacies. All day long they beset the drogueman's door when he was at home, or lay in ambush for him when he went out; and so great became at last the persecution, that at every new disembarking at Nauplia, he used to be seized with a fit of the ague.

There is a danger in doing things too well. What was first volunteered as an extraordinary feat, is soon assigned as an every day task. I once happened to dismiss one of these troublesome visitors too dexterously; and from that time it became my regular office. The appointment, it is true, could not be in better hands. Without troubling the drogueman for particular instructions, or annoying him with awkward messages, painful to the delicacy of a man who would rather have been thought only allied to Jove, I knew at once when a new face presented itself at the door, by its cut and dimensions, whether it could conveniently be suffered to pass the threshold or not; and on finding it either too long or too wide, or too red or too shining, or otherwise inadmissible or questionable, I resolutely defended the pass committed to my care, was as formidably repulsive as Cerberus himself, and minded not even a little scuffle in the cause: sure of never being taxed by my master for disrespect to his blood. Hence it happened that once or twice, on the drogueman's expressing a fear that certain of these visitors might call, I had the pleasure to inform him that they had called, and would call no more; after which, whenever a stranger was announced, the answer, "Let Anastasius go to him," was quite sufficient to explain the reception he was to meet with, and the way his importunities were to be treated.

By thus anticipating my master's sentiments, I rose to such a degree of favour that often, having in public caused Turks of the highest rank to stare at his haughtiness, he would in private put his humble cafedjee[5] in no fear but from his excess of familiarity; for frequently it left me almost unable to bear in mind the old preceptor's caution, and to refrain from overstepping my station. One evening, after one conversation, "Anastasius," said the drogueman, "I told the Pasha to-day what a graceless stripling I had picked up. He will see you tomorrow."

A person so terrible as this Pasha, and who so filled the world with the mere sound of his name, must, I thought, equal Homer's heroes in size. I estimated his stature at the least at eight feet; and accordingly, when ushered into his presence, kept looking up at the ceiling till I nearly fell over a little man squatted on the floor, whom I only recognised by the commotion which my heedlessness excited, as the formidable Hassan. I knew not whether the Pasha felt nettled at the abruptness of my approach or had been discomposed before; but when, ready to sink into the ground with dismay, I stepped back to repair my blunder, and kiss the hem of his garment, he no more heeded me than the dust of his feet which I respectfully brought to my forehead. Mavroyeni soon perceived that the moment was inauspicious, and made me a sign to withdraw. I immediately slunk away.

There is something in my nature which revolts at every act of humiliation performed towards a fellow creature. Nothing but the extreme kindness of Mavroyeni could reconcile me to my servile situation; and his indulgence had made me expect equal caresses from Hassan himself: "I only stoop," thought I, when appearing before him, "to rise the higher." But when I found myself left in the dust, in which I had been cringing, without gaining any thing by my submission but a contemptuous look, how deep in my heart sunk the mortification! Scarce could I contain myself while hurrying out of the room. On the very threshold I burst into a flood of tears.

Fresh constraint, however, soon again became necessary. My fellow attendants, to whom I had been boasting of my summons, were all waiting in a row, to know the result of my visit. Lest its luckless termination should make them too happy, I had to convert my sobs into smiles, at the inexpressible graciousness of my reception.

The principal tribes of the rebellious Arnaoots, the Beckiarees, established to the number of about ten thousand in the very capital of Morea, kept its governor, Mehemet Pasha, as some supposed, a willing prisoner. Hassan, ere he engaged in actual hostilities, once more offered them, on condition of immediately quitting the country, an unqualified pardon; but the hardened banditti, whether confiding in their numbers or other less apparent means of averting the blow, rejected all compromise, intrenched themselves under the walls of the city, and bade defiance to the Pasha's forces.

Probably they expected to awe him by this show of resolution. They were deceived. On the tenth of June, about noon, Hassan set out with four thousand picked men for Tripolizza, and continued on the march the whole night. Mavroyeni followed the Pasha, and I followed Mavroyene. In my capacity of Greek, and still more of cafadjee, I had not the least hope of personally contending with the foe, and all my solace was the chance of a sly thrust at some run-away, But my master, desirous to let me have my share of all the good things that offered, after whispering something in the Pasha's ear, suddenly turned round to me: "Anastasius," he cried, "I have obtained his highness's permission for you to shoulder a musket, and to join in the fight, like an Osmanlee."[6]

The favour, no doubt, was inestimable; but its suddenness somewhat confounded me. I felt, however, that I must seem delighted, and though with something of a flutter about my heart, endeavoured to look all joy in the face. In order to confirm my assurance of unutterable satisfaction, I kept singing all the way, – though, now and then, perhaps, a little out of tune. But let it be recollected what I was: – a Greek, in whose unlicensed hand a musket had been deemed, until that moment, a sacrilege, and who had only learnt by stealth to take aim at a sparrow.

I shall therefore not attempt to deny that when the early dawn showed in front of our column, between ourselves and Tripolizza, at the distance of a few hundred yards the whole Albanese encampment, my stout heart began to beat; and that when, the next moment, I heard Hassan give orders for the charge, breath seemed for a moment to forsake my frame. Shame, however, supplied the place of bravery. The danger which I could not avoid I determined not to think of; and, following the example of the more experienced warriors around me, I swallowed in a hurried manner several copious draughts of a certain nameless liquor, which, on particular occasions, the High-admiral wisely allowed himself to distribute among his followers; whereupon, whether it be that the inspiring potation did its duty, or that courage is infectious like cowardice, my heart, the very moment before almost sunk to my heels, rebounded with such energy, that in its ebullitions of bravery, I could scarce refrain from breaking from the ranks, and engaging some hero of the adverse party in single combat, even before the line was formed; – and when the trumpet sounded the charge, when the onset began, and the whole body of cavalry at once rushed forward, causing the earth to shake under the horses' hoofs, such grew my delirium, that I scarce saw, heard, or felt; much less had senses to think.

Mavroyeni had taken care to confide his cafedjee, excellently mounted, to a trusty spahee, whose side he enjoined me not to quit. But at that moment not heaven itself could have prevented my giving the reins to my warlike spirit. The cloud of smoke which arose soon baffling the vigilance of my guardian, I gave him the slip, and spurring my steed with all my might, at once plunged into the thickest of the fray. There, finding the loading of my pistols too tedious a process, I began hacking and hewing with my yatagan;[7] – consoling myself for any mistake I might make in the objects of my ire, with the thought that my blows never could fall amiss, where all alike were enemies to Christianity, and oppressors of the Greeks. If upon this principle I hit one or two of our men, too much engaged to heed whence came the compliment, I made amends by cutting down as grim an Arnaoot as ever wore red whiskers, in the very act of measuring one of our saphees for a back-handed blow; and by this feat, so happily timed, and more happily observed, gained prodigious credit. It elated me to such a degree, that, thinking myself quite invulnerable, I was going next to rush headlong amidst the only little knot of Lalleotes which still maintained its ground, – when my guardian, again catching a glimpse of my person, grasped me by the arm, and, spite of my despair at not seeing the end of the affair in which I had taken such an active part, began dragging me away: but the rout of the Arnaoots becoming decisive just at that very moment, he listened to the entreaties of those who had witnessed my behaviour, and again let me go. I darted forward like an arrow from the bow, and gave chase to the now dispersing foe.

Foremost in the attack, I was soon foremost in the pursuit. Among the Albanians flying before us like chaff before the wind two particularly caught my eye, while apart from the rest they sought concealment behind a small patch of furzes. Steadfastly watching their progress, and tracing their route by the motion of the bushes, I left the rest of the troop, to follow this promising scene. Fortunately my fugitives, instead of turning short upon me to punish my imprudence, in their panic only pushed forward, until the hindmost getting entangled among the briars, presented his side to the contents of my carbine, and bit the dust; while the other only ran the faster for his comrade's groans.

My great ambition had been to take a prisoner, – to possess a slave. I therefore left the disabled man, as secure, to his own meditations, and with my biggest voice called on his companion to surrender. Luckily he did not even look round at the stripling who addressed him; but presently, leaping down a little eminence, disappeared in a thicket, where I thought it prudent to give up the hazardous chase.

I now returned to the fellow whom I had left writhing on the ground, apparently at the last gasp; and when sufficiently near, lest there should still lurk about him some latent spark of life, which might only wait to spend itself in a last home thrust, swiftly sprung forward, and for fear of foul play, put an extinguisher upon it, ere I ventured to take any other liberties with his person. This done, I deliberately proceeded to the work of spoliation. With a hand all trembling with joy, I first took the silver mounted pistols, and glittering poniard, and costly yatagan; I next collected the massy knobs of the jacket, and clasps of the buskins, and still more valuable sequins lying perdue in the folds of the sash; and lastly, feeling my appetite for plunder increase in proportion as it was gratified, thought it such a pity to leave any part of so showy an attire a prey to corruption, that I undressed the dead man completely.

When, however, the business which engaged all my attention was entirely achieved, and that human body, of which, in the eagerness for its spoil, I had only thus far noticed the separate limbs one by one, as I stripped them, all at once struck my sight in its dimensions, as it lay naked before me – when I contemplated that fine athletic frame, but moment before full of life and vigour unto its fingers' ends, now rendered an insensible corpse by the random shot of a raw youth whom in close combat its little finger might have crushed, I could not help feeling, mixed with my exultation, a sort of shame, as if for a cowardly advantage obtained over a superior being; and in order to make a kind of atonement to the shade of an Epirote – of a kinsman – I exclaimed with outstretched hands, "Cursed be the paltry dust, which turns the warrior's arm into a mere engine, and striking from afar an invisible blow, carries death no one knows whence, to no one knows whom; levels the strong with the weak, the brave with the dastardly; and, enabling the feeblest hand to wield its fatal lightning, makes the conqueror slay without anger, and the conquered die without glory!"

On the very point of departing after this sort of expiatory effusion, with my heavy but valuable trophy huddled on my back, the thought struck me that I might incur a suspicion of sporting plumes not my own, unless I brought my vouchers. With that view I began detaching from my Arnaoot's shaggy skull both the ears, as pledges for the remainder of the head, when I should be at leisure to collect it; but considering how many gleaners stalked the harvest field, and that if I lost my own head, none other might be found to make me amends, I determined to take at once all I meant to keep. The work was a tough one, and the operator at best still a bungler, but I succeeded at last; – and, now, in an ecstacy of delight, though almost afraid to look at my bundle, I returned to our party – for ever cured, by an almost instantaneous transition to temerity, of every sentiment of fear. Indeed such remained for some time the ferment of my spirits, that, while I carried my load on one arm, I kept brandishing my sword with the other, still eager to lay about me, and to cut down whomsoever I met.

My master, – already informed of my prowess, and on the look-out for my return, – seeing me arrive thus fierce and turbulent, immediately cried out: "Bravo, Anastasius! At your first outset, you are become a complete hero. – But," added he, laughing, "since the fight is over, and the enemy routed, suppose you put up your sword, and wash your face!'

The advice was seasonable. I had in the heat of the engagement received, I knew not how, a cut across the jaw, of which the scar remains to this day, and shows a shining white ridge across my strong black beard.

The head[8] which, in imitation of my companions, I laid before the Pasha, he only treated it as a football; – an usage which made me feel vexed for its dignity and my own: but when the whole harvest was got in, he ordered the produce to be built into the base of a handsome pyramid. The remaining Arnaoots of the peninsula, cut off at the dervens, afterwards supplied its top, and thus afforded the inhabitants of Tripolizza a most agreeable vista, which they enjoy to this day. One of our men, indeed, attempted to keep back from the common store a skull of his own collecting, meaning to turn it into a drinking cup for private use: but the Pasha severely censured an idea "so disgraceful," he observed, "to a civilised nation like the Turks;" and was near making its author, in punishment for his offence, contribute to the building materials from his own stock. As for myself, when I came to offer my mite, I found the same Hassan, before so supercilious, all condescension. Bravery was for him the first of virtues: some said the only one! – Mine he paid in ready money, with a handful of sequins; adding: "You are a lad of spirit; and if you will but become a true believer, you may rely on me for promotion."

At this flattering offer, my heart rose to my lips. At once I would have answered: "Moslemin, or heathen, or whatever your highness pleases!" – but a look from my master stopped my complying speech. I read in it a positive prohibition, and durst not disobey. Prostrating myself on the ground, I begged the Pasha would command his servant anything but to renounce his precious faith. This behaviour had the good luck not to displease the Visier, and much to gratify the interpreter. It entirely gained me the heart of a nephew of Mavroyeni, his uncle's agent, named Stephan; – a man who was said to keep his accounts between this world and the next much more even than his older relation. Indeed, so little had the drogueman the reputation of being tenacious on the score of religion, that I could not refrain from asking him, the first instant we were alone together, "why he should thus have stood in the way of his servant's fortune?"

"You fool," was his answer, "I only stood in the way of your ruin. Had you accepted the High-admiral's proposal, you would immediately have received some inferior appointment, and in that you would have been left to waste the remainder of your life. Your first promotion would have been your last. Despised by the Turks and shunned by the Greeks, you would have found support nowhere; and must henceforth have lived not only degraded, but, what is worse, forgotten. Has it never struck you," added he in a whisper, and as afraid of being overheard, "that if much were to be gained by a Christian turning Moslemin, there are others beside yourself sufficiently reasonable not to stick at the difference between Kyrie eleison, and Allah, Illah, Allah?[9]

This observation set all reply at defiance. I laid by my sword, and resumed my coffee-tray.

The interior of the Morea being liberated from the Albanians, Hassan determined to spend the remainder of the season in clearing its seas of the Maynotes. A strong detachment was sent with instructions to force the passes of mount Taygetus, the abode of those miscreants; and our encampment was in the mean time removed from the plain of Argos to that of Nauplia. Precisely the small slip of this otherwise delightful valley which is closest to the city, and extends under the tremendous rock of the Palamida, had, by the sea water constantly oozing in, been rendered a swamp, vying for noxious exhalations with the opposite morass of Lerna. Hassan, while waiting the issue of the expedition to Mayno, resolved, without knowing much of the garden of the Hesperides, to make this pestilential nook its fac-simile, – and, by the way of restoring to their pristine innocence and purity the somewhat deteriorated minds of his Arnaoot prisoners, had them conveyed on shore every morning, chained two and two, to forward this rural design. Hands that never yet had wielded any thing but weapons of war and destruction, were now reluctantly seen to grasp instruments of peace and husbandry, and to exchange the sword and the carbine for the rake and the spade; and men only accustomed to cut and clip human limbs, gnashed their teeth with rage, at being compelled to prune orange-trees, and to tie up carnations.

Like other distinguished personages, Hassan had his enemies in the capital. They represented his attempt on the impregnable fastnesses of Mayno as a mad scheme; they ceased not to inveigh against his extortions: but the crime they dwelt upon with peculiar eloquence and pathos, was his atrocity in employing Mohammedan captives to lay out his vile shrubberies; and one morning that Hassan, in the midst of his works, was inhaling in copious streams the incense of his courtiers vying in compliments on his taste, came a fulminating hatti-sherif from the Porte, to enjoin the immediate liberation of all his prisoners, and the return of his squadron to Constantinople.

Vain would be the attempt to paint the Pasha's rage. Striking his forehead with the imperial mandate, he swore he would obey its commands – would deliver his prisoners from their bondage: but only in death! and ordered them to be marshalled for immediate execution. The signal was given; and at each waving of his hand fell a head. Every beholder looked aghast, but none durst breathe even a syllable of intercession for the victims. Fifteen heads already lay gasping amid the parterres which their wearers had planted; and seemed only a prelude to the fall of as many hundreds: when Mavroyeni at last stepped forward, and, throwing himself at his master's feet, begged he would have mercy, not on the culprits, who deserved their fate, but on his own innocent lilies and jasmines, which had done nothing to deserve being deluged in blood, instead of moistened only by the dews from heaven.

Perhaps the Pasha himself had already begun to reflect, not on the cruelty of his conduct, but on its consequences; – perhaps he was not sorry for an excuse to desist from his rash vow. His jocularity, between each new act of the disgusting spectacle, might only in reality be intended to slacken the progress of the slaughter. The flowers were pitied, the massacre stopped, the garden abandoned, and the not yet pollarded Arnaoots conveyed to the passes out of the Morea, there to be turned loose upon the reminder of the Turkish empire.

By the sacrifice of a few of the purses which he had collected, Hassan still obtained leave only to resign the command of the Morea to Hadgee Ibrahim, his own kehaya:[10] a man who, in turns pilgrim at Mecca, chief of banditti in Roumili,[11] slave-merchant on the Black Sea, and soldier at the Dardanelles, was by no means the Pasha's unapt representative; but who nevertheless was only allowed to succeed him with the subordinate rank of Moohassil,[12] – the exhausted state of the Peninsula disabling it from supporting, in a governor, the burthensome weight of the three tails.

The news of the entire failure of the Maynote expedition became the signal for our departure. In my impatience to behold the capital I had been counting the days and hours till we should sail, and had been frightened by many a report of our wintering at Nauplia. Inexpressible therefore was my joy when, on the fifteenth of November 1779, I actually saw the anchors heaving, and the sails unfurled.

Behold me now at sea a second time, not like the first on board a paltry trading vessel, only surrounded by tarred sailors, and myself toiling like a galley slave, but in a superb three-decker – a positive moving city on the waves; basking in the sunshine of a vizier of the first class; viewing, whichever way I turned my eyes, glittering officers and guards; and having nothing myself to do but to wonder at all I saw. This I did abundantly. Not a hole or corner of the vessel was left unexplored; and, though, exceedingly wroth on board the Venetian at being obliged to bear a part in working the ship, which I then thought an intolerable drudgery, I here, on the contrary, from being very much discouraged by the sailors in my attempts to assist them, found no pleasure so great; and was constantly lending a hand in setting the sails, bracing the yards, and imitating like a monkey all I saw others do. Frequently, when my master sent for me to my berth below, I was up in the main top; and I seldom came down from this favourite station, except to listen open-mouthed on the carriage of a gun to the glowing descriptions of the wonders and delights of the capital – the city by pre-eminence – which some one or other of my companions was constantly praising. It seemed to me, though the wind continued unabatingly fair, that we never were to reach this earthly paradise.

On one occasion indeed the current of my thoughts, thus far uninterruptedly directed towards Stambool,[13] experienced a sudden stop, a total reflux. The intellectual tide, till then only flowing in one direction, at once ebbed, and set the contrary way. It was when we came in sight of my native land, of my beloved Chios. While rapidly sailing before the wind along its verdant shores, a pang shot to my heart, – an indescribable yearning seized upon my soul. At the back of that ridge of purple crags which I could almost touch with my hand, lived my aged parents; lived, sighed – perhaps, sighed no longer – my injured Helena, the first loved of my heart! Were not the rocky screen betwixt, I might actually at that instant behold their now melancholy homes, and less than an hour, I might restore the mourning tenants to their wonted serenity. I might receive and bestow the embraces of love and of duty; I might again possess the united blessings of those whom I had so cruelly abandoned: I might tell them. "Anastasius has fought, Anastasius has vanquished, Anastasius returns to you. He returns to deposit at your adored feet, and to sacrifice to your love and your pardon, the laurels he has gathered, and the praises and promises he has gained." "Now is," thought I – "but soon irretrievably to vanish – the moment in which to recover kindred, country, peace of mind, and connubial happiness. If again cast away, they must be lost for ever!"

Frantic at this thought, I hastily left the deck, and hurried to the drogueman, to entreat that I might be put ashore, and allowed to return among my friends.

On what trifling circumstances depends the fate of our lives! Had I felt less anxious, I should have succeeded: I should have reached my master's presence, have preferred my petition, have obtained my suit, have been reinstated in my filial privileges, and probably at this time have been the happy father of a numerous progeny, with the soothing prospect of a tranquil and respected old age.

A nail-head made the difference! – A nail-head causes me, by remote consequences, at the distance of many years, to die in a strange land a premature and painful death, unowned by a friend, unwept by a child! This unfortunate iron (on which may lie all my sins) not being sufficiently clenched, protruded most unwarrantably from the steps of the cabin. Several times already it had caught my flowing dress; and each time condemned to decapitation, it had only been reprieved from sheer thoughtlessness. In the eagerness of the moment, I hooked it with my shaksheer,[14] as I ran down stairs, and losing my balance, fell, and struck my skull against the floor of the cabin.

Senseless from the shock, I only recovered to find myself lying on the deck, with my head in the lap of one of the Pasha's tshawooshes. The first thing upon which my eyes opened was the officer's vest, – one of those gorgeous specimens of embroidery, which I had so greedily coveted, and had so fully determined some day to obtain: the first thing I heard was a condescending message of inquiry from the Pasha himself! So much glare dazzled my senses; so great an honour overpowered my weak brain. For some time, indeed, I scarce could remember what had occupied my thoughts prior to my accident. All in my mind was confusion and darkness; and when I again began with some clearness to retrace my ideas, the contact was too immediate with one species of object near my heart, not to feel the attractions of other more distant treasures, weak in comparison. It now seemed to me a womanly act to cast away all the fruit of the perils I had past, of the reputation I had gained, and of the favour I had earned; – to exchange the fame and greatness that awaited me, for obscurity and oblivion; to prefer to the destinies of the eagle, soaring from region to region, those of the worm, content to die in the same clod of clay in which he was born, and perhaps crushed to death before his time, by the more bold and aspiring. I knew I should be laughed at by all on board, only for hinting such a whim; and, on further reflection, I even felt it a filial duty to seek at Constantinople that rank, which might be so powerful a protection to my parents on their little island.

Still, however, some inward doubt remained. As soon as I was able to move, I rose, and ran to the side of the ship, to see what way she had been making since my accident, and whether there still was time to execute my design. Chios had already dwindled away into a scarce visible speck. The magnet ceased to act; my lately excited feelings subsided, and my no longer distracted mind gradually resumed its former hopes, its vanities, and its ambition. Its current again, as before, only flowed whether our prow was tending. Stambool again became, as before, its polar star; – and if some natural regrets still arose in my mind at intervals, the new and bustling scene which ensued, during the few days we lay at anchor before Mitylene and Tenedos, completely dispelled them. These days appeared to me so many ages, only from their delaying our arrival in the capital.

At last we entered the Boghaz![15] Stunned by the incessant thundering of the almost uninterrupted succession of batteries, which line the whole of the shore, I felt not the less as if sharing all the honour of their salutes, and could scarce repress my joy and exultation. In a few hours I was to behold that celebrated city, whose origin lay hid in the obscurity of ages, whose ancient greatness had often been the theme of my infant wonder, and whose humiliation under the Othoman yoke I had, in concert with my didaskalos[16] of Chios, frequently lamented with tears; but which – even in its present degraded state, and groaning under the despotism of the Turks – had from a child been the final object of all my views and wishes.

A most favourable wind continued to swell our sails. Our mighty keel shot rapidly through the waves of the Propontis, foaming before our prow. Every instant the vessel seemed to advance with accelerated speed; as if – become animated – it felt the near approach to its place of rest; and at last Constantinople rose, in all its grandeur, before us.

With eyes riveted on the expanding splendours I watched, as they rose out of the bosom of the surrounding waters, the pointed minarets, the swelling cupolas, and the innumerable habitations, either stretching along the jagged shore, and reflecting their image in the mirror of the deep, or creeping up the crested mountain, and tracing their outline on the expanse of sky. At first agglomerated in a single confused mass, the lesser parts of this immense whole seemed, as we advanced, by degrees to unfold, to disengage themselves from each other, and to grow into various groups, divided by wide chasms and deep indentures, – until at last the clusters, thus far distantly connected, became transformed, as if by magic, into three distinct cities,[17] each individually of prodigious extent, and each separated from the other two by a wide arm of that sea whose silver tide encompassed their base, and made its vast circuit rest half on Europe, and half on Asia. Entranced by the magnificent spectacle, I felt as if all the faculties of my soul were insufficient fully to embrace its glories: I hardly retained power to breathe; and almost apprehended that in doing so, I might dispel the gorgeous vision, and find its whole vast fabric only a delusive dream!

CHAPTER IV

It was with difficulty that I could collect my scattered senses when the time came to step down into the nut-shell, all azure and gold, which waited to convey the drogueman's suite to Fanar, where, with the other principal Greeks, Mavroyeni had his residence. Each stroke of the oar, after we had pushed off from the ship, made our light caïck[1] glide by some new palace, more splendid than those which preceded it; and every fresh edifice I beheld, grander in its appearance than the former, was immediately set down in my mind as my master's habitation. I began to feel uneasy when I perceived that we had passed the handsomest district, and were advancing towards a less showy quarter. My pangs increased as we were made to step ashore on a mean-looking quay, and to turn into a narrow dirty lane; and I attained the acme of my dismay, when, arrived opposite a house of dark and dingy hue, apparently crumbling to pieces with age and neglect,[2] I was told that there lived the lord Mavroyeni. At first I tried to persuade myself that my companions were joking; but, too soon assured they only spoke the truth, I entered with a fainting heart. A new surprise awaited me within. That mean fir-wood case of such forbidding exterior, contained rooms furnished in all the splendour of eastern magnificence. Persian carpets covered the floors, Genoa velvets covered the walls, and gilt trellis work overcast the lofty ceilings. Clouds of rich perfumes rose on all sides from silver censers; and soon I found that this dismal outside appearance was an homage paid by the cunning of the Greek gentry to the fanaticism of the Turkish mob, impatient of whatever may, in Christians, savour of luxury and ostentation. The persons of the Fanariote grandees were of a piece with their habitations. Within doors, sinking under the weight of rich furs, costly shawls, jewels, and trinkets, they went forth into the streets wrapped in coarse, and dingy, and often thread-bare clothing.

My arrival in the capital was almost immediately followed by an advancement from my private situation, to a more public office. Whether the drogueman of the Capitan-pasha thought it unbecoming for a sprig of his own body – a drogueman's son – to appear in the capacity of a domestic, or whether he conceived that a taooshan like himself, unconnected with his rivals in office, and entirely dependent on his nod, was, in point of trust-worthiness, the next thing to a mamluke;[3] or whether, finally, he considered my acquirements and my capabilities, as above being confined within the compass of a coffee-tray, or the extent of a Persian pipe, he had scarce time to look about him, ere he conferred upon me the employment – or rather the dignity – of relieving him in some of the lesser details of his business. These chiefly consisted in attending every day at the arsenal, there to introduce to the High-admiral the persons and to interpret the petitions, of Greeks and of foreigners; for in the style of Turkish diplomacy, a Christian ambassador demanding an audience was introduced as a suppliant preferring a suit.

While, to perform the duties of his office, Mavroyeni himself held his usual station in the Capitan-pasha's own apartment, I was installed in a small adjoining room, where I had to hear, to understand if I could, or, whether I understood or not, to set down and to condense into the shortest possible written abstract, the long stories of petitioners, and the endless dialogues of disputants; a duty, which I always performed the better in proportion as I understood the business before me the less. It was here I learnt that art of generalising my ideas, so esteemed, as I am told, among Frank[4] philosophers.

Undoubtedly, had the choice been laid before me, I should have preferred the truncheon to the pen. But the drogueman had not the former in his gift; and the tedium of the latter was materially relieved by certain circumstances attached to its exercise. For it soon became notorious that nothing assisted me so much in giving weight to a case, as a few sequins slipped from sheer absence of mind between the pages of the report; and in this respect the difference between my master and myself only consisted in his receiving purses,[5] where I received single pieces.

Still, to one who loved money only as a means of pleasure, my confinement could not but be irksome; and the moment Mavroyeni disappeared I too used to break my levees, and to saunter about. Whenever my master was employed by the Pasha in some long-winded expedition, I proceeded to spend the money already earned in the Tchartchees and Bezesteens,[6] or to procure new customers for my new shop, by boasting in the coffee-houses and taverns of my influence in higher quarters. Was Mavroyeni, on the contrary, only to make a short absence, I contented myself with taking a turn round the precincts of the arsenal.

In one of these rambles, I remember being shown two highly esteemed productions of the pictorial art, presented by the drogueman to the Pasha. They were representations of two of Hassan's most memorable achievements: the surprisal of the Russians at Lemnos, and the bombardment of Daher at Acre. In these chef-d'oeuvres all was depicted with the utmost faithfulness – the vessels, the batteries, the guns, the very balls whizzing through the air, and the shells falling on the buildings. One feature alone was omitted in compliment to Turkish prejudice; a mere trifle, no doubt, in the eyes of the painter – the combatants themselves! – but this very circumstance – as I told the Turkish officer my *cicerone* – so far from lessening its value, was, in my opinion, the most judicious thing I had ever beheld. The great point in works of art, my language-master at Chios had assured me, was only to bring forward the leading objects, the essential supporters of the action; and to discard all insignificant and superfluous accessories. Now, what was it in engagements by land or by water did all the execution? The men? – by no means! They only stood aloof. It was the shells, the bullets, the grapeshot. These therefore filled the whole foreground more properly.

So much did the acuteness of this remark delight the officer, that in his rapture, he clapped his broad whiskers on my face, and swore I was the only sensible Greek he ever had met with. It was evident that he knew not a countryman of mine, whom I found one morning in excessive wrath with a Perote artist – a Frank, – for having painted him a Madonna with such force of light and shade, as absolutely to stand out from the canvas. He swore it was a scandalous production; – almost as bad as an image! and the poor artist could not even obtain praise for his talent much less, payment for his labour.

I had been several weeks at Constantinople without yet seeing my patron's lady. Not that, like Turkish wives, she was kept secluded in a harem,[7] but, on the contrary, because, in order to enjoy greater freedom, she preferred spending her autumn at a villa on the Bosphorus. One afternoon Mavroyeni took me to Therapiah[8] in his caïck, and I was there presented to the domina. She happened to be sunning her plump charms on the quay. Nothing could exceed the stateliness of her appearance; and has she not been somewhat broader than she was long, her carriage would have been very dignified. Half a dozen surrounding attendants had no other employment but to support her august person; much too important to support itself on ordinary occasions. One walked on before with a peacock-tail fan, to keep the flies from her glossy face; and another behind, to shake the dust off her still more lustrous gown.

An untoward accident was fated to happen, just as every thing seemed disposed to strike a new comer with all possible awe and admiration. At the furthest outlet of the channel, in the middle of its silvery expanse, and on the verge of the horizon, was descried a dark speck that looked endowed with motion. Rapidly the opaque body advanced, skimming the fleecy surface of the waters; and, as it approached, it increased in size and consequence. Its wide extending fins dipped into the waves like the pinions of the swallow, while its sharp and prominent beak cut its way through the billows like the shark or the sword-fish. All eyes were riveted upon the threatening monster, and presently no one but myself any longer remained in ignorance of its nature. It stood confessed, – O horror! – not exactly a dragon come to devour our princess on the sea-shore, like another Andromeda, in order to give me an opportunity of signalizing my gallantry as her Perseus; but something full as savage, and much more inglorious: the Bostandgee-bashee[9] in his police boat, coming to nibble at the trains of the Greek princesses, which exceeded the standard of the Turkish sumptuary laws. At this terrific sight, the arms of the six suivantes all dropped with one accord by their sides, and with them dropped to the ground their mistress's train. The snow-white ermine swept the dust of the road; while its wearer – who just before had appeared scarce able to move without assistance – suddenly recovered the entire use of her short legs, and waddled away by herself as nimbly as any duck pursued by a kite, until the friendly screen of a wall enabled her to stop, to face about, and to take breath after the immense exertion.

As soon as the terrified party had safely reached the house, the fault of the precipitate retreat was laid on an impending shower. I had the impudence – fool that I was – to run and search for a cloud. The only one I could find was the gathering on the lady's own brow; and my officiousness got me a look in that quarter, which boded more storms than ever lashed the Bosphorus in March.

What could the company do, in the uncertain state of the sky, but collect round the tandoor?[10] – that safe refuge against the winter's rigours, that eastern nondescript, which in the angle of the mitred sofa holds a middle character between the table and the bed, and underneath whose gaudy coverlet all the legs of the snug party converge round a pot of lighted charcoal, there to stew for the evening. Like the rest, I crept under the bedclothes.

This was my first admission to a gossiping party of quality; and I must in justice to its members confess that it yielded not to those of inferior ranks. In the course of an hour or two I heard a very reasonable quantity of scandal. There was no recent occurrence in church or state, army or navy, boards or bed-chambers, the Bab-humayoon,[11] or the backstairs but was properly collected, combined, compared, dissected, analyzed, and circulated. I now for the first time learnt, to my infinite satisfaction, both the precise offence of the last vizier beheaded, and the precise length of the last feridjee[12] curtailed. I was informed in the same breath, how the great Morosi managed his principality, and how the little Manolacki conducted his courtship; how the Patriarch had quarrelled with the Archons,[13] and how the Spatar[14] had beaten his wife; how the mortgages of the church were redeeming, and how the slipper-money[15] of the Sultans was engaged: and so I confidently heard it asserted by a gentleman on my right, that the conference between a certain Ambassador and the Reïs-effende[16] would produce a new war; and by the lady on my left, that the meeting between a certain archimandrite and his ghostly daughter would produce a new christening, that I no longer doubted that the fumes of the brazier over which we sat, must have all the oracular virtues which issued from the cave of Delphi. On going to bed I expected from them very surprising effects, but to my disappointment, I experienced none other than a dream, in which I beheld the Sultan pounding the Grand Mufti in a mortar,[17] and the pope of Rome standing by, crying Bravo! – "Bravo," echoed I with all my might, – when my voice waking me just in time, I got up to return to my master in the capital.

"Well, Anastasius," said the drogueman to me, as we were cleaving the waves of the Bosphorus, "how do you like our Constantinople life?"

"Very much;" was the answer evidently expected, but which I did not give, – feeling a little edified with my visit to Therepiah, where I had had my share of the second-hand insolence, which the Fanariotes take very quietly from the Turks, only to put it off less quietly among the taooshans. "Not at all;" was therefore the short reply I made.

The drogueman stared. I felt I had been too laconic. "Were the rest of the Greeks I see here," added I, "at all like your highness, the place would indeed be a paradise; but this capital seems to change the nature of whatever it harbours; and my countrymen, so gay, so light-hearted at Chios, seem at the Fanar at once dull and important. Besides, the difference made between Christians and Mohammedans here is too great, too mortifying. The few Moslemen of Chios mingle with its rayahs on a footing of equality. They almost reckon it a favour to be admitted to their junketings. But here, the very noblest of the Greeks – your highness alone excepted – are daily exposed to the insults of the meanest Turk. Were it not for my principles, I would rather be a Turkish porter than a Greek prince."

Mavroyeni looked thoughtful. After a little pause, "You mistake, Anastasius," replied he, "in thinking the Greek of Constantinople different from the Greek of Chios. Our nation is everywhere the same. The same at Petersburg as at Cairo; the same now that it was twenty centuries ago."

I stared in my turn.

"What I say," continued my master, "is perfectly true. The complexion of the modern Greek may receive a different cast from different surrounding objects: the core still is the same as in the days of Pericles. Credulity, versatility, and thirst of distinctions from the earliest periods formed, still form, the basis of the Greek character; and the dissimilarity in the external appearance of the nation arises, not from any radical change in its temper and disposition, but only from the incidental variation in the means through which the same propensities are to be gratified. The ancient Greeks worshipped an hundred gods, the modern Greeks adore as many saints. The ancient Greeks believed in oracles and prodigies, in incantations and spells; the modern Greeks have faith in relics and miracles, in amulets and divinations. The ancient Greeks brought rich offerings and gifts to the shrines of their deities, for the purpose of obtaining success in war and pre-eminence in peace; the modern Greeks hang up dirty rags round the sanctuaries of their saints, to shake off an ague or to propitiate a mistress. The former were staunch patriots at home, and subtle courtiers in Persia; the latter defy the Turks in Mayno, and fawn upon them at the Fanar. Besides, was not every commonwealth of ancient Greece as much a prey to cabals and factions as every community of modern Greece? Does not every modern Greek preserve the same desire for supremacy, the same readiness to undermine by every means fair or foul his competitors, which was displayed by his ancestors? Do not the Turks of the present day resemble the Romans of past ages in their respect for the ingenuity, and at the same time, in their contempt for the character of their Greek subjects? And does the Greek of the Fanar show the least inferiority to the Greek of the Piraeus in quickness of perception, in fluency of tongue, and in fondness for quibbles, for disputation, and for sophistry? – Believe me, the very difference between the Greeks of time past and the present day, arises only from their thorough resemblance; from that equal pliability of temper, and faculties in both, which has ever made them receive with equal readiness the impression of every mould and the impulse of every agent. When patriotism, public spirit, and pre-eminence in the arts, science, literature, and warfare, were the road to distinction, the Greeks shone the first of patriots, of heroes, of painters, of poets, and of philosophers. Now that craft and subtlety, adulation and intrigue are the only paths to greatness, these same Greeks are – what you see them!"

To me it mattered little, whether the modern Greeks resembled the ancient or not, as long as I was not reckoned on a footing with my neighbours the Fanariotes. I therefore paid Mavroyeni a compliment on his oratory, and let the subject drop; still muttering to nyself, "Stambool was a detestable place!"

It remained not always so. The Fanariotes – whose defect is not want of quicksightedness – soon perceived that I was a great favourite of the favourite par excellence: and as no ramifications of this genus, however minute, were to be neglected, I began to enjoy my due share of adulation and consequence. Those who before were deaf when I spoke to them, now addressed me the first; and the identical joke which formerly left the muscles of every face unmoved, now had the power to set a whole table in a roar. With my situation my manners underwent a total change. The rude exterior of the islander had been changed among the caleondjees[18] of the Capitan-pasha, for a swaggering braggadocio air. The martial strut was now laid aside for the smooth simpering smile of the courtier. Instead of spluttering out my unpolished sentences by half dozens in a breath, as if I had more words crammed in my throat than could issue one by one from my mouth, I now practised with a nonchalant air to drop only now and then a significant monosyllable, so profound in its meaning that no one could get at it; – and as to the mother tongue, the Romaïc[19] idiom, it was no longer to be used, except interlarded with such scraps of French, Italian, and Turkish, as to render it almost unintelligible to the vulgar auditor. Athwart my borrowed languor and effeminacy, however, the native vigour and raciness of the soil would break forth occasionally with such energetic bursts, as both astonished and delighted the Fanariote fair. To them my rough-cast homage presented an acceptable contrast to the mawkish tenderness of their everyday admirers. My freedom passed for naïveté, my neglect of forms evinced a flattering devoutness, and my rustic exterior promised affections more robust and lasting than could be expected from the sickly natives of a large capital. Flattered by the men, and smiled upon by the women, I now said to myself –"Stambool is a charming place!"

So great, indeed, did I become the fashion, that, had my fastidiousness been less, I might have adapted my courtships, as our great men suit their pelisses, to the different seasons of the year: for, while autumn still continued to pour forth her golden treasures, a grocer's fair spouse – herself the image of ripeness and plenty – offered to feed my good-will with figs and raisins, to pay in comfits for the sweets of my converse, and to support the ardour of my affections with rosoglio and spice: when winter began to chill the blood, the sleek helpmate of the furrier would fain have dispelled my freezing coldness even at the expense of all her husband's rarest ermines; and, when returning spring enamelled every field with fresh flowers, I beheld at my feet a whole bevy of beauties, fresh as the violet and the daisy, and, to own the truth, not much more exalted in the scale of human flowerets: – but comfits were only lures for boys; ermine had no charms, except as the gab of royalty; and beauty itself lost its attractions in my eyes, when destitute of rank and fashion.

The first lady possessed of these latter attributes whom I found disposed to cast an eye of compassion on my sufferings, was of the devout order, and the very domina who had excited the oracular ingenuity of one of the party, on my first visit to Therapiah. The worthy archimandrite, to whom were entrusted her spiritual concerns, had, on the application of her husband, been exiled by the Patriarch to the holy mountain,[20] in order to pursue his spiritual mediations with less interruption. The lady, now finding that even the long beard of a priest was unable to screen her reputation, resolved to try whether the beardless face of a boy would protect it.

A first success obtained in a distinguished quarter from real preference leads to others granted by vanity. But with my fashion increased my fastidiousness. All could not catch that laid snares for me; nor could all keep that caught me. My favour was precarious, and – a little tyrant in love – I treated the tender passion quite in the Turkish style.

Still I continued undistinguished, nay, unheeded, by the proud Theophania. Not even by accident could the looks of this lofty woman descend to my level. She appeared unconscious that a being so insignificant as myself existed, filled its portion of space, and breathed the same air with her noble lungs. If she wished to move from one part of the room to another, and I happened to stand in her way, her hand would mechanically push me aside, without the participation of her mind, like a chair or a table; while her averted eye was directed to some more distant point of space. In vain might I lay myself out for her approbation, – I could not even obtain her satire. The very ridicule of Theophania would have been too much notice from one so low as me. It was positive condescension in her, one day when in an humbler quarter I showed myself insatiate of adulation, to turn round to me and with some impatience to say, "it is the privilege of the great, sir, to receive praise: the insignificant should be at the trouble of praising themselves!" – So violent indeed was her temper, and so sarcastic her conversation with individuals of every rank and degree, that even the most distinguished among the Fanariotes only approached her with fear and trembling, and, as soon as the indispensable rites of politeness had been performed, hastened away, ere, like the drones in a hive, they felt the sting of this intractable bee. The shafts of Cupid she had usually turned aside by her petulance; but the few times they happened to draw blood, she had loved as others hate.

Undismayed by these difficulties, I swore she would be at the feet of the taooshan whom she vouchsafed not to suffer at her own, and thenceforward bent the whole force of my genius towards attracting her attention, and exciting her interest. When therefore she, who at first had feared to disgrace her pretty pouting lips with the mere sound of my name, began to abuse my person and my character with most loquacious virulence, I considered my triumph as secure. "Theophania," cried I, – though not yet loud enough to be heard by herself – "you only pursue me with contemptuous looks, to feast your eye on my person; and you only load me with opprobrious epithets, to fix your mind on my image!"

If at last – which love and discretion forbid me ever boasting! – the prize rewarded my pains, yet troublesome was its tenure. The Euxine passes not more quickly from tranquillity to storms, than from serenity to passion changed my tempestuous and variable mistress. One moment, infatuated to perfect forgetfulness of her pride and station, she would clasp my knees in ecstacy, and humbling herself unto my very feet, glory in her debasement; the next, choking with rage, she would suddenly start up again, rail at her degradation, wonder what she saw in me to admire, and charge me, on my life, to disclose by what spell I had compelled her affections; but again, after having heaped upon me every direst execration which her fertile fancy could suggest, her passion would take another turn, and, bursting into a flood of tears, she would conjure me by all that was most sacred, if I could not return her love, at least to pity her agony, and assist in breaking the charm I had wrought, by rendering myself purposedly as hateful as possible.

What more could I do than I did? The only thing she ever saw me coax were my own little budding mustachios, whose education and growth I watched over with the tenderness of an anxious parent: the only thing she ever heard me praise, were the qualities to which she had the least pretension; self-command, endurance, meekness.

The preferences I felt in other quarters I freely owned; and the consolations I found, when she banished me her presence, I regularly enumerated. In my vulgar exultation (for vulgar it was) I treated with the familiarity of a clown, one who had been used to the deference of a queen; and to all such as had formerly suffered from Theophania's insolence, I boasted of being their avenger. Yet, in spite of my conduct her love lessened not; it only became more conspicuous; it afforded a sneering public a richer treat; and at mass every eye in the church seemed constantly vibrating between the grated gallery above, where Theophania sat with the other women, and the part of the nave below where, by her express desire, I took my station, in order that she might see me during her devout prayers.

Let man make his confidential friend of no woman, except such an one as he cannot possibly make his mistress; – namely, his mother, his sister, or his aunt. If she happen not to stand with him in any of these forbidden degrees, be she ever so old, or ugly, or infirm, she will end by feeling disappointed; and will accuse her unsuspecting friend of both too much and too little reserve.

A quiet demure looking woman – one of those persons with whom one feels as much at ease the first time of seeing them as with an old acquaintance – once or twice so good-naturedly cautioned me against the consequences, when on the point of imprudently courting public censure, that I determined professedly to open to her my whole heart and circumstances. Why not? "She herself had renounced all love engagements. They gave more trouble than they were worth; and she infinitely preferred to the feverish enjoyments of passion the calm pleasures of friendship – that is, of stable male relationships, which could depend upon. A tenderer intercourse she only contemplated in others, at a distance, by way of amusement, and in order to study human nature in its different varieties and shades. As to female friendship, she held it in the contempt it deserved." The looks of this good lady had informed me that she perfectly knew all my doings. Giving her my confidence, therefore, was only binding her to discretion; and at first I saw every reason to congratulate myself upon this determination. The tone of my new friend with me was that of a mother with her son; overflowing only with parental tenderness. Her whole mind seemed only bent upon keeping an unexperienced youth out of difficulties. But I soon found that from her appeals to my prudence, the company present was always excepted. Incensed by this discovery, I spoke in anger and was answered with asperity. We parted, no more to meet in friendship; – but I continued not the less to live in the remembrance of this excellent person.

Theophania's husband held one of the highest offices at the court of Moldavia. He was wont to date his days of repose from those of my attentions to his wife. He could have raised a statue to my merits from sheer gratitude, were statues ever raised in modern times from such an antiquated motive. All he prayed for was the permission to keep his eyes shut; – and this was precisely the only favour which my little friend would not grant him. Qualified for the task she undertook by my former confidence, she kindly forced upon him such irrefragable proofs of his wife's imprudence, as permitted him no longer to be blind to her conduct.

I was so accustomed always to be the last in my appointments with Theophania, that one day in the verdant valley of Kiad-hané,[21] the favourite haunt of the Cupids of Constantinople, I felt rather nettled at finding myself, though much after my time, the first at the place of rendezvous. Still I waited, and waited on; until impatience began to fan my languid flame, and Theophania's star began to mount. Alas! While I was trying to cool my ardour by contemplating the gurgling brook, in which the weeping willow was lightly dipping its delicate spray, as if striving to steal a last parting caress from the stream that fled its embrace, little did I imagine that the proud Theophania was jogging along in a rumbling kotshi – screaming until she was able to scream no longer – to the borders of the Black Sea; thence to be conveyed in an open-boat – much too sick with the motion even to scold – to the port of Galatsch, where a stout mule waited to carry her, bumping in a wicker basket, to the presence of her loving husband! He gave her a tender embrace, assured her she had decided vocation for the monastic life, and accordingly whisked her off the next morning to the most secluded convent in the province of Valachia; where, I understand, she has continued ever since, fasting, praying, and scolding, by turns. As soon as I heard of her adventure, I failed not to thank my little friend for the great service she had unintentionally rendered me.

My own day of retribution from the hands of my master was approaching. Neither my affair with Theophania, not even, I believe, my daily neglect of my duties, was the cause of my disgrace. It was the cloud, the fatal cloud, which I could not see when the Bostandjee-bashee passed by Therapiah, but which nothing could expel from *madame's* angered mind, except my dismission. Her husband would have preferred to have kept me; but, among the tongues he commanded, that of his loving helpmate had never in the family been numbered. He neither could stop it, nor yet had acquired the facility of listening to its explosions, as to the softer murmur of a mill. He therefore might rule in great affairs abroad, but always ended by obeying in little matters at home: content to save his credit by pretending to do from choice what he did from necessity.

One evening, after playing truant the whole day, I went up to submit to the accustomed lecture. Instead of blustering as usual, Mavroyeni asked in the most placid tone imaginable the cause of my long absence. I now gave myself up for lost beyond redemption. It was precisely the tone which the drogueman was wont to assume, when, fully resolved to have no further dealings with the person who had offended him, he deemed reproach an useless waste of breath. Still I made out a little story, to which Mavroyeni listened very patiently, – after which, without further reply, but pointing towards the door, he desired me to walk out, and never to walk in again.

I knew him too well to have the least hope of his recalling a sentence uttered in this manner. My only remaining solicitude, therefore, was to make a dignified retreat. After a profound bow – of defiance rather than of respect – I strutted away, carrying my head so high, that I knocked it against the soffit of the door.

But in spite of my seeming indifference, I felt injured, if not degraded; for, in surveying my conduct, I only took into account the last drop that rose above the brim; the rest was hid within the vessel.

I need not observe that what to me appeared the height of injustice, was deemed by the rest of the family only a tardy act of bare equity. Such as it was, however, it caused great jubilation, and in the twinkling of an eye, the whole Fanar was informed of the secretary's disgrace: – only it was ascribed to my having, with a pistol in one hand, and a sword in the other, made such proposals to madame la droguemane, as she could not possibly listen to – from her husband's clerk.

Eavesdropping never was among my fancies. Nor was I fond enough of puzzles, to put together broken sentences, which in general may be made to bear any signification; but one's own name is a great stumbling-block in the way of one's discretion: and when, crossing a dark passage as I went out of the house, I heard mine pronounced with great vehemence, the sound acted like a talisman. It riveted me to the spot. I stopped to hear my panegyric. All I could collect, however, was only the abundantly hated, while in the fresh zeal of my service I chose to perform more than was set down for me, and to do better than others, I had since retrieved my character in the family by mending my ways, and neglecting my business. On that account I now carried away a certain portion of good will. The party present regretted my fall; but the chief orator consoled himself by thinking me such a daring and dexterous fellow, that, happen what might, I was always sure to come down upon my legs.

"Amen!" cried I, walking out; "I accept the welcome omen!"

CHAPTER V

As the night was already well advanced, I went, till the next morning, to one of those temples of hospitality ever opened to the stranger who sues for admission with a silver tongue. It was sheer churlishness in me, no doubt, to defer for so many hours affording my numerous friends the often wished-for opportunity of testifying the sincerity of their regard. As soon, however, as the sun had risen high enough to shine upon its testimonials, I had determined no longer to delay their happiness. I even resolved, in order that no one should complain of being omitted, to begin my visits methodically at one end of the Fanar, and not to leave off until I had reached the other. In the course of this experimental round I found the warmth of my well-wishers precisely in an inverse ratio to their means. The higher classes made it a matter of conscience, not to receive a servant discarded by his master. Those of a lower degree expressed their willingness to continue as friends as long as I had a piastre left; only reserving to themselves the privilege of dropping me, the moment their poor assistance became of real consequence. Nothing however stopped me in my circuit, until I had knocked at the last door in the district; – for I still bore in mind the last words I had heard under my master's roof, and wished to preserve an authentic record of my obligations to each of my friends. When no one remained to apply to I cast up the total sum, and finding it a cipher, wished them all at the devil, and crossed over to Galata.[1]

I here got, for my money, a new set of cronies; – jolly souls, who, not possessing a para[2] of their own in the world, never inquired what others were worth, but lived from hand to mouth, banished care, and set melancholy at defiance. They initiated me into a lower and more riotous species of intemperance than the decorum of my former situation permitted. Every day we met in some of the taverns of the neighbourhood, where my new friends contributed their share of the entertainment in sallies at the expense of my old ones – and I, in ready cash. It was quite consoling, to hear them how they pitied the droguemen, for losing such a treasure as myself; how they laughed at my wit even before I spoke, and how they drank every instant to my health, and the success of my schemes. No day passed without a party of pleasure being proposed, for the sole purpose of keeping up my spirits: and, lest I should not be aware how entirely they all joined in it for my sake, no one ever ventured to inquire the cost. Indeed, so far from presuming to offend my delicacy by requesting to share in the expense, they thought it a proper compliment to my liberality to borrow from me whatever money they wanted. Not for the world would they give another the preference!

As soon as my finances were exhausted, my companions of course disappeared; not, however – to do them justice – from choice, but from sheer necessity, and because, having been entirely supported by me, they now had to shift for themselves. When my embarrassment became known, one person only came forward to relieve me, and that a female too, and one who had not much reason to be pleased with my proceedings – the little grocer's wife, whose figs and raisins I had disdained. Hearing an exaggerated account of my distress, and thinking me absolutely starving, she trundled away with all her pristine affection still next her heart, and a large pot of marmalade under each arm. These, and all else her shop contained, she pressed me to dispose of. Too proud to owe to charity what I could not earn by love, I pointed to my dress, which had cost a great deal, and was still, in its ruins, worth a few sequins, and begged she would not urge me. "I will not receive," cried I, "where I can make no return; but when you thought I wanted bread, you brought me conserve of roses; and if any fresh ones ever strew my path, the deed shall be found recorded in the very kernel of my heart!"

Without leaving the poor little woman time to answer so flowery a speech, I ran off to the only one of my dispersed associates whom I knew where to find. I wanted his advice, and felt sure that he would not refuse what even those who will nothing else often bestow with such readiness.

An ascent of about fifty steps brought me to his exalted abode. Its tenant might truly be said to look down on the world. To him it was a journey to descend to the level of his fellow-citizens; and he therefore conformed but little to their hours. Just at mid-day signor Vasili was awaking from his night's repose. On entering his aerial apartment I still found him sprawling on his couch, – stretching one arm, putting one leg to the ground, rubbing his eyes, and giving such a yawn that I thought he would have swallowed at least half of Constantinople, spread out like a map before him. At my unlooked-for visit he stared, shook himself as if to be certain he was not dreaming, and disposed his ears in silence to listen to my story.

"I came," – I said, – "to ask how people lived, who had not any ostensible means of subsistence?" This feat Vasili had performed so long, that it never struck him it could puzzle any body. He therefore still continued some time staring at me in utter silence as before, in order to collect his thoughts. At last, jumping up in such a fury as almost to startle me, he seized hold of my arm, and led me to the window. The prospect from it extended over the immense city of Stambool unto its utmost boundaries, and showed the inside like a prodigious ant's nest, where, far below the eye, myriads of little insects were bestirring themselves, crossing and jostling each other in every possible direction. I praised the view, said it was undoubtedly delightful to the eye, but still I could not see how it was to feed an empty stomach. "It may teach how to fill it with something else though," cried my friend Vasili, – now for the first time breaking his portentous silence. "Of the thousands you behold in those streets, on those quays, in those boats, on the land, and on the water, scarce one half knew this morning how to get a meal at noon, and a place of rest at night; yet I will engage that every blockhead of them by this time has broken his fast, and will find a hole to sleep in! Why therefore should you fail, but from possessing too superior abilities? Only scare not away your invention by your fears, and – depend upon it! – some means of livelihood will present themselves! However, what leisure I can give to help such measures forward, I shall willingly bestow."

So saying, Vasili thrust his hand in his pocket, and hauled forth a heap of the smallest coin of the realm. This treasure he poured on the sofa, and divided into three equal parts. Then, laying his finger on each in succession, "the first," said he, "we shall drink together this morning, in order to whet our invention; the next I reserve for my own wants tomorrow; the third is yours, until you find it particularly convenient to repay me.

Your brain will by that means have an entire holiday, before you need call upon your wits for your livelihood; and, when you are thus upon a par with myself, the deuce is in it if you cannot do as well!"

I thanked my generous friend; but, just as we sailed forth to fulfil the first article of this particular treaty, he cast his eye upon my attire. It was no longer the flowing robe of the Fanar – the anteree[3] of state: I had exchanged that for the more dashing short dress of my last intimates. A rich embroidery covered the seams, and a costly velvet formed the ground-work. "I am thinking," said Vasili, "that your present wardrobe ill suits your purpose. Who can fancy a purse, stiff with gold outside, to be empty within? Supposing, therefore, that on this occasion we give business precedence over pleasure, and, reversing the dreams of the alchymists, change gold into baser substances. We may afterwards adjourn to a tavern, to drink success to your metamorphosis. The showiest caterpillar, you know, must become a chrysalis ere it can soar as a butterfly."

I could have dispensed with the chrysalis state: for, though poor, I still liked to look well; but I yielded to my friend's arguments, and hied with him to Sultan-Bayzid[4] to change the outward man. While we were looking for something suitable to our purpose, in stepped a worthy Israelite, who came like ourselves, not to sell, but to buy. A still decent beneesh – but of a dusky hue – hidden under a heap of gaudier dresses, seemed to catch his fancy; which the salesman no sooner perceived than all the powers of his oratory were summoned to extol the article in question. He had better have been modest about its merits. The Jew – both by nature and by cultivation adept in the business – now put upon his mettle, at once began to pour forth such a torrent of profound observations on the art of old clothes dealing, that the seller was glad at last to give him the cloak for nothing, ere he let all the bystanders into every deepest mystery of the trade.

In truth, it was diamond cutting diamond. The Hebrew had himself professed, the elegant quarter of Hash-keui,[5] the noble trade of old clothesman, till bankruptcy forced him to quit his district and his business. Having early in life served an Esculapius of his own nation, with whom he learnt a few terms of medicine, he now resolved to turn physician himself. The thing was easy enough at Constantinople, where a man need only stalk about in a furred cap[6] and a dark-coloured gown, followed by an attendant with a small square chest, to have all the men hold out their wrists, and all the women put out their tongues to him – in consultation.

The cap had already been provided. The beneesh was immediately put on, and the very attendant chosen *in petto*. For, to the hawk's eye of my Israelite, my anxious look at once bespoke me the very thing he wanted. Calling me aside, he made the proposal without much ceremony. I was ostensibly to be his servant, but, in reality, his partner. Even that clause, however, could not sweeten the nauseous draught. I felt so indignant at being proposed to for an apothecary's apprentice, that, without making any answer, I went and imparted the impertinent offer to my friend Vasili. But in that quarter I found little sympathy. "See," said he, laughing, "how fortune throws herself in your way. I wish you joy of your good luck." This speech I was willing to take as a joke, but I found it to be serious; and, more incensed than before, "Sooner," I cried, "if all other trades fail, would I, in one of those coarse and dingy Lahse[7] jackets there, work for my bread in the fields! The earth cannot degrade its children, and no one requires a character to plough the ground." "True," replied Vasili; "but one may require a constitution, though; and who in their senses, pray, would take such a spindle-shanked fellow as you are just now, with a face as pale as a turnip already, and an eye round which 'rake' is written in most legible black letters, to dig his garden for him? Ere you had half done, he would expect to have your own grave to dig! For my part, I would try what requires neither stock, nor capital, nor labour, nor even science, as I take it, nor any thing but the impudence of which you possess a sufficient stock; were it only for fun, and to see what no one but a physician ever sees: – for, more potent than gold, medicine will open to you the deepest recesses of the harem; and who can tell but, like our friend Lorenzo,[8] you may feel sultanas' pulses."

This was setting the masquerade in its most tempting light. It tickled my fancy; and I struck the bargain with the Jew. He was to carry his own Galen, in the shape of the best half of an old missal, stolen from a capuchin; I undertook the medicine chest, with all its pills of starch, and all its powders of pipe-clay. The only thing I insisted upon as a *sine qua non* in the treaty, was not to appear in my character in any of the streets I had before frequented; and to this ultimatum the Jew readily enough agreed. Matters thus settled between us, I somewhat dolefully exchanged my gaudy apparel for a dress in unison with that of my principal, and, after vainly begging in gratitude for my friend Vasili's advice, to have the honour of making upon him my first experiment in my new profession, walked away with my grotesque patron.

Immediately we began stalking through all the lanes and by-streets of the capital; I, with a pace exactly regulated by that of my new master, who walked before me, and both of us turning our heads constantly from right to left and from left to right, like weathercocks, to watch every call from a door or signal from a window; but full as much on the alert to avoid old faces as to court the notice of new ones. Now and then, when we had time for idle chat, I used to advise Yacoob, – that was my principal's name, – to provide himself with a proper license for killing the Grand Signor's subjects, in the shape of a diploma from Hekim-bashee.[9] He denied not the expediency of the measure, but he always found some pretence for denying the performance. At first his poverty prevented the purchase; afterwards, the pressure of business, and so long did we go on, without any inconvenience from the neglect of the said formality, that at last we began to think we never should feel the want of it, and totally forgot there was such a person as the Hekim-bashee.

Ours was an off-hand method of practice. As all cases were pretty much alike in reference to our skill, a single feel of the pulse generally decided the most difficult treatments. Our patients – chiefly of the industrious class – could not afford long illnesses, and these we certainly prevented. What most annoyed us was the headstrong obstinacy of some individuals, who sometimes insisted that they still felt disordered, when we positively assured them they were cured. Had they been killed instead, they would have complained! Still more disagreeable incidents occasionally occurred. Called in one day to a woman in convulsions, Yacoob, I know not why, prescribed a remedy which the Turks regard as an insult. In a rage the woman flew at him, and bit off half his ear. It was all I could do to save the other half. Another day (a Mohammedan festival), a set of merry-making Osmanlees insisted on Yacoob putting on an European dress, which they carried about on a pole, that they might kick him through the streets as a Frank; and though he actually refused a fee for gratifying their whim, he nevertheless was made to go through the whole ceremony.

I remember a quieter, but more impressive scene. One evening, as we were returning from the Blacquernes,[10] an old woman threw herself in our way, and taking hold of my master's garment, dragged him almost by main force after her into a mean-looking habitation just by, where lay on a couch, apparently at the last gasp, a man of foreign features. "I have brought a physician," said the female to the patient, "who, perhaps, may relieve you." "Why will you," answered he faintly – "still persist to feed idle hopes! I have lived an outcast: suffer me at least to die in peace; nor disturb my last moments by vain illusions. My soul pants to rejoin the supreme Spirit; arrest not its flight: it would only be delaying my eternal bliss!"

As the stranger spoke these words – which struck even Yacoob sufficiently to make him suspend his professional grimace – the last beams of the setting sun darted across the casement of the window upon his pale, yet swarthy features. Thus visited, he seemed for a moment to revive. "I have always," said he, "considered my fate as connected with the great luminary that rules the creation. I have always paid it due worship, and firmly believed I could not breathe my last whilst its rays shone upon me. Carry me therefore out, that I may take my last farewell of the heavenly ruler of my earthly destinies!"

We all rushed forward to obey the mandate: but the stairs being too narrow, the woman only opened the window, and placed the dying man before it, so as to enjoy the full view of the glorious orb, just in the act of dropping beneath the horizon. He remained a few moments in silent adoration; and mechanically we all joined him in fixing our eyes on the object of his worship. It set in all its splendour; and when its golden disk had entirely disappeared, we looked round at the Parsee. He too had sunk into everlasting rest.

Our easy successes amongst the lower orders made us by degrees aspire to higher patients. We took to attending the poor gratis, in order to appear qualified to try the constitutions of the rich; and, by appearing to have respectable customers, we got them. A Beglier-bey[11] of Roumili, – the great-grandson of a Sultan, on the mother's side (for, on the father's, such filiations are stifled in the birth), was passing through Constantinople. One of his Armenian grooms chose to thank Yacoob for having been relieved by nature from a troublesome quinsy, and recommended him to his master's kehaya. The kehaya also – in spite of Yacoob's attendance – got the better of his rheumatism, and praised us to the head eunuch. The head eunuch, left by us as we found him, spoke of us in high terms to his master; and the Visier, on being seized with an indigestion for which he had laboured very hard, himself condescended to send for us. He however determined to have two strings to his bow, and to consult the stars as well as the faculty: so that my master found himself pitted against a moonedjim,[12] who recommended an emetic, while Yacoob insisted on a contrary remedy. The Visier, determined to be right, slyly took both, thinking thus to make the opposite opinions meet. The medicines certainly did; and by their conflict, kept us for a while in as violent a perspiration as the Pasha himself. As however the disorder only proceeded from too free an indulgence of a good appetite, the double remedy, though a little violent, in the end proved beneficial; and after suffering a few sympathetic pangs, we ultimately reaped both reputation and profit from our treatment of this three-tailed patient.

Thus we were enabled to quit our itinerant mode of life, and to set up near Backtche-capoossee[13] a shop of decent appearance, furnished with jars and phials of all sorts and sizes. These we inscribed with the names of the most costly medicines, while the insides bore witness to their rarity. Instead of going in pursuit of patients, we now waited till they came or sent. In the course of his practice my principal had discovered that, if some ailments will obey a face furrowed with age, youth and freshness best dispel certain others; and these he left to my sole management.

Our Visier (he was ours, body and soul) had his two regular wives – fixtures in the capital. But to his home establishment he added a lighter travelling equipage of half a dozen slaves, Circassians and others. Among this latter troop, the stag-eyes Fathmé shone like the full moon among the stars. Besides her patron of eighty or thereabouts, this fair one boasted two other equally strenuous admirers; the black eunuch who guarded the harem, and the old governess who kept its contents in order. These two personages used to devote half their time to the cares of their own persons, and the other half to watching that of their rival. Both having intrusted us with their health, each took an opportunity of hinting how agreeable I might make myself, by putting that of the other beyond the reach of contingencies. It was a glorious hint! Without going the whole length of the modest request, I might contrive to keep signor Suleiman and signora Zelidah confined to their beds, while I made inquiries after the health of their prisoners; but unlooked for incidents marred this bright scheme.

Disappointed at Yacoob's not being able to restore him at fourscore to the vigour of forty, the Visier had, unknown to his Jew doctor, called in a new ally; – the very person whose lynx-eye Yacoob dreaded more the than spectacles of all the imperial moonedjims put together, namely, the chief physician of the Seraglio. Just as my master was coming in triumphantly one morning to his patron, with a phial of soap-suds and cinnamon which he swore would renovate the last defunct Mufti himself, he unexpectedly beheld the crabbed visage of the crusty Trisetene the very first thing on the threshold. Poor Yacoob looked as if he had seen the Medusa in person! He however had presence of mind enough left to dash his phial to pieces, and then to be in despair at the accident. It afforded him an opportunity of making an immediate retreat, under the pretence of running home to repair the grievous loss; but with the full determination never more to go near the Pasha's door. This availed him little. The old devil of a Tristene – who at his exit had sent after him the ugliest grin I ever beheld, – satisfied that we practised unlawfully, denounced our doings to the president of the killing college. The Visier, – the more incensed at being duped, from the pleasure he promised himself in bringing together two such luminaries of the profession, – threw in his weight against us, and the consequence was our being sentenced to an exemplary punishment. As we sat brooding over the misfortune of the Pasha's proving less a fool than we thought, a posse of police myrmidons invaded our shop, and summoned us to prison. These gentlemen, however, as usual, began their official functions by emptying all our phials and gallipots into their capacious stomachs. This proceeding, and its natural consequences, caused us a short respite.

While our guardians were engaged, a new set was to be sent for: but these conveyed us without further delay to the place of our confinement. The very hour which I had destined for consoling the fair Fathmé in her prison saw me ushered into that of the Bagnio.[14]

CHAPTER VI

The vast and high enclosure of the Bagnio, situated contiguously to the arsenal and the docks, contains a little world of its own, but a world of wailing. One part is tenanted by the prisoners made on board the enemy's ships, who, with an iron ring round their legs, await in this dismal repository their transference on board the Turkish fleet. This part may only be called a sort of purgatory. The other is hell in perfection. It is the larger division, filled with the natural subjects of the Grand Signor whom their real or supposed misdemeanours have brought to this abode of unavailing tears. Here are confined alike the ragged beggar urged by famine to steal a loaf, and the rich banker instigated by avarice to deny a deposit; the bandit who uses open violence, and the baker who employs false weights; the land robber and the pirate of the seas, the assassin and the cheat. Here, as in the infernal regions, are mingled natives of every country – Turks, Greeks, Armenians, Jews, and Gipsies; and are confounded individuals of every creed – the Mohammedan, the Christian, the Hebrew, and the Heathen. Here the proud and the humble, the opulent and the necessitous, are reduced to the direst of equalities, the equality of torture. But I err: for should some hapless victim – perhaps guilty of no other crime but that of having excited the Sultan's cupidity – still wear on his entrance the livery of better days, his more decent appearance will only expose him to harsher treatment. Loaded with the heaviest fetters, linked to the most loathsome of malefactors, he is compelled to purchase every alleviation of his burthen, every mitigation of his pain, at the most exorbitant price; until the total exhaustion of his slender store has acquired him the privilege of being at least on a level with the lowest of his fellow sufferers, and spared additional torments, no longer lucrative to their inflicters.

Every day a capital fertile in crimes pours new offenders into this dread receptacle; and its high walls and deep recesses resound every instant with imprecations and curses, uttered in all the idioms of the Othoman empire. Deep moans and dismal yells leave not its frightful echoes a moment's repose. From morning till night and from night till morning, the ear is stunned with the clang of chains, which the galley-slaves wear while confined to their cells, and which they still drag about when toiling at their tasks. Linked together two and two for life, should they sink under their sufferings, they still continued unsevered after death; and the man doomed to live on, drags after him the corpse of his dead companion. In no direction can the eye escape the spectacle of atrocious punishments and of indescribable agonies. Here perhaps you see a wretch whose stiffened limbs refuse their office, stop suddenly short in the midst of his labour, and, as if already impassible, defy the stripes that lay open his flesh, and wait in total immobility the last merciful blow that is to end his misery; while, there, you view his companion foaming with rage and madness, turn against his own person with desperate hands, tear his clotted hair, rend his bleeding bosom, and strike his skull until it burst against the wall of his dungeon.

A long unpunished pirate, a liberated galley-slave, Achmet-reïs by name, was the fiend of hell who by his ingenuity in contriving new tortures, and his infernal delight in beholding new sufferings, had deserved to become the chief inspector of this place, and the chief minister of its terrors. His joys were great, but they were not yet complete. Only permitted thus far to exercise his craft on mortals, he was still obliged to calculate what degree of agony of the human frame could bear, and to proportion his inflictions to man's powers of suffering, lest, by dispatching his victims too soon, he should defeat his own aim. He was not yet received among his brother dæmons, in the blissful abodes where torments do not kill, and where pangs may be increased in an infinite ratio.

Of this truth the very hour of my arrival had afforded him a sorely lamented proof! An Armenian cashier, suspected of withholding from the Sultan – sole heir to all his officers – the deposit of a deceased Pasha, had just been delivered over into Achmet's hands; and many were the days of bliss to which the executioner looked forward in the diligent performance of his office. On the very first application of the rack, out of sheer malice, the Seraff expired!

Two days later the whole of Achmet's prospects of sublunary happiness were near coming to a close. Some wretches, driven by his cruelty to a state of madness, had sworn his destruction. Their hands, tied behind their backs, could be of no use to them in effecting their purpose: – they determined to crush him with their bodies. All at the same instant fell with their whole weight upon the executioner, or upon their companions already heaped upon the monster, in hopes of burying his corpse under a living tumulus. But Achmet's good star prevailed. Ere yet his suffocation was completed soldiers rescued the miscreant. He recovered, to wreak on his disappointed enemies his fiercest vengeance. Their punishment was dreadful! Sanguinary but not cruel, prone to shed blood in anger, yet shuddering at torture, I was horror-struck at the scene, and the yells of the victims still ring in my ears.

Characters meet at large in the world, which may almost count as sure their meeting again, some time or other, within the narrow precincts of the Bagnio. Of this species was the captain of the Maynote pirates, who took our Venetian cutter. He now occupied his winter quarters among the galley-slaves. Though I had had but little time on our first interview to cultivate his acquaintance, I could not help remembering that from the moment his tall commanding figure rose above the side of our vessel, and stepped on board, my stars had assumed a milder aspect, and my situation had been improved. Each, therefore, was glad of the *rencontre*; each expressed his sincere pleasure at meeting the other; each politely hoped the other might be destined to make a long sojourn in the place.

There are men so gifted, that in whatever situation fate may place them, they still inspire a certain awe and respect, and, though fallen through dint of adverse circumstances into the most abject condition, still retain over all round them an innate superiority. Of this sort was Mackari. He had been one of the chieftains of that small tribe of mountaineers, pent up in the peninsula of Mayno, who like greater nations claim dominion over the seas that gird their native rocks. Mackari, therefore, had only considered himself as acting conformably to his natural right in capturing the vessels that trespassed on his domain, without purchasing his permission; and in his conduct he discerned neither injustice nor treachery. Hence his lofty soul still preserved all its dignity amid his fallen fortunes. Patient under every insult, unruffled by direst torture, he was never heard to utter a sigh, to offer a remonstrance, or to beg a mitigation of the agonies inflicted on him. Even when his keepers, unable to wrest from his scornful lip the smallest acknowledgement of their ingenuity in torturing, began to doubt their powers, and – irritated by his very forbearance – resolved to conquer by a last and highest outrage his immoveable firmness; when with weights and pullies they forced down to the ground that countenance which, serene in the midst of suffering, seemed only fit to face the heavens; when they compelled him, whose mental independence defied all their means of coercion, constantly to behold the fetters that contracted his body, they only succeeded to depress his earthly frame; they were not able to lower his unbending spirit. Still calm, still serene as before, he only smiled at the fresh chains, with which he was loaded; and at each new fetter added to his former shackles, his mind only seemed to take a loftier flight.

Yet, impassible as he appeared to his own woes, was he most feelingly alive to those of his companions. Of every new hardship with which they were threatened, he uniformly stood forward to court the preference; and while his fortitude awed into silence the useless complaints of his troop, his self-devotion still relieved its real misery. One day, when a ferocious soldier was going to fell with his club the comrade of Mackari's fetters, whom his manacled hands could not save from the blow, he opposed to the frightful weapon all he could command – his arm, which, broken by the stroke, fell by his side a wreck.

Thus did the Maynote captain's former crew still view in their chief, though loaded with irons like themselves, not only the master to whom they continued to pay all the obedience they could show, but the protector on whom they depended for all the comfort they could receive. His very keepers were unable in his sight to shake off the awe felt by all who approached him. They confessed by their fears their nothingness in his presence: they scarce could revive a sufficient sense of security from all the fetters which they had heaped upon their victim. In vain would he himself with a bitter and disdainful smile point to his forlorn state, and ask what they apprehended from one on whom they might trample with impunity? The mere sound of his voice seemed to belie his words. It was the roar of a lion, dreaded even through the bars of his cage. And when his shackles were loosened in order that his daily labours might begin; when Mackari was enabled to raise for a moment his long depressed head; when his majestic brow soared above the humbler height of his tallest companions, – he looked like the cedar of Lebanon, which, though scathed by the lightning from heaven, still overtops all the trees in the forest; and the wretches to whose care he was committed used immediately to recede to a fearful distance.

Unendowed with any of the forebearance of the Maynote chief, I had scarcely been an hour in the Bagnio before I began to measure with my eye the heights of its walls, to consider the strength of its gates, and to count the number of its guards. A good natured fellow-sufferer, who guessed my thoughts, called me aside. "Take care what you do," whispered he; "there is danger in even looking at these walls. The mere suspicion of a plan to escape from this place meets with the severest punishment; the execution is impossible. Should you have succeeded so far as to clear every impediment, every barrier, every sentinel; should you have reached the very heart of the city; should you in its seemingly impenetrable vortex think yourself most secure from any search, you have yet achieved nothing; you have not advanced a single step toward your liberation. Many inmates of the Bagnio, possessing families in the city, enjoy unrestrained egress on the express condition of bringing back the missing, or of taking their place. The most active and watchful of the spies they employ are stationed precisely wherever the security from discovery seems the greatest; and the sufferings of those whose attempts at evasion have been baffled by their vigilance are so cruelly aggravated, that a man must have lost all hope of any other deliverance on this side the grave, ere he attempt so desperate a mode of regaining his freedom."

Not such was my case. As soon as, recovering from my first dismay, I had begun to cast my eye around, it had been arrested by a neat little spire with a handsome gilded top, peeping over the battlements of the western enclosure, and which somehow struck me as an old acquaintance. No wonder that it should! It crowned that very pavilion of the arsenal where the drogueman held his office; where sat Mavroyeni; where I myself had performed with applause my first part on the stage of the capital. An immediate gleam of hope beamed from its golden ball, and glanced on my mind. "How!" thought I, "Mavroyeni, my old master, shall spend all his mornings within a stone's throw of the place in which pines his Anastasius; shall only be impeded by the thickness of the wall from seeing his hapless favourite; shall almost in the midst of his business hear the moans of his suffering servant, and, if applied to, can he refuse to relieve me? – Impossible! He needs only know where I am, and what miseries I experience, to restore me, not perhaps to his pristine favour, but to the common privilege of living, or at least dying, where I choose."

My only doubt was whether I should demean myself so far as to implore his intercession. This scruple, however, one of my satellites soon helped me to get over by an opportune application of his switch – only to keep his hand in practice – just as I sat down in deep deliberation. Accordingly I adjured the first fellow-prisoner who was liberated, by all that he held sacred, to acquaint the drogueman with my confinement, and to lay before him my petition. I must confess that there was nothing the good-natured creature did not promise in his joy to do for me; but there I imagined his generosity stopped. Though he had sworn that the sun should not set before he spoke on my behalf, the sun set and rose, and set and rose again, and nothing more was heard of the fate of my request. I hereupon repeated it to another person allowed to leave the Bagnio, and after him a third; and to a fourth; but always with the same result. All professed equal readiness to serve me, but all were either alike forgetful of their promise, or unsuccessful in their application; for no notice was taken of me by Mavroyeni. In vain I lingered day after day in feverish expectation: in vain I questioned every new face that appeared. No one knew anything of my business; no one had heard my name mentioned. At last I became convinced that the drogueman was determined to leave me to my fate, and resolved to give up all further hopes of being freed, at least by the hand of man. I say "by the hand of man" – for a higher power was beginning to manifest its awful presence, which held out a prospect of speedy release, not only to me, but to the whole Bagnio.

This was the plague.

The scourge had been expected for some time. By several of the prisoners had the frightful hag, its harbinger, been distinctly seen hovering with her bat's wings over her drear abode, and with her hooked talons numbering one by one her intended but unsuspecting victims. In the silence of the night she had been heard leisurely calling them by their names, knocking at their several doors, and marking with livid spots the damp walls of their cells.[1]

Nothing but the visitation of this destructive monster seemed wanting to complete the horrors which surrounded me: – for if even, when only stalking forth among men free to fly from its approach and to shrink from its contact, the gaunt spectre mows down whole nations like the ripe corn in the field, it may be imagined what havoc ensues when it is permitted to burst forth from the inmost bowels of hell, in the midst of wretches close-wedged in their dungeons or linked together at their tasks, whom it must trample down to the last, ere it can find a vent in space. It is there that – with a focus of infection ready formed, a train of miasma ready laid on every side – though this prime minister of death strike at random, it never misses its aim, and its progress outstrips the quickness of lightning or of thought. It is there that even those who thus far retain full possession of health, already calculate the hours they still may live; that those who today drag to their last abode their lifeless companions, tomorrow are laid beside them; and that those who are dying, make themselves pillows of the bodies not yet cold of those already dead. It is there we may behold the grim destroyer in one place awaited in gloomy silence, in another encountered with fell imprecations, here implored with anxious cries, there welcomed with eager thanks, and now perhaps received with convulsive laughter and mockery, by such as, trying to drink away its terrors, totter on the brink of the grave from drunkenness as well as from disease.

The before busy beehive of the Bagnio, therefore, soon became a dreadful solitude. Its spacious enclosures, so lately teeming with tenants of every description, now began to present a void still more frightful than its former fulness. Universal silence pervaded those endless galleries, but a few days before re-echoing with the confused din of thousands of prisoners, fighting for an inch of ground on which to lay their aching heads; and nothing any longer appeared that wore a human shape, except here and there some livid skeleton, which, as if again cast up by the grave, slowly crept along the clammy walls. When however the dire disease had devoured all that could offer food to its voracity, it gradually fell like the flame which has consumed its fuel; and at last become extinct. What few miserable remains of the former population of the Bagnio had escaped its fury, were again restored to the regular sufferings of the place, suspended during the utmost height of the desolation.

I was among those scantly relics. I who, indifferent to life, had never stopped to avoid the shafts of death, even when they flew thickest around me, had more than once laid my finger on the livid wound they inflicted, had probed it as it festered, I yet remained unhurt: for sometimes the plague is a magnanimous enemy, whose blood running cold ere it is tainted, lacks the energy necessary to repel the infection when at hand, it will pass him by who dares its utmost fury, and advances undaunted to meet its raised dart.

Not that my old master Yacoob can be quoted as another instance in point. He too escaped, indeed: but it was from anything but excess of courage. Probably the plague thought his former campaigns in her cause as an old clothesman, should not be forgotten in his later acts of hostility as a physician. Little trusting, however, to the generosity of his old ally, who might consider the obligation fully repaid by the ample stock of goods she had occasionally procured him, his mind had, during the progress of the progress of the disease, brought forth nothing but plans of evasion. Each later device indeed miscarried, as all the former contrivances had done before it; but this was only to give birth to some plan still later and more preposterous. One day, astride on the lofty summit of the outer wall which surrounds the prison, he had nearly given his enfeebled guardians the slip, by softly letting himself down upon a heap of rubbish thrown up outside as if on purpose to break his fall, when, most unluckily espied, he was hauled down to receive a hundred lashes on the soles of his feet, for the nimble use he had made of them. This castigation, if inflicted, must have ended his troubles. Fortunately he had laboured before under a suspicion of madness; and so violent a paroxysm of raving now suddenly seized him, that some of the by-standers began to think an hospital fitter for his residence than a prison. The sacredness of insanity saved his skin. The keepers durst not execute the sentence passed upon him; and Achmet, to whom a treat in his own way was since the ravages of the plague become quite a rarity, walked off sorely disappointed, and devoutly praying God to deliver the Bagnio from such madmen!

Yacoob's contrivances to be released from his confinement did not end here. He had got by heart all the prayers of the Mohammedans, and secretly made himself perfect in all the accompanying gestures. One morning, after he had attracted the eye of the Turkish visitor of some distinction, he suddenly fell on his face, crying: "he saw the prophet, and was not only bidden by him to embrace Islamism,[2] but actually instructed how to perform its rites;" – of which indeed he forthwith acquitted himself with great dexterity. The bait took with the stranger; but the farce was laughed at by the familiars of the place, who told Yacoob he might go to the mosque if he chose, but reminded him that there was one in the Bagnio. This damped his religious ardour, and the vision sneaked off, as visions do. Still did he from time to time repeat his grimaces; and he was always observed to invoke Allah most lustily when a stranger came in sight. It was curious to see the holy silence with which on these occasions he went through his namaz,[3] until large drops of perspiration trickled down his greasy face. No disappointments had power to stop these pious but unavailing exercises.

He and I herded little together. The ordinary companion of my toil was a young Greek, nearly of my own age, but, from his less elevated stature, his rounder features, and his more delicate complexion, seemingly three or four years younger. His dress, though at the time rather the worse for wear, preserved an appearance of something beyond mere neatness, or even costliness; it had a sort of studied, and what would be called in Christendom theatrical elegance. His gait and manners corresponded. They too wore, not an air of quality, but a species of *recherché* carried beyond natural grace. This artificial exterior, this refinement of appearance, were the more remarkable from the simplicity of mind, the singleness of heart, on which they seemed superstructed. The varnish penetrated not beyond the surface. Yet there it adhered pertinaciously, and amidst sentiments of sincerest piety, Anagnosti never fell upon his knees to say his prayers, without an air, and never rose from his devotions, without a grace. He himself, when aware of these superfluous ornaments, blushed, and would have given all he possessed to shake them off: but they clung to him in his own despite. Sometimes I used to rally him on the semblance of affectation so little suited to our abode, and so discordant to his real character. "Is it my fault?" cried he one day. "If the plant has so long been trained to formal symmetry, can the utmost neglect itself immediately recall its primitive ease and wildness? The subject, as you may have observed, is one which I think of reluctantly, and hitherto have avoided with care: but your good nature assures me of your pity. Hear my story, and judge."

CHAPTER VII

"My father," continued Anagnosti, "was proësti[1] of Stavro: Phoenea gave birth to my revered mother…"

"No doubt," cried I, interrupting him, "all the world knows those two important places; but fancy me very ignorant, and tell me where they lie?"

"Near Corinth," answered the youth, somewhat surprised and resumed his tale.

"The inhabitants of Phoenea," said he, – "justly boast of their proficiency in the mysteries of divination. This art formed my mother's principal portion. Unfortunately her skill made her foresee every calamity, but it found a cure for none; and she spent her life in bewailing her sorrowful endowments. Those of my father were of a different cast. They consisted not so much in doubling present evils by the fear of future mischiefs, as in making the best of the ills under which we unavoidably laboured. When therefore one evening a troop of Arnaoots – in order to pay themselves for the unwelcome protection they had afforded us against the Russians – plundered our house, made fire-wood of our olive-trees, and turned out our cattle into our vineyard, my much respected father observed how fortunate was this misfortune, as we possessed at Salonica a rich relation who would do better for us than we could do for ourselves – unless, as my mother added with a shake of the head, he should be dead or ruined.

"This kinsman we determined to seek out. Leaving our patrimony at the mercy of the waywode, as an acknowledgement for his trouble in selling us to the robbers, we bade adieu to our native land – which never had looked more lovely than it did at that moment – and set out upon our journey. My father trusted for our travelling expenses to the charity with which he was sure Providence would inspire every mortal we met, while my mother trembled lest we should only meet banditti. If any thing could move the hardest heart, it certainly was our procession. Imagine, first, a man already in years, loaded with scanty wrecks of his property; next, a woman, pale, emaciated and borne down by illness, with a baby at the breast, and leading another by the hand, hardly able to follow; while, myself between two little girls, one of ten and one of twelve, in a most tattered condition, brought up the rear. We did not beg, for we knew not the way; but we looked wretchedness itself: and sometimes we found relief, and to those that bestowed it, we gave in return all we had to give, – our blessing. As however we advanced on the journey, we began to need less assistance. This my mother had said would happen, and she herself was the one that accomplished her prediction. Sinking under her grief she turned out of the path, sat down upon a stone, and urged us to proceed – for she could go no further. I threw my arms round her neck, tried to cheer her, and sobbed. 'O my Anagnosti;' said she, as she pressed my little fingers within her clammy hand, and fixed on my countenance her anxious boding look, -'O my curly-headed boy! Remember your poor mother's last words; let others fear their foes; you, my sweet innocent, beware only of your friends!' Then, in convulsive agony, she clasped me to her breast, laid down her head, and died.

"Much as my mother's weakness had retarded our progress, her decease was the only event in which my father could not at first see any advantage. Long he wept for his loss, and at last, assisted by us all, he dug a grave by the road-side. In it was buried my poor mother, – all but this lock of hair, which shall only return to dust with her child.

"Just as we again set forward from the dismal spot, the baby, which had long been pining, expired for want of sustenance. We would not divide in death what in life had thus far still been as one; and turning back, deposited the child in the lap of its parent: – they sleep together!

"My father now observed, 'it was better for my mother to be dead than to suffer; and my little brother was provided for.' Still he never ceased to weep until we arrived at Volo. A lady of that place, who had lost an only child, took such a fancy to my rosy face that she begged to have it. Her nauseous kisses had stamped it hers already! After my mother's, could I bear them? My father too was but indifferently inclined to part with his Anagnosti – the only one of his children who in all his looks and sayings reminded him of his Zoe: but he was poor, he thought that his loss would be my advantage, and he only proceeded on with the other three. I stayed, to cry and be kissed.

"At Salonica my father found that his affluent relation had died a bankrupt, as my mother had foretold. 'This,' he observed, 'must make him return to the labours of the field, which after all, were the healthiest.' Alas! in the damp deleterious country to whose climate he was unaccustomed, they carried him off. It was what my mother knew would happen. In a quarrel between my father and his waywode, she had heard the spiteful wretch wish his worthier neighbour a seven year's ague.[2] The disease only took seven months to bring him to the grave; and this he thought a great mercy. While ill too, he remembered that one day in the fields, on suddenly turning round, he had seen his fellow-labourers, jealous of a stranger, stamp on his shadow. How could he after that be expected to live? At the last gasp, his eyes lit up at the thoughts of rejoining his Zoe! – and his poor Anagnosti, he was sure, would not long stay behind. Charitable persons took in the other little orphans: I sent them the few pence I had collected: but alas, my little hoard was lost by the way!

"My own good fortune lasted not. The old lady at Volo who had promised to adopt me, changed her fondness into aversion when she found how dearly I loved to play in puddles, and how little I liked to be kissed. She scolded me for being a boy; and sighed to think what a tidy little girl she might have had in my place, who never for an instant would have quitted her side. The first of these faults I acknowledged, and observed that she might have been aware of it before; and as for the other grievance, I told her 'if I could not always stay by her side, I could do the next best thing, which was never to go near her again.' She made no reply and I ran away.

"As I had always promised the Holy Virgin faithfully to divide with her whatever I might earn, I made no doubt that she would direct me well in my search for a livelihood. I cannot think she did; though it might be for my good. She made me engage on board a Hydriote[3] laden with corn for the Black Sea. A single family formed the crew, from the captain down to the lowest cabin-boy. But to that family poor Anagnosti belonged not; and when all the rest of the sailors used in a calm to dance on the deck, I alone was left out to listen to their mirth in the hold. Alas, I have since had dancing enough! At the time, however, I thought the hardship so great, that on my knees I begged the captain to let me too have my share of dancing, and to flog me afterwards as much as he pleased. Had he granted my petition, I might not have had leisure to discover, as I did, how ill a sailor's task suited my abilities, or agreed with my duty to the Panagia. I therefore resolved to abandon my amphibious life. The moment we touched at Constantinople I took to my heels, not doubting to find an easy substance in a place where, as I had heard, the streets were paved with silver, and the houses roofed with gold. For two long days I waded knee-deep in mire – sleeping at night among the cinders of the public baths, and waking in the morning without a morsel of bread to break my fast. So great became my hunger, that, at a sudden turn which brought me opposite a cook-shop near the Tophana,[4] the sight of a plate of kiebabs[5] hot from the oven almost bereft me of my senses. Not daring to approach, I involuntarily fell on my knees, and half worshipped the dear hissing cutlets at a respectful distance. An ill-looking fellow saw the action, and guessing the motive, told me, 'if I was hungry to come along with him; – I should not want for bread, as he was a baker.' He wanted a shop-boy; and hard as it might seem for the son of proësti of Stavro to sell rolls at Constantinople, my stomach audibly groaned the words: 'necessity had no law!'

"My apprenticeship was short. The very second day of my ministry, after a flying visit from a Turk, my master came up to me, and said 'he liked me so well that he had determined immediately to give me a share in the business; and I had nothing to do – whoever might call – but to say that the concern was my own.' On this my principal ran out, leaving me in astonishment at my speedy promotion.

"A person did call, and I did say that the concern was my own: but as that person was the Stambool Effende,[6] who had set apart that day for weighing the weights and for measuring the measures of the different tradesmen, the deficiency he found in ours made him – though very condescending and familiar at first – end by ordering that I should be dealt by as I dealt by my loaves; namely, baked in my own oven. In this consisted the chief advantage I was to derive from the partnership.

"My cries of 'aman'[7] at this intemperate sentence, brought out the whole neighbourhood. It well knew my master's character, vouched for mine without knowing it, and through dint of strenuous intercession moved the Effende to such excess of lenity, as, in regard for my innocence, only to order me three dozen strokes on the soles of my feet.

"The change, undoubtedly, was to my advantage: yet did I feel so angry that I swore rather to go without bread all the days of my life, than ever again to trust a baker. Lame as I was I tried to hobble away. An odd-looking man, who had been eyeing me all along from head to foot, asked me whether I loved dancing. The question seemed insulting; but, lest I should commit myself, I neither answered yes or no. 'You have been ill-used' – added he – 'My compassionate heart moves me to take you home, there to cure your bruises.' I fancied not the man's countenance, but my feet told me not to mind his face, and I saw the less of it as he took me on his back. While riding along I conceived very sinister forebodings; but when set down where we stopped I smiled at my fears. Nothing could look less terrific than the place of my destination. Around the walls hung suspended by elegant cords and tassels, cymbals, guitars, and other musical instruments, beautifully inlaid with mother of pearl. The richest dresses were airing in the windows, and if the habitation resembled any one thing more than the another, it was a temple of mirth. In fact, when, restored by wholesome applications both outward and inward, I asked what return I could make for so much hospitality? the answer was, 'to dance'.

"I immediately began capering. But this was not the thing meant. My host – a Greek of Scyra – had in his youth been a dancer by profession. Age having stiffened his joints, he now gained his livelihood by giving suppleness to younger limbs. He had a number of boys whom he trained to perform ballets in the conacks or palaces of the great. His eye had been caught by my nimbleness when about to be put in the oven, and he roused my ambition by pledging himself to make me a first-rate dancer,

"The greatest natural genius still requires cultivation. For a while I toiled beyond all belief. But as I never attempted a difficult step without addressing the Panagia, I succeeded at last. I may say without vanity that I acquired the perfection of the art. The exactness of my poise, the precision of my movements, the apparent ease with which I performed the most difficult steps, were pronounced positively sublime. From the ends of my fingers to the tip of my toes, all was expression. The best connoisseurs declared that in me alone they had found the poetry of the heel; and my very shadow was lighter than other people's shadows. But I do not wish to praise myself!

"That I became celebrated, I need not tell. Every other dancer was voted execrable. Whenever I appeared, I was stunned with applause before I moved a step; and the spectators were entranced at my performance of what in others would have been hissed: for it was not always that I exerted my best abilities. With indifferent judges I would scarcely stir; and even with the best I sometimes had my bad days, when all the coaxing in the world could not draw out my powers. I once felt so ill in reality, that another dancer was sent out in my clothes, who, accomplishing with evident effort what I performed with ease, made the blockheads declare that I never yet had danced as well as I did that evening.

"My emoluments kept pace with my celebrity. At each pause in my exhibitions my forehead used to be studded with gold coins,[8] and at the conclusion of the performance, heaps of sequins showered from all sides into my spangled cap. Who then could have fancied me otherwise than happy? But it is one thing to divert others, and it is another to taste of joy one's self! The constant fatigue, the sense of dependence, the fear of not succeeding, the liability to the humours of a capricious audience, the danger of losing the attention of novelty, the chance of being eclipsed by some abler competitor, are alone dreadful drawbacks on a profession like mine. Yet with me they were minor evils. Keener sufferings peculiar to myself assailed me, and that in general by preference just when my situation seemed most enviable; for it was almost always in the intoxication and flurry of spirits produced by the exertions I made, by the bravos I excited, and by the crowds of people, the glare of lights, and the din of instruments I moved among, that the image of my diseased mother, as she appeared in her last moments, would rise with most distinctness to my heated fancy. And often have I between the several acts of entertainment, retired to some lonely corner to weep at liberty, while the whole assembly seemed in ecstasies of pleasure. It is true that if dancing produced melancholy, melancholy more than once in its turn produced dancing. Sometimes, in the sort of frenzy brought out by the clang of a full band, I have started up, and, like the Mewlewi derwishes,[9] have reeled round a room full of people, until, completely exhausted, I fell senseless on the floor.

"To add to the discomforts of my situation, I was not even allowed to retain the hard-earned fruits of my labour. Of the gold which I gained by the sweat of my brow not a para remained my own, except what in the evening, when I crossed the cemetery of Galata, I had the address to slip into a hollow tree or to drop behind a mouldering tombstone, where the crows often were the first to find my little store. The moment I got home from our nightly exhibition I was regularly searched, and every farthing found about me went into my master's pocket, as his pay for my board, lodging, and maintenance. Enraged at his illiberality, I one evening threw my gilt jacket in his face, saying, I wished to keep nothing that was his, but would go and exercise my talent, naked as I stood, on my own account. Hereupon the vampire – the odious blood-sucker – brought against me such a bill for bestowing that talent of which he said I wanted to rob him, as must have left me all my life a mere drudge – a puppet moving at his nod, – had I not determined to settle the account in my own way.

"In fact, now clearly discerning the whole drift of the hospitality which the Scyrote had so kindly afforded me I henceforth watched my opportunity to slip away from the ballet-master at Galata, as I had done from the lady at Volo, the Hydriote captain, and the fraudulent baker. This was not an easy matter. Our master was vigilance personified, and never allowed me to go out of his sight. An accident befriended me. One of my companions had long cherished the greatest envy of my superiority. In a *pas-de-deux* which we performed together as a lover and his mistress, he kicked my shins; I boxed his ears; he retorted by breaking on my head the guitar with which he was serenading me, and scratching my face in such a manner that the next time the troop went out, I was left at home as unfit to be seen. Whatever might ail my head, my heels were in good order; I took to them as usual, and never stopped till I had reached the quarter most remote from where the Scyrote lived.

"Here I might dance on my own account as much as I pleased, but found nobody to dance to except the lowest rabble. In retiring out of my master's latitude I had out-stepped my own vantage-ground. From exhibiting in palaces to assemblies of the great, amid showers of gold, I was reduced to toil in taverns for the amusement of ruffians, who thought a few paras a very liberal reward, after perhaps mortifying my pride into the bargain, by invidious comparisons with some arrant posture-maker. Obliged to lower the tone of my performance to the standard of my new patrons, I lost all that finish and delicacy of movement for which my dancing had been celebrated, and dwindled into little better than a tumbler.

"Nor was this all. One night, after drudging to amuse a set of brutes, I met with such ill treatment from the Bacchantes their companions, as to make me expect with my poor lyre the end of Orpheus. Thank God! The Panagia – knowing how observant I always had been of her festivals – protected me even against her own sex, and my poor life was saved, little worth as it was. This signal escape led me to serious reflections.

"I had always been punctual in my prayers, both before dancing and after; and had as yet committed no very heinous sin, save once on a fast-day eating some nice yaoort,[10] which a Turk gave me after a long performance; but I did not know what worse might happen in my daily intercourse with infidels; and I determined to avoid the danger by quitting a profession, which, if distinguished, is also dangerous, and full of hazard to one's faith and morals.

"Alas! it was too late to execute my good intentions! My special admirers, brought into contact at a tavern with the professed supporters of a rival dancer, the two factions came to a pitched battle, in which a life or two were lost, while I – the innocent cause of the disturbance – was taken up by the patrole, and thrown into this place of wretchedness; more than ever convinced of the truth of all my honoured mother's predictions: – for what were the old lady of Volo, who washed her hands of me when I would kiss her no longer; the Hydriote captain, who would not let me dance with my messmates, after giving me shelter on board his ship; the baker who first fed, and next slily destined me to a snug corner in his oven; the Scyrote, who cured, who entertained, and afterwards robbed me of all my lawful gains; and the caleondjees, who went about my zealous champions, in order to get me almost torn to pieces limb by limb, and locked up in the Bagnio – but so many persons, all professing themselves my staunch and trusty friends! And such is the horror with which the word now inspires me, that, were I hear the Panagia herself say she was my friend, great as hitherto has been the holy lady's goodness, I should expect her to end by playing me some scurvy trick!"

Here ended my companion's tale – the faithful picture of his mind, in which moral rectitude and affection were strangely combined with conceit, credulity and bigotry. In the wide range of social intercourse this odd mixture might not perhaps have taken much hold on my harder compound; nor should I greatly have coveted an intimacy with the character of a stage-dancer grafted on a peasant; but in the narrow precincts of the Bagnio fastidiousness wears out, and constant propinquity produced different sentiments; and the more, as athwart Anagnosti's apparent facility of temper and tenderness of heart there broke forth a sort of determined sturdiness on certain points, which all the laxity of his education and companions had never removed, and which, inclined as one might be to smile at his studied exterior, induced a sort of respect for the stuff within. Insensibly, therefore, an attachment grew between us, which, though it daily increased, gave my companion no alarm, until one day I remarked how great an alleviation our misery had derived from our friendship. At this unguarded speech Anagnosti turned pale. "Friendship!" repeated he; "Say not so! It will again bring me ill fortune. Like the rest of my friends, you will ultimately be my bane."

"Words," answered I, laughing, "cannot alter the nature of things. We certainly at this moment are friends, and warm ones too: for I believe each would willingly lay down his life for the other; and even if the dangers of friendship should now make us resolve to become bitter enemies, it would already be too late: – already would the present evil fail to ensure redemption from the future one! – The mischief is done; the spell is upon you."

"Then," said Anagnosti, after ruminating a little, "if we cannot be less than friends, let us be more! Let us become brothers; let religion sanctify our intimacy, so as to divest it of its dangers;" – and upon this he proposed to me the solemn ceremony,[11] which, in our church, united two friends of either sex in the face of the altar by solemn vows, gives them in the endearing appellation of brothers or sisters, and imposes upon them the sacred obligation to stand by each other in life and death.

Anagnosti, though he certainly had in his different avocations run away as often as he had stood his ground, and had derived from his last mode of life a certain outward twinge of effeminacy, yet in reality was as brave as affectionate. He had more than once resisted his guardians most manfully in their unjust behests; he had even defended his new friend at the risk of his life: – for, one day that, disabled by illness, I lay at the mercy of every aggressor, he had wrested from a fellow slave the dagger levelled at my breast for the sake of the worn-out capote on my back; and from his disposition there was every reason to expect that the fruits and burdens of our alliance would ever be equally shared. The first day therefore that we could obtain the permission, we went to the priest in the Bagnio, and desired the holy man, after a short service which our straitened means permitted, to accomplish the indissoluble union. At first the venerable papas treated the request as a jest. "The practice," he said, "was quite obsolete, except among the most barbarous clans of the remotest provinces. Epirotes, and other savages who like them lived in eternal strife, might indeed still retain such old customs[12], but the people at Constantinople were sufficiently employed in minding their own concerns, without gratuitously engaging to risk their lives for others." This remonstrance producing no effect, the priest warned us more earnestly to consider the consequences, before we irrevocably bound ourselves by so serious an engagement. Still we insisted, and he at last complied. He enveloped us in the sacred veil, symbol of the holy ties we contracted; and made us swear on our knees, in the face of Heaven, to share together like brothers, while we breathed, both good and adverse fortune.

The solemn vow pronounced, and Heaven fervently implored to bless it, we again rose. I shook Agagnosti by the hand, and could not refrain from saying, "though now brothers, still friends as before."

He involuntarily shuddered. All his fears recurred; and on casting off the sacred zone, we found on it a fresh stain of blood. How it came there neither of us could guess. Both searched for the cause: none could be discovered; and we at last forgot the evil omen.

The very period which saw our intimacy indissolubly riveted, was fated to be that of our separation. Whether at the time of my imprisonment the length of my detention had been fixed; or whether (as I afterwards suspected) Mavroyeni, while apparently rejecting my application, in reality had procured my deliverance, – one morning, when I least expected my freedom. I was bidden to quit the Bagnio. I say "bidden;" for, thinking the thing optional, I at first, in conformity with my sacred engagement, refused to accept the boon offered, unless shared by my friend. But I now found myself as little allowed to stay in, as I had before been to stay out of the Bagnio, at my pleasure. I must resume my liberty whether I chose or not, and was very near being driven by force out of prison, – a somewhat unusual circumstance! Anagnosti tried to sweeten the bitterness of my release, by observing that it might be rendered instrumental in procuring his own. "Remember." said he, "that in losing you, I lose all. O Anastasius, O my – *friend!* remember,"...

Here his sobs interrupted his speech, and the guards, tired of our tedious leave-taking, tore us asunder. After proceeding on a few yards, I turned round to cast one more last look after my companion: but already the gates had been shut behind me; and I went forth – shaking off indeed the dust of my prison, and with all Constantinople before me, – but without a single particle of that rapturous joy of heart, which I always fancied must crown the hour of my liberation.

CHAPTER VIII

To enjoy liberty one must live, and to live one must eat, and I had not a para in the world to purchase me a meal. In this embarrassing situation I thought of my old patron. If he really had procured my freedom, it was proper to thank him; if not, it was still wise to do so. In the first case, he might be induced by my sense of past kindness to seek still greater claims to my future gratitude, – since benefactors often resemble gamblers, who double their stakes rather than lose the benefit of a first throw; and in the latter case, the thanks I gave for imaginary services would make the drogueman wish to deserve them by real obligations. Gratitude I had often found most productive when it preceded the benefit. Besides I had my friend Anagnosti to intercede for and I was desirous to strike the iron while it was hot.

Most willingly would I have smartened myself up for the visit. Not only a tattered appearance smooths the way but indifferently athwart the out-post of pampered domestics, who guard the approaches of the great man's citadel; it often makes the master himself ashamed of his petitioner. The rich are ever ready to accuse the poor of wanting proper respect, when they offend the fastidious eye of pride by the display of their wretchedness. The utmost I could do, however, was to arrange my rags gracefully; and – repeating to myself, as I strutted along, that a man's innate dignity of mien and manners were a sufficient passport even to the presence of a king – I boldly went to the Fanar, and with the least tremor knocked at Mavroyeni's door.

It certainly opened at my summons, but not to let me enter. The porter who answered, holding it cautiously ajar, contrived to fill the open aperture with his own person, until he had most leisurely surveyed mine. While thus examined, I recognised in my surveyor an old acquaintance. So it seems he did in me: for when I asked to see his master, he banged the door in my face, without a syllable of reply. It was just what I myself had done a dozen times, when with Mavroyeni at Argos. The uncouthness of the janitor's reception, therefore, I thought, must originate higher. Servants behaved not thus, unless they felt their conduct sanctioned by their masters: for dependants know the antipathies of their patrons by instinct. "Hie thee hence, therefore, Anastasius," exclaimed I; "thou hast no longer any business near this threshold:" and hereupon I walked away.

At that instant the same door burst open again, and almost flew off its hinges. I looked back. It was to let out Mavroyeni himself. Convinced that an attempt to accost him would only expose me to fresh mortifications, I now felt as solicitous to avoid his eye as I had been before to be admitted to his presence. Hastily drawing back my head, I passed on, or rather ran away, as if it had been an ignominy even to be seen near the drogueman's abode.

Heated with my race, I rushed into the first coffee-house on my way, and observing a large bowl of hoshab[1] most invitingly set out on the counter, greedily lifted it to my lips, and gulped down the icy beverage. I had no earthly means of payment; but heaven came to my assistance. Exhausted with inanition, I felt too weak to resist the sudden chill: it struck me to the heart. I reeled backwards, and fell senseless on the floor.

How long the fit lasted I am unable to tell. All I know is, that when my senses returned I found myself in a smart jog trot, bumping at the back of a hamal, and travelling in this inconvenient posture at the rate of a league an hour, up one dirty lane and down another; – but whither, was beyond my power to guess.

I therefore made free to ask the question, and was but little pleased with the information obtained. Convicted in the shop by my sudden seizure of a confirmed plague, the master had only felt desirous to get rid as soon as possible of so unwelcome a customer, and had called in the porter aforesaid, to convey me to hospital. Thither I was speeding as fast as another man's legs could carry my person: for even during the above account my bearer slackened not his pace, but kept jogging on as lustily as before.

I took the liberty of representing that there was mistake in the case. However weak and exhausted, I was totally free from any infectious disorder. "Nothing more likely," answered the hamal; "but he has paid for the job, and must earn his fare;" and upon this he only grasped me somewhat tighter than he had done before, for fear that being less ill than he imagined, I might contrive more easily to give him the slip. In vain I insisted upon being let loose, and excused from going where, if I brought not the plague, I was sure to find it. My expostulations were of no avail; and I therefore tried to liberate myself by pummelling my vehicle with all my might: – but the feeble impression of my unnerved fist on the rough hide of my obstinate beast, instead of making him throw me off, only served to quicken his pace.

I now resorted to the last means of salvation in my power, fixed my claws in the brawny throat of the miscreant, and squeezed him almost to suffocation. Finding his load became too troublesome, he at last let me slip down from his back to the ground, swore I was the most refractory piece of goods he ever had carried, and left me, in order to seek elsewhere an easier fare.

One street appeared to me as good as another die in: – and my present sensations foreboded nothing else. I crawled to a stepping-stone near the place where I had been deposited, and on that pillow resigned myself to my fate.

So near in fact seemed my exit, that a novelist writing my history would have availed himself of the circumstance happily to terminate his first volume, and to leave me irretrievably for dead in the opinion of his reader, until my unexpected resurrection at the beginning of volume the second. Writing in the first person, I cannot keep my friends in this state of agreeable suspense, or conceal from them one single moment that I lived on: but it was for some time in this wretchedness, as would not even leave the most fastidious critic any pretence to find fault with the proceeding. One man passed by me, and another, and another, and several stopped and looked; but, when their curiosity was satisfied, all went on again, only shrugging up their shoulders. No one of my sex offered me the least assistance. At last came two females. For several minutes ere they reached my resting-place, their incessant loquacity had warned me of their approach; but I was too ill to look up, and had closed my eyes. "Bless me," said the one, "I see something alive there!" "Bless me," said the other, "and so do I!" "A man!" cried the first. "A handsome youth I declare!" cried the second. "Unwell," rejoined the little one: "Dying, I fear," resumed the tall one. "How like Anastasius!" exclaimed the former. "Himself, as I live!" replied the latter. "Then, indeed," continued the other, in a sagacious whisper, "I am very much afraid, neighbour, that he is not dying, but only dead drunk." – Enviable effects of a good name!

My character was now to me a matter of life and death. "No," said I, therefore – making an effort to speak, but in a scarce audible voice; – "it is not drunkenness that oppresses me: it is suffering – it is starvation."

At this speech, the women both scream out in astonishment; both talk at the same time. They want to know the how, the when, the where. "Torment me not with questions," cried I; "but if you have any humanity, get me conveyed to St. Demetrius.[2] Pay the five piastres required for my admission; and expect not to be repaid in this world." Saying this, I again fainted away.

The first perception which followed this second fit, was that of an entirely new change of objects. The women had succeeded in their humane endeavours, and I was lying under a filthy coverlet, on a filthy pallet, in the filthy hospital in question, next to a dead man, whose pulse the would-be physician of the place was just in the act of feeling, – assuring some by-standers that it was perfectly quiet, and no longer showed any symptom of fever.

I shall not finish the picture of the disgusting abode, where nevertheless I had been introduced only out of sheer humanity. Suffice to say that under its hospitable roof every nuisance found a home, medicine alone excepted. A scanty charity was the chief support of the institution, and an unwieldy governor the chief object supported. Yet, after a fair contest between my constitution and my pleurisy, in which neither side received the least assistance from doubtful prescriptions, the former got the better. The father of nine helpless orphans expired by my side, and I recovered.

It was during my convalescence that I most forcibly felt the wretchedness of my receptacle: it was during my convalescence, also, that I most fully owned my unworthyness of a better. "But," cried I, tossing about on my hard couch, "the deadliest poisons compose the most salutiferous medicines, and the direst calamities produce the best resolves. It will be my own fault if I rise not from this bed of sickness and suffering, both wiser and worthier!" Thus I spoke while my pulse still beat low, and my passions were still weak.

At last came the day which I fancied would never come – that of my release from the hospital. It dawned about a month after I had entered the dismal place. I sallied forth at mid-day; and indescribable was the rapture with which I first again breathed a pure air, and beheld the whole expanse of an azure sky.

Still was I as much as ever at a loss how to subsist. Absorbed in this weighty consideration I slowly walked down the hill of St. Demetrius, when I fancied I discerned at a distance a caravan of travellers, who, with a slow and steady pace were advancing towards Pera, the residence of the Franks at Constantinople. I mechanically quickened my steps, in order to survey the procession more closely.

First in the order of march came a clumsy calash, stowed as full as it could hold of wondering travellers; next came a heavy araba,[3] loaded with as many trunks, portmanteaus, parcels, and packages, as it could well carry; and lastly led up the rear a grim-looking Tartar,[4] keeping order among half a dozen Frank servants of every description, jogging heavily along on their worn-out jades. At this sight the droguemanic blood began to speak within me. "These are strangers, Anastasius," it whispered: "be thou their interpreter, and thy livelihood is secured." I obeyed the inward voice as an inspiration from heaven, and, after smartening myself up a little, approached the first carriage.

"Welcome to Pera, excellencies!" said I, with a profound bow, to the party within. At these words up started two gaunt figures in nightcaps, with spectacles on their noses, and German pipes in their mouths – whose respective corners still kept mechanically puffing whiffs of smoke at each other. The first action which followed was to lay their hands on the blunderbusses hung about the carriage; but, seeing me alone, on foot, they seemed after some consultation to think they might venture not to fire, and only kept staring at me in profound silence. I therefore repeated my salute in a more articulate manner, and again said, "Welcome, excellencies, to Pera, where you are most anxiously expected. As you will probably want a skilful interpreter, give me leave to recommend a most unexceptionable person – I mean myself. Respectable references, I know, are indispensable in a place where every one is on the watch to impose upon the unwary traveller; but such I think I can name. As to what character they may give me; *that*," added I with a modest bow, – "*that* it would ill become your humble servant himself to enlarge upon."

At so Christian-like a speech, uttered in the very heart of Turkey, the travellers grinned from ear to ear with delight. It produced another short consultation; after which the two chiefs cried out in chorus: "*Qui chai pesoin*," and bade me mount by their side. This enabled me, after a little compliment on Germany their birthplace, and on their proficiency in the French idiom, immediately to enter upon the duties of my office – for which I thought myself sufficiently qualified, by the squibs which I had heard the drogueman of the Porte, Morosi, let off, in company with my patron, at the diplomatic corps of Pera.

"This edifice," said I, pointing to the first building of note in the suburb which we met in our way, "is the palace of the Ich-oglans – the Sultan's pages. It is the most fruitful seminary of favourites, of Pashas, and of Sultanas' husbands.[5] In that direction lives that most respectable of characters the Imperial internuncio[6] – the Baron Herbert; who, with all the shrewdness of a thorough-paced minister, combines all the playful simplicity of a child. Further on dwells the French ambassador Monsieur de Choi-seul-Gouffier – a very great man in little things; and opposite him lives his antagonist in taste, politics and country, the English envoy Sir Robert Ainslie – of whom the world maintains exactly the reverse. Quite at the bottom of the street, likewise facing each other, live the envoys of Russia and Sweden.[7] The former I feel bound to respect, whatever be his merit; the latter really possesses much. He is an Armenian, who writes in French a history of Turkey. He has lately made with his bookseller an exchange profitable to both, – he having given his manuscript, and the other his daughter: that is to say, the Armenian a single voluminous work, and the Frenchman a brief epitome of his whole shop. Wedged in between the palaces of Spain and Portugal is that of the Dutch ambassador, whose name, Vandendiddem-totgelder,[8] is almost too long for these short autumn days; and whose head is thought to be almost as long as his name: inasmuch as he regularly receives, twice a week, the Leyden gazette; which renders him beyond all controversy the best informed of the whole Christian *Corps Diplomatique*, with regard to Turkish politics. You see, gentlemen, the representatives of all the potentates of Christendom, from Petersburg to Lisbon, and from Stockholm to Naples, are here penned together in this single narrow street, where they have the advantage of living as far as possible from the Turks among whom they come to reside, and of watching all day long the motions of their own colleagues, from their most distant journeys to the sublime Porte, to their most ordinary visits to the recesses of their gardens."

These little specimens of my *savoir-dire* seemed to please my German friends. They immediately noted them down in their huge memorandum books, which, no more than their short pipes, were ever left an instant unemployed. Scarce had the party stepped into the inn which I was allowed to recommend, when they engaged me for the whole fortnight which they meant to devote to the survey of the Turkish capital.

My travellers were of the true inquisitive sort. Every body used to fly at their approach; a circumstance highly favourable to my interest. Under the notion of always applying for information at the fountain-head, they would stop the surliest Turk they met, to ask why Moslemen locked up their women. One day they begged the Imperial minister, at his own table, to tell them confidentially whether Austria was to be trusted. They were very solicitous to know from the Russian envoy the number of Catherine's lovers: and they pressed hard for an audience of the Kislar Aga,[9] only to inquire whence came the best black eunuchs. Had they been in the company of the Grand Mufti, they certainly would have asked his honest opinion of the missions of Mohammed; and they would scarce have neglected the opportunity, had it offered, of inquiring of the Sultan himself, whether he was legitimate heir to the Califate, as he asserted. In consequence of this straight-forward system I was every moment obliged to interfere, and to pledge myself for the guiltless intentions of our travellers. The statistics of the empire, its government, politics, finances, &c. they indeed troubled themselves little about. All such things they thought might be learnt much more compendiously at home from the Leipsic gazetteer; but the botany and mineralogy of the country were what they studied both with body and soul. Every day we brought home from our excursions such heaps of what the ignorant chose to call hay and stones, that the wags whom we met on our way used to ask whether these were for food and lodging; while the more fanatical among the Turks swore we carried away patterns of the country, in order to sell it to infidels; and one party, by way of giving us enough of what we wanted, was near stoning us to death. Hereupon, to elude observation, my cunning travellers determined to dress after the country fashion: but this only made bad worse; for they wore their new garb so awkwardly, that the natives began to think they put it on in mockery, and were frequently near stripping them to the skin; independent of which, whenever they went out, they got so entangled in their shaksheers and trousers, their shawls and their papooshes, that our progress might be traced by the mere relics of their habiliments which strewed the road. Sole manager both of the home and foreign department, I however tried to give all possible respectability to their appearance, and never would suffer their dignity to be committed by paltry savings; at the same time, that, to show them how careful I was of their money, I took care sometimes to detain them an hour or two in driving a close bargain about a few paras, – especially when I saw them in a hurry. Accordingly, if they had any fault to find with me, it was for my over-scrupulous economy. That failing alone excepted they thought me a treasure; and so I certainly found them.

The fortnight of their intended stay having elapsed, they were all impatience to depart. Out of pure regard for science I contrived to prolong their sojourn another fortnight, by various little delays, which with a little industry I brought about in the most natural way imaginable, but which I joined them in lamenting exceedingly: and when at last they set off – which I saw with very sincere regret – I was left by them in possession of a most flattering testimonial of my zeal and fidelity. As to their behaviour to me, its liberality might be sufficiently inferred from the change in my appearance.

This first experiment gave me a taste for the tergiumanic life. It also increased my means of success in that department. Till I took up my residence at Pera, I had little intercourse with that odd race of people yclept Franks, except though the stray specimens that now and then crossed the harbour, on a visit of curiosity or business to Constantinople. I now got acquainted with their ways, while they became familiarised with my person. This gradually procured me the advantage of seeing and serving, in my new capacity, samples of almost every nation of Europe. Thus I formed a sort of polyglot collection of certificates of my own ability and merits, which I filed very neatly on a red tape according to the order of their dates, and to a sight of which I treated every new comer whom I thought worthy of that distinction.

Once, however, the lofty manner and the imperious tone of an English traveller, newly arrived, completely deceived me. From his fastidiousness I made no doubt I was addressing some great Mylordo: it was a button-maker to whom I had the honour of bowing. He came red hot from a place called Birmingham, to show the Turks samples of his manufacture. Unfortunately Turks wear no buttons, at least such as he dealt in; at which discovery he felt exceedingly wroth. My ill fated back was destined to feel the first brunt of his ill humour. After spending nearly two hours in spelling every word of every one of my certificates – "This then," said he in a scarce intelligible idiom, which he fancied to be French, "is the evidence of your deserts?" "It is," answered I, with an inclination of the head. "And I am to make it the rule of my behaviour?" "If your Excellency be pleased to have that goodness," replied I, smirking most agreeably. "Very well," resumed the traitor, never moving a muscle of his insipid countenance, "My Excellency will have that goodness." And up he gets, gravely walks – without uttering another syllable – to the door, turns the key in the lock, takes a little bit of a pistol scarce five inches long – also from Birmingham, I suppose – out of his pocket, snatches up a cudgel as thick as my wrist, and turning short upon me, who stood wondering in what this strange interlude was to end, holds the pistol to my throat, and lays the cane across my back.

This operation performed to his satisfaction: "It was No. 5," coolly said the miscreant, "whose contents I thought it right to comply with first; as being written by one of my countrymen, and because I make it a rule, in every species of business, to get the worst part over first. Had you understood our language – as an interpreter by profession ought – you might have known the certificate in question to be a solemn adjuration to all the writer's countrymen, to treat you as I have had the pleasure of doing; and all that remains for you to perform is to give me a regular receipt, such as I may have to show."

The pistol was still tickling my throat, I, jammed up against the wall, and the button-maker six feet high, and as strong as a horse. All, therefore, I could do in the way of heroism would have been to have let him blow out my brains at once; – after which, adieu my turn, at least here below! I therefore signed, had the satisfaction of seeing the receipt neatly folded up and deposited in a little red morocco pocket-book with silver clasps, was offered a sequin for the exercise I had afforded, took the money, and, leaving the button-maker to write home what mean rascals the Greeks were, departed fully impressed with the usefulness of learning languages.

Almost every evening the man of the buttons used to walk from Pera, where he had lodgings, to a merchant's at Galata, from whence he frequently returned home pretty late at night, without any escort, – trusting to his small pocket instrument, and to his colossal structure, for his safety. A dexterous thrust, at an unexpected turn, might easily have sent him to the shades below; but this would not have sufficed to assuage my thirst for revenge. I wished to inflict a shame more deep, more lasting than my own, and which, like Prometheus's vulture, should keep gnawing the traitor's heart while he lived. His great ambition at Constantinople was to boast the good graces of some Turkish female – young or old, fair or ugly, no matter! On this laudable wish I founded my scheme.

Muffled up in the feridjee which conceals the figure of the Mohammedan fair, and the veil which covers the face, I went and seated myself immediately after dusk, on one of the tombstones of the extensive cemetery of Galata, where my traveller had to pass.

He soon arrived, and, as I expected, stopped to survey the lonely fair one, whose appearance seemed to invite a comforter. The bait took. My friend, on his nearer approach, aware that his pantomime was more intelligible than his idiom, had recourse to the universal language: he held up a sequin, – and on the strength of this gift became more enterprising. Profane hands are laid on my veil. I resist: – but by way of compromise for keeping concealed my features, I show my necklace, my bracelets, my girdle. In an infantine manner I slip the manacles from my own wrists over those of my amorous shepherd, and, before his suspicions were aroused, have the satisfaction to see him fast bound in chains, not only of airy love, but of good solid brass; and with a soft lisp wish him joy of being at once handcuffed and pinioned. It was now I showed my face, and drew out my handjar[10]. Perceiving an inclination to remonstrate, "No noise," cried I, "or you die; but return me the receipt." Unable to stir, my prisoner in a surly tone bade me take it myself. I did so, and thanked him; "but," added I, "as we have not here – as with you – all the conveniences of writing, accept the acknowledgement of the poor and illiterate:" saying which, I drew the holy mark of the cross after the Greek form, neatly but indelibly, with the button-maker's own sequin, on his clumsy forehead; poured into the wound some of the gunpowder out of his pouch; and, apologizing for the poorness of the entertainment, bade him good night, and walked off.

A troop of caleondjees of my acquaintance, reeling home from a tavern, happened to come up just as I retired, and took all that I had left. The next morning the man of buttons departed from Constantinople without sound of trumpet, before sunrise; and never since has been heard of in the Turkish dominions.

This little frolic, at the expense of the English speculator, recommended me to a French chevalier, come to Stambool on a visit to his kinsman the ambassador. The lively young gentleman swore he wanted no other certificate of my character than my prowess. His object in undertaking the long journey to Turkey seemed to be to play on the guitar, and to compose French love songs. Twice a week a messenger of the embassy was despatched to Paris, with M. de Vial's effusions, in order that his friends at home might see how he employed his time abroad. *Par contre,* he had determined, as soon as he returned to France and found himself at leisure, to write a detailed account of Turkey – rather however as it ought to be, than as it was. For M. de Vial disapproved of the Othoman system *in toto*: and hence he deemed it sheer loss of time to visit the curiosities of its capital. The only thing he could have liked – had he not been busy wearing the romeïka – was an *affaire de coeur* with the favourite Sultana; and for a long while he continued exceedingly anxious to give the ladies of the imperial harem a fete on the Black Sea; but that project failing, from their sending no answers to his notes, he wondered who could bear the dowdies of Constantinople, that had seen the *Trois Sultanes* of Marmontel at the Paris opera. In truth M. De Vial had no patience with the barbarians. Their language was gibberish, *ou l'on n'entendait rien*; and they had so little *savoir vivre*, that they let their heads be chopped off like cabbage tops. Desirous, however, of treating them to a sight of the last Paris fashions, he decked out his nether man in pea-green coloured cloth, and got himself chastised by a hot-headed emir,[11] for thus profaning the forbidden colour – almost too sacred with the Turks for the head itself. In his turn M. de Vial sent the cousin of Mohammed a challenge, with which the emir lit his pipe. At last, after a whole day uselessly employed in ogling the Sultana mother through a huge telescope, from the tower of Galata, the chevalier felt seized with a desperate fit of ennui, laid in a reasonable stock of embroidered handkerchiefs, to throw to the Paris belles after a Turkish fashion which the Turks know nothing of, and determined to bid adieu to Pera. My services and talents he transferred, ere he went, to a flaxen-headed Swedish baron, whose ruddy face had inflamed the susceptible heart of the droguemaness of the Venetian mission, and who was so highly favoured by his doting mistress, that every night she allowed him to pay her whole loss at *tresette*. This lady was an uncommon proficient in writing. Proud of an accomplishment which so few of her colleagues possessed, she used every morning to fire at her lover a little billet-doux of three or four pages. These refreshing epistles I came to call for as regularly as for the water from the well, the moment the husband was supposed to have gone forth to the Reïs-effende, with the scarce shorter memorials of the Serenissima Republica – at that period any thing but serene. This same husband, though only four feet high, presumed to be jealous; and the correspondence, therefore, was to be kept from his knowledge – a circumstance which rendered my office of Mercury of some trust.

I acted accordingly. Tired of being postman without pay, I one day hinted to the lady that I should expect some species of acknowledgment for my trouble. Madame D–i was one of those fair ones for whom Cupid must dip his dart in gold, or they recoiled unfelt. She resented my freedom, called me a lowborn fellow, and forbade me her presence. The tide of amorous billets now ceased to flow for want of a channel. Nothing but my forgiveness of the insult could make it resume its course. On the part of the lady, accordingly, advances were soon made towards a reconciliation, and on mine, every spark of resentment was magnanimously extinguished until further occasion. I saw myself reinstated in my daily office.

The Hyperborean lover – not quite so brisk a correspondent as his mistress – used to answer about one letter in three or four. This, however, is the course of a few weeks began to form a very respectable amatory collection. The pink-edged, perfumed epistles – regularly endorsed – were all deposited by the delighted droguemaness in a little mother-of-pearl casket, which she kept for the benefit of her heirs by the side of her reliquary. From one of those strange incidents which will happen in the course of things, this casket, though most carefully locked up, fell into my hands; but no contrivance of mine could conjure the key out of the lady's unfathomable pocket. She used to sleep with the huge receptacle under her pillow, in order to obtain pleasant dreams. It mattered little: I had no sort of curiosity to peruse the correspondence. I contented myself with carefully wrapping up the box, sealing the cover, and begging the signor drogueman – that is to say, the signora's husband – to keep the parcel in trust for me, as most valuable property, and such as could not be committed to fitter hands. The rod thus kept suspended over his faithless spouse, the reward of my discretion past and future was demanded with becoming humility; and, to do Madame D–i justice, when she found that no other way of extricating herself was left, she showed every readiness to listen to the voice of reason.

By some accident, however, the baron got wind of these transactions, and, so far from feeling flattered as he ought to have been, with the anxiety which his mistress evinced to recover his letters, had the ingratitude to cavil about the mode, and left the fair one to find what consolation she could in the re-perusal of his correspondence. Jupiter's retreat became the signal for that of Mercury. I wanted nothing more of the commonwealth of Venice, and, with a mock farewell, left the droguemaness punished alike in her pride and her avarice.

CHAPTER IX

No sooner had my various little trades rendered me a person of some substance, than I began to think of purchasing a berath:[1] I mean one of those patents of exemption from the rigour of Turkish despotism, which the Sultan originally granted to foreign ministers, in behalf only of such rayahs as they had occasion to engage in their immediate service, but which these excellent economists now readily sell to whatever other subjects of the Grand Signor are disposed to pay the current price for the article. To a youth like me it was highly desirable to possess a paper, through whose magic power a native might in the very capital of his natural sovereign outstep the limits of his jurisdiction, brave his authority, put himself on the footing of a stranger, and, from being heretofore an Armenian or a Greek, at once find himself transformed into a reputed Italian, or German, or Frenchman, wear the gaudiest colours in competition with the Turks themselves, and strut about the streets in that *summum bonum*, a pair of yellow papooshes.

The thing had been put into my head by an Italian missionary of the Propaganda, who, considering me as a sort of stray from the Greeks, had determined to stow me safely within the pale of the Romans. On first perceiving his drift I gave his pious exertions small encouragement; observing that early habits, as well as belief as of action, could only be rooted out later in life, either by the most irresistible arguments, or the most palpable interest to adopt different tenets. To this remark the missionary only replied that he had a very general acquaintance at Pera, and, consequently, possessed many opportunities of recommending a well-disposed youth to travellers. The observation was in point. Impressed with its full weight I began to indulge the padre Ambrogio, whenever I happened to be out of place, with a little conference on the disputed articles; and for every Greek variation of the Latin creed which I yielded up, he used to find me a new situation. Unfortunately the discussion of the Greek liturgy ran so parallel with that of the signora D–i's correspondence, and the interviews with the friar were so interwoven with those of the lady, that I sometimes confounded the two subjects, and more than once, in a fit of absence, let padre Ambrogio into the mysteries of my negotiation, instead of learning from him those of his faith. The ghostly conferences, however, only ceased entirely when the friar very nefariously disappointed me, in favour of another neophyte, of an excellent employment for which I had sacrificed the whole procession according to the Greeks. Hearing of this flagrant act of bad faith, I called upon him in a very great passion; told him I again disbelieved all that he enticed me to believe; and, leaving him exceedingly dismayed at my unexpected rebellion, went to dispel the confusion in my head by a walk on the road to Dolma-backtché.

The snow which had lain several days on the ground having entirely disappeared, I met a good many people taking the air; but who all looked, I thought, as if like me they had been bewildered by some friar or derwish. At last came a woman of rank, accompanied by a long train of females. The pavement being narrow, I stood up against the wall to let her pass. As she brushed by me, her hand, gently pressing against the back of mine, gave me reason to think that I had not been unnoticed. A gay adventure seldom found me slow to engage in it, be what it might the peril of the enterprise. I therefore let the lively group trot on a few yards, and then turned back hastily myself, in the manner of a person who recollects having left something behind. Thus, without casting right or left a single glance which might savour of design, I gave the lady an opportunity of minutely scrutinising my appearance, should she be disposed to cultivate my merits. That done, I crossed over to the other side, and stole away into a by-lane, for fear of rousing the suspicions of her suite.

The next day, however, I failed not at the same hour to take a walk in the same street, and again did the same the next day, and the next; in the full expectation, each time, of meeting with some faithful Iris, commissioned to give me the verbal assurance of my good fortune.

During a whole week, my punctuality continued without the least abatement. As sure as the clock struck one I used to sally forth, and display my handsomely attired person before every woman, young or old, fair or ugly, who bore the least appearance of coming on my business. Vain and fruitless diligence! The busier females passed on without noticing my disconsolate figure at all; the less diligent baggages, who remarked my airs and graces, only answered them with laughing. Some, who had become familiar with my forlorn perambulations, ironically pitied me for the cruelty of my mistress. It was worse when two or three *goules*, that haunted the same street, seriously undertook to console me under my disappointment, and put me in the greater fright, lest, by their unconcealed advances in the broad glare of day, that they should drive away any messenger of love that might be on the wing.

At last I lost all patience, and was going in good earnest to execute the resolution fifty times solemnly taken, and as often again broken, of giving up the vain pursuit, when, just as for the last time I paced down the oft-trodden pavement, looking anxiously round on all sides to see what good tidings might still be in the wind, I perceived a Jewess – seemingly on the alert with myself – who eyed me with a promising air. I coughed once or twice; and this signal inducing the old dame to approach, we opened a parley. My answers tallying with her private tokens, she soon became confidential.

"You must know," said she, "I am a tradeswoman, one who goes about to ladies' houses to provide them with…"

"What signifies, my dear," cried I, interrupting her – "what you are, and what you provide your customers with? That speaks for itself. Only tell me who the lady is, who graciously condescends to make me the object of your embassy."

"The lady," answered the Jewess, "is the young wife of an old Turkish effendee of very high rank. Her own birth and fortune made her parents stipulate that her spouse should have no other wife but herself. Nor has he; but while he adheres to the letter of the agreement, he violates its spirit, in short, he totally neglects his handsome helpmate. This the fair Esmé properly resents – and…"

"And in me," – cried I, interrupting my informer, – "she will find the avenger she deserves. Let us forthwith go!"

"Gently, gently." now whispered the old beldam, "It is not thus that matters of this sort are conducted. If the lady, by whom I have the honour of being employed, were one of your ordinary women on whom the wind blows as freely as on the weeds of the desert, all would be easy enough. Females who go out at all hours to the bath, and to the market-place, and to the bezesteen, or to visit their friends, do whatever they please. But cadin Esmé is none of those, I warrant you. This exalted fair one has in her apartment baths of marble and gold; twenty slaves are always ready at her nod to execute whatever whim may cross her fancy; the richest goods of every country are brought from every quarter to be spread out before her at her toilet; her own chamber opens on gardens whose roses make those of Sheeraz look pale. In short – poor thing! – she can find nothing to want abroad; and when she does go out, it seems rather for the sole purpose of seeing how superior is all that she leaves at home. Then she generally only travels about in a close carriage. Her visits are confined to two or three of her near relations; and she so seldom finds an excuse for stirring out on foot, that the day you met her was the first time these six months she had stepped across her old threshold. Even when she indulges in a little excursion of the sort, she only moves, as you see, accompanied by a swarm of servants, or rather, of spies."

"You only add fuel to my flame," cried I. "The more difficult the enterprise, the nobler the victory!" – and immediately we fell to discussing the ways and means. A hundred different schemes were alternately proposed and rejected. At last a contrivance was hit upon, only liable to half a dozen radical objections. Still it was the best, and therefore adopted. A friend of the Jewess's, equipped as a woman of rank, was to spend the day on a visit to the lady Esmé, whose husband could not, during that period, intrude upon the privacy of his wife's apartment. Esmé would thus obtain an opportunity of slipping out in the attire of a slave, of stopping at the Jewess's abode, there to put on Greek habiliments, and of thence going to meet me at some selected house in Galata. After the interview, she would have nothing to do but to resume her Turkish dress, in order to release by her return her pretended visitor. The plan required some preparation, and the day after the next was fixed upon for its execution.

Matters being thus all apparently settled: – "One word more," added the Jewess. "You are aware that we embark upon an adventure of life and death. In this nether world the joys of paradise can only be sipped with the secrecy of the grave. The least indiscretion brings ruin to us all."

I begged my instructress to make herself easy on that score; – "and," added I in turn, "there is one circumstance which the lady may not be sorry to learn; namely, that in me she will find a youth not only of the greatest discretion, but of the most respectable birth and connections."

I thought the peal of laughter never would have ended, into which the old hag brought out at this intimation. "And pray," cried she, "do you think the fair Esmé is in love with you for your musty ancestors, or means to show you off to her acquaintances? For my part, I mistook you for little better than a porter. If you be a prince, so much the worse! It will require consideration." – Here the beldam hobbled off.

"Can I have marred my hopes by my vanity?" thought I, after the woman was gone. But though this idea gave me a little uneasiness, it prevented me from not from bestowing the utmost pains, on the day appointed, in adorning my person, ere I went to the place conveniently situated for watching the entrance of the party into the house agreed upon.

Here minute after minute rolled on, without my perceiving the least symptom of the looked-for couple. But what I clearly discerned instead, were loud titterings behind a latticed window, which presently left no doubt in my mind that the whole interview was a mere waggery of some of the females who had found me out, and were determined to have a laugh at my expense. The very description of the lady's grandeur now made that matter palpable by its exaggeration; and I held myself assured that the greatest real danger I had to apprehend was that of becoming the laughing-stock of the whole district. In this conviction I cursed my credulity, and set my wits to work, in order to devise how I might turn the joke against its authors, – when a faint murmur made me look round, and behold two females, carefully muffled up, glide into the place of our appointment.

"Shall I follow or not?" was now my only thought, – "and take my chance of whatever good or evil may offer?"

The Jewess suffered not my suspense to last. Coming out again: – "What are you waiting for?" whispered she impatiently into my ear; and, without staying for my answer, took me by the hand and led me up stairs, where, having bidden me not to be frightened, she left me, and ran down again to keep watch while I remained.

By some strange perverseness of human nature, the Jewess's seemingly superfluous caution had the contrary effect from that which was intended; and, combined with Esmé's apparent backwardness to throw off her feridjee, made me fancy I had been entrapped with a monster. Full of this idea, I cursed the Israelite for leaving me thus committed, would have given the world to have seen her return, even with the account of some most urgent danger, and stood riveted near the door like a statue, – until my expectant fair one, losing all patience, tore off her envelopes more in anger than in love, and convinced me of my error in doubting her attractions.

As her wrath did not continue inexorable, I trust I may pass over the remaining details of the interview, without any great violation of my duty as a biographer: – they presented strong features of resemblance with many others of the same description; and in truth, though the rare beauties of my mistress – her soft black eyes, her coral lips, and her carriage more graceful than the movements of the sailing swan, – might have obtained at other times a more elaborate encomium, thoughts of a sedater hue occupy my mind at present.

Irksome as I had thought the departure of the Jewess, I thought her return still a thousand times more barbarous, when, ere we had time to think of her existence, she reappeared, and with relentless cruelty summoned us to separate.

It seemed as if we had only just met; and it also seemed as if we were never to meet again. For the expedient resorted to could not be repeated; and our faculties were too bewildered to think of any other. Like people just awaking from a rapturous dream, or rather just shaking off a deep intoxication, we reeled about, lost in a maze of confused feelings, and able to reflect neither on the past, the present, nor the future. The vain attempt to think was soon given up, and we settled to communicate through the channel of the Israelite, when our minds should be sobered by separation. At the moment of parting, however, and when casting on each other the last farewell glance: – "What can I do," cried the grateful Esmé, "to repay my more than preserver, my sovereign, and my god; what gifts worth acceptance can I bestow? Take this, and this, and this: it is nothing to what I owe for the felicity conferred; it is all I can give in return;" and so saying, she tore off her richest jewels, and heaped upon me – in spite of my resistance – strings of pearls, clasps of rubies, and girdles of diamonds.

"And do you then imagine," cried I, "that one, honoured by your smiles, can expect or can want a recompense of this sort?"

"What signifies," replied the fair one, "what you expected or what you want! – You wanted not the poor recluse Esmé, when you vouchsafed to come to me. I have my burden of gratitude to lessen. For my sake, I must give, and for mine you must receive."

Still I refused. But a cloud began to gather on the brow thus far serene: gleams of ominous lightning flashed from those eyes that before glowed only with unmixed tenderness. "I see it," cried Esmé. "You love me not. You fear to take an earnest. You intend not to return to my arms!" – and upon this she tore her jetty locks. The Jewess now stepped forward. "For God's sake," said she, "pocket all, as I do. It may cost us our lives thus to stand on ceremony." I therefore yielded, took the proffered gifts, for this magnanimous act received a last rapturous glance, and tore myself away.

Scarce deigning to lower my looks to the earth, scarce feeling the ground that bore my feet, gliding along on invisible pinions, rather than walking, I proceeded at random, intoxicated with my good fortune. In my own mind I soared at that moment above all the monarchs of the globe. Constantinople seemed too small to contain my exultation, and, oppressed within its walls by the excess of my happiness, I went forth at the gates, and poured out into the country the ebullitions of my joy, and the ferment of my spirits.

Here, however, let me for an instant interrupt the thread of my subject, in order to observe that, though my courtships have thus far occupied a great portion of my narrative, it is not the history of my loves, but that of my life, which I wish to record. Instead, therefore, of detailing the scheme through means of which was effected our next meeting, and the many others which followed, I shall only in general state that each interview seemed to increase the fondness of my mistress. Every circumstance of my situation which gradually unfolded itself to her knowledge, only gave me new attraction in her eyes. Above all she delighted in that inferiority of my condition to her own, which enabled me to become indebted for ease, affluence, and whatever else appeared desirable, to her sole affection. Hers was the mighty bliss of giving me all I possessed; of making me all I was.

Out of compliment to her taste, I bestowed upon my person the utmost attention. The berath which before I had coveted I now failed not to purchase, and the gold I accepted for the sake of peace, I laid out in such a way as to make the liberalities of the donor yield her eyes at least an ample return. Every time I appeared in her presence, it was with some fresh improvement in my ostensible person. Now and then, indeed, too plentiful supplies proved hostile to my prudence; but if an opulence to which I had not been accustomed often got me into scrapes, it always got me out again; nor left me, like modern friends, in the difficulties into which it had lured me. In one of my midnight orgies – for instance, – being summoned by the patrole before the waywode, "I was actually on my way to his worship," I forthwith exclaimed, "in order to discharge an old debt. Pray, gentlemen, have the goodness to take charge of these few sequins: but only pay them at your convenience;" – and immediately my freedom was restored to me with a hundred bows and scrapes. In another frolicsome mood, making so great a noise on the canal that the Bostanjee-bashee had me handcuffed in spite of my berath – on the plea that it was too dark to read it: – "I have heard," I cried, "that a fine carbuncle will throw out as much light as a lamp. Vouchsafe, mighty sir, to try the experiment with this ring;" – and all at once the officer saw so clearly I was a berathlee, as to grant me the entire range of the Bosphorus.

These occasional frolics were necessary to keep up my spirits under the depression which they began to experience. For my intrigue cast upon my free agency a constraint which I had never felt before. I, who until that period knew not what it was to abstain or to conceal; who, even with the haughtiness of the archondessas of the Fanar used to assert my liberty, and to mock the fair one's rage, now felt anxious, with the prisoner of a harem, to dissemble the least act of inconstancy, however unpremeditated. Nor let it be supposed that this conduct proceeded from any fear of stopping the lady's bounty It is true that where I gave my love, and would have given my utmost largess, had the means been mine, I scrupled not, with the affections, to receive the gifts of my wealthy mistress: but all the gold of Peru could not have purchased my person, had not my heart fully ratified the bargain; and Esmé owed to her situation – not to my selfishness – a consideration which never yet had accompanied my preferences. The archon's wife, a free agent like myself, like me had been mistress of her choice, and where I sinned against her, had possessed all the means to retaliate. It was not so with Esmé. She was a helpless captive, who could not punish my offences by following my example. What with the one seemed a justifiable proceeding, with the other became wanton cruelty.

And most acutely would the fair Mohammedan have felt any unnecessary wound inflicted by my hand: most alive was her susceptible mind to all the fellest pangs of jealousy. "When first I loved you," she said, "you had never beheld me, you knew not whether I was fair or hideous, you could not harbour the least spark of reciprocal affection; you might, without the smallest sacrifice on your part, for ever have kept out of my sight, and left my hopeless flame, unfed, to die away. This indeed – had not your heart been free, and able to return all the warmth of my feelings – honour, justice, and humanity required. You acted otherwise: ere yet you felt a spark of reciprocal tenderness, you threw yourself purposely in my way; you sedulously nourished my passion, and you have carried my madness to that pitch where it must find yours commensurate, or end in my perdition. You now are bound to sustain the affection which you have gratuitously raised: you are pledged to save me from despair. If, after having fanned my love into a resistless blaze, you should think of forsaking me, I die; but the blow by which I fall – that same blow shall kill us both."

The same blow did not kill both! For when long impunity had made me so daring as to invade the effendee's own roof; when suspicions arose in her husband's mind which he resolved to verify; when on he rushed to his harem; when right and left flew the women's slippers, placed as a spell on the threshold; when open burst the door of the sanctuary, and jealousy carried its search into the inmost recesses of the gynecaeum; when what became of the hapless Esmé, heaven, the effendee, and the Black Sea alone can tell, – not a hair of my head received the smallest injury. That very impetuosity of my enemy which seemed to doom me to certain and immediate destruction, proved the means of my preservation. In the very act of making my escape, the door which turned back upon its hinges turned back upon my person, and concealed the intruder behind its friendly screen, till the effendee and his troop had passed by. I then slipped away, unperceived by any creature within. Some slaves, however, who kept watch on the outside, seeing me run and in evident confusion, set up a hue and cry. Finding they gave me chase, I darted into a mosque, whose open gate seemed to invite my entrance. All I wanted was to throw my pursuers off the scent. A few old Moslemen were in the djamee[2] mumbling their evening prayers; and while the mob outside howled for the adulterer, the congregation within began to scream at the yaoor. Thus placed between two fires, all hope of escape forsook me. I felt as if I must – but for some special miracle – soon be torn to pieces!

One human measure only remained to save my life. I drew my dagger, threw my cloak over my face, leaned my back against the mihrab[3], and cried, "I am a Moslemin!"

If there existed not even any positive evidence of guilt having found its way at all into the effendee's harem, still less did there exist any direct proof of my being the offender. All that could be alleged against me was merely circumstantial. So far from being found in the wife's faithless arms, I had not been caught under the injured husband's roof. At most I had displayed my activity somewhat near the dwelling disturbed; but, though this might be reason enough to massacre an infidel, a follower of the true faith – however recent his conversion – demanded greater respect.

From the moment therefore in which I invoked the name of the Prophet, every breath of accusation was hushed, every hand became suspended. A magic power seemed to arrest the daggers on my breast. A fanatical mob instantly took under its protection the new, the fervent proselyte.

But this proselyte I had bound myself to be. I had proclaimed myself one of the faithful; and on the spot, in the very mosque, I went through the various forms which mark the reclaimed infidel, and announce his admission into the bosom of Islamism.

CHAPTER X

Historians often err in attributing to a single great cause the effect of many minute circumstances combined. My sagacious biographer, for instance, would not fail to place my abjuration of the Christian faith entirely and solely to the account of my intrigue with a Turkish fair one, and the desperate alternative between life and death which ensued. Nothing could be more erroneous. The seemingly bold measure had long been preparing *in petto*; and the unexpected dilemma to which I was reduced may only be said to have fixed the period for its execution.

There had arrived at Pera a foreigner whom I shall call Eugenius. His ostensible object was to acquire the ancient lore of the East, in return for which he most liberally dealt out the new creed of the West. I cannot better describe him than as the antipode to father Ambrogio. For as the one was a missionary of a society for the propagation of belief, so was the other an emissary of a sect for the diffusion of disbelief. He mediated indeed a pilgrimage to the holy land, but with the view to prove more scientifically the fatuity of all thing holy. Reason, philosophy and universal toleration were the only objects of his reverence; and some of his tenets which I picked up by the way had in them something plausible to my mind, and, if not true, seemed to my inexperience *ben trovati*. He conceived that there might exist offences between man and man, such as adultery, murder, &c. of blacker dye than the imperfect performance of certain devout practices – eating pork, steaks in Lent included; and, above all, he thought that whatever number of crimes a man might, on using his utmost diligence, crowd in the short span of this life, they still might possibly be atoned for in the next by only five hundred thousand million of centuries (he would not abate a single second) of the most excruciating torture; though this period was absolutely nothing compared to eternity. As to his other tenets, they were too heinous to mention.

Ere father Ambrogio was aware that Eugenius broached such abominable doctrines, he had introduced me to him in the quality of drogueman, or rather of cicerone; and the tone in which I was received might have made the father suspect that all was not right. But the father's range of intellectual vision extended not further than his own nose,[1] and that nose was a snub one.

"It was you quibbling, sophistical Greeks," cried Eugenius laughing, "who, proud at the commencement of the Christian era of your recently imported Gnosticism, perverted by its mystic doctrine the simple tenets of Christianity. It was you who, ever preferring the improbable and the marvellous to the natural and the probable, have contended for taking in a literal, and therefore in an absurd sense, a thousand expressions which in the phraseology of the East were only meant as figurative and symbolical; and it was you who have set the baneful example of admitting, in religious matters, the most extraordinary deviations from the course of nature and from human experience, on such partial and questionable evidence, as, in the ordinary affairs of man, and in a modern court of justice, would not be received on the most common and probable occurrence."

Father Ambrogio, who conceived that every reflection upon the Greeks must be in favour of the Romans, was delighted with this speech, and, as he went away, earnestly recommended to me to treasure up in my memory all the sagacious sayings of the wise man whom I had the happiness to serve.

But it was not long before he changed his mind. The very next day, when I called on Eugenius, I found padre Ambrogio in most angry discussion with him about the doctrine of Divine clemency, which the friar could not abide. Eugenius at last was obliged to say in his laughing way, that since the father appeared so incurably anxious for endless punishment, all he could do for him was to pray that, by a single exception in his favour, he at least might be damned for all eternity. Father Ambrogio, who never laughed, and who hated Eugenius the more for always laughing, upon this speech left the room: but the next time he met me alone, he very seriously cautioned me against one who, he was sure, was the devil incarnate.

"If so," thought I, "he preaches against his own trade; and his principal is little obliged to him for making his dominion a mere leasehold, instead of a perpetuity." Meanwhile I resolved not to be too sure, and, when Eugenius took off his clothes, watched whether I could perceive the cloven foot. Nothing appearing at all like it, and his disposition seeming gentle, obliging and humane, I began to be fond of his company, – until, from liking the man, I unfortunately by degrees came not to dislike some parts of the doctrine of which he was the apostle.

Eugenius differed in one respect from his brethren of the new school. While they wished to subvert all former systems *in toto*, ere they began to re-edify according to their new plan, he, on the contrary, only contended for the appeal of reason on points of internal faith, and urged, in external practices, the propriety of conforming to the established worship; – and this, not from selfish but philanthropic motives: "for," said he, "while the vulgar retain a peculiar belief, they will close their eyes and hearts against whatever practical good those wish to do them who join not in their creed; and should they, in imitation of their betters, give up some of their idle tenets, – unable immediately, like those they imitate, to replace the checks of superstition by the powers of reason – they will only from bad lapse into worse, let loose the reins to their passions, and exchange errors for crimes."

Now, in conformity to this doctrine of my master, what could be clearer than that it behoved me, where the Koran was become the supreme law, – as a quiet orderly citizen, zealous in support of the establishment – with all possible speed to become a Mohammedan? Should there happen to be any personal advantage connected with this public duty; should my conforming to it open the door to places and preferments from which I otherwise must remain shut out; should it raise me from the rank of the vanquished to that of the victors, and enable me, instead of being treated with contempt by the Turkish beggar, to elbow the Greek prince, was that my fault? or could it be a motive to abstain from what was right, that it was also profitable?

The arguments appeared to me so conclusive, that I had only been watching for an opportunity to throw off the contemptuous appellation of Nazarene, and to become associated to the great aristocracy of Islamism, some time before the fair Esmé lent the peculiar grace of her accent to its Allah, Illah, Allah; and though, for the credit of my sincerity, I would wish my conversion not exactly to have taken place at the particular moment at which the light of truth happened to shine upon me, yet, all things considered, I thought it wiser not to quibble about punctilios, than to be sewed in a sack, and served up for breakfast to some Turkish shark.

Thus it was that the doctrine of pure reason ended in making me a Mohammedan: – but with a pang I quitted for the strange sound of Selim my old and beloved name of Anastasius, given me by my father, and so often sweetly repeated by my Helena.

I was scarce a Mohammedan skin deep, when I again met padre Ambrogio, whom since my affair with Esmé I had entirely lost sight of, and who knew not my apostasy.

"Son," said he in a placid tone, "we are all at times prone to passion. I myself, meek as you now see me, have had my unguarded moments: but it is impossible that you should not wish to achieve the glorious work so well begun. Suppose therefore we resume our spiritual exercises. You are already so far advanced in the right road, that we cannot fail ultimately to make you an exemplary Roman Catholic."

"Father," answered I, "what may ultimately happen, it is not in man to foresee: meantime, since we met last, another trifling impediment has arisen to my embracing the Latin creed. I am become a Moslemin."

At this unlooked-for obstacle, father Ambrogio started back full three yards. "Holy virgin!" exclaimed he, "how could you make such a mistake?"

Not caring to assign the true cause; "I wanted," said I, "to secure in the next world a little harem of black-eyed girls."

At this speech father Ambrogio fetched a deep sigh; and began to muse, looking alternately at his habit and mine. – "Well!" said he, after a pause; "at least you are no longer a Greek, and this is something;" and hereupon he departed, – wondering, I suppose, where, in his paradise, Mohammed meant to dispose of the angels whose eyes were blue.

I never was very ambitious of learning, but my new godfather, a formal Turkish grey-beard, could not brook my total ignorance of my new religion. "You are not here among Scheyis,"[2] said he, "who under the name of Mohammedans live the lives of yaoors, drink wine as freely as we swallow opium, and make as little scruple of having in their possession paintings of pretty faces,[3] as if at the day of judgment they were not to find souls for all those bodies of their own creating. You are – Allah be praised! – among strict and orthodox Sunnees; and, however an old believer may have had time to forget his creed, a young neophyte should have it at his fingers' ends."

So I had to learn my catechism afresh. Great indeed was my need to expostulate: – but all I could obtain was to be provided with a teacher who, for my twenty paras a lesson, should put me in the way of passing over the bridge Seerath[4] as speedily as possible. And this I was promised.

Nothing therefore could exceed my surprise, when in walked the gravest of the whole grave body of doctors of law – the very pink and quintessence of true believers; one who would not miss saying his namaz regularly four times a day, three hundred and sixty days in the year,[5] for all the treasures of Devas:[6] who, to obtain the epithet of hafeez,[7] had learnt his whole Koran by heart unto the last stop; and who, not satisfied with praying to God like other people, had linked himself to a set of dancing derwishes, for the sole purpose of addressing the Diety with more effect in a sugar-loaf cap, and spinning round the room like a top: – a personage who, in a devout fit, would plump down upon his knees in the midst of the most crowded street, without turning his head round before he had finished the last reekath[8] of his orison if all Constantinople were trembling in an earthquake; who, considering all amusements as equally heinous, made no difference between a game of chess or mangala and illicit attentions to one's own great-grandmother, and once, in his devout fury, with his enormous chaplet positively demolished Karagheuz[9] in the midst of his drollery; a personage who, at the end of Ramadan,[10] looked like a walking spectre, and the very last time of his fast absolutely doubled its length, only for having snuffed up with pleasure, before the hours of abstinence were over, the fumes of a kiebab on its passage out of a cook-shop: a personage who had an absolute horror of all representations of the human figure – those of Saint Mark on the Venetian sequin only exempted: a personage, in fine, who already was surnamed in his own district the wely or saint; and whom all his neighbours were dying to see dead, only that they might hang their rags round his grave, and so get cured of the ague.

When this reverent moollah[11] first made his appearance, his face was still bedewed with tears of sympathy, occasioned by a most heart-rending scene of domestic woe, which his charitable hand had just assuaged. In an adjoining street, he had found, stretched out on the bare pavement, a whole miserable family – father, mother, brothers, sisters, together with at least a dozen children of tender age – in a state of complete starvation. The very description of such a piteous sight harrowed up my soul. Lest however the holy man should incur a suspicion of having been betrayed into a weakness so reprehensible as that of pity for the human species – for which he felt all the contempt it deserved, and which he never presumed to solace under any of the visitations inflicted by Providence, – I should add that the wretched objects of his present compassion were of that less reprobated sort, the canine species! They belonged to those troops of unowned dogs which the Turks of Constantinople allow to live in the streets on the public bounty, in order to have the pleasure of seeing them bark at Christians whom their Frank dress betrays. To these, and other beings of the irrational genus, were confined the benefactions of my tutor; but, if his own species had few obligations to acknowledge from him, he was recorded as having purchased the liberty of three hundred and fifty canary birds in cages, granted pensions to the baker and butcher for the maintenance of fifty cats, and left at least a dozen dogs, whom he found on the pavé, handsomely provided for in his will.

No sooner was my venerable instructor comfortably seated on his heels in the angle of my sofa, than, looking around him with an air of complacency, as if he liked my lodgings, that, provided he only took his station there for two hours every day, he pledged himself before the end of the first year to instruct me thoroughly in all the diversities of the four orthodox rituals – the Hanefy, Schafey, Hanbaly, and Maleky; together with all that belonged to the ninety-nine epithets of the Deity, represented by the ninety-nine beads of the chaplet. In the space of another twelvemonth he ventured to hope that he might go over with me the principal difference between the two hundred and eighty most canonised mufessirs or commentators on the Koran, as well as examine the two hundred and thirty articles of the creed, concerning which theologians disagree; and in the third year of our course, he promised to enable me completely to refute all the objections which the Alewys and other dissenters made to the Sunnee creed; and to give me a general idea of the tenets of the seventy-two leading heretical sects, from that of Ata-hakem-Mookanna, or the one-eyed prophet with the golden mask, to Khand-Hassan, the fanatic who ate pork and drank wine in the public-place like any Christian; so as, through dint of so much diligence, on the fourth and last year to have nothing to do but to go over the whole again, and imprint it indelibly on my memory. By way of a little foretaste of the method of disputation in which he promised to instruct me, he took up one of the controversial points; first raised his own objections against it; and then – as he had an indubitable right to do with his undisputed property – again completely overset them by the irresistible force of his arguments; after which – having entirely silenced his adversary, he rose, equally proud of the acuteness of his own rhetoric, and charmed with the sagacity with which I had listened.

The truth is I had fallen asleep; for which reason, when I suddenly awoke on the din of his argumentation ceasing, I shook my head with a profound air, and by way of showing how much in earnest I meant to be, with a very wise look said I could not give my unqualified assent until I heard both sides of the question. Thus far I had heard neither.

This determination rather surprised my doctor, who seemed to have relied on my faculty of implicit credence. "Hear both sides of the question?" exclaimed he in utter astonishment. "Why, that is just the way never to come to a conclusion, and to remain in suspense all the days of one's life! Wise men first adopt an opinion, and then learn to defend it. For my part I make it a rule never to hear but one side; and so do all who wish to settle their belief."

The thing had never occurred to me before; but I thought it had in it a something plausible, which at any rate made me resolve not to lengthen the four years' course by idle doubts. Accordingly in the first three lessons I agreed to every thing the doctor said or meant to say, even before he opened his mouth, and only wondered how things so simple, for instance, as the Prophet's ascent to the third heaven on the horse Borak, with a peacock's tail and a woman's face (I mean the horse), could be called into question. Unfortunately, when in the fourth lesson the moollah asserted that Islam was destined to pervade the whole globe, a preposterous longing seized me to show my learning. I asked how that could be, when, as Eugenius had asserted, an uninterrupted day of several months put the fast of Ramadan wholly out the question near the poles? This difficulty, which the doctor could not solve, of course put him into a great rage. He reddened, rubbed his forehead, repeated my query, and at last told me in a violent perspiration, that if I mixed travellers' tales with theology, he must give up my instruction.

I was too happy to take him at his word; instantly paid what I owed for the lessons received; and begged henceforth to remain in contented ignorance. Lest however I should appear petulant to my godfather, I went and desired him to find me a moolah that was reasonable.

"A moollah that is reasonable!" exclaimed an old gentleman present, who happened to belong to the order himself. "Why, young man, that is a most unreasonable request. The Koran itself declares the ink of the leaned to be equal in value to the blood of martyrs; and where will a single drop be shed in disputation, if all agree to be reasonable? But come," added he, laughing, "I will undertake, without fee, to teach you in one word all that is necessary to appear a thorough bred Moslemin; and if you doubt my receipt, you may even get a fethwa of the Mufty, if you please, to confirm its efficacy. Whenever you meet with an infidel, abuse him with all your might, and no one will doubt you are yourself a stanch believer." I promised to follow the advice.

CHAPTER XI

Stern winter had breathed his last: his churlish progeny had fled. The waves were no longer lashed by storms, nor was the earth fettered by frost. Constantinople hailed the day, revered alike by Greeks and Turks, when St. George opens in state the gaudy portals of the spring. The north wind had ceased to howl through Stambool's thin habitations. Mild zephyr reigned alone; and as his fragrant breath went forth in gentle sighs, the white winding-sheet of snow shrunk on the swelling mountain, while a soft and verdant carpet of young herbage spread along the hollow valley. The taller trees of the forest might still slumber awhile: the lesser shrubs and plants of the garden were all waking, to resume their summer robes of rich and varied dye. Blushing blossoms crowned their heads, and every transient gale was loaded with their fragrance. Over fields enamelled with the crimson anemone fluttered millions of azure butterflies, just broke forth from their shells with the flowers on which they fed, and hardly able yet to unfurl their wings in air: while on every bough was heard some feathered songster, hailing the new season of joy and love. The very steeds of the imperial stables, liberated that day from their dark winter stalls, measured with mad delight the verdant mead of Kiadhane, while their joyful neighing re-echoed from the hills around. Under each dazzling portico reflected in the Bosphorus were seen groups of Ich-oglans and pages, sporting their new spring suits, like gilded beetles, in the sun. All eyes seemed riveted on the Othoman fleet, which in gay and gallant trim issued forth from the harbour, and, with every snowy sail swelling in the breeze, majestically advanced towards Marmora's wider basin, there to commence its yearly cruise through the mazy Archipelago. Of the immense population of Constantinople a part was skimming in barges glittering like gold-fish, the scarce ruffled surface of the channel, while the remainder gaily sauntered on the fringed terraces that overhang its mirror, and in the woody vales that branch out from its banks. On all sides resounded the tuneful lyre, and the noisy cymbal, animating the steps of the joyous dancers. Nature and art, the human race and the brute creation, seemed alike to enjoy in every form of diversified festivity, the epoch when recommence the hopes, the labours, and the delights of summer.

I too was one of the mirthful throng. In company with a few Osmanlees, not the most rigid of their race, I had been indulging in the orgies of the day outside the gate of Selivria. Somewhat flushed with the juice of the berry which Bacchus first planted in my country, we were returning toward the Top Capoossee,[1] when close behind us came prancing an exceeding bad horseman mounted on a worse steed. At Constantinople it often occurs that an old menial, whose rambles never extended beyond the village of St. Stephens, and whose foot never pressed a stirrup, is rewarded for his domestic services by a military fief or zeeameth,[2] at ten or twenty days journey from the capital. He then first learns to ride in the plains outside the gate of Andrinople, – in order that he may know how to cling to his saddle, when constrained to present himself before his distant vassals. Of this description seemed to be the equestrian whose pleasure it was to annoy us. Proud of his newly acquired horsemanship, he was incessantly in our way, now trotting, now prancing, now galloping at full speed; so as to keep us involved in a cloud of dust, with the additional advantage of expecting every instant a nearer participation in the horse's kicks and curvetings. Whether we went slow or fast, or turned to the right or to the left to avoid him, still he haunted us like our shadow; or, as if for a moment he seemed to have taken his leave, it was only to raise a fallacious hope, and to return to the charge, like the forest fly, when least expected. Vexatious as was the fellow's behaviour, my either less irritable or more sober companions agreed not to notice it. They would have nothing to do, they said, with a saucy green-head, only amenable before his own officers, and sure to be supported – be his behaviour what it might – by all his comrades. Less patient, or less awed by the Prophet's kindred, I swore I would grapple with the emir, and soil with the crimson of his own blood, the green rag round his thick skull, upon which he presumed with such insolence, – when, guessing my intentions, he buried his sharp stirrups[3] in his lank and harassed steed, and scampered away: but not before he had succeeded in what seemed throughout to be the sole aim of all his labour; namely, in bespattering me from head to foot with all the mud of almost the only puddle which the sun's daily increasing power had left in the road.

Who that – in the full pride of an entire new suit, of which the colour has long been pondered over, the stuff chosen after infinite consideration, the making only entrusted to the most skilful artists, the fitting tried in all its various stages, and the final possession obtained only at the very period destined for its display – is fated to see the work of so much thought and labour irretrievably spoilt in its first bloom, and ere yet the world has been dazzled by its splendour; – who, I say, that is fated to undergo such a trial, ever preserved his temper unruffled, and was blessed with feelings sufficiently torpid to abstain from falling out even with blind undesigning chance?

Then fancy my impatient spirit submitted to this trial, and that by the unprovoked malice of a fellow mortal! But a few moments before, alas! the vest of purple broad cloth, the velvet jacket of emerald green, the scarlet bernoos[4] lined with sky-blue satin, and the ample trousers of a blushing lilac, still shone through the mazy net-work of gold cast over every seam, in the full perfection of their primitive purity. After parading their beauties all day long, like a peacock, in the country, I was only going homewards to display them all the evening, to still greater advantage, in the most brilliant coffee-houses in the town, when all my honours felt blasted in the bud, and – every item of my gay attire was made to drip with a black offensive mud; so that I looked like a once gaudy tulip, whose erect splendour has been crushed by some ass's heedless hoof. Such was my indignation at the insult, and still more at the escape of the culprit, that I felt a positive want of some luckless wight, on whom to vent my ungovernable rage.

At that inauspicious moment, who should suddenly start up, as from the very bowels of the earth, but Anagnosti, whom I had left a prisoner in the Bagnio!

On quitting that hideous place, I was fully determined not to let an hour elapse without applying for my friend's liberation, nor to rest until I had procured it. For that purpose chiefly I had gone to Mavroyeni. The reader may remember how I was received at his door. The fainting fit which followed this ineffectual visit, the illness in the hospital, and the indigence I had to encounter on first being thrown anew upon the world, were circumstances which combined to prevent for several weeks all furtherance of my design. When my condition improved, other impediments arose. I then thought it advisable to wait until I had earned a character, had acquired friends among the Franks, and had purchased the berath which might give greater independence to my movements in behalf of a rayah. These desiderata came in due time, but with them also unfortunately came the infatuation of my Turkish amour, during which I was obliged, for my mistress's sake, carefully to avoid attracting public attention; and this affair only ended in that apostasy which made me, bold as I was, dread the reproachful sight of Anagnosti, – of him whose faith neither fear, nor interest, nor even pleasure had had power to shake. Yet I had not abandoned my purpose; and had determined, the very day after St. George, to undertake the seemingly arduous work of my friend's release, when he thus unexpectedly crossed my way.

The very presence of Anagnosti – of Anagnosti so long neglected in his forlorn situation, and of Anagnosti freed at last from his fetters without my assistance – was in itself a severe rebuke. Convicted by my friend's enlargement of a culpable neglect, I almost regretted his liberation as premature. I felt it as an event expressly brought about to shame me. Though in reality the poor youth only came from celebrating – somewhere more devoutly no doubt – the same festival[5] with myself, he seemed only to rush thus full upon me, while yet ignorant of his liberty and unprepared for his appearance, in order to take me by surprise, and to enjoy my confusion.

And this idea, mortifying in itself, became doubly galling at a moment when, had even my conscience proclaimed me Anagnosti's sole deliverer, I still would have wished to be spared all expression of his gratitude. Thrown among Osmanlees proud of their untainted blood, I had just asserted a perfect equality with my lofty companions. I had sworn indeed that I was *not* one of those Candiote Turks[6] who, though three parts Greek, are yet regarded as amongst the highest mettled of the Sultan's Mohammedan subjects: but I had sworn to this truth in a jesting tone; had in consequence been disbelieved as I wished, and had thus found means to combine with pretensions to strict veracity, the benefit of a lie: I had even, in conformity with the moolah's advice, most vehemently abused the whole race of Christian dogs; and, in the midst of my success and exultation, I now stood most unexpectedly confronted with the only person who must, by his familiar address, not only overturn the whole fabric of my raising, but proclaim me a mere renegade, – a downright outcast from the Bagnio!

A circumstance so provoking – so subversive of all my views and wishes – was sufficient to give Anagnosti, in my already ruffled mind, the character of an enemy rather than a friend. The instant I perceived him, shame set my cheek on fire; I tried to avoid his irksome notice: – but already I had caught his watchful eye.

In this situation I felt that a mere retreating movement would only invite a more eager advance; and conceived that nothing but a coolness so marked on my part as to chill on that of Anagnosti every demonstration of warmth, and perhaps even to make him scorn in his contempt of me all signs of recognition, could save me from his fearful familiarity. Upon this principle, instead of either darting forward to meet his embrace, or shrinking his approach, I stopped suddenly short, stood entirely motionless, and, with all the dignity of the turban, merely put out my hand, to receive the homage of his respectful lip.

His first glance, alighting only on my features, made him rush forward to press me to his bosom. His second look, falling on my dress and companions, again arrested his progress, and seemed to rivet him to the ground. Hence, judging him sufficiently awed by my appearance, I now ventured to utter some condescending expressions; but my words he heeded not. Keeping his haggard eyes fixed on my person, he asked me whether a spell fascinated my senses, or whether in reality I was become…a Moslemin, he would have said; but the hateful appellation he had not power to utter. Not caring for the completion of the sentence – "be Selim what he may," I hastily cried, "proceed thou, without fear."

The pious ceremonies of the morning had even carried beyond its usual exalted pitch my friend's religious enthusiasm. At this mortifying speech, resentment of my neglect, indignation at my apostasy, wounded pride, and disappointed affection took possession of his soul.

"Fear!" exclaimed he, – repeating my last words with an hysteric laugh; while his eye darted lightning, and his lip curled up in scorn; – "Fear suits only the deserter of his country and his God!"

So proud a taunt completed the rising ferment of my blood. Enraged at the invective; still more enraged at its coming from a rayah, from a man of mean appearance, and in the presence of sneering Osmanlees. I mechanically thrust my hand in my girdle, and drew out my handjar. It was an unmeaning and half involuntary action: I had no fatal purpose; I intended not – no! upon the solemn word of one again prostrate before the cross – I intended not to hurt a hair of my friend's sacred head. A flourish, to dazzle the Osmanlee eyes which were watching all my motions, was all I had in view. Frantic, Anagnosti rushed forward and fell, – fell upon the too diligently sharpened weapon! Feeling that its point had entered, he with one hand pressed it home to his heart, while with the other he struck me convulsively away. The dagger – slipping through my palsied fingers – remained, as he intended, deep buried in his side.

Leisurely he drew it out, and with a sort of complacency viewed his blood as it trickled from the blade: but presently, his eyes filling with tears, – tears not flowing from his present sufferings, but from the remembrance of things gone by – "O my mother, my mother," he exclaimed, "thy dying words prove true! My friends alone have been my perdition; and the small crimson speck found on the bands of our brotherhood is grown into a stream that now gushes from my heart! – but at least, Anastasius," added he, with a look which pierced my very soul, – "I have prevented him who made a vow to defend me to his last dying breath, from being himself the destroyer of my wretched life. When released from the Bagnio through the kindness of strangers, I wondered what event caused the neglect of my friend, wondered why Anastasius alone had abandoned his Anagnosti. Alas! I knew not that thou hadst forsaken thy God! – May he pardon thee as I do. Life to me has long been bitterness; death is a welcome guest: I rejoin those who love me, – and in a better place. Already, methinks, watching my flight, they stretch out their arms from heaven to their dying Anagnosti. Thou, – if there be in thy breast one spark of pity left for him thou once namedst thy brother; for him to whom a holy tie, a sacred vow…Ah! Suffer not the starving hounds in the street…See a little hallowed earth thrown over my wretched corpse."

These words were his last: he staggered; his body fell lifeless across the highway – and his spotless soul flew to heaven.

In the day of battle, so mighty are the preparations for hurling death at thousands; by so many are shafts of the grim destroyer expected, launched, and felt; so rapidly are the slain often followed by their slayers, and the mourners by their mourners, the harvest of the grave, however dire and sudden, scarce finds leisure to be noted; and no longer appals an imagination already dizzy with excitement, or stunned with repeated blows:– but, when, in the hour of mirth and revelry, a single frame of exquisite perfection is, by some unforeseen shaft of fate, suddenly snatched away from the gay scene, and in the full exercise of all its energies transformed to a limp of insensible clay; when we behold it stretched out, equally unconscious of insult and of pity, in the kindred dust – how drear, how awful is the sudden change!

Then add that this frame thus transformed was that of a friend – that of my brother; – and that my own thrice cursed dagger had wrought the deadly change!

Oppressed at this spectacle beyond the power of a human pen to describe, I long continued fixed in intent amazement on the spot; I long continued gazing on my friend's lifeless form; and at last – late at night, and after every curious bystander had insensibly dropped off – returned, exhausted with anguish, into the city, by the same gate through which in the morning I had sought the country, brimful of thoughtless mirth.

Such indeed was now my soul! I felt the hand of the Almighty growing heavy on me. I felt the long series of chastisements beginning which awaited my apostasy. Precisely where the religion of my fathers had imposed upon me the most sacred ties, where by my change I had most grievously sinned against its high behests, and where the punishment of my infidelity must give my heart the deepest wound, there the first blow had been struck! It was because I had abandoned my God that I had been doomed to lose my friend – the friend to whom I had been sworn in his holy name! – and doomed to lose that friend by my own baleful hand! And so great became, from the bitter taste of its first fruits, the sense of my guilt, that, could I only have avoided the dismal fate of an utter outcast, forced for ever to fly from home and country, I should willingly have forfeited all else which I possessed, even now to abjure my new errors and to return to my forsaken faith. Nor did any fear of the consequences which awaited my rashness mix itself with the feelings called forth by my misfortune. Had I been even more unquestionably guilty of the premeditated murder of an infidel, my life, as a Moslemin, could run no risk from the award of the Turkish law. But the numerous circle which had witnessed the scene united in asserting my entire innocence of the deed which I bewailed: and, when on the morning ensuing I presented myself of my own accord at the nearest mekkiemé[7] to take my trial, the cadee, after exchanging a few words with his naïb,[8] dismissed me fully acquitted.

Not so my own conscience! Loud and ceaseless were its upbraidings. "Thy dagger," it cried, "has been lifted on thy friend; it killed thy brother; it has struck him to the heart, whom it ought to have defended while thy hand could grasp its hilt; its accursed edge has cut through the holiest of engagements, and doomed to destruction the sincerest piety and the tenderest affection. To the last day of thy life, the wound inflicted by thee on Anagnosti shall continue to fester in thine own distracted bosom: it shall remain fresh and green when his mouldering remains have fallen into the dust; it shall follow thee beyond the grave; it shall make thee dread to meet thy friend even in the regions of eternal bliss, – if it should not eternally close against thee their inexorable doors."

To hush the relentless monitor, to honour my ill fated friend's remains and to appease his shade, I did all that I now could do. I not only had his body carried to the grave in splendid procession, masses performed for his unspotted soul, the boiled wheat[9] handed round among the congregation, the purest marble sought for a gorgeous tombstone; I myself – clothed as I was in Mohammed's hateful livery – followed at a distance the dismal pomp, with my garments soiled, my feet bare, and my head strewed with ashes. From an obscure aisle in the church I beheld the solemn service; saw on the field of death the pale stiff corpse lowered into its narrow cell, and hoping to exhaust sorrow's bitter cup, at night, when all mankind hushed its griefs, went back to my friend's final resting-place, lay down upon his silent grave, and watered with my tears the fresh raised hollow mound.

In vain! Nor my tears nor my sorrows could avail. No offerings nor penance could purchase me repose. Wherever I went, the beginning of our friendship and its issue still alike rose in view; the fatal spot of blood still danced before my steps, and the reeking dagger hovered before my aching eyes. In the silent darkness of the night I saw the pale phantom of my friend stalk round my watchful couch, covered with gore and dust; and even during the unavailing riots of the day, I still beheld the spectre rise above the festive board, glare on me with piteous look, and hand me whatever I attempted to reach. But whatever it presented seemed blasted at its touch. To my wine it gave the taste of blood, and to my bread the rank flavour of death!

I who before had set at nought even the sober creed of the sage, now sought comfort in the silly superstitions of the vulgar. I made offerings to the inexorable Fates. I supplicated the awful *Moirai*[10] to withhold from me their scourges. Thinking by swift motion to fly from the vision which every where pursued my steps, I bestrode the swiftest coursers, and roamed the country over. I flew across hill and dale, both early in the morning and late at night – now descending headlong the steep banks of the Propontis, now rushing along the rugged shores of the Euxine.

Among my acquaintance was a rich Armenian. The fondness for handsome horses, prevalent among his nation, in him was a perfect passion; but a passion which the jealous laws of the Turks only suffered a rayah to indulge in secret. He might keep, at immense cost, the most magnificent coursers that came from his own country: bestride them he durst not – except in his stalls. To ride and to enjoy them he was obliged to hire some mean Mohammedan; and, as the noble animals often wanted exercise, he was glad to assist me in flying from my sorrows, by giving me the unrestrained use of his costly stud.

Thus enjoying the command of the fleetest horses and the most active grooms, I took care that neither should lack exercise. I devoted my whole time to drawing the bow, and flinging the djereed.[11] Nowhere was I seen, but at the Oc-meidan and in the Hippodrome;[12] where I endeavoured to raise my oppressed spirits, by sending them on wing after a barbed arrow or a staff that cleft the hair. In order to concentrate on one point all my faculties and feelings, I used to set myself a task. I resolved to hit a particular mark at an assigned distance, and I left not the spot until I had performed the feat. This practice gave me a dexterity in warlike exercises, of which at a later period I reaped the benefit. At the time of its acquirement, the swiftest motion of my body was not sufficient to afford my mind repose. The instant I vaulted into my saddle, the gaunt spectre of death leaped up behind me. I might walk or I might gallop, saunter along or fly at full speed; yet would the avenging spirit alike goad my galled heart, and with his iron grip wring my breast to suffocation. If for an instant I breathed more freely – if sometimes I conceived a transient hope that my gloom was wearing out, it soon proved a mere delusion; and even in the Neotia's swamps, and where autumn sears the leaf, the sun's enfeebled rays find not greater difficulty to pierce the chilling mist, than did the least glimpse of hilarity to penetrate the shroud of anguish which surrounded my heart.

As a last and desperate resource, I tried to drive away my frightful visions by gayer dreams, the children of drowsy opium. I found my way to the great mart of that deleterious drug, the Theriakee tchartchee.[13] There, in elegant coffee-houses, adorned with trellised awnings, the dose of delusion is measured out to each customer according to his wishes. But, lest its visitors should forget to what place they were hying, directly facing its painted porticoes stands the great receptacle of mental imbecility, erected by Sultan Suleiman for the use of his capital.

In this tchartchee might be seen any day a numerous collection of those whom private sorrows have driven to a public exhibition of insanity. There each reeling idiot might take his neighbour by the hand, and say: "Brother, and what ailed thee, to seek so dire a cure?" There did I with the rest of its familiars now take my habitual station in my solitary niche, like an insensible motionless idol, sitting with sightless eyeballs staring on vacuity.

One day, as I lay in less entire absence than usual under the purple vines of the porch, admiring the gold-tipped domes of the majestic Sulimanye, the appearance of an old man with a snow-white beard, reclining on the coach beside me, caught my attention. Half plunged in stupor, he every now and then burst out into a wild laugh, occasioned by the grotesque phantasms which the ample dose of madjoon[14] he had just swallowed was sending up to his brain. I sat contemplating him with mixed curiosity and dismay, when, as if for a moment roused from his torpor, he took me by the hand, and fixing on my countenance his dim vacant eyes, said in an impressive tone: "Young man, thy days are yet few; take the advice of one who, alas! has counted many. Lose no time; hie thee hence, nor cast behind one lingering look: but if thou hast not the strength, why tarry even here? Thy journey is but half-achieved. At once go to that large mansion before thee. It is thy ultimate destination; and by thus beginning where thou must end at last, thou mayest at least save both thy time and thy money."

The old man here fell back into his apathy, but I was roused effectually. I resolved to renounce the slow poison of whose havoc my neighbour presented so woeful a specimen; and, in order not to preserve even a momento of the sin I abjured, presented him, as a reward for his advice, with the little golden receptacle of the pernicious drug which I used to make my solace. He took the bauble without appearing sensible of the gift, while I, running into the middle of the square, pronounced with outstretched hands[15] against the execrable market where insanity was sold by the ounce, a solemn malediction.

The curse, I believe, took effect. Certain it is that with me seemed to depart for ever the prosperity of the Theriakee tchartchee. From the day I turned my back on its fatal abodes, the use of wine and spirits may be said in Constantinople to have superseded that of opium. Every succeeding year has seen the trade of madjoon decline faster, and the customers of those that sell it diminish more rapidly. The old worshippers of the poppy juice have dropped off like the leaves in autumn, and no young devotees have sprung up in their stead. The preparation has not even preserved its adherents among those men of the law, formerly anxious to combine, through means of a drug that may be taken unperceived, the pleasures of intoxication with the honours of sobriety.

CHAPTER XII

By degrees my purse, exhausted in the daily purchase of ready-made mirth, had – by the ill-wearing of that commodity – begun to partake of the depression of my spirits; and on this occasion I found pecuniary embarrassments an excellent remedy for a settled melancholy. When a man knows not how to support life, he has little leisure for feeding sorrow. To replenish, however, my empty coffers, I commenced upon a novel pursuit, which, if it completed the waste of present resources, made me amends by the brilliancy it cast over my future prospects.

This I shall explain.

My melancholy, my retirement, and my endeavours to find relief from my sorrow in superstitious practices, had brought me in contact with a personage who long since had exchanged the society of man for habitual converse with spirits, and who, disclaiming all further intercourse with the inhabitants of the earth, employed himself solely in cultivating an extensive acquaintance in the different regions of the heavens. The only easy and familiar chit-chat in which my friend Derwish might be said to indulge was with the stars. His accurate information respecting the various occurrences in the firmament, it is true, gave him so superior an insight into the affairs of this globe itself, that he could not help feeling mortified as well as surprised, at seeing both in potentates and private individuals so unaccountable a backwardness to profit by his wisdom: for he was as fond of giving advice as those who have not the stars to back their opinion; – and indeed, who more capable than Derwish of directing every concern of man? He understood the composition of cabalistic sentences capable of baffling the subtlest witchcraft, and disarming the most determined evil eye: he could tell to a second the precise period for every critical measure, from the giving a battle, to the taking a dose of rhubarb; and in casting nativities and predicting seasons, the Venice calendar itself must yield to the all comprehending Derwish. It is well known what innumerable little devils float in air, always on watch, when people inadvertently yawn, to whip into their mouths and slip down their throats, when they make sad intestine commotion in their stomachs. These he possessed the art of expelling with rare success, and, soon preparing to soar far beyond his former flights, he was at the eve, when I made his acquaintance, of a discovery which promised mines of wealth to whoever might choose to join him in its pursuit. It consisted in ascertaining by the itching of one's fingers what heaps of gold lay buried under those ancient piles which – like the arches of Backtchékeui,[1] the ruins of Greece, and the pyramids of Egypt – are mistaken by the ignorant for aqueducts, and temples, and mausolea, but by the wise are known to be the secret treasuries of the Constantines, the Suleimans, and the Pharaohs of old. The exact situation of the deposits known, what so easy as to pull down buildings over them!

Ere, however, this measure could be quite accomplished, other resources, less splendid no doubt, but more acceptable, and in which Eblis[2] had no hand, lent me their seasonable aid.

One day when walking through Galata with a brother in distress; "See," said I to my companion, "all those bales of costly goods tossed about on the quay like common ware! For whom think you they are landing? Why, for some old churl, to be sure, immured in his dingy counting-house, and who perhaps will never behold with his own eyes either their contents, or even their final produce. Fortune reserves all her favours for those who only know their amount by a cipher more or less in their ledger. Young fellows like us, who would proclaims their bounty by sound of trumpet, and sow its golden fruits far and wide in the world, the churlish prude leaves to starve."

"Fortune, gentlemen," observed the caravokeiri[3] of the ship, who had overheard my speech, "cannot, if she be a lady, dislike her votaries more than other females do, for being young: but perhaps, like other ladies, to be won, she must be courted."

I now recognised in the captain one of our islanders: he knew me before. "You, sir," added he, "might have had the goddess in question on your own terms as much as any body. Who so petted as you were by your worthy deceased mother?"

"What! My mother dead?" exclaimed I, both shocked and surprised.

"To be sure," rejoined the reïs; "and had she known where to find you, ere that accident happened, who doubts that she would have left her wealth to you rather than to that cross-grained minx – pardon my boldness – your elder sister?"

"All left to my eldest sister?" cried I, drying up the tears that had began to flow profusely. "Ah, if I too had but scolded her all the day long! – That at least is a proceeding which shows attention, and, it seems, meets the adequate thanks. Or rather," – added I, on thinking of her ruinous lenity with regard to my youthful aberrations – "if she had but scolded me, when I deserved reproof! But she has gone to a better place than her son must hope to see her in: Peace be to my own soul, as it is sure to be hers!"

"It would not much perhaps disturb its repose," observed my companion, "to make a little inroad on that of your sister, and try, in your quality as Moslemin, which went furthest, your mother's partiality or that of the law."

Next to her mother and her husband, Roxana (now the eldest female of the family) had always made me the favourite object of her ill humour. I owed her a longer score of petty spies, than I had hoped ever to pay off. It would have been a pleasure for me to hustle her out of the inheritance, had it even been for a stranger. Finding, therefore, that the accumulated produce of my mother's estate at Naxia was in the hands of a merchant in Constantinople, and in ready cash, I went to claim it. My sole regret on my way was my not having provided sacks and porters to carry away the whole treasure at once.

There was little occasion for such a hurry. At first my mother's fortune seemed little easier to get at than the wealth of the Pharaohs, which my friend Derwish meant slily to pocket, by displacing the pyramids. In order to obtain the much-valued memorial, I found legal forms to go through, certificates to sign, petitions to present, securities to give, and accounts to settle, which only allowed me at the end of several weeks to pocket my money, or, rather the half of my money which had not been melted away in the interval, in law expenses, merchants' commissions, presents distributed among men in power, and fees paid to men in office. Even that half, however, my necessities rendered a most welcome supply.

To the landed property of Naxia I could only enforce my right by personal appearance; and a little voyage round the Archipelago seemed to promise a pleasing as well as a profitable change of scene. Accordingly I bargained for my passage in a Greek vessel bound for Ragusa, but which was intended to touch at Chios. I should thus once more behold, under the protection of the turban, my home and friends: and, having gratified that wish, an open boat could easily convey me, whenever I pleased, from my father's birthplace to my mother's native shore.

With all these arrangements settled in my mind, I sent my luggage on board; meaning myself to go by Gallipoli, where the sacoleva[4] was to ballast. Already, with one foot in the stirrup, was I taking my last leave of all my acquaintance, collected in a merry circle around me, when from a distance resounded a loud cry of – "Stop him, stop him!" Accordingly I was going to set off as fast as possible – cursing the fellow who had girt my saddle ill, and now detained me to rectify his awkwardness – when, ere I could get away, who should burst through the opening crowd and seize my bridle like one frantic, but the stargazer Derwish!

"Can you," said he in an angry whisper – almost biting my ear, – "can you think of going after a paltry rabbit warren, when placed by my skills on the very threshold of the all the treasures of the universe?"

"Friend," answered I, "accuse the stars; they have been so dilatory in performing their promises, that I disclaim all further engagement with their highnesses."

"Foolish impatience of youth!" resumed Derwish. "But if hope cannot stop you, at least listen to fear. For your sake I have spent the whole night on my roof, watching your perplexing planet. It looks all spleen and malice. Therefore at any rate go not till Saturday. Besides, who in his senses sets upon a journey on any other day of the week?"

"Every day is auspicious," replied I, laughing, "to those who go after money."

"Hark!" exclaimed the persevering stargazer, "there is the muezzeem[5] of Sultan Achmet, just calling to prayers. Before you go, say your namaz." "I have said it three times over," replied I. – "And the bag of garlic against witchcraft?" – "There it dangles from my horse's throat." – "And the amulets against the evil eye?" – "Head, stomach, arms, all are stiff with them." "I see," observed my friend, deeply sighing, "you have done every thing for yourself: now do something for me, whom you desert with all my excavations on my hands. It will cost less than fifty thousand piastres only to undermine the aqueduct, and I have not five paras in the world! Give me at least in advance a couple of sequins."

Derwish had now completely worn out my patience. In order to get rid of him – "This good gentleman," cried I to the bystanders, "only wants to deprive the capital of every drop of water. Pray assist him in this good work, as I have not time to stop." Derwish at these words grew frightened; he let go my reins, and slunk away. I rode off, rested during the heat of the day at a village on the road, and in the evening arrived at Gallipoli.

The captain having already taken in his ballast, we set sail immediately. At the Dardanelles the vessel was detained several hours by private jobs of the crew, of which the custom-house officers unconsciously bore the blame. Just as we got under sail again, an Israelite, who had heroically determined to go by water whither he could not get by land, begged admittance. He pleaded poverty so piteously that no other conditions were attached to the granting of the favour he sued for, save the diversion which he might afford. Another Jew, seeing his countryman so readily taken in, begged hard for the same boon; but the sailors, thinking they had provided sufficient pastime for the voyage, now became obdurate, and, when the supplicant attempted to creep up the sides of the vessel, stoutly beat him off. In this ungracious operation no one was more active than his brother Jew, who, concealed behind the sailors, gave him with his stick the last decisive rap over the knuckles, which put an end to his attempts. I could not help noticing this want of charity in one who had experienced ours so recently; but on imparting to Mordecai my feelings on that subject, I found that he was acting from the very impulse of that virtue in which I thought him deficient. The other Jew, he informed us, was an arrant rogue, and, if admitted, no one could tell what mischief he might do.

We now thought ourselves secure from further intrusion, when a light wherry, skimming the waters like a swallow, shot alongside us, and flung upon our deck, without even a show of waiting for our permission, a smart caleondjee, whose high behest was to be conveyed to Tenedos. The captain immediately bowed submission.

In this new passenger I soon recognised a personage with whom I had made acquaintance on board the Turkish fleet, during the expedition to the Morea. Never had we met since the failure of the attempt on Mayno. The consequential marine therefore felt great pleasure in boasting of the more successful cruise against the same nest of pirates, undertaken the ensuing year. The delights with which he described how the Moohassil of the Morea forced the little peninsula by land, and the Capitan-pasha blockaded it by sea; and how the inhabitants, driven by the one out of their strong holds, fell with their boats into the clutches of the other, could only be exceeded by the rapture with which he painted the males all hanged, and the women and children all drowned, in order to reconcile them to the Turkish yoke. – "You," he concluded, "who are going to take possession of your estates, mean henceforth, I suppose, to lead a sober country life, and have done with all such frolics. May you prosper! For my part, I hate innocent amusements, and want a little vice to season my pleasures!" Tenedos now being near, my friend called for the boat, and got himself rowed ashore; while I wished him at parting a great deal of pleasure, with all manner of vice.

The current had faithfully escorted our vessel out of the straits; but – having seen us fairly launched into the open sea, it now made a deep obeisance, and bade us farewell; leaving our further conveyance to the care of the winds. These apparently had business elsewhere: at least, they attended not our summons; and for several days we were left to confront a dead calm.

Should any one be so fortunate as to have had no acquaintance before with the monster ennui, the most favourable without doubt for witnessing all its powers, is, when on board a small boat in a sea almost boundless, one lies for hours watching a cloudless sky for a breeze which stays away, and a waveless sea for a ripple which chooses not to come. In this situation, while all else is entirely at a stand, time itself seems to roll on so heavily, that, though every hour of one's short life runs wholly to waste, one still wishes that waste to be more rapid. I who could only exist in a bustle and thrive in a whirlwind, found myself so completely weighed down by this obstinate stillness of every surrounding element, as almost to gasp for breath; to persuade myself that even a sense of pain would be a welcome relief from so horrible a tedium, and at last to cry out in an evil moment, "O for an end to this misery, even by the worst storm which the heavens have in store!"

Just such a storm happened to be within hearing. It took me at my word. Scarce had I uttered the wish, than it hastened with all possible alacrity to attend the invitation. A white fleece arose in the distant sky; a dark streak shot across the furthest wave; a breeze was felt. This breeze became a gale, and this gale grew to a hurricane. Angry clouds, gathering on all sides, began to travel in every opposite direction. They met, they crossed, and stopped each other as if to parley, until the whole heavenly vault became a continuous mass of darkness. It would have been difficult to decide which howled the most dismally, the frightened sailors, in the act of lowering the yards, closing the hatchways, and clearing the deck, or the frightful blast, while mocking their petty endeavours, and tearing and tumbling every thing about our ears. It kept lashing the roaring waves, until they alternately hove us up to the sky, or almost left us aground at the bottom of the sea.

When the tempest became so furious that a crew ten times more numerous than ours would have found ample employment, each sailor wisely left off his work, to fall upon his knees, and say his prayers. Had Saint Spiridion, the protector-general of ships in distress, been ears all over, he scarce could have heard or have heeded half the vows addressed to him on this occasion. But the more we prayed the more the blast increased, until our ship must inevitably have sunk, had not sailors at last most providentially hit upon an infallible expedient for appeasing the tempest.

The Jew – content with making sport for us most handsomely on the deck during the whole of the fine weather – had, at the very first lowering of the sky, taken care to dive into the hold. Entirely forgotten for a while, he happened just to be remembered at this critical period. All now plainly saw the whole cause of the hurricane, – but with it also the remedy. The Hebrew must be sacrificed to appease the angry waves.

From his very hiding-place the wretch heard his doom. He strove to creep between the stones of the ballast: but had he nestled, like a toad, in their heart, he could not have escaped. He was dragged upon the deck, to be tossed into the sea. When indeed absolutely held over the brink of eternity, he begged to ransom his life for that article of which he had pretended to be entirely destitute – for money; and offered, first, one piastre, then two, then five, then five and twenty! The sum was tempting: – but existence was at stake with the sailors themselves, and gold had lost its power. They let the Hebrew drop.

Meanwhile I had fancied that the storm began to slacken, – wherefore, catching the sinking wretch by his coat; "Hark ye, palikaria,"[6] said I to the crew, "the question is not what the cheating scoundrel may deserve; it is only what further evils we may suffer by bringing him to punishment. Now, if the mere sight of his uncouth figure is sufficient to frighten the sea into these fits, what will she do when his whole ugly carcass – skin and all – is crammed down her throat? Worse – depend upon it, than when, on a similar occasion, she threw up near Saint Irene, amidst fire and flames, a raging volcano! Let us therefore appease the ruffled elements by only quietly squeezing the miscreant's soul – doubtless composed of good sequins – out of his dirty body. In my quality as Moslemin, I fear I must encumber myself with half the load."

The wind having slackened by this time, the proposal was approved of by a majority: the few that looked askance at me were frowned into silence; and the Jew, tossed back into the vessel, was submitted to our search.

His vest, trousers, and shirt – attacked first – yielded nothing. His enormous belt, therefore, became the next object of scrutiny: – and for fear of losing aught of the wealth its weight bespoke, we spread a small ihram[7] on the deck, ere we began its dissection.

Scarce was its paunch opened, by the most delicate puncture which the point of my sabre could inflict, than out rushed with resistless impetuosity such a stream of clattering coin, as lasted full five minutes ere it was quite exhausted: – but the highest pieces were paras, and the whole amount of the heap scarce a piastre.

The sailors turned pale with disappointment: nor was I myself greatly pleased. "Son of Satan and of the witch of Endor," exclaimed I with a furious gesture, "do you wish me to treat your own body like your belt, and to seek for your treasure in your bowels?" Mordecai was not put to the trouble of answering; for, on clawing his head to give it a shake, his caul remained in my hands – a positive musket-proof helmet of conglomerate sequins! I now had my cue, and it struck me that, where the head was so well furnished, the heel might also be worth investigating. – Like the dirty caul, the clumsy buskins offered a solid stratum of gold!

As soon as stripped of his pelf, the Jew begged to be killed outright: – he was worth nothing now! We thought otherwise. Another vessel hailing us at that moment for some water, we sent two casks: – in one of them was Mordecai.

The gale, which had not entirely fallen, soon carried us full sail into the straits of Chios, and the distant sound of bells, so long unheard, again struck my ears. Though now become a Mohammedan, it affected me with inexpressible rapture. The impression of approaching home, however, as it strengthened became sadder. From what I still hoped to find under the paternal roof, I turned my thoughts to what I was to find no more. My mother had not been the wisest of mothers: as a son I owed her not unlimited gratitude. Instead of skimming off the dross of my disposition, she had, by injudicious treatment, only added new alloy to its ore, and then cast the compound away, as utterly worthless: yet she had been my mother; and however lightly all the later ties of choice or of chance were wont to sit upon my mind – however often I may wantonly have broken the social bands of friendship and of love – the primary claims of nature and of instinct seemed, spite of my own reasoning, still to maintain their roots firm in my heart.

Absorbed in my musing, I found myself opposite the town of Chios, ere I fancied it in sight. A boat from the Island soon took me ashore. When setting foot on the beach, I threw myself on my knees, with both hands gathered up the loved dust of my native land, and, bringing it with ecstasy to my lips; "Ah, my own paternal soil!" cried I in wild rapture; "defiled as thou art by the tread of rank barbarians, and by the yoke of ruthless Tartars, still do I bear thee devout worship; still does thy arid surface more entrance my longing eyes than all the gilded domes of Eyoob, and all the gaudy gardens of Sultanieh!"[8]

As, advancing with hurried steps, I beheld in quick succession the various stops endeared by the incidents of my early years, the agitation of my mind still increased. Here was the corner of the quay where, with other boys of my age, I used to watch the ships unloading. There, at the turn of the street, stood the house in which on St. John's eve we played at Kleidon rysika.[9] A little further on I passed by the abode of our ancient paramana,[10] whose nursery tales I still could listen to with pleasure. Right over the way my eye fell on the fatal window whence, at Easter, a whole load of broken pots and pans – the wrecks of a twelvemonth – fell on my devoted head[11]. Ere I had quite done looking – with some still remaining fright – at its threatening aperture, I stumbled over the steps of the cross old papadia's[12] hovel, whose flesh-pot I filled one day with glue, in revenge for her complaints of my prior frolics. I was still inwardly laughing at the remembrance of her fruitless attempts to unclose her toothless gums, after tasting her broth, when I grazed the stone seat of a house where…but at present pass we on! Suffice to say that out of the open entrance of this forlorn mansion there seemed to rush a chilling blast, which, hastily as I darted by, changed the warm moisture on my forehead into a clammy dew!

In this way did an uninterrupted chain of recollections carry me from the water-side to my parental threshold. There all seemed solitude and desolation. The only acquaintance remaining – the only being which gave me welcome, was Xeno the old dog, procured when a puppy from the consul, and reared by myself. Many a time he had stood sentinel during my meetings with the donor's daughter; and when I fled from my home, I had been obliged to tie him to a post on the quay, lest he should follow me to the ship, and betray me by his fidelity. He still seemed to remember his old master, looked up in my face as if to say, "what had he done to be thus deserted;" and, wagging his tail, licked my hand. His joyous yelping brought down an unknown female of uncourteous appearance, who asked my business. Having told her its nature, she desired me to go to the garden in the Campo, where the signor drogueman at present resided.

The objects I met in my way to the country were no less interesting than those which I had passed in the town. But in the one as in the other, I perceived a change which quite confounded all my calculations. Every thing still stood in the same place, and still preserved the same shape as before; but the dimensions of every object appeared totally altered. What I thought I had left huge, gigantic, vast as the tower of Babel, now to my infinite surprise seemed paltry, diminutive, reduced to the size of a child's plaything. Houses, gardens, hills and dales, all looked as if, since my childhood, they had shrunk to half their primitive size. A few steps brought me to the end of what I thought covered acres; and what formerly I fancied reared its head in the sky, now hardly rose out of the ground. I had left my home, impressed with the magnitude of every object: to the first images imprinted in my memory, I had assimilated all the vaster scenes which I had since beheld; and only now I first perceived the difference, and from the comparison, thought what I saw even smaller than it was.

My long strides soon brought me abreast with a little man, advanced in years, who was hobbling on before me. The few additional wrinkles that furrowed his face could not prevent my recognising in him the Signor Polizoï, an old friend of the family; while to his failing eyesight, my change from boy to man left me an entire stranger. As I must in that capacity have the more to learn, he seemed to increase in the same proportion the natural communicativeness of his disposition. At my request he went regularly over all the members of the paternal house, until he came to a certain graceless youth named Anastasius, who – he informed me in a sort of confidential whisper – was the saddest reprobate that ever had disgraced Chios; insomuch that even he, Polizoï – a primate as he was – never felt safe from his pranks, while yet only a mere boy; and if he met him now, would, he verily believed, die with positive terror.

Far be from me all suspicion of an intent to commit murder, in acquainting the old gentleman that this dreaded reprobate actually stood before him. Thunderstruck at the intelligence, he stared at me some time in horror; then suddenly wheeled about, and scampered away. My calling to him to quiet his apprehensions, till I grew hoarse, could neither bring him back, nor stop his progress. Some block of stone I fancy was more persuasive; for I heard a loud tumble, and would have gone to his assistance, when the sight of our door drove all other thoughts away.

I paused a few seconds on the threshold. Signor Polizoï's speech had taught me to expect little kindness; "and might it not," thought I, "be preferable to fancy what was best, than to be certain of the worst?" But *that* worst – filial piety suggested – "I might make the best by my change of deportment!" I therefore entered.

As I ascended the steps and, near the trellis of the landing, caught my father's voice, grown tremulous with age, my heart began to throb. He was conversing with his friends, and the ceaseless grinding of the water-wheel[13] in the yard prevented his hearing my approach. Unprepared, he saw me stand before him. Perceiving his surprise at the appearance of one in the Moslemin dress walking in thus familiarly: "Sir," said I, "you see your son," At these words my father started: – yet he seemed moved, and made a sort of gesture to bid me welcome; but again suddenly checking himself, as he caught my brother Constantine's eye eagerly scanning his countenance: "the sons I know," observed he drily, "when they greet me, begin by kissing my hands: I know none other, Perhaps you are only come to wrest from them their remaining property, and to leave me, in my old age, to beg my bread."

I was going to make the only fit reply in my power; – to throw myself on the ground; to kiss, not my father's hands, but his feet; to beg his blessing, and to renounce his property: when my ungracious brother stepped in between the purpose and the deed, to mar all my good content. "I made no doubt," said he in a brutal tone, "that after disgracing your family by your conduct, you would also wish to brave it by your presence; but truly you should avoid the air of Christian houses. It can do you no good, and to us your breath is pestilence."

At another time such a speech would instantly have been resented. But I felt this the decisive moment of my life. I stood at the turn between good and evil. I determined to repress my rising wrath, though I should choke in the attempt.

"Sir," said I to my father, – looking earnestly in his face, while the tears ran down my cheek, "is it your pleasure that I should be treated thus?"

This unexpected appeal to his feelings seemed for a moment to stagger my not yet impenetrable parent. But whether it was that he felt awed by my brother, who ruled him with a rod of iron, or that his own heart had ceased to plead for Anastasius; "Stanco," said he coldly, "is in the right. You ought ere this to have perceived that your company is not acceptable. We can have nothing to interchange with each other. Go, therefore, and disturb us no longer."

At these harsh words my heart swelled till it was ready to burst. Lest my enemies should have the pleasure of beholding me unmanned, I turned away, and leaned over the stone parapet. Had Constantine not been by, I should have made another attempt to soothe my less inexorable father. In the presence of this unnatural relation I knew it must be fruitless. Yet I lingered on. I could not bring myself to depart. I still hoped to be called back. Alas! I only stayed to hear my brother propose, in an audible whisper, to have me thrown out.

Turned out of my father's house! It was too much. I rushed away!

Sacred walls of the parental mansion, I call you to witness! By your moaning echoes denounce me a wretch to all future ages: be the name of Anastasius in my native land the name of guilt, and among foreign nations a title of disgrace, if I entered not your sacred threshold with feelings of love, of peace, and of submission! They were rejected : they were spurned. Let those thank themselves for other sentiments, who strove to obtain them!

In three strides I cleared – I do not know how – the fourteen steps of the stone flight at whose top I had lingered; and got out at the gate. Then, turning round to the unkind habitation, I stopped, once more to contemplate – but for the last time – its well remembered features, whose former smiles now were changed into everlasting frowns! "Dear abode," exclaimed I, "where first I received the boon of life, too soon become irksome, adieu for ever! Anastasius shall no more approach thy loved shade! If he do, may it prove to his perjured soul the shade of death!" This said, I hurried away, as if pursued by all the fiends of hell; and in less than half an hour again reached the town.

Ah! how often does it happen in life, that the most blissful moments of our return to a long left home are those only that just precede the instant of arrival; those during which the imagination still is allowed to paint in its own unblended colours the promised sweets of our reception! How often, after this glowing picture of the phantasy, does the reality which follows appear cold and dreary! How often do even those who grieved to see us depart, grieve more to see us return; and how often do we ourselves encounter nothing but sorrow, on again beholding the once happy, joyous, promoters of our own hilarity, now mournful, disappointed, and themselves needing what consolation we may bring!

CHAPTER XIII

The visit to my father was not the only fearful duty I had to perform. Another and more appalling task remained to be achieved. Of this, however, the nature was such as no longer to leave room either for hope or fear. I knew the worst, and grievously did that worst oppress my heart. Helena, my first love – Helena was no more! At Constantinople, in the heyday of my devotion to the fair Esmé, I had heard her mournful fate. The moment my flight from Chios was known, she made a full confession. To avoid unavailing exposure, the consul sent her for change of air to Samos. There she was attended by one of those nuns of St. Ursula who, in our islands, double the merit of their chastity by disclaiming the defence of a convent. Wretched from the first, Helena, as the hour of maternal anguish approached, became every day more impressed with the idea that she should not survive it. In this persuasion she wrote me a letter, which she confided to the nun; and soon became the unhappy mother of a lifeless child. In conformity with her foreboding fears, or rather, perhaps, in consequence of her apprehensions, she only survived the birth of her babe a few hours. The nun had made a solemn promise not to part with her trust except into my own hands. She however sent me word at Constantinople that it only waited my return to my deserted home. Hearing that she now lived on my own island, and only a short distance from the town, I went to claim the melancholy bequest. I found Sister Agnes at home, and alone. The people with whom she boarded were gone to a neighbouring fair.

The nun had heard me described as a fair complexioned Greek boy, with a smooth skin and flowing locks. No wonder therefore that in the swarthy rough-skinned Moslemin, with forehead bare and shaded lip, she could not recognise the original of her fancied portrait. The first sight of my fierce figure, standing unannounced before the lonely maiden, made her start with evident surprise; but when I showed her a note from Anastasius – whose hand-writing, treasured up by her friend, had met her eye before – she became more composed, and gave me the history of Helena's sufferings. Touched with a sense of shame for the ruin heaped by my lawlessness upon this innocent girl, I had determined, while I remained in the presence of her friend, not to deposit my assumed character, but to hear the tale of woe to the end with pretended unconcern. Soon, however, unbidden tears would start, and began to flow so fast, that, for fear of betraying my feelings I hid my face in my cloak. Even that could not conceal from the quick-sighted nun the anguish which throbbed beneath the gaudy mantle. "I wonder not, sir," said she, "to see you moved. In truth the story is touching, and calculated to affect even the stout heart of an Osmanlee. But, to behold such deep emotion in a stranger! While the author of so much woe, while Anastasius himself –"

Here all control over my tongue forsook me. "I am that Anastasius," cried I; "could you a moment doubt it?"

The nun appeared confounded. Shuddering with horror at finding herself thus unconsciously in the actual presence of him whom she looked upon as her friend's murderer – as little less than a devil incarnate, a complete fiend – she darted at me the gesture of anathema, and to the dread sign added such dire imprecations, that I could not help mechanically uncovering my breast, and wetting it with the moisture of my lips,[1] to avert the evil influence. This action, however, did not prevent a torrent of more explicit abuse from following the first vague explosion of anger; and a full quarter of an hour did sister Agnes rant, and rave, and curse, ere I could find an opportunity of claiming the letter I had been promised. With a hand still trembling with rage she at last took it out of a small casket, and bade me read – with compunction if I could – the last words of my lovely and murdered mistress.

They were these:

"I neither reproach you with my ruin, which was my own fault, nor with your want of love, which was not yours. It depends not on ourselves to love; but it does to be merciful, and you were inhuman: you deliberately pierced that heart in which you were worshipped; and of this deed I die. On a foreign shore I soon shall breathe my last, and my wretched father, who expected in me the comfort of his old age, shall see me no more. Thanks be to God! The author of my unfortunate existence shall not have to blush at the sight of his daughter; nor shall I, wont to look up with the confidence of innocence, have to avert my eyes from a parent. For the unfortunate offspring – I dare not say of our love – which perhaps may survive me, I must not claim a father's care. You have trod under foot the duties which you owed her who in the eyes of heaven was your wife, and had committed no offence except loving you so ardently. My child will be abandoned to the hands of strangers; will live in contempt, and die in misery. But should heaven bestow upon you the pledges of a less requited affection, fear, ah fear lest my infant's wrongs be visited upon them! Yet, if the last words of a wretch, who is afraid her love will only cease with her life, can find entrance into your impenetrable heart, ah, Anastasius! Ah, my Anastasius! Repent of your sins, run not from crime to crime, and revenge not my woes so severely on yourself, as to render it impossible that we should ever meet again!"

The time that had intervened between the writing and the perusal of this letter might already be counted in years. The fair writer had ceased, not only to exist, but to be the subject of the public talk. The guilty boy to whom it was addressed, revolving years had made a man. The event of which he was the worthless hero had been forgotten even in the district where it took place, for more recent adventures; and the very ink of the admonition had already become pale. Still did my heart feel every sentence of the appeal as if yet in all the freshness of its first inditing. It forgot the lapse of time, and became filled at once with sadness as sincere and profound as if Helena's last despairing sighs still were breathing on my ear. Keeping the sacred characters pressed to my lips, I struck my heaving bosom, and flung myself on the floor. "Here," cried I, "let me lie, and commune undisturbed with my wretched soul; here let me shed tears of blood for her whom I first learnt to prize, when through my fault I had lost her for ever!"

Had sister Agnes known the omnipotence of mercy; had my penitent, my humble suit been unconditionally granted, who knows what richer fruits my first contrition might by degrees have borne? None such were in store for the destroyer of Helena! The nun, the fatal nun, more impelled by vanity than by friendship, more anxious to see my sex humbled than her own exalted, was not satisfied with my writhing under the reproaches of my own conscience, unless I also smarted from the sting of her viper tongue. So keenly did she sharpen its dart, so many little punctures did she one by one inflict, so much venom did she pour into every fresh wound, that resentment at last left not room for regret, and instead of slowly rising with resolves of amendment, I hastily started up with schemes of revenge. A mean ungenerous triumph over one already prostrate, I swore should meet with an adequate punishment.

How this was inflicted; how sister Agnes, who had witnessed the last and direst effects of my unworthiness, – whose curses still pursued me fresh and green, though time had already long faded the less wrathful farewell of her friend, – was made to blush herself; but to blush at my contemptuous forbearance, let the humbled nun herself explain. All I wanted was, after the haughty dame has sneeringly exclaimed, "You of all men!" to be able in my turn to retort in the same tone, "And you of all women!"

Notwithstanding the ill success of my visit to my father, I had not given up all hopes of being restored to his favour. Knowing the uselessness of any attempt at a conciliatory interview, with my brother as the mediator, I penned a letter replete with every possible offer of submission and sacrifice consistent with my safety as a follower of Islam, and sent the supplicating words to their destination by a common friend. Independent of the force of paternal feelings in the head of the family, I depended upon the suggestions of policy in the younger branches. Hatred prevailed over prudence, and I received no answer. After lingering several days in fruitless expectation, I at last prepared to leave Chios.

Ever since the sight of home had revived ancient recollections, and with them the remorse for ancient misdeeds, I had panted for a journey to Samos, there to perform on the lonely grave of my Helena the sad rites of contrition and penance. On the morning of my own birthday I proceeded to the not distant island, whose privileged earth held the sacred deposit; landed on its rocky shore early in the afternoon, and, ere the evening cast its lengthened shadows around, reached the hallowed spot, sole object of my visit.

The sun's departing rays were just gliding from the moss-grown tomb. I approached it with awe; strewed upon it the wild flowers which had grown in its shade, bedewed its silent stones with tears of grief and remorse, and over the ill-fated treasure underneath, poured out my heart's bitter anguish in alternate groans and prayers. The whole night Helena's gravestone was my pillow; and early the next morning, ere yet the orb of day rose out of the sparkling wave – making my dagger my pen – I traced on the dusky slab as on a recording scroll, my Christian, my Grecian, my old ANASTASIUS; filled in the deep sunk characters with the hot stream drawn from my bosom; and, exclaiming: "with the purple of my blood I sign the marriage contract:[2] I make thee mine in death, and mine in life hereafter!" for the last time imprinted my quivering lips on the cold on the cold marble, and rushed away from death's receptacle, which I had made my nuptial couch.

By this expiatory visit I felt my heart somewhat relieved. I thought my Helena might, from the higher regions where she dwelt, have viewed if not in forgiveness, at least in pity, my tardy atonement; and with a lightness of soul to which I long had been a stranger, I proceeded to Paros, and there spent a day or two with some of my old kinsmen. Dull stupid islanders as they were, they entertained me not the less kindly for being out of favour at Stambool, and when I went on to Naxos, actually expressed a wish that I might visit them there again!

At Naxos reigned supreme, under the wide spreading wing of Hassan-pasha's all powerful protection, my maternal cousin Marco Poiti, heir to all the favour enjoyed at the arsenal, before him, by the papas his uncle, and sole epitrope[3] of the Greek villages which cover the island. From every one of these individually might this wily and ambitious personage be said to wage an incessant warfare against the Latin inhabitants of the city; and if the Grimaldis, the Giustinianis and the Barozzis of yore caused Marco's forefathers to groan under the weight of the Venetian yoke, amply did Marco now make the miserable relics of these proud families pay for the sins of their slumbering ancestors. He kept them absolutely shut up in their citadel and towers. Fearful of letting down their draw-bridges to take a stroll in the fields, they envied their own flocks of pigeons the liberty of their roamings, and seemed perched up in their lofty habitations, for no other purpose than to have a better bird's eye view of their adversary, leisurely walking forth to skim the fatness of the land, and going his rounds among the peasantry, to reap the country's choicest fruits, and to levy his tithe on its fine wines, its fragrant oils, and its rich honey, – while they had often nothing else to beguile gnawing hunger, but the treat offered their eyes in the mouldering insignia of their ancestors, clumsily carved over their gloomy gates. Such was their dread of Marco's hostility and power, that, whenever he made a trip to Constantinople, the whole nobility of Naxos took to their beds, in expectation of some new avaniah.[4]

Of his own villages Marco was the idol. Like other idols indeed he was not to be worshipped empty-handed. But he hated the Latins so cordially, that it was universally allowed he must feel an unbounded love for his Greek countrymen. The more, therefore, in his management of the haratsch and other contributions to the Turks, he squeezed out their inmost substance, the more he was thanked for his disinterestedness and public spirit. If Marco had any private foibles, they were, like those of other great men, deemed more than atoned for by his public virtues. This was his own opinion also; and it even appeared, as he observed, to be that of the higher powers themselves; from the frequent interpositions of Providence in his favour, and the almost miraculous manner in which his greatest enemies had been disabled from putting their wicked purposes against him in execution, by almost always disappearing – nobody knew how or where – just the juncture when he seemed exposed to the greatest danger, or involved in the most inextricable difficulties.

It was from a kinsman thus mighty and thus fortunate that, within his own dominions, I, a poor unprotected stranger, had to claim an estate, which he called my mother's indeed, but which, for upward of five and twenty years, he had taken care to nurse as his own. My first point for consideration therefore on landing was, whether I should at once offer to him my unwelcome visage, or first keep myself in abeyance until I had tried my ground. It was not exactly the dictates of reason which decided my conduct. During the conflict in my mind, I filled, by way of assisting my judgment, a cup of that delicious muscadel in which, I was credibly assured, Theseus had on that very spot pledged the too tender Ariadné: but just when in contact with my lips, the still untasted glass slipped through my fingers, as the hero did through those of the nymph. "I accept the favourable omen!" cried I, (to my Frank readers it might not appear such) – and resolved to dare my antagonist at once. "Let me seem to fear no one," was my maxim "and some may fear me!"

Upon this I immediately set out for the village of Trimalia, where the primate resided. He was employed with his men in the fields. The day being sultry, I threw off my cloak in corner of the house, and went out with a servant in search of his master. We found Marco on a little knoll under an old olive tree, in the midst of his farmers, finishing his midday meal. He appeared to be eating with uncommon relish a crust of black barley bread, and enlarging with great earnestness on its peculiar excellence and flavour, when my salutation interrupted the eulogy.

My tone was civil but decided. I told his primateship that, in conformity to the established custom of informing near relations of especial calamities, I had thought it my duty to acquaint him with the misfortune which had befallen me of turning Mohammedan; and added how very much I regretted my being obliged, out of respect for my new religion, to claim my mother's estate, till then entrusted to his management. This circumstance he regretted as sincerely as myself; and the more, when I hinted how absolutely my particular situation prohibited my disregarding the partiality of the Moslemin law to its new proselytes; and expiated upon the powerful support I was promised by the Turkish ministers in the task of maintaining my privilege – and which, to say a truth, I a little exaggerated. At the conclusion of my speech, however, I assured my cousin that I did not think my obligations to my new creed so very strict, but that I might consider myself warranted in some degree to proportion my facility in passing old and intricate accounts, to the alacrity I found in giving up the trust.

Much against my expectation, my relation expressed entire readiness to conform to circumstances. No exception was taken to any part of my statement. Nay, my avowed determination to disregard all opposition seemed rather to increase Marco's apparent cordiality and frankness. He even pressed me so earnestly to take up my abode with him, during my stay at Naxos, that I found some difficulty in handsomely declining the offer. But my obstinacy was equal to his solicitation, and after fixing the time the next day when I was to return and enter upon business, I at last took my leave, and bent my steps towards the town.

Scarce had I measured three hundred yards, when I remembered the cloak which I had left behind. Returning back to the house the shortest way across the fields, my path led me by the side of a thick lentiscus hedge, which surrounded the garden. To this my cousin had by this time retired with his confidential agent, for the purpose of more private conversation. As I approached, I could not help hearing my own name uttered with such emphasis, that I was tempted to stop, and indulge for a few minutes in the contemplation of the beautiful shrubs which formed the inclosure. Meanwhile Marco was proceeding with the conversation. "Cannot you understand, " said he to his confidant (in rather a louder tone than became so wary a personage), "that if I had attempted at once to oppose his claim, he would immediately have resorted to the most effective means for enforcing his demands; and the world would infallibly have joined him in condemning my proceedings: whereas, by admitting his title in the gross, I begin by lulling asleep his suspicions, gain credit with others for fair dealing, and then, by every quibble about the items, and every delay in the forms of the law, defeat his purpose in detail, and tire out his very heart, before he gets from me a single inch of the estate?" This plan of campaign seemed so well worth a cloak, however handsome, that I left mine for the present unclaimed, and, wheeling about, went straight into the town.

But I had my cue for the interview of the next day. When therefore I found in the course of its proceedings, that the more Marco explained, the less I understood, and that certainly I was much less master of the subject at the conclusion of the sitting than I thought myself at the opening, I rather abruptly broke off the conference, and rising, said in the smoothest tone I was master of: "Hark ye, cousin; I make no doubt that you have brought forward every quibble concerning the items, and equally mean to use every delay in the forms of law, which belong to so able a diplomatist: but this I would have you remember, that when, thanks to its unraveller, a business is become so thoroughly entangled as to defy the keenest intellect, I know but of one way to cut the knot asunder; and that," added I, pointing to my yatagan, "is with a good Damascus blade; – and so fare ye well."

Marco was fonder of diplomacy than of fighting. He knew his cousin to be a desperate fellow, and he began to think his agent a traitor. In this double apprehension, he delivered over the whole concern into my hands; including every deed, bill and receipt, accumulated upon the estate since the last clearance of the deluge. "What a thing it is," thought I, "to show a little mettle!"

But I soon found that by mine I had got more than enough. Many of the transactions relative to the property, in the way Marco had managed them, were to be inexplicable enigmas, and this the scoundrel knew. The moment I was proclaimed sole possessor of the estate, and sole respondent for every claim relating to it, there came upon me a host of creditors of every description, from the bishop who had witnessed my mother's will to the Moiro-logistri[5] who had wept at her funeral, all of whom I verily believe Marco had kept back on purpose for the occasion. With this posse constantly at my heels I did not know which way to turn myself. My cousin Marco meanwhile was all at once become so discreet as to decline interfering even in the smallest trifle, or offering his opinion on the simplest question, until he had the satisfaction of seeing me fairly worn out with business and perplexity. He then ventured to suggest that the science of accounts did not seem to be the acquirement most congenial to my disposition, and proposed – but with the sole view of relieving me – to take over the estate entirely, for a round sum of money. Convinced, by this time, that every fresh step I took in the management would only lead to fresh confusion, I became vastly more tractable, and so, after a little demur, agreed to have the property valued. This was done by arbitrators, all so very liberal in their concessions on my part, that the estate was estimated at about half its real worth. But this half was rendered in ready cash; and taking into consideration what most men who drive bargains seem entirely to overlook, – the waste of time, temper, and breath, in standing out for more than is willingly conceded, – I accepted the sum offered, signed the proper receipts, put my capital into my bag, and took leave of Marco to return to the town.

Whether or not I might think the money too little to take, Marco still thought it too much to part with. Most kindly he had stationed two of his trustiest myrmidons in a narrow lane just outside his gate, in order to rid me of the burden as soon as possible. At my going he so earnestly recommended the utmost caution, and so pathetically lamented the unsafeness of the path, that it struck me he must have good authority for his surmises, and considered I could not show my sense of his solicitude more effectually, than be avoiding altogether the road to which he gave so ill a character. Accordingly I waited not even till I was out of my cousin's premises, but, as soon as out of his sight, jumped nimbly over a hedge, and soon got entirely clear of his outpost. I might never have more than surmised the favour intended for me, had I not learnt all the particulars of the scheme the very next day from his deputy. This worthy person, having been drubbed by his master for not stopping me, came to demand a compliment for the civility of his forbearance. "Then you really saw me pass by?" said I to him. – "Yes." – "And intentionally permitted my escape?" – "No doubt." – "Nor let me go home unmolested, only because you could not help it?" – "No indeed." – "If so," exclaimed I, "heaven forbid I should encourage disobedience in servants! You were sent by your principal to rob me, and you ought to have done as you were bidden. Here is all the compliment I can in conscience make." Upon which I gave the fellow a second drubbing, and desired him to inform his master of my proceeding: but this he neglected.

From that day forward, however, I thought it prudent not to take long walks by myself in the country; nor to put the obedience of my cousin Marco's servants a second time to the test. I remained chiefly among the Latin inhabitants of the castle, until a conveyance should offer for some other place, which only seldom occurs in an island destitute of harbour, and rarely visited by ships. But my time hung far from heavy on my hands. I was treated among the Catholics, in my quality of Moslemin, with very great deference. The chancellor held my stirrup; the fiscal lit my pipe; and the archbishop – an entertaining old capuchin – used, when I went out, to mumble prayers in his chapel for my safe return. I paid these civilities in Constantinople news. What I brought not, I made; but this only rendered it the more novel and acceptable. All I regretted was occasioning a schism between church and state. I had spread the report of a secret correspondence between the Grand Signor and the Pope on an intended conversion of the former to the Catholic faith; and upon this the chancellor and the archbishop quarrelled who should sign the address of congratulation. Before the question was decided, a khirlangitsch[6] of the admiralty, which had spent the summer in a fruitless chase of the Maltese corsairs, cast anchor at St. Mary's in the neighbouring island of Paros, and induced me to take my departure. Just on setting out, however, a perhaps too fastidious scruple arose in my mind. I did not like to go without making my cousin Marco some acknowledgement for his last mark of attention, however unsuccessful it had been. Five or six honest lads were come from the khirlangitsch to fetch me away in their boat. With a handful of Marco's own piastres I made it worth their while to convey to the primate my leave taking in the most cordial manner. But as my cousin had taught me by his example how necessary it is for the master's eye to watch delicate commissions, I superintended the business myself. From the high bank of the lane which led to Marco's fields, I had the satisfaction not only of seeing my cousin soundly bastinadoed, but of condoling with him as pathetically as he had done with me, on the unsafeness of the path. This performed, ere he had time to get up and crawl home I bid him adieu, scampered away with my associates to the boat which lay waiting under a cliff only a few hundred yards off, and was rowed to Parrecchia. From that port I got in a few hours, across the mountains, to St. Mary's, and on board the khirlangitsch.

CHAPTER XIV

The cutter which touched at Paros so conveniently, was on its way to receive the annual contribution of part of the circumjacent islands, and was to finish its cruise at Rhodes. This destination perfectly suited my purpose. In want of occupation, and without any precise aim, Rhodes promised a scene of interest to which I hastened with pleasure.

As my former connections with the arsenal gave me a certain predilection for whatever belonged to the navy, I speedily formed an acquaintance with one of the tchawooshes of the Captain-pasha, who like myself was only a passenger. Aly was his name, and Crete his country. This latter circumstance added much, in my eyes, to the merit of his society. The Turks of Candia, by their constant intermarriages with Greek women to whom they permit every latitude of worship, became divested of much of their Mohammedan asperity, and Aly, himself half Greek, was not entitled to any great prejudice against me for being only half a Turk. In the refinements of his toilet, however, Aly tchawoosh might be considered as a finished Osmanlee. Nothing could exceed the exquisite taste of his apparel. His turban attracted the eye less even by the costliness of texture than by the elegance of form. A band of green and gold tissue, diagonally crossing the forehead, was made with studious ease completely to conceal one ear, and as completely to display the other. From its fringed extremity always hung suspended like a tassel, a rose or carnation, which, while it kept caressing the wearer's broad and muscular throat, sent up its fragrance to his disdainful nostril. An hour every day was the shortest time allotted to the culture of his adored mustachios, and to the various rites which these idols of his vain-glorious heart demanded – such as changing their hue from a bright flaxen to a jetty black, perfuming them with rose and amber, smoothing their straggling hairs, and giving their taper ends a smart and graceful curve. Another hour was spent in refreshing the scarlet dye of his lips, and tinting the dark shade of his eyelids, as well as in practising the most fascinating smile and the archest leer which the Terzhana[1] could display. His dress of the finest broad-cloth and velvet, made after the most dashing Barbary cut, was covered all over with gold embroidery, so thickly embossed as to appear almost massive. His chest, uncovered down to the girdle, and his arms bared up to the shoulder, displayed all the bright polish of his skin. His capote was draped so as with infinite grace to break the too formal symmetry of his costume. In short, his handjar with its gilt handle, his watch with its concealed miniature, his tobacco pouch of knitted gold, his pipe mounted in opaque amber, and his pistols with diamond-cut hilt, were all in the style of the most consummate *petit maître*; and if, spite of all my pains, my friend Aly was not without exception the handsomest man in the Othoman empire, none could deny his being one of the best dressed. His air and manner harmonized with his attire. A confident look, an insolent and sneering tone, and an indolent yet swaggering gait, bespoke him to be, what indeed it was his utmost ambition to appear, a thorough rake. Noisy, drunken, quarrelsome, and expert alike in the exercise of the bow (the weapon of his country), and in that of the handjar, he possessed every one of the accomplishments of those heroes chiefly met with on the quays of Constantinople and the other principal seaports of the Othoman empire, whom a modest woman avoids, and to whom a respectable man always give way.

Intimacies are soon contracted at sea; and Aly was too vain to keep up much reserve. He soon favoured me with an account of some of his adventures! "My dear fellow," said he one day, "I would have you know that from my earliest infancy I always had the most decided taste for idleness; and this ruling passion of my heart has never ceased increasing. The only agreeable occupation I could ever devise was doing nothing. Whatever lures were held out to me by fortune lost all their charms to my eye, the moment the pursuit required the least exertion. Not for an empire would I give up my dear laziness. At the same time, next to doing nothing, my chief delight always consisted in spending a great deal of money. Unfortunately I was not one of the privileged few who can afford to indulge both these tastes at once. My luck, however, made me succeed in some little commissions from the governor of Canea, which gained me his good will: and his good will in its turn gained me an employment, in which I was enabled to enjoy my two chief conditions of earthly happiness, if not together, at least alternately. It was that of tchawoosh or messenger of the Captain-pasha. You know the lives these gentry lead; you also know the scanty wages they receive: and you moreover know the splendid figure they are expected to make. I have always suspected our grandees, so profuse in their presents to other people's servants, and so niggardly in their salaries to their own followers, of having struck a secret agreement with each other, by which each was to support his neighbour's retinue instead of his own. It is but justice to us to say, that we do all in our power to give effect to this contract; for you cannot but remember how, at Terzhana, we lie in wait for every hapless stranger whose evil stars inflict upon him business with our Pasha; what fees we exact for every audience he craves, and for every favour he receives. The utmost produce, however, of the fines levied in the capital, would but indifferently defray the expenses of our apparel, board, &c. were it not for the chance of being each in our turn intrusted with some lucrative commission in the provinces.

"For my part, I never, till I saw my wishes fulfilled, ceased praying to Allah both morning and evening, that he might be pleased to whisper in the Pasha's ear a word in my favour, and make him employ his faithful servant Aly as his representative in some lucrative negotiation. The occasion on which my prayers were granted was this. Certain Speciote[2] adventurers had waylaid a Greek vessel bound for Ancona, and not yet knowing – poor souls – the difference 'twixt good and evil, had in the innocence of their hearts sold both cargo and ship in their own native place, among their own fellow-citizens, all more or less engaged in the same primitive sort of profession with themselves. On an application from the owners of the vessel, I was sent to Specia to recover the property, and to bring to justice the culprits. We gentlemen of the short dress carry little ballast, and when we have a prize in view, know the value of time. I no sooner had received my instructions than I hoisted my pennant, and set sail. Not that my journey was quite as expeditious as my departure was prompt. Ships at sea sail not always as the crow flies. Besides, one has often to seek a conveyance, as chance may offer it. In addition to which, I thought it would be showing a proper respect for the grand Admiral my patron, to represent his person in some of the smaller islands on my way. This cost him nothing, nor me either. Everywhere I found board and lodging gratis. I was made welcome to all the necessaries of life, – among the foremost of which I reckoned its superfluities, – and, at my departure, never failed to receive a small present for the honour conferred on the place; for which I always took care, in return, to promise my protection.

"By my deliberate mode of proceeding, I gave the fame of my approach time to precede me to Specia; for I did not wish to take any unfair advantage of its inhabitants, by coming in upon them unawares, and before they had had sufficient leisure to prepare for my reception. The island is so small, and its population so scanty, that, but for some little management of this sort, I could not have avoided stumbling upon the poor wretches whom I was sent in quest of, at the very first step; and this, considering how essential it was to them to avoid my sight, would have been most unhandsome. Such was the confidence which I inspired by the humanity of this proceeding, that the plunderers of the merchantmen did not even seek concealment on the news of my actual arrival, but treated me with an openness of behaviour quite equal to my own. To have taken advantage of such frankness of conduct I must have been callous to all liberal feelings. As the rogues assured me therefore upon their honour, that they had already ate and drank three-fourths of the produce of their prize, I only exacted restitution of the fourth which remained. Not wishing, however, to mortify my employers by restoring to them so small a portion of their property, I put it into my own pocket. My conciliatory spirit gained me universal esteem; and the inhabitants – all more or less liable to the same errors – showered upon me from all quarters presents of all descriptions: sheep, kids, fowls, and other live, as well as dead stock. Just as I was considering to what market I should carry my perquisities, this vessel hove in sight. I thought the opportunity a good one for disposing of my provision and my person; and thence it happens that you find me going onwards to Rhodes, instead of returning back to Constantinople."

"And do you not fear," said I, "that the grand Admiral may some day discover your exploits?" "No," replied the Candiote. "He lays his account with them beforehand. He knows he cannot furnish his hall with forty or fifty strapping fellows stiff with gold lace, and ready to break their necks at his nod, for nothing but a miserable dish of pilaff; and like a man of sense, he suffers his Greek subjects to maintain fellows, by whom they think it an honour to be soundly cudgelled."

A young sailor boy of the district of Sphachia[3] – whose inhabitants consider themselves as the only descendants of the ancient Cretans, and are shepherds in their mountains half the year, and pirates at sea the other half – stood by, listening to Aly's narrative. "You Sphachiote scoundrels," added the tchawoosch, turning sharply upon him, "may thank your stars that your Sultana is fond of your cream cheeses. Many a well deserved avaniah does her favour save you from – you and your blessed malkiané.[4] The last gentle correction you had, I think, was in the Russian war, when the expedition from the Canea left not a soul alive in any of your villages."

"Found none to kill, you mean;" answered the boy. "Our men were on board the Russian vessels, and our women and children in the mountains with their flocks. This you knew, or you durst not come."

Aly began to knit his brow, – and the more, as he saw me entertained. Wishing however to prevent a quarrel: "Who," cried I laughing, "ever wants a broken head, that can get plunder without a scratch on his little finger? For my part I always prefer maruading when the owner is from home; were it only to save the goods from being knocked about."

In this sort of conversation passed away the time, until we came in sight of the island of Scyra. "What have we here?" cried I. "A town like a sugar-loaf, built on the model of a derwish's cap; with the church at the top, by way of a tuft! It must be strange enough to step from one's garret into one neighbour's cellar! Though I should be afraid that a walk, begun on two legs, here might end on all fours."

"This happens the oftener," observed Aly, "as the inhabitants are by disposition stately, and fond of strutting about in long robes, in which the unevenness of their ground often makes them get entangled. Surely you must know that Scyra is the great nursery of men and maid servants of Pera. Two sacolevas, loaded only with this article, go to the capital regularly every year; and no Scyrote returns home till he can live on his island in comfort. This comfort consists in milking their goats and grinding their barley in all the cast-off finery of their masters and mistresses, with feathered heads, and furred tails. When they meet, they treat each other with the forms and ceremonious language of people of quality. The first time I visited the island, I witnessed a salutation in the street between two ladies whom I took for princesses. It begun very well, but it ended with one being rolled in the mire by a jackass, and the other riding away upon a pig, which had got entangled among the folds of her trailing drapery."

The captain of our khirlangitsch had to receive the contribution of the little islet of Serpho. On going shore for that purpose, he proceeded straight to the hospice of an old capuchin. A sort of attraction subsisted between these two grey-beards. From the heaviness of their intellects, I suppose it was only that of gravitation; for it ended in mere bodily juxtaposition, and scarce ever was a word or idea interchanged. Still did its constancy give their mutual regard quite a romantic air. Nowhere but in the friar's dingy cell would the Bey receive in state the salutation and the tribute money of the Greek primates, whose troop presently made its appearance. All its members had their hands crossed on their stomachs, and their features composed into as a demure form as possible. The whole Greek community of the island, men, women, and children, formed the long train of procession.

No sooner had it arrived within hearing of the Captain, than the coryphaeus of the party stopped short, hemmed, coughed, and commenced his harangue. With singular aptitude of simile he compared the whiskered Bey to an angel of light, and with equal consistency, he besought him not to diffuse darkness over the land by exacting a contribution which its inhabitants could not pay. The pleas for exemption consisted in a catalogue of calamities, of which pirates, floods, short crops, earthquakes and conflagrations were the least!

"All *that*, gentlemen," answered the Bey in his Barbaresque idiom, fetching a sentimental sigh, "no doubt very true and very miserable; but, sun set, you put no tribute here," and he pointed to his pouch –"me put bastinado there," added he, pointing to their backs.

At these appalling words, the whole troop, epitrope and commoners, joined in a full chorus of lamentations. When they could squeeze out no more tears, they beat their breasts, and uttered the most piteous groans. Finding all this of no avail, and the Bey as obdurate as ever, they at last retired, hanging their heads, and like men led out for execution.

The sun was still above the horizon when the troop returned, with faces as dolorous as before. They only brought half the sum required; affirming with greater oaths than ever, that if they were to be pounded in a mortar, they could not produce another aspre.

"Me believe that," said the Bey, "and me therefore sorry me obliged to perform my promise. Me however begin with signor epitrope, in due respect for his rank. Him me not dare give less than fifty strokes. Up with his lordship's heels!" added he, turning to one of his attendants, "and begin."

All now cried for mercy, and swore that, if but allowed five minutes more, they would try to bring the complement, were they to wrest it from the bowels of the earth.

The Bey assented, and the troop again retired; but it was only to make a full stop at the first turn of the road, and there to lug out from under their cloaks the entire sum demanded, neatly tied up in bags. With this reserve they returned, and delivered it. The Bey made the proper apologies to the epitrope, and the party was dismissed.

They now in a close phalanx walked slowly home, with the most dejected and miserable look; but they had not gone a hundred yards, when they met some friends returning from a wedding, preceded by music. Both parties stopped, a parley ensued, and presently the whole procession, the epitrope the foremost, spread out their arms, and began to dance the romeika! Attracted by the sounds of the instruments, the Bey went to the window, and beholding the merry scene; "Mirar papas," said he to the friar in lingua franca; "mi parler bono, canaglia senza fede piandgir; ma mi bastonar, mi far pagar, subito ballar et cantar."

Not quite so gay were my friend Aly's accompaniments, when our ship lay rocking on the waves to the music of the roaring winds. On those occasions there was anything but grace in his movements or melody in his utterance. He had not even the pretension to heroism at sea. The slightest ruffling of its surface made him as quiet as a lamb. To his noisy insolent tone immediately succeeded the most piteous and subdued look and manner. Aware himself how altered a man he became in rough weather, he used, at the first breeze, to slink away like the moulting peacock, and conceal himself in some hole or corner, where he lay speechless while the motion lasted: – nor until the sea resumed its tranquillity did Aly re-appear on the deck. How glad he was to see Rhodes need not be told. He almost plumped into the waves in his impatience to step into the boat. But even ashore, he still awhile wore a languid look, which made all the acquaintance he met ask him ironically, "with what fair one of the islands he had left in pledge his spirits?"

My reader has already classed me among those vulgar beings, who take a greater interest in the living occurrences of the passing day, than in the dead letter of remote ages. As a Greek, I ever found but little motive for exultation in any research which led me to compare the present with the past. Still I had leant – where, I cannot tell – that Rhodes belonged not to the Turks from the days of the deluge; that it had once obeyed a Christian order of knighthood, of noble blood, high spirit, enthusiastic devotion, and undaunted bravery; that a handful of these valiant warriors had defended it an entire twelvemonth against the whole force of the Othoman empire; and that the Moslemen at last only found an entrance to the citadel over the bodies of its brave defenders, fallen, to the last man, in the long contested breach.

The outside of the ancient fortress – once the chief theatre of these brilliant and bloody achievements – might be seen from every part of the quay, towering high above the modern city. Its wide ramparts, its lofty bulwarks, its crested batteries of a black and rugged stone, deprived as they now were of the once thundering engines of fire and destruction, looked like the silenced crater of an extinct volcano, still frowning upon the fertile plain below, though its devastating powers are no longer feared.

"Let us go," said I to Aly, "and examine this object of so much strife, which Osmanlees knew how to wrest from the hands of the infidel, but know not how to preserve from the injuries of time." "Let us go," echoed Aly, who expected some opportunity to play the tchawoosh: and accordingly we went.

Though now thrown open to all, the formidable enclosure still seems guarded by an invisible power. Few ever enter its precincts; and, on passing its massy gates, I felt struck with inexpressible awe.

Monuments that already have been so long in a state of progressive decay, as less to retain the regular forms of art than they resume the ruder semblance of nature; as to offer less of a mode of existence gone by than of a new one commencing; less of lapse into death than of return to a different shape of life; less of dissolution than of regeneration: as again on all sides to let in through their crumbling walls the broad glare of day; again every where to show their mouldering joints clothed in fresh vegetation, and again, at every step, to display their mazy precincts tenanted by the buzzing insect, and the blithe chirping bird, – such monuments have their gloom irradiated by at least an equal portion of gaiety; and resemble the human frame so entirely returned to its original dust, as to preserve no trace of its former lineaments, and only to break forth afresh from its kindred clay, in the shape of plants and flowers more luxuriant and more gaudy.

But edifices, whose abandonment by man has been so recent that they still bear about them the marks of death and mourning, still preserve undiminished their funereal darkness, still remain the uninvaded property of solitude and silence; that their outlines scarce are indented by the sharp tooth of time, or their surface varied by the softer impressions of the weatherstain; that their precincts offer yet the smallest transition from unmixed death and dereliction, to a new modification of life and a new order of inhabitants; that they say in distinct terms to the beholder: "It was but yesterday we still resounded with the din of business, and the song of joy," – such edifices preserve their sadness unaltered; they chill the sense, oppress the heart, and make the blood run cold: for they resemble the human body just abandoned by the vivifying soul; just stiffened into an insensible and ghastly corpse; just displaying the first awful signs of fast approaching corruption.

And of such mansions was composed the scene before me. The broad square, the stately palace, the solemn chapel, once re-echoing with the clang of arms, the bustle of trade, the boastings of youth, and the peal of devotion, looked as if the blood scarce was clotted which had stained their massy walls, and the sounds still must vibrate in air, which had circulated through their lofty passages; – as if one still might discern at a distance the dying voices of their departing tenants: though the death-like stillness of the nearer objects was only broken by the plaintive murmur of the pensive turtle dove, nestling in the jagged battlements, or the measured bound of some stone, slowly severed from them by the hand of time, and dropping with hollow din through the yawning vaults.

Contemplating the great names, the sadly eventful dates and the proud armorial bearings, still shining in marble of resplendent whiteness on the black honey-combed walls, like the few memorable persons and periods that still continue to soar in light among the general obscurity of times long past: thinking on the noble ancestry, the high blood, the martial character, and the monastic life of the illustrious youth – the flower of Europe – whose abodes, whose history, and whose habits these monuments so clearly marked, I experienced a new and hitherto unfelt emotion. I envied the heroes who, after a life of religion, of warfare, and of glory, slaughtered in the very breach they defended, now slept in peace and renown, leaving after them names ever young and ever flourishing in the hearts of grateful Europe. I wished that I too had been among these noble few; that I too had sprinkled these edifices with my heart's fullest tide; that I too had fallen in these ramparts, and had filled these yawning chasms with my body. In the enthusiasm of the moment I wished that I too might now be nothing more than a spirit; but a spirit entitled to haunt this august spot as the scene of my past achievements, and to say to other inferior and wandering ghosts: "Here I lived, here I died, here I immortalized my name!"

Disposed, by the comparisons which these ideas suggested, to repine at my own country, condition and parentage, I sat down on the prostrate trunk of a pillar; and there lamented the hard lot of man, who, so far from being able to adapt his circumstances to his faculties, is often, with a spirit equal to the highest station, left to linger in the lowest. In my despondency my eye caught a piece of broken marble, gorgeously emblazoned with chivalresque insignia: – but, if the side which lay uppermost displayed the plumed crest of a Gothic knight, the reverse still bore the remains of an Hellenic inscription. It was a work and a record of the ancient Greeks, and had no doubt been brought from the opposite shore, where the ruins of Cnidus furnished the knights of Rhodes with an ample quarry for the monuments of their feudal vanity. At this sight, my own national pride returned in all its force. "And does it then belong to me, " cried I, – the dormant energies of my mind all again aroused and starting up – "to envy the borrowed greatness of Goths and barbarians, only able in their fullest pomp to adorn themselves with the cast-off feathers of my own ancestors! Am I not a Greek? And what Grecian blood, even where remotest from the source and running in the smallest rills, is not nobler than the base stream that flows through the veins of these children of the West, whose proudest boast it is to trace their names to the obscurity of ignorance and the night of barbarism; whose oldest houses only date as of yesterday, and whose highest achievement are the exploits of the savages?"

My friend Aly was not a person to sympathize with my feelings on this occasion. From his very first entrance into this dark abode, his mind had misgiven him. Turning as pale as if again at sea, and in a storm, he cried out: "What can you mean to do among these ugly ruins? The place is too dreary even for an appointment with a Goule." All the time during which I stood considering the various objects that successively attracted my attention, he had continued most impatient to return; and when, after my first round, he saw me sit down composedly on an old broken pillar, there to follow up at leisure the train of my reflections, he fell into complete despair. "What can this confounded son of a Greek jabberer be muttering to himself, as if possessed," I overheard him say, – "and that in a place where people should keep calling to each other with all their might, in order to frighten away evil spirits?" and after various surmises, it seemed he at last settled it in his mind, that I was brewing some incantation, and going to treat him to a dance of spectres. At this idea his teeth began to chatter; he looked round for a way by which he might escape; but, after several trials, all equally abortive, he at last convinced himself as well as me that he had not the courage to retrace his steps alone.

The only thing left for him to do, therefore, was to exert his utmost arts of persuasion, and prevail upon me to bear him company. Ere his fear had risen to its highest pitch, he had ventured for a moment to quit my side. He now became so pressing to show me what he had seen on that occasion, and was pleased to call the prettiest prospect imaginable, that at last I consented to follow him, merely to get rid of his importunities; but fully expecting to be shown some dunghill, or burying-ground, or other object equally extraordinary and agreeable. My surprise therefore was great, when, from a projecting bastion, I really beheld a most delightful view of the city's gay and busy suburbs, stretching with their gardens full of orange and date trees, along the winding beach.

"There now!" cried Aly in a coaxing tone, on perceiving the bait to take, "who in his senses would stay another moment among these black and frightening dungeons – in which all the company I could start consisted of as sociable a party of vipers and of scorpions as one would wish to join, – that had the faculty to go and investigate all the innumerable species of delight contained in that knot of little snow-white dwellings down below?" and hereupon he began to enumerate on his fingers such a wondrous list of all the good things of this world, which might probably be found in the aforesaid habitations, that my mouth, by degrees, watered at the catalogue; and, to Aly's inexpressible satisfaction, I at last took him under my arm, and left the castle to explore the beach.

My curiosity was soon satisfied, but my newly acquired taste for travelling only received fresh excitement. From our conversation by the way, Aly had given me a longing desire to visit Egypt, to which country I had now performed more than half the distance from Constantinople; and the commander of the khirlangitsch had raised that desire to the highest pitch, by his description of the advancement which I might hope for in the land of the Mamlukes. "Egypt," he observed, "always was the cradle of revolutions and the patrimony of strangers; always welcomed the wanderers who had no predilection for any particular soil, or attachment to any particular home. – At present more than ever," he added, "it holds out irresistible attractions to the bold adventurer, who seeks his fortune in strife and confusion. To external appearances, indeed, the country slumbers in the profoundest peace. No one would guess, on a superficial glance, that the least convulsion threatened to disturb its tranquillity. The utmost wish of the two parties who divide the supreme sway seems thus far confined to measuring each other's strength, and watching each other's movements with the eye. But this apparent serenity is only the calm which precedes the storm. The various elements, all preparing soon to fall asunder and to assume new combinations, are ready at a moment's warning to burst out into open strife, – uncertain when the trump of war may sound as the signal for battle. Meanwhile each party most eagerly seeks to increase the number of its adherents by every new sword's-man of tried enterprise and courage, disposed to embrace its cause. Under these circumstances a youth like you, – Greek by birth, and Mohammedan from choice – is already beforehand half a Mamluke, and, handsome, vigorous and warlike, still adds to his skill in martial exercises the more uncommon qualification of expertness in languages and readiness at his pen, – wields the hollow reed as ably as the heavy spear, and can execute a delicate commission as dexterously as a dangerous mandate, – is a treasure for which all must contend. He need only show himself on the spot, to ensure opposite factions vying which shall by the most brilliant offer enlist him in their foremost ranks."

At this tempting picture, I sighed. The Bey guessed my thoughts. "I see," said he, "what you want, and I can supply it. Suleiman, one of the most distinguished among the present rulers of Egypt, is my particular friend. The number of his Mamlukes has been extremely reduced by the late destructive plague. He seeks every means by which to recruit his house. For this purpose, his kehaya at Constantinople, knowing the number of ports and islands I would have to visit, gave me an express commission to engage for his patron whatever youth of promise I might find. I have watched you during the voyage. You are resolute, sensible, and, as I deem, not likely to demur at trifles; and, if you like the scheme, I will give you the recommendations to my old friend which these qualities deserve."

I bowed, expressed my delight at the commander's good opinion, and accepted his offer. Elate at the idea of not only seeing fruitful Egypt, but perhaps myself some day shining in its annals, I immediately sought a vessel in which to take my passage; and embarked the same day.

As the coast of Rhodes receded from my view, my heart beat high with eagerness and with hope. It seemed to me as if thus far I had only been trifling away my existence in contemptible pursuits, and in a contracted sphere. I was now, for the first time, going to take a flight worthy of the flight of my pinions. – Wide views, noble prospects, vast plans of fortune and of fame, all at once, as if by the drawing of a curtain, expanded to my enraptured view!

CHAPTER XV

The sacoleva which carried Anastasius and his fortunes was first to touch at Castel-rosso, there to take the firewood for Alexandria. The captain seemed to have no acquaintance whatever with the coast for which we were bound; nor could any of his crew boast less ignorance; but they all agreed that Providence was great; and in order to set the greatness of Providence in its fullest light, they always kept as close as possible to a shore set round with hidden reefs, and teeming with avowed pirates.

On the second day of our departure Castel-rosso came in sight. We were just going to double the most advanced promontory of the island, and to cast anchor for the night behind its projecting cliffs, when on our last tack there suddenly appeared ahead of us, close in with the shore, a long dark object of suspicious form, though the dusk prevented our discerning its precise nature. It lay in the water as still as a rock, but it bore all the appearance of being filled with life. At this sight our carvokiera grew as pale as a ghost; and all the crew showed equal signs of courage. “A bad way this,” cried I, “to meet danger! The pirates cannot see more of us than we do of them: let us at least try what a show of resolution may effect.” And hereupon I got our whole artillery brought upon deck, and prepared for a warm engagement. The moment we thought ourselves within musket shot of the enemy I gave the signal for firing. “If the compliment produce nothing else,” thought I, “it will at least make the scoundrels turn out, and show their strength,” Off went our first volley, and after it every eye – expecting immediately to see the hostile boat in the utmost bustle. So far, however, from changing her position, she deigned not even to return our salute. Half surprised and half piqued, we repeat our fire: but our second is not more noticed than the first. Still more amazed, we give a third broadside. Even this makes no impression. But with the seeming shyness of the enemy our own bravery rises. We now approach near enough to be within speaking distance, and a fourth time discharge every gun and swivel into the hostile deck. In short, we continue incessantly firing, without experiencing the smallest retaliation, till, by degrees, this very impassibility of the enemy causes an alarm of a new species: – for we now fancied ourselves under the influence of some spell; we supposed that we beheld nothing but an unsubstantial vision; we became convinced that we were fighting only with the phantom of a ship; which presently would either explode or vanish away – either blow us up in the air, or draw us after it into the fathomless abyss. As however neither happened, and the vessel seemed equally little inclined to rise or to sink, we at last agreed that the very few men which she contained must all have been killed by our very first broadside. We therefore suspended all further hostilities during the remainder of the night, proposing as soon as the dawn appeared to remove the dead bodies, and to divide the spoils.

The dawn at last did appear, and as soon as it was sufficiently advanced to light up the scene, showed to our straining eyes, in the object of the whole night’s strenuous fighting, a small rock in the sea, which from the peculiarity of its shape actually bears the name of the Galley. We regretted all the ball and powder, and agreed not to boast of our intrepidity: but our modesty was, in spite of our caution, put to the blush. The whole island of Castel-rosso had been alarmed by the incessant firing; every part of the shore was lined with spectators; and the moment we landed, they all crowded round our party, and with loud cheers wished us joy for having silenced the enemy.

Having laden our wood, we pursued our voyage. It seemed an eternity in duration. Our crew knew no other mode of sailing than right before the wind; and the least cloud that arose made them put into the first inlet they could reach, wholly heedless of the risk of splitting upon a rock, or running aground upon a shoal. Coasting from one headland to another, we slowly crept round every cape or promontory on our way; and there scarce exists a single creek, I believe, in or outside the Satalian bay, which we did not successively visit. When the wind increased to what was called a fortuna, the sailors could only think of praying and lighting tapers before the Panagia; and as soon as fair weather returned, they could only dance and play upon the guitar; nor ever thought of repairing the damage done to the ship, until reminded of it by a fresh storm. Still was the first part of our journey, compared with the latter, the flight of the swallow contrasted with the creeping of the tortoise. In the latitude of the Damiat, fate seemed to have fixed us to the spot for life; and as we thought ourselves doomed never to pass the eastern outlet of the Nile, even with the assistance of some more experienced sailors whom we there got on board. Every inch the feeble breeze enabled us to advance, the strong current as regularly drove us back; so that on our starboard tack we invariably lost all we had gained on the larboard. Day after day at sunrise we had the satisfaction to find ourselves just in the same place from whence we had parted at sunset the evening before. The fatal mouth of the stream seemed to breathe a fascination which no earthly power could overcome!

An aerial one at last flew to our assistance. It arose on the fifth day of our vain attempts, in the shape of a siroc sufficiently strong to cope with the current. Backed by the burning blast, we doubled the point of the Delta in the very teeth of the perverse tide, and thus approached the goal. Even before we could discern the sandy shore on which it stands, we beheld the town of Alexandria, crowned with minarets and encircled with date trees.

In its quality of Grecian property, our vessel cast anchor in the new harbour; the old being reserved for stanch Musselmen keels. Hell itself, as the bourn of a long sea voyage, would have appeared to me a very habitable place; Alexandria seemed heaven. In its melancholy mounds of barren sand I could only see pleasing swells, and in its dismal ruins a picturesque ruggedness. Its inhabitants, ready to assume any hue or form at will, were a sort of human chameleons: but chameleons may afford entertainment by their constant changes. To me the contrast between the liveliness of the Alexandrians and the solemn stupidity of the Turks seemed quite enchanting. As I went to secure my night's lodging at an okkal,[1] I was every instant arrested by their wit and repartee. "How pleasant to must be to reside here!" said I to myself. "Gay people are always so good-natured!"

The words had scarcely dropped from my lips, when I heard at some distance a loud and increasing clamour, which I supposed to be that of some rejoicing or festival. Presently appeared an immense crowd of people of every age and description – men, women, and children – rending the air with their shouts. In the midst of the motley assemblage advanced in a separate cluster a chosen band, trailing after them in procession, with louder howlings than the rest, the city weights and scales.

"What means this ceremony?" said I, accosting one of the actors in this novel scene; "for what purposes are these instruments travelling?" – "For the purpose of gibbeting the chief of the customs, a Syriac Christian, on the very instrument of his malpractices;" hastily answered the fellow, impatient at the detention.

"And has the law weighed, and found him wanting?" – "How could it help doing so," was the reply, "when we all demanded his punishment? We insisted on the sharallah, – the justice of God; and the cadee himself thought us too many not to be in the right. So we are going to execute the sentence."

Having now carried his courtesy to the utmost stretch, the man bade me adieu, for fear of further questions, and ran after his companions, who already were out of sight. For my part, I contented myself with inwardly praying to Allah that I might be preserved from his justice; and particularly at Alexandria.

My apartment at the okkal secured for the night, I went to a native of the place who followed the various trades of ship agent, interpreter, and pilot, in order to obtain from him a conveyance to Raschid.[2] In his youth, the bustling personage had served on board Marseillese, Venetian, and Leghorn traders. He spoke with equal fluency the Turkish, the Arabic, the Greek, the Provencal, and the lingua Franca. On entering his small abode, where he sat with open door in readiness to receive strangers, I found him gravely discussing with a Franciscan monk, over a bottle of rakie,[3] the relative merits of Islamism and of popery.

"Hark ye, father," said he, speaking with such a volubility of tongue and violence of gesture, that at first I thought him in a tremendous passion, "I do not mean to pass myself off for the most squeamish of Moslemen. In my long intercourse with infidels (begging your pardon) I have been obliged occasionally to relax a little from the rigour of our practices; sometimes, when time ran short, to mumble half a prayer instead of a whole one; and when water was scarce, to perform my ablutions to the wrist only instead of to the elbows; nor did I always remember, when a good joint was smoking on the table, and I sharp set in consequence of a long fast, to inquire before I fell to, whether the beast had been stabbed by a knife or knocked down with a hatchet. But, thank God! I have never been a rank heathen – a kafr. I never, like you, believed in scores of Gods, nor worshipped idols of wood and brass."

"Merciful Father," cried the friar – setting down the rakie, already in contact with his lips: – "nor I neither, nor any of us! How can you say such things?"

"How can I?" answered the Alexandrian, "but from having witnessed them with my own eyes! Who among you, I beg, thinks of celebrating a festival, building a mosque, addressing a prayer, vowing a present, imparting a wish, or expressing a wish, or expressing a want to any but St. Anthony of Padua, St. Francis of Assisi, St. John, St. James, St. Peter, St. Paul, St. Agnes, St. Catherine, St. Cecilia, or any other of the saints and saintesses, whose interference quite leaves Providence a cipher, and whose number exceeds that of days set apart to worship them? In whose name but in that of these officious go-betweens are your oxen, and your sheep, and your poultry, and your very pigs blessed by the priest at the church door? In whose honour but theirs do you suspend over your altars silver tokens of broken heads and hearts, of children born, and grown people mended? Can your cook so much as bake his meat, but by favour of St. Lawrence? – delighted, it seems, to be reminded of his own broiling on a gridiron! And as to worshipping wooden images, – have I not seen whole shoals of Nazarenes leave the nicest, whitest little flaxen-headed madonnas which your toy-shops could produce, at home quite neglected, to travel barefoot perhaps five hundred leagues to some old mouldering figure, as ugly as a scarecrow, and as black as negro; which strange fancy you will allow could only arise from some peculiar virtue assigned to the latter image, – since, how should they otherwise try to extract it, by rubbing their noddle against its greasy pate?"

"As to that, child," replied the friar – taking a fresh sip of his rakie, and pursing up his mouth like one who is going to give an unanswerable answer, – "it is only on the score of superior resemblance to the saint, that certain images are preferred. All the world knows that the holy Virgin sat for her picture by St. Luke: and we may suppose she wishes to distinguish the originals by some peculiar mark of her divine favour."

"Well!" exclaimed the Alexandrian, in astonishment; "if this same virgin had been offered to me as a wife!" but again checking himself: "and pray," added he, "your other saints, have they also each had his painter?"

"No doubt," replied the Franciscan. "All great personages with us sit for their portraits. I myself have sat, both as Cupid and a friar."

The factor now got up, and fetching a little parcel which he gave to the padre: "There," said he, "are the St. Domingo beans you wanted. They are the very best I could find in the market. You may safely send them to your friends in Christendom, and be sure that, when well roasted, like St. Laurence aforesaid, they will drink them for pure Mokha, and admire how superior they are in flavour to the vile West Indian coffee." Upon this, he slapped the father on the back, dismissed him, and asked my business. I had made signs to him before not to break off the discussion, which I thought rather diverting.

On stating my intention to go to Raschid, he agreed for my passage on board one of the country djerms.[4] It was to sail early the next morning; and at the appointed time, I went to secure my berth.

The boat seemed chiefly loaded with live stock; and by far the noisiest article of that description was a lot of female slaves, selected from among a ship load bought for sale to Alexandria. A sharp *grego-maestro*, which kept blowing in our teeth all day long, and at dusk forced us to anchor before Bekier, enabled me to form some estimate of the value of this cargo. In the small place where we were all huddled pell mell, the rolling produced by the storm afforded me every opportunity I could wish for of forming an acquaintance with such of the ladies as looked most sociable; nor did our innocent chit chat suffer any interruption from the watchfulness of their keeper, who, horribly sea-sick, lay speechless in the hold, and never opened his mouth for any purpose at all calculated to interrupt our conversation. His charge, inured to the sea by the voyage of the Euxine and the Mediterranean, only laughed at his distress, and, in defiance of winds and waves, chattered away like magpies. A Tcherkassian damsel, whose large black eyes seemed quite determined not to suffer from the concealment of her other charms, chiefly attracted my attention. She rewarded my notice with her utmost confidence, and gave me the rude sketch of her rough adventures.

"One evening," said she, "when I was in bed, and pretended to be asleep, my parents began to talk as usual, about the trouble I gave them. My mother wished me far away. My father observed nothing was so easy as to fulfil that wish. A Turkish merchant, who used every two or three years to come and collect slaves in our country, had arrived that very day; and assuredly it was fairer that those who had had all the expense, should have the profit of me, rather than the neighbouring Tartars, who were every day carrying off some of our girls to sell to the Turks. My mother – somewhat fond of contradiction – now changed her tone, and would not hear of parting with her only daughter. But my father, telling her she was always perverse, offered her an alternative between what she liked better than keeping, and what she disliked worse than losing me, – a cask of brandy or a sound cudgelling. She took the spirits and gave up the child. The next day I was carried to the merchant. After a great deal of haggling, he bought, or rather accepted me in exchange for arms, apparel, and sweet meats. I was stowed on board a small vessel, with a number of other slaves picked up in various parts. Most of them had been sold by their landlords in payment for rent. The ship proved so leaky that we never expected to reach Stambool. By a miracle, however, we got there; – at least, so I was told: for I never saw anything of the place, except the huge ugly khan in which we were housed. Our owner had us taught here the various accomplishments required for a ready sale – the Mohammedan religion, music, and dancing. Every day customers of all descriptions used to come and cheapen some among us. The price set on me was what few could afford: but my time meanwhile passed comfortably. I had plenty to eat, heaps of fine clothes, and a looking-glass to myself. I should have been quite happy but for the dread of being bought by the Grand Signor who, they say, has so many wives, that he does not know what to do with them, and, though as old as Methusalem, yet must have a new one for Christmas. Think of being laid on the shelf at the death of this old spindle-shanks, as useless lumber, in an ancient seraglio with tremendously high walls – there to remain for life neither single nor married! This fate I escaped. The kehaya of Yousoof-Bey of Cairo bought me for his master, with some of my companions. We were immediately shipped off in a very comfortable vessel; hardly ever had a whipping during the whole voyage; and here we are, on the eve, thank God! of reaching our final destination. To me it promises a paradise. I wish I could say as much in favour of my companions. But, poor things! they were only, as it were, thrown into the bargain; and I fear will remain all their lives mere drudges!"

This last piece of intelligence, though conveyed in a very low whisper, did not escape the quick ears of the damsels for whom Hamida expressed such unacceptable compassion. I thought it would have occasioned an immediate engagement. With one accord the whole party rose up from their mattresses, and, gathering round the frightened Hamida, abused her for telling such falsehoods – she! a low-bred Tcherkassian, without faith, fat, or manners – of Georgians like them, who at home used every day to go to mass, and had as much victuals as ever they wished to eat! But Hamida's own mettle rose at the base insinuation, and facing her assailants boldly; "It signifies much truly," replied she in an ironical tone, "from what country we come, when none of us will ever see it again; and whether we had much or little of our religion, when we all have renounced it alike! And as to our fat – which is the most material point – that must be seen to be judged of."

"Then, let it," replied all the others in chorus; "and trust to us for seeing nothing!" and immediately they all fell upon poor Hamida, forcibly tore open her feridjee, and displayed her bosom. It might not answer the utmost amplitude of Asiatic ideas, but I confess, though I looked hard, I perceived no deficiency.

Even before this exhibition, the keeper of the ladies had cast sundry savage glances our way. He now contrived, sick as he was, to crawl unperceived among the busy group, and only announced his presence by unexpectedly laying about him with such energy as not only to separate the combatants, but to send them slinking away to the furthest corner of the hold. He then lay down before them, and thus formed an effectual mediator for the prevention of further disputes.

No one remained on the field of battle except the spectators: namely, myself, and a single female as different from our Circassian as night is from day: an Abyssinain negro woman. Manumitted by her last master, the dusky nymph had nobody to whom she was accountable for her conversation but herself, feared not the interruptions of a keeper's lash, and seemed determined to avail herself to the full of her advantages. She began by informing me, most prolixly, of all her concerns, past, present, and future. At first, she told me, her stars had looked but coolly upon her. She had been carried to Constantinople in winter, had suffered much from chilblains, and had been married to a black eunuch. But the husband died, the chilblains healed, the summer came, and lovers began, like bees, to buzz about the black rose. "Still," continued she, "as I now was rich, I resolved again to quit the cold climate of Constantinople, and gradually to re-approach the milder temperature of Sennaar. Perhaps, thought I, in my way, at Alexandria, I may chance to find among the Mawgarees[5] some proper husband for my money, to make amends for my former empty honours. Nothing, however, worthy the acceptance of the widow of Ibrahim-Aga offered; and I am now moving onward to Cairo, where, wholly independent of your insipid whites, I am quite sure of suitably matching my own colour, – unless, " added she, with a significant glance, "something very tempting should offer by the way."

That this something actually had offered, and that every objection to the insipidity of whites had been overcome, I soon felt convinced by the lady's *oeillades*. Certain of her own approval, she did not in the least seem to trouble herself about any possible objecttion on my part; and her advances presently became so marked, that I owed the greatest obligation to the timely interposition of the Boghaz. This formidable sand-bank, which muzzles the mouth of the Nile, was announced at a most critical moment. Immediately every other passion yielded to terror. The Circassians screamed, the Turks fainted, and the negress turned as pale as she was able. Even after the peril was surmounted, all thoughts of taking the citadel by storm seemed laid aside; and the siege dwindled into a mere blockade, which lasted till we got to Raschid.

The abrupt transition from the yellow aridity of Alexandria to the verdant freshness of Rosetta, rising on the margin of a beautiful river, and embosomed in orange, in sycamore, and date trees, might give a taste of Elysium. I spent a whole day in a jasmine arbour, eating bananas, and drinking the juices of the sugar-cane; and, after having thus truly tasted the sweets of Raschid, re-embarked on board a maash,[6] destined to sail up the river, and to land us at Cairo. It resembled Noah's ark; was filled with beasts of every description, and surrounded by an universal flood. As far as the eye could reach, the waters of the Nile suffered nothing to rise above their surface but the walls of towns and villages, looking on their artificial platforms, as if floating in trays on the liquid plane. Among the strange animals which our barge conveyed across this immense plash, shone conspicuous from the bright yellow of his glossy skin, a short bloated biped, who, on a head scarce peeping over his shoulders, wore, perfectly poised, a huge flat turban, which gave the *tout-ensemble* the complete proportions of a toadstool; and truly, in the eyes of the other natives, this natural production seemed to be very much held in equal estimation with a fungus. An Osmanlee of Cairo – a man of unusual information of his country, and of open pleasant manners – seeing the wonder with which I contemplated this figure, whispered me: "Coobd is the name these people bear, and they trace their descent from the ancient Egyptians; but they have changed the object of worship from cats and onions to gold; and the only hieroglyphics they preserve are those in their scrutoires, which secure to them the exclusive knowledge of the size, produce, and boundaries of all the cultivable tracts of the country. Nor is this, in their hands, a mere speculative and barren science. It ensures them the stewardship of all the property of their Mohammedan masters. More conversant in arms than in arithmetic, we cannot dispense with this vermin, though it lives upon our best substance; and every Moslemin of any rank or wealth, from the Schaich-el-belled[7] who farms the whole territorial contribution of Egypt, to the smallest Aga of a village, has his Coobtic steward or writer, whose accounts he understands just as much as the Coobd understands the language of his own prayers. He only knows that he is cheated, and has no way to help himself."

Night, meantime, had begun to cast its veil even over the nearest objects, when, on a sudden turn of the river, we all at once beheld at a distance before us a most splendid spectacle. The left bank of the Nile seemed for a considerable space in an entire blaze, and the luminous streak which edged the winding shore, producing by its reflection a parallel line of light in the mirror of the stream, made the whole resemble a riband edged with fire. It glittered more brilliantly from the surrounding darkness. The spot which it skirts resounded with the incessant clang of cymbals, of kettle-drums, and other musical instruments; and, as we approached near enough to discern in the fairy spectacle the effects of a most extensive illumination, the shouts and song of innumerable voices met the ear. The place thus distinguished was Mektoobes, famous in all seasons for its gaiety, and at this particular period engaged in the festival of its patron Schaich, which drew together the population of all the surrounding districts. For almost a mile the quay was lined with barges, so closely wedged that one might walk from deck to deck; while the interior of the town was rendered as light as day by thousands of lamps; some winding in lofty spirals to the summit of the minarets, others thrown in long festoons from pinnacle to pinnacle, other again expanding in wreaths, in sheaves, and other fanciful forms. As we drew nearer the eye was not more dazzled by the glare of light, than the ear was stunned by the din of instruments. At every corner of a street a different band of musicians played a different tune, in hopes of drowning all the others in its noise; and in every open space some different troop of singers, dancers, tumblers, sorcerers, or fortune-tellers exhibited their different sorts of feats, with a view to eclipse all the rest. Here a string of awalis[8] strained their windpipes in tremulous quavers, until they grew as hoarse as the frogs in the neighbouring ditches; and there a knot of ghazie[9] distorted their limbs into as uncouth postures as if they had been frogs themselves; and while one portion of our passengers stood watching the tricks of a juggler, whose troop of performers consisted in a basket full of serpents, another portion sat gaping at the feats of a rival mountebank, whose *chef d'oeuvre* was turning water into blood, and earth into vermin. I speak not of the female charmers, who preferred for the exhibition of their fascinations the darker places, where they excelled in emptying of its last para the closest purse. Of these Syrens, our Coobd might give the best account. He had been missing almost from the moment we went ashore; and no one could guess what witchery had conjured him away, until we all got back to our barge. It was there he first reappeared among us; and the first thing he did was to untie his pouch, in order to ascertain the damage it had sustained. A sequin was the utmost he rated it at; and that was just twice as much as, by his own account, the thrifty personage ever had spent on similar aberrations. What was his horror when he found that, by an art exactly contrary to that of the alchymists, the ladies whose leger-de-main tricks he had been too curiously investigating, had converted all his gold into base metal. His purse indeed, externally, preserved its full size and weight; but alas, the contents had experienced a sad transmutation! His gold was all turned to brass!

At any other period, the adventures of the Mektoobes and the misfortunes of the Coobd would have furnished materials for conversations till we reached Cairo; but at this moment the mind of no Egyptian born was sufficiently disengaged for such idle talk. A topic of higher, more universal, and more vital interest engaged every thought, and dwelt on every lip; absorbed the whole mind of man, woman, and child; and was sure, whatever other subject most foreign from it might accidentally be started, ultimately, by imperceptible steps, to regain full possession of every receptacle of thought and words!

This was the rise of the Nile, – the phenomenon on whose measure and degree depended, throughout Egypt, the serious difference between plenty and famine; and whose increase, perceptible inch by inch and sometimes rapid, sometimes slow, sometimes wholly at a stand, kept, while it lasted, every eye on the stretch, and every mind in a fever.

In vain, as a stranger not yet imbued with the spirit of the universal subject, I now and then tried to turn the conversation into another channel. The slimy ducts that carried the muddy waves of the Nile to the furthest limits of the country, were the only channel which my hearers could contemplate. When I talked of Hassan's expedition to the Morea, a person on my right observed it must have happened the year when the river only rose fifteen cubits; when I hoped to engage the attention of the company by describing the splendours of the Sultan's court, a man on my left asked whose office it was to bring him the daily intelligence of the Nile's increase; and when I extolled the beauty of our islands, some one, who till that instant had never opened his lips, sighed to think they had no rivers to rise like the Nile. I now despaired of any other general conversation, and, in order to hear the last of the ruling topic, took my Osmanlee friend aside, supplicated as a favour that he would first say all his imagination could suggest concerning the Nile and all its branches, and would then vouchsafe to give me a little sketch of the politics of Egypt. This he readily undertook, and as his information on that subject may render more intelligible my own subsequent adventures in that country, I shall here transfer it to the reader – in substance more than in form – and with such additions and emendations as I subsequently derived from my own observation.

CHAPTER XVI

"Egypt," said (or said not) my Osmanlee, "after its conquest by Omar, first obeyed a race of Arab sovereigns called Kaliphs. To these succeeded, on its occupation by Selah-el-din, a race of Tartar princes denominated Sultans.

"It was the early practice prevailing in every country under Tartar government, to leave the cultivation of the ground to the free-born peasant, and to employ the prisoner taken in war, and the purchased slave, in domestic and personal services alone. When, however, in their southward progress the Tartar swarms came in contact with black and woolly-haired nations, they varied the destination of the new slaves according to their colour. The more pliant and pacific negro, foreign in habits as in looks from the purchaser, was under the name of Abd or domestic servant confined to household duties, and was never kept for defence. Admitted to the highest posts in the household, he could attain no advancement in the state. The more warlike white slaves on the contrary, not infrequently the neighbour, nay the relation of his master in the country whence both derived their origin, and considered as more able to wield a patron's authority, and more fit to represent his person, was under the name of Mamluke, trained up to arms as well as to attendance. While in his master's house, he served him not only as his domestic but as his military guard and defender, and when manumitted, he became entitled to aspire to the highest dignities in the army and the state. The custom of raising military slaves or Mamlukes to eminent employments has prevailed wherever throughout Europe, Asia, or Africa, a Tartar dynasty has arisen. Indeed, slaves of this description were deployed by Tartar sovereigns as their generals and their ministers in preference to freemen, whether of the conquered or even of the conquering race. Torn up by the root from their native soil, strangers to that into which they were transplanted, unconnected with the body at large either of the vanquished or of the vanquishers, deriving their existence, their support, their greatness from their master alone, raised by his will, and at his nod again reduced to their original nothingness, they appeared of all descriptions of men the least formidable to a despotic ruler. In their hands the power which an absolute monarch is obliged to delegate in all its fullness to each of ministers down to the last and the least, seemed most exempt from the danger of being turned against its author.

"No device, however, has yet been discovered by which a single hand can long continue to hold undivided an absolute sway over an extensive country. He who must singly withstand the pressure of many, is doomed at last to fall. Thus it fared with Selah-el-din's successors. The Mamlukes entrusted by them with the command of provinces, amended their original insulation by their subsequent leagues. They set aside their legitimate sovereign, and established a military government in a republican form. Each of the fourteen provinces of Egypt was governed by its own Bey. These lesser chiefs used to assemble in council under a president called Schaich-el-belled, or chief of the country. In this Divan were enacted by plurality of votes the decrees for the common welfare of all, and each Bey presided in his own department over their due execution.

"From its first origin and throughout all its later vicissitudes, this republic of Beys has been perpetuated by means unexampled to the same extent in any other country, – namely, by an uninterrupted importation of strange slaves, transformed by degrees into rulers of Egypt. Not that, as foreigners have sometimes imagined, the constitution of the Egyptian commonwealth prohibited by any positive law natives, freemen, and the actual progeny of prior rulers from participating in the government of the country: not that any express ordination ever reserved the succession of power and the exercise of authority exclusively to strangers and to slaves. Throughout every period of the domination of the Beys, instances have existed of individuals who were neither slaves nor strangers, but free-born Mohammedan Turks, nay, sons of Mamlukes and of Beys, being allowed to attain the highest employments in the state. Three generations of Beys shone in the family of Beloofi: at this moment, Ibrahim, our Schaich-el-belled, boasts of the great destinies that await his son Matzook; and at some future day you yourself, who as far as I know were never bought nor sold, may, unless prevented by prior claims, become one of our Beys.

"But a concurrence of circumstances has nearly effected what no law ever expressly decreed. According to our customs the prolific period of youth is spent by the Mamluke under his master's roof in forced singleness, and in the society of none but his fellow soldiers. His constitution, more liable to the enervating tendency of the climate in proportion as it derives from its more bracing native atmosphere a greater natural fullness, and succulence, is weakened, perhaps his very imagination allows him to quit his master's house, and to enjoy the comforts of the connubial state. No sooner indeed is he gifted with freedom than he seeks a wife, were it only to acquire in the sacredness of the harem a security for his person, and a sanctuary for his property: but even on this occasion his pride and his prejudice lead him to spurn from his embrace the woman of the country, whose seasoned constitution might counteract the effects of his debilitated system, and suffer him to form an alliance only with some female slave of his own nation, on whom the climate exerts the same enervating influence. Seldom does any progeny arise from these too well assorted marriages; or, if blessed with offspring, and such as attains maturity, it is in general too degenerate in body and too imbecile in mind, to hold, and to defend the parental authority against a host of sturdier competitors: and for want of a sufficiency of natural heirs to succeed to their possessions and their power, the rulers of Egypt have throughout every period of their history been obliged to seek in fresh slaves imported from their own native realms, the heirs to their wealth and the successors to their dominion.

"Among these creatures of servitude and devotees to ambition, the Abases, the Tcherkassians, and the youths of Odeshé and of Gurgistan[1] are in general the most esteemed, as being the nearest in blood to their patrons, and the most eminent in corporal endowments and warlike accomplishments. Renegadoes themselves, their masters make it a rule, more in compliance with custom than out of respect for religion, to raise no servant to any employment who is not by birth or from choice a Mohammedan. But this condition fulfilled, whatever native of any country north of Egypt is willing to owe his existence and advancement to his patron, may aspire to all the advantages which an

Egyptian grandee can bestow. The Bey connects with the artificial relationship between master and slave all the reciprocal duties, nay attaches to it all the reciprocal appellations, that belongs to the natural ties of which he lives bereft: he calls his Mamlukes his children, and hears them call him their father. According to the measure of their attachment, their deserts, or their favour in his eyes, he promotes them successively, while yet in bondage, to all the honourable offices in his household, from that of a simple body guard, to that of hasnadar or treasurer; and, when manumitted, to all the dignities in the state at his disposal, from that of a single Aga, to that of Kiashef,[2] and Bey, and Schaich-el-belled. During his lifetime he marries them to whatever female relations of his own he can discover, and at his death he leaves them heirs to his wealth and his offices. So much are these adoptive children considered the natural heirs to all their patron's property, that his very wives, and sisters, and daughters devolve to them, according to the date of their creation and the eminence of their rank; and the greater the number of such creatures, devoted to his service, defending his person, devouring his property, and raised by his patronage to wealth and to dignities a man in power possesses, the more the lustre reflected from these satellites that move around him, swells his pride, increases his own importance, and extends his own sway. It is by the vast circumference of its base that we estimate the height of the mountain.

"Such is in Egypt the inertness of the native, and such the insulation of the country, encompassed on all sides by seas and by deserts, that the domination of the Beys, though only continued by slaves, by renegadoes, and by strangers – by men foreswearing every tie of country, of blood, of sex, and of religion, and presenting every form of anarchy, civil war, and murder by steel and by poison – yet subsisted near two centuries, without being wrested from the feeble hands that held it, either by an indigenous subject, or by a foreign invader.

"At last, however, the sway of the Mamlukes seemed destined to decline. In the year 923 of the hegira, Selim, Sultan of the Turks, invaded Egypt, conquered the land of Beys, hung their chief, and degraded his body: the former rulers of the country were reduced to the rank of collectors of its revenue. Attached to different provinces, they and their kiashefs became the farmers of the territorial contribution; while their chief, the Schaich-el-belled, was alone fixed at Cairo under the watchful eye of the Sultan's own Visier.

"As an intermediate power between the Mamlukes and the Pasha, the conqueror created a provincial militia. It was destined to support the financial operations of the Beys, and to restrain the political influence of the Visier. It is true that these troops swore submission to severe regulations. Confined to the citadels of Cairo and of Djirdgé, they were to exercise no trade, lest they should lose their martial spirit, and to possess no land, lest they should acquire a local interest. Great privileges, however, made amends for these restrictions; since, in order to render his military force independent of his representative, the Sultan allowed its adgiaklees, or chiefs, to enact in their own private councils the laws necessary for the welfare of the corps.

"No human power, however, can be so nicely poised, but that a little excess in some quarter will by degrees determine all further weight to flow to the same side; until the balance be at last wholly destroyed. Stationary in the country, and commanding a formidable force, the chiefs of the militia soon began to resist indiscriminately every order of a Pasha, liable to constant removals, and the bearer of unsupported mandates: they ended by compelling him to sanction in the name of the sovereign the statutes decreed in their own. A prisoner in the castle, while suffered to remain at Cairo, he no sooner gave the least offence, than he was dismissed without delay.

"The Beys were held in still more open and degrading subjection: for the Schaich-el-belled was made, on days of ceremony, to hold the stirrup to the Aga of the janissaries. Even the subjects of the Porte at large experienced at the hands of this lawless soldiery the direst oppression. They could only escape its rapacity by enlisting in its corps: but in proportion as the candidate for this honour was wealthier, and thus exposed to greater extortions, he obtained less easily the immunity which he more urgently wanted. One half of his fortune was generally the price of his security during his life, and at his death the other half devolved to the regiment in which he was enrolled; nor, if a rich individual had by some means succeeded to elude while he lived the burdensome boom, could his good fortune while he had breath, on his demise avail his heirs. In default of a real engagement a forged contract was soon produced, and promptly acted upon.

"Thus did the militia of Egypt, in spite of the Sultan's edict, soon absorb all its personal property: nor was it long, ere, by a still more glaring infraction of their rules, the odgiaklees became possessors of most of the land: – but if their power at first thus gained them inordinate wealth, that wealth again, by a just retribution, served to undermine their power; and just as the Nile, after rising till it overflows the country – . . . ."

"At this ominous simile I took fright, put my finger on the narrator's lips, and earnestly entreated that he would tell his tale in a straight-forward manner, without tropes or figures – especially about the Nile.

"He smiled and thus proceeded: – "By becoming landed proprietors, the members of the militia had rendered themselves accountable in one sense to those very Beys who were amenable to them in another: but there remained no longer an equal security for the discharge of the mutual obligation. While by the enrolment in their corps of every able soldier himself requiring a stipend, the militia was become at once enfeebled at the heart and unwieldy at its extremities, the Beys seemed to have regained all the strength which their antagonists had lost: for the Mamluke tribe – that indestructible plague of Egypt, that weed always alive, and at every new subversion of a more artificial system again springing up in all its former luxuriance – had, by constant fresh supplies, meanwhile recovered all its vigour.

"Thus the different departments of the state, intended by Selim to check each other's pressure, became totally confounded; or rather, their offices were exchanged, their interests reversed, and the supremacy made to flow back into its pristine channels. While the militia insensibly spread over the surface of the land, to attend to its culture, the Beys again flocked to Cairo, to resume their cabals: when the odgiaklees had erst given to their creatures the employments of the Beys, the Beys now gave to their freedmen the rank of odgiaklees: the public revenue, before squandered by the soldiery, now became wasted by the Mamlukes; and what power remained in the hands of the Sultan's forces, was no longer employed to resist but to protect the Sultan's enemies. The spider was left to weave its web in silence over those gilded vaults, which had once re-echoed with the fierce debate of commanders; and the Pasha, who formerly had only feared the power of the militia, now only trembled at the name of the Beys.

"Scarce however had his revolution been perfected, when the daring Aly, Bey and Schaich-el-belled, succeeded in wresting its fruits out of the hands of its authors. Renouncing his allegiance to the Porte, and contracting an alliance with the Russians, he awed into silence his colleagues, and reserved every office for his own adoptive children. He sent his son Ismail to sack Damascus, and his son Hassan to pillage Djedda; while he kept his eldest son Mohamed at home, to bear as he could the whole weight of his favours: and great it was; – for he honoured him with the hand of his sister, sent for purposely from Georgia; he heaped upon such riches as to cause him to be surnamed Aboo-dahab, or the father of gold; and he endowed him with sufficient power to create his own dependants Beys: insomuch that at last Aboo-dahab, disabled by his patron from rising any higher, except by stepping on his patron's neck, slew him, in order that his work might be completed.

"Nor was Aboo-dahab disappointed in this purpose. Named Schaich-el-belled by his own Beys, and chosen Pasha by the grateful Porte, he offered the first example in Egypt, as he did the last, of all the grandeur which the country could bestow, and all the authority which the Sultan can give, united in the same person: – but his joy was short! Intoxicated unto madness by these too copious draughts of successful ambition, his blood began to ferment; his fluids turned to poison; a raging fever struck his brain; and in the midst of Acre, which he had taken by storm, and delivered up to pillage, one day saw him resplendent with glory , and the next a livid corpse.

"No sooner had Aboo-dahab breathed his last, than his Mamlukes hastened back to Cairo to divide his spoil. Ibrahim, the eldest Bey of his creation, obtained with the place of Schaich-el-Belled the widow of Aly. Mourad, the second in rank of the Beys named by Mohammed, married his patron's own relic. The other Beys of Mohammed's recent house, Osman, Mustapha, Suleiman, and the two Ayoobs, took, according to their rank and seniority, what else remained to be divided.

"The younger children of Mohammed's ill requited patron, Ismail and Hassan, who shared not in their eldest brother's ingratitude, had, on Aly's death, fled to Upper Egypt. There they remained quiet during the short period of Aboo-dahab's reign; but gained strength by the alliance with two great Arab Schaichs; those of Esneh and Negaddi. Thus reinforced, they determined not to suffer Mohammed's children to supersede the remaining sons of Aly himself, and marched directly to Cairo. Ibrahim, Mourad, and their party, had not yet had leisure to prepare for the attack. With all their followers they passed through the citadel, situated on the utmost verge of the mount Mokhadem; gained the defiles of that range of mountains which extends along the right bank of the Nile into upper Egypt, and there took that station, which their antagonist had just quitted to occupy their own at Cairo.

"Ismail, received in the capital with acclamation, and immediately installed as Schaich-el-belled by a Pasha, prompt to confer the title on whoever held the place, lost no time in clearing his residence of all lurking leaven of sedition. Two old Beys yet breathed, owned by no party still in being, but supposed secretly to favour that of Ibrahim. They had, nevertheless, when Ismail entered Cairo, remained in the capital, – either prevented from quitting it by their infirmities, or relying for protection on their age. They were friends, and saw each other familiarly. But when Sogeir came to pay his court, Ismail exacted, in proof of his loyalty, the head of Abderahman; and Sogeir bowed submission. In the midst of the customary reminiscences which formed the conversation of men who had outlived all their contemporaries, Sigeir dropped his chaplet: Abderahman stopped to pick it up; and Sogeir plunged his dagger into his colleague's side. His feeble hand, however, could not give a life thrust, and Abderahman, intended to be laid prostrate for ever, rose from the blow, and struggled with his adversary. The surrounding Mamlukes viewed unmoved two men, seemingly united during half a century in the closest bonds of friendship, contend which should first bereave the other by violence of the few remaining sparks of life almost extinct, – should first draw from the other's heart the few remaining drops of an almost stagnant tide, and should first thrust the other into that grave, on whose brink both were tottering. This feat Sogeir achieved. He then crawled back to the Schlaich with the head demanded; but, exhausted with the fight, fell dead in the act of presenting the prize.

"Ibrahim and Mourad remained not much longer in upper Egypt than Ismail and Hassan had done before them. With the assistance of the Arab Schaichs of Farshoot and of Dendera, they descended from Djirdge, and demanded re-admittance in Cairo. Ismail consented, in hopes of more effectually ending the struggle by treachery. With the concurrence of Ezedlee the Pasha, his antagonists were to be murdered in the citadel, in full Divan. Hassan, however, dissatisfied with the small share of power ceded to him by Ismail, thought he now had the means for ever to secure the gratitude of the adverse party. He warned its leaders of the plot; and the same night Ibrahim and Mourad with all their adherents again evacuated Cairo. As soon as they had passed the gates, they proclaimed all reconciliation with Ismail henceforth at an end, and went back to their old post at Djirdge. Here they fortified themselves, and determined to reduce the capital by famine. All provisions which descended the Nile were interrupted, and Ismail at last found himself obliged by the impending scarcity to collect his few troops, to march southward, and to give his rivals battle. It was Hassan who gave them the victory, by going over to their side in the midst of the combat. Ismail immediately fled back to Cairo.

"The Schaich-el-belled's popularity in the capital had been annihilated by his exactions. Closely pursued, he felt his situation desperate. In haste he loaded his camels with his treasure, abandoned his honours, and crossed the desert as a fugitive. At Gaze he embarked for Stambool, to seek assistance from the Porte.

"As Ismail went out at one gate of the city, Ibrahim and Mourad rushed in at the other. Content to resume their former station, they impeded not their enemy's convenient flight. After reinstating themselves in all their offices, they strengthened their party and rewarded their adherents, by making a considerable promotion of Beys and of Kiashefs.

"Hassan himself gained the least by his defection. This Bey, surnamed Djeddawee from the sacking of that city, was among those unfortunate individuals who with the greatest physical bravery, entirely want moral resolution and steadiness; by their waverings and changes forfeit the confidence of all parties, and to every faction alike appear more desirable in the character of avowed enemies, than in that of seeming friends. Whatever sacrifices he might make to the cause he espoused, they were uniformly attributed to interested motives; truth from his lips was received as falsehood; and generosity in his behaviour could only be viewed as cunning. The bare circumstance of his asserting a fact caused it to be discredited, and his being the author of a scheme sufficed for its rejection. Thus situated, he always found the thanks of his associates short of his pretensions, failed not soon to accuse his colleagues of black ingratitude, and scarce had joined the party, when he afresh meditated a change. His most ordinary converse necessarily degenerated into a tissue of dissimulation and fraud which produced an illusion; and his life became a series of intrigues and of cabals which brought him no benefit.

"Tired of his complaints and fearing his fickleness, the sons of Mohammed resolved to stop his reproaches by cutting short his career. The Saturday exercises in the place of Roumaili were fixed upon to execute the purpose.

"The exercise of the djereed was over. One of Mourad's Mamlukes enters the lists for the game of the jar.[3] He advances in the circle, takes aim, fires, and misses. A second darts forward, and equally fails. A third now tries in his turn: his ball goes wider still than the former from the pretended mark; but it strikes the real one, – for it grazes the turban of Djeddawee. Every bystander loudly laments the accident. The Bey alone saw the intent: he saw his death-warrant signed. Immediately he calls round him his Mamlukes, and from their closed pressed circle raises the cry of war and the sword of defiance. His suite all draw their sabres: so do Mohammed's children. The games cease; the fight commences: the few remaining adherents of Ismail join the banners of Hassan.

"Three entire days did every street of Cairo in turns become the field of battle. Three entire days did every stone of the capital stream with blood. At last Hassan felt his strength give way, and saw his supporters fall off one by one. On the point of being overwhelmed by his enemy's superior force, he gathers together a small troop which he still could rely upon, and breaks through the very midst of his assailants. With a speed which nothing could slacken, he gains the vast suburb of Boolak, on the Nile, and there seeks shelter in the house of an old friend, of the Schaich Damanhoori. The sanctity even of that distant asylum is disregarded, and the approach invested, a few minutes after its gates had received the noble fugitive.

"For a while however, entrenching himself behind the enclosure of his fortress, Hassan gallantly stands the siege, from every window and battlement of the edifice pours down upon Mourad's satellites every species of murderous implement, and makes many a foe atone with his life for the relentless pursuit. But after more than an hour's strenuous defence, he beholds from the top of the building the door burst open, and the entire torrent rush in at once. He now resolves to quit the hopeless contest, and to save himself by flight. Mounting on the terrace no longer secure, he thence clambers on the roof of a neighbouring house. From that, passes on to the next, and in this manner vaults from terrace to terrace,[4] and climbs from roof to roof – sometimes scaling almost inaccessible heights, at others leaping down awful precipices, and at others again clearing frightful chasms – till at last he gains the furthermost of the habitations that form a connected cluster. Here he finds his aerial progress stopped; and from the summit of this final promontory again is compelled to descend to the regions below, and to return to the level of his pursuers. From the terrace he lets himself down into the attics; from these into a lower floor: gains the top of the stairs, runs down a hundred steps, reaches the hall, and opens the entrance door. In the very porch stood sentinel a hostile Mamluke of gigantic stature, waiting his arrival to intercept his passage: him he fells with his sabre at a single blow, and mounting the Mamluke's own steed, he rides back at full speed to Cairo. But at every turn his antagonists were watching. They soon espy his escape: and in a moment he heard the whole troop again close at his heels. Danger seemed to lend him wings. He reaches Cairo the first, – though scarce by the distance of a pistol shot. Clearing the crowded entrance of the city, and pushing up the main street, he rushes, as soon as opportunity favours, into the midst of the most populous and busy district; runs up one narrow lane, and down another. As he enters a new division, he causes its gates to be shut behind him, in order to delay the progress of his pursuers. Meeting a string of camels carrying water, he rends open the skins with his dagger, to increase the slippery smoothness of the pavement. Coming up with a file of arabas, conveying a wedding, he tilts over the wagons to bar the passage. No throng of human beings, however great, stops his career. His yatagan cuts its way through the thickest cluster of passengers. Overthrowing some, trampling others under foot, he still advances unslackened in his speed. Every where warning shouts announce his approach; every where screams of terror precede his rapid steps. At sight of him the horror-struck mob flies in every direction like chaff before the hurricane; and his wide circuit frequently bringing him back to the same places in which he had appeared before – but each time more pale, and ghastly, and covered with blood than before – he at last begins to be viewed as his own ghost, still continuing the flight of the body. It was a stupendous thing to behold a vast capital, successively filled throughout each of its numerous quarters, from one end to the other, with ever increasing terror and dismay, by the appearance of a single man, – and that man himself a fugitive, only darting by like a meteor; just heard, just seen, and then again disappearing.

"Hassan's strength now begins to fail him. His horse is ready to drop. His pursuers, – who for a while had lost his track, – guided by the clamour of the mob at his appearance, again recover the scent. They gain ground upon him so fast, that nothing seems capable any longer of saving him from becoming their victim.

"He now bethinks himself of one last desperate expedient. The house of his most inveterate enemy, – of Ibrahim, the Schaich-el-belled – had just risen in sight. He springs from his exhausted steed, no longer able to move, and, summoning all his remaining strength, runs to this perilous abode, and gains with difficulty its frowning portal. Entering the reluctant gates, he forces his way athwart the bevy of astonished pages, who in vain try to stop the intruder; and makes straight for the holy of holies, for the women's apartment. Pushing away right and left the eunuchs, the slaves, and the guards, stationed to defend the entrance to the entrance to the gynecaeum, he bursts open the prohibited door, advances through the labyrinth of narrow passages, and at last, after many wanderings, reaches the very centre of the sanctuary.

"Here, totally exhausted, and faint with fatigue and loss of blood from many a wound inflicted by a distant carbine, Djiddawee at last stops, lies down on the rich carpet his ensanguined sword, and viewing before him that mightiest of her sex, the sister of Aly, the widow of Mohammed, and the wife of Ibrahim – risen from her seat in mute astonishment, – he throws himself prostrate at her feet, clasps the hem of her embroidered garment, and implores her all-powerful protection.

"What could Ash-har do? when a son of her brother, and a brother of her first husband, humbled to the dust, implored her to save his life!

"She swore to protect him, while he remained in her sight; and in her presence none durst lift his hand against the supplicant. Even Ibrahim her husband consented to respect his hated existence, until he again should go forth from the shadow of his roof.

"But Mourad appears! Furious from his numerous disappointments and Hassan's hair-breadth escapes, he demands possession of his victim, or threatens to abandon his party. The Schaich-el-belled wavers, and at last consents to cast a stain upon his character, in order to satisfy his colleague. In defiance of the laws of hospitality he insists on Hassan's quitting his habitation, content to receive a safeguard to the frontiers of Egypt. The Bey was not in a condition to decline the specious offer. Accompanied by a numerous escort, he takes leave and departs. But what is his new dismay, when he leans on the road that his destination is the very town in Arabia, once the scene of his devastations! To turn him adrift among the injured populace of Djedda was to devote him to a death more cruel than the fate from which he had fled. On the least resistance, however, to the mandate of his enemies, he was to be killed on the spot. He therefore feigned acquiescence and suffered himself quietly to be conveyed to Suez, and there to be embarked for the harbour of Meccah. At sea he might by surprise have slain a few of his conductors, but in so rash an attempt he must soon have been overpowered by the rest. He devised a better plan. In the darkness of the night he fell upon the reïs himself, the moment sleep closed his eyelids; and with his arm round the pilot's throat and his pistol to his heart, he forced him to steer for the African coast, and for the port of Cosseir. There, under the favour of a mob whom the cry of a son of Aly soon collected round the boat, ready for his defence, he disembarked, by forced marches gained Akmim, and from that place plunged into the desert. In a few days he reached the tents of his former Arab allies. Under their wing he took shelter: the fame of his wonderful escape spread in all directions: – at last it reached Cairo, and the wreck of his party, remaining in that capital, insensibly withdrew, and joined, high up the Nile, its imperishable leader.

"Ismail, on his arrival at Constantinople, has found the Porte too deeply engaged in war with Austria, to involve itself in fresh hostilities with Egypt. Tired of consuming his time in fruitless expectation, and his wealth in unproductive bribes, he at last re-embarked, landed at Derne, and through the oasis of Sewa, rejoined Hassan near the

Cataracts. Either chief had gained too little by deserting the other, not to meet his former rival with willing heart half way. Common disappointment for this time riveted the union of the Beys. They agreed to consign to oblivion the past, and for the future never more to abandon each other."

"Thus far," – added my Osmanlee, – "the engagement has remained inviolate. Three years and more the sturdy veterans have continued to live together in undisturbed possession of Es-souan, the furthest place in Said, on this side the falls. Too weak to molest the chiefs at Cairo, and too near the confines of Nubia to fear their molestation, they are watched, but are left quiet. All the land on either side the river, their small district excepted, obeys Ibrahim and Mourad. These chiefs reign supreme at Cairo, and heavy is the yoke which they impose upon the provinces. But it bears alike on every one, and therefore appears less galling than the partial miseries of a civil war. People pray for an oppression which prevents their being torn limb from limb, in the strife of contending parties."

Here ended the long narration of my Caireen friend, – and high time it was. Already rose in sight the vast pyramids to the right, and the castle of Cairo on our left. Each passenger began to collect his parcels: and scarce half an hour more elapsed, ere we cast anchor at Boollak, and stepped ashore. Our little party broke up, and every one of its members went his different way. My new friend and myself walked on together to Cairo.

NOTES

CHAPTER I

1 p.1. *Jubbee*: flowing gown, generally worn in the Levant, by men of sedentary habits and professions.
2 p.1. *Drogueman:* official interpreter employed by Franks in their conferences with the Mohammedans.
3 p.1. *Agrumi*: Italian denomination used in the Levant for every species of fruit of the orange and lemon kind.
4 p.1. *An Ipsariote rëis*: or master of a merchant vessel from the island of Ipsara..
5 p.2. *Hamal*: the Turkish for porter.
6 p.2. *Caloyera*: a nun, as Caloyer means a friar.
7 p.4. *Moselemin*: a true believer; title assumed by the Mohammedans.
8 p.4. *Papas*: Greek priest.
9 p.4. *Panagia*: the All-holy! The Virgin.
10 p.4. *The Mitre*: the cap of the Greek priesthood.
11 p.5. *Yaoor*: infidel; word of abuse frequently used by the Turks in reference to Christians.
12 p.5. *The Russian war*: namely, that which ended in 1774, by the peace of Kainardgee.
13 p.6. *The slim Perote dress*: that worn by the Greek women of Pera, and of the continental provinces; wholly different from that of the islands.
14 p.8. *Caravan:* word applied in the Levant to voyages of merchant ships, as well as to land journeys of merchants and goods.
15 p. 9. *Maynote*: native of the Penisula of Mayno, whose inhabitants are almost all pirates.
16 p.10. *Capitan-pasha*: Commander in Chief of the Turkish Navy.
17 p.10. *Arnaoot*: Turkish name given to the Albanians who profess the Mohammedan religion; and form the body guard of many of the Turkish Pashas.
18 p.10. *Caravellas*: frigates.

CHAPTER II

1 p.11. *Codgea-bashees*: chiefs of the Greek communities, accountable to the Turkish governors for the contribution imposed on their districts.
2 p.11. *Lacedemon and Christianopolis*: two Greek bishoprics in the Morea, thus denominated.
3 p.11. *Buskined hero*: the Albanians wear buskins or rather greaves of cloth or velvet, often richly embroidered and adorned with silver clasps.
4 p.12. *Rayas*: subjects of the Porte, not Mohammedan, who pay the capitation tax: such as Greeks, Armenians, Jews, and Gipsies.
5 p.12. *Grand Visier*: All Pashas, before whom are carried the three horse-tails, have the title of Visier: but the head of that distinguished body, the lieutenant of the Grand Signor, who represents him in his councils, and commands his armies, is called by the Turks Vezir Azem, by the Franks Grand Visier.
6 p.13. *Waynode*: Turkish farmer of the revenue of a district.
7 p.13. *Haratsh-tickets*: vouchers for the payment of the haratch or poll-tax, due by all rayahs.
8 p.14. *Cadee*: Turkish judge.
9 p.15. *Spahees*: Turkish holders of military fiefs, which oblige them to join the army, mounted at their own expense.
10 p.16. *Taooshan*: hare; epithet given to the Greek islanders.
11 p.16. *Fanar*: district of Constantinople, where chiefly reside the Greeks of the higher class.

CHAPTER III

1 p.18. *Tergiuman*: the Turkish for Drogueman.
2 p.18. *Beneesh*: cloth vestment worn over the jubbee on occasions of ceremony.
3 p.18. *Calpack*: cap worn by rayahs.
4 p.18. *Tshawooshes*: ushers and messengers of men in office.
5 p.20. *Cafedjee*: the servant who in Greek and Turkish houses hands round the coffee.
6 p.21. *Osmanlee*: follower of Osman or Othoman, the founder of the Turkish or Othoman empire: – epithet which sounds as agreeable to its bearers, as the name of Turks is offensive to them.
7 p.22. *Yatagan:* Turkish sabre, worn in the belt or sash.
8 p.23. *The head, &c.* It is customary among the Turks after a battle to give a reward for every head of an enemy that is brought to the commander.
9 p.24. *The difference between Kyrie-eleison and Allah Illah Allah*: Greek and Mohammedan forms of prayer or invocation.
10 p.25. *Kehaya*: official agent of a public personage in Turkey.
11 p.25. *Roumili*: the Greeks of the lower Empire affected to call themselves Romans, their language the Romaic, and their country Romania, which the Turks have changed into Roumili.
12 p.25. *Moohassil*: a governor of a province, inferior in rank and power to a Pasha.
13 p.26. *Stambool*: the Turkish corruption of the Greek, pronounced by them ees teen bolin; and used to denote their going to the city.
14 p.27. *Shaksheer*: ample breeches made of cloth.
15 p.27. *The Boghaz*: generic Turkish for straits; here applied to those of the Dardanelles.
16 p.27. *Didaskalos:* a teacher.
17 p.28. *Three distinct Cities*: namely Constantinople, Galata, and Scutari.

CHAPTER IV

1 p.29. *Caïck:* light and elegant wherry, plying about the quays of Constantinople.
2 p.29. *A house of dark and dingy hue, apparently crumbling to pieces with age and neglect:* The former circumstance being in consequence of the sumptuary laws imposed by the Turks upon the Greeks; the latter in consequence of the Greeks often affecting poverty in order to avoid being heavily taxed by their tyrants.
3 p.29. *A Mamluke*: name given among Mohammedans to such white slaves as are destined to be gradually promoted to offices of importance within doors and without.
4 p.30. *Frank philosophers*: all Europeans not rayas, and therefore considered as strangers in Turkey, are called Franks or Franguee, their country Franguestan, and the corrupt idiom composed of their various languages current along the Mohammedan shores of the Mediterranean, *lingua franca.*
5 p.30. *Purses*: denomination for a sum of five thousand piastres.
6 p.30. *Tchartchees and Bezesteens*: places in Turkish cities, distinct from the habitations of the merchants, in which they keep and sell their wares.
7 p.30. *Harem:* the Turkish name for the apartment of women: Seraglio or Serai meaning palace in general.
8 p.31. *Therapiah*: one of the villages on the Bosphorus which the Greeks of quality make their country residences.
9 p.31. *The Bostandjee Bashee*: officer who acts as ranger of the Sultan's demesne, and superintends the police of the waters about Constantinople.
10 p.31. *Tandoor*: a square table placed in the angle of the sofa, with a brazier underneath and a rich counterpane over it, under which, in Greek houses, in cold weather, the company creep towards each other.

11 p.32. *Bab-Humayoon*: the imperial gate or principal entrance of the Sultan's palace at Constantinople.
12 p.32. *Feridjee*: cloth worn out of doors by the Greek and Turkish women of Constantinople.
13 p.32. *Archons*: denominations assumed by the principal Greeks.
14 p.32. *Spatar*: sword-bearer; one of the principal officers at the courts of the Hospodars of Moldavia and Valachia, which are formed on the model of the ancient Greek court of Constantinople.
15 p.32. *Slipper money of the Sultanas*: in Turkish Peshmalik: equivalent to our pin-money.
16 p.32. *Reïs Effende*: the Turkish secretary of state for foreign affairs.
17 p.32. *Pounding the grand Mufti in a mortar*: according to the ancient mode of capital punishment inflicted on the heads of the law, whose blood it was deemed irreverend to shed.
18 p.33. *Caleondjees*: marines from caleon, a galley.
19 p.34. *Romaïc*: the modern Greek: as Hellenic means the ancient Greek.
20 p.34. *The Holy Mountain*: mount Athos; that beautiful promontory now infected by twenty-two Greek convents.
21 p.36. *Kiad-hané*: public walk near Constantinople, called by the Franks *Les Eaux douces.*

CHAPTER V

1 p.39. *Galata*: suburb divided from Constantinople by the harbour; and occupying the base of the hill of which Pera crowns the summit.
2 p.39. *Para*: a small Turkish coin.
3 p.41. *The anteree*: part of the long dress of men of sedentary professions.
4 p.41. *Sultan-Bayezid*: one of the Imperial mosques at Constantinople, near which is held the market of second hand apparel.
5 p.41. *Hash-keui*: suburb of Constantinople, where the Jews live.
6 p.41. *Furred cap*: which the droguemen wear when in fiocchi, and the physicians habitually.
7 p.41. *Lahse jacket*: the Lahses or inhabitants of the northern shores of Asia Minor are chiefly employed at Constantinople in garden work.
8 p.42. *Lorenzo*: Nucciola; a Raguseen; physician to the Seraglio, and only very lately (as I find in Mr. Turner's account) beheaded, in his eightieth year, by order of his chief patient, Abd-ool-Hameed.
9 p.42. *Hekim-bashee*: chief of the college of physicians.
10 p.43. *Blacquernes*: a remote district of Constantinople.
11 p.43. *A Beglier-bey*: or Bey of Beys; a title given to the Pashas of Roumili and of Anadoly.
12 p.43. *Moonedjim*: astrologer.
13 p.44. *Backtche-capoossee*: the garden gate; one of the gates of Constantinople.
14 p.45. *Bagnio*: the vast enclosure near the arsenal, which serves as a prison to the Christian captives, and the Turkish and Rayah criminals.

CHAPTER VI

1 p.50. This description of the plague is conformable to the modern Greek personification of that disease.
2 p.51. *Islamism*: the true belief, according to Mohammedan doctrine.
3 p.51. *Namaz*: the chief prayer of the Mohammedans.

CHAPTER VII

1 p.53. *Proesti*: the Greek primate of a district.
2 p.54. *A seven years' ague*: the liberal wish of an enemy in a country replete with *mal aria.*
3 p.54. *Hydriote*: from the island of Hydra; chiefly inhabited by sailors and shipowners, who, at the beginning of the revolution, when France was shut out from the Baltic, supplied her with corn from the Archipelago.
4 p.55. *Tophana*: the cannon foundery, which gives its name to a handsome quay near Galata.
5 p.55. *Kiebabs*: mutton steaks, sold in cookshops at Constaninople.
6 p.55. *Stambool Effendee*: inspector of the police of the capital.
7 p.55. *My cries of "aman"*: of mercy or pardon.
8 p.56. *My forehead used to be studded with gold coins*: Turkish mode of rewarding public dancers and singers.
9 p.57. *The Mewlewi Derwishes*: sort of Turkish friars, whose devout exercises consist in twirling round like tops.
10 p.58. *Yaoort*: a sort of Turkish cream cheese.
11 p.59. *The solemn ceremony*: still in use in Albania and along the eastern shore of the Adriatic.
12 p.60. *Epirotes might retain such old customs*: under the denominations of *probratimi* for the men, and *prosestrini* for the women.

CHAPTER VIII

1 p.61. *Hoshab*: a beverage made of fruit of various kinds.
2 p.63. *St. Demetrius*: remote suburb of Constantinople, where the Greeks have a hospital.
3 p.63. *Araba*: Turkish wagon.
4 p.64. *Tartar*: the Mohammedan messengers in the service of the Porte are called Tartars, or more properly Tatars, as the gate porters in France used to be called *Suisses*, from their original extraction.
5 p.64. *Sultana's husbands*: the Sultan's sisters and daughters – whom consequently he cannot espouse – are alone called Sultanas: his wives or concubines never assume that title, appropriated exclusively to the Imperial blood.
6 p.64. *Internuncio*: title given to the Austrian minister at Constantinople, in order to avoid conflicts of etiquette. Baron Herbert Rathkeal was equally venerated by Turks and by Christians.
7 p.64. *Envoy of Sweden*: Mouradgea d'Ohson; an Armenian by birth, originally drogueman to the Swedish mission; and author of a celebrated work on the Othoman Empire.
8 p.65. Anastasius sometimes spells Frank names very incorrectly. On inquiry I find that of the gentleman in question to be Vanden Dedem tot Gelder.
9 p.65. *Kislar Aga*: chief of the black eunuchs: a personage possessed of vast power and patronage: being entrusted with the administration of all the religious foundations of the Turkish Empire, of which the revenues are immense.
10 p.67. *Handjar*: Turkish poniard.
11 p.68. *Emir*: or Shereef: name given to the descendants of Mohammed's daughter, who in every city of the empire have their own distinctive tribunals, and the exclusive privilege of wearing turbans of the sacred colour: namely, green.

CHAPTER IX

1 p.70. *Berath*: Foreign ministers being often obliged to employ rayahs as their domestics, originally obtained for them patents of exemption from the jurisdiction of the Porte, which they now find it more profitable to sell.
2 p.76. *Djamee*: name given to the mosques founded by Sultans.
3 p.76. *The Mihrab*: or altar.

CHAPTER X

1 p.77. *Extended not farther than his nose. – Il ne voyoit pas plus loin que son nez.*
2 p.79. *Scheyis*: the two special sects among the Mohammedans are the Sunnees and the Scheyis; and as the difference between them is small, so is the hatred proportionably intense. The Turks are all Sunnees, the Persians all Scheyis: the former are more fanatical, and the latter are more superstitious.
3 p.79. *Pretty faces*: the Persians admit representations of human figures in their books of poetry, which the Turks hold in abhorrence.
4 p.79. *The bridge Seerath*: over which the souls of the elect glide into heaven; while those of the damned tumble from it into hell.
5 p.79. *Three hundred and sixty days in the year*: the Mohammedan months are lunar.
6 p.79. *Devas*: the Mohammedan spirits that guard subterraneous treasures.
7 p.79. *Hafeez*: holy, but in a less degree than the Wely or saint.
8 p.80. *Reekath*: a division of the Mohammedan prayer.
9 p.80. *Karaghuez*: black-eyes; the principal personage in a Turkish puppetshow resembling the *Ombres Chinoises*.
10 p.80. *Ramadan*: or Ramazan: the month during which the Mohammedans fast all day, and feast all night. While the sun remains above the horizon they dare not even refresh themselves with a drop of water or a whiff of tobacco.
11 p.80. *Moollah*: generic name for the doctors of law, who according to the Mohammedan system are doctors of divinity; inasmuch as the Mohammedan law is entirely founded on the Koran.

CHAPTER XI

1 p.83. *Top Capoossee*: cannon gate: one of the gates of Constantinople.
2 p.83. *Zeeameth*: denomination of the military fiefs which ought to supply the regular cavalry of the Othoman empire, but by frequent abuse pass into the hands of women and children, who find substitutes.
3 p.84. *Sharp stirrups*: which with the Turks perform the office of spurs.
4 p.84. *Bernoos*: cloak worn by the Barbaresques, by naval characters, and by those who adopt the short dress.
5 p.85. *The same festival*: outside the Top Capoossee there is a holy well much resorted to by the Greeks on the day of St. George's Festival.
6 p.85. *Candiote Turks*: reckoned peculiarly brave and dashing, though often intermarrying with Greek women, whom they suffer to retain their religion.
7 p.87. *Mekkiemé*: Turkish hall of justice.
8 p.87. *Naib*: the cadee's clerk.
9 p.88. *The boiled wheat*: or colyva, distributed by the Greeks at burials.
10 p.88. *Moirai*: The Fates, who in some of the Greek islands are still worshipped with superstitious rites.

11 p.89. *Djereed:* a staff, which the Turks make it one of their sports to fling at each other with prodigious force on horseback.
12 p.89. *Oc-Meidan and Hippodrome*: the first the place of arrows; the latter, still called by the Turks At-Meidan, or the place of horses.
13 p.89. *Theriakee Tchartchee*: place where the lovers of opium used to resort. On one side of it rises the superb mosque built by Suleiman the 3rd; and in front stands the hospital for insane persons.
14 p.89. *Madjoon*: Turkish name for opium.
15 p.90. *With outstretched hands*: the Greeks still utter their imprecations with outstretched hands and fingers.

CHAPTER XII

1 p.91. *The arches of Backtche Keui*: magnificent aqueduct near the village of that name built under the Greek emperors, in the pointed style, and which still supplies Constantinople abundantly with water..
2 p.91. *Eblis*: his satanic majesty.
3 p.92. *Caravokeiri*: master of a merchant vessel.
4 p.93. *Sacoleva*: a small merchant ship.
5 p.93. *Muezzeem:* person who among the Turks cries the hour of prayer from the top of the minarets. Sultan Achmet is a magnificent mosque at Constantinople, built by that sovereign, and the only one which has six minarets.
6 p.95. *Palikaria*: my brave fellows!
7 p.96. *Ihram:* a small floor carpet, used chiefly by the Turks for prayers.
8 p.97. *Eyoob and Sultanieh*: the former a beautiful suburb, the latter a delightful valley near Constantinople.
9 p.97. *Kleidon Rysika*: the game of drawing lots by means of keys.
10 p.97. *Paramana*: nurse.
11 p.97. It is the custom among the Greek Islanders to preserve the broken vessels of a twelvemonth, in order to throw them away in a single heap at Christmas.
12 p.97. *Papadia*: the wife of a papas, or priest.
13 p.98. The ceaseless grinding of the water-wheel: used in the gardens of Chio to irrigate the numerous plantations of orange-trees.

CHAPTER XIII

1 p.101 *With the moisture of my lips*: a superstitious process supposed to avert the influence of the evil eye or other ominous circumstances.
2 p.102. *With the purple of my own blood I sign, &c.*: alluding, I suppose, to the custom of the Greek emperors of signing their names with purple.
3 p.103 *Epitrope*: primate in a Greek community.
4 p.103 *Avaniah*: name given to a contribution imposed by Turks on rayahs, on some unfounded pretence.
5 p.105. *Moiro logistri*: the hired female who in some of the Greek islands still follows a funeral, singing the praises, and bewailing the loss of the deceased.
6 p.106. *Kirlangitsch*: properly a swallow; a Turkish sloop of war.

CHAPTER XIV

1 p.108. *Terzhana*: the admiralty.
2 p.109. *Speciote*: from the island of Specia.

3 p.110. *Sphachia*: district on the coast of Crete, forming the dower of one of the Sultanas, and whose inhabitants combine the pastoral and piratical life.

4 p.110. *Malkiané*: fief of the nature of an *apanage*.

CHAPTER XV

1 p.119. *Okkal*: name for an inn or caravan-seraï, in Egypt.

2 p.120. *Raschid*: Rosetta.

3 p.120. *Rakie*: an ardent spirit.

4 p.121. *Djerms*: small country vessels.

5 p.123. *The Mawgarbees*: men from Garbieh, or the West; name given to the Barbaresques.

6 p.124. *Maash*: covered passage boats that sail up and down the Nile.

7 p.124. *Schaich-el-belled*: chief of the country, or rather land; title given alike to the chief of the whole body of Beys of Egypt and to the chief among the notables of a small district.

8 p.125. *Awalis*: plural for Almé; public female singers.

9 p.125. *Ghazie*: female public dancer.

CHAPTER XVI

1 p.128. *Gurgistan*: Georgia.

2 p.129. *Kiashef*: an officer commanding part of a province under a Bey; though, like the handsomest

3 p.133. *The jar*: an earthen vessel which, in one of their martial sports, the Mamlukes try to hit.

4 p.133. *From terrace to terrace*: the houses at Cairo are all flat-roofed; and each peculiar district of the city is separated from the neighbouring ones, by its particular gate, which is kept shut at night.

VOLUME II

CHAPTER I.

From the brilliant descriptions given me of the celebrated Masr[1] – of the kalish[2] that runs through its centre, and of the birkets[3] that adorn its outskirts – I expected, if not an earthly, at least an aquatic paradise. On first reaching this vaunted city, I saw nothing but filth and ruins on the outside, and filth and misery within. "So much!" exclaimed I, thinking of Aly Tshawoosh, "for travellers' tales!"

"So too," said I, "echoed my companion the Caïreen – somewhat nettled – "on entering Stambool!" The retort startled me in my turn. "Heavens and earth!" was my answer, "would you compare Cairo with Constantinople? Where can you find the least resemblance? Is it between the vile swamps which here have confounded the river with its banks, and the verdant hills which there hem in the very sea? between the yellow muddy stream here treasured up for refreshment in sooty pitchers, and the crystal rills there gushing forth from golden fountains? or finally between the smoke dried men, tattooed women, and blear-eyed bloated children of this overgrown beggarly place, and our population of patriarchs, of houries, and of cherubs? In Constantinople the very cemeteries of the dead look like portions of elysium; here the habitations of the living already seem charnel-houses."

"With us each gem has its foil," observed drily my friend; "and we admire our beauties the more from the relief produced by that very circumstance. Suspend your judgment on our comforts till you see the palaces of our Beys."

This was not to be my destiny immediately. I had observed the haughty looks and gorgeous apparel of the meanest of the Mamlukes who condescended to mix among the populace; and wished to avoid the privileged cast, until I might vie in my appearance at least with its minor members. I therefore was content to sleep the first night at a khan; and the next morning prepared for presenting my letters. Keeping my friend Aly before my eyes as my model, I put on my gayest attire; and when fully equipped for my visit, viewed myself in a looking glass with such complacency, that I began at last to apprehend the fate of Narcissus; and for fear of catching the evil eye from myself, tried to spit in my own face;[4] deeming an extraordinary case to require an extraordinary remedy.

This exploit performed – not without some labour – I sallied forth, feeling quite secure as to what might happen. A fellow in the street, himself totally deprived of eyesight, showed me the way with the utmost readiness to Suleiman's palace. The grandeur of its portal, far from damping my confidence rather elevated my pride, by promising a theatre worthy of my ambition. Bounding like a ball, I ascended its spacious stairs, paced the long gallery, and entered the hall of audience. Perceiving the Bey, seated in the angle of his sofa at the upper end of the room, I boldly advanced, – retorting the supercilious and scrutinizing looks of the gay youths who lined the passage, – and when arrived near their patron, put my hand to the ground, to my forehead and my lips, and presented my credentials with every possible grace.

Throughout the East, grandees, when first addressed, preserve an impenetrable countenance. Their internal emotions lie concealed under a mask of stone. Thus they avoid committing themselves, as they must in some measure be liable to do, were they even to express the reverse of what they feel. Still I fancied I could discern athwart the Bey's immoveable features, such an impression, produced by my first address, as left me little cause for uneasiness. Once or twice, while one of his eyes affected most diligently to run over the recommendatory lines, I caught the other straying from the paper and stealing a sly survey of my person, with an air of most encouraging approbation. Having at last, – apparently with great toil, – completed the perusal of the long epistle, Suleiman laid it by him on the sofa, wiped his face, and bade me welcome. "My friend Othman Bey," said he, moving his little hands in unison with his speech, "describes you as possessed of valuable talents, and I feel anxious to acquire a claim to your services. Unfortunately," added he in a lower tone, after beckoning to his attendants to retire out of hearing, "our Mamlukes, with all their excellent qualities, are somewhat addicted to idleness, to deceit, and to treachery, and extremely jealous of all whom they look upon as intruders: nor dare we openly brave these little weaknesses, or confer on a stranger what these our adopted children consider as their rightful honours. Indeed, the stranger himself would soon have cause to rue the unavailing favour. I therefore do not immediately give you in my house a definite office. But stay as a guest, a friend, a household counsellor; and in time the thing I wish may be managed. God be praised, you are not at least a native Turk! Like us, you are an Islamite from choice."

After this little preamble the Bey proceeded to try me on the nature and extent of my acquirements; and, as he was not sorry that his Mamlukes should have an opportunity – which occurred but seldom – of witnessing his own vast erudition, he made signs to them to return within hearing distance, during the examination. An Italian missionary had once given him a dictionary, as a book replete with short and pithy stories; and in its sedulous perusal the Bey had contrived to pick up a considerable assortment of technical terms of art and science, which he employed as it pleased Providence. Of the things themselves whose appellations he had learnt, he seemed to have no more idea than the huge Angora cat which sat purring by his side; and an elementary chaos of astronomy, tactics, geography, mythology and medicine, all huddled together at random in his brain, flowed in most picturesque confusion from his lips. Extensive therefore as certainly was the general outline of his attainments, it still left me room to fill up a few intervening blanks, in such a way as to give a very favourable opinion of my own knowledge; without however presuming so far on its superiority as to tell his highness point blank that England, for instance, lay not contiguous to India, – as he had imagined from their constant warfare; or that Voltaire had never been Pope of Rome, – as he had inferred from the frequent juxtapositions of these personages in his missionary's anecdotes. With all this forbearance, however, my course of practical education at the arsenal, joined to the speculative topics I had heard discussed at Pera, still enabled me to pass myself off in the meridian of Cairo for a youth of no common accomplishments;

and at every answer I gave to Suleiman's subtle queries, he failed not to assume a profound look, and, after some little apparent meditation, to exclaim in an emphatic tone "good, very good, excellent, admirable! In time you will know as much as I do!" The only thing which seemed to give a little offence was my affirming peremptorily that the earth revolved round the sun, and not the sun round the earth. At this bold assertion, so contrary to my usual caution, the Bey looked as if he suspected me of a design to play upon his credulity; and I could only get out of the difficulty into which my pride of learning had led me, by assuring him that it was among us a very common belief; which he nevertheless still wondered that so sensible a fellow as I seemed to be, should have adopted.

When satisfied with the exalted idea which he doubted not he had given me of his own learning, Suleiman by degrees descended to more familiar topics; and I now was surprised in my turn to find a man so utterly ignorant in matters of general information, at the same time so much at home in all that concerned the immediate interests of his country and station. But, like many other people, the Bey prized his knowledge in proportion to its rarity, and seemed to value most that of which he possessed the least. He threw out all his questions about the politics of the Porte in so careless a manner, and seemed so little to heed my answers, that an indifferent by-stander would have sworn, the most vital subjects to Suleiman were just those which weighed the least in his mind.

Having exhausted every topic of more immediate importance to himself, – "You have been long at Stambool," said he at last, "and therefore cannot fail to know all about Franguestan.[5] What bone, pray, are those Christian dogs now contending for? Do they think they possess enough upon the earth: or are they planning some expedition to the moon? Blind as they be, poor creatures! they bustle about as eagerly as those that can see!" I assured him that this blindness and bustle had increased to such a degree, that, from one end of Europe to the other, every potentate was actually at the present moment disposing of his neighbour's property, as if it had been his own![6]

Book-learning and general politics might afford a pretty pastime; but with a race like the Mamlukes, whose chiefs as well as meanest individuals, were always required to be on the alert, and ready alike for attack, for defence, and for retreat, skill in the exercise of the carbine, the pistol, and the sabre were the essential and indispensable qualifications of every candidate for preferment. In respect of these military accomplishments also Othman Bey had in his letter mentioned me with praise; but I perceived in Suleiman a conviction that the same human being could not possess talents so opposite and so varied. When therefore I begged permission to join the next day in the martial sports of his Mamlukes, he strongly tried to dissuade me, lest I should only expose myself: but my perseverance conquered. He at last consented, though evidently concerned at my obstinacy, and pitying my rashness. Not so his young Mamlukes! They were delighted with anticipations of the sorry figure I should make among their expert and dashing troop; and significant glances circulated round every part of the room. The morrow was to be a day of merriment.

At the appointed hour on that morrow I went to the Bey's palace, and found the whole household assembled in the court-yard, ready to sally forth. We soon marched out in grand procession; but when I enquired whither we were going, not a creature knew. The Beys are too fearful to trust their followers with so important a secret. Not until the whole party is turned adrift in the fields does the serrah, or domestic charged with the camp apparatus, receive intelligence of the destined halting place. Off he then sets, on his dromedary, to make his preparations: the rest follow with loud clamour; and when the place of destination is reached, the Mamlukes immediately dispose themselves in a spacious ring round the ground.

The Koobbet-el-haue proved to be the spot selected; and I suspected the Bey of a secret wish to verify his forebodings, when I understood it to be the most trying ground about Cairo for martial exercises. In order to judge how it lay, I hung back at first, as if not daring to enter the lists with men so distinguished for their skill and address: but of course, the less alacrity I showed, the more I was pressed to expose myself. "The youngsters knew, it was in sheer compassion upon their inferiority, that I did not choose to come forward. But my backwardness would not serve me: I stood engaged, and my modesty must be put to the blush."

As if only reluctantly urged on by these ironical observations, I at last, in seeming trepidation, snatched up a djereed. In order to render my incapacity the more palpable, the most indifferent performer of the set was pitted against me. Off went my adversary's staff! and after it every eye. Spite of my indifferent steed, I avoided the blow, and the harmless stick only raised a cloud of dust. All wondered at my escape. In my turn I flung the wooden weapon, but not with similar effect. It reached its destination, and most unequivocally delivered its errand. The astonishment of the spectators redoubled, and my antagonist, dismounted, limped in rage out of the circle. The rest of his companions now began to suspect that it was not a tyro's task to contend with the new comer. The more skilful players took their turn. They had little better success; and the first exclamations of surprise gradually subsided in speechless disappointment and dismay. Every voice was hushed, and every lip bleeding with bites of vexation.

I had the good fortune to show equal dexterity in the use of the pistol and the sabre. The jar flew in pieces, and the felt[7] was cut through and through. In the Koobbet-el-haue at Cairo I thus first reaped the fruits of the exercises performed in the Oc-Meidan of Constantinople, and the dejection of spirits which led me to the one, prepared the way for the triumph which I obtained in the other. So high rose in an instant my reputation, that the Bey himself proposed to try his hand against me. I had heard him described as an indifferent performer. I could have no doubt that, equal as my skill appeared to that of Suleiman's ablest Mamlukes, I had little to fear from their master. Yet did every person present seem to revive at the bare proposal of the match. "How is this?" thought I: – but a moment's reflection gave me the clue to the phenomenon. "Ah rogues!" I inwardly exclaimed – on penetrating the new drift of my friends – "to see me victorious is now precisely what you wish for, in order that I may irretrievably lose the favour of the Bey. But take leave of your hopes! Selim not only knows when to play well, but also when to play ill;" and in fact, I took such uncommon pains for this prudent purpose, that, on quitting the field, Suleiman pronounced me by far the best player next to himself he knew in Cairo, and the one he liked most to engage with; and, on returning home, definitively took me into his service. Fearful, however, of putting me at once on the footing of the favoured cast, he placed me for the present among his seratches.[8] My salary was trifling; but who among the followers of Beys of Egypt, depended upon his wages for his emolument?

Suleiman possessed, in addition to the numerous Mamluke sprigs ingrafted upon the family tree, one male, and sundry female suckers, directly sprung from the stock. To his female offspring Suleiman seemed attached: the male shoot no one could accuse him of spoiling, at least by excess of fondness. He considered the Bey-zadé as a perfect cipher. Seldom he deigned to enquire after his health: never to demand his presence. "What interest," would he say, "can I take in a plant on which all culture is thrown away? Why cherish a reed, too feeble to support my increasing age? What I lay out on a conceited idiot, who forgets his deficiencies only to remember his birth, I lay out to utter loss: I even expend it without reaping empty thanks! Are not then my gifts more wisely bestowed on men whom I cherish for their intrinsic merit, and who reward me with their gratitude?" To this mode of reasoning, I, for one, could not possibly object!

Various were the sorts of merit which, in the eyes of my patron, took precedence of kindred. Valour, capacity, zeal, each obtained their share of superior esteem: but the quality rated above all others was a pair of ruddy cheeks. Among many other instances of their paramount influence, a young fellow from Odesché, remarkable for his stupidity and peevishness, had just superseded in the Bey's favour, and in the place of Tchibookdjee,[9] a Georgian esteemed for his good qualities by all his companions; and that, for no other earthly reason which any one could discover, except that his face looked like a ripe Damascus peach. Suleiman himself saw nothing singular in this fancy. "People," he said, "value a tulip, a shawl, a ruby, a canary-bird, a horse, for the brightness of their hue: they dress up their domestics in the gaudiest colours! Why then should they not be as particular about their faces? and choose their attendants by the same rule as their flower-pots; since both alike are destined to furnish their chamber! For my part, it is my delight, when I cast my eyes around, to view a long row of handsome busts; and I think I may be permitted to be as fastidious about the hue of my pages, as my neighbour Ayoob is about that of his pipe-sticks!"

Fortunately, the new comer possessed not in his complexion wherewithal to make any very valuable addition to Suleiman's collection, as it must have kept me at home much oftener than I liked, for fear of disturbing the set. So far from my hues being any longer of a pure and primitive description, they were rather become what painters might call neutral tints, and such as could not, by their absence, leave the smallest sensible gap in the Bey's prismatic scale. Scarce a day therefore passed without my allowing myself – in company with some of the younger Mamlukes of our house – time to visit Maallim[10] Ibrahim, Maallim Yacoob, Maallim Yoossef, or some other of the Maallims, or writers of the Coobtic persuasion, who lived round the lake Yusbekieh.[11] They assisted us in keeping up some of our good old Christian customs; for they never would let us depart without reviving our spirits with a few glasses of rakie: "in order," they said, "to keep out of our stomachs all the water that surrounded us." This good purpose however, they sometimes overshot; for one evening my companion and myself took so copious a dose of the antidote, that on returning home, we no longer could distinguish the path from the canal that ran along side of it; and so fell into the ditch, which was full to the brink. My companion first pulled me in, and I afterwards pulled him out; and he felt so thankful for this trifling compliment, that from that moment we became sworn friends. Some of the other Mamlukes, indeed, wished to sow the seeds of discord between us; but in vain they tried to damp the ardour of an attachment begun in a ditch.

Rashooan was my comrade's name: Gurgistan his country. He possessed in an eminent degree all the qualities in which Mamlukes excel. Equally active and vigorous, he could break the most unruly horse; leaped a ditch (when sober) with the agility of a deer; brought his steed to a dead stand in the midst of the swiftest race; and wielded with equal dexterity, the scimitar, the musket, and the pistol.

One day I found him describing in glowing terms to a knot of his companions the glories of his native soil. Its flowers, fruits, verdure, streams, men, women, and even, I think, tobacco-stoppers, were, according to his account, positively of a different nature from those of every other country; and could he but once more behold this land of wonders, he would resign his breath contented! "I did not know, Rashooan," said I, when the party separated, "that you so grievously regretted your native country." "Nor I neither," was his answer; "and between ourselves, I pray to God every morning that I may never see it again. Fine horses, rich caparisons, costly armour, sumptuous apparel, Egyptian grooms, and Negro slaves, would be a sad exchange for a life of hard labour and poverty; and for what purpose? Only to find myself forgotton by my parents, and recognized by nobody but a landlord who would sell me again, as he sold me before! I have lost my relish for simplicity, and am weaned from mother nature. But my imagination got the better, just now, of my sober senses, and besides it is not amiss, now and then, to remind these pert coxcombs that they are only savages, and that I am a Georgian."

Scarce had Rashooan uttered these words, when two or three of Suleiman's younger Mamlukes came running to us, and addressing my friend, said: "Either something very good, or very bad, is hanging over you. We have left Othaman kiachef closeted with the Bey, and you are the theme of their discourse. Both repeated your name frequently with considerable vehemence." "Ah!" answered Rashooan, "if any thing extraordinary awaits me, it is sure to be bad. I never was fortunate myself; nor ever brought good fortune to others! When a boy I was sent among the Kabardahs. Kind people! My host adopted me as his child; his wife sealed the act with the milk from her own breast; and his sons swore to treat me as a brother. What was the consequence? Tartars carried me off, my adopted kinsmen fell in my defence, and I was sold to the Turks. I now am a slave by habit as well as from necessity, and no longer wish to be free: the chance therefore is that I am doomed to have my liberty."

Other Mamlukes now brought Rashooan word that his presence was commanded. Sighing he went, and in about half an hour returned to us with a countenance clouded by sadness, "Selim," said he, "I leave you: for ever I must leave the house of Suleiman."

"What motive," cried I, "can induce the Bey to part with a favourite?"

"Listen," answered Rashooan. "Othman kiachef had an elder brother in Georgia, settled at a distant place. The kiachef has just discovered that I am that brother's son. He has consequently requested of Suleiman to purchase me. But, as you may suppose, our patron did not think himself warranted by any circumstance, however singular, to listen to the proposal. 'Such a disgrace,' cried he, 'as that of bartering my Mamluke for money shall lie neither on his head nor on mine. Suleiman may inflict death on an undutiful son, but his enemies shall never say he exchanged him for gold!'"

"Othman upon this looked exceedingly dejected, and Suleiman for awhile seemed rather to enjoy his distress. At last he proceeded thus: "Since, however, Rashooan is your nephew, God forbid I should keep him from his uncle's longing arms. Receive the young man as my gift, and let the donor ever remain near your heart."

"Othman," pursued the Georgian, "would fain have excused himself from accepting me in the burthensome form of a present; but unable to obtain his nephew on any other terms, he submits. I therefore leave you; I leave all that is dear to me! Torn in my childhood from my natural friends, I now in my youth am wrested from all my adoptive brethren. But the will of God be done!"

We accompanied Rashooan back to the palace, where he took an affectionate leave of his patron and his friends. All regretted the young Mamluke sincerely; and Suleiman himself appeared greatly moved. Little did he foresee what luck his gift one day would bring him!

The removal of Rashooan left me fewer inducements for rambling, and this was fortunate; for every day the Bey could less endure my absence. I was his cyclopoedia, and whatever puzzled his sagacious brain – whether a paragraph on Egypt in an old Vienna gazette, or the site of Cairo in a worn-out Nurnberg map; whether the arranging of a microscope presented by a traveller, or the telling of the weather by a barometer extorted from a Jew; whether the construction of a barge, or the design of a keoschk – all was referred to me, as to the oracle in chief: so that many a time, when there occurred what seemed inexplicable riddles to Mamluke intellects, I could only escape my part of Œdipus, by my insufficient proficiency in the language of the Egyptian sphinx; and my ignoreance of the Arabic saved my credit for information on many other subjects. The Bey, however, recommended me to the tuition of a schaich, bred in the college of El-Azhar,[12] not doubting that, when once taught all the refinements of the Caïreen idiom, I should no longer be at a loss for an answer on any topic whatsoever. He thought me a positive abyss of science; and in truth it would have been difficult to discover on what foundation bottomed my knowledge. Whenever I feared that its want of solid foundation might become palpable, I diverted the Bey's attention by some piece of flattery. Not that I ever condescended to perform so inferior an office in the endless departments of adulation, as that of administering to Suleiman his daily dose of crude unmodified incense, which, in common with all other grandees, he had from long and inveterate habit come to regard – like his daily pill of opium – as an absolute necessary to his constitution; and therefore took as a thing he could not well dispense with, but no longer either derived much exhilaration from, or felt much gratitude for. The task of cramming him with this insipid sort of panegyric I left to the vulgar herd of attendants. Mine was the nicer office of exciting the Bey's appetite ere I gratified it, and of heightening the flavour of the destined draught by that little previous fermentation which I often had found to give spirit to the flattest beverage. I therefore usually began by putting my patron, by some point blank contradiction, into a violent rage. To yield afterwards to the force and perspicuity of his arguments was perfectly irresistible: it gave my patron all the pleasure of a complete surprise, and me, all the appearance of a sturdy sincerity!

Such pains to please deserved a recompense, and the reward was liberally bestowed; but in a mode nearly as circuitous as that in which the reward had been earned. Suleiman naturally abhorred a direct gift: what he usually granted to his favourites, was an opportunity of grinding other favourites already provided for, – of laying under contribution some dependant or client. He would send me, for instance, to inform some rich Jew protégé that he had been thinking of him all day, or some wealthy Christian tradesman that he had been dreaming of him all night; and truly I had never before experienced such a solid way of thinking, or such golden dreams! As an additional favour, he introduced me to all his most distinguished colleagues; particularly to Ibrahim-Bey Sogeir, to Moustapha-Bey Skanderani, and to Ayoob-Bey the great. This latter was pleased to express great regret that the commander of the kirlangitsch should not have addressed me, at the outset, to himself.

On first entering Suleiman's house I had found the envy of his Mamlukes entirely centred in the Tchibookdgee. It was hard to digest so marked a preference shown a native of Odesché, whatever might be the colour of his cheeks. But when I, who was not even a purchased slave, became the Bey's right hand, only for practising a few foreign juggling tricks – as they were politely termed – even the favourite was thought aggrieved, and began to be pitied. Accustomed to dissimulation, he however preserved with me an exterior of civility, tempered only by a few cutting remarks so expressed as to seem to arise from sheer kindness; until a favorable opportunity at last offered of letting loose upon me all his malice.

Suleiman had been rather too eager one day in exhibiting his prowess at the djereed. Over-heated with an exercise too violent for his age, he returned home greatly indisposed. His illness soon became so violent a fever that his life was thought in danger; and his hakem in ordinary, at his slender wit's ends, no longer knew what to do. All his Mamlukes stood aghast round their patron, expecting every hour to be his last. I was looking on with the rest, when all at once it occurred to me that I need not remain an idle spectator. Eugenius my French instructor at Pera, whose strong mind lodged in but a weakly sort of a body, had on occasions derived relief from an English powder, which he always kept with him. Of this panacea he had at parting given me a few papers, as a valuable present. But Anastasius in health never remembered that Anastasius might fall ill, and the medicine was abandoned to whoever chose to try its efficacy: an occurrence the more frequent as the result of the experiment always was favourable. It however now struck me that, possibly, among my clothes, there might be some powders left which might save the Bey's life, and make my own fortune.

Full of this idea, I broke through the circle, burst out of the room, and ran, with a throbbing heart, to my own chamber to look for the medicine. But where to find it I know not! Every corner of my box was ransacked, every hole of my room was searched, every article of my apparel was turned over fifty times, without my being able to discover the least symptom of the tiny blue papers for which I was hunting. At last I gave over to search, considered the case as hopeless, and went down stairs again, to resume my forlorn station in the sick chamber, where even during my short absence matters were grown worse. Scarce had I entered, than I recollected that in tumbling over my wardrobe I had perceived the blade of an old rusty handjar – a keep-sake from Aly – thrust half way out of the sheath, and had met with some resistance on trying to push it home. In the flurry of my spirits, I had only curst the rusty weapon; but, on recurring to the circumstance, a glimpse of hope flashed upon me. Aly had taken one of my powders after his sea-sickness, and the handjar had been his acknowledgment for the relief obtained. I ran back to my chamber, probed the scabbard to the bottom, and from the very point of the implement of death drew forth the last dose of my restorative of life and health, – probably thus untidily stowed away in some thoughtless moment. Wrapping up the precious medicine in an embroidered handkerchief, I ran down again to the Bey; gave him – for fear the simple truth should sound too homely in his ears – a pompous account of the singular personage to whom I owed the gift; expatiated on the incalculable rarity and wonderful powers of the medicine itself; and ended by imploring him to take perhaps the last dose of this powder of life existing on the whole terraqueous globe!

Most ready was my patron to try its efficacy; but I had seen him swallow other medicine of less vital importance with an ill grace, and spit out three good quarters and a half. Fearful lest he should serve in the same manner what I considered his sole remaining chance of existence, I went for some palatable vehicle in which to secure a safe transit to the powder.

Though scarcely absent two minutes, I found on my return the face of affairs entirely changed! The Tchibookdgee had employed the short period of my absence to insinuate that the medicine probably was a poison, and the giver a rogue. Of late, I had been much with Ayoob-Bey. Ayoob indeed was Suleiman's most intimate friend! But what were Mamluke friendships? And my evident confusion, my wildness, and my running in and out, clearly bespoke a guilty mind. When full of exultation and hope I offered the draught, the Bey pushed it aside, and, without giving any reason, said he would take no more physic. This declaration was in itself sufficiently stunning; but much of the mischief it implied might depend upon its particular author. – I cast my eye leisurely round the Mamluke circle: the Tchibookdgee looked away; I guessed the truth, and trembled.

It now became necessary to insure my own safety. I therefore said with firmness: “This powder has some other virtues beside that of expelling fever: it exposes calumny. Since my patron rejects its healing powers, let it at least bear witness to his Selim’s heart; – and may God forgive the unfaithful servant who suffers the waste of what might have saved his master’s life!”

Saying this, I carried the cup to my lips. My speech had restored to the Bey his former confidence. With all the eagerness which his debility permitted, he interposed his trembling had between the rim and my mouth, wrested from me the draught, and, whispering to the Tchibookdgee in a faultering accent: “he cannot be a poisoner,” at one gulp poured down his throat the whole contents.

In my eagerness to do good, I certainly had not sufficiently proportioned the dose to the weakness of the patient. Instead of finding relief, he felt greater oppression: and soon his constitution appeared utterly unable to struggle with the medicine. The Mamlukes, upon this, renewed all their former surmises, and spoke their sentiments so loudly in the Bey’s hearing, that they seemed quite determined to justify their imputations, cost what it might, and, in default of real poison, to kill their patron through the fear of it. My life seemed to hang by a thread! – Had I dared, I should have mounted my horse and rode away, without waiting the issue; but I saw myself watched on all sides, and I knew that on the smallest attempt to make my escape, I must be cut down on the spot. Meantime a death-like paleness overspread the Bey’s countenance: his features became fixed, and his breath ceased to perceptible. This was the critical moment. I gazed on his countenance, like one whose own life depended on its changes. At last a slight dew broke out upon his forehead: – plentiful relief soon followed and enabled the system to throw off the weight which oppressed it, and the fever abated! From that instant the Bey’s illness took a favourable turn. Every hour showed an improvement on the preceding; and in a short time after being to all appearance in the agony of death, Suleiman was on his legs again, as well as ever; while, – as had been predicted at the Fanar, – I fell upon mine at last, and stood proclaimed the saver of his life.

CHAPTER II.

On the occasion of his recovery from the first alarming illness which he had yet experienced, Suleiman took with its vanquisher a less circuitous mode than usual of showing his gratitude. He made me at once, by a direct grant, Multezim or proprietor of a district containing several villages near Djarrah; and Selim Aga thus became a man of substance. But this favour inflamed to such a degree the jealousy and murmurings of the Bey's Mamlukes, that he would at last, I believe, gladly have seen me in the condition from which I rescued him, and that, without the benefit of Eugenius's powders. An urgent summons into his presence was the consequence. The moment I appeared: "Selim," he cried, "you prescribed the other day for me: I must now prescribe for you!"

I thanked my patron, and assured him that the pleasure of seeing his health restored, had put mine beyond the reach of accident.

"You mistake," resumed the Bey. "I see by your face that you are ill, – very ill indeed! The air of Cairo disagrees with you. Take my advice, and change it immediately for that of the province in which your property lies."

It was something to find that I was not expected to swallow a positive dose, which I feared might cure all my ailments too effectually. Still I considered the prescription as indicating something critical in my case, and exclaimed: "Say at once, Sir, that I have lost your favour; say at once you banish me your presence; say that my enemies have prevailed!"

"To prove you mistaken," replied the Bey, "to prove that I lose not so soon all sense of gratitude, I add to my former gift a new one; I name you Caïmakam[1] of Samanhood. It is a delightful place, and your residence in your own district will season you to the climate. On your return, you will appear less a stranger among us."

From some lips, "I advise," implies "I command." My only business therefore was to go where bidden, as soon as invested with the insignia of my office.

Meanwhile, behold me now become Selim-Caïmakam! and by the indefeasible privilege of always rising one step at least above one's real rank, giving myself by anticipation all the airs of Selim-Kiachef. Not a single rayah had the misfortune to meet me in the street, whom my mokhadam[2] forced not to jump from off his long-eared steed, and humbly to salute me in the mire. The great fat Frank merchants indeed, showed themselves as yet more firm in their seats, and these I thus far only indulge in the pleasure of bespattering them from head to foot, *en passant*, while I promised myself ampler satisfaction on their persons at some later period. These were the follies of my youth; – and would that they had been the worst for which my riper years have had to blush!

Suleiman's regular bazirghian[3] was the merchant on whom chiefly devolved the honour of fitting me out for my lieutenancy. I chose at his shop broad-cloths, shawls, silks, muslins, armour, &c., sufficient for the equipage of a Bey. These I paid for in orders on my villages; and as the term of payment was distant, so was the price of the goods proportionably high. My indignation therefore exceeded all bounds, when, alarmed at my increasing requisitions, the wary trader at last swore – with great apparent concern – that he had not a strip left of the articles I wanted. A piece of information so little expected, put me under the disagreeable necessity of secretly watching the entrance of some customer of more established credit into Zohrab's shop, when, gliding in after him, and finding the whole counter covered with the choicest specimens of the very goods which I had in vain demanded, I congratulated the merchant on his seasonable supply, swept away the whole assortment, and resold what I could spare from my own private use.

Spite of Suleiman's impatience to see me gone, I was determined to witness at Cairo the opening of the Kalish. Rather than lose that festivity, I chose to sprain my ancle, and limped to the show. Among the costly articles which I had brought to grace my accession to my government, shone pre-eminent a fine Samoor[4] pelisse. This costly fur I was dying to display at the fete; and caught a cold on purpose to wrap myself in it in the midst of the dog-days: nor did I stir a step except in my pelisse. The very mob raved of its beauty; and one youth in particular beheld it with such eyes of adoration, that, unable to possess himself of the whole, he cut off the left sleeve, while it hung dangling at my back, and bore it away as a relic. It was mortifying to learn my loss from some persons behind me, in the very midst of my happiness. The sleeve indeed might be replaced, but the pelisse could no longer be worn that day, and with a deep sigh I sent it home. Scarce, however, had its mangled body reached my door, than after it walked in the severed limb. Dropped in the confusion of the place by the thief, the precious fragment had been picked up by an honest fellow, who, by the greatest good luck, happened to be a tailor into the bargain, and offered to wield his needle with such diligence, as in a trice to enable the Signor Caïmakam to resume his robe of state. The honest fellow's services were accepted: the cloak was given him, and he retired to work in a little back chamber.

Unluckily this room – besides a door – also had a window; and, having come in at the one, my friend chose, for variety, to go out at the other. On my looking in to hasten the business, tailor, cloak and sleeve, had disappeared together, nor have they ever since been heard of. I applied to the Schaich or chief of robbers at Cairo, who, for a certain consideration undertakes to restore stolen goods; and during the sultriest season of the year had every day fifty pelisses of cat and rabbit skin brought me to examine; but not one of samoor!

Spite of my loss I proceeded on my journey. According to the custom of the country, I was accompanied by some of the fellahs[5] of my own estate, to serve me as a sort of hostages for the good behaviour of my remaining serfs; and, in addition to these had by way of retinue, four black slaves for the service of my person; three hawarees or Barbaresque horsemen for the protection of my vassals, half a dozen kawasses,[6] to clear my way of canaille, and four or five saïs, or grooms, to take care of my stud. This latter consisted, besides the steeds we mounted, of three or four fine led horses for show, as many mules for use, and a dromedary for flight, should circumstances render a retrograde movement expedient. As to asses for incognito expeditions, they were, thank God! to be found at every turn. This little assortment of bipeds and quadrupeds, –

extended on as long a line as possible, – formed a very respectable procession, and quite sufficient to make passengers enquire, and have an opportunity of learning, that it was Selim Caïmakam on his way to his government.

I began my journey by land, and spite of the humble entreaties of the Schaichs and Shehoods[7] of the different places where I halted, preferred pitching my tents in the open air, to lodging in the close and miserable hovels of the towns and villages; but I took care that the inhabitants should lose nothing by the great man keeping aloof: and consoled them by sending for as much provision of every sort as I could manage to consume or carry. The Schaich-el-belled of each district is obliged to supply the public officers on their route at the expense of the district; in consequence of which excellent regulation I should never have given up the more economical way of travelling by land, for the more expensive conveyance by water, had not some of the kiachefs on my way been most inconveniently engaged in hostility with the neighbouring Arabs. This rendered part of the road insecure; and as I had but an inadequate force, I resolved, after three or four days march along the banks of the Nile, to contend with its adverse current; myself in a light khandgea,[8] which went on before, and the bulk of my equipage in a larger and heavier boat behind.

In consequence of the adventure of my pelisse, I had conceived the erroneous notion that the thieves of Cairo far excelled in skill those of the provinces. This opinion, so injurious to the latter, I had occasion to correct. One evening, advancing with a fresh breeze pretty rapidly against the stream, our ears were suddenly struck by the noise of a heavy body, plumping into the waves; and inexpressible was my surprise and concern when, running to the stern of the boat, I beheld this body to be that of my best mare,; and when I saw the faithless Noorshah whom I thought I had left tied fast by the legs, swimming away to the land with all her might. Unable to guess the cause of this strange freak, I did all in my power to entice the beast back. In vain! – As if bewitched, the more she heard me call the faster she swam; so that at last I gave orders to tack and row after the fugitive with all possible speed. Noorshah however reached the bank about fifty yards in advance of her old master, and no sooner had she touched the shore, than out came the secret, in the shape of a thief; who, to my inexpressible horror, started up from behind the animal, cut the strings that confined its legs, pressed its loins with his own bandy shanks, and scampered off. By diving all the way, the scoundrel had contrived unperceived to reach the boat, had crept by favour of the dusk into the hold, had slipped under the mare, and, then, by raising his back under her belly, had tilted her over into the water; when, confined as were her extremities, it became an easy task to pushed her to the land. Unfortunately the boasted speed of the animal put out of question all chance of successful pursuit; and Noorshah was placed in my memory together with the pelisse, among the things that had been.

At Mamfloot I again quitted the khandgea. Only five or six days journey now separated me from my new district, which bordered upon the province of Djirdgé; and the road bore a good character.

On the third morning, however, passing near a mean looking village of mere mud hovels, I began to doubt its claims. All the inhabitants, young and old, were under arms; some carrying clubs, others stones, and, the most distinguished a rusty sword, or a worn-out matchlock. The enemy against whom they marched, drawn out in most martial array on the brow of an eminence hard by, were the inhabitants of the next village; and inquiring into the cause of hostilities, all the information I could get, was that nobody knew the date of its first beginning. The origin of the hereditary animosity between the two districts lay concealed in the obscurity of ages; but its virulence remained not the less impaired: it had been laudably kept up by as many subsequent injuries and retaliations as other business permitted; and to my great edification I understood that, however totally the first cause of the enmity might be forgotten, it was only the more implacable on that account.

Though gratified by so praise-worthy a spirit, I yet took the liberty to represent that, even supposing the happiness of the community to be beyond enduring, I still thought that certain regular drawbacks – such as contributions to the Sultan, taxes imposed by the Beys, provisions claimed by travelling officers like myself, exactions of avaricious landlords, depredations committed by wandering Arabs, and yearly encroachments of the sand on the cultivable soil, together with the incidental circumstances of locusts, plague, imperfect irrigation, mortality and famine – might, upon the whole, qualify it sufficiently, without the gratuitous addition of civil warfare and bloodshed between neighbours, begun without a cause, and carried on without an object!

This civil remonstrance, I rejoiced to find, and made a great impression. Not a single objection was raised, and my speech – frequently interrupted by cries of: "listen listen!" seemed to obtain universal approbation. The auditors thanked me humbly for my good advice: when I departed, they remained for a considerable time immovable on the spot; and only after I and mine were quite out of sight they proceeded on, and gave their enemies (as I have since understood) the bloodiest battle on record in their annals.

After nearly four weeks spent on the road, I found myself, to my great satisfaction, performing the last stage of my tedious journey. In the midst of a deep reverie I was suddenly aroused by the loud shouts of my suite at the sight of my capital. Already delighted with these welcome sounds, I expected to be soon still more so by the appearance of my subjects, drawn out in due state to meet their new governor, with drums beating and colours flying. "How long they must have been watching my arrival!" thought I, and spurred my horse, straining both eyes and ears to discover some distant stir; but no symptom of bustle being yet discernible, I again slackened my pace, in order to give leisure for the procession to advance. Vain considerateness! I might proceed as slow as I pleased, not a creature appeared to welcome my arrival; and I had to enter my capital unhonoured with the smallest notice. Matters mended not even as I penetrated deeper into the town; though at every street or lane which I successively entered, I still entertained fresh hopes of some tardy demonstration of respect. On the contrary, the place looked peculiarly forlorn. Every door and window was as empty as if the city had been visited by the plague; and the inhabitants, so far from impeding my passage by their congratulations seemed rather to have all fled from their homes, at my approach. Inconceivably mortified, I fell into a state of such complete abstraction that I no longer at all minded what I was about, but crossed my capital (which to say the truth was among the largest) through and through; after a few more turnings and windings, issued forth again at the opposite extremity from that at which I had entered, into the open country; and, leaving my residence wholly behind me, continued, on in full march toward the Saïd. In fact, I might have proceeded in this way to the very end of the world, had not all at once a prodigious clamour assailed my ears, a hundred yards or two in my rear. It was not less than all the Schaichs, Shehoods and notables of the place, who, seeing me thus contemptuously turn my back upon my new subjects, and run away from my government, were in full cry at my heels, to stop my strange career. Unfortunately the discord of their shouts had the contrary effect from that which they intended. Imagining it in my abstraction to be some fray in which I had no concern, I only spurred on my horse the faster, and the more pertinaciously the procession pursued me, the harder I galloped. At last one of my own suite, who in the interval had learnt the truth, got me to hear him, and rectified my mistake. My subjects, poor creatures! had only appeared remiss from an excess of loyalty. Apprised that, I drew near, they had, early in the morning, taken their station where they expected me to enter their city: – totally forgetting a bad pass in the road, which compelled me to make a circuit, and thereby obliged my subjects to run after the governor, instead of advancing in due state to meet him face to face. Matters now were soon brought to an amicable understanding, and I turned back without any other ill consequence arising from the mistake, except that of the whole procession – governor and governed – entering the town the wrong end foremost.

It had been sheer modesty in me not to expect a capital at least equal to Raschid or the Fooah. When therefore, on looking round, I saw what a place I was in, the first thing I did was to accuse Suleiman of having treated me with disrespect. It was only by degrees that I came to more reasonable sentiments; – time only taught me that mine was a situation not of amusement but of profit; but by degrees my docile intellect became so thoroughly imbued with this principle, that, through dint of unabating diligence, I was at last able to tell to a fraction of a para what each feddan of ground might yield, and each head of man or beast thereto belonging be chargeable for, whether to the Multezim, the lieutenant, the governor, or the miri.[9]

After these severer studies, letting leases, imposing contributions, levying fines, receiving presents, and inflicting penalties were only my pastimes. Indeed, as the Egyptian fellah makes it a matter of conscience never to pay his rent, until compelled by main force, and wears the stripes he has incurred in his resistance as badges of honour, my very financial operations sometimes afforded me an opportunity for indulging in my warlike propensities: not but what my genius – even in its fullest exertions in that line – still shrunk into absolute insignificance before that of my Coobtic writer, who, with a salary of six medeens a day, and a large family to maintain, had become, by mere savings, as rich as a Sultan's seraf. It is true that whenever he drew a para out of his vest, it was as if he tore his very vitals out of his bosom. Once I tried to make myself master of his accounts, but I might as soon have attempted to find my way in the labyrinth of Crete. When I complained of this worthy personage to my confidential servant, I found little sympathy. Seyed shrugged up his shoulders; said it might be tiresome to be cheated, but it was the regular practice. If the Coobd cheated the Multezim, did not the Multezim in the same way cheat the Caïmakam, and the Caïmakam the Kiachef, and the Kiachef the Bey, and the Bey the Schaich-el-belled, and the Schaich-el-belled the Pasha, and the Pasha the Porte, and the Porte the Sultan? who, he was very sure, cheated Allah himself, when he assumed the title of Kaliph of the faithful.

The only thing I could see through tolerably were the decisions of the cadee, which I sometimes went to witness at the mekkiemé. In Egypt as elsewhere, the conjugal union seemed to be in all its various stages the most universal source of discord, and subject of litigation. One day there appeared a fair one, entitled thus far only to the blushing honours of a bride who, on being conducted in state to her bridegroom, had been refused admittance, and had found herself compelled to return as she went. Another day came a wife regularly installed. She, poor woman! had been dispossessed less openly, but of rights already exercised, and now claimed her long unpaid dues with arrears of interest : and on another occasion in walked a mourning widow; who, still as much in love with her dead husband as while he was alive, only demanded the empty gratification of nightly visiting his grave, unimpeded by her churlish relations. She was pretty: her grief affected me, and once or twice I went to the scene of her affliction, to mix my tears with hers.

In Europe, they say, the law demands a long apprenticeship: it is not so among Mohammedans. The Koran and its commentaries decided every case, – from a point of faith to a right of gutter – in a few seconds. The form of trial is simple. Every man pleads his own cause: and wonderful is the readiness of the Egyptians in finding answers to every interrogatory, excuses for every action, witnesses to every fact, and sureties for every engagement. I remember a poor fellow who, called upon for his respondents, and having none on earth, had recourse to heaven. Imam Aly was the one he chose: nor dared the other contracting party, albeit a little startled, both at the distance of the saint's abode and at the difficulty of enforcing his appearance, refuse so respectable a security.

My stay was long enough in my lieutenancy to find the subject of discourse which once had appeared to me the most tiresome, become the most interesting in the world. I mean, the rise of the Nile. So far from wishing never more to hear of it, I could think of no other. Yet was it this season a source of no very cheering contemplation. The river – as if in a trance – displayed such unusual tardiness in rising, that soon every district trembled lest its waters should fail of attaining the requisite height. Nothing was heard but lamentations and complaints. One came to tell me of canals which had no chance of receiving a drop of moisture; another of such as had been drained prematurely of their insufficient contents. Here the legal period for cutting a dam had been wholly disregarded; there a single field had been flooded at the expence of a whole district: every where it seemed as if the dread of a scarcity had made man exert his utmost ingenuity to render a famine unavoidable.

I now became haunted by the phantom of drought, the most dreary that stalks over Egypt's rich domain. My thoughts by day, and my dreams by night equally presented to me its ever extending, blasting form, followed by the whole train of its frightful offspring: unirrigated tracts, fields remaining fallow, insufficient crops, farmers unable to pay their contributions, peasants abandoning their villages, whole troops of fellahs leaving their possessions and their homes to till the land of the stranger, impositions to remit, short rents to receive for the Bey; and the Caïmakam alone held accountable for all the deficiencies of nature, and all the waywardness of man. O! how earnestly did I now pray for some lucky incident, which might release me from my stewardship and responsibility! But of such a piece of good fortune I entertained no hopes.

It however came, and when it came it failed of its promised pleasure. One morning, as I sat puzzling over some of my writer's explanations, in walked a smooth-spoken gentleman, who, in a civil tone, informed me that he came to take my place; and, lest I should doubt his word, handed me an injunction from the Bey to return forthwith to Cairo. This unlooked for recall produced such a revolution in my sentiments, that I now would gladly have given just as much to retain, as I would have done the instant before to get rid of, my trust. It is true that to my concern for what I left was to be added my apprehension of what I might find. So sudden a removal, so little accounted for, savoured of a disgrace. I doubted not but my enemies had improved my absence to undermine my favour. The Tchibookdje was evidently at the bottom of the whole affair; and as I had already vowed the insidious pipe-bearer an eternal hatred, I could now only add the vow of a speedy revenge.

Absorbed in my meditations on the best mode of executing what, but for the consequences, was feasible a thousand ways, I one day, on my homeward journey, rode on so fast as to get entirely out of sight of my suite, when suddenly I found myself breast to breast with a troop of Bedoween Arabs, whose low dusky tents, pitched behind a sand hill, had remained concealed from my view, till I almost stumbled over them. The same instant the chief of the tribe, followed by half a dozen of its ragged members, advanced upon me with couched spears, demanding either a hundred sequins for my passage, or all I had. Neither of these proposals suited me; but my retinue amounted not to one-forth of that of the Arabs, and it seemed quite certain that if it came to blows, we must have the worst of the fray. Without therefore advancing, but without either answering the summons, I turned round to the foremost of my escort who by this time had approached within reach, and bid them fill a basket with ball and cartridge. This ammunition I sent the Bedoweens: telling them at the same time it was the only coin in which I paid impositions; but if not content with the quantity offered, they might, as soon as my army came up, have as much more as they could carry away: and that, sent by the speediest conveyance. This rodomontade took effect. The Schaich received the gift with thanks, filled the basket in return with superexcellent dates, and bade me pass on, with the salutation of peace. This latter I most readily returned; nor waited until my army should be in sight, to hurry with all possible speed out of that of the Arabs.

Brooding all the way to Cairo over the cause of my recall, I could scarce avoid, on my entrance into the capital, reading in every countenance the confirmation of my disgrace. This idea made me conceal my own features in my shawl, till I reached the palace. There, meeting at the gate an old and confidential comrade, I for the first time gave vent to my apprehensions, and by way of obtaining, without asking it, more explicit information respecting the manoeuvres of the Tchibookdjee, cried out: "I was come to look after Osman." – "God forbid!" was the only answer I received.

But these few words, with the addition of an ominous smile, sufficed to complete the subversion of my senses. – I rushed up stairs, flew into the Bey's apartment, and hardly allowing myself time to breathe, or to perform a respectful salutation: "Sir," cried I in scarce articulate sounds, "Osman, I know, will never cease his machinations, until he has entirely ruined me in your esteem!"

"If so," coolly answered the Bey; "your knowledge far exceeds in its reach even what I imagined; nor did I think poor Osman still continued to disturb your repose, after being himself laid for ever to rest."

"How!" replied I, – my ideas now all completely subverted – "is Osman dead?" "And what else," replied the Bey, "do you think could have made me send for you in such haste? What but the means of now conferring upon you without any obstacle……? but you are too much agitated to listen at present. I must wait until to morrow to unfold my designs. Meanwhile, go, and compose yourself."

I went, but whether I obeyed the sequel of the injunction, need scarcely be told. My imagination, always ardent enough, had been set in a complete blaze; and burning with impatience to learn my new destinies, I only felt my agitation changed in its object without being in the least diminished in its intensity. The whole night I kept racking my feverish brain to clothe into some definite shape the Bey's vague and desultory hints; and in my anxious wish for the day that was to clear up the mystery, I began to think night had overslept herself, and the morning, pregnant with my future fate, would never arrive.

At last it duly shone upon the world, I was summoned to my patron's chamber, and gave him no cause to complain of my dilatoriness. Left with the Bey in much-portending tête-à-tête, he looked at me, smiled to see the impatience depicted in my countenance, hemmed twice or thrice for no purpose but to increase the fever of my spirits, and having asked me some trifling questions, which I answered without well knowing what they were – at last began his discourse.

CHAPTER III.

"Selim," – said Suleiman, in all the solemnity of a set speech, – "you have seen our two leaders, and seldom, I should think, can have observed two personages more unlike both in mind and in body. The short spare form, the mild countenance, the insinuating address, the cautious calculating turn of the Scaich-el-belled could not find a greater contract than in the ferocious features, the colossal frame, the voice of thunder, the violent temper, the fearlessness of danger, the impatience of control, and the prodigality of disposition of his blustering colleague. Little union might be expected between qualities so dissimilar; and, in fact, the public at large, which sees Ibrahim ever prefer artifice to force and negotiation to war, while Mourad openly professes to hold in his sword his only instrument of persuasion, regards these two chiefs as constantly on the eve of rupture, and about to hoist the standard of interminable enmity. We can only, when Ibrahim and Mourad affect to be at variance, view in their reciprocal strictures upon each other studied sallies carefully rehearsed beforehand by the performers, with a view to mask their schemes, and to mislead their rivals. Each appreciates in his heart at its true value that difference of disposition from the other, which gives him in his associate precisely all he wants in himself, and makes Mourad cut asunder the knot which Ibrahim cannot untie, as it again enables Ibrahim to cure by his management the wounds which Mourad has inflicted by his rashness. Thus it is that the dissimilar qualities of the two chiefs – like the gold and the steel of a Damascus blade – only form a closer amalgam, and leave less hopes of those chasms and fissures in their union, at which competitors insinuate themselves to divide the party, to drive its members asunder, and to rise on its ruins."

"Some of us therefore, – Ibrahim Bey Sogeir, Osman-Bey Tcherkavi, Moustapha-Bey Skanderani, Ayoob-Bey the lesser, and myself, – have at last come to a determination to bring these all-grasping leaders by main force to a more equal division of the spoil; and even Ayoob-Bey Kebir, Youssouf-Bey, and Ismaïl-Bey Sogeir, though they still seem to waver, only do so, in order that they may sell their co-operation at a higher price. Their irresolute and doubtful conduct, however, would have made us put off the execution of our design until it had had time to acquire greater consistency, did not the present juncture offer advantages which perhaps may never hereafter recur. Ismaïl and Hassan, after their long sleep at Es-souan, are at last awake, and preparing for a descent to Cairo. Aware how little our assistance is to be depended on, should the capital be made the field of battle, the leaders have thought it advisable to hush the storm, if possible, in its cradle, and Mourad is going to march to the Saïd, while Ibrahim stays to awe us at Cairo. Thus separated from his colleague, and deprived of half his strength, the Schaich-el-belled must, if strenuously attacked, yield to our united force: and in order to be in readiness for the day of trial, we all are busy recalling with the least possible shew our adherents from the different provinces. This made me so abruptly summon you from your government, without much considering whether your recall might not for the moment wear the air of a disgrace. You now know the great secret for which your presence was wanted; and all that I have to add is the strongest recommendation that it may never pass your lips."

Here my patron – rising from his seat – marked the end of his discourse. The conclusion fell somewhat short of my expectations. Great undoubtedly to one like me was the satisfaction of learning that all the world was going to unsheathe sword and dagger: but still I had looked forward to the disclosure of some more directly personal advantage. It however occurred to me that whatever new favour Suleiman might destine his servant was probably deferred to a later conference, on very purpose lest it should appear the consequence only of his necessities; which circumstance being made due allowance for, I humbly thanked him for his expenditure of breath, made every requisite profession of attachment, fidelity and zeal, and respectfully retired.

A slave of Ayoob's had been waiting for my appearance near the gate of the palace. The moment I went forth, he came up to me, and rather in a mysterious manner whispered an invitation to his master's palace, which I obeyed with alacrity.

As soon as Ayoob saw me: "Signor Caïmakam," cried he in his eager way – wholly unlike that of his brethren – true volcanos wrapt in snow – "a most extraordinary occurrence has happened. It is still a secret to all, save the parties concerned; and you are the first stranger to learn the wonderful event!

"You know," continued he after a short pause to fetch breath, "that since I cannot have my Mamlukes of my own blood, I at least spare neither money nor pains to have them of my own country – my beloved Gurgistan. Doomed to live and to die in this distant land, whoever comes from the country of my birth seems to me a relation. Not many days ago my harem was enriched with a new bud reared in the parent soil. In order to save the maiden from the rapacity of her landlord, her friends were going to put her under the protection of a husband's name, at the tender age of eleven: but already they had deferred their purpose too long. Her wedding day was fixed, when an armed troop carried her off; and made her a slave ere she had time to become a wife."

"Brought hither to adorn my garden, this lovely rose of the East became my favourite flower: yet had I the forbearance, ere with eager hand I placed it in my bosom, to observe our sacred custom, – to enquire on what stem it had grown, and what walls had sheltered its infancy from the rough blasts of heaven, and the rude touch of man? Selim – would you believe it? in my slave, I found a sister!"

"The virgin blushing before me, was my own father's daughter: was a young and solitary shoot, which, long after the elder branches had been severed from the parent stock, had sprung up to shade the withering top with fresh and tender foliage. For the first time during my twenty years sojourn in Egypt, I heard the voice of kindred, and felt the ties of blood."

"But what is all this to you? Perhaps you are thinking? Listen!"

Here Ayoob gave me nearly the same sketch of the state of affairs, and of the views of the party as Suleiman had done before: except that he spoke of himself as more decided in his sentiments than he had been represented by my patron. I began to fear that I was twice in one day fated to be inveigled, by a hope of personal advantage, into listening to a long detail of other people's concerns. But mark the sequel!

"At a moment so critical" – continued Ayoob – "I naturally feel anxious to surround myself with men who to such bravery as comes and goes not with the fumes of hashish,[1] add such intelligence and skill as may render that courage useful. Of men of this description, small, alas! is the number; but you are one, and I may now freely urge your devoting your future existence to my house, since it affords me – God be praised! – the means of rewarding your services.

"The husband my sister lost in Gurgistan we must find for her at Cairo; yet what man among my own Mamlukes worthy of the honour of so great an alliance, and able at the same time to requite it by undivided attention? The elder individuals of my household already are already established; and the younger have not yet accomplished their probation. To you, therefore, I offer Zelidah's youthful hand; to you, who may become my own support as well as my sister's solace! Let me however add, that I never should have made the proposal, while Suleiman your old patron continued faithful to his promise; but since – for what reason I know not – he resigns his claims upon a faithful servant, I, without scruple, offer you all I can bestow, – an alliance with my blood, a share in my honours, and a home in my house."

At this overture, I felt utterly confounded. It filled me with pleasure, but at the same time with anxiety. I knew not how to choose between the brilliant offer which came unexpectedly, and the expected favours as yet unbestowed. I dared not hope that Suleiman's thus far undisclosed designs would ever gratify my ambition beyond Ayoob's avowed intentions; but then again, I saw no means of attaching myself to Ayoob, without setting at nought the debt of gratitude, and the duties of the allegiance which I owed to Suleiman. In this dilemma between the certain and the promised boon, I magnanimously determined to make the proposals of the strange Bey, in the first instance, instrumental only in bringing to the test the munificence of my own patron – reserving their final acceptance or refusal for a later period; and in a speech brimful of those high-flown nothings called thanks, begged Ayoob's permission to ask Suleiman's consent, ere I changed my allegiance: observing that so far from my favour at home being on the decline, it stood higher than ever; and, in order to confirm this assertion, representing, by a little transposition only of the future to the past, those honours which I still expected, as already come to pass, and only for political purposes kept as yet unpublished.

Ayoob seemed not much to relish the idea of having his splendid offers accepted conditionally, or his liberality submitted to the discussion of a rival, and swore by his beard he though it very strange: but seeing me immoveable on this point, "Then go," said he at last, "since you will be so obstinate; but remind Suleiman that if he stops the current of my intended bounty, his own should make you unbounded amends; and above all, stay not long. An hour is the utmost I can bear to be left with my richest gifts thus hanging unaccepted on my hands.

I promised to return in much less time; and flew home as on the wings of lightning, to communicate to my patron the substance of the interview with his colleague. On hearing of his offers, he reddened, and seemed offended. "By the head of our holy Prophet," he cried in a tone of bitterness, "my brother Ayoob uses me ill: but these are times in which we must hush our resentments; and *this* Ayoob knows! You, Selim, I cannot blame: his offers took you by surprise, and you could not stop your ears. I however feel happy that, ere my rival made his proposal, I hinted the new favours with which I myself purposed to crown your zeal. You might otherwise suspect me of only acting from the fear of being out-bidden. Now mark me. My oldest kiachef, Mocktar, is married you know to my first born daughter. My second kiachef to her sister next in age. My other children, already set forth into the world, are provided for in different ways adequate to their deserts. Thank God! I have been able to make all my freedmen lords! My haznadar,[2] – first in rank of those still under my roof, – I cannot yet afford to part with, and I do not wish to conceal from you that had Osman lived, his name would have graced the nuptial son, sang in honour of my youngest girl. But Providence has called him away, and none of his comrades are yet entitled to an alliance with my blood. I may therefore indulge the suggestions of my heart by giving you my only remaining daughter. It is true, the man she marries must possess a public rank: but this also I give. I name you kiachef. Remember, however, that as my favours are great, so will your duties be arduous. – Of our intended plan of insurrection, the success may depend in great measure upon your devotion, your skill, and your activity!"

To this hour I value rank: it is reverenced by fools; and fools form the major number. In the first aspirings of youth, so vast an accession of honours as that offered me by Suleiman almost overpowered my senses. It scarce left me able to make my patron the proper acknowledgement for his liberality, ere I retired out of his sight, to give vent to my emotions.

"I shall then see myself a kiachef!" exclaimed I aloud, whirling round like a top, in an ecstasy of joy: "I shall then, every time I stir out, behold dancing before me those dear damasked spears which I so often have coveted! I shall appear abroad only with a handsome retinue, and at home possess my own separate establishment and harem! No longer a mere graft on a strange tree, I shall cast my own roots in the soil, and on my own independent stem bear my own separate fruits. This chin of mine shall henceforth cease to be kept close mown, and shall put forth unrestrained its most luxuriant crops!"[3] And immediately, with the eagerness of the husbandman, eager to ascertain whether in his field the budding blade comes up close and strong, I ran to the glass to see whether my broad jaw promised to bear a thick and handsome beard; already coaxed and perfumed in anticipation the still sleek unclothed skin, traced in imagination the symmetric outline of its future jetty fringe, and wondered how the new appendage would become the remainder of my features!

My raptures lasted some time ere I remembered that I had promised Ayoob an immediate answer; and soon as my memory returned, my imagination began to wander; – I became suddenly seized with a romantic fit. The substantial advantages were nearly balanced on the rival offers; but as honour threw its additional weight into the scale of my patron, I took it into my foolish head, that beauty must preponderate in that of Ayoob. In short I persuaded myself that Zelidah – by birth a Georgian, by condition a slave – must be as superior in personal charms to Khadidgé, a daughter of Egypt, and a descendant of rulers, as the fairest lily is to the dusky bulrush; and determined, at every risk, to see Ayoob's sister, ere I decided.

A Jewess of my acquaintance was the chief purveyor of female finery for Ayoob's harem. I went straight to this useful person, and made her instantly collect some of the richest stuffs she could find. I then put on the blue shift and chequered veil of the Egyptian women of the lower order; and in Sarah's unassuming suite, loaded with all her packages, proceeded to Ayoob's palace – now and then sharply reproved by the way, for my long strides and strapping gait.

Zelidah, when we arrived, was unfortunately in the bath, and Signora Sarah had to wait. In order to be less conspicuous the while, I squatted myself down on the floor, in the darkest part of the room. Even this had too much light to conceal me from Ayoob, who, whether informed of the entrance of a suspicious figure, or from some other cause, himself unexpectedly made his appearance, as if to see his sister. The moment his eye fell upon the bundle into which I had transformed myself, his countenance changed, his brow became contracted, and he rushed out again, muttering to himself some words of ungracious import, and not at all complimentary to somebody's mother.[4] At this ill-boding symptom, the Jewess turned pale, and striking her breast: "I have brought," cried she, "the thing I should not have come with, and have left behind what I meant to have brought! Go, Dalla; run home; fetch the tissue we were talking of; and return not without it."

Scarce had the words been uttered, when heavy footsteps were heard to approach the place. Active as she was, Dalla had but just time to make her escape, and to reach the outer gate without hindrance. Running home as fast as possible, I cast off my disguise, and immediately hastened back to Ayoob in my own proper form and character.

With many apologies for the unavoidable delay, I now solemnly declined the Bey's offers, but in terms full of regret, of gratitude, and of protestations. The answer was in the same strain, though, as I thought, delivered somewhat coolly, and in a ruffled manner: and I afterwards understood from the Jewess, who had bravely remained at her post, that, in less than half a minute after I had made my exit, Ayoob reappeared in the harem followed by a host of black eunuchs, and looking blacker than any of his suite. He again cast round an enquiring eye; and in seeming disappointment asked what was become of the Egyptian woman. Sarah told off-hand some just possible story, and, expressing a shrewd doubt of her servant's finding the stuff she wanted, went home herself; too glad at encountering no impediment! Thus ended my courtship with the fair Zelidah!

The instant Suleiman's intentions in my behalf became known; the greatest discontent shewed itself among his Mamlukes. "Their patron," they asserted, "had no right to give his daughters to any but Mamlukes, or to make Mamlukes any but purchased slaves. Othman-Bey Aboo-seïf and Achmet-Bey el Sukari, Turks by nature, and Beys by the favour of Ibrahim Kehya, though precedents, were not examples. The oftener such abuses occurred, the more they ought to be resisted." At last losing my temper at these repeated murmurings, I went hot with passion to complain to my patron. "Sir," cried I, "your Mamlukes judge me unworthy of your favours. Permit me to make them repent of their insolence – equally insulting to yourself and to your servant – or suffer me to renounce your kindness, and bid Egypt farewell."

At these words the Bey only stared full in my face, and set up a loud laugh; but perceiving that I joined not in his mirth, and continued immoveably grave, he too by degrees dropped his assumed gaiety, and in a serious tone replied, "If, Selim, you really feel desirous to leave me, go! Why should I detain your person, when I cannot prevent the estrangement of your mind? But," continued he, raising his voice until it sounded like thunder, while he darted looks fierce as lightning round the Mamluke circle, "I acknowledge not yet my slaves as my masters. Let them harmlessly sharpen with kohl,[5] the soft glances of their eyes, but let them repress the more offensive sallies of their tongues. Too soon may the voice of this presumptuous cast cease to be he heard in Cairo! Too soon may we be too happy to replenish our thinning ranks with men, not worthy to gird on the sabre of him whom these young fools abuse!"

This speech – supported by a letter from Suleiman's kehaya at Constantinople, read aloud to the by-standers, in which the agent actually complained that the slave market was empty, that the Russian she-emperor had out of mere spite made the Padi-shah,[6] renounce the living tribute yearly claimed from the Crimea; and that it was feared the whole world meant soon to be at peace – gave me some comfort, and my enemies more discretion.

My marriage being fixed, the wedding soon was announced. Meanwhile, every hour intervening seemed an age. I longed to possess a wife who, if she could not be an object of love, must be an earnest of promotion; and I was dying to have in a harem of my own, a sanctuary, where, even though my person should be proscribed, my wealth still must remain inviolate, and my dear sequins undisturbed!

All things being ready for my nuptials, the ceremony began. My bride was conducted to the bath in state, lest the world should remain in ignorance of her cleanliness. Properly steamed, stretched out and pumiced, she next went through the labours of a toilet so exquisite, that on its completion not one among her beauties remained nature's own! Several hours were employed in twisting her hair into the semblance of whipcord, in adding to the one hundred and fifty plaits which adhered to her own head, two hundred and fifty braids more, the produce of other scalps; and these were into an edifice at once so elegant and so weighty, that she could have wished for a second head, merely for common use. A pair of eyebrows sufficiently notable in themselves, were only dismissed the artificer's hands, after being shaped into two exact semicircles; and a pair of eyes, expressive enough without foreign assistance, were not deemed to possess all their requisite powers until framed in two black cases of surmeh.[7] Henna,[8] the symbol of joy, which already had been most liberally bestowed upon the epistles which communicated my marriage to my patron's numerous clients, was lavished in still greater profusion on my bride's own plump and lustrous person; and made it emulate the colour which no doubt Isis displayed, when doomed to roam through Egypt's plains in the undignified shape of a red cow. After all these pains, taken for the sake of beauty, the lady was, on the score of modesty, wrapped up in so many veils impervious to the eye, as scarce to escape suffocation; but the most celebrated awalis of the capital took care to inform the assistants in their epithalamiums, of the vastness of the charms and the splendour of the jewels, which they were not allowed to gratify their sight.

I do not know how, at the nuptial feast, with the prospect of all these attractions before me, and in the midst of all the bustle of the dance, all the din of music, and all the glare of the lights, I insensibly fell into a reverie, composed of at least as many gloomy as cheerful thoughts; – but so it was!

"Here," said my wandering mind, "am I, the youngest son of a petty Drogueman in an island of the Archipelago; I, at one time fallen so much beneath the level of my own destiny as in vain to seek the situation of a menial, become the master of a host of slaves, the son to a Bey of Egypt, and the governor of a province; – – in other words, already occupying a station far beyond what at one time my most sanguine dreams durst have promised me; and yet regarding that elevation only as a stepping stone to a station infinitely more exalted, – to that of Bey; nay, who knows – of Schaich-el-belled itself!

"But, by what a series of toils and sacrifices, and perils I may be doomed to purchase these honours, who also can tell? Alas! do I not on the very threshold of a career, strewed with as many thorns as roses, begin by yielding up my person, perhaps to an unseemly female, and my freedom, to a domestic tyrant. For well I know the conditions of marrying a patron's daughter! And what labours, what snares, what treachery may be the offspring of this splendid union, may accompany every step in the road of my advancement, I know not yet. But the die is cast: and I must wait the issue of the game!"

A shake, prolonged by the chief of the singing damsels with the most consummate skill, through every note of the gamut, until it drew forth such a pearl of taïbs or bravas as made the room shake, roused me from my unseasonable meditations; and brought back my mind to where sat my body. Presently a pretty Almé,[9] inviting me to make her tamboureen resound with the clang of my gold, threw my thoughts into a totally new channel. I now became impatient for the moment that was to disclose to my sight the partner of my future life; and in this disposition obeyed with eagerness the damsel who, delivering me from these tiresome amusements, summoned me away from the noisy hall of mirth to the silent sanctuary of Hymen. With awe and anxiety I passed its threshold, and was ushered into the presence of her, on whose qualities of person and of mind must depend so great a portion of my future fate. The mysterious veil which till then had concealed her, – face, form and all – from my inquisitive eye, fell at her feet; and I saw –

"What?" wonders perhaps the curious reader. "An angel of light, sent from the highest heavens, on purpose to make my earthly dwelling a paradise?"

"Oh no! that would have been too unreasonable an addition to my good fortune."

"An ugly little monster, then; sufficient, were this earth and heaven, to convert it into a hell? – A being calculated to stamp on each endearment all the merit of martyrdom?"

"Alas! is it then decreed that the human mind must always, from one extreme, run straight into the other? like the ball whose recoil is ever proportioned to the violence with which we see it projected! And are there not a sufficient number of individuals in the world neither handsome nor ugly!

Of my spouse at least I do not know what else could have been said with due adherence to truth. Her face was neither of a description to excite, in defiance of reason, a very extravagant passion; nor yet of a species to damp, in despite of duty, a more legitimate ardour. Like other plants kept carefully secluded from the beneficial aspect of the sun, this prisoner of the harem certainly had a sickly pallid hue. Bounded by its sable locks, her wan colourless face might aptly be compared to the moon surrounded by darkness: but then again from the midst of this unvaried expanse, her large languishing black eyes shot forth glances like lightning when it pierces the clouds; and, as virtue is its own reward, the assurances of unbounded devotion which may situation called for, tarried not to diffuse over Khadidgé's countenance some of that animation which alone seemed wanting to class her, if not with the Helenas and the Cleopatras of two thousand years ago, at least with the prettiest of the mongrel race, which at present grace the land of Egypt.

But ere, from the hour when I first beheld my spouse, the sun had completed one single, of its daily revolutions, not a doubt remained on my mind, that I had obtained, instead of a mistress, a master. I had only changed my allegiance from the father to the daughter, and from a lord's dependant, was become a lady's slave. Nor was even the general rule, applicable to whatever Mamluke married his patron's offspring, modified by the peculiar disposition of the Lady Khadidgé! Quite the reverse! Within a most delicate frame the young lady concealed a most unbending mind. The least breath of air seemed capable of annihilating her person, but no breath of man had any power to influence her will. Already in the first coyness of the bride, there lurked more of pride than of timidity; and in the subsequent altered conduct of the wife, there shone forth an exaction of dues, rather than surrender of affections. Jealousy indeed Khadidgé felt, and in all its force; but it was of that contracted sort which fears the loss of a tangible property rather than that of a mental tenure; – of that sort which in a man rests satisfied when he has locked up his wife. As Khadidgé could not, consistent with custom, in the same way lock up her husband, she took care not only to let me have no female retinue of my own, but to keep concealed from my view all the nymphs of her own suite, that might divert my feelings from their legitimate current. The instant my footsteps were heard near the gynecæum, all its inmates short of sixty used to hide themselves or fly, leaving me with my lady in awful tête-à-tête. In one instance indeed the anxiety of the attendants to obey their instructions defeated its own purpose. A young and pretty slave, unable to get away in time, took the desperate resolution of creeping under a clothes basket in the very middle of the room through which I had to pass. In the dark I fell headlong over the awkwardly placed utensil; and in my rage grasped with such violence the bundle which had caused my downfall, that, ere I recognised its nature, my ever watchful spouse found her fair slave in my arms. In vain I pleaded ignorance of what I thus had grasped. The pretty Zuleika – never more beheld – seemed to have dissolved into air.

"And Anastasius the impatient of control" me-thinks exclaims my reader, "submitted tamely to such egregious tyranny!"

Alas! already had the climate of Egypt begun to exert over my energies its enervating influence: already had I imbibed all the languor with which its watery exhalations by degrees affect foreigners: already was I, in point of listnessness and apathy, a perfect match for my indolent helpmate. While she lay all day long motionless on her sofa at one end of the house, I lay all day long, equally motionless, in my recess at the other end; and if she could scarce accomplish the labour of clapping her hands for a slave,[10] to hold a rose or jessamine up to her nose, I could hardly go through the exertion of calling an attendant, to sprinkle some fragrant essence over my beard. Hour after hour I used to sit, inaccessible to visitors, in a sort of trelliced birdcage, suspended over the kalish, puffing clouds of perfume through a pipe cooled in rose water; and deeming an anteree thin as a cobweb too heavy clothing for my delicate person.

I felt the more anxious to enjoy the moments of repose still within my reach, as I considered the days of toil to be at hand. The rumour of Ismaïl and Hassan's impending descent every day acquired new strength; and the preparations of Mourad for a southward march every day became more active. But the whole was a bubble, and it burst at last. Misunderstandings arose between the exiles in the Saïd and the Arab Schaichs on whose alliance they depended. The quarrel rose at last to such a height that the Bedoween troops already with the Beys, again retired into the desert. The expedition to Cairo therefore was given up; and with the plot fell the counter plot. On all sides affairs seemed to assume, for a season at least, an aspect more calm and serene.

Meanwhile I had secured my Kiacheflik as well as my spouse; and finding that for some time to come I was not likely to be called out on actual service, I felt it incumbent upon me to act like other governors, who annually visit their provinces, and spend a few weeks in the agreeable occupation of regulating the police and levying the contributions of their various districts. For the purpose of appearing in my government with proper éclat, I mortgaged one year's income of my estate, took an affectionate leave of my patron, sighed with my wife over the duties of my station, and set out to riot in the luxury of receiving presents, and imposing avaniahs.

CHAPTER IV

According to custom, I journeyed slowly. The tent from which I set out in the morning was, by more diligent attendants, pitched before my arrival, where I had settled to stop for the evening. Frequently during my march I assumed some disguise. Sometimes it was that of a travelling Syrian, sometimes of a Barbaresque, and sometimes of an Arab, enveloped in his abbah.[1] – Thus fearless of observation, and aloof from any suite, I amused myself in prowling about the country, and peeping into the peasants' hovels. My servants, indeed, discouraged this mode of travelling: they never ceased to express their uneasiness at their lord's thus exposing his precious person; but the more good reasons they gave for my staying with my retinue, the further I extended my rambles. I wanted to see all that passed; and if the master's eye be the best, the master's garb I knew to be the worst for making discoveries. My trouble seldom went unrewarded. In one place, the village Schaichs, mistaking me for the kiachef's caterer, offered bribes of fattened fowls, to make me swear by the Prophet to an absolute famine. In another, the town folks, honouring me with the office of the great man's steward, promised me ten paras in piastre on whatever sums I disbursed for his account; and in a third, where I passed for an entire stranger to the travelling officer, they proposed a joint concern in plundering his equipage. Here an Arab, who was abusing a fellah for preparing the service of a Mamluke to the freedom of the desert, appealed to me as to a brother Arab, for the justice of his reproach; and there a peasant, who was describing to a townsman the rapacity of the kiachef's people, referred to me as to a fellow peasant, for the truth of his assertion.

One day in my solitary rambles I met on its way to the river, a family of villagers consisting of three generations and upwards: for besides grandfather, father and sons, several of the daughters seemed burdened with more than the babes they bore on their backs. An ihram in rags, an old mat torn to pieces, and an assortment of pitchers worthy of an antiquarian's collection, were the travelling relics of the deserted home. A few head of consumptive cattle formed the van, and a worn-out plough closed the procession, and a plough all in pieces closed its rear.

"Whence come you, good people?" cried I, addressing the patriarch of the family?

"From the Feyoum," was his answer.

"And you leave the native soil, to seek the bread of strangers?"

"Soon I shall be called away, and my son will not be able to redeem his inheritance. Must he wait to be driven from the land his father tilled?"

"Whence arises your distress?"

"From God and man, in conjunction. Every year the waters of the Nile make less way in our kalish; and every year the sands of the desert creep further over our fields. Egypt's soil, instead of crops, will soon only bear corpses! Can we then fly too soon?"

"And let those that stay behind bear the burden of the absent?"

"Those we leave to-day would have left us to morrow."

"Who is your lord?"

"Even that we scarce can tell. One day it is the Sultan, in whose name we are taxed; another the Beys, who are employed to tax us, or the delegates of those Beys, throughout all their numberless subdivisions and stages; another the Multezim or owner, who accounts with the Beys; another the Arab Schaich, who rents the land of the owner. All call themselves our masters, while we can pay them tribute; all deny their being so, when we want their protection!"

My retinue now came in sight, "Hark ye," added I therefore in haste, "servants should not betray servants; but here come the masters. Take this,therefore, and go;" and hereupon I gave the party to the amount of a piastre; begging they might not huzza, lest the lord should heart the noise.

Scarce had I, at the ensuing halting place, sat down to my welcome supper, when in burst a fellah, dragging by the sleeve another of the same class. "This rogue," said the first, "is the man who last year stole your lordship's mare." Of course the heavy charge was most solemnly denied; but not minding what I considered as a thing of course, "Scoundrel," said I to the accused, "had you been content at least with only taking my black mare! but to rob me of my white one!" "The white one!" exclaimed the man! "As Allah is my witness, I never once came near her!" "No more you did," was my reply "for there she stands: but the black one you stole I find, and for her you shall swing!"

I was still exulting in my ingenuity on this occasion, when, passing by a Latin hospice on the outskirts of the town, my ear was assailed by the most piteous groans; and looking through a latticed window, I discerned their cause in the shape of a flagellation, which a lusty friar was inflicting with his knotty girdle, not on his own sturdy back, but on the much less powerful shoulders of a little yellow Coobd, whom he forcibly held down, before him. Doubting the efficacy of this mode of instilling a doctrine, I interposed, and inquired of the missionary the reason of this paternal correction.

"While we distributed rice," replied the friar, "this fellow chose to become a catholic; now that supplies grow scarce, and that we hardly have enough for ourselves, he brings me back his chaplet, and cries: "no pilaf, no pope!"

The conduct of the little Coobd I certainly could not approve; but it reminded me of my own toward padre Ambrogio. I conceived a fellow-feeling for the defenceless sufferer, and released him from the clutches of his ghostly corrector. Thus it was that to my former achievements I added those of a true knight-errant, and, in my own mind, became another Antar.

Knight-errantry, however, was entirely set aside as soon as I came within the pale of my own jurisdiction; – though perhaps it might there have been asserted to the best purpose. Nothing could give me a more indifferent opinion of the condition of my vassals than the first hovel within my domain which I entered. In the mud of the doorway lay weltering – affected in various degrees with the rheum that was to end in total blindness – five or six bloated brats, quite naked, and fighting for a bit of mouldy millet cake, the size of my little finger. Further on in the cabin sat over a heap of buffalo's dung, and quite enveloped in its offensive smoke, a female spectre, mother of these gaunt abortions, who, on seeing a stranger, tore the only rag from off her body, to cover with it her face; and at the most distant extremity of the hovel, stood the head of the dismal family, burying the bag of rice intended for its support in the earth that formed the floor. One more spade full, thrown over the store, would have completed its concealment when I made my appearance. At this awful sight, the spade dropped out of the peasant's hands; and the rag he called his turban, rose a full inch from his head.

"Be composed, my friend," cried I, "it is not the enemy that is coming, it is your own governor."

"Alas!" replied the man, "will not the kiachef devour my rice – and can the Bedoween do more? But since you have seen the heap, take half, and mention not the other, or we must all perish!"

"Come," rejoined I, "for once keep the whole; but when my writer calls for my tribute, remember I know your hiding place, and think not your honour engaged to let yourself be cut in stripes before you pay the rent you owe!"

At the words I departed, leaving the fellah motionless with astonishment at having seen his kiachef, without paying for the sight.

"And this, then," thought I, "is the land which its infatuated natives boast to be the finest on the earth; where they would rather die of want, than live in plenty elsewhere. That it has a hidden charm, I needs must believe, since all obey its attraction; but where it lies, I cannot yet discover. I am now in the very heart of that Feyoom so famous for its roses, and all that yet has struck my senses is the smell of its cow-dung!"

Arrived at the place of my residence, I immediately set about receiving with all proper dignity the homage and the presents of my subjects. My writer took special care that none of my vassals should have to complain of my forgetfulness. To each he sent a summons to welcome their lord; and his invitations were addressed not only to the aboriginal and stationary cultivators of the soil, but also to the Arab Schaichs, who occasionally here and there rented a district. The liberality of these latter on this occasion exhibited various shades of difference. The first of my Bedawee[2] tenants who attended my summons, gave me, over and above the tribute due, two camels, a dromedary, and fifty fat sheep, with fleeces white as snow. "This begins well," thought I. The second produced for my acceptance a present of a different hue: – two jolly Abyssinian damsels of the most complying temper: observing "that even ivory looked insipid, unless contrasted with ebony." The third only presented his landlord with a lean steed; but then he was of noble blood, and his pedigree so long that it would have reached to Cairo. "Even this is not much amiss," said I to myself. A fourth Arab chief now made his appearance, who gave me not a single para beyond the stipulated rent; and to him I only grew somewhat reconciled, when there came a fifth, who raised such a commotion, that I would willingly have remitted all he owed me with a handsome consideration on my side into the bargain, to see a hundred leagues of imperviable desert separate our respective jurisdictions.

I had left the lady Khadidgé my wife fully occupied in collecting every species of amulet and charm, and recommending herself to the efficacy of every form of devout orison and practice, in vogue either among Mussulmen or Christians, for the purpose of seeing her waist lose on my return its perverse slimness: but, except on the score of progeny, felt with respect to my spouse in the most happy security, when unexpectedly an express arrived from Cairo, with the sad tidings that she had not only been seized with a sudden illness, but was actually considered as in very great danger. As, however, the sapient Moslemin Esculapius, called in on the occasion, had decided upon the case without seeing the patient, on the mere evidence of a bit of silk thread tied round her wrist, I chose not implicitly to trust to his report, and immediately set off myself with all speed for the capital; – resolved that some Frank physician should, if possible, cure my wife, even at the risk of seeing her; and only puzzled how to bring about so desperate a measure!

Alas! It was written that I myself should behold her no more! Just before the last stage of my journey, the breath of life had left her for ever! My speed only brought me home in time to hear the dismal howlings that were raised on my youthful helpmate's decease. At my first alighting in the court yard of the house of mourning, a fresh peal of woolliah-woes louder than any former, went forth from every window, by way of appropriate greeting; and, without much preparation, gave me the first notice of my heavy loss. I was next dragged by force of arms to the place where lay an insensible corpse, she whom my last parting look had left elate in all the pride of youth, of health and of power. Dazzling tissues hung suspended from the bier, plates of gold encircled the coffin, and flowers of every hue filled the air with their fragrance, embowered the glittering chest, as if to mock, or to render more dismal by their gaudiness, the foul corruption at work within. "O Khadidgé," cried I, at the appalling sight, "too soon has thy tale been told: too soon hast thou glided by like a noonday shadow; too soon has the rough wind of death swept away the just expanding blossom of thy existence!" and was hereupon going to perform some demonstration of respectful regret: – but already the attendants had begun to chide me, that I thus rudely kept the black and blue angels of the tomb waiting for their new guest. I therefore let the funeral proceed without further interruption, lest Azrail and his host should render me accountable for the delay.

My myrtles now faded – my only remaining shade now depending on the mournful cypress, I went and deposited my grief at Suleiman's feet. A good deal afflicted himself, he yet preserved his wonted placidity of manner, and assured me that his sentiments in my behalf would ever remain unchanged. I thanked him for saying so; but felt that I had lost the surest pledge to his favour, and was tempted to apply the Greek saying: "Welcome this misfortune, so it come but single!"

A Mamluke seldom finds much leisure for mourning. Scarce had I composed myself for the purpose, when my retirement was invaded by a rumour that the expedition against the Beys of Upper Egypt, a few months before unexpectedly abandoned, had been as unexpectedly resumed. It soon was followed by a strange report that Maurad had actually set out on his march for Es-souan. This event would only have afforded us a subject for rejoicing, had not the Signor Mourad, – whether with the view of reserving for his own adherents all the profits of the campaign, or in the idea of leaving Ibrahim provided in his absence with sufficient means of defence, – contented himself with only taking on this occasion his own troops, instead of all those at Cairo which belonged to his party; whence the Schaich-el-belled retained a larger force at his disposal, than was desirable for the success of our plan. Still, despairing of a more favourable opportunity, we determined to put the scheme forthwith into execution; and a meeting of all the principal confederates was convened at Ayoob's palace, to determine upon the best mode of proceeding.

When it came to my turn to give my opinion, I proposed rushing at once with all our host upon the Schaich-el-belled surprising him in his palace ere any assistance could reach him from the citadel, and running every hazard in order to secure his person. No hint whatever was to be given him of the least dissatisfaction lurking in our breasts; above all, no proposal of any sort was to be made nor no step to be taken that could put the wily chief in any way upon his guard, ere this purpose was accomplished. When once fairly in our power, Ibrahim must submit to whatever terms, and grant whatever securities, we chose to prescribe.

Several of the party, and among others Suleiman my patron, felt the expediency of this decisive conduct; and supported my proposal with all their influence: but Ayoob as strenuously opposed it. He would not hear of proceeding, as he called it, to extremities with the head of the corps, till less galling measures had been tried; and when I reproached him with faint-heartedness, looked significantly, first at me, then at the further corner of the room, and at last cried out in angry tone, "that at least he never yet had fled from any place in women's clothes."

Encouraged by the sentiments of this leading personage, some of the lesser members of our party now in their turn opposed my scheme with all the resolution of cowardice; and the boldest measure which could obtain the assent of the majority, was that of marching out of Cairo, collecting all our forces in the Koobbet-el-haue, and from our camp sending Ibrahim the option of compliance with our terms, or immediate and interminable warfare. On this poor and spiritless conclusion of the meeting, Suleiman in his wrath rent his garment, I shrugged up my shoulders, and the few that had common sense, considered our affairs as lost.

According to the plan resolved upon, as soon as Mourad was supposed to be sufficiently advanced on his way to the Saïd, we bravely rushed out of the capital, pitched our camp under the city walls, and deputed Saleh, the ablest of Ayoob's Kiachefs, to lay before Ibrahim our long list of grievances. On the first blush of the business, the Schaich-el-belled appeared more frightened and more disposed to grant redress, than I durst have hoped. He seemed ready to accede to any terms; and only wanted, – he assured us, – clearly to understand what were our wishes. Those who had insisted on gentle measures now triumphed, and looked all exultation. In the course of the negotiation, it is true, their confidence in their sagacity abated a little. The first panic of the chief seemed gradually to subside: he showed symptoms of returning resolution; and contrived to make the affair drag on a long while after the expected period, ere he came to a conclusion. At length, however, he agreed to our demands; the treaty was put into writing, and emissaries went out in every direction to collect such of the Schaich-el-belled's creatures as were to be our securities. We only waited for the hostages, triumphantly to enter the city, and take possession of the government.

All at once a most appalling report spread through the camp! while we were quietly drawn up under one extremity of the city, Mourad, it was said, had with all his forces re-entered its precincts at the other. Informed on his march of our insurrection, – which perhaps its only object had been to bring about prematurely, – he had redescended the left bank of the river, crossed over at Djizeh, and resumed his post at Cairo, ere the enormous circuit of this city had permitted our receiving the least intimation of his precipitate return; and the very messenger who was to have brought us the pledges for the fulfilment of the treaty, brought the first authentic intelligence that all negotiation was at an end! "Tell my friends without the gates," were the last words addressed to this personage by Ibrahim, "that since they have taken the trouble to quit Cairo of their own accord, they have nothing to do now but to make the best of their way to Upper Egypt. Mourad, my colleague, is less enduring than I am."

We looked aghast; but followed the Schaich-el-belled's advice. Raising our camp without a moment's delay, we glided in haste behind Mount Mokhadem, and during four days marched without interruption along the back of the rugged ridge of which it forms the extremity. Then crossing its uneven width, we on the fifth morning gained the river. This, too, we passed, and soon, on its western bank, reached the town of Minieh.

Here we fixed our head quarters. Our position afforded us every convenience for what was next in our wishes to ruling at Cairo – namely, starving the capital by intercepting its supplies. To contribute to this laudable purpose as effectually as possible, I stationed my own little troop in the vicinity of Ash-Moonin, where I had opportunities of making good captures, and of manifesting a laudable impartiality. The times in truth admitted not of nice distinctions between friends and foes: besides which there lurked about me – I know not why – a pre-sentiment, that my sojourn in Egypt was drawing to a close. I therefore determined to make the most of my time while I staid. Summer insects sting sharpest in autumn, when they begin to grow weak.

Still was it my study that the little offerings of my friends should appear the sole result of their own liberality. Receiving intelligence one day that a rich Coobd of Cairo was to be on the road, I took special care to greet him on his passage. "I knew your intentions, my worthy friend," said I, "of travelling this way with all your money and jewels; and for old friendship's sake immediately scoured the country, that you might meet with no extortion." Davood was all thanks. "Set bounds to your gratitude," resumed I; "the two hundred sequins you destine me for my trouble I positively will not take. All I can consent to is to accept an hundred." Davood began to remonstrate. "No words," cried I, "but the sequins; for the robbers still are near!" So thought Davood, and paid the money.

CHAPTER V.

Hunger, they say, drives the wolf out of the forest: it certainly in the year eighty-three drove the Schaich-el-belled out of Cairo – but with a full determination to clear the banks of the Nile, of which we entirely impeded the navigation. Some surprise indeed was created by thus seeing the two leaders exchange offices and characters: for while Ibrahim sallied forth in warlike trim to attack the enemy, Mourad remained in the capital a tranquil spectator of the fray. The conclusion, however, shewed that for once Mourad had foiled Ibrahim with his own weapons. During the march of the Schaich-el-belled, his colleague negotiated so successfully with the Sultan's Pasha, that he induced the Visier to invest two of his Mamlukes – Osman Kiachef surnamed Tamboordgi, and Mohammed Kiachef called Elfi – with the rank of Beys.

This proceeding of Mourad's appeared so suspicious to Ibrahim, that he began to fear lest his colleague might be meditating the same game which he himself had played before; and having drawn him out of Cairo, might shut its gates against his re-entrance, as he had shut them against ours. He therefore change his plan, or at least seemed to do so; and made this occurrence the pretext for sparing us the battle which he probably never had intended to give. Instead of waging savage war, he proposed terms of peace. Our leaders judged it prudent to meet his advances; and in October of the same year Ibrahim reinstated our whole party in Cairo.

Mourad now in his turn sullenly marched out; but we at first heeded not much his pettishness: as it is far from a rare occurrence for the rulers of Egypt to agree most amicably upon a rupture. The apparently impending hostilities afford each party a pretence for imposing on its adherents and clients extraordinary contributions; and when the last para for the warlike preparations is paid; lo and behold! the world is gladdened with the news of a reconciliation.

On this occasion, however, Mourad protracted the shew of warfare somewhat longer than usual; and indeed acted his part with such truth of imitation, as almost to impress us with the idea of the reality: for not only he actually retired into the Saïd, but there continued with such earnestness the task which we had undertaken of destroying the supplies of the capital in their very sources, that Ibrahim at last began to think the joke too serious, and in order to appease his rival, again sent us fresh notice to quit the capital. It was unpleasant to be thus bandied to and fro; but at this juncture braving Ibrahim would have been braving the whole force in the citadel, ready to move at his command. Thus deprived of every hope of successful resistance, we agreed to obey; but only with the view of executing a scheme proposed many times and as often rejected, of coalescing in the Saïd with Ismaïl and Hassan.

I was at home when the resolution of our Beys to quit Cairo reached me. Immediately on receiving it I collected all that was most valuable in my harem, and while the beasts of burthen were loading, walked over the various apartments of my abode, as one who bestows a last look on friends he leaves for ever. "Happen what may," exclaimed I, "here I have at least enjoyed a few moments of ease and quiet, whose existence fate has no power to expunge from the records of time! Should I, while I live, enjoy no other, my mind will revert to these with a grateful recollection!" All now being ready, I joined my patron, and with the rest of our party marched out of the city.

In the full confidence that Ibrahim must make the peace offering required of him, Mourad had re-descended from the Saïd along the eastern banks of the Nile, and had returned to the vicinity of Cairo. From the heights of the Mokhadem he saw our troop wind along the plain. He had the vantage ground, and thought the moment propitious for exterminating our hostile body at a blow.

To rush down the hill with all his force, and attack us like a lion who sees an unsuspecting prey, was the work of an instant. Fortunately his superior numbers were exhausted by a long march, while our fewer men all were fresh. We therefore received the shock of the first onset without giving way, and a bloody combat immediately ensued.

As usual, the Mamlukes of each different house at first remained in close order round their chiefs; and I therefore fought next my patron, until, wounded in the shoulder, he was carried to the rear, when I acquired greater latitude of movements. spying in the thickest of the fight a son of Osman's, to whom, for many a treacherous action, I long had owed an adequate return, I took aim at him while firing his carbine, and lodged a ball in his side, which made him bite the dust. One of Elfi's hairbrained children instantly sprung forward to revenge his friend's death, and made a thrust at his slayer. I received the stroke on my yatagan, and with a well timed blow sent him too reeling out of the field. He scarce had gone fifty yards, ere he fainted and fell. Another myrmidon of Mourad's now advanced: Assad was his name. Proud of his size and strength, he deemed himself secure of victory before he fought; and in order to give greater splendour to his triumph, prefaced his assault with the most insulting language. The clash of swords soon followed; and here again mine proved the better blade. My adversary's sabre was shivered in his hand, and himself unhorsed and brought to the ground. Maddened by his previous taunts I was going to dispatch him; but he expressed such contrition and begged mercy so piteously, that I agreed, though reluctantly, to spare his worthless life. Scarce had I turned my head to call to my people, when the wretch, deliberately taking aim, fired his pistol at me. The ball grazed my cheek and only tore my turban. I now dismounted to plunge my dagger to the scoundrel's heart; but in the very act of lifting my poniard, a bullet struck my hand, and paralysed my fingers. I dropped my handjar; and Assad – with a sudden jerk tearing himself away from my Mamlukes, who already were seizing hold of the traitor, – darted afresh amid the thickest of the combat, and slunk out of sight.

In despair at this grievous disappointment, I now vaulted back into my saddle, but, from the uselessness of my left hand, was unable either to hold my reins or wield my fire arms. Soon therefore my horse, unsupported by his rider, came down completely. Thrown off and lamed by the fall, I was obliged for some time to defend myself against a Mamluke enemy with one knee to the ground. While with my yatagan I parried his unceasing blows, another of his party tried to ride over and trample me to death: but spite of his rider's urging voice and stirrup, the generous steed refused to obey, and my own horse who had got upon his legs again, now exhausted with loss of blood, fell dead by my side, and served me as a rampart. Yet still my helpless state must soon have left me at the mercy of my well-mounted adversary, had not at this juncture my own Mamlukes dashed through the adverse current, and come to my assistance. One of them struck my enemy in the loins. He fell backward in his saddle, was immediately pulled off his horse, and I raised up and mounted in his stead. I could however only hold my reins with my teeth, and guide my courser with my sword, while raging with the thirst of vengeance, I flew from rank to rank to seek the traitor Assad.

Already the falling dusk seemed to deny every act of personal animosity, and to permit a continuance only of random blows and general slaughter. My search therefore was fruitless! Ere yet, however, the closing night had dropped its sable curtain entirely over the combat, a colossal form, soaring like the spirit of evil, caught my searching eye. Instantly I threw myself down, stooped close to the ground, penetrated athwart the surrounding phalanx, and, while the haughty chief was giving a signal, struck at his face one single furious blow. A second must have wrought my own death. I therefore tarried not, but, under my horse's belly, assisted by the darkness, made my escape. At this instant a loud and long shout of terror announced to all his men that Mourad was wounded; and his hated blood drawn by me, formed the last event of the expiring battle.

Our principal apprehension had been all along lest Ibrahim, appraised of the engagement, should sally forth, and support his colleague with the troops from the citadel. Probably he wished not to render his rival's success too complete; and Mourad himself, now having had enough of fighting, no longer opposed our retreat. He entered the city, while we, gathering up our most distinguished dead, to be consigned to vulgar earth on the road, continued our march uninterruptedly all night. Suleiman, who suffered much from his wound, was carried in a litter, and I, with my hand in a sling, and my leg bandaged up, figured on a jaded hack. I regretted the richly caparisoned steed of my enemy Assad, which I one moment had regarded as mine; I still more grievously regretted the home-thrust of my dagger, which I hoped to have made his: but my successful aim at Mourad himself, the ugly gash imprinted on his rugged jaw, and the streams of blood gushing from his hateful face, though sights which I had not had leisure to enjoy in the original, were a rich treat for my imagination!

Several years had elapsed between the first combat I witnessed, and this last engagement. In both I was allowed to have shewn some valour: but how different were the sentiments which, on these different occasions, nerved my arm! In the fight against the Arnaoots, I only obeyed a vague desire to gain applause, and to vent the empty ferment of my youthful ambition. I fought the foe, as I would have hunted the beast of prey: no personal rancour gave venom to the wounds I dealt. Here, on the contrary, every feeling of personal interest, animosity and revenge directed my aim, and dwelt on my blows. After hewing down my enemy, I greedily contemplated his fall, and could almost have wished to turn my weapon round and round in his wound: my soul seemed to thirst after his blood as after a refreshing stream; and when the hot spring gushed from Mourad's own swelling veins, I could have dared death itself to riot in the crimson tide!

Just at the period when the animosity between the insurgents and the chiefs of Cairo was at its height; when both parties had sealed their enmity with their blood; when all chance of reconciliation seemed for ever at an end, arose that never-ailing healer of internal feuds, the fear of an external enemy. A report, bearing the stamp of undoubted authority, suddenly spread itself through Cairo, that Hassan was making immense preparations at Constantinople for re-instating Ismaïl. Immediately the terrified leaders sent after our fugitive troop proposals of mutual forgiveness. The bearers, entrusted with no less credentials than Mourad's own ring and chaplet, reached us the sixth day of our march, in the midst of the mountains. The sole indispensable condition of the reconciliation they offered, was a sacrifice of a few of our Beys' trustiest followers, whose spoil was wanted to feed the rapacity of their own Mamlukes. It is true, the interests of these very adherents had been the ostensible pretext of the rupture: but they were readily given up as a peace offering, when deemed the only obstacle to renewed harmony.

Among the appointments to be ceded was mine. Suleiman indeed proposed a commutation; but whether Mourad knew the author of his wound, or from whatever other cause, he would hear of no exchange. My father-in-law therefore ended like other politicians by yielding to circumstances. He declared himself unable alone to resist the importunities of all the other Beys, and I was summoned to give up my possessions. Thus were realized the effects which I apprehended from the loss of my wife.

My patron had only yielded, he said, to superior force; I thought it fair to follow his example. When therefore the storm burst forth, I gathered together my trustiest followers, and, instead of returning to Cairo, and expressing my readiness to be stripped, – as I was expected in deference to higher interests, to do, – struck across the country, passed the river, and reached my Kiacheflik. There, intrenched in the best manner I was able, I bade my antagonists take the trouble of turning me out.

During a whole mouth they seemed averse from the task, until at last I thought myself forgotten; but on the fifth week after my arrival, I received intelligence that my successor was coming. He was accompanied by a force so very superior to what I could muster, that I gave up the Kiacheflik for lost, and only resolved to make the new Kiachef pay a handsome admission fee. Collecting all my cash, jewels, and other valuables, I loaded with them half a dozen camels and dromedaries, freed my slaves, gave away my fixtures, and followed by my small troop of faithful Mamlukes, posted myself in ambush a few leagues from the town, in a place where I knew the enemy must pass. It was an elevated plain, advantageously suited for my purpose. In front rose a hillock covered with ruined koobbees[1], cactus hedges and date trees, which screened us completely, while behind lay an open country, and a kalish, with a bridge of boats and boards, which secured our retreat.

After a whole night of tedious expectation, we early in the morning heard the tramp of horsemen, and presently the enemy came in sight. By his loose and straggling order of march it was plain that he had no suspicion of our design: and soon the troop approached so near our masked battery, that we could discern the features of every individual. Heavens! how my heart bounded when in the chief, – in the stranger who came to dispossess me, – I recognized the identical Assad who had tried to take away my life, as my reward for saving his own. I immediately made a signal to my followers to leave in my own hands the soothing task of just revenge, took the best aim I was able, and fired. A general discharge instantaneously followed: but I had the inexpressible satisfaction of seeing Assad fall first, though several of his troop soon bit the dust around him. The remainder, unable to guess the force of their invisible assailants, immediately took flight, and dispersed in all directions.

Save the place which my men occupied, there was not a spot in sight where the fugitives could halt and rally. The rout of those that remained sound, therefore, enabled me to approach the wounded. Assad, though weltering in his blood, was still alive: but already the angel of death flapped his dark wings over the traitor's brow. Hearing footsteps advance, he made an effort to raise his head, probably in hopes of approaching succour: but beholding, but recognizing only me, he felt that no hopes remained, and gave a shriek of despair. Life was flowing out so fast, that I had only to stand still, – my arms folded in each other, – and with a steadfast eye to watch its departure. One instant I saw my vanquished foe, agitated by an unceasing tremor, open his eyes and dart at me a glance of impotent rage: but soon he averted them again, then gnashed his teeth, convulsively clenched his fist, and expired. I spurned the lifeless wretch with my foot.

Wishing now for nothing more, I only sought the speediest retreat, fell back in all haste, and got to the westward of the beaten track, into the boundless desert. Several of my camels were intercepted by the Arabs, and my men suffered cruelly from missing a well: but falling in soon after with the Nubian caravan, our distress was relieved, though at the expence of half my remaining treasure. At last, after performing a prodigious circuit, during which we experienced incredible hardships, we contrived to reach Es-souan, and joined the exiled Beys, Ismaïl and Hassan. Never had the insurgents, even when in most open hostility with the chiefs of Cairo, formed a common cause with the party in the Saïd. Too deeply rooted a jealousy divided the houses of Mohammed and of Aly. The first and only attempt at an union of interests was that which followed the battle of the Mokhadem, and was foiled by the reconciliation of which I became the victim. At enmity now with every party in the capital, I was well received by the Beys of upper Egypt. I confirmed to them the welcome intelligence of the Capitan-Pasha's preparations, and engaged soon to return with Ismaïl to Cairo. Meantime, apprehending that I might, in spite of appearances, be deemed a spy only upon the ex-Schaich-el-belled, I made over to him my few remaining Mamlukes, and, rid of this burthen, determined to withdraw from Egypt, until the Grand Admiral should actually be on his way. Having however still some goods and valuables, I kept my design a secret, lest my kind friends should make my property a keep-sake. After a few short rambles, to wean them by degrees from the pleasure of seeing me, I at last undertook a longer flight. On a fine star-light night, of which there is no lack near the Cataracts, accompanied only by two trusty servants mounted like myself on dromedaries, we slipped away and again plunged in the desert.

By a forced march I reached Gieneh. Its Kiachef had formerly been my friend, and what deserves to be recorded, still shewed himself my well wisher. He gave me letters for his lieutenant at Aïdab. I travelled across the sands to this seaport, by the Franks called Cosseir, and found its road full of Zaïms[2] from Djedda, freighted for Suez, but which had lost the season. One of them I engaged to carry me across the Red Sea; and bidding Egypt, with its plagues as well as its blessings, – its mud and misery, its locusts and lizards, as well as its perfumed rice and purple dates, its golden grapes and azure nileh[3], – a reluctant adieu, with heavy heart embarked.

The vessel was wretched, and the passage stormy; but after expecting to founder on every coral reef in our way, we at last providentially ran safe into Djedda harbour. On stepping, after so many perils by land and by water, on the Arab shore, I could not help exclaiming: "My native land has renounced me; the country of my adoption has cast me off: be thou, O strange soil, the wanderer's less fickle friend!"

I had left a storm gathering in Egypt, of which I since have thanked God I witnessed not the bursting. Already previous to my departure the consequence of the scarcity had begun to appear in many places: but it was only after I left the country that famine attained its full force; and such was, in spite of every expedient of human wisdom, or appeal to Divine mercy, the progressive fury of the scourge, that at last the Schaichs and other regular ministers of worship, – supposing the Deity to have become deaf to their entreaties, or incensed at their presumption, – no longer themselves ventured to implore offended Heaven, and henceforth only addressed the Almighty through the interceding voices of tender infants; in hopes that, though callous to the sufferings of corrupt man, Providence still might listen to the supplications of untainted childhood, and grant the innocent prayers of babes, what it denied to the agonizing cry of beings hardened in sin. Led by the Imams to the tops of the highest minarets, little creatures from five to ten years of age there raised to Heaven their pure hands and feeble voices; and while all the countless myriads of Cairo, collected round the foot of these lofty structures, observed a profound and mournful silence, they alone were heard to lisp from their slender summits entreaties for Divine mercy. Nor did even they continue to implore a fertility, which no longer could save the thousands of starving wretches already in the pangs of death. They only begged that a general pestilence might speedily deliver them from their lingering and painful agony: and when, from the gilded spires, throughout every district of the immense Masr, thousands of infantine voices went forth the same instant to implore the same sad boon, the whole vast population below with half extinguished voices jointly answered, "so be it!"

The humble request God in his mercy granted. The plague followed the scarcity, and the contagion completed with the famine had begun. The human form was swept away from the surface of the land, like the shadows of darkness which the dawn puts to flight. Town, and villages, and hamlets innumerable were bereft of their tenants to a man. The living became too few to bury the dead. Their own houses remained their cemeteries. Where long strings of coffins at first had issued forth, not a solitary funeral any longer appeared. Hundreds of families, who had fled from famine to Syria, were overtaken by the plague in the midst of their journey, and with their dead bodies marked their route through the desert. Egypt, smitten by the two fold visitation, almost ceased to appear inhabited; and both plagues at last disappeared, for want of further victims to slay.

CHAPTER VI.

I was near the Holy City, and had all my time at my disposal. Could it be better employed than in seizing so favourable an opportunity of acquiring the title and the prerogatives of a hadjee[1]? I therefore determined to perform in its utmost strictness, the pilgrimage imposed on all true believers; and no sooner had set foot on shore at Djedda, than I immediately proceeded on to Mekkah, where I achieved in solitude my first round of devotions at the Kaaba[2]. It is true that, as on this globe at least the holiest places are not always the most agreeable, I again returned as fast back to Djedda; but it was only to wait until the Coorban Bayram[3] should bring together at Mekkah the whole assemblage of caravans and pilgrims; when I purposed to revisit the ruby of Paradise, and to join the great body of hadjees, in the more solemn rites performed at that period under its shadow.

Even in the busier seaport of Djedda itself, it must be owned, my pursuits scarce soared above the amusements of a paltry coffee-house, where I went every morning to smoke my pipe, drink my cup of kishr[4], and play my game of chess with a famous hand from Surat; always hoping to return my adversary's infallible checkmate. These harmless pastimes were varied by a turn on the quay to see the unlading of goods and monsters from the Red Sea; and by the monotonous tales of a poor Schaich of the neighbourhood, who, for my paras, procured me, if not any very delightful waking visions, at least some very sound naps.

An accidental *rencontre* with an inhabitant of Djedda, Sidi Malek, for whom I had recovered at Cairo some property, purloined by Hassan's people on their visit to his city, promised me a little change of scene. Our first meeting was in the street. "I know," exclaimed Malek on seeing me, "that this would be a day of rejoicing! The word Allah, heard the first thing in the morning, never fails to bring good fortune! I shall not however think mine complete until you leave your okkal, and take up your abode under my roof." So easy a mode of making my friend happy I could not in conscience decline. I collected my things, and followed Malek to his habitation.

My acceptance of the Sidi's hospitalities, however, soon turned out a greater burthen than I had suspected. According to Derwish, the star gazer at Constantinople, whom I left meditating how to undermine the aqueduct, it was only the most distinguished among the heavenly bodies that troubled themselves about the fate of man: but in the opinion of Malek, every stone, beast, and plant on the surface of the earth, presumed to meddle with our destiny. Nothing animated or inanimate could be named which exerted not over our being a mysterious influence. From every occurrence, however trivial, some omen might be extracted, if one only knew the way; and that way my friend Malek was determined to find out, cost what it might. Not that, in the course of his research, he ever dreamt of looking for such connections between cause and effect, as must arise from the intrinsic nature of things, and the palpable relationships between divers objects of the creation: Such a course would have been derogatory to the dignity of his pursuit. His science only admitted what was totally out of the course of nature, and beyond the reach of human understanding. The occult virtues which Malek sought in objects, were always precisely those which common sense would never have hit upon. Every secret agency was to have in it a something savouring of a prodigy, which chance alone could disclose. Accordingly, the less foundation there appeared for a peculiar belief, the more pertinaciously Malek clung to it; and while he looked upon men of real science – astronomers, physicians, and mathematicians, – as paltry geniuses who could not penetrate beyond the surface of things, he considered astrologers, jugglers and mountebanks, as the only men of real and sublime talents. To Aristotle and Galen he would probably have given but an indifferent reception, but the most errant fortune-teller might under his roof call for whatever he pleased. His house was a sort of asylum for all decayed mountebanks. One party, out of gratitude for his kindness, recommended another: and though in other respects rather a strict Mohammedan, Sidi Malek immediately made a favourite of every dirty Jew, Gentile, or Christian, who had the least pretensions to occult knowledge. The impostor ever found a hearty welcome while he condescended to accept of the Sidi's hospitalities, and never was dismissed without a handsome viaticum. "Because weak man happens to err in one particular, can he be right in no other?" Malek used to ask; and on the strength of this truth, he believed every lie that was uttered.

While merely theoretical, these opinions might have been entertaining enough, but reduced into practice, they rendered Malek's society very irksome. His own conversation was incoherent, mysterious, and often unintelligible; and he took it much amiss when his friends wished to converse on what they understood. On the least appearance of incredulity with respect to his favorite tenets, his passion knew no bounds. Always on the watch for every chance word or gesture that might be construed into a prognostic, either good or bad, he was constantly floating between idle hopes and silly fears, and conceived the strangest predilections or the most unfounded antipathies. My nose unfortunately had a curve which promised uncommon capabilities for the occult sciences, if but properly cultivated, and Malek determined they should not lie fallow for want of any pains which he could bestow.

The Sidi's stationary oracle was a soothsayer of established repute, residing in one of the remotest suburbs of Djedda, and who seldom condescended to visit from home, but waited to be worshipped in his own cave or temple. For the sake of peace, I suffered myself to be conducted to this personage, the odour of whose fame, I was told, extended all the world over. It might be so: – and certain it is that I was nearly suffocated on entering his den. To say the truth, however, this sanctuary smelt more of things below, than of the stars above; but I had promised to introduce myself, and accordingly groped my way till I reached the inmost recesses of the unsavoury abode.

There I found the wizard seated in state on an old clothes-chest. A stuffed crocodile canopied his head; a serpent's skin of large dimensions was spread under his feet. On every part of the wall glittered potent charms and formidable spells. They had their names written over them for the information of the beholder, and hair of unborn Dives,[5] heart of maiden vipers, liver of the bird Roc[6], fat of dromedary's hunch, and bladders filled with the wind Simoom[7], were among the least rare and curious. Of the wizzard's own form and features so little was discernible, that I almost doubted whether he had any. An immense pair of spectacles filled up all the space between his cloak and his turban. These spectacles were in constant motion, like a weathercock, from left to right and from right to left, between a celestial globe robbed of half its constellations by the worms, and a Venice almanack despoiled of half its pages by the wear and tear of fingers. Before the astrologer lay expanded his table of nativities.

Opposite the master shone with a reflected light his apprentice, crouched, like a marmoset, on a low stool. This youth, with his little pair of round sparkling eyes immoveably fixed on his principal, sat watching all his gestures, and never stirred from his station, except to hand him his compasses, to turn his globe, or to pick up his spectacles, which for want of the support of a nose, came off every moment. After each of these evolutions he immediately ran back to his pedestal, and resumed his immoveable attitude until the next call for his activity. So complete a silence was maintained all the time on both sides, that one would have sworn every motion of this pantomime must have been pre-concerted.

Fearful of disturbing the influence of some planet, or confusing the calculations of some nativity, I myself remained a while silent and motionless at the entrance of the sanctuary; but finding that I might stay there till doomsday, if I waited for an invitation to advance, I at last grew impatient, marched up to the wizard, put my mouth to his ear, and roared out as loud as I could: "I suppose I am addressing the learned Schaich-Aly."

Upon this, the astrologer gave a start, like one suddenly roused from some profound meditation, turned his head slowly round, as if it moved by clockwork, and after first leisurely surveying me several times from head to foot, and again from foot to head, at last said in a snuffling but emphatic tone, drawling every word in order to make what was not short in itself longer still: "If you mean the celebrated Schaich Abou Salech, Ibn-Mohammed, Ibn-Aly el Djeddawee el Schafeï, Schaich[8] of the flowery mosque, and the cream of the astrologers of the age, who holds familiar converse with the stars, and to whom the moon herself imparts all her secrets; I am he!"

"And if you should happen to want the best beloved of the pupils of this luminary of the world, the young bud of the science of which he is the full blown pride, the nascent dawn of this meridian splendour," added from his pedestal the little marmoset – "I am he!"

"Hail," answered I, "to the full blown pride of astrology, and hail to its nascent bud! May they be pleased to inform me what I am, whence I come, whither I am going, and whether or not I may hope to recover what I have lately lost?"

"Young man," replied the wizard, "you lump together a heap of questions, each of which, singly, would take a twelvemonth to answer at length. Besides, it is not in my own person I inform people of such things. You cannot be ignorant that the voice of prophecy has ceased with the holy one of Mekkah. I am but the humble interpreter of the stars. It is true that my vast knowledge of these celestial oracles enables me to understand their language as clearly as my mother tongue; and that is what enables me to know to a tittle all that was, and is, and is to be. I therefore may forthwith, if you please, ascertain from the chance opening of the holy book, in what way the Heavenly bodies choose to be interrogated."

I agreed. The Doctor performed his ablutions, and the dawn of his meridian spleen-dour shook the dust off his gown. Thus cleansed, at least externally, he mumbled a prayer or two, and then with great solemnity opened the Koran.

"Child," said he, after having inspected the page, "the admirable and important chapter on which Providence has willed the eye of its servant to fall, treats of the balance Wézn[9]. This proves in the clearest manner – but, ere I proceed further, what do you mean to pay me?"

"Two piastres," was my answer; thinking this a handsome remuneration. Not so the wizard: the most grievous of insults could not have put him into a greater rage. "Two piastres!" exclaimed he; "why, in the quietest of times, and when a man's fortune might almost be told him blindfold, this would scarce have been an aspre each adventure; and now that the world is all turned topsy turvy, that men do not know whether they stand on their heads or their heels; now that women wage war, Kings turn philosophers, and high priests stroll about the country; now that the Grand Lama of Tibet takes a turn to Pekin, and the Pope of Rome travels post to Vienna – to offer such a fee! insolent, absurd, preposterous!"

I let the astrologer's passion cool a little first, and then resumed the negotiation. After a good deal of altercation it ended in Ibn-Mohammed, Ibn-Aly el-Schafeï undertaking to reveal my destiny in two days, for the important sum of one sequin.

At the appointed time I returned, but found not Schaich Aly, as before, in solitary mediation. He stood surrounded by a whole line of customers; and one he was abusing with such intemperance, as seemed to terrify all the rest, and make them apprehend their own fortunes would fare the worse for the incident. "Wretch!" he cried; "to apply me for charms to rid your house of vermin, as if I was in league with vipers and with scorpions! Go to the wandering Santons that ply in the cross ways, and presume not again to appear in the presence of one whom the very skies treat with reverence."

The frightened peasant retired, and the remainder received the devout and wonderful sentences, which only required being kept carefully sealed up, to procure the bearer every species of bliss.

The levee thus dispatched, the wizard turned to me. "I have completed your business," cried he, handing me a dirty scrawl. "But it has been with incredible toil. I cannot conceive what you have done to the stars. At the bare mention of your name they all began to laugh. It has cost me a whole night's labour to bring them to their senses. Instead of one sequin, I ought to have a dozen."

"Not one single aspre," replied I, glancing over the paper, and throwing it in the wizzard's face. "The beginning informs me that I shall certainly die young, provided I do not grow old, and cannot fail to marry, unless I die single; and as to the end, it has no meaning at all!"

"It has a great deal of meaning," relied the now infuriated star-gazer; – grinning like an afrite[10] – "for it means that you certainly will be hanged."

"It then also means," replied I, "that I need not pay a farthing; for, if I am not hanged, you have written a parcel of lies, undeserving of a fee; and, if I am equally to swing, whether I pay or not, I may as well save my money, and give you a drubbing into the bargain." So saying I laid on; and the young bud of science, who tried to protect his master, came in for his share of my bounty. All intercourse with the constellations now being at an end, I walked, off, threatened alternately with the justice of the stars, and with that of the Cadee.

I thought it best to tell Malek at once how I had behaved to his astrologer. He began to think less favourably of my docility, and our friendship somewhat cooled. Fortunately the season of the festivals was at hand, and I returned to Mekkah, to witness the arrival of the pilgrims.

At Cairo I had viewed the departure of the caravan from the Birket-el-hadj,[11] as a species of public rejoicing. The whole of the night which preceded the raising of the tents, the camp, resplendent with the light of millions of lamps, and re-echoing with the sound of thousands of musical instruments, seemed the special abode of mirth and pleasure; and the ensuing morning the pilgrims, fresh, gay, full of ardour, and prancing along the road, looked like a procession of the elect, going to take possession of Paradise.

Alas, how different was the appearance of this same caravan, after a long and fatiguing march across the desert, on its arrival at Mekkah! Wan, pale, worn out with fatigue and thirst, incrusted with a thick coat of dust and perspiration, they who composed it seemed scarce able to crawl to the place of their destination. The end of their journey looked like that of their earthly existence; or rather, one might have fancied their bodies already smitten by the spirit of the desert, and their ghosts come disembodied to accomplish their vow.

Among the arrivals were some of my Egyptian friends; but their sufferings had so altered them, that they were obliged to syllable their names, ere I could bring their persons to my recollection. One had almost lost his eyesight, another scarce preserved a remnant of his before slender intellect, and a third was, in consequence of constant alarms, become subject to such spasmodic movements, that he believed himself obliged to hold his head fast by the ears, lest it should turn round like a top on his body!

The holy house of Mekkah offers nearly the same difference from that of Loretto, which the Mussulman character does from that of the Franks. Every body knows the Santa Casa to be a whirligig sort of thing, which in its roving disposition, changed its abode half a dozen times before it could finally settle. The Kaaba, on the contrary, is a steady demure sort of a house, which, from the day the angels placed it where it stands, never manifested the least inclination to move. Accordingly, even Mohamed dared not meddle with its well established reputation. It firmly stood its ground in spite of his reform, and to this day remains the chief object of the worship of his followers.

Seven times I walked round the holy pile in full procession, and seven times kissed the black stone, which the Angel Gabriel brought from Paradise, (I did not enquire why) to figure in its south-west corner. I next went to the valley of Menah to renounce Satan and his works, by flinging a pebble over my left shoulder; nor did I fail to fill a pitcher with the brackish water of the well Zem-Zem, to quench the thirst of the soul. But what I prized beyond all other things were the parings of the besom that had swept the tabernacle, which I purchased from the Shereef of Mekkah,[12] to cleanse the impurities of the heart, and which, if mine were not all wiped away, failed of doing its duty.

My spiritual concerns thus attended to, I turned to my temporal affairs, and made an exchange of some of the property which I brought from Egypt, for other and more suitable articles; for be it known, that the festivals of the holy house end in a fair, held in the innumerable tents that encircle it like a girdle, and which brings together merchants and goods from the most opposite extremities of the old hemisphere – very properly making even the worship of Mammon contribute to support the temple of the Lord.

From Mekkah I proceeded with the whole body of the pilgrims to Medinah, a place somewhat less holy but infinitely more agreeable. There (still intent on deeds of holiness) I bargained for a little bit of the fringe which had adorned the Prophet's tomb; but found the unconscionable vender ask a price I scarce would have given for Mohammed's own two front teeth, kept in the holy treasury at Constantinople. Fringeless, therefore, I went on to Damascus, with the principal division of the caravan, headed by the celebrated miscreant Djezzar[13], Pasha of Acre.

No extraordinary events that year signalized the homeward journey of the Hadj:[14] for I reckon not as such the hundreds of camels that died every day of fatigue on the road, to the great annoyance of the schaich of Sardieh who furnished them, and to the great delight of his loyal subjects, who cut them up and ate them; and still less do I reckon as such the thousands of pilgrims that gave up the ghost from the same cause, to the annoyance I fear of no one but themselves; and to the unspeakable satisfaction of the conducting Pasha, to whom their property devolves.

For my own part, as I observed mortality to be, some how, rifest among the richest pilgrims, and was still possessed of some valuable luggage myself, I continued during the whole of the journey particularly careful of my health. I ate no made dishes, knowing them to be heating; and abstained from brewed beverage, as apt to attack the bowels: but preferred the simplest fare, however coarse, and drank plain water, though ever so muddy. By means of this regimen I escaped – thank God! – all the bad effects of the journey. A more difficult task than that of avoiding the consequence of the climate, was in my opinion that of eluding the overpowering attentions of the Bosniac guard[15] of the Emir Hadj. These gentlemen were paid for protecting the property of the pilgrims, and it is but doing them justice to say, they could scarcely have acted otherwise than they did, if it had been their own. A Deli-bash[16] of the Pasha's in particular, used to shew such solicitude about my equipage, that not one article of it would have escaped his vigilance, or been suffered to remain out of his box, had I not, early in the business, bethought myself of recommending to him, as more worthy his attention, the luggage of a wealthy Turkish merchant, which, infinitely heavier, assuredly much more required being lightened.

The only one of my companions whom I trusted was a Cypriote. Like myself a Greek by birth, he had like me embraced Islamism from choice: but with this difference, that love had been my motive, revenge his. He had turned Mohammedan for the sole purpose of being qualified to return to another Mohammedan, without breach of etiquette, the favour of a drubbing. No sooner was he admitted into the bosom of Islamism, than he ran to discharge the debt; and paid it with such ample interest, that his creditor was never heard to utter a single syllable of complaint. To do penance for this petulance, as he said; or rather, to withdraw from the scene of this achievement, as I believe, he undertook the pilgrimage. From Cyprus he embarked for Jaffa, from Jaffa crossed over to Suez, and at Suez took shipping with a flotilla of Hadjees bound for Djedda. "Huddled together so thick" – said he – "that we found not room to lie down, in boats so rotten that we expected to split on every coral reef, on which our ignorant sailors chose to run, I never expected to reach land again; and I do not know whether I owe my being saved from a watery grave to Mohammed or to the Virgin; as, for fear of a mistake, I addressed my prayers to both. This however I do know, that, having once got upon terra firma again, I mean – please God! – never more to trust myself on the water. I have conceived such a horror of that element, that Mohammedan, and, what is mere, Hadjee as I now am, I can scarce prevail upon myself to drink a drop of any thing but wine."

My friend Mahmood, however, was destined more justly to appreciate the comforts of travelling on dry land, when a three weeks journey across the sands of Arabia had killed off with fatigue and heat about a fourth of our caravan. Almost become transparent with loss of flesh, he now swore he would rather a thousand tines be swallowed up at once by a wave, than be mummified by inches.

On entering the Pashalik of Damascus, the scene changed completely. Each league, as we advanced, now brought some improvement in our condition. First came to meet us the supply of fresh provisions from Trabloos; next the convoy from Palestine; and when, soon after, we entered the fertile plains of Hauran, I felt as if ushered at once from the burning bowels of hell, into the flowery fields of Elysium. Indeed, on first beholding from a small eminence, after a month's wearisome march through sands almost red hot, the glassy pool of Mardin, encircled by its verdant banks, such was the fit of hydro – not phobia – but mania, which came upon me, that had I been within reach of the lovely puddle, I would have plunged into it headlong, – dress, armour and all!

The privations of a pilgrimage are not necessary to render Damascus a true Paradise. Groves of orange and apricot and plum trees inbosom its walls, limpid fountains sparkle in all its habitations; and so much did its beauties, animate and inanimate, its exquisite confectionary, and its cool sherbets delight my eye and palate, that I purposed making it my abode, until I should hear further of the High-admiral's motions. Purified by my pilgrimage, I thought I could afford to run up a new score of little peccadilloes; and though in the course of three weeks I saw the forty thousand Hadjees with whom I had entered Damascus again disappear almost to a man, I still continued without the smallest intention of stirring, until I found that I had reckoned without my host – I mean without Djezzar, the eternal Pasha.

One Friday morning, after my devotions, just as I stepped out of the mosque, my eye happened to be caught by one of those celestial beings, found in large cities, who anticipating the office of the Houris of Paradise, have no objection to cast a ray of bliss on the existence of mortal man. Unfortunately, my eagerness to pursue the rapid motion of the flitting form of brightness, made me overlook some nearer but less attractive objects, which stood in my way. Foremost among these happened to be a little man, who, walking up the steps of the mosque, just as I rushed down, was so much below my line of sight, directed straight forward, that only perceived his proximity by the violence with which I came in contact with his person, and occasioned his downfall. I should more properly have said, his fear of a downfall; since I had the address to catch him in my arms, and to twirl him round like a top, so as to break the force of the shock, and only to lay him neatly down on his seat upon the steps, without having received the smallest injury.

Great as was my hurry, I felt unable to proceed, until I had looked round, as one always does, to see whom I thus had disposed of in the least disagreeable manner I could help. I found it to be a personage dressed after the Turkish fashion indeed, but evident, in the very Christian like manner in which his Mohammedan apparel was huddled on, a Frank in disguise. In short, I had run foul of an inquisitive traveller, come to have a sly peep at a mosque, noted in the empire for being kept peculiarly sacred from the intrusion of infidels; and who certainly expected not his curiosity to meet with so providential a punishment.

I always piqued myself upon my good breeding, especially to strangers; and I felt particularly anxious to display it to one who might report of me in Franguestan. For which reason I turned back, and laying hold of the short person of the traveller in the readiest way for righting it – I lifted him up like an oil jar, and so set him on end again; at the same time reversing his position for the benefit of his curiosity, and turning his face towards the entrance of the mosque which he was come to view.

I do not know by what strange bias in his mind, to be pushed down should have appeared to him a misfortune to be born with, while to be set on his legs again was taken for an indignity, which called for every expression of the most outrageous resentment. Perhaps it was from the superiority of size and strength it implied on my part. But so it was; and instead of thanks for an act of which my hurry still increased the merit, I got nothing for my pains but abuse, the more galling, since the courtesy which caused it had made me lose sight of the object of my pursuit. It is true that in his passion, my traveller resorted for epithets to the German tongue; but I had learnt with my friends at Pera, the fundamental words of that language, and perfectly understood every term of commendation he was pleased to bestow. I therefore ran back, and, in order to undo what I had obtained so little gratitude for doing, again gently laid him down upon his seat as before, in the very place from which I had raised him; at the same time begging his pardon for my presumption in having lent my unwelcome assistance to rectify his position. A fat friar of the Latin hospice tolerated at Damascus, who accompanied the stranger through the city as Cicerone, but had prudently kept aloof while his guest made the attempt on the mosque, saw from a distance the last operation, and not knowing the cause, took it into his head that I was ill-treating his friend; upon which he ran to his rescue.

Padre Giacomo happened – from some private cause or other, connected by the damascenes with the magic art – to be in great estimation with the Pasha; and thence had the confidence to abuse me in his turn, not like the traveller, in an outlandish language, but in good Arabic, intelligible to every bystander. This materially altered the case. To be thus, in the midst of Damascus, and in the hearing of a numerous audience, publickly insulted, and that by a Capuchin, was not to be borne. "See," cried I therefore to the mob, "what it is to have an old woman for a Sultan, who grants firmans[17] to Christian dogs," (my politeness had by this time given way a little) "to come and spy disguised in our own dress the nakedness of our land; in order that their Crals[18] may know how to conquer it! But glory be to the Prophet, and down with the Yaoors!"

"Yes, down with the Yaoors; and let us go and drown them," answered the ready mob.

This proposal even exceeded my wishes. But once I had saved a Jew from a watery grave, and I thought I might have equal success with a brace of Christians. "No, no," cried I therefore; "the Arabs would think that inhospitable. Let us only disable these infidels from passing themselves off for Mussulmen, by stripping them of their mustachios and their beard. They will look as ridiculous again when shaved, as they would do merely drowned." So thought the mob. My friends consequently were taken to the nearest barber, seated, lathered, shaved, and dismissed.

But the bristles of the Capuchin's beard were fated to become thorns in my side. The Pasha took up the affair. He could neither bear to be without his friend the friar, nor to see him in his presence with a beardless chin. I very soon got hints of the unwholesomeness of the Damascus air; and of all physicians I wished least for Djezzar to be let blood by. Having picked up a good number of the country sword-blades, remarkable for their fine temper, I resolved to convert my steel into gold in the capital. There also I should be more in the way of watching the Grand Admiral's motions; and I doubted not that an ex-Kiachef, hostile to Ibrahim and Mourad, would easily obtain rank in the Sultan's army. I therefore packed up my little property, and the very evening after the warning slept at Salieh.

The next morning I proceeded with a caravan to Trabloos, and there embarked for Stambool on board a vessel from Alexandria. The cargo consists of black slaves. The richest article was a little Negro, who had been furnished with his passport for the harem by an old Coobd in the Saïd, purveyor to my patron Suleiman. Though the only one of twenty who had escaped alive, poor little blackie looked very unhappy. To consol him, I used to prognosticate his becoming some day Kislar-Aga; when he would have all the beauties of the Seraglio under his command! "Alas!" answered he, "of what use will it be to me?" "Of what use?" I replied, "Why to whip them to be sure; and so to vent your spleen!"

CHAPTER VII.

A certain number of years had now elapsed since I left Mavroyeni; and changes more potent than even those which time effects had taken place in my circumstances. I was not only from a boy become a man, but from a Greek a Mohammedan, and from a person of no note whatever, an individual who had filled no inconsiderable character in the world's varied drama. I had acted a part both in negotiation and in warfare. I no longer either thought myself an inferior to the drogueman of the Arsenal, or stood in need of his protection. It was doubtless for the latter reason that, when arrived at Constantinople, I no longer felt any hesitation to call at his door. Little acquainted, however, with the revolutions which might have happened in a place so fertile in storms as the Fanar, I thought it prudent, ere I ventured upon my visit, to collect some information respecting my old patron, lest, seeking his abode too abruptly, I should be conducted to a burying ground or a dungeon.

"Friend," answered the old messmate to whom I addressed my inquiries; "Mavroyeni is no longer to be found at the Arsenal."

"I understand," replied I – motioned with my hand, as if to say: "he is shortened by the part above the neck."

"Not yet," resumed my informer, "but in a fair way of being so. He is at present Hospodar of Valachia."

"Hospodar of Valachia!" exclaimed I, starting back at least three paces. "What! Nicholas Mavroyeni – a mere man of the Islands, a rank taooshan! – has he then at last been able to wriggle himself into the fairest of the two Greek provinces; and that, in the very teeth of every Ipsilandi, Morosi, Callimacqui and Souzzo whom the Fanar could muster to oppose his intrusion?"

"He has;" rejoined Notara. "After having been, during fifteen years and upwards, regularly threatened every day at the Terzhaneh, by the Grand Admiral, with being kicked out of office, he has only left the place of drogueman of the fleet, to step into the very highest situation which a Greek can attain in the Turkish empire; and that, without any stipulation for the purchase of the principality, without any compromise as to the length of his tenure, without any restriction or engagement as to the persons he was to promote. Fettered by no clause or limitation whatsoever, he has distanced all his rivals and swept away the whole stake single-handed."

I begged my friend to inform me how this miracle had been accomplished.

"You must remember," replied he, "that Russia never acted with more hostility towards Turkey than after the peace. But the Muscovites were governed by a man in petticoats, and we, ruled by old women in turbans. Haleel-Hamid Visier, and after him Shaheen-Aly Visier, seemed determined to abide every insult of the northern virago. At last, however, the interview between Joseph and Catherine opened the Sultan's eyes. Abd-ool-Hameed felt that his sacrifices would not preserve peace, and must diminish the chance of a successful war. He dismissed the pacific Shaheen, and looked about for a more enterprising and warlike Visier. The only one in the whole Empire that could be found to suit his views, was Youssoof, the water-carrier of Smirna, the caleondgee of the fleet, the counsellor and right hand of the Capitan-Pasha, the defender of the Boghaz against the Russians, the Moohasseel of the Morea, and finally, the supreme Visier of the Otthoman empire.

Youssoof in his turn felt the necessity of confiding the government of a province so important and so much exposed as Valachia, to none but a man of resolution and bravery. Such an one was not to be found among the merchant-princes of the Fanar; but such an one he knew his old comrade in the service of the Capitan-Pasha, Mavroyeni, to be. He therefore proposed him. In vain did all the Fanariotes for once cordially unite to prevent his nomination. In vain did they put forward their tool, Petracki, the seraff[1] of the mint. This zealous agent might spend more money to prevent an election to a principality, than ever had been wasted to obtain one: it availed nothing. Mavroyeni was invested; and when, in the act of receiving at the hands of the supreme Visier the marks of his dignity, he begged as the single favour which was wanting to complete his bliss, the head of the seraf; that boon also was granted. On going out of the audience chamber, – by way of a delicate attention – Petracki's bleeding head was made to roll at his fee.

"Mavroyeni is now gone in the fullness of his glory to take possession of his principality. Perhaps, however, what he regarded as the last testimonial of his elevation may prove the first step to his downfall. It is secretly whispered that the late Sultan Mustapha had confided several millions of piastres to Petracki for the use of his son Selim, during the reign of Abd-ool-Hameed his brother. This deposit is necessarily involved in the general fate of the seraff's confiscated property. But Selim some day must come to the throne, and he will not fail to remember the loss he sustained through Mavroyeni."

On hearing all this, my first impulse was to pay the patron of my youth a visit in his principality: but my second thoughts presented my stake in Egypt, as the one most worth following up. However, the Capitan-Pasha being as yet far from ready for his expedition, I determined, in the meantime, to indulge in the supreme pleasure of the Italians; the *far niente.*

At Chios, an intimacy had long subsisted between my father and another Greek merchant, by name Mavrocordato. His extraction was honorable: friends traced his pedigree to a younger branch of the Imperial Palaeologi: history allowed him the later and more certain honour of being related to Princes of Valachia; the first of whom, invested by the Porte, bore the same name. He was a man of most respectable character: nay, while burthened with so numerous a family, that the most rigorous parsimony could only ensure to each of its members a very moderate provision, he even enjoyed the reputation of being particularly liberal, and seemed contented, so the expenses of the twelvemonth did not exceed the comings in of the year. But – strange to tell! – no sooner had he, through a fatal contagion, lost all his children save one, in whom consequently was to centre his whole inheritance, than a total revolution took place in his conduct. The possibility of leaving this only heir extremely opulent now for the first time seizing hold of his imagination, gave it a new bias, and bred a desire for riches, before unfelt. He who, while in moderate circumstances, had been generous to a proverb, now all at once when he saw his hoard accumulate, became saving, retrenched many of the innocent luxuries in which he formerly indulged, and began to toil for the acquirement of superfluous wealth, with a devotion often before sharply censured in others by himself while only possessed of a sufficiency. Still, however, he was at no time suspected of encreasing his gains by dishonourable means, nor could he be accused of sordid avarice. He might be said to live below his income, but he ranked not among those embecile misers who, during their life-time, starve the very heir whom they destine at their death to revel in their riches. No expense was spared for the education of Spiridion; and even for the pleasures of this beloved son, Mavrocordato would often outstep his own notions of discretion.

The intimacy between Mavrocordato and my father had produced a habitual intercourse between Spiridion and myself. It could not be called friendship, it was scarce even entitled to the appellation of companionship: for there existed between us a difference of two years – a prodigious one at our age, – and sufficient to make me look upon the son of Mavrocordato as by no means fit to join in my youthful sports. Our connection might be described as composed of protectorship on my part, and of deference on that of Spiridion. I led him in my train, spoke to him in a tone of authority, and gave myself the airs of his tutor. The fag of the party when I associated with boys of my own standing, my protégé was only allowed to contribute to my pastimes, when I found myself destitute of other resource. But flattered by being admitted in any form under my auspices to the diversions of his older playmates, Spiridion asked not for more, contemplated me with sentiments of veneration, felt honoured by my commands, and executed all my high behests with a zeal and promptitude amounting to perfect devotion. To employ in my concerns any other boy but him was on my part a sign of displeasure, and to himself a subject of mortification. It was he who, whenever we went on a marauding expedition, was sent forward as a scout to explore the ground; who, when we stripped an orchard, kept watch until we had secured the booty; and who, whatever exploit we engaged in, generally paid the penalty, while we carried off the fruits. But the sufferings he earned in our service he ever bore most manfully, and his firmness in submitting to any punishment rather than betray our confidence, was truly heroic. In return, I always sustained my part as his protector; defended him against every other boy, allowed none of my comrades to assume over him the least authority, and would have made any one who, in my presence, had presumed to correct him, long remember the castigation which would have followed such an offence.

Still, however, spite of the public countenance with which I honoured Mavrocordato's son, the father would not have grieved to have seen us less together. For a time he kept us as much asunder as his own frequent intercourse with my own sire would permit: but an event took place, which, in the midst of all Mavrocordato's attempts to dissolve us, riveted our friendship more closely than ever.

I had headed a large troop of my companions in a swimming party, when one of the lesser boys, spying some way off a small boat upon the beach, set it afloat, leaped in with Spiridion, and rowed out to a considerable distance. Suddenly there arose a violent squall. The truants grew frightened, they lost their presence of mind, mismanaged the boat, and overset it. Much fatigued with a good hour's splashing in the water, I had just finished putting on my clothes, when an universal shout of terror made me raise my eyes, and see the two children struggling with the waves!

Spiridion's companion was a tolerable swimmer, and rapidly approached the beach. No one felt the least alarm for him: but Spiridion himself, who had laid hold of an oar for support, seemed on the point of sinking. Already encumbered with my clothes, I called out to my still naked companions to jump in and save my charge. "Who dares?" was all the answer I got.

Dressed as I was, I now myself plunged into the sea, swam to Spiridion, and succeeded in throwing to him one end of my sash, while I held the other fast between my teeth. Supporting the child in this way, I tried to regain the beach. It was still a good way off, when some of my comrades seeing me appear faint and overwhelmed with my load, at last took courage, and threw themselves into the water to swim to my assistance. But I had got too far unassisted to accept of their tardy succour, and resolved to achieve the task alone, or perish in the attempt. Collecting all my remaining strength, I pushed away my officious playmates, and invoking my protecting saints, strained every still obedient nerve for a final exertion. It exceeded my powers: held back by the weight of Spiridion, I felt myself going down. In this situation, was I by a perseverance which could do my friend no good, to share his untimely end? or by yielding to the suggestions of prudence, at least to save my own life? – Reason, I suppose, would have said: "Save yourself."

Luckily, the dilemma never struck me. I had resigned myself to death, when an enormous billow, which only seemed advancing to swallow us up, flung me upon a shoal just hidden by the waves, of which I had no knowledge. I found means with one arm to cling to the rock, while with the other I grasped my poor Spirro. Thus we remained above water, until a boat, which just before had put off to meet me, reached the reef, took us in, and brought us on shore.

Mavrocordato happened to walk with my father on the quay when the accident took place. Apprised of his son's danger, he had arrived in sight half frantic with terror, just as, floundering on the waves, I threw out my sash to Spiridion. He had gone through all the agonies of every subsequent crisis, until he saw us safely landed on the beach. Immediately he ran, or rather flew to the spot, and even before he noticed his child, clasped me convulsively in his arms, as the saviour both of the son and the father.

These expressions died away on my ear. Exhausted with fatigue, I had fainted, and lay half an hour bereft of all perception. But on recovering my senses I still found Mavrocordato by my side, ministering to my relief, while poor Spirro was drenching my cold features with his tears.

As soon as his father saw me sufficiently collected, he resumed his boundless thanks, only interrupting them to lay on his son a most positive injunction ever to treat me as a brother; and in the face of all around, and of heaven itself, he took a solemn engagement, strengthened by every most sacred oath, henceforth to consider me as his second child. "Happen what may, Anastasius," he cried, sobbing with emotion, "rest secure that I shall never abandon you;" and indeed, from that day, Mavrocordato seemed to have no second object of solicitude, (his son always remaining the first) except to palliate my frequent offences. Many a time he redeemed my sins with the sums he would have denied to the gratification of his own fancies; and, had he been at home when the ripening effects of my imprudent conduct made me become a voluntary exile, I might not perhaps have fled as I did from my natural parent and from my adoptive father.

Since my abandonment of home I had lost sight of Mavrocordato and his son. When I wanted assistance most at Constantinople, and might have derived the greatest benefit from the performance of their promise, Mavrocordato happened to be gone on business to Trieste or to Vienna, I did not know which; and just before I went to Chios, he had entirely quitted that island – a theatre too confined from his extending concerns – and had come to settle at Stambool.

In a capital of that description the love of riches soon begets the love of sway. Mavrocordato, who before only wished to leave his son distinguished for wealth, now aspired at beholding him eminent in rank and dignity. In short, he aimed at nothing less than seeing him some day Bey of Valachia or Moldavia; and all his endeavours now tended to forming the requisite connections at the Fanar. Unfortunately he had not the lungs which ambition requires. Accustomed to inhale the pure mountain air of Chios, he found the confined atmosphere of the capital ill agree with his health. Accordingly, while he only retained at Constantinople a small recess for business, he bought in the country, close to the beautiful village of Kandilly, the villa of a proscribed visier for his residence. It was there that, in one of my excursions, chance again threw me in the way of my adoptive father.

There were two things in this *rencontre* which surprised me, and to many will appear incredible: the first was that Mavrocordato had not toiled like a galley-slave for his son, while a boy, only to fall out with him, when grown a man; the other, that he did not consider, because nine or ten years had elapsed since I saved that son's life, the natural term of a father's gratitude as wholly expired: nor did he even think that all the promises made to a Christian must fall away on the misguided wretch becoming a Mohammedan. When indeed Mavrocordato learnt that, for reasons good or bad, I had changed my religion, he looked a little dismayed, but soon recovering: "The will of God," he cried, "be done!" and invited me not the less as cordially to his mansion as if I could publicly have pledged him in the wine of his own growing. Perhaps a person who, in my situation, could raise himself to rank, and had found means to save money, might not to a mind of Mavrocordato's prudent cast, after all, appear wholly destitute of some laudable ingredients in his disposition. At least my host received me as if he had thought so; and the very same day wrote to my father, to acquaint him with his *rencontre*, his pleasure, and his grief.

Many letters between Stambool and Chios – I suspect – are intercepted by the Tritons and the Nereids, curious to know what passes above water; but Mavrocordato's epistle was left by these submarine gossips to take its course. There even came to it as speedy an answer as the diligence of man could indite, or the breath of a favorably disposed servant of Eolus waft to its destination. My host was conjured in it, by every tie of ancient friendship, and every motive of religion, to spare no pains in recalling a stray sheep into the way of salvation. A postscript, longer by half a page than the letter, stated that, should my adjuration of my errors compel me to quit the Turkish dominions, I should find my wants provided for in whatever nearest part of Christendom I might make my abode. These assurances moved me to tears. "Blessed be my aged parent!" cried I. "When permitted by those that surround him, he still feels anxious for the welfare of his Anastasius!" "And so do your brothers," answered old Mavrocordato. "They had rather even that you should return to your faith than to your island. So they write." – At this speech a dark cloud again overcast the transient sunshine of my heart.

As to Mavrocordato, he enquired not into the motives, he only considered the merits of the request. At all times he had been religiously inclined: but he had extended the sphere of his devotion, since he had contracted that of his liberality. He gave more to God as he gave less to man; no doubt expecting the stake in Heaven to bear the higher interest. The arduous and delicate commission entrusted to his prudence, he undertook, not as a mere act of duty toward a friend, but as an effectual means of working his own eternal bliss. Had he been offered the nursing of a visier's estate, instead of the rekindling of a taooshan's extinguished faith, he could not have engaged with more zeal in the business. I believe he would have paid me to become once more a Christian, had I been in want of money: but finding that all I stood in need of was good advice, he determined not to spare it, and only considered how he might best administer most plentifully the unwelcome potion. Cunningly therefore he bethought himself of making his solicitude for my temporal concerns the means of advancing his spiritual aim; and actually offered to manage my property for me to the best advantage, free both from commission and from brokerage! The thing was in itself worth accepting, be what they might the conditions annexed to it. I left my casket in Mavrocordato's custody, empowered him to sell its contents to the greatest profit, and even accepted, at his urgent request, of an apartment under his roof.

Still he at first only ventured upon the performance of the task, to which all this was preparatory, with a very tender hand. He feared to excite my impatience of control, or my jealousy of independence, and carefully abstained from all that might savour of the tone of a pedagogue, or the authority of a parent. My well bred host contented himself with throwing out, when opportunities offered, such delicate hints and such round about insinuations as left it easy, at my pleasure either to avoid their hitting, to take off their point, or to let their whole weight fall unnoticed beside me.

At last, however, Mavrocordato began to find out that this over cautious mode of proceeding did not advance his purpose. Accordingly he resolved upon a more open and undisguised mode of attack. He now on all occasions enlarged upon the reprehensibleness of my conduct, and the danger of my evil courses; constantly represented me as standing on the very brink of perdition, and never met me, at home or abroad, without significantly shaking his head, uttering a deep groan, and inflicting upon me so vehement a lecture, that, whatever he might say, I could never think myself obliged to him for it. This new method, therefore, succeeded still worse than the former. Instead of not minding my host, I now carefully avoided his company. Though still nominally an inmate in his house at Kandilly, I was oftener to be found at the furthest end of Constantinople: and always out in the morning before he came from his office, and seldom returned at night, ere he retired to bed, it was but on very extraordinary occasions that I indulged him with the sight of his very discreet guest.

A third plan of operations was then resorted to. In the idea that the son, from less disparity of age, and greater means of watching my behaviour, might succeed in the scheme in which his father failed, Mavrocordato now committed the whole labour of my conversion to Spiridion.

This, undoubtedly, evinced a thorough confidence in the steadiness of the youth. Even spotless purity might risk, unless composed of very hard and impenetrable stuff, to contract in the office of cleansing such extreme moral foulness as mine a few unavoidable stains.

Independent even of the danger to which the purpose of the father exposed the son, perhaps the son was the person most unfit to forward the design of the father. I do not mean on the score of insufficient interest in my welfare. Far from it! – In the exuberance of life's early spring, the holy ties of friendship strike root too deeply in the soul, and entwine themselves too closely round every fibre of the heart, to be enfeebled, or broken, by later separations or storms. The intimacies of that happy epoch, as they procede, also survive all the more interested connections of a maturer age; and Spiridion's early devotion to the companion of his childhood had not only kindled up anew, but again glowed in his breast with all its former ardour. Spite of my manifold failings, he loved me at Constantinople as he had done at Chios: but the scope of his understanding, so greatly exceeding that of his father's, prevented his wishes for my weal from being exclusively directed to the single narrow point, in which centred all the views of the latter. If he more than emulated Mavrocordato in his solicitude to see me renounce my old sins, he was far from feeling equal anxiety for my adjuring my new worship.

Spiridion had received from nature an expansive mind. It had resisted all the contracting powers of a Greek education. In vain might its glance be obstructed by the opaque blinds of ignorance, its flights impeded by the leaden trammels of prejudice: it could see through the one, and soar above the other. As greater efforts were made to hem in on all sides his powerful faculties, they seemed only to derive superior strength from their concentration, and to break with greater force through their insufficient barriers. While with all his canvass spread to the breeze of the passing hour the father sailed down the muddy tide of the Fanar, the son would retire to his closet, there to imbibe long draughts of wisdom at the pure spring of philosophy: and as, where literary discourse was despised or was prohibited, men do not peruse books merely to quote sentences, he found more leisure to ruminate upon his reading, and to digest his volumes. Hence his understanding rose far above the level of his age and country: for in those days modern Greece had not yet attained that miraculous emancipation from the bondage of error and superstition, so vauntingly set forth, I am told, by the P – 's and the C – 's of the present more enlightened period; and in the more than Cimmerian darkness which surrounded him, Spiridion was almost the only person I could have named, with whom morality weighed more than dogma, and who attached greater importance to inward goodness than to outward practices.

His behaviour and his exhortations to me wore the stamp of this peculiar frame of mind. He did not indeed say in explicit terms: "Those articles of faith, those forms of worship, which affect not the heart, and influence not the conduct, are of little importance;" the deference he bore his father forbade such a speech: but, while he more faintly urged, and only in the tone of an irksome task, an ostentatious abjuration of Islamism, which might only rid the mosque of a bad Moslemin, in order to throw a worse Christian back upon the church; – while he deprecated with all his might the scandalous spectacle of a man running backward and forward between Mekkah and Jerusalem, between the Cross and the Kaaba – sometimes kneeling to the one, and sometimes prostrate before the other – while he ventured to believe that even a good Moslemin might still enter heaven, though with different credentials and at a different gate, he insisted with all the strength of his faculties and all the warmth of his heart upon those moral duties commanded by the Koran as well as the Gospel; he admitted of no mode of compounding for those actions on which depend not only our own happiness, but the good or evil condition of our fellow-creatures; he ceased not to depict with all his eloquence and to urge with all his rhetoric the beauty of rectitude and the wisdom of goodness; nay, he spoke of the charm which purity of mind and dignity of manners throw over our sublunary existence with such earnestness and such unction, as if he wished me to adopt them not from cold conviction but from positive taste, and to regard myself as sacrificing my terrestrial happiness, not in adopting but in rejecting the restraints of decorum and of principle. Whether with some real foundation for his opinion, or only from the partial medium of friendship and of gratitude through which he viewed my character, he often would say he observed in me a singular and romantic turn of mind, capable of becoming as enthusiastic in the cause of virtue as it had been unrestrained in the career of vice. He believed that the same energy and boldness which, while wasted in fostering my evil passions, had made me seek distinction in all that was profligate and base, when employed to resist their sway, might render me pre-eminent in all that was exalted and noble; and he therefore felt all that eagerness for enlisting me in the cause of moral excellence which was natural to one, who, himself totally devoted to its charms, wished to extend its empire by procuring it a powerful new champion. It is true, the prodigious change in me from the extreme of ill to the extreme of good, Spiridion rightly considered as attainable only through immense efforts; and he regarded the victory over my thus far ungovernable temper, the triumph over my hitherto exclusively cherished vices, as an achievement no less arduous than it was desirable; but that very circumstance, by rendering the success as glorious to conqueror as it was beneficial to the conquered, added a new stimulus to my friend's yearnings in my behalf. It made him feel a pride on his own account, as he felt an interest on mine, in the accomplishment of the task he had set himself. For he too was of an ambitious mind, and more desirous of success as success was more difficult.

The zeal which from the first outset in his undertaking still grew as he advanced in his labours – as the very obstacles he met with, forced him to devote his time, his attention and his powers more exclusively to his favourite purpose; as, by keeping his mind more stedfastly fixed upon, more thoroughly absorbed in this single object he weaned it more entirely from all other pursuits; as in short, by the pains already bestowed, he felt more committed not to cast them away in a pusillanimous dereliction of his plan, ere he reaped fruits worthy of his perseverance; and he toiled and toiled until at last all his other views and occupations yielded to that of my sole amendment; until he devoted to my reformation alone all the faculties of his understanding, and all the energies of his heart; until he no longer seemed placed by Providence on this globe for any other purpose but that of making me a worthy member of society; and until – almost working himself up in his honest enthusiasm, into a belief that he had been appointed by the Almighty as my guardian angel – he held himself responsible to his Creator and to his conscience for my conduct, and bound by the very gifts he possessed, to devote his whole existence to the purpose of making mine a blessing. To see me wise, to see me happy, and that, through his exertions; nay, to sacrifice, if necessary, his own repose and felicity on this globe to mine, became the only bliss Spiridion aspired to on this earth! Indeed, so fully had he identified his fate with mine or rather, so entirely had he reduced himself to the rank of a mere instrument of my salvation, – not indeed by mere faith or even devout practices, but by an entire reformation of my conduct, – that, had the irrevocable decrees of fate destined one of us only to be accepted among the host of Heaven, I verily believe he would, with all his ardour for excellence, have submitted to stoop to the bitter fruits of sin, in order that Anastasius might not be the one discarded from the realms of bliss eternal!

CHAPTER VIII.

With a temper such as mine, Spiridion was perhaps, in spite of all his zeal – and I may add, all his abilities – one of the persons worst calculated in some respects, not only to succeed in the more contracted purpose of his father, but even in his own more extended and more liberal design: not only to obtain from me a public and ostentatious return to my faith, but even a more private though more sincere relinquishment of the failings.

For in truth – up to the moment when my young friend undertook my reformation – what was I? – A being of mere instinct; a child over whom the cravings of the sense still reigned uncontrolled; and which, like all children, still acknowledged no subjection save to superior strength; still could be made to obey the voice of reason, or even to weigh the dictates of caution, by no other means than those of physical compulsion; still must as it were, have his submission to the rules of society and the requisites of the established order rendered a habit through dint of force, ere it could become an act of choice; but who, while thus still weak in intellect, wholly matured nevertheless in bodily might, nay, possessing with the mental imbecility of childhood more than the ordinary corporeal endowments of grown up man, required to find even more than the ordinary gifts of body in other surrounding individuals ere he could be awed into an external allegiance to social institutions; and though he might like other children, in some degree be allured to good by the imitative bias implanted in our natures, but like all children, was only disposed to make those the models of his conduct, who had begun by making themselves the masters of my imagination, and to take counsel where I felt a previous deference for the person of the counsellor.

And thus far, alas! such had been the example and conduct of my chief associates as only to increase my natural aversion from the shackles of civilization, and my repugnance to the mere approach of those who bore them with meekness. Gregarious, indeed, though not sociable, I loved not positively to prowl in solitary majesty through the unreclaimed wilds of nature; I felt that some species of companionship was unavoidable, even for the mere purpose of assuaging the cravings of the sense; but, like those rude tenants of the forest, not yet themselves lured into subjection by civilized man, I only loved to herd with beings wild, indocile, and unbridled; I shunned every fellow-creature already entrapped in the snares of society; and could only bear to appear linked by choice with such as, ever prone like myself to deride every symptom of order, and to despise every show of decency, were not less anxiously avoided by the sober and steady part of the community than the untamed lion or the unbroken colt. Call it effrontery, or call it bashfulness – temerity or cowardice – I only felt at ease, only thought myself safe as it were from the infection of contented slavery, with men who bade defiance to every precept of morality, and to every injunction of the law; and the more an individual shewed himself broken into a ready compliance with all the requisites of social institutions, and fearful to outstep the received manners and customs of his neighbours, the more I dreaded and avoided him on that very score as a dangerous person, a confederate in the great plot against my natural rights and liberties, and a rancorous though secret enemy, who only coaxed and caressed, in order to betray me to his associates, and to throw with more certainty the fatal noose round my neck.

Add to this that, still wholly averse from the most distant thoughts of quitting Islamism, still elate with all the pride of the turban, I shrunk from the idea of appearing guided in any degree by one not like myself of the privileged cast, and would sooner have seemed to take lesson or example from a Turkish beggar than from a Greek archon.

Now, of the qualifications which a desposition, such as that of the worthy individual here depicted in his ghostly director, who possessed fewer, and on the contrary, of the attributes which must disqualify their owner for the office of guiding a pupil of that description, who reckoned more than my friend Spiridion? Even in point of person he wanted some of the conditions most indispensable to the success of his undertaking. His figure was elegantly moulded indeed; but, far from possessing the size and strength requisite to support insolence in their possessor and to curb it in others, he was rather under-sized, and the son of Mavrocordato appeared by my side like the willow by the side of the cedar. Again: his features were in as perfect symmetry as Grecian blood could make them; but his countenance, unarmed with that look of boldness and daring which represses the brazen stare of audacity and defiance, habitually only expressed gentleness, nay even timidity: and if bursts of indignation or of rapture would sometimes change its mildness into something so lofty and commanding as to awe any mind not yet wholly impenetrable, still could the purely intellectual ray which shot from it make little impression where – as in most of my associates – all was mere unmixed matter. His manners, too, were elegant and refined: but the more they breathed that elevation and dignity calculated to charm a well educated circle, the less they partook of that coarse and vulgar *dash* necessary to please men of blunted feelings and vitiated taste. Reserved, instead of forward, he never had a chance of making the force of reason silence the force of lungs; and, too proud to be conceited, too conscious of his worth to announce his claims to notice, he was only by people who, apt themselves greatly to presume upon nothing and unable to understand a behaviour wholly different, praised – if at all – for discreet and becoming humanity.

The sombre livery of Christianity too, by rendering my friend a dark spot – almost a blemish – in the brilliant circles of Islamism, increased tenfold every difficulty of his arduous task: for while his modest exterior could not prevent me, who knew his inward excellence from fearing his watchful eye, and feeling restrained by his observing presence, it emboldened low-bred wretches to treat him with a rudeness, the pain of which I shared. Hence, though I could not but venerate Spiridion's character, I mostly felt averse to his company, and so far from meeting the advances of the too unexceptional youth, discouraged his assiduity. Sometimes, when he pressed me to make him my associate and my confident, I used only to answer jestingly, and say: "How can I possibly live with you or introduce you to those with whom I live – you, who have not one idea in common with then; whose very language seems a different idiom, as unintelligible to them as theirs is to you; who stare at every unguarded expression, shrink from every spirited proposal, and groan at every bolder frolic: who stay as the door where others walk in, remain sober while others revel in festivity, keep watch where others slumber, and have the folly to be wise where others have the wisdom to court folly!" At other times I spoke more seriously, and warned the youth in sober earnest against wasting his valuable gifts in the fruitless attempt to reform one, by long habit too deeply sunk in sin to shake off the allegiance. "How can you, Spiridion," would I ask, "with your excellent understanding, expect any good from a wretch so thoroughly broken into every species of evil, so suppled by long practice into every form of vice, so loose in all his mental hinges, so dislocated in all his moral joints, that all his inclinations turn with equal facility toward wrong as toward right? The very transcendency of your merit, – my all good, all perfect friend! – leaves you a far less chance of inoculating me with the smallest particle of righteous feeling, than might have befallen a person of inferior worth, less proudly soaring above my own level, and whom I could have met half way. You and I are too far asunder in the scale of beings, ever to come in contact together either in this world or the next." And hereupon, in order to prove my assertion by illustrations taken from facts, and to enjoy Spiridion's surprise and horror, I would commence the braggadocio of vice, and give my friend such details of my iniquity as made him raise meekly to heaven his dark expressive eyes; until, unable any longer to bear the revolting tale, he would start up, run to me, put his hand on my lips, and supplicate me to spare at least him, if not myself.

It was not long, however, before even Spiridion felt that nothing was so inimical to the success of his scheme as a forbidding fastidiousness. He therefore tried to shake off his prudery, at least in appearance, to conquer his too evident disgust at the tone and manner of my habitual associates, and to bring himself down more nearly to their level. In short, he gave up his refined pursuits and his regular habits, for the honour of holding in my esteem the same rank with a set of blustering profligates. Upon the sublime principles of seducing me to virtue, he became the patient witness of all my vices. He followed me to those temples were Aphrodite wears no veil, in order to preach to me decency; and more than once in the orgies he assisted at, he narrowly escaped being the reeling victim to his own fervour for opening my eyes to the loathsomeness of intoxication.

Even this effected not the wished-for purpose. Libertinism, as well as refinement, requires its apprenticeship. It is not the attainment of a single day, and sits as awkwardly on the wearer as fastidiousness, where – only stimulated by the lips – it flows not from the heart. Wherever Spiridion followed in my train, he failed alike to catch the spirit of the place and the tone of the company. His best attempts at extravagance only looked like demureness run mad; and if his endeavours to do as others did, and to set my gayer friends at their ease, had any effect at all, it was only that of making them, while he was by, look as stiff and constrained as himself. The moment his name was announced, every countenance fell, and every lip was sealed up. Adieu from that moment to all that lightness of heart, all that flow of spirits, without which vice itself, only pursued with the dullness of a task, loses its seductive gloss, and for want of a brilliant exterior to dazzle the eye, shews all its inward foulness. Instead of rendering my associates pleased with him, Spiridion only contrived to put them out of conceit with themselves. The genuine sons of mirth and revelry dreaded the intrusion of this false brother. Abashed at the mere sight of one to whose manners they were strangers, and to whose behaviour they had no clue, they insensibly in his company – without themselvest knowing why – lost all their assurance, and felt their air of boldness and defiance, degenerate into a subdued and humble manner. Not but that they strove to resist the novel influence. Fearful lest in his presence they should appear to have lost their wonted tone, they even talked louder than usual, were wittier, made more jests, ironically wished me joy of my new friend, and complained of his repartee, as too much for their dullness: but aside and by stealth, they frowned at me for having brought an extinguisher among their jovial troop; and I myself wished from the bottom of my heart that Spiridion had remained a complete saint, rather than have become half a sinner; for no purpose but to spoil all the sport of genuine honest rakes!

But what of all this! Be a man ever so sturdy a hater of what is good and wise, still, if fated day after day to witness in another the most unabating solicitude for his reformation, the most untiring efforts to seduce him to virtue, and these endeavours proceeding, not from interested motives, nor even from a wish to display superiority, but solely from so ardent a desire to procure a beloved object's lasting welfare, that the monitor would even with pleasure sacrifice his own happiness to that of his friend: if, above all, forced to own that the symptoms of this solicitude, never shown in intrusive advice, irksome reproof, and acrimonious censure, only appear in the keenest watchfulness, the gentlest persuasion, the most exulting looks at each instance of success, and the most evident dejection at every failure in the benevolent attempt, so as not even to leave him a pretence to feign anger and to fly from his monitor; – he must have in his composition materials still harder and more compact than mine, to remain wholly unpenetrated by so deep a devotion and so flattering a testimonial, lurking under reproof itself; and to feel no wish, however transient, that it should cost him less to reward with an amendment in his manner so deep a devotion: he will in spite of himself repay such constant sacrifices, at least by something more than cold and unprolific.

It is true, no person wont to combine cause and effect, could expect that in a vortex of unceasing dissipation, hurried on without intermission to excesses of every description, my heart, volatile by nature, and by constant friction somewhat blunted in its feelings, should return with equal intensity Spiridion's affection. My regard necessarily must have intermittences, display fits and starts, and be interrupted by intervals of forgetfulness, nay of coolness. In the pursuit of pleasure I would shun the sight of the young Greek, in the intoxication of enjoyment I would neglect his society, in the frenzy of passion I would hide myself from his view as from that of an unwelcome monitor; but still did his daily converse here and there drop a seed of tenderness and compunction in my bosom; and this seed – often unheeded at first, and resembling the corn which, in order to germinate, must for a while be screened from the rays of that sun, indispensable to its subsequent development, failed not to spring up when his immediate presence no longer obstructed the more general survey of his noble conduct and beneficent precepts. In the midst of the raillery at Spiridion's expence with which I tried to keep up the unconcern and independence of my mind, I conceived for him a real and deep rooted attachment; and, though we rarely associated together in my hours of joy, the moment I felt the least grief or disappointment – the instant the faithlessness of a mistress, the treachery of a companion, or the superciliousness of a grandee cast the least cloud over my happiness – I darted past all my ephemeral friends, to pour my feelings and my sorrows into the bosom of their sole legitimate depositary. From his lips alone I expected the balm of consolation; and though long and distant were my flights, still would I ever ultimately return to Spiridion's arms, as the stork, from the furthermost regions of the globe, returns to her wonted nest.

My growing regard for Spiridion, and my admiration of his worth, awoke in my breast the first cry of conscience, and the first risings of shame. In the presence of my friend I would sometimes repress the rashness of my temper, and regret the violence of my passions. I blushed for the vices in which I had formerly exulted. For the first time in my life I took pains to excuse my errors, and laid down plans for rooting out my ill-propensities. I went so far as actually to meditate a general reform; nor did I at any time put off the execution to a very distant period. If I carried not immediately my good intentions into effect, if inveterate habit frequently made me relapse into my evil doings, still did I no longer find in the commission that zest, that unalloyed pleasure which they used to afford me. I felt the bitterness of remorse follow the sweets of indulgence. So great was the revolution in my sentiments, that it often made me contemplate with envy the calm dignity of Spiridion's life and occupations, which before I had treated with contempt. Looking over him, when he would hurry the completion of some noble work, or lay by the pursuit of some interesting study, in compliance with my eagerness for some low or trivial pastime, I often could not help repining at the difference of our disposition. "Ah," said I, "Spiridion! why was it not my fate to be brought up like you! – In me, too, nature had implanted many a rich and varied germ. Cultivation might have made them expand into all that was useful and beautiful. Fragrant blossoms might have been grafted on my stock full of vigour and sap, luxurious fruits might have adorned my branches: but, alas! I was born in a desert, I grew up remote from the sun-shine of civilization, and I put forth only wild and fruitless boughs, distorted by ceaseless storms, and casting wide around them a drear and deadly shade!"

Nor was this all! Whenever Spiridion parted from me to go into the presence of his God, to prostrate himself before his Maker, and to listen with devout attention to the loud hymns sung in praise of his Saviour; whenever, in conjunction with all his assembled countrymen he addressed, through the mediation of holy ministers, his supplications to Heaven in the language and with the forms left him by his forefathers, and which once had been mine; whenever, in his doubts and perplexities, he derived comfort from performing the awful signs of his creed, and attending the sacred rites of his ancient religion, I panted to follow him to the place of my old worship, to kneel down by his side before the holy doors[1] of the sanctuary, and to join in his ardent and heartfelt devotions at the altar of Christ! I repined at the solace he was receiving, and of which I had deprived myself; regretted that change which only permitted me an open, a public, and a solemn approach to my Creator and my Judge in a strange house, under a spurious garb, and in a language not my own; loathed the Moslemin rites which, converting every act of devotion I panted to perform into a solemn mummery, bereft my appeal of its earnestness, my prayers of their unction, and my worship of its sanctity; and secretly vowed, – should I not be able immediately to re-enter the pale of church I had abandoned – at least some day before my death to compel the holy gates to open to my supplications, and again to admit within the dread precincts now closed against the renegade, my sighs of shame, of contrition and of penitence!

Thus did the gentle timidity of Spiridion end by making a deep impression on my obdurate heart, and resemble the frequent falling drop, which by slow degrees hollows out the hardest stone. That empire over my will, which the young Greek never would have obtained had he attempted to assume the least authority, he, by an almost unreserved submission to my own caprice, now for many an hour held undisputed.

It is however true, that the utmost actual amendment in my ways still remained prodigiously short of the quantity requisite to form a particularly valuable member of society. The effect of Spiridion's exhortations rarely went beyond good resolutions. Seldom did they ripen into actual realities; at least of such a nature as to claim peculiar praise. The occasions on which I expressed the strongest determination to become a new being, were often those on which I relapsed into some old sin with more impetuosity than ever. The very contrition, however, which followed the misdeed, was already, in one who before gloried in evil, a great step towards good; and the power in Spiridion to produce that feeling, the sign of a vast hold obtained over my wayward soul.

How great however was the toil, how constant the watching of my friend, to retain that feeble sway over my furious passions, which he had with such labour acquired! What unceasing terror he felt lest my perverse instinct should again recover its noxious preponderance over my still weak and giddy reason. How he trembled for fear of seeing me, like a young tiger half tamed, at the faintest scent of blood or glimpse of the forest, resume all my sanguinary yearnings and all my roving inclinations, break my fetters, recover my ferocity, and forfeit all the fruits of my tedious education.

And but too often still were all his sinister forebodings on the point of being realized! But too often still would I sigh at the remembrance of those days, when no monitor from within checked the freedom of my will and actions; when, if the voice of pleasure called, or the spur of instinct urged, no second thought, no extraneous consideration held me back; when above all no subsequent reflection, no dread of reproof embittered the image of the joys I had snatched from the fleeting wing of time, and had made my own beyond recalling. Often still would I say to myself – "because a little Greek, who is neither my relation nor my master, happens to owe to me his life, is he entitled to rob me of my liberty; or because his mind is by nature's own ordination so well regulated as without effort or sacrifice to pursue a steady course, must my soul, which that same nature has been pleased to render fiery, impetuous, turbulent, and without rule or measure in its motions, be, through dint of the utmost violence, forced into the same even pace?" Often, from feelings of contrition for my offences, I relapsed into feelings of indignation at the shackles imposed upon my will. I railed at Spiridion for thwarting my inclinations, and at myself, for submitting to his yoke. The influence he had gained over my mind only appeared to me an usurpation, and the restraint he put upon my passions a tyranny. The fear I felt of his reproaches, and the care I took to avoid his displeasure, no longer seemed to me aught but a wanton surrender of my rightful independence, a disgraceful prostration of my freedom, which made me weep with anguish, or rather with rage. "Is it I, is it Anastasius," I exclaimed, "who suffers the silly and minute formalities of society, like the small but numerous threads and meshes of a net, to confine every limb, and to impede every motion? Is it I who have lost all free agency, and like a puppet can only obey the pleasure of another?" And at these mortifying thoughts, shame burned in my cheek, and anger sat quivering on my lips.

I then resolved to tear asunder my slight yet heavy trammels, to assert my ancient freedom, and afresh to roam at liberty. The passions, long restrained, again broke loose with tenfold fury; and the act, intended to manifest my recovered liberty, was always some extravagance, far exceeding the most outrageous of my former follies.

My friend, on these occasions, seemed lost in despair. Breathless, except when now and then a deep sigh forced its way from the inmost of his soul – like the slow bubble, which rises from the very bottom of the seemingly motionless pool, – he hung his head in gloomy silence; while, proud of my feat, and like the steed turned loose in the meadow, I snorted, shook my mane, and looked round with fierce and taunting eye; until, after a certain time, the effervescence of my blood again subsiding, I returned to a sense of my folly, felt contrition for my excesses, and blushed at my bravado. Then again I execrated my ungovernable temper, beat in anguish my throbbing breast, convulsively grasped my friend's retiring hand, and, by confessing how little I deserved it, in the end obtained his forgiveness. Spiridion, who, the moment before, had renounced all hopes of my reform, now again began with fresh ardour to toil at his chimera.

The father's less pertinacious dream meanwhile had subsided. Spiridion still might expect some day to bring me to the path of virtue, Mavrocordato clearly saw that he was not the person destined to lead me back into that of the Greek church. He almost began to think it possible that, instead of his son's reclaiming me to Christianity, I might end by seducing his son to Mohammedanism. At any rate, he now deemed the free admittance of a personage of my description into the interior of his family, as equally injurious to the moral character of that son, and to the commercial credit of his house. He first endeavoured to intimate this new opinion to me by a studied coolness and reserve, totally different from his former warmth of manner. Unluckily, as I never had courted his favour, I heeded not the change, nor considered the caprice of the sire, as a reason for withdrawing my countenance from the unoffending son. Mavrocordato therefore was at last obliged to be more explicit.

I had one evening made myself rather conspicuous at Kandilly. The next morning, as I was sitting with Spiridion, in walked his father, who had staid from his office on purpose. He enquired very civilly after my health, hoped I had not caught cold, and then apprized me in terms polite but peremptory, that his occupations not longer permitted him to manage my property, nor his view to cultivate my society; returned me the remains of my deposit, which my frequent draughts had greatly reduced, presented me with an exquisitely penned abstract of my account, which he begged me to cast up at my leisure; recommended me to look out for a lodging more convenient for my purposes, and to drop an intimacy with his son, of use to neither; and taking his leave, wished me all manner of happiness.

However politely Mavrocordato's compliment might be turned as to the form, I could not help thinking it very rude as to the matter. His behaviour seemed to me both unfair and unhandsome. In fact, was I the one that had made the first advances to this purse-proud merchant? or had he, on the contrary, first sought of me a renewal of intimacy? – He might have left me alone if he had chosen. I asked not of him any attention; I expected not any civility: I should have been perfectly contented if the accidental meeting had ended, as it had begun, in the market-place. But to invite me to his house, to press upon me his hospitalities, to admit of no denial to his solicitations! and all this only in order that he might end the farce by turning me out of doors, which I hardly ever vouchsafed to enter: and that without the least preparation or warning! – It was what I could not brook, and what I promised myself some day to resent. Meantime, I determined not to trespass another instant on the forbearance of one so anxious to recall his bounty, and spite of all Spiridion's entreaties that I should at least stay the night, and all his endeavours to convince me that his father could not mean things as I understood them, I walked out. Nor did I, until launched into the very middle of the street, stop to consider how I was to dispose of my person and my casket. Then indeed I felt a little at a loss, and could have liked to walk in again. But this my pride forbade.

I had not ruminated half a minute before I wondered how I could have felt any embarrassment at all. Within a stone's throw of Mavrocordato lived the fittest person to succeed him as depositary of my fortune: namely his most rancorous enemy, – an Armenian, and a cashier, who hated him with all the cordiality of one whose commercial schemes had been less successful than his own. There was no species of mischief which the envious Aïdin had not attempted to do his more fortunate or more skilful neighbour. First, he had endeavoured to ruin him by representing his wealth as a mere fabrication. Unable to succeed this way, he took the contrary method, and laid snares no longer against his credit, but against his like, by accusing him of having doubled his fortune through means of the treasure of a beheaded Visier, found concealed in his garden. But he was fated to be foiled alike in the most opposite attempts. For when, in order to circumstantiate his evidence, he showed the officers of the fisc the place in the Greek's garden, where from his window he had with his own eyes seen him dig out the ponderous chests filled with gold and jewels, something more ponderous was found still unremoved; namely, such an immense and continuous stratum of solid rock, as without being great mineralogists, the very satellites of the hazné judged to have lain there undisturbed since the flood.

Now, the personage who had been at all these pains to stamp himself a rogue was the one whom I sagaciously selected for the depositary of my money; – nor shone my judgment less conspicuously in disposing of my person.

CHAPTER IX.

My worldly affairs thus prudently arranged, I attendee to my spiritual concerns; and, to compensate for not eating caviar during the Greek Lent, properly fasted during the Turkish Ramadan. Every one knows how trying that month is to the temper of the good Mohammedan. As long as the sun lingers above the horizon, he dares not refresh himself with the least morsel of food, the least drop of liquor, or even the least whiff of tobacco. His whole occupation consists in counting his beads, and in contemplating the slow moving hand of his timepiece, until the moment when the luminary of the world is pleased to release him from his abstinence, by withdrawing its irksome orb from his sight. Sufficiently disagreeable as it might appear for every purpose of salvation, when it falls in winter, the month of the Ramadan seems absolutely invented for the destruction of the Moslemin species, when the precession of the lunar months brings it round to the longest and hottest days of summer. It is then that the Christian, rising from a plenteous meal, if he has common prudence, avoids all intercourse whatever with the fasting Turk, whose devout stomach, void of all but sourness and bile, grumbles loudly over each chance-medley of the sort as over malice prepense, rises in anger at the supposed insult, and vents its acrimony in bitter invectives.

Sometimes a demure Moslemin may be seen looking anxiously round on all sides, to ascertain that he is not watched. The moment he thinks himself unobserved, he turns the corner of some of the Christian streets of Pera or Galata, and ascends the infidel hill[1]. Led on as it were by mere listlessness from one turn to another, the gentleman still advances, until perverse chance brings him just opposite a confectioner's or a pastry-cook's shop. From sheer absence of mind he indeed steps in, but he buys nothing. Allah forbid! He only from pure curiosity examines the various eatables laid out on the counter. He handles, he weighs them, he asks their names, their price, and their ingredients. What is this? What do you call that? Where does that other come from? Thus discoursing to while away time, he by little and little reaches the inner extremity of the shop; and finding himself at the entrance of the recess, in which by mere accident happens to have been set out – as if in readiness for some expected visitor – a choice collation of all than can recruit an exhausted stomach, he enters it from mere thoughtlessness, and without the least intention. Without the least intention also the pasty cook, the moment he sees his friend slunk into the dainty closet, turns upon him the key of the door, and slips into his pocket. Perhaps he even goes out on a message, and half an hour or so elapses ere he remembers his unaccountable act of forgetfulness. He however at last recollects his prisoner, who all the while would have made a furious outcry, but has abstained, lest he should unjustly be suspected of having gone in for the purpose of tasting the forbidden fruit. The Greek unlocks the door with every expression of apology and regret; the Turk walks out in high dudgeon, severely rebukes the vender of cakes, and returns home weaker with inanition than ever. But when the pastry-cook looks into his recess, to put things in order, he finds, by a wonderful piece of magic, the pies condensed into piastres, and the sugarplums transformed into sequins.

I suppose my new banker suspected me of some times dealing in this unlawful sorcery, and wished to destroy the transmutations in their very source. He disappeared with my casket. On the twentieth day of the Ramadan I found myself with a tremendous appetite, five sequins in my pocket, and not a farthing elsewhere.

Ever since my final exit from Mavrocordato's house, Spiridion had kept completely aloof from me, and I had not once seen my till then inseparable friend. That he was a dutiful son, I knew; that he would not openly fly in the face of his father's commands, I had expected; but I was not prepared to find that where his friend was concerned, he would conform to his parent's orders with such scrupulous punctuality. It mortified me; and as prompt as ever to value things only when forbidden, I now began to long for the youth's company: "After all, how preferable," thought I, "was his society to any other. What information he possessed, what knowledge he imparted! How full of resource was his mind, and of variety his conversation! How different from the empty rattle of men whose ideas never moved out of a single narrow circle, and whose efforts at jocoseness absolutely sickened with repetition. How many more acute observations on life at large he used to make, who only seemed to view its storms and whirlwinds from a narrow estuary deep inland, than those who sailed down its fullest tide. The very reflection of his own excellence cast a lustre upon those who associated with him. They felt greater self-esteem from being in his company;" – and I could not forgive myself for so wantonly forfeiting what was so valuable in itself, and so willingly bestowed!

Yet, if even prior to the loss of all I possessed I had felt too proud to seek one who shunned me, it may well be supposed that since that event I should more than ever spurn all attempts at renewing the intercourse. However great my distress might be, I would rather have thrown myself upon the generosity of an absolute stranger, than upon the kindness of a forgetful friend.

Whatever I might have imagined, such a friend the son of Mavrocordato was not born to be. Two days had scarce elapsed since the retreat of the Armenian, when, as I lay despondingly on my couch, who should I see standing beside me, like a cheering vision, but my still true Spiridion! The disappearance of the banker had soon been published, and amply commented upon, in the commercial world. My friend knew my little property to be in his hands. He had immediately enquired into my circumstances; and apprised of my ruin, had come to my relief.

His pecuniary offers he found me unwilling to accept. "Your friendship, Spiridion," cried I, "is dearer to me than ever; but away with your purse! It offends my eyes. I love you too well to become your debtor."

"Selim;" replied the son of Mavrocordato, "if what affection bestows demands a return of gratitude, believe me, it is too late to escape the irksome burthen. You are already too deeply in my debt for all the anxiety you have cost me. In the scale in which your reformation has outweighed all consideration of my own repose, in which your welfare has preponderated over all my interests and schemes in life, a handful of paltry gold is but a speck of dust – an atom devoid of weight!"

I felt the truth of this speech, bade my foolish pride be silent, and accepted the money. "This gift," exclaimed I, clasping the purse with both hands, and placing it next my heart, "will enable me to prove that your friendship has not been thrown away; that the seeds you toiled to sow, though slow to rise, have sprung up at last: their fruits will soon appear. Henceforth, Spiridion, I tear from my bosom every root of evil; henceforth I renounce all the pleasures of vice; henceforth I become a new man, thy boast, thy credit, and thy glory!"

These words, the first of the sort my friend had ever heard me utter, sounded in his ears like music from heaven. Tears of emotion started from his eyes, he embraced me with convulsive rapture. What more could he wish for? His long sought triumph was complete; and like men on the morrow of a victory which terminates a toilsome war, we had only to sit down and discuss at leisure the new plan of life, suitable to my new resolutions. Upon this we enlarged as upon a delightful dream soon to be realised, until, fearing to stay longer, Spiridion at last rose to tear himself away from me.

Evening was stealing on, and darkness beginning to let loose all the hounds of hell that shunned the light of day. It was scarce safe for Spiridion to return home without some escort. "Stay, Spirro," said I; "this once let me be permitted to accompany you. Even your father, just now, I am sure, would wish to know me by your side." Spiridion consented.

Our way lay by a coffee-house, the favourite resort of those against whom other doors were shut. On the threshold stood lounging a boy – the son of a Capidgee[2] of the Porte, – with whom I had already before once or twice had a tift. Achmet was his name, insolence his profession. His behaviour had made him the pest of the whole neighbourhood. As soon as he spied us: "What," cried he; "the old inseparables again risen from the dead! See how the hound lugs the hog by the ears!" At these insulting words I felt the blood rush in my face; rage convulsed my whole body: I grasped my handjar; but at the same instant the remembrance of my recent promise to my friend flashed across my mind; and, smothering my indignation, I silently hurried on.

Spiridion, who had turned pale with anticipation of the consequences of so grievous an insult, observed the struggle in my bosom: "Anastasius," said he, "I see all, and I thank you. But suffer me to pursue my way alone. In the land where my ancestors held the sceptre, I am become thy reproach."

"What, Spiridion," replied I "when you come to save me, I, leave you in danger! I, leave you exposed to the insult of the bigot, and the blows of the ruffian? Never!" And spite of my friend's entreaties, I continued by his side until his own door opened to afford him safety. I then pressed his hand, bade him farewell, and returned my own way.

The lateness of the hour quickened my pace. In the most lonely part of the road I overtook Achmet, likewise on his way home, and passed by the swaggering coxcomb.

His sagacity had construed into fear my preceding endurance. Accordingly, his insolence only increased. "Coward," exclaimed he, "you run too fast for me to take the pains of pursuing you. But I depute this messenger to give you my errand;" and on my looking round to see what he meant I felt a huge stone graze my ear. But for the motion of turning round my head, it must have broken my jaw.

Human patience could endure no longer. I faced the ruffian. Each lifted his hand, but my dagger went first to the heart. My antagonist fell without a groan. I paused a while, – but he had ceased to breathe! Raising the lifeless body, I threw it over a wall into an adjoining cemetery, and walked off.

No mortal had beheld the conflict: but the prior provocation had had all Kandilly for a witness. What the darkness of the night awhile concealed, the dawn of the next day could not fail to bring to light: and to no one but me would the deed be imputed. Achmet indeed was abhorred, but his parents were respected. Having, therefore, much to apprehend from the law, and little means to purchase justice, I determined not to try which would carry the day.

Still, however, before I abandoned for ever the abode and the vicinity of my friend, I determined to see him once more. By another way, I ran back to his house. For the first time since his door had been shut against me, I knocked. He recognized my hand. It was the signal I used to give when, coming in late from my evening rambles, I feared to disturb his father. He himself opened to me.

"Spiridion," said I, "but an hour ago, I pledged all I could pledge to make you witness in me an entire reform. Alas, it is no longer time! I only return so soon to bid you adieu for ever. Forget me; forget a wretch whom his ill fate pursues; and thank heaven you thus are rid of one on whom misfortune has set its mark!"

I then told him what had happened; mentioned where I meant to go; and imploring the Almighty to shower on my tender, my last, my only friend, his choicest blessings, once more pressed to my arms the companion of my childhood, and broke away.

But little time was requisite to deliver over the few articles I left behind me, into the care of my hostess, to saddle my horse, and to ride to Iskiudar.[3] There I crossed the channel, entered Constantinople just at the dawn of day, and traversing its long and still empty streets from end to end, went out again at the gate of Andrinople, across field and common gained the western road, and about the middle of the day, reached the town of Rodosto.

In this out of the way place, I thought myself safe, at least for a few hours; and feeling much fatigued, went to a kind of coffee-house, asked for a private room, and lay down on the floor to take a little rest. I had scarce began to dose, when I was suddenly roused by a loud knocking; and by a sort of rumour, immediately ensuing, of which I seemed the object.

I listened, though without getting up, and for some time could only confusedly make out enquiries on one side, and answers on the other. At last one sentence distinctly struck my ear, uttered by some one of the party within. "He is up stairs and alone:" it sufficed for my information. Nothing could be more evident than that my exploit had been discovered and my footsteps traced. The only thing now left for me to do, was to sell my devoted life as dear as possible. Already was the posse hurrying up stairs, and approaching my door. I drew my yatagan, and cried out with all my might: "Whoever enters, dies!" But such was the noise outside, that my threat remained unheard. – at least it was not heeded. The door burst open: In rushed my pursuer, and down fell my sword – upon my own Spiridion!

The sight of my friend had not been able entirely to stop my uplifted arm; but it broke the force of the blow. The weapon fell innocuous: and Spiridion, at first quite breathless, and unable to utter a syllable by degrees recovered his breath, sat down, and spoke as follows:

"You are surprised, Anastasius, to see me again: but listen. When last night, after your departure, I lay down – amazed at what had happened – to reflect upon your conduct and my duties, I persuaded myself that, among those contending in my breast, the more recent obligations contracted towards a friend ought to yield to the prior claims of a parent; and confirmed myself the more in this idea, as all my wishes leaned the other way. The struggle indeed between inclination and reason was long and fierce; but at last I began to conceive a hope that the impulse to follow you, at first almost irresistible, had been entirely conquered. In vain, however, I sought repose – in vain tried to close my eyes in sleep. My mind found no rest, and a feeling of inexpressible anguish invaded my body. While I lay, oppressed by an insufferable weight, but unable to stir and throw it off, my door gently opened, and without the least noise, a form glided in which approached my bed side. It was that of my mother – of her whom I loved, and lost the first!"

"My son," it said, looking sternly in my face, and with an air of settled melancholy, which thrilled me to the heart, "vows of gratitude are recorded by angels, and only demons blot them out. He who at this moment – breaking the solemn silence of the night – with his horse's heavy hoof shakes the ground over my head, saved thy life at the risk of his own, in days that seem forgotten. For having saved it a second time, a second time his own is threatened – not by nature, but by man. In return for his first deeds of love, my son, thy very father once made thee promise to regard him as a brother, and thou wouldest, now that their sum is doubled, leave that brother to perish as a lonely, friendless outcast!"

"Here the dread shade ceased to speak. But much as I tried to answer, I had not the power. My jaw was of stone, and my tongue cleaved to my mouth. The vision disappeared. A loud clap like thunder shook to dust my imaginary fetters. I started up, and obeyed the voice from heaven!"

Spiridion said no more. I looked at him in astonishment. "Is it you," I cried, "my friend! – you, till now so inaccessible to every form of superstition, – that canst mistake the dream of an agitated mind, or the nightmare of a suffering frame for a voice from above? Ah! ere you give way to such delusions, reflect but one moment on what may be the consequence. Consider who you are, what destines await you. Think that on you depends the happiness of an affectionate parent, and the preservation of a noble family; that for you are reserved the respect of dependants, the wealth of relations, and the honours of the world: think that I, on the contrary, am a wretch, ruined in fortune and in fame, long ago rejected by his friends and family, now renounced by his fellow citizens, and proscribed by the laws of his country; then say to yourself that between us no further society can subsist, no common interests can be maintained; that far from offering to follow my fate, it is your business to fly from my society as from a pestilence, and to avoid the contagion of my breath, which must at last involve all that remain within its reach. I myself could not allow you to barter your advantages against my wretchedness; could not permit the sufferings of my friend to encrease the sins already on my head! I myself must implore you to remember your now grieving father, and to forget for ever, the lost, the miserable Anastasius."

"Cruel friend!" replied Spiridion, "talk not to me of the world! Was I ever elate with its blandishments, or solicitous for its distinctions? My father indeed – but who more earnestly than he ever urged my prior duty to my God? Who oftener dwelt upon the paramount sacredness of the engagements contracted with Heaven? Let then the vision I beheld have been real, or have arisen only within the compass of my heated brain; still has it spoken what I must accomplish; still dare I not desert my brother. Since then heaven wills you to go, I must not stay behind. Under Hassan's banners my friend purposes afresh in Egypt to pursue the path of fame. Well! – with him I may go; with him I too may run the race of glory! We shall fight side by side. Perhaps I may some day save your life, as you once saved mine. Perhaps, vouchsafed the bliss to shed my blood for my friend, I may die on his bosom the death of the brave! Or, if Providence should guard us both, should permit both to live, – triumphant with thee, I shall with thee return; and with thine lay my laurels at my exulting father's feet! Does not Mavrocordato himself – prizing his son's elevation beyond that son's existence – destine me to those high offices, whose approach is over daggers, and whose end is the bowstring? Thus already inured to danger ere I encounter my rivals, I shall with greater confidence commence the struggle, and with greater vigour contend for the prize, sought by a father's ambition under a son's borrowed name!"

"No, Spiridion," answered I, "it shall not be! In accompanying me, thou goest not to renown; thou goest only to disgrace, perhaps to perdition. Thou assumest the appearance of my accomplice. Thou coverest with dishonour a thus far spotless name. Thanks to my conduct, I am alone in the world; I belong to no one else; I am a twig torn from its stem, that strikes no root, and bears no blossom. My existence goes for nothing in the sum of earthly things! My lonely fate involves no other destiny! The weed of my sterile existence any one may pluck up, may tear, may cast upon a dunghill, – and no loss be felt, no regret expressed, no cognizance taken of the deed, no tear, save by thee, shed over my remains, nor any flower, save by thee, planted on my lonely grave! Of what importance is it where I may wander, or what may become of me? But thou, to plunge headlong from the summit of earthly blessings into the abyss in which already I already lie prostrate; thou, to mix thy fair name with the foulness of mine – no, no, it cannot, it shall not be!"

Here the young Greek's tone and manner at once entirely changed. "Anastasius," cried he with a rage so concentrated it almost looked like calmness: "you may spurn me from your side, you may proceed without me. But mark the consequence. I return to Constantinople, I go before the judge, and in the face of the whole public I proclaim myself what I am, – the murderer of Achmet!"

It now was evident that emotion and fatigue, acting on a susceptible frame, and a mind always exalted, had produced in Spiridion that degree of excitement which rendered further opposition dangerous. I thought it best for the present to give way; bowed, and submitted.

On my first arrival at Rodosto, I had desired my horse might be sold for me, and a boat hired to continue my journey. In their excessive zeal for my service the good people of the house had parted with my steed for half his value, and had taken a boat at double the usual fare: but it was not a time to mind minute miscalculations. The boatmen were waiting, I stepped in, and Spiridion followed. Before the sun had set, the wind, in conjunction with the current, carried us out of the Boghaz into the open sea.

Just as we launched into the wide basin of the Archipelago, the sun's brilliant disk was majestically dropping behind the distant crags of Athos, whose gigantic and insulated mass, alone dimly beheld soaring above the silver wave, looked like the huge spirit of the deep, emerged from its dark caverns to survey his domain. With the last departing rays of the orb of day also died away the breeze, leaving the liquid plain as smooth as a mirror.

The monotonous sound of the oar, falling upon the waters in slow and steady cadence, now remained the only sound which broke the universal silence, and insensibly its solemn and regular return disposed me to ruminate on my portion of life already wound off.

"How whimsical a thing," thought I, "is man's immutable destiny! How variously seem contrasted its most proximate vicissitudes, and yet how intimately are linked its furthest incidents: by how many anterior minute and hidden agencies is often irresistibly produced the last and sole ostensible cause of the weightiest events! How entirely is the will that seems spontaneously to urge us on, an unavoidable offspring of circumstances wholly independent of that will, since prior to the very existence of the being whom it sways! A fair form arises in Damascus; and this form, flitting through the distant streets, and just caught by my eye as it vanishes away – this form, never before or since beheld – makes me throw down a Frank on the steps of the mosque, crop a friar's beard in a barber's shop, seek refuge from a Syrian Pasha's wrath in Constantinople's vortex, incur in protecting an old friend the insolence of a stranger, rid the world of a ruffian for threatening my own life, and again abandon Stambool to fly – God only yet knows to what remote part of this ill conditioned globe!"

"How fearfully above all blood begets blood! Had I not many years before slain a Greek under the walls of the capital, I should not have split Mamluke blood under the battlements of Cairo, nor by a recoil as distant as the first impulse, again have shed Turkish blood in Constantinople's suburbs."

"But stay; in this filiation of slaughter was I entirely passive? Had my own temper no share in the sanguinary parentage? Did not the untowardness of my own disposition give fertility to otherwise barren circumstances? If at one time I durst have owned a friend, at another could have pardoned an enemy, at a third have held in the contempt he deserved a silly coxcomb, had not the treble generation of murders been stifled in the birth, the causes that brought them forth remained childless, and the black offsprings wasted away in the vast womb of time?"

"True indeed! But that if; that indispensable condition of the more favorable alternative, – what prevented its growing into a reality? What mixed up with my temper those fiery, those combustible ingredients, always ready to explode, to drive away every suggestion of reason, and to raise my hand ere my mind could check the blow? – was it myself? Certainly not: for if, at my outset in life, the option had been given me, how gladly would I have received, instead of a bias to evil and its bitter fruits, an inclination to good and its beneficial consequences!"

"But to whom," I exclaimed inwardly, "is such an option granted? In whom does not the inclination preponderate either on the side of good or evil, only according to the examples beheld, the lessons taught, the circumstances experienced, the very constitution inherited from parents, and the elements imbibed from climate and from food, prior to the first dawn of individual volition? However prone man may be to think himself endowed with free agency, as soon as his actions correspond with his own wishes; however much he may forget that those very wishes are not free; however much he may regard his will as spontaneous, from its being often so nicely poised between agencies so numerous, so complex, so minute, so intimately connected with every most distant circumstance, that it yields irresistibly to impulses of which the precise period, and place, and boundary, and existence even cannot be definitely recognized, it is not the less true that – unpossessed of the smallest component particle of body or of intellect, of will or of knowledge, of sensation or of thought, which, if his Maker be really the sole creator, upholder, and mover of the universe, is not an emanation from, a part of that very Maker: incapable of performing the most trifling action or conceiving the most transient desire, which, if there be a single first cause of all sensible effects, does not proceed originally from the express will of that first cause alone; liable to no temptation of which the first seeds have not been sown by that first cause itself; and fraught by that first cause alone with the strength which resists, or the weakness which yields to their blandishments – man is from his first breath unto his last as wholly passive an instrument in the hands of Providence as the insentient plant, or the unorganized mineral; conforms as fully to the irresistible decrees of heaven in doing what is blamed, as in performing what is praised; becomes guilty of as flagrant an act of rebellion to his ruler in attempting to decline the task of evil as that of good set down for him; or rather – where he most fancies he rebels against, still most implicitly obeys that ceaseless ruler; and leaves heaven itself as exclusively accountable for the mischiefs of the moral world as it is for those of the mere physical creation, – for the destruction caused by conquerors and statesmen, as for the havoc produced by earthquakes, floods, hurricanes, famines, and pestilence. To eat and be eaten by each other is the business assigned us here below by our Maker himself; – and, much as I may regret the greatness of my appetite, how can I more restrain it than the wolf or the vulture?"

At this somewhat disheartening period of my reasoning, a new light flashed suddenly upon me. It struck my sublime intellect that, if Omnipotence had not merely permitted, but had itself positively ordained, on this transient globe of waiting, good to be mixed with evil, production with destruction, knowledge with error, and happiness with suffering, this ordination was only a more palpable effect of Almighty goodness than any other apparently more desirable disposition could have been: – that so far from this temporary conflict of interests and passions being decreed for the cruel purpose of punishing the man who yields to temptations which need not have assailed him, it was in reality only with the benevolent design of teaching creatures all destined for ultimate felicity, through the means of some intervening sufferings, that which a state perfect from the beginning could not have taught, – namely, the eternal difference between evil and good, ignorance and knowledge, misery and happiness: in order that they might thus, through the unceasing comparison of their opposite effects, more forcefully feel when attained the ineffable bliss of that new existence where good is to be freed from evil, and joy to reign without the alloy of pain.

But man will never be satisfied; – for even in this arrangement (liberal as it seemed upon the whole) I still perceived a clause at which to cavil. I still thought that those ill-fated wretches, selected as it were from their very birth and wholly without their consent, for the purpose of serving, through the mischiefs they were doomed to perform, and the miseries they were destined to suffer, as examples, as warnings, as foils to the rest of mankind, might have reason to complain of partiality in the decrees of Providence, at least during its present temporary dispensations; – unless indeed, as seemed fair, those unfortunate evil doers in this world, were to be made adequate amends in the next, by an additional share of rewards and of glory. But, as I was not at all sure of such a compensation being intended; as, on the contrary, I almost feared that there might still be in store for these unfortunates, even hereafter, a sort of fiery process, for the sole purpose of purifying and bringing them to the precise standard of perfection, requisite to associate with the elect by right of birth, I began to feel wroth at being myself (as I suspected) among those pitiable wretches, forced to perform all manner of mischief for the general benefit; repined at the mortifying part allotted to me on this vilely got up stage, and wholly lost what little patience I thus far had evinced in following up my cue. In short, I determined no longer to forfeit the certain for the uncertain; but immediately to throw off my compulsory character, and – whatever punishment I might incur for my disobedience, – forthwith to become a very pattern of virtue, in spite of heaven itself!

But alas! I found there is no contending with the powers above; I soon discovered that the scheme which I was meditating is more easily planned than executed. Spiridion, whom till that moment I had looked upon as my good demon, – as the angel appointed to guard me from evil, – was in reality the spirit destined to scare me from good. Perceiving the strong labour in my mind, he lost his usual caution, and, in the mistaken idea of availing himself of the propitious moment, commenced so dark a picture of my vices, ere my virtuous resolves were well matured, that my self-love – that infernal and ever watchful sprite – suddenly felt alarmed, flapped its raven wings, and took the field. At once the current of the salutary reflections, spontaneously sprung up in my breast, became totally stopped by the fear lest my companion might think me subdued by a sense of my forlorn situation. Angrily interrupting his lecture: "I agree," cried I, "to the society of a friend, not to the admonitions of a preceptor. It is unfair to get me into a small boat out at sea, in order to pursue me with lectures from which I cannot escape!"

This sally, though it made Spiridion smile, still left me ruffled; and a little after, when my friend, after spreading out our little provision, looked for a knife, I offered him my handjar, still crimsoned with Achmet's blood. He said nothing, and only turned away his head. But as he leaned over the sides of the boat, I saw big tears drop into the waves. Night, meanwhile, had stolen on, and our little silent skiff, filled with mourning, and encompassed by darkness, looked like the barge which carries to the regions of wailing the souls of the damned.

The hours of darkness passed without further discourse, but early in the morning Spiridion, thinking me more calm, ventured on what he called another appeal to my reason. The very word deprived me of what little I had left. "Appeal to my affections," exclaimed I: "bid me do one thing or leave another for the love I bear you, but talk not to me of reason. I hold the cursed gift in abhorrence. It is the source of all our errors, the mother of all our mischiefs. The brute, who has only instinct to guide him, is sure to act right: but human beings, with their miserable reason, are always acting wrong, and acting wrong through the persuasions of that reason itself. For, if they are liable to evil passions of which brutes have no conception; if they experience avarice, and ambition, and pride – those feelings most fertile in crimes and in havock among the human species, – to what do they owe this unfortunate distinction, but to the impulse of a reasoning faculty which happens to mistake its way! And if they have been able to accomplish mischief beyond what brutes could have imagined; if they have succeeded, for instance, to double on this globe, through such inventions as printing, cookery, and gunpowder, the three evils of infidelity, disease, and premature dissolution, what again have they to thank for the advantage but their inestimable reason? It is no doubt in mercy to the human species, that of all its baneful faculties, that of reason, on which it prides itself most, should have been made to develop the last, and to slumber the oftenest."

"I suppose, then," said Spiridion, "it is only for fear of appearing too reasonable, that you, who do not think yourself accountable to heaven, and, indeed, are not over nice how you act by your neighbour, yet make your neighbour pay so dearly for any injury he may attempt to do you?"

"Listen," replied I. "As to the duties between man and man; if my life or happiness depend upon the bread, or money, or jewel which happen without my consent to be in my neighbour's hands, assuredly I do not see why I should so far prefer his interests to my own, as to leave them there, if I can do better for myself. Upon the same principle I defend against my neighbours what I already have gotten; and, as I ward off impending injuries, so I retaliate injuries received, to prevent a repetition; but in all this I feel no ill humour towards my neighbour, allow him a complete reciprocity of rights against myself, and, though I should even occasionally find it necessary to kill, in order to settle whose right shall prevail, I presume not to blame, and think myself not entitled to punish."

"Indeed!" cried Spiridion archly; "and when would you, pray, first think chastisement lawful?"

"As soon," answered I, "as by an express, or even tacit, but acknowledged agreement between certain individuals, each had ceded to the rest his natural indefinite right over their persons and properties, in return for other definite concessions, at once more restricted and more advantageous; and had voluntarily submitted to certain penalties on infringing this agreement."

"Well said!" exclaimed my friend, "You have described the social compact, – the source of every law, the cement of every state; and, since you not only have acknowledged its sacredness, but subscribed to its terms, by claiming its support both as subject and as ruler, what more have you to do, but henceforth to abide, while this empire subsists, by all its stipulations?"

Here I rubbed my eyes. "Am I alive," cried I, "and awake; and do I hear a Greek, and under the yoke of the Turks, talk of a social compact, – of an agreement intended for mutual benefit, support and protection, – as of a thing actually subsisting; as of a thing that should regulate his conduct to his masters? Ah! Had I only discovered the faintest trace of any such agreement between Christianity and Islamism, and had I found, in those for whose security it was framed, the least disposition to enforce its terms, and to resist its infraction, who would have been more proud than myself of remaining a Greek, of standing by oppressed countrymen, and of maintaining the glorious struggle to the last drop of my blood! But it was because in these realms the contract, if ever it existed, had been perverted, – or rather – had been torn, rent asunder, cast away! because my countrymen, – as if fascinated by the despot's crooked cipher, – had themselves preferred implicit submission to the restoration of an obliterated text; and because, not content with themselves going quietly to slaughter, when I claimed their defence, they only bade me do likewise, that, no longer either benefited or bound by the broken engagement, I left the community from which I in vain expected support, for that from which I hoped for effectual protection, – until, equally disgusted with the brutal stupidity of the rulers, as with the servile apathy of the ruled, and seeing in every system, whether of conquered or of conquerors, equal disorganisation and ruin, I at last resolved to resume my rights of nature, and the primeval state of warfare against all worth attacking!"

Here Spiridion looked, or pretended to look as if he thought he might be among those entitled to this distinction, and would now gladly have rid me of his company if he could. *That* being impossible, he vouchsafed to answer me. "Men," he cried, "so violently enamoured of their natural liberty, or rather licence, should at once remove themselves from the pale of civil society; nor disturb those who are satisfied with what *they* disapprove."

"Spiridion," I replied, "that is easily said; but is it as easily done? Far as that society has spread its insidious snares, has it so much as left a single small spot on earth, where those yet unborn who should dislike its partial regulations, may find room to retire to the enjoyment of their birth-right? Or if there be any such asylum remaining in the wilds of Tartary or the wastes of America, has not society, at any rate, so monopolized all the means of disentangling oneself from its mazes, as to render the gaining these blissful abodes next to impossible? Must we not possess land-caravans, or vessels, licences and passports, even to fly to the loneliness of the desert, together with a strength of body and of mind, of which the social institutions take care to deprive us, ere we suspect their dangerous power? They cut our claws, they clip our wings, and then they cry out with a smile of derision: "poor pinioned eagle, fly if thou list!" The man who is not wealthy can only escape from society through the gates of death. Nor does he every where, I am told, dare to approach even these bodily and honestly. He must, in some countries, smuggle himself out of the world by stealth, and embark for his journey under false colours, lest his body be made accountable for the roving disposition of his soul!"

In this sort of conversation did we while away our time in the boat. I knew that some of my arguments could not bear minute scrutiny; but I felt less solicitous to seek the shortest road to truth, as it must abridge our discussions, and leave us to all the irksomeness of a passage, which grew more tedious in proportion as our sentiments became less discordant.

CHAPTER X.

After a coasting voyage of three or four days, some ominous appearances in the sky made us veer about, and enter that most beautiful of harbours Port Caloné, on the island of Mitylene, where the olive tree, growing almost out of the sea, again dips its pendant boughs in the briny tide which laves its knotty roots. "Had it not been written," exclaimed I, as we stepped ashore, "that this brain of mine should be stewing under a huge turban, instead of freely venting its superfluous heat from under a slight skull cap, what a fine opportunity there would now be, midway as we are between the three hundred rich friars of Nea-Moni,[1] and the three thousand poor friars of Agios-Oros, to turn thrifty myself, and exchange the thoughtless prodigality of the sinner, who stakes eternal happiness against a few years of jollity, for the calculating conduct of the saint, who inflicts upon himself just enough of privation and torture in this life, to purchase a perpetuity of bliss hereafter; – or again, had it been written that you should wear the turban as well as myself, how profitably we might spend our time in this boat slashing our arms and legs; in order to mix our blood, and ever after to be bound to each other both in body and soul, and sure of a companion in hell as in heaven. But I wrap my brains in muslin, and you in sheep-skin; and so our souls must – whether they choose or not – after they quit this frame, go miles asunder; and while they remain in these paltry bodies, we have nothing to do – since we cannot pass our lives rowing through the Archipelago, – but to consider how we may dispose of our persons to the best advantage, or at least where we may convey them with the least inconvenience."

"All this," said Spiridion, "I suppose you are already fully determined upon in your own mind."

"I am;" was my reply; – "but still I want your advice. You must know that in my humble opinion this eternal Capitan-Pasha, whom I am for ever talking of and waiting for, may be longer going to his new harvest-field, than my poor old father to his last home; and therefore, as we are approaching my native island, and the attraction begins to operate, I should like, wind and weather serving, with so many sins on my head and so many enemies at my heels, to crave my sire's last forgiveness and blessing. It would lighten my burthen, and strengthen my soul, which sickens and wants such a cordial."

My motives for visiting the *fior di levante*[2] silenced all Spiridion's objections to going where he himself still had so many connections. We agreed to cross the mountains which separated us from the town of Mitylene, and there to hire a swifter vessel for the remainder of our journey. Like Orestes, I was to wander about from place to place, trying to expiate my guilt, while Spiridion – my Pylades, had nothing to do but to watch me, in case I went mad.

Arrived in the city and on the quay, the first figure that struck me was a person, like myself going to embark – of whose features my mind seemed to retain a faint recollection. On closer examination I found the gentleman to be an inhabitant of my native town; upon which I accosted him, and inquired the news of Chio. Eight or nine years had altered my features considerably more than his, of which the already long fixed wrinkles had only acquired a little more depth and sharpness. He therefore answered me as a stranger. His account was not the less minute; but throughout the whole narrative not a syllable was mentioned of the only thing I cared about, namely, my own family, which somehow I had expected would have figured foremost. At last, losing all patience: "And Dimitri Sotiri," said I, "what may he be doing at this time?"

"You come from distant parts, sir," answered the gentleman, smiling agreeably; "otherwise you would know that signor Sotiri has been dead this fortnight. I myself attended the funeral, and a noble one it was; – more sweetmeats consumed than at half a dozen weddings! But you turn pale, sir! Is any thing the matter with you?"

"Nothing, nothing," cried I – trying to contain myself – "but a little giddiness to which I am subject;" – and laying hold of a post for my support: – "who," resumed I, "carried the body?"

"His two sons, of course."

"There was a third."

"Aye, so there was; – and, though absent in person, present enough in name. Sotiri talked of no one else during his illness!"

"What was it he said!"

"Why, faith! that is what no body can tell. Constantine and his brother maintained it was all raving."

"Has that third brother been heard of?"

"Troth! people talk differently. Some say he is a great man, – a Bey of Egypt; others, a positive beggar at Constantinople. An acquaintance of mine, a man who seldom speaks any thing but the truth, swears he met him the other day in one of the streets of Galata, all in rags, and absolutely begging charity. My friend was going to give it in the shape of good advice, but the spark said that was not what he wanted, and turned away. As to his brothers, they report all that is bad of him. Their father never could silence their tongues; and though it is likely enough that all they say is true, yet every body cries shame to her people talk in that way of their own blood. It is what should be left to strangers. With the mischief they have made, it may be as much as his life is worth, for Signor Anastasius, or Selim, as they call him, to shew his face among us. The Turks' fingers itch to throw the first stone at him, as much as those of the Christians; although they say his is a hadjee, and has been to Mekkah. But none need fear his trying to come to Chios. I'll lay my life on it he is dead long ago!"

"No," exclaimed I, as if suddenly awaking from a deep trance, and grasping the affrighted talker by the wrist; "he is not! and since you are going to Chios, and may be glad to carry a piece of news – tell them, Anastasius still lives; tell them they soon shall see him; and tell them he comes to resent his wrongs, and to claim his rightful property!"

Spiridion, alarmed at this sally, interrupted the conversation. Taking the Chiote by the left hand, while I still held him tight by the other, he pointed to his boatmen, who were making signs of impatience at his delay. Nothing he wished for so much himself as to be gone. Disentangling his hands hastily from our grasp, he gave us an awkward half strangled salutation, and sped to his barge.

As soon as he was out of hearing: "Is this," said Spiridion, shaking his head: "the way in which a son should mourn for his father?"

I could only stammer out: "My brothers, my brothers!" – Spiridion let the first emotion pass; and when he saw me more composed, spoke as follows.

"I see, Anastasius, you still meditate some outrage; of what nature I know not, nor wish to hear. But of this I think it right to apprise you: if, impressed with a sense of all the forbearance you stand in need of yourself, you show equal lenity to your kindred; if, forgetting every injury, you only appear among them to speak words of peace; if, above all, you renounce every advantage bestowed by the partial laws of Islamism, you have my friendship for ever. But if, on the contrary, you only return to your country to insult the ashes of your father, to devour the little substance of your brothers, and to justify the disgrace stamped in your birthplace on your name, I stay here, I leave you to run your race of shame alone, and I abandon for ever all solicitude about your welfare!"

"Spiridion;" answered I, "you know that covetousness is not the vice of my hart. But do you blame just resentment; do you wish calumny to remain unpunished?"

"And are you then so irreproachable;" asked the son of Mavrocordato, "as to leave so much room for injustice in the accounts concerning you, and to render every unfavourable representation of your proceedings an unbearable calumny? – But be that as it may; promise to do what I ask, or be content to see me withdraw on the spot from the pain of witnessing your future errors, and the disgrace of sharing in your yet unborn crimes."

"I will not," replied I, "bind myself by a promise. I should appear to have taken the engagement, unmindful of its weight, and only to fulfil reluctantly an irksome task, because I had unguardedly pledged my word to perform it. I wish at least to acquire all the merit of acting right, by retaining the power of acting wrong. Only go with me as far as Chios. When there, if I should behave ill, it will then still be not too late to leave me."

"Then once more go we on!" cried my friend, in a tone half confident, half fearful; "once more be the day yours; – but beware!"

I now strewed ashes on my turban, took the gloss off my glittering vest, and put on the signs of mourning. After this we engaged another boat, and in a short time reached our destination.

There was no necessity in Chios to announce my arrival. On my very first landing I found every minor topic eclipsed by the more important subject of my speedy coming. Already had my brothers found means to stir up the whole town against me. Already was every inhabitant up in arms, to prevent the renegade from reducing his nearest kindred to beggary. So loud was the cry of defiance, that, on stepping ashore, I found it expedient to go straight to the Mekkiemé. Safe in the hall of justice, I had my brothers summoned.

Spiridion did not know what to think of my proceeding. Questioned by his anxious looks, I made him signs to be silent: but though he unclosed not his lips, it was easy to see his heart trembled between hope and fear.

For my part, without giving the least hint of my intentions, without noticing the crowd collected to survey my person and to watch my behaviour, without satisfying the curiosity or correcting the errors of the bystanders, who aloud, at my very elbow, imparted to each other their surmises, I stood haughty, unmoved and silent, waiting the appearance of my worthy pair of brothers.

At last they made their entrance; and never certainly did men take less trouble to conceal the ill-humour they felt at seeing an unexpected relation. Without addressing me even in the words of anger, they went and took their station on one side of the hall, while I stood on the opposite side. There – pale, sullen, dejected, and now and then casting upon me a lowering look of mingled rage and despair – they awaited, without uttering a word, the legal injunction they expected, to surrender the paternal estate.

I own that for some time I enjoyed their dismay. It was the only pleasure they could afford me. Having indulged in it till the zest evaporated, I at last broke the long protracted silence. "My brothers," said I, "you are aware of my claims upon you; and you likewise are conscious of your conduct to me. In your own minds, therefore, you dare not cherish the smallest particle of hope, that I should surrender in your favour any portion of my right. Yet what you dare not expect, I of my own accord perform. I here publickly relinquish my privilege. Take each your third of the paternal property: and only leave me that portion which would have belonged to me as a Christian, and which I can but ill spare. That done, mourn for your sins, and repent of your injustice."

To describe the effect these words produced on the audience would be impossible. Those who before considered me as a devil incarnate, now of course regarded me as an angel from heaven. The hall resounded with loud applause. Nothing was heard but praises of my generosity; and my brothers themselves, stunned by so unexpected a turn in their situation, were reluctantly forced to join in the general cry. They thanked me, but in such a way as made it doubtful whether they more rejoiced at recovering their property, or regretted retracting their abuse.

I took no notice of their coolness, but, leaving the mekkiemé, went straight to the paternal house. My progress looked like a triumphal march: all that had witnessed my behaviour in the hall of justice, and all whom we met on the way, joined the procession. Having reached the steps of the mansion, I turned round and saluted the company. In its turn, the assembly honoured me with fresh cheers, intermixed with a few observations on my brothers, which at least showed they were not overlooked. I expressed my unmixed gratitude, and retired to a private chamber, where I was glad to sit down and rest my wearied mind.

While every one else had been loud in praise of my conduct, the son of Mavrocordato alone had not uttered a syllable. As soon as we were by ourselves, he threw his arms round my neck, and attempted to speak: but in vain! His emotion was too great for utterance. He could only gaze on me with overflowing eyes. To see his Anastasius, who thus far had caused him nothing but anguish, had afforded him no employment but to conceal his errors, all at once become the theme of universal admiration; to find his friendship thus justified, his perseverance thus rewarded, – what a moment for his feelings! Even while speechless for want of breath, his exulting look seemed to say, "Well, my friend, are you now sorry that you followed my advice?"

If, however, Spiridion's first thoughts were for his friend, his second were for his father. Till that moment, a more urgent subject of anxiety had occupied his mind. This being set at rest, he took up the other. "Ah, my tender parent," exclaimed he, "why cannot you witness my success, or rather your own! For I act in your name; I but accomplish your vows. Alas! while I triumph, you still remain in anguish. Yet shall you not suffer longer than a grateful son can help."

Hereupon, he proposed to go out and inquire for the means of sending a letter. Already he had dispatched a few lines from Rodosto to make his father easy respecting his disappearance. On my agreeing to the thing, we went forth. As we crossed the esplanade of the castle, I perceived a dark cloud gather on my friend's brow. His eyes seemed to dart out of his head, and to remain riveted on the quay. I turned mine the same way, but saw nothing to account for Spiridion's perturbation. At last, changing colour, and pressing my arm: we are traced," he cried, "see Marco coming towards us!" This person was his father's steward – an old and confidential servant. "Let us go," rejoined he, "and meet him. I have done nothing for which I ought to blush."

Marco saw his young master advancing. He hobbled on to meet him, and with a respectful salutation, presented a letter which he took out of his bosom.

Spiridion, with a trembling hand, broke the seal and read: then paused, ruminated, and read all over again. At last, trying to speak with more composure than he felt; "Your instructions, Marco," said he, "were to trace me, to follow me, and to hand me this letter. Your commission is performed. I have in great measure answered my father by anticipation from Rodosto: what remains, I shall go and complete. I now am able to convey the welcome information that the adopted brother whom he committed to my care, is become worthy of his kindness, and, like me, only wants his prayers and his blessings."

"Sir," answered Marco, in a firm but respectful tone: "My instructions went further than you state. I am bearer of letters to the despots,[3] the bishops, and the proëstis of our different islands. They import that I am to see you safe home. But even had I not received express orders to that purpose, could I find the courage to reappear before your worthy parent, unaccompanied by the son for whom he grieves? Ah, sir – ah, my dear young master! – already from the anguish he has suffered, his precious life hangs by a mere thread. Seeing me return alone would certainly break his heart!"

"Hark ye, Marco," relied Spiridion, pacing backward and forward in an agitation which almost bordered upon frenzy: "My father gave me a charge which he cannot at will recall. It was witnessed by heaven, and was recorded by angels! In conformity with his solemn commands, and in compliance with my sacred promise, I have toiled at my task. God knows I have not spared myself. But on the eve of completion, I cannot, must not, give up my work unfinished. On my head would lie, to the end of time, the sins of a brother unreclaimed. If there you urge me no further, but quietly return to

Kandilly, I pledge my honour, nay, if you wish it, I take a solemn oath, that all on my part shall end to my father's satisfaction. If you refuse me, the soul I stand pledged for shall not be lost alone; two shall plunge together into ruin everlasting. I run to the first mosque, and, whatever be the consequence – may it fall upon your head!"

"Sir," replied Marco, "I grieve at this issue of my commission; but the will of God be done! Many years have I lived under your kind roof, many an hour have I had you in my arms, as an infant, as a child, as a boy. From the day on which you first lisped the feelings of your affectionate heart, to that on which you left your home, never have I known your promise fail. The word of Spiridion always was that of truth! I therefore submit. I return alone: yet may I hope you will deign to let me carry to your father a few lines of comfort from your own beloved hands."

Spiridion, in running home to comply with the request, only performed what he already had promised. I, meanwhile, remained alone with Marco, and availed myself of the opportunity to question him respecting the reports of Kandilly. They were more satisfactory than I could have hoped.

When, on the morning after my departure, the son of the Capidgee was found, already taking his last sleep in the proper place, the public cemetery, no one suspected me of being the public benefactor who had introduced him to the silent, sedate sort of company, in which he for the first time spent the night, inasmuch as he was notorious for his outrageous conduct, and, at the time I met him, had several other quarrels on his hands, much more public than the one for which he suffered: but every body agreed that whoever had taken the trouble of ridding the neighbourhood of the nuisance, rather deserved thanks than blame. As to my disappearance, a sufficient cause for it was charitably found in the very natural wish of a needy adventurer to fleece a wealthy heir.

These particulars left me an opening to return to Constantinople, whenever I liked. I ran to relate them to Spiridion, ere he concluded his letter; and they relieved his mind completely. He pledged himself soon to bring back to his father two sons instead of one; and on this assurance old Marco took his leave. I proceeded to settle with my brothers respecting the succession.

Had I quietly stepped into an undisputed property, and found nothing to do but to mourn to my heart's content for the loss of a parent, I would have fulfilled with the utmost punctuality all the observances of grief. Sadness really possessed my soul, and I had constantly before my eyes my poor father, in his illness wishing to see his Anastasius, to forgive him, and to die in his arms; and perhaps in his last moments, and when I would have gone to the world's end for his blessing, pierced to the heart by exaggerated accounts of my unfeeling and incorrigible profligacy. But if mere business accords but ill with sorrow, nothing is so sure to drive melancholy away altogether as strife and bickerings; and my brothers were much too considerate not to afford me every distraction of this sort which they could think of. Theirs was a malice which no kindness of mine could assuage; and the moment my formal renunciation of their portions made them conceive all cause either for hope or fear on my score at an end, their ill-concealed hatred again broke out in all its pristine virulence. They not only cavilled about every most trifling article of the property, they even attempted to deprive my conduct of all its little merit, by roundly asserting that I had only acted from pusillanimity, and sacrificed a part to make sure of the remainder. Constantine was the leader in every altercation. Eustathius, more indolent, contented himself with giving his unlimited approbation to whatever his brother (and that meant Constantine alone) thought proper to do.

Thus were all the ancient wounds afresh torn open and made to fester. Spiridion tried in vain to interpose. He only got for his trouble taunts from his antagonists, and reproaches from me. "Why had he meddled at all? Why had he made it a point with me to behave kindly to unnatural brothers, whose injustice, but for his interference, would have met with its deserts."

And yet, notwithstanding my murmurings, did I to a certain degree restrain myself; not from any real moderation, but from the wish that my assumed forbearance might encourage my adversaries to so extreme a pitch of ill conduct, as to render their provocations evident to all the world, and to justify any step prompted by my legitimate resentment. Nor did this period seem far distant. Whether from an idea that they had daunted me by their haughty tone, or from an absolute intoxication of brutality, they by degrees cast away all pretensions to decency. The more I forced myself to appear calm and composed, the more they encreased in the grossness of their insults.

All wondered at my patience; all beheld me with admiration. When my brothers allowed themselves every licence of language – almost every latitude of gesture – all stared to see me content myself with turning up my eyes to heaven like a saint cast among savages. Even those least acquainted with the irascible temper I had to restrain, cited me on this occasion as a perfect model of meekness and forbearance. He only who with unwearied vigilance watched each change of my countenance, and could penetrate each emotion of my heart, was not to be deceived. One day, when Constantine even exceeded his usual insolence, and I, my customary forbearance, I caught him expressing by an almost imperceptible shake of the head, his distrust of my tranquillity. His suspicions were spoken too intelligibly for me to pass over. "What do you fear," cried I, as soon as my brothers were out of hearing? "Do you not see me laugh at their meanness? "Ah!" replied Spiridion, fetching a deep sigh: "you may laugh with your lips; but laughter reaches not your eyes, and fell resentment rankles in your heart.

My friend was right. Suppressed anger had already curdled my blood, and clogged the whole circulation of my humours. Ere yet he had done speaking a sudden shivering rushed through my frame, my teeth began to chatter, and my limbs to shake. In an instant all my strength seemed to forsake me.

Since my sojourn at Chios, I had resumed my old travelling custom of carrying my pistols, duly loaded, in my belt. Many in Turkey always wear them thus when out of the capital. As they now impeded my breathing, I took them out, and laid them on the sofa. Scarce was I disencumbered of my weapons when my knees began to tremble; a dark curtain seemed to drop over my eyes, – and I fell senseless on the couch.

I continued some time bereft of all perception. On its return I found myself stretched out at full length where I had fallen, with all the accompaniments of one duly convicted of a decided and lasting illness. A regular physician of the place was feeling my pulse, and going to pronounce on my case; and as my first return to my senses was marked by a fierce struggle with my Esculapius, I was at once judged to be in a violent delirium, and in imminent danger. Sentence was pronounced accordingly, and every internal medicine, and every external application prescribed, which could torture the human body and stomach. All the bystanders conceived me in the agonies of death, and civilly expressed their regret, at the short stay I made among them.

To myself these politenesses seemed premature. The sudden transitions from heat to cold, the suppressed perspiration, the fatigue of body and the anxiety of mind during the journey, were quite sufficient in my own opinion, to bring on a strong paroxysm of fever, without death being the necessary consequence. I however deemed it expedient to assent to all the doctor said, in order that he might say no more. It afforded Spiridion an excuse for turning out the company, and procuring me a little quiet. He alone stayed to nurse me.

"What a pity," muttered I to myself, when I thought no one heard me, "that that last dose of the English powders of mine, should have been wasted in Egypt on that traitor my father-in-law!" Spiridion lost not a syllable of the soliloquy. "There are foreign vessels in the harbour," he cried. "Possibly they may have some;" and he immediately ran out to enquire.

Meanwhile my brothers had received from the departed visitors the agreeable intelligence of my being at the last gasp. They hastened up to me eager with curiosity and hope; and finding my door ajar and unguarded, slipped in with the least possible noise. I however had discerned their steps on the stairs, and immediately – before they entered the room – assumed the appearance of one in the act of resigning his last breath. Constantine was the first to approach. On tip toe he came to my bedside in order to ascertain whether his joy was founded, ere he gave it full scope. With that laudable view he examined me most minutely from head to foot, raised and let fall my arms and legs, moved his hand before my eyes, put his ear to my mouth, first addressed me in a low whisper, then audibly, then shouting with all his might, as if he suspected I might not be in earnest.

Most manfully did I stand the whole ordeal. Nothing could make me wince or move a muscle; and my affectionate brother at last acquired the grateful conviction, that if not quite dead yet, I had at least already lost all perception, and could not fail soon to depart for ever. He no longer delayed conveying the agreeable intelligence to the discreet Eustathius, who, the hindmost on all other occasions, on this also had not ventured beyond the door, and there stood, in breathless expectation, waiting the result of the scrutiny; and perhaps also watching the condition of the outposts.

"Stathi;" said Constantine, with sort of subdued exultation; "there is some warmth still about him, – but depend upon it he cannot last!"

"Ah!" exclaimed the wary Stathi, shaking his head, "worse than he, I fear, have recovered!" and he fetched a deep sigh at the thought!

"True," answered Constantine; "and as we are alone, and have every presumption in our favour, why not make sure work, and crush the snake at once!" And so saying, he laid his hands on my throat, and attempted to strangle me.

This was doing things in a grand style! Not stopping at half measures. I conceived for my brother a veneration, unfelt before, almost thought it a pity to interrupt him in his spirited proceeding, and would have let the farce go on, could I, at its conclusion, have revived at my own pleasure. *That* not being the case, I was reluctantly forced to notice the intended favour, and weak as I felt, to defend myself as well as I could, against my two stout assailants; for Stathi too had now advanced to lend a hand; and it was evident that having once begun, they would not, if they any way could help it, leave their work unfinished.

My fire arms lay concealed, but within reach. With one hand I seized Constantine's wrist, and with the other a pistol: "Ah, brother! Ah, fiend!" I cried, – and fired.

Never yet had I missed my aim, even when I held not my prey in my grasp. But at my first sign of life Constantine had started, and, content to leave his jubbee in my possession, had disengaged his person. My hand, besides, trembled with the effects of the fever, – perhaps even with some instinctive sense of the dire office it was performing, and – the miscreant only received the ball in his shoulder.

Uttering a dreadful yell, he made a spring at the door, and darted out. Ere I could find my other pistol, Eustathius too had made good his retreat. Both were out of sight in an instant, but not out of hearing. My ears bore witness to Stathi's tumbling down stairs, with such violence and outcry, as to make me entertain hopes that neither of them had entirely escaped the merited retribution.

As soon as, after a few dying murmurs, all was again hushed in silence, – "now," thought I, "for the tête-à-tête with Spiridion! According to custom, he will lay the whole blame on me. He will deem my good brothers' intentions all very wise and proper; well see much sound reason in them, and will not be content, I suppose, until I go to them with a halter round my neck, beg pardon for my impatience in stopping their proceedings, and humbly supplicate them to put their design into execution!"

Meanwhile, the report of the pistols had a second time collected the whole neighbourhood round my door. But, if pronounced delirious before, I now was supposed to be under the influence of a frenzy so outrageous, that no one durst step across my threshold. The curious contented themselves with forming a blockade outside the room, each holding himself in readiness to fall back, and to shove his neighbour in his place, should I make an unexpected sally.

This state of things continued until Spiridion's return. His expedition had been unsuccessful. When he appeared, so many officious friends sprung forward to tell him what had happened in his absence, that it would have been utterly impossible for him to understand a single word of the matter, supposing even that the relaters themselves had known the truth. But my brothers, to whom they were indebted for all their information, had, in their hurry, dropped the trifling circumstance of their attempt upon my life, in which the affair began. Despairing, therefore, to make any thing of the confused and contradictory accounts with which he was stunned, Spiridion at last pushed aside the crowd, and, to the utter astonishment of all – entered my room undaunted and alone!

He found me seated on the sofa, with my face in my hands, and my elbows on my knees, overwhelmed more with disappointment than with shame, and incapable either of raising my eyes or of unclosing my lips. Thus I remained, wholly unmindful of his entrance, until, after some time contemplating me in silent earnestness, he at last took a seat beside me, and spoke.

"Selim," said he, "am I to believe these people? are you really out of your mind; or rather, as I apprehend, perfectly in your senses?"

"In my perfect senses," answered I, "with all the composure of which I was master. My hand was raised to punish demons. This time they have escaped! – But what is not yet, may be!"

"Never, never," cried he, "while I have life. – Rather than that you should hurt your brothers, my breast shall interpose."

"Then through your breast," I exclaimed, "must I strike them."

Spiridion here rose. "Anastasius," said he, calmly, "I feel but little wish to live: not however at they hands must I receive my death blow! My bosom may be pierced by thy speech, but let it remain sacred from thy sword. The world must not have it to say that thou couldest plunge they dagger into the heart of thy friend. The crime would be as idle as it would appear heinous. If my presence be a burthen to thee, say but the word, and I go."

"I never desired you to stay," cried I in a sullen tone.

"Very well," rejoined Spiridion. "You speak plain. Yet, ere I act accordingly, once more, and for the last time, I appeal from Anastasius blinded by passion to Anastasius restored to reason. In an hour hence I return and repeat the same question. If the answer be the same – then farewell, and for ever!"

At these words Spiridion went out, and tranquillized the gentlemen drawn up in the passage with respect to my situation. On my friend's assurances they all rushed in, and teased me with so many questions, and with so much advice, that they almost made me lose the little wits I had left. Their annoyance still lasted, when, at the expiration of the hour, Spiridion returned. Without seeking it, he had gained so universal a sway by his dignified demeanour, that at his desire all retired. The room being cleared of strangers, he took me by the hand, and finding that the symptoms of bodily disorder had subsided, he looked sternly in my face, and spoke thus.

"This, Anastasius, is at last the moment which must decide my resolution. The solemn vow is irrevocably spoken; and according to what you now answer, I may stay, or I must leave you for ever. Do you swear by all that is holy to renounce your impious revenge, or do you prefer to be released from my society? – If the last, utter not, I beseech you, the ungracious word. Only withdraw your hand."

Undoubtedly this would have been the moment for thoroughly explaining the business with my brothers, of which my friend knew but half, and of which that half more than doubled my guilt. Not aware that my own life had been attempted first, and ignorant that I acted in my own defence, Spiridion considered my illness as a pretence, or, at any rate, my firing as a premeditated scheme. It would have been easy to remove his error: – had not my bare word sufficed, Constantine's torn garment would have born witness to the struggle. But after my solemn promise at Mitylene, I considered the bare suspicion as so injurious to my honour, that my offended pride forbade my undeceiving my friend or clearing my character. I pulled away my hand, and Spiridion walked out. Yet God knows I did not wish to lose him!

As soon as he had left me, I paced up and down the room with a hurried step. After a few turns I went out to fetch breath on the quay. An hour's air and exercise changed the current of my ideas. I felt regret for my obstinacy and fear of its consequences. With the utmost speed I ran home, and up to Spiridion's chamber.

He was closing his portmanteau. The things about the floor had disappeared. All looked empty, orderly, and desolate.

"What means this," cried I, affecting more surprise than I felt.

"Only," replied Spiridion, "that what I said, I do."

"Ah my friend, my real brother," exclaimed I, "do you then, in sad earnest, purpose to leave me? Cursed be my tongue, which uttered what my heart had no share in; and cursed be my hand, which confirmed the untruths of my tongue!"

"Anastasius," now said Spiridion, seating himself upon his little bundle, "fancy not your last words and actions to have been the sole and primary cause of a long formed and long resisted resolution. Its origin dates far higher. The unkind speeches and gestures of this day only gave the final impulse!

"From children we were brothers in love. When you rescued me from death, the day that all our companions stood palsied by fear, gratitude only riveted affection's prior links; – and duty, I hoped, had rendered them indissoluble, when my father himself named you his second son! Many years his commands of fraternal kindness to his Spiridion's preserver remained without fruit – you yourself best know how. Yet was the deep-rooted attachment of childhood never replaced by more recent friendships; and when I again beheld you at Constantinople, my feelings for my Anastasius still preserved all their freshness unfaded. Evil inclinations of no ordinary magnitude, indeed, I saw mixed with your better qualities; but I thought that, if freed from their alloy, your virtue too would eclipse ordinary virtue; and I imagined an unbounded devotion might enable me to become the instrument of so noble a reformation. I resolved to save from perdition your soul, as you had saved my body; and I prayed the Almighty to bless the undertaking. Some return on myself also, some selfish feelings perhaps were mixed with my wishes for your welfare. I could not help fancying that, regenerated through me, you would become my support and my consolation in the irksome race I am destined to run; that in your turn, you might assist me in the struggles and dangers that strew the rugged path, through which I am destined to journey. In short, I hope that, each blessed in the other, we should toil through life together, and that when shone forth our last day, which ever was summoned first should only die in the other's loved arms. Great as were the pains you took to expose my presumption and to dispel my foolish dream, long did my soul firmly cling to its fond chimera; long did my heart hug it as a thing too precious to part with!"

"But there are lights that even strike the blind. Reluctantly though irresistibly I have at last been forced to see that no arguments, no persuasion, no labour of mine have power to control the passions which enslave you; and that however I may strive, I still must leave you ungovernable, and you still must leave me wretched as before. Much as I tried to avert my eyes from the fatal truth, I have at last yielded to the painful conviction that, sooner or later, we still must end in separating for ever; and that, by trying to put off the evil day by struggling for a short and transient respite, I can only at last drink the cup with greater bitterness. I therefore submit to the decrees of Heaven: I bow to the will of Providence in flying from thee, as I erst hoped to fulfil it by following thy footsteps. In sadness I go; but I go, and for ever! Far from thee I henceforth shall live; and far from thee it will be my fate to die! Yet, Selim, thou art young still. What the anxious warnings of friendship could not perform, the leaden hand of time may achieve. It may allay the ferment of thy passions, clear away the impurities of thy heart, and, – though I shall not witness the blissful change, – still make thee great and virtuous. This happy consummation God in his goodness grant!"

"Ah, Spiridion," cried I, clasping my friend in my arms, "you cannot, you shall not leave me thus!" But he – fearing his own weakness – in order to render a relapse impossible: "On my head be God's eternal curse, be that of my aged father!" he exclaimed, "if I do not immediately return to my paternal roof!"

I now felt all remonstrance to be fruitless. "You are right," replied I. "The game could not go on between us. The stakes were not even. Loaded with the gifts of Providence, and accountable to your fellow creatures for their use, you may not squander your ample means on a barren soil, nor seek ruin with a reprobate whom you cannot save. Yet, if once Anastasius did possess your love, and still returns all your affection; if that wretch, that reprobate, in the midst of all his errors, never ceased to reverence your virtues; if his spirit, undaunted by all else, stooped to you, and worshipped you alone – oh Spiridion, listen! At present that, bereft of all hope, indeed weaned of all wish to hear a sentence repealed on which depends your peace, he for ever renounces the happiness of your society, nay, urges you himself to fly his baneful presence, at least grant this only last request; grant what he, who never yet humbled himself before mortal man, implores of you on his bended knee: tell him – lay this unction to his sickening soul to now – that you do not hold him in utter detestation; that on leaving him to return no more, you at least feel a pang; and when – all earthly things gone by like unsubstantial shadows – comes the day of your reward in heaven for the good deeds done on this earth; when, before the throne of Mercy, arrayed in all your worth, you receive your well-earned meed of ineffable joy, cast back one look of pity on the wretch who, overwhelmed by the weight of his guilt, sinks while you rise to glory. Speak for him to your Maker one poor word of intercession: and beg he may not fall so low in the abyss of wretchedness, but that from an immeasurable distance he still may behold, and be consoled by your bliss!"

"Here or hereafter," cried Spiridion, "if I forget you, may heaven forsake me!" – and bending down his head, he wept aloud.

After some time he rose up, and wiping away his tears: “I have made you,” said he, “a promise to hold good for eternity; now, in your turn, make me a promise for a short space of time.”

“Any promise you please,” I answered.

“What a temptation that!" rejoined my friend. – “But I shall not abuse your confidence. I shall not ask what you cannot perform. It was only a trifling favour I wanted for mutual mitigation of pain. Take this watch,” he added, giving me the one he wore; “and count just twenty minutes ere you stir from this spot.” – saying which, he took up his parcel, and walked to the door. I tried to remonstrate and to stop him; but, gently pushing me aside, – “You have promised,” he cried, and instantly disappeared.

I ran after my friend as far as my pledged honour would permit – to the threshold of my room, and there called him back with loud and repeated eries: but in vain! Spell-bound by my promise, I stood motionless on the utmost verge of my apartment, with ears stretched out to catch each fleeting sound, and eyes riveted on the hands of my watch. At first I perceived some commotion, some distant bustle in the house, some running backward and forward; but very soon all these noises sunk away in a dreary and lasting silence. Yet were there several long minutes wanting of the point marked on the inexorable dial for my release. Each of these appeared an entire age, composed of many lesser periods of endless duration; and all the time I kept my eyes straining on the figures, as if my bare look could quicken by its motion the impulse of the hands. At last they approached the goal, glided over the last second, and attained the long wished-for term! – I now dart forward like an arrow: I run, I leap, I fly; first, through the house, from room to room; next, on finding all deserted within, out into the street, and lastly to the quay.

There I perceive nothing but an indifferent and gaping crowd, which my eyes in vain interrogate, and which gives me no satisfactory answer. Where-ever I look, no Spiridion appears!

Fearfully I at last cast my eye on the wave; and after an anxious search among the shipping in the road, spy, already far away, a small caïck, which, with stress of sails and oars, seems steering towards Tchesmé. A young man, I was told, for whom the caïck lay waiting, had been seen to step in, with his face wrapped in his shawl; and immediately the boat was pushed off, and cleft the billows with such speed, as already to appear little more than a mere speck.

The young man was Spiridion, – and my first impulse, to go after him. I called for another barge; but while it was preparing, soberer thoughts drove away my first design.

Why in fact follow a friend determined to fly from me! – Was not his purpose irrevocably fixed? Went he not back to his father and his home? Was he not right in doing so? Did not the happiness of his life depend upon this measure; was I to impede his progress, or to increase his parting pangs, and that from a mere selfish feeling? For what now could he gain, by aught that I could say or do?

Immediately I gave up the short-lived project, and having paid for the trouble I occasioned, walked away, and sought on the beach a more retired spot, in which to vent my sorrows. Distracted by so many opposite feelings that I scarce seemed to feel at all,

I threw myself on the ground, and moistened with my tears the sand on which I lay. "All now," cried I, "to me is at an end; my abode is become a desert, my life a scene of solitude, my very existence a blot in the creation!" – and hereupon I struck my breast, until, exhausted by my grief, I grew somewhat more quiet, and began my song of sorrow.

In the midst of my melancholy ditty I remembered that, together with his watch, Spiridion had slipped into my hands a pocket-book, which, not knowing what to do with, I had thrust into my bosom. I now pulled out the toy. It might contain some farewell token; some last and sacred behest.

A few words had indeed been written on one of the leaves but had been rubbed out again. The only uncancelled manuscript I could find, and to which the case seemed intended as a vehicle, was a loose slip of paper, an order to the bearer – but to what amount I know not: for without looking at the figures, I tore the draft to pieces, and scattered the useless fragments in the wind. No sooner however had I done so, than I regretted my precipitation. The sum was nothing! I never meant to claim it; but the last signature of my friend in my behalf, – what to me could be equally precious? As of many other things, however, I felt its value when too late! Already had the surf washed away the last remnant of the paper.

I now pressed to my lips the empty book. "Last remembrance," exclaimed I, "of a friend for ever lost, be thou my sole unceasing companion. Lie ever next to my heart. Continue its ægis against all evil passions. Preserve me henceforth, not from grief, but from sin!"

This said, I started up, and left the lonely spot: but as I returned among the bustling throng, my sadness increased. Why did I any longer tarry in my native land? How could I face my countrymen, abandoned as I was by my friend? "Ah," cried I, "since I have him no more to guide and to support me, let me fly from Chios, as from the place of my shame. Let me seek refuge in Egypt, at Algiers, in France, – or wherever else men acquire fame by destroying each other! There let me in the din of arms forget friendship's silenced voice; there pass my days in strife, there conquer, or there die!"

Conformably to this resolution I determined not to stay for the completion of the settlement with which had commenced my worst misfortune, but left my full powers with a friend, or in other words, sold my birth-right to a schemer, for an immediate sum. The same act rid me of my troubles, and began those of my brothers: a circumstance which they probably only learnt after my departure, as, in consequence of their ill-fated attempt, both kept their beds; – not entirely from choice, however, – Constantine having got a broken arm in the conflict, and Eustathius a dislocated hip. These were the only incidents which gave me any comfort.

As for me, I took my passage to Cyprus, where I thought I might join the Turkish fleet in its way to Egypt; and in the act of embarking, called down upon my head the utmost wrath of heaven, if ever I set foot in my native land again.

Spiridion, by the way of Smyrna, speedily reached his home, and his father's longing arms. Whether from fatigue or from mere disappointment, he fell into a state of languor, which long threatened a fatal termination. But time and corporeal debility at last blunted the sting of mental suffering. Insensibly health returned, and with health, a calm hilarity. The youth then resumed, never more to abandon it, the steady regular mode of life which only for my sake had been interrupted. In good time he married a young lady of noble blood and distinguished beauty, and became the happy father of a lovely family.

Mavrocordato, as observed before, had destined his son to run the perilous race of ambition; and, had he never known the fear of losing that darling son, would with difficulty have been diverted from his purpose. But while Spiridion's fate hung suspended between life and death, his father too strongly felt the blessing of his existence, and the value of his happiness, any longer to stake them against perilous honours, difficult to attain, and hollow when possessed. His desires became sobered, and his views less aspiring: he determined to prefer the certainty of his son's bliss, to the probable misery of his grandeur; and vowed, so heaven but left him his child, never more to abuse a father's authority, by goading him on to dangerous distinctions. Thence, indeed, Mavrocordato obtained not, like the Giccas, the Callimackis and others, the advantage of boasting that their nearest of kin had been bowstringed on a throne; but this misfortune he bore with becoming resignation. As to Spiridion, content to move in the sphere of a wealthy merchant, he employed his daily growing riches in diffusing around him happiness and prosperity. His life resembled the course of a majestic stream, whose deep but tranquil waters, winding their ample way through fertile plains and flowery meads, as they advance still receive from new rills fresh increase, while at each step also they bestow more profusely all the fruits of industry, and all the blessings of plenty.

Far different was the similitude borne by my roving life. Seeking my fortune in strife, not in harmony; making havock, not culture, the means of my support; and engaged, not in the steady pursuit of a regular profession, but in a wild wandering flight from one career to another; sometimes prosperous, and oftener unfortunate; now in unavailing plenty, and now again in pinching want, I at best resembled the blustering mountain torrent, which, only acquiring might and substance during the war of the elements, as soon as they cease their strife, again subsides in a mean rill; in times of serenity shews no trace of its existence, save in the havock of darker days brought to light; and so far from in its fullness diffusing more benefits than in its penury, only effects greater mischief as it receives ampler supplies. While still near its source in the upper regions of the globe, this ill-favoured offspring of the clouds – hurried over fell and precipice – only presents a sucession of fierce struggles, furious falls and impracticable shallows; when further advanced in its impetuous career, and rushing with tremendous roar into the fertile plain below, it seems indeed determined to seek a full recompence for all former restraint; – it disregards all rights, destroys all property, and levelling fence and boundary, annihilates crops, habitations and life: but throughout the whole of its wild uncertain progress, from where it first bubbles up near the sky, to where it finally plunges into the vast abyss of the deep, it equally remains a curse to the regions it pervades!

CHAPTER XI.

The paroxysm of fever which seized me at Chios, had, in the hurry of the strange and rapidly succeeding events which it gave rise to, been entirely forgotten. I was therefore surprised when, on board the ship, I experienced a second attack more violent than the first; and was still more mortified when I found that, so far from being allowed to drop the acquaintance, I had thenceforth to consider the unwelcome intruder as my regular guest. Its visits were repeated with most irksome punctuality every third day during the whole of the passage; and this passage seemed to have no end.

Oh! how long appeared those sleepless nights, in which I felt no change of motion in the ship, but what was caused by its rolling from side to side, or pitching from end to end; in which every object suspended round my narrow birth – my clothes, my lamp, my person, and the very shadow they cast on the wainscot – never ceased rocking from right to left, and from left to right; obeying an impulse as resistless as it was monotonous, and which found its equally monotonous response in the periodical creaking of the hulk, straining of the mast, swaying of the yards, and flapping of the sails and tackle. How slowly approached those mornings which were neither announced by the crowing of the cock, nor hailed by the twittering of the swallow, and whose dead and universal silence was only broken by our own harsh discord, added to that of the howling winds, and roaring waves! How often I anxiously looked out at my narrow loop-hole, to see whether the stars had yet lost their trembling radiance, and whether the horizon yet reddened with the approaching dawn! My mind suffered with my body; and during those tedious hours, the depression of disease made me survey with deep contrition the errors of days past, and form sincere resolution for my future life. They lasted with unremitting continuance – until health and strength returned.

This happened at Cyprus. That island which gives agues to so many, cured my tertian completely; or perhaps transferred it to some other luckless wight, opportunely in the way to catch it as it left me. I was, however, only just convalescent, and had scarce let my bed, when, from the heights above Larneca, Hassan's armament was described five or six leagues out at sea, in full sail for Egypt. That fleet, which I had so long expected, now cleft the wave almost under my eyes, without its proximity enabling me to join the nearest vessel of the squadron.

Fortunately I had another string to my bow; but ere I proceed to tell by which way I returned to the land of the Mamlukes, I must premise a few words concerning what happened there after my departure.

I have already mentioned, I think, that in Aly-Bey's time, an alliance had been proposed between Petersburg and Cairo. This project the Autocratrix of all the Russians failed not to resume as soon as she saw Ibrahim and Mourad in firm possession of the supreme authority. Her wish was to obtain from the Beys the port of Alexandria; an object of the greatest importance to her future maritime operations against the Turks. In return, she offered to afford these turbulent leaders every assistance in their design of shaking off the yoke of the Sultan; and the Russian Consul-general at Alexandria,

Thonus by name, was entrusted with the negotiation. He had the facility of corresponding with the rulers of Cairo through the medium of a Russian subject, become a renegade, a Mamluke, and a Bey, under the appellation of Khassim. On the other hand, he found indissolubly united again him the consuls of the other European powers in Egypt, who, whether friendly to the Porte or not, were all alike hostile to the plan of giving up to the Russians so important a harbour as Alexandria. Thonus undertook to defeat their opposition by the simple expedient of removing their persons. A petty quarrel had arisen between Mourad and the commercial diplomatists, respecting some trifling repairs to the Latin hospice at Alexandria. This slight spark of misunderstanding the crafty Livonian contrived to fan into so furious a blaze, that the consuls no longer thought themselves safe on land, and determined to take refuge at sea. Their intention was to sail in a body to Constantinople; and this design, sedulously by Thonus – who suffered not the fears of his friends to relax – would soon have been fulfilled to that gentleman's utmost wish, had not Ibrahim, alarmed at the consequences of the dispute, sent them an express, to efface by his concessions the outrages of his colleague. Already were the consuls on board, and in the act of weighing anchor, when, stopped by this trusty agent, the exulting Thonus had the mortification to see them return on shore, and resume their situations.

Ibrahim's conciliatory measures, however, came too late to prevent the interference of the Porte. On the first blush of the business, the consuls, apprehensive of violence on the part of the Beys, had dispatched an express to lay their complaints before the Sultan; and Abd-ool-Hameed had determined to resent the insult offered by the rulers of Egypt to the strangers under his special protection, in an exemplary manner. Had it suited the convenience of the Porte to remain at peace with its vassals, the representatives of all the potentates of Europe, flogged round Mourad's hall, would have obtained no other redress than an exhortation to mutual forgiveness of injuries; but the Divan wished to humble the rebellious Beys, and it therefore expressed the utmost readiness to resent their behaviour to the high offended personages. In vain did these worthy individuals themselves, as soon as they no longer entertained any apprehension for the safety of their persons, try to undo what they had done, and to prevent a rupture injurious to their interests. In vain did they write to assure the ministers that they had been premature in their fright, and forgiven their enemies, like true Christians as they were: – Hassan Capitan-Pasha, who was a Turk, and moreover had never yet found, in his varied expeditions, an opportunity of exploring the fertile plains of Egypt, expected too plentiful a harvest, if not of laurels, at least of piastres from this business, to let the quarrel be hushed up; and, under Abd-ool-Hameed, the wishes of this favourite were law. The Divan, therefore, in answer to the pacific protestations of the consuls, only observed that they were much too lenient, could not be overlooked, and that they must have satisfaction whether they chose it or not; and hereupon proclaimed the Beys outlaws; and ordered an armament to be fitted out against them.

A shew of negotiation had, however, been kept up, and had to a certain degree succeeded in lulling asleep the apprehensions of the Mamlukes, when, on the sixth of July 1786, the squadron which I had beheld with longing eyes from the coast of Cyprus, appeared before Alexandria. It consisted of six ships of the line, four frigates, some gunboats, and forty or fifty kirlangitshes, and other small craft capable of going up the river to Cairo. These vessels carried six hundred chosen Arnaoots from the interior of Epirus, as brave as well armed, and about five thousand raw recruits from every corner of the Archipelago, possessed of neither arms, courage, nor discipline. To this small force the Grand-Admiral added at Alexandria about three thousand Maugarbees, or Barbaresques, very lightly equipped. Of cavalry, the species of troops most wanted against the Mamlukes, Hassan's armament was entirely destitute; but the Asiatic Pashas of Oorfa, of Haleb, of Trabloos and others, had been ordered to bring with all expedition from their respective governments more horse than were wanted to Belbeïs, near the Syrian confines of Egypt, there to wait the Grand Admiral's further orders.

These orders were indeed dispatched the day that the commander in chief reached Rosetta: but their execution experienced some difficulty, in as much as the Pasha or Oorfa was not arrived yet at the place of rendezvous, and all the others had, immediately after Hassan's departure from Constantinople, been entirely countermanded. The ministers were in daily expectation of a war in the North, and felt unwilling to waste all their resources in the south.

Hassan, thus disappointed, resolved to compensate for want of numbers, by celerity of movements, and began to ascend the Nile on the last day of July. The land troops marched along the banks of the river, while the flotilla advanced abreast with their foremost ranks on the stream.

When the intelligence of the Capitan-Pasha's operations reached Cairo, the greatest unanimity took place among the Beys as to their sense of danger, but the greatest diversity of opinions as to the mode of repelling it. Ibrahim was for submission, Mourad for resistance; and no medium being hit upon between these two extremes, the former retired into the Saïd to avoid the imputation of rebellion, while the latter marched into Lower Egypt to oppose force by force.

The fourth day of August witnessed the meeting of the two armies near Mentoobes. Mourad with his well-mounted Mamlukes, all mail without, and all ardour within, felt secure of an easy victory over the Grand-admiral's ill equipped foot soldiers. He had neither taken into his account the artillery they were flanked by on the stream, nor the swamps through which he must march, to attack them on its banks. Received, on his first onset, with a tremendous discharge of cannon from the boats, his troops were immediately thrown into confusion. Even the safety of flight was denied them. Sinking with the weight of their accoutrements up to their horses bellies into the rice grounds that formed the field of battle, they became motionless, and were slaughtered at pleasure by Hassan's naked infantry, which might have walked on the wind. The few Mamlukes that escaped, immediately fell back upon Cairo; but finding the gates of the citadel shut against them by the Sultan's Visier, they only traversed the city, and joined Ibrahim in Upper Egypt.

Hassan entered without further opposition the defenceless capital, and received the homage of the country. He took up his abode in Ibrahim's palace at Kasr-el-aïni, and conferred on the long exiled Ismaïl, come from the Saïd to meet him, his long vacated office of Schaich-el-belled. Djeddawee's more dubious loyalty was less splendidly rewarded; and Yeyen-Visier, the obsequious tool of every party in power, was dismissed from his place: it was reserved for the Pasha of Oorfa, conductor of the Asiatic troops.

This personage, Abdi by name, had been Pasha of Haleb. Turned out of that city by its janissaries, jealous of his Koordish body-guard[1], he had just been consoled for his loss by the government of Oorfa, when he received orders to march with all the force he could collect from Diarbekeer to Egypt. As nothing had been said about provisions, he resolved to trust for his supplies to the plunder of the districts through which he had to pass; and as he only had to traverse Syria from end to end, in its greatest length, he just contrived to spend, for want of subsistence, the whole summer on his march.

Nothing could have happened more conveniently for a man who, like me, wished to go from Cyprus to Egypt. It afforded the readiest means of making up for the loss of my passage on board the fleet on my right, by joining the army advancing on my left. A boat conveyed me from Larneca to Trabloos; and thence forward I found the track of Abdi's troops too distinctly marked by their devastations to miss the way. I however could only overtake the Pasha near Nabloos in Palestine, where I reached him in the best possible disposition for glory; that is to say – not valuing life a straw. Had I been inclined to fastidiousness, I might have found some fault with the appearance of my competitors for warlike fame. They pursued its career unencumbered by superfluities. The best equipped among the Pasha's troops were his own bodyguard of Koordish horse, who, under the denomination of dellis[2], still exercised their old trade of banditti, and plundered every friend on their march to the enemy. To this body of about eight hundred men was added another of about six-hundred Spahees, in very indifferent condition. The infantry was composed of about five-hundred Maugarbees, who looked as if they could be led to victory by nothing but famine. In fact, this ravenous horde only resembled a swarm of locusts, who suddenly appear in a region as if driven by an evil wind, fall on whatever spot offers the most abundant harvest, devour all its crops, and, when they find nothing further to consume, rise again, only to lay waste the fields next in succession. As long as there remained in a place a single article to take away or to devour, the Pasha thought not of stirring. The complete denudation of all around him, became the signal for departure: but the tents were again pitched in whatever nearest district admitted of the same proceeding. The march was lengthened only when such deserts intervened as offered neither provision nor plunder. Every where, before the approaching army, the inhabitants abandoned their villages, carrying with them all that was portable to the mountains; so that every new region we came to looked as if we had been there already, and left us no means of marking our route but by the destruction of the fixtures; and from the lengthy shape of Syria, and the direction of the march, no district escaped the devastating scourge.

Besides the general claim which my former rank in Egypt gave me to the attention of a commander in the pay of the Porte, I carried particular letters to Abdi from the governor of Larneca. Accordingly, I was promised the reversion of whatever eligible appointment might become vacant, and meanwhile stepped into the place of a captain of

Dellis[2], most fortunately killed the very morning of my arrival, by some peasants in ambush.

On calling over the muster roll of my corps, I found not a single baïak[3] possessed of half its complement of men. Each was a grand skeleton composed of lesser skeletons; and never did troops, at the opening of a campaign, more resemble soldiers returning from the wars. This remark, however, I kept to myself. As a new comer, I took it for granted that my predecessor knew what he was about (except indeed when he got killed); and resolved not to begin by breaking through established customs. Quietly, therefore, pocketing the surplus of the pay, and selling the supernumerary rations, I gained the love and esteem of all my fellow officers. We agreed that Hassan would not give us more fighting than was necessary; and it would be wrong to tempt him to imprudences by too marital an appearance. The only thing I took care of was to be well mounted myself. But the horses and accoutrements which I purchased, having drained me of most of my remaining cash, I was obliged to draw for my other expences on the present holder of my kiacheflik, – whoever that might be.

At Gaza we made our scanty provisions for the great desert. Very ample ones were left in it for the vultures. Belbeïs saw us arrive at last, not in May indeed, but in September; and from that place of general rendezvous, were not a soul met us, we marched on to Cairo.

It was here that an edifying scene of mutual astonishment took place, in Hassan at the smallness of our force, and in us, at the absolute nothingness of his. In fact, we had never had many more troops, while he had disbanded half the men he brought, to pocket their pay.

Nothing could equal the change of scene which Cairo presented from what I had known it before. I had left it a Mamluke city – I found it a Turkish camp. Every object indicated a change of masters and of regulations. Turkish detachments patrolled the streets, Turkish piquets occupied the places; and those porticoes of the Grandees' palaces which formerly witnessed the Mamlukes driving away with their naboods the famished Egyptians, now saw the Osmanlees treat the Mamlukes with scarce more respect. My friend Aly-Tshawoosh, whom I had the pleasure of finding with the Capitan-Pasha – but somewhat impaired in flesh, in spirits, and in brilliancy of appearance – took me to the house where I was billeted. "What," said I, on seeing it; "am I to lodge with my old acquaintance Sidi-Emin, who had such a praiseworthy horror of usury? And when his friends wanted money thought nothing of obliging them by buying their old slippers at a hundred piastres in ready cash, so they only, in return, bought his new ones at a thousand, payable in three months! – I shall be glad to shake hands with the worthy man."

"Ah!" cried Aly, "you will only shake hands with his ghost. But that you may make sure of. It stalks all night about its old mansion."

And good reason it had for being disturbed. The reader may remember the dreadful famine which I left hanging over Egypt. Emin, on this occasion, was one of the provident. During the years of plenty he had laid by for those of want. But, like the ant, he laboured for himself, and cared not to share his savings with the idle. Though his granaries groaned under their loads of corn, he saw unmoved the thousands of wretches who every day perished with hunger under their very walls. When the bodies of the suffers choaked up the entrances of his store houses, he still refused to unbar their surly gates, until the corn had reached the exorbitant price fixed by his avarice. This is at last attained; – and now, exulting at the thoughts of the millions he should make in a few hours, Emin took his keys, and opened his vaults. But O horror, O dismay! Instead of the mountains of golden wheat he had accumulated, he only beheld heaps of nauseous rottenness. An avenging worm had penetrated into the abodes fortified against famished man! A grub had fattened on the food withheld from the starving wretch! While the clamour of despair resounded without, a loathsome insect had in silence achieved with the work of justice. It had wrought Emin's punishment in darkness, while his crimes shone in the light of heaven! The miser's wealth was destroyed, the monster's hopes were all blasted! At the dire spectacle he uttered not a word. He only a few minutes contemplated the infected mass with the fixed eye of despair; then fell, – fell flat on his face upon the putrid heap. God had smitten him! On raising his prostrate body, life had fled. Like his corn, his frame was become a mass of corruption!

I had the pleasure to find Mavroyeni's former place of drogueman of the fleet, occupied by his nephew Stephan. This youth's character presented a singularity among Greeks in public situations, wondered at by all, and disapproved of by most, – that of being a perfectly honest man. His enemies rejoiced at it, though his friends still kept hoping that he was not too old to mend. Meanwhile the acquaintance, begun between us in the Morea, ripened at Cairo into a real mutual regard. I say mutual – for though Stephan did not always think well of my conduct, he valued my sincerity.

The strongest proof of attachment, however, which I received in Egypt, was from my quondam Mamlukes, whom I had ceded to Ismaïl at Es-souan, and now found established with the reinstated Schaich-el-belled in the capital. At the time of my flight, they seemed perfectly satisfied with the transfer; and indeed, had they now thought it incumbent upon them to leave the Schaich-el-belled, and to return to their old patron, they must have been great losers by the change. But so excessive became, on seeing me again, their generous wrath at thinking I had given up their services, that they could not even bear to remember that they once had belonged to me.

As to the Capitan-Pasha himself, his memory was more retentive. He not only remembered having seen me in the Morea; he even remembered the proposal he made me after the affair of Tripolezza. When again presented to him: "you would have acted more wisely," said he, "to have embraced the true faith for the sake of a patron, than for the love of a mistress; and perhaps you might have found the service of the Sultan more profitable than that of the Beys. You have lost much time and gained few friends. But you are young still, and what is more, you are brave: if you would not let me lay the foundation of your fortune, I still may raise the fabric to a desirable height." And so saying, he recommended me to his kehaya; who grinned a ghastly smile of obedience and of spite.

The government of Egypt being completely organized by the installation of Abdi Pasha in the office of Visier, and all the forces having arrived that could be looked for,

Hassan at last began to busy himself about the long talked of expedition to Upper Egypt, in pursuit of the rebels. Resolved not to stir himself from his commodious quarters in the capital, he gave the supreme command to his kehaya. The troops destined for the expedition were to rendezvous at Atter-el-nebbi, a place on the Nile, a little above Cairo. As before, the land force was to follow the banks of the river, and to be supported by the flotilla. Hassan's favour enabled me to exchange my ragged Koords for a fine body of Arnaoots; and in honour of my new soldiers I furbished up my old Epirote pedigree, and my presumptive descent from Achilles and from Alexander. The former indeed they knew little about, but the name of the latter all to a man remembered, and only maintained, in opposition to my doctrine, that he had fought the Doge of Venice; – which, in fact, he had.[4] Including the militia of the country, supplied by the citadel of Cairo, our force might amount to six thousand men; and I could not help thinking Hassan rather over-rated our chance of success, when at parting he recommended to us in a flowery speech, to bring back the days when the Schaich-el-belled held the stirrup to the Aga of the Janissaries, and when the Pasha of the Porte hung up the Beys at pleasure, under the gate of the castle: – a wish at which Ismaïl, now surnamed Kbir, or the Great, Aly-Bey-Defterdar, Mohammed-Bey-Mab-dool, Rodoan-Bey the bold, and several other Beys present, I thought, winced a little.

As usual, our army depended for its subsistence on the plunder of the provinces through which we had to pass. This circumstance alone would have retarded our coming up with Mourad; but what still more increased the difficulty of closing with this chief, was his own good management. He had profited by his discomfiture in the Delta. Instead of advancing to give us battle, he, on the contrary, kept constantly retreating before us; now and then just letting his rear appear in sight, to keep up the ardour of the pursuit. We discovered his drift – somewhat late however – when at Sioot we found the waters too low to permit the further progress of our flotilla, and thus were obliged to proceed onwards, deprived of the support of our floating battery. With a diminished strength, we only reached the rebels at Djirdgé, where they had all the advantage of the ground. Their position was admirable. Backed by the walls and garrison of the city, they had in front a long declivity of hard even ground, where their excellent horses and impenetrable coats of mail were as much in their favour as they had been against them in the swamps of the Delta. They rushed upon us like a cataract, and it soon became evident on which side the scale would turn. Our rout began among the Asiatics. The brave Arnaoots alone kept awhile the victory in suspense. Still anxious for the credit of my former corps, I set some Epirotes at the heels of the Dellis, and kept them wedged in between two fires. This concern for other people's honour cost me dear. A pistol-shot struck my hip, which certainly came not from the enemy. It brought me not the less to the ground; and I must have died from loss of blood, or have been trampled under foot, had not one of my trusty Albanians thought me dead already. He judged it a pity that my handsome armour should become the spoil of rebels, and approached to strip me; when, to his great dismay, he found me still alive. For a second or two he seemed to consider whether he should not realize his surmise; but my good stars prevailed. Shrugging up his shoulders, as if to say, it was not his fault, he took me in his arms, carried me off the field, bound up my wounds, and left me in the care of two of his comrades, themselves disabled from continuing to support a more active part in the engagement.

Meantime our commander, seeing the rout become general, sounded the retreat. Fortunately the enemy had determined only to act on the defensive, in order not to cut off all opening to a reconciliation. Mourad, content with the advantage gained, abstained from pursuing us. Thanks to his moderation, we experienced in our flight no other molestation than that of the Arabs and fellahs, whose crops we had destroyed on our progress. At Sioot we rejoined our flotilla; and thence returned to Cairo in a plight, which even the Mamlukes reinstated by Hassan could view without breaking their hearts. The assistance of a rival is seldom forgiven.

After a certain period Mourad's Arab allies, tired of the protracted war, as usual withdrew from the contest; and Mourad, deprived of half his strength, no longer appeared averse to a negotiation. Of this disposition Hassan availed himself to draw him down to Djizeh, when again he sent his Kehaya in pursuit of the Bey. Cured of my wound, I joined the expedition, and on the eighth of January 1787, we crossed the Nile. The flotilla on this occasion was out of the question; the river being at its lowest, and the commander of the Caleondgees dismissed: for Hassan suffered not his officers to rob without his participation.

At the news of our approach, Mourad again fell back; but we came up with him at Sioot, where he was forced to halt, to face about, an to receive us. His position was exactly the reverse of that at Djirdgé. Instead of occupying the top of a long declivity, of which we filled the bottom, his army was drawn out at the bottom of an extended slope, of which we occupied the summit; and instead of having immediately in his rear a high wall to cover his movements, he only had a deep ditch to cut off his retreat. The consequence was, that when we fell upon him as he had done before upon us, with all the impetus of a down hill charge, we almost immediately drove his troops backward into the fosse, where, tumbling head over heels in the mud, they left us no trouble but that of dispatching them at leisure.

Of my old patron, who sided with the rebels, I hitherto have made no mention. The edge of the ravine, down whose slope the Mamlukes were rolling, gave me the first glimpse of his venerable figure. He was curvetting mid-way the long declivity, surrounded by his retinue. The sight roused all my dormant feelings of relationship, and others not less warm; and I became most irresistibly anxious to join my father-in-law, to embrace, nay, to keep him entirely with me! Calling to my best men, I shewed them the Bey, and proposed a bold push for so valuable a prize. They fired at the thoughts, and off we set! I was within ten yards of his person, and already in imagination hugging him most tenderly, when some of his guards, perceiving our drift, gave the alarm. Immediately his whole house closed in upon him, and our purpose miscarried. I retired not, however, empty handed. We had penetrated so far into the Mamluke knot, that I was enabled to seize by the arm and to carry off, what at the time was nearest Suleiman's heart, his tootoondjee.[5] This young fellow I consigned to some of my servants in the rear, and having seen him safe in their custody, again returned to business.

The chase of a young Mamluke, whose shewy accoutrements caught my eye, had inadvertently drawn me out to some distance from my men, when another Mamluke of more advanced age and greater powers – till then concealed behind a small eminence – suddenly darted forward between us. The contest now lay with the new comer, and his agility already rendered the issue more doubtful. But when a third Mamluke of colossal size – a kiachef of my ancient patron – found means by a dexterous circuit to join his comrade, my situation seemed desperate. It was plain that a scheme had been concerted to entrap me; – and unable single handed to contend with two such formidable antagonists, whom others still were approaching, I gave myself up for lost, and only resolved to sell my life as dear as possible.

To my inexpressible surprise, just as I rushed forward, as I thought, to certain death, the new comer made signals for a truce, which his comrade immediately obeying, I did the same. I stopped short, still however remaining on my guard, and watching every motion of my enemies, in order to make my escape should an opportunity offer. The kiachef perceived my apprehensions. "Fear not," he cried: "your life is indeed in our hands; but we seek not your death; we want your prisoner. Restore Suleiman's tootoondjee, and in return take this handjar studded with diamonds, this order on the Bey's harem at Cairo for two thousand sequins, and this signet of our patron's to corroborate his draft."

All this was vastly better than to be butchered at Sioot: I accepted the offer. Meanwhile some of my Arnaoots, who had perceived my danger, were coming up. I cried to them, as soon as within hearing, to bring back the prisoner. One went on the errand, and the others waited at my signal. The Tootoondjee was delivered over, and the ransom placed in my hands. With this rich spoil, the thing I feared most was to return to my own men. Fortunately, they were full-handed themselves, and I rejoined our troops safe and sound – just in time to see the remnant of the enemy's force, which had escaped the ditch, in full flight towards the Saïd.

Our troops were so exhausted, that we spent the night where we had won the day. The next morning, ere we marched, I walked over the field of battle. Beholding on all sides sturdy limbs locked in death, which but the day before had turned my blows with all the energies of life, lips closed in eternal silence, which had stunned me with their clamour; and eye-balls fixed in sightless glare when, when met by mine, had sent forth flashes of lightning; – unable to avoid treading upon the mangled bodies of some who often had attempted to crush me with their very look, and now could not keep away the already busy vultures, – I felt a strange delight! I contemplated with a bitter satisfaction that unavoidable lot of all mankind, that doom of mortality which none can escape, that precariousness of life hanging alike over king and over beggar, thanks to which, if I could not be sure of a single instant before me, no more was the proudest of my antagonists certain of not being the next moment a clod of clay, a mass of corruption, a feast for worms, a heap of dust; thanks to which, if any rival had over me a temporary advantage, it was, however great, a trifle, a nothing, in the contemplation of the common fate awaiting all with equal certainty, and to all coming too soon; and thanks to which, finally, if I could not reach the very top of fortune's wheel, or for the present carry my head quite as high as some of my more successful opponents, I knew that their's must ultimately lie as low as mine!

"Poor speechless unresisting object!" cried I, lifting up by the ears one whose taunting language of the day before still rung gratingly in mine, "thou art now not only below me, or the meanest of my slaves; thou art worse than the live dog that licked thy hand, or the very worm that crawls to thy corpse as to his meal; he harbours joy, thou feelest not even my abuse and my scorn!"

Though we did not absolutely stay in the agreeable spot which occasioned these reflections, we seemed loth for a time to move beyond its influence. Want of money to pay his troops prevented our commander from proceeding in good earnest in pursuit of the rebels, until the month of May. We then made a sudden move; but as soon as we came in sight of Mourad's men, they crossed the river and retreated into Nubia. Arrived at the Cataracts, heat, want and disease stopped our further progress. We admired the falls, turned about, and marched back to Cairo.

CHAPTER XII.

By this time Hassan had, through penalties, confiscations and other such processes, reaped all the real fruits he expected from his expedition. He knew the utter impossibility of exterminating a set of men who always kept open a retreat where they were secure from pursuit; and he now made the approaching rupture between the Porte and Russia a pretence for conveying his armament back to Constantinople. On the twenty-fourth of July, 1787, therefore, he signed a treaty with the rebel Beys, by which he left them in full possession of the country from Barbieh to the frontiers of Nubia. All below these limits was to be prohibited ground. For the observance of this treaty they consented to give as hostages four of their party – my old friend Ayoob-Bey, Osman-Bey-Tamboordgi, and two other Beys of recent creation, Abderaham and Husseïn. These important Mamlukes had leave, however, to remain at Cairo, under the eyes of the Visier.

The quartetto soon arrived, and I failed not to call upon Ayoob. He had strongly reprobated at the time Suleiman's conduct in giving me up, an assured me he wondered not to see a man of my mettle, after such treatment, return to Egypt in so different a character. I was glad in my turn to find an opportunity of doing a chief, who formerly had distinguished me in a most flattering manner, a very signal piece of service. Some expressions, dropped by the Capitan-Pasha, had made me surmise that some foul play was intended to the hostage Beys. I need not say by what means I verified my suspicion; but I forthwith went and apprized Ayoob of his danger. His gratitude for this act led him to offer me a handsome present, which I declined.

Meanwhile Hassan had got every thing in readiness for his departure. He confirmed Abdi-Pasha in his place of Visier, and Ismaïl Bey in his rank as Schaich-el-belled. On his Kehaya, whose name likewise was Ismaïl, he conferred the situation of his Wekil, or agent at Cairo. After these and other appointments, he assembled in the citadel a solemn Divan, gave, in a set speech, a pompous detail of the incalculable benefits he had bestowed on Egypt, and terminated the sitting by inviting the four hostage Beys, against the faith of treaties, to follow him to Constantinople. Osman, Abderaham, and Husseïn, taken by surprise, were obliged to accept his proffered hospitality. Ayoob, more on his guard, had taken his precautions, and had given instructions to his Mamlukes. The summons had scarce dropped from Hassan's lips, ere he rushed out, and, assisted by his suite, sought refuge in Ibrahim's harem. Hassan durst not, in defiance of his own solemn promise, drag him from so respected a sanctuary. He was left at Cairo in possession of all his honours.

Those which Hassan offered to my choice, were to remain in the citadel of Cairo, commander of the corps of Arnaoots, or to go back to Constantinople, and obtain promotion in the expected war. Admiring neither the Visier, the Schaich-el-belled, nor the wekil, and wishing much to try Valachia, and to rejoin Mavroyeni, I accepted the latter. The ransom of Suleiman's Tootoondjee, duly paid on presenting his order, the well lined belt of a Mamluke whom I had disrobed at Sioot, and the liquidation of certain old claims at Cairo, which I employed those ready accountants my Arnaoots to settle, had gone a good way towards repairing my shattered finances. The last evening of my stay at Cairo added another figure to the balance of my capital. As I passed through a narrow lane, an ill-looking fellow suddenly stopped me, and drew out a dagger. I started back: but instead of the point he turned to me the hilt, left the handjar in my hands, and disappeared. The weapon was covered with emeralds, and of considerable value. I had seen it before, on grand occasions, sparkle in Ayoob's girdle. – Hassan never saw it in mine.

Nothing remarkable occurred on the journey down the Nile. On the 21st of October we weighed anchor from Alexandria. Our voyage was prosperous, our reception at Constantinople indifferent. The mob of the capital, it seems, had promised itself the agreeable spectacle of the heads of the Egyptian Beys stuck on the battlements of the Bab-Humayoom, and cared little to see us only bring back our own. To ourselves, however, this was a source of some satisfaction; and the more, as we brought, besides, wherewithal to fortify our minds against idle clamour.

Even after Spiridion and I had parted for ever, my friend had not dismissed all solicitude in my behalf. Fearing lest the obscurity which hung over Achmet's death might not always succeed in preventing its influence over my fate, should I return to Stambool, he had, during my campaign in Egypt, negotiated with the family of the deceased a legal renunciation of its vindictive rights. At first indeed his proposal greatly shocked the mourning parents. "What! sell the life of a relation, of a son, for money! – No, never! Were the earth to swallow them up on the spot, they must, they would have blood for blood! – At any rate, they could only compound, with the executioner's axe on the culprit's neck!" By degrees, however, they came round to more reasonable sentiments. The event was nearly forgotten, the loss small, the chance of discovering the offender still less, and the sum offered considerable. With many ifs and buts, they at last signed so formal an act of forgiveness, that I might, if I liked, have added to my other titles that of slayer of Kara Achmet.

I needed not this new proof of kindness, to feel ill at ease until I had embraced my friend. Fearful, however, of taking him by surprise, perhaps at an unseasonable moment, I sent to enquire whether my visit would be acceptable. The precaution seemed a wise one. Just then was pending the negotiation with the lady, who soon after bestowed upon him her fair hand. Her parents only objected his former intimacy with a notorious profligate and a renegado. Had I shown myself at that juncture, and taken advantage of Spiridion's friendship to appear in his company, the match would have been broken off. It was even requisite, I understood, for the advancement of the business, that the coolness arisen between us should be openly expressed. A hint of this circumstance having been given me, I acted accordingly and in bitter terms of Spiridion's leaving me at Chio; but privately I sent him, as a token of friendship, a fine Arabian, accompanied by a few lines of affection and of thanks. Unavowed proceedings always turn out ill, however well meant! Whether the messenger thought the horse would betray the giver, or whether the horse ran away with the messenger, neither they nor the letter reached their destination; and long after, I heard that Spiridion had felt hurt at my seeming neglect.

Returning one day from witnessing – with infinite satisfaction – to what degree the Franks, who accuse the Greeks of meanness, can excel themselves in that useful quality; how they can humble themselves, even in persons of the representatives of their sovereigns, before the paltriest of the Sultan's officers; and how at their public audiences these pliant envoys of European powers will put up with any indignity from the lowest Turkish rabble, for the sake of maintaining a constant intercourse with a nation which returns their advances with contempt – I happened to meet a face no longer young, which put me in mind of an old vow, not the less sacred from the lowly station of its object. It was that made to the little grocer's wife, who in the days of my first distress had come to my relief with conserve of roses. In her own later career – poor soul! – bitters had succeeded sweets. The new French style of cookery, and the white sauces introduced with the revolutionary principles among the Greeks of fashion, had exploded the spice and comfits, staple ingredients of the darker complexioned dishes, the delight of their forefathers. The grocer consequently was become a bankrupt, had died of grief in the midst of his unsold dainties, and had left his consort to struggle with misfortunes, which required a species of consolation more solid and less sentimental than that which I once administered to a mourning widow in Egypt. I should not have mentioned the visit which I paid for this purpose, and the real pleasure I derived from the relief I was able to afford, but that my friends, justly solicitous about my unsullied fame, might remark that I had at an early period of my history recorded a solemn engagement, and no where had mentioned its fulfilment.

Let us return to matters of more importance. Though from the first instant of his elevation, Youssoof-Visier had been preparing the rupture with Russia, the war broke out without any formal declaration. On the 18th of August, 1787, the Russian Embassador found himself unexpectedly complimented with a lodging at the sultan's expense in the Seven-Towers[1], and the Turkish troops stationed at Ockzakow, made an attack upon the fortress of Kinburn, when the garrison thought itself in profound peace. The fullest success of these petty manœuvres could not have made amends for the imputation of bad faith which they fixed upon the Turks; their failure only added disgrace to discomfiture. They gave the Emperor of Austria a plausible excuse for joining the Russians, and for declaring war against the Porte, on the 9th February, 1788. This event seemed to mark Valachia for the seat of the ensuing campaign. It increased my wish to take a share in its hazards; and I obtained from Hassan-Pasha letters both for Youssoof and for Mavroyeni. Encamped at Daood-Pasha, the supreme Visier had already hoisted the sacred standard of the Prophet, and was collecting round it the grand army of the faithful, for the defence of the empire. I intended to visit the Commander in chief on my way, but aware of my moderate dimensions, and expecting to make a greater figure on the smaller theatre of Valachia, I purposed to tarry only with Mavroyeni.

Neither personage, however, was to be favoured with my company the very first instant my credentials were signed: such unnecessary diligence would have bespoken an anxiety in their behalf somewhat too flattering. With my letters in my pocket, I gave three days more to the dissipation of the capital; and satisfied with having, through dint of unexampled diligence, compassed as much pleasure as so short a period would allow, proceeded without further delay on the less perilous road to open warfare and destruction. My equipage was light. It consisted of what articles my horse could carry in addition to my person; for, unable to afford a long string of attendants, I trusted more for safety to a perfectly unobtrusive appearance, than by a small and insufficient retinue.

Though I had seen camps before, that of the Visier-Azem, with all its want of order, struck me as very magnificent. The central object, the tent of the commander – with its avenues of pillars and standards, its gilding and draperies – looked a most imposing mass: but its tenant disappointed me. I had formerly known Youssoof as Hassan's kehaya. He was then quoted for the erect majesty of his mien, and for the jetty lustre of his ample beard. The personage to whom I was introduced at Daood-Pasha, on the contrary, had the grey hairs of age and the stoop of infirmity. "Heavens!" thought I, "can this be the same man whom I formerly admired; can seven years so pull down the sturdiest human frame? would they make of me so woeful a ruin?" – And it was a relief to my mind when I heard that Youssoof, in order to encrease the gravity of his appearance, used similar arts for the purpose of looking old and infirm, to those which others employ for that of appearing young and active.

With the other attributes of age, Youssoof seemed to have acquired its garrulity. I thought there never would have been an end to his enquiries after Hassan-Pasha. The Grand-Admiral's health, his looks, his spirits, were each separately made the theme of long and repeated expressions of solicitude: and at each favourable reply, Youssoof blessed Allah for the good news with such studied emphasis, that I judged the Visier's affection for his ancient patron, and the Capitan-Pasha's regard for his overgrown favourite, to have sunk nearly to the same level. Base coin is always shewy!

As soon as Youssoof had added his contribution to my letters for Mavroyeni, I proceeded on my journey. The supreme Visier himself was soon to break up his first station, and to halt successively at divers other marked places, in order to give the Zaïms and Timariotes of all the different provinces of Roumili an opportunity of re-inforcing his army: and I was unwilling, by unnecessary delay, to encounter on the road more than I could help of the small detachments of true believers, expected soon to obey from all quarters the invitation of Mohammed's vicar![2]

From Daood-Pasha I met nothing in a questionable shape until I reached Erekli. There appearances became more terrific. On going out at the gate of that city after dusk, and turning the corner of the spacious burying-ground which extends close under its walls, my horse suddenly stopped, and in defiance of all my efforts to urge him on, stood wildly looking towards the tombs, and trembling like a leaf. "So!" thought I, at these symptoms of terror; "the Gouls are abroad; the spirits of the dead hold their revels; the living are unwelcome here!" And in fact, I soon perceived, by the light of the moon, a number of deep and threatening shadows in human form glide along the marble gravestones. The spectres seemed to move hand in hand round the funereal mounds, sometimes separating, then again forming clusters, then totally disappearing under ground. Presently sounds too arose from the hollow earth: confused murmurs pervaded the place; and at last a whole swarm of ghastly figures sprung up close to my horse, – no longer indeed unsubstantial phantoms, but seeming from their emaciated form and pallid hue, the very corpses of the dead arisen from their coffins. Immediately they encircled me with a hideous yell.

No sooner, however, was the frightful ring completed, than my apprehensions of the deceased vanished in my fears of the living; and I no longer thought myself in the company of spectres, but in that of banditti. Accordingly, clapping both stirrups to my horse, I was going to break through the threatening circle, when I perceived that none of the party were armed, or at least had any weapon more formidable than a stick, or a pair of crutches; that there were as many women and children in the ranks as men; and that more than two thirds of the troop were halt, blind, or paralytic.

There is, gentle reader, a district in the Morea, whose inhabitants are, to a man, beggars by profession. Every year, as soon as they have sown their fields, these industrious members of society abandon their villages until harvest time, and sally forth, on a begging circuit, through the different provinces of Roumili. The elders and chiefs of the community plan the route, divide the provinces, and allot to each detachment its ground. They shorten or prolong their sojourn in the different places they visit, according as the mine of charity is rich, and has been more or less explored. Through wastes where little is to be gleaned large troops travel in close order, but on approaching fruitful districts the swarms again divide and spread. According to his peculiar talent, each individual undertakes the heart-rending tale of mental woe, or the disgusting display of bodily suffering. "His wife and children died of hunger by the road side, after being burnt out of house and home;" – or, "he has an incurable leprosy in every joint;" – or, "he is actually giving up the ghost for want of a morsel of food!" Old traders grown rich by their indigence, sell out to young beginners; and the children of the society remain in common, so that each female may in turns be provided with a pair of fatherless twins, to be duly pinched to tears, and made lustily to roar out whenever compassionate people are in sight. Unceasing warfare is kept up with interlopers from other quarters, who trespass on the domain of this regularly organized band. Among its members, a dislocated limb, or a disgusting disease, are esteemed peculiar blessings; and hereditary complaint is a sort of an estate, and if conspicuous, and such as to resist the officious remedies of the charitable, confers rank, and may be called a badge of nobility. But even those who have the misfortune to labour under the most incurable state of health and vigour, are dexterous, if not radically to correct this perverseness of nature, at least to remove its untoward external appearance. They excel in the manufacturer of counterfeit wounds and mock diseases; and the convulsions of a demoniac are graceful movements to their spontaneous fits.

The troop with which I had the luck to fall in, had destined Erekli for the next day's scene of action. Its worthy members were taking among the tombs a comfortable night's rest, previous to the morning's labours. Already had most of the party sunk into soft slumbers on the pillows of the fresh laid graves, when the tramp of my horse, resounding among the hollow vaults, and reverberated by the sculptured slabs, roused, and made them start up, and surround me as has been seen. Their clamour was only the eleemosynary ditty, which, from long habit, they kept mumbling even in their sleep.

Moved with compassion at the sight of so much sufferings, I determined at once to remove all these accumulated ills, and for this purpose began to lay lustily about me, with my good long ox-hide whip. It would have gladdened a feeling heart to see what a salutary and immediate effect this application had. At the very first flourish, the lame found the use of their legs, the blind recovered their sight, and the deaf and dumb a Stentorian voice. A poor decrepid creature, doubled with age and infirmity, straightening as if by magic, became all at once as nimble as a stag: a man shaped like a dromedary, slipped his hunch without missing it; and a woman, eighteen months at least gone with child, stumbling over a grave stone, brought to light a truss of straw!

The fright of my friends, however, was not of long duration. By degrees they began to fancy, that, though I was armed and on horseback, and they were unarmed and on foot, yet in the dark, and among heaps of grave-stones, thirty or forty had a chance against one. In this notion they again rallied, and soon sticks and stones whizzed about my ears as thick as hail. I now found I had to deal with a set of ungrateful rogues, who, so far from thanking me for the miraculous cure I had performed, only requited good with evil. It therefore seemed time to leave them to their fate, and to scamper off; by which means I soon got out of sight, and a very little while after, out of hearing of the vollies of abuse which accompanied the repeated showers of stones.

The crossing of the Balkan, – which rose in sight soon after – would, I suppose, have been a delightful treat to one who preferred the remains of a former worn out world to the good things of the present renovated globe, and a petrified oyster or cabbage to fare of easier digestion. For my part, who felt more anxious to know the end of things than their origin, I was very glad when I found Mount Hemus fairly left behind me, and still more so when before me I beheld winding in ample sweeps the wide waters of the Danube. My raptures still encreased on setting foot, after crossing the turbid stream, in the plains of Valachia.

In order to profit as much as possible by the benefits of Christendom, and to evince the estimation in which I still held its institutions, I purposed sleeping the first night of my entrance within its pale, at a monastery. I had heard of one on the road, where the caloyers lived well, and could spare a way-faring man a few crumbs from their table, and a corner in their dormitory. On my arrival I found my design forestalled. The convent had been invaded, only an hour before, by a set of Frank travellers, who carried peremptory orders from the provincial government to inconvenience at their pleasure every place on the road.

I say, invaded: for between masters, servants, interpreters, couriers, mikmandars[3] and janissaries, there were no less I think than twenty or thirty individuals; and for many of the least important among them singly, the place appeared much too small. The very monks had been turned out of their cells to make room for the strangers.

At first I took for granted that so mighty a removal of human bodies from the place of their birth must have an adequate end; and that the head of the party could be no less than the ambassador of some great Christian potentate, come to transact affairs of the utmost importance with the Porte; and resigned myself in consequence to lay my own diminished head where I could: but on discreetly seeking to have my surmises confirmed by a sort of courier half Swiss half Italian, who, in a gibberish between both was giving directions to the Greek steward of the convent who understood neither, I could only discover that the *padrone* was a young gentleman of great fortune, who, tired of having every thing at home in the most comfortable style for nothing but the trouble of issuing his commands, was thus wandering about the world, for no other purpose but to enjoy the variety of now and then going to bed without his supper, or getting up without having gone to bed. Constantinople was to be his first halting place on the journey; but whether from thence he was to go by land to China, or by sea to Peru, was not yet decided.

I now began to think it somewhat hard that in the Sultan's own dominions, one of his faithful subjects, travelling on real business, and who had lived long enough not to think going to bed on an empty stomach, or to think sleeping in the fields a desirable variety, should be thus kept on the *pavé* by strangers who only came to burthen us with their ennui: and accordingly desired my informer to go and remonstrate in my name with his master, respecting the unreasonable monopoly he was exercising – fully determined, should the negociation prove inefficient, to resort to more energetic measures for obtaining redress. I knew that, to whatever extremities I might proceed, the Greeks would remain neutral, and I feared not the Franks. All I apprehended was, that the servant might not deliver my message in terms sufficiently forcible; and I therefore soon followed myself – highly incensed at the supposed indignity I was suffering – and bolted into his excellency's dingy chamber, just as the courier had concluded his speech.

To find all complacency, where one expects nothing but resistance, and is prepared only for using proportionate force, occasions a shock similar to that of sinking into a down pillow where one had laid ones account with finding a seat of impenetrable stone; and this sort of shock I experienced, when received by a young man of the most prepossessing appearance, only intent upon knowing in what way he could most effectually accommodate myself and all my suite; and ending by inviting me to partake of his own indifferent supper, which, he added, his companion had just stepped down to hasten.

Thus courteously addressed, my answer was made to correspond, and nothing ensued but a conflict of civilities. It was only interrupted by my going out again to look after my said suite – namely, my horse, – ere I gave myself up for the remainder of the evening to the pleasure of conversing with so charming and well bred a host.

His invitation to the strange traveller at the gate had, meanwhile, gone abroad among his own retinue; and before I was able to return from my excursion, it was my good fortune to overhear the impression it produced on his companion, still engaged in bustling below stairs. This somewhat less hospitable personage was pleased loudly to wonder what pleasure Mr. T – could find in courting every adventurer, Turk or Christian, with whom chance brought him in contact on the road; and grievously moaned over the selfish vanity which made a man of his sense unfeelingly put his friends out of their way, merely to have his politeness admired by utter strangers.

The remark fortunately affected not my appetite. When the smoking evidences of the amiable companion's industry appeared on the table, I paid them not the less every compliment in my power; and was only the more intent upon diverting their author from the nefarious purpose of being himself the first again to destroy the various fruits of his labour, by forcing upon him a thousand little attentions, for which, in his heart, he would have wished to box my ears. From this proceeding lengthened the meal but little. I soon perceived that my host – overcome with the fatigue of the journey – though striving to the utmost to entertain his guest, was scarce in a condition to receive from that guest an adequate return; and therefore speedily proposed a separation – in which I was most warmly seconded by his companion, who, sated at last, now sagaciously observed that, as they were to rise betimes, they had better go to their rest.

As far as his own share was concerned, it is but doing the gentleman in question justice, to state that he spared nothing to promote this laudable object. He kept to himself a mattress, which might have accommodated three more of his fellow travellers, and left these – not *friends*, I suppose – unceremoniously enough to lie on the bare tiles: but in spite of this precaution the nimble tenants of the place, whose supper was only just beginning, kept *il signor compagno* awake. This misfortune caused him to groan so loudly and so incessantly all night, that no one else within hearing was permitted to enjoy the repose which had forsaken this important personage. I heartily regretted his fine feelings, and wished he had had some of the selfishness of his patron.

The moment the Frank party was off, the caloyers were released from the forced confinement in which all, except the superior, had been held during their stay. I thought this black gentleman looked at me distrustfully, for having displayed Frankish freedoms under the Muslim turban, and feared he might make some report at Bucharest to my disadvantage. The impression was to be done away. Taking him therefore aside, I honestly confessed that I was not only a Greek – which my speech confirmed – but a disguised emissary from Russia, come to sound the disposition of the Greek papases in favour of Ekatharina![4] Hereupon his heart opened: he expressed his admiration of the Empress, in particular for her laudable perseverance in the privations of widowhood; and earnestly entreated me to inform her by the first opportunity what a staunch friend she had in Father Kyrillos; dwelling much all the while upon the means of corresponding with the well affected to that sovereign, throughout Valachia, afforded by his convent, – a hint by no means lost upon me, when afterwards I had troops to quarter, and contributions to levy.

Continuing my journey, absorbed in reflections which were greatly favoured by my slow progress through endless bogs, I scarce perceived a personage who came from whither I was going, until he pulled up his steed to consider me more at leisure. I returned him the compliment, though his equipage little deserved it, and "Selim!" on his part, and, "Condilly!" on mine, we roared out at the same instant.

This Signor Condilly, originally a Roman Catholic, had first married a sister of Mavroyeni's, and consequently a Greek. On her demise he showed his grief by embracing the Greek creed himself, and marrying a Roman Catholic. Her he left to go into a monastery; and the convent he fled from to take a third wife, younger than the two former. He had treated his sovereigns as he had done his consorts. When Venetian Consul at the Canéa, he sold the interests of the republic to the Turks; and when employed for the Turks at Zante, he betrayed them to the Venetians. I had known him at Constantinople, where he gave himself as much airs as if he carried Jove's thunder in his sleeve, and entertained his friends with stories so long and tiresome, that they would have make the very moon split her face with yawning. On Mavroyeni's appointment to the principality of Valachia, he sent this worthy brother-in-law on before him to Bucharest, as his Caïmakam; and when he came himself, he appointed Condilly his cupbearer: nor had I heard, when we met, of any later change.

"Whither bound, Georgacki," cried I, "for the capital or for the army?"

"For whatever place" was his reply, "I may be invited to. You see me at large again!"

"That misfortune," rejoined I, "you seem to be used to; but how happened this last speedy dismissal?"

"Who can tell?" exclaimed Condilly with a shrug of the shoulders, "Not I at least! – When a man has his familiar sprite, with whom alone he takes counsel, we poor mortals must be contented to remain in ignorance. People do what they please, when they act by inspiration. You must have heard of the wealthy Vakareskolo, the Croesus of boyars,[5] who thought himself so secure from being fleeced, by never appearing at court, and declining all dangerous distinctions. Well! – has not Mavroyeni, by means of his invisible counsellor, at last hunted him out, and sent to him to say that the humble should be exalted, and that his very disinterestedness made it necessary, for the good of the country, that he should assume some high and responsible office!"

"The Bey found not the same reason, I presume, for securing the permanence of my worthy informant's services?" was my reply.

"His household demon," rejoined Condilly, "lately put it into his head that his Greek name was a base corruption; that he was descended from the ancient Venetian family of Morosini: and its Latin translation, Maurocenus, is now the name he insists on being addressed by. My tongue once made an unlucky slip; I called him by that of his forefathers; – and for this offence he condemned me, his kinsman, his counsellor, and his cup-bearer – who tasted every drop of his wine – to bread and water in the salt-mines! Had I remained there long, I must have become pickled alive, and so have died a vampire, even without excommunication, and have sucked his blood, as he does that of others. For that reason only, I suppose, he let me out at last, on condition of leaving Valachia. But, O how I shall talk, as soon as I am past the frontier!"

To me it seemed that Signor Condilly waited not till that period to execute his threat. Loth, however, to lose time in conversation where I was sure not to hear a word of truth: "Hark ye, Georgacki," cried I, "you, who are going, may be right to talk, but I, who am coming, would do wrong to listen. You have been long enough in the world to know that the atmosphere of one out of favour is infectious, and cannot take it amiss if you are done by as you would do by others. So adieu! and fare ye well!"

At these words I pushed on. The cup-bearer called after me, to say that, for all my caution, he would take upon himself to bespeak the horses for my own return. I did not stop to retort, but made what speed I could, and the same evening reached Bucharest.

CHAPTER XIII.

From the first moment of the rupture with Austria, Mavroyeni, expecting Valachia to become the theatre of the war, had sent his useless princess and her still more useless train back to Constantinople; – a wise measure, I thought, where *real* clouds were gathering! In order to defray the expenses requisite for the defence of the principality, he had levied enormous contributions, not only on the laity, but on the clergy, who, as ministers of peace, could not conceive what they had to do with the war, and thought their task fulfilled when they had prayed for the safety of the country. He had, moreover, banished to Turkey, or put in durance on the spot, such of the boyars and others – no matter what their rank – whom he suspected of a secret understanding with Austria. Among the passes or ravines which form the only communication athwart the formidable barrier of mountains that separate Transilvania from the land of the Roumoums,[1] he had distributed seven or eight thousand Seïmen, or provincial troops. Through his care, Bucharest, a city of immense extent, lying in an almost dead flat, for whose defence nature had done nothing, and art could do but little, bade as formidable defence to an enemy as its situation permitted. Each khan within its circuit was converted into a battery, and each convent into a fortress. The very archiepiscopal palace, and the cathedral, situated on the only eminence favourable for defence, were, to the inexpressible horror of the Valachians, transformed into a citadel. Soldiers quartered where priests used to say mass, cannon balls heaped up where stood the cross, and muskets and sabres piled where had been raised the host, completed the dismay of the natives.

It was in the midst of all this bustle of warlike preparations that I entered Bucharest. At its gates nothing was seen but groups of moaning families going out, and detachments of turbulent soldiers marching in; and wherever I stopped within its precincts, no other discourse met my ear but that of banishments, confiscations, fines, imprisonments, recruitings, fortifications, and plans of attack and of defence. "Good!" said I to myself; "this martial discord is music to my ears! It promises plenty of what I most want: dear delightful confusion! Born to live in troubled waters, again I breathe, again I feel in my element!" – and every officer of state whose favour seemed expiring, every grandee of the court, whose fall was announced, I only considered as kindly making room for me. My feelings somewhat resembled those of the sagacious birds called vultures, who, the moment the battle begins to rage, flap their wings, exult, and already in imagination revel in their promised feast!

When, however, – the first tumult of the sense allayed – I sat down quietly in my lodging, to consider how I should best proceed, my reflections assumed a soberer hue, and my expectations gradually fell to a less exalted pitch. "I am now," thought I, "in a place where I possess not a friend, nor even an acquaintance; where all must consider me as an intruder against whom it is their business to unite; and, in that place, at the mercy of a single man, and that man, Mavroyeni! – Mavroyeni! even in his first dependent state often uncontrollable, and ruled by caprice rather than by cool reason, and who now, after so long thirsting in a state of servility for the despotic sway he has at last obtained, every hour drinks unto intoxication of the honeyed cup of power. It is true, I bear within my own breast the qualities which his situation renders most valuable, and I carry in my pocket the recommendations which his interest obliges him most to respect. The commands in my favour of the two rulers of the state – by sea and by land – would, with any other person in his place, leave me no further trouble, than that of announcing myself and my wishes! And I moreover know Mavroyeni sufficiently lenient in religious matters, not to regard my apostacy as a great bar to my promotion, even in his Greek principality: "but," added I, in order to restrain the too sanguine hopes founded on these considerations, "may he not retain an unfavourable impression of my youthful pranks, and my insolent mode of quitting his service? May he not, with still more probability, feel hurt at my long estrangement from his person, my long apparent disdain of his protection, my long obstinacy in seeking my fortune any where upon earth rather than under the shelter of his wing!" – So often had his wayward temper only turned the more restive, for being more sharply reined, that, in order to shew his independence, it was likely he might make the very weight of my recommendations, a motive for treating me with the greater coolness. I therefore – spite of my expectations – prepared my mind for the possibility of an indifferent reception, and resolved only to advance in so cautious a manner, as not to stand much committed should I meet with a rebuff.

In this spirit, – so far from dressing for my first audience of Mavroyeni as I had done for my first interview with Suleiman; so far from informing every passenger as I went along, by the importance of my looks, that I was going to court; from announcing in an authoritative tone, on my arrival at the palace, that I carried letters from the Grand Visier, the Lord High Admiral, and the Drogueman of the navy, – I rather ran into the opposite extreme, and by way of pitching my tone at the outset in such a key as I might be sure not to have to lower afterwards, came in so modest a dress, crept into the audience chamber in so quiet a manner, and, having delivered my message in a scarce audible voice, stood so demurely with my hands in my sleeves at the further end of the room, that I scarce was noticed by a troop of gentlemen of far higher apparent pretensions, who held their more conspicuous station in the middle of the apartment, and bore such a prodigious air of self importance, that their very yawnings (which were both frequent and loud) had in them a something grand and imposing; while their conversation – chiefly intended, it should seem, for the benefit of distant hearers, – ran entirely upon the last joke of the Ban of Crayova, the last remark of the Cameraz, and the last witticism of the Spatar!

I had heard that in some place or other the humble were to be exalted: but this certainly was not in Mavroyeni's anti-room. Its familiars seemed of a sort not easily to give a stranger credit for higher claims than he chose to divulge, but, on the contrary, to indulge a man desirous of remaining in the back ground, to the utmost of his wishes in this to them strange propensity. It is true, they vouchsafed now and then to honour me with their attention, so far as to eye me from head to foot, – but it was with any thing but a look of invitation to join their noble group. This silent scrutiny was even carried to such a length, that at last my patience forsook me, and I began, in my turn, to stare at the starers with sufficient steadiness gradually to disconcert all their petulance, and to make them fall from their haughty self-sufficient look, into an appearance of downright constraint – until at last one of the set, determined to beat me out of the field, detached himself from the cluster, came over to where I stood with a sort of mock civility, and asked me in a simpering tone, whether the company had the honour of my approbation?

I was going to answer "No," without circumlocution, – when suddenly the door of the inner room opened, and the party fell back to range themselves round the room in a respectful circle, in the middle of which the gentleman usher advanced to select whom he should first introduce to his Highness.

Each was striving to obtain that distinction, by straining to protrude the upper part of his body a few inches before that of his neighbour; – for as to me, I did not at that critical moment come into consideration at all, and would have been entirely forgotten, had I not informed the usher of my presence, by holding over the heads of those that pressed before me certain talismanic papers, at the sight of which the officer pushed the crowd aside to let me pass. I now handed to him my credentials to be taken to the prince; and as I delivered my letters, amused myself with naming the writers one by one.

Being, on the strength of so respectable an introduction, immediately let in, I left my anti-room friends nearly as composed as if a thunder-bold had just exploded among them. One half looked pale as ashes, the other red as crimson; and every one seemed intent only upon how he should repair his imprudence most dexterously on the re-appearance of the great man in disguise.

Though my call was speedy, my reception was not the more promising. Mavroyeni, at first, deigned not even to greet me with that look of surprise with which I had laid my account, but went on with the different occupations in which I found him engaged, as if unaware of my presence; leaving me full leisure mean time to mark the havoc made by ambition more than by age in his originally hard and homely features. In fact, the ruling passion seemed to have increased to such a degree the obliquity which the natural dimness of his right eye had produced in the motions of the other, as to have rendered his a perfectly *sinister* look, in every sense of the word. He always eyed one askance! Those to whom he stood opposite, his eye glanced beside; and to fix his interlocutor, he turned his face away from him. It is true, that the lower features of that same face in some measure made amends for the defects of those above. His jet black beard and mustachios, of which he took great care, encompassed lips whose smile was as pleasing as the frown of his dark brow was terrific; and these lips in their turn disclosed, when he spoke, two rows of teeth as white as snow, which no man could be more ready to show on all occasions.

For some time after my entrance, however, they were only uncased in the process of dictating a letter of three pages to the Reïs-Effendee: and not until he had finished this and all his other business – paring his nails included – with the utmost composure, did he seem to perceive that I stood before him, tired of watching his left eye, and of commencing bows all stifled in the birth. At last, when he had fairly exhausted his own occupations and my patience, he cast a look my way, and appeared to see me; but it was only to ask in a gruff and snappish manner – while pointing to my poor letters flung unopened on the sofa, "Whether it was I who had brought that load of papers?" –

I bowed again, and said it was, but only as the person entrusted with its conveyance. "For well I know," added I, "that with your Highness neither interest avails, nor even talent, when presumptuously relying on its own merit, and without the sunshine of your spontaneous favour, Heaven directed towards its possessor!"

This compliment to the Bey's independence smoothed the bristles round his heart. His features immediately relaxed; and I thought I could clearly discern athwart what they retained of outward rigidity, an inward smile of approbation. At last his satisfaction even broke out in words. "Right," he cried, "my will alone is my law! If you were the angel Gabriel, descended from the highest heaven, you must hit my fancy, ere you obtain my favour, – at least here in Valachia. But," – added he, wholly unbending, "you know I always liked you in spite of your pranks; nay, perhaps even the better for them. You were clever as a lad, and I trust years have given you discretion without blunting your spirit. Tell me, – for I know you have been Kiachef in Egypt, – how you got that rank; and how you contrived to lose it?"

Thus invited, I gave the Bey a sketch of my principal adventures, – not indeed drawn with the entire unreserve of these memoirs, but in which, without startling Mavroyeni's belief by an improbable account of my excessive wisdom or virtue, I yet only touched upon my follies and vices with the tender hand of a friend, whose blame is less severe than the praise of an enemy. The last occurrence which I mentioned was the first of my entrance into the Beys' dominions, the meeting with Condilly.

"He was going to Turkey," said I. – "Not so," answered Mavroyeni. "he was speeding to Vienna: he only made a circuit to deceive me. It was not worth the while. I ever knew him do more harm to his friends than to his enemies; and so I ordered that every pass might be opened to him. With you I mean to do the reverse."

I assured the Bey I should remain a willing prisoner; and finding that nothing more was wanting of me for the present, made my bow and retired.

Meantime my seemingly interminable audience had fully confirmed the idea of my importance in the anti-room. The mystery which hung over my character only served, like the vapours which envelope a mountain, to magnify my seeming grandeur; and when I stole back among my friends in sheep skin, I found that during my absence they had had high words about me: each reproaching the rest for his own incivility. No sooner did they perceive my return, than they all dropped some incidental remark, intended to smooth the way to a more direct address. The gentleman who had the first turned a deaf ear to my salutation had lost his hearing from a cold; the one who had laughed at me most openly, had been able to think of nothing but a domestic misfortune which quite distracted his senses; and as to the one who attacked me in articulate speech, he always made it a point, when he saw a stranger of quality anxious to remain incognito, of doing something or other to favour the scheme.

Having thus each dropped his little propitiatory sentence, but without the smallest intention – poor innocent souls! – of its being overheard, they now all with the utmost surprise perceived me standing before them, immediately bowed in the most gracious manner, and all speaking together, ventured in the most obsequious terms to express...... but what? – is the thing I am unable to tell, as without stopping to hear it, I left the cringing circle to divide among them a single supercilious glance cast upon the whole troop collectively, and then turning on my heel, very quietly walked off.

The next day I received from Mavroyeni a summons to a pleasure-garden formed by him the year before, outside the city. "A good omen this," thought I, – "His villa is the place where he deposits his Beyship at the entrance gate;" and truly, among his tulips and ranunculuses, his temper seemed, chameleon like, to reflect a somewhat gayer hue. It was almost *couleur de rose*, and not perhaps the less resembling the queen of flowers, because it had a lurking thorn. Through Mavroyeni's transient gaiety of manner and conversation might still be discerned the stationary weight which oppressed his heart, as through the fleeting waters of the stream you see the rocks that lie motionless below. The whole drift of the Prince's apparently unpremeditated discourse tended indirectly to find out how he was spoken of by the world at large. "Nothing," he observed, "was so entertaining as to hear what people say of one: and no body had such opportunities of knowing as a stranger who mixed in every set, and whom no party yet mistrusted. Often an indifferent new comer heard sentiments drop by chance from the lip, which the person most deeply interested, could not wring from the heart."

"Sir!" answered I with great gravity, "Suleiman[2] the Just, of glorious memory, when his subjects disapproved of his measures, used to cut off not only the tongues of the railers, but also the ears of the listeners."

"Sensible Suleiman!" exclaimed the Bey, sighing: "but I, who am not the supreme ruler of the empire, may make it my amusement to hear the various opinions on the merits of my administration."

"What can your Highness expect to hear," answered I – somewhat doubtful of the intensity of that pleasure, where every one of those opinions uniformly ended in abuse – "but that all who make your actions the theme of their discourse vie in expressions of equal veneration?"

"Which of my virtues are dwelt upon most at length," resumed Mavroyeni: my clemency, or my contempt for money?"

This was a home question: it sounded like taking flattery by storm; though thus abruptly assailed from the most vulnerable quarter, she could scarce avoid inflicting wounds, even with the utmost wish to caress. I looked at Mavroyeni to find out whether, perchance, he only intended the query as a trap to catch the flatterer. His countenance gave me no clue; his features were immoveable.

"Sir," said I therefore: "every one knows the natural humanity of your disposition; every one is persuaded that if, in your conduct, you depart in the least from the dictates of clemency, your tender soul regrets what your trying situation commands.'

"I see;" rejoined Mavroyeni with a gesture of impatience, "I can extract nothing from you. Now at least let me show I can spare your information. Let me tell you myself what people say. They call me – a monster of rapaciousness and cruelty,"

I looked surprised.

"Yes," repeated the Bey, raising his voice; "they call me as covetous as hell, and as merciless as Satan: and though you try to look astonished, you know it full well. But what you may not perhaps know quite so fully, is, that for being what I am, I deserve public thanks."

Here my surprise became real, and I therefore concealed it.

"Two things," rejoined Mavroyeni, "I assume, which you will scarcely deny."......

I was going to say: "Certainly not;" but I stopped myself in time.

"The first," he continued, "is that this province must be defended; and the second, that no man in the empire is fit to defend it but myself."

I bowed assent.

"Now!" added the Prince; "how am I to fortify my province against invasion, without money; and how, without money, am I to keep myself in my province? Without the sums necessary to raise soldiers and batteries, the Austrians march into Bucharest next month; and without the sums requisite to fee the Capitan-Pasha, the Visier and the Sultan, I am turned out of my principality next year. Let then my avarice light on the heads of my employers. With them, my generosity would be my only crime."

"Again; – as to cruelty," resumed he, having paused to breathe. "For what purpose, do you think, has the Porte made, in my favour, the hitherto unexampled exception to its rules, of joining the rank of a Turkish Seraskier[3] to the prerogatives of a Greek Hospodar? For what purpose has the Porte allowed me to command in the field several thousands of Moslemin soldiers? but for that of enabling me to avert the extraordinary perils that hang over this province, by extraordinary vigour! If I then find that from all the various peculiarities in my situation, as a native of the Isles, as the subject of a Mohammedan master, and as myself a follower of the Christian religion, I have every body against me, as well within the very heart of my principality as beyond its boundaries; if I see the Greek who hates me as an intruder, the Valachian who wishes for the Austrians, and the Mussulman who looks down upon me as a Yaoor and a Rayah, all unite in praying for my subversion; if I have to defend myself against the jealousy of the first, the treachery of the second, and the fanaticism of the last; if I know that the least lenity, considered as weakness, will only encourage their audacity, and hasten my ruin; and if I also know that with me must perish my province, – is it not my duty to my sovereign and my province, by an extraordinary pressure to cement the jarring elements ready to fall asunder; and must I not, neglecting the petty forms of the law to do the speedier justice, wherever I can, pinion the suspected, paralyse the traitor, and cut off the criminal?"

Here Mavroyeni again stopped to draw breath, and to see what effect his oratory produced; and having established, to his satisfaction, the entire propriety of picking pockets, and chopping off heads, without waiting to ask the owner's leave, he passed from his affairs to mine.

"You have much employed my thoughts," said he, "since your arrival. Unfortunately, by the capitulation of these provinces, it is as difficult for a Mohammedan to find promotion in Valachia, as it is elsewhere in Turkey for a Greek. Few are the offices to which Turks may be appointed; and yet I should like to give you something good in itself, and something too that might not remove you too far from my person. To combine these conditions, is a purpose which I have turned every way in my mind. In short, convinced that, with your talent, it only depends on your will to succeed in any line, I make you my Divan-Effende.[4] It is only exchanging the sword for the pen."

A mere trifle, thought I: – the same turn of the wrist will do to cut a flourish on paper and on the face of an enemy; and it would only be fancying myself in the field, marshalling a parcel of soldiers, when I sat in my closet symmetrising a heap of words, and that for the same purpose too – namely, of defending ourselves, and of attacking our enemies. The ministers of the Porte would be delighted with their new correspondent, and my epistles could not fail to be preserved as models of a diplomatic style for the use of future ages!

Too well, however, I knew the Bey's fondness for extraordinary measures to express my surprise at the proposal. "Sir," said I, bowing respectfully, "your Highness has performed so many other wonders, that I consider the additional miracle of making me all at once a sober steady secretary, squatted all day long upon his heels, squaring lines and rounding periods, as only to depend upon your will: and as my forte in the Turkish language has hitherto been confined to the vulgar dialect, I mean this very minute to go and study the court phraseology, in order that the grandees of the capital may have no fault to find with our provincial dispatches."

These suggestions made the Bey reflect a little. As I prepared to take my leave: "Stop," cried he; "on second thoughts, I may do better in making you my Besh-lee Aga. You will have the command of my troop of janissaries; you will see the orders of the Sultan carried to the different districts; you will provide escorts for the great officers of the Porte; and all that, I know, you will manage to perfection. It is true, you will have to preside in a sort of court of justice, and to decide in all differences between Mohammedans and Rayahs, according to the Mussulman code. But what of that! Where God gives an employment, he gives the requisite capacity. My Postelnic makes an excellent secretary of state; – for not knowing how to sign his name. I find no fault with my Vestiaris, in his place of treasurer, though he never learnt the rule of three; and as to my Spatar, is he a worse minister of police, I pray, for knowing practically how at night windows are broken and riots made in the streets? You will do like all the rest: provide yourself with a clerk who gets less pay, and knows more of the business than the principal; and in every doubtful case of law, always presume the Mohammedan to be in the right; and give verdict in his favour."

I bowed as before. In truth, I liked the place of Besh-lee Aga as little as that of Divan-Effendee: but I trusted to the Bey's own mutability of temper for again changing his plan. I knew the only certain way to make him persist in it, was to remonstrate. I therefore silently retired.

The next day I was again summoned. The wind meantime had, as I expected, shifted to another quarter. "Skanavi," – cried the Prince, as soon as he saw me, "thinks you will make but an indifferent judge after all. He is sure, he says, you will never look grave enough in the hall, nor consent to let your mustachios turn down instead of up. I myself cannot conceive what made you so anxious for the employment. Take my word for it, the command of my Arnaoots will suit you much better."

This happened to be so exactly what I thought myself, that I now felt fain to argue the point, in order to have the nail more securely clenched; but, as the mere act of revolving the expediency of this measure in my mind gave me an appearance of hesitating, it answered all the purpose. "No words!" exclaimed the Bey. "I know what suits you much better than you can pretend to do yourself. Here is your commission made out already. Take it; go home, and thank God and the bog-fever which has left so fine a vacancy for you to step into. Your promotion will cause a few heart-burnings, – but I soon depend upon a good dose of leaden pills to cure them."

I now threw myself at the Bey's feet to thank him for his favours, and went to assume the insignia, and to perform the duties, of my new station. Acquaintance was soon made with the officers of my corps; and obedience somewhat later enforced among the privates. Many had been haïdoots or banditti before they became soldiers, and seemed likely to end as they had begun; but though they at first looked at me rather askance, we in time came – and without needing the court phraseology – to a proper understanding.

Of one who like me expected to be but little stationary, no great establishment was required. Leaving to prince Brankovano to lie in state alive in gilt keoschks, amidst troops of female slaves, I contented myself with a firwood hut for my habitation, and a few gypsies for my domestics. It is the fashion to abuse that chattering, lying, thieving, nimble race, who, invoking Mohammed among the Turks, and the Holy Virgin among the Christians, make shift in Valachia to extract gold with equal dexterity from the filth of its cities, and from the pure crystal of its mountain streams, and, if they were all to drive their wagons elsewhere, would leave the province without singers, dancers, fiddlers, fortune-tellers, tinkers, blacksmiths, or grooms. For my part, I did not dislike their attendance. Too much despised to be honest, but too timid to commit atrocious crimes, I found them lively, entertaining, and sure to succeed in whatever requires more address than courage, and more dexterity than labour.

The disorganisation of the Otthoman empire often obliges the sovereign to enforce by stratagem that absolute right over the lives of his immediate servants, which the constitution admits; and thence does the government of the Turks frequently present a strange contrast of apparent perfidy with real good faith. Its scrupulous observance of treaties is proverbial; and has been most powerfully exemplified in the Greek provinces of Valachia and Moldavia. When they surrendered to the Turkish arms, they stipulated the preservation of Greek worship and rulers; nor has the letter of the capitulation ever been violated. The governors may have been changed from the nobles of the country to the merchants of the Fanar; from men entitled to the situation by their descent, to individuals only invested with the office in consideration of their treasures; but to this day in both provinces the steeple soars above the minaret, and the worshippers of Christ take precedence of the followers of Mohammed: I mean as far as the internal organization is concerned; for with regard to external allegiance, the Greek Hospodar holds his power of his sovereign by the same tenure as the Turkish Pasha. A despot in his province, he still remains the slave of the Padi-shah, and his head may at any time be included among those with which the Sultan sometimes adorns the outer gate of the seraglio – a circumstance which, with some, might be considered as a small drawback upon the felicity of possessing a court, modelled in all its departments upon that of the Greek Emperors.

With each new Bey a whole new flight of officers of state and courtiers comes from Constantinople. They are generally the relations of their sovereign, unto the twentieth degree. Mavroyeni, however, – averring that these family leeches, the nearer their own blood was, the harder they sucked, – had fewer hanging about him than any of his predecessors. My arrival therefore formed a desirable addition to the intimate circle. Scarce a day passed that I was not sent for by the prince, to contribute my share to his entertainment. He distrusted the Greeks and he feared the Turks. I was an amphibious animal, which he considered as equally destitute of the fins of the one and the fangs of the other. "Selim," he used to say, "will neither bite me, nor slip through my fingers."

This degree of favour, however, was not without its inconveniences. Nothing could exceed the variableness of the Prince's temper. Sometimes all calm and sunshine, it was at others more stormy and boisterous than the Black Sea in March. Its changes chiefly depended on the news from Constantinople. Whenever a messenger arrived from the Porte, I used to keep out of the way, until the object of his mission had transpired. One day I found the Bey as desponding as if the old hag had come in person to warn him. "See," cried he in a tone of despair, "what I have got here!" – I expected to behold nothing less than a hatti-sherif purporting his recall. It was only a Vienna gazette; and the whole misfortune consisted in an article, dated from Bucharest, in which, it must be owned, he was somewhat roughly handled. "This ribaldry;" exclaimed Mavroyeni, "composed in a garret on the Danube, for the entertainment of a day, will be preserved by the scribblers of Germany, in their monthly, quarterly, and annual journals; will be, by the writers of the rest of Europe, chronicled as an authentic document and will finally receive endless durability in carefully written histories, intended to go down to the latest posterity as accurate pictures of the present times. Strangers will defame my character to all future ages, and not one of my countrymen will waste a drop of ink in my vindication. Ah! why was I cast among so vile a race: why was I born in such a miserable epoch! I had some generosity, some honest pride, some noble sentiments in my composition; and it was only when I found modesty confounded with incapacity, and humility considered as meanness; when I saw virtue excite more distrust than vice, and successful vice usurp the praise of virtue, that I cast off qualities which could only prove stumbling blocks in my way, and that, like the rest,

I became insidious, vindictive, and faithless: but on others fall the weight of my sins: on others the responsibility of my good dispositions depraved!"

It may be inferred from this speech, that one of Mavroyeni's great weaknesses was a desire to make a figure in history; and many were the things he did with no other view but that of their being recorded. Many also were those which on that account he enjoyed, though abstractedly they had nothing else very enjoyable in them. When an earthquake happened, or an inundation, or a fire, which laid waste half the capital, he would rub his hands and cry out with evident marks of glee; "Materials for the annals of my reign! Posterity will say – this happened in the days of Prince Maurocenus;" – and in order that posterity might say this, he would himself, I believe, like Nero, have set fire to his capital. This thirst for posthumous notoriety gave all his actions a sort of theatrical turn, which appeared quite an anomaly in a Hospodar of Valachia, and made him do things which in Christendom would have been cried up to the skies, and here made him pass for insane. Nothing frightened him so much as an anonymous threat of being turned into ridicule, or mentioned in a slighting manner in some Frank publication: and I know of two or three heads that were left on their shoulders, not in consideration of what the owners might feel, but of what the journalists might write. Sometimes he thought of imitating prince Kondemir, and composing the history of his time himself, in order to make sure of appearing in it as he wished; but for this he had not leisure yet, and put it off till after the war. At other times he talked of dubbing me his historiographer; but then I was not serious enough, and might make my readers laugh. At other times he had thoughts of sending for some French savant; but their heads seemed all turned by the revolution in their country, and they might raise the cry of liberty in Turkey. Meanwhile he never failed to distinguish by his attentions whomsoever he thought likely to give him celebrity in verse or prose. Bucharest would have become a nest of writers of odes and sonnets, had not sometimes the Bey's fancy been difficult to hit. For, occasionally, amidst the most lavish praise, a single word would provoke his wrath; and that word the author would be sent to correct in the salt-mines. This place was a greater damper to poetic ardour, and nipped many a bright effusion in the bud. Nothing, however, under ground or above, could daunt the courage of a little hunchback poet, who conceived himself destined to restore in modern Greece the pure Hellenic taste. This lofty son of Apollo was admitted to present to the Bey an ode composed in his honour on the Pindaric plan. In conformity to his model he had dispatched the prince's praise in half a dozen words, and had then passed over to the Lisbon earthquake, and the fall of Babylon, which served to eke out the remainder of his performance with as many rumbling sentences as he wanted. This, however, suited not exactly Mavroyeni's less classical ideas; and the poet, finding he did not make the impression he expected, begged of the Bey to expunge what he disliked; whereupon the Bey tore all away, save his name, observing, that that alone would say more than any rhymer could express.

The author united in his single person all the irascibility of a poet and a hunchback. He said nothing; but he sold his habitation, disposed of his movables, and retired to the Austrian states. As soon as out of Mavroyeni's reach, he wrote him a letter, to state that he had intended to make him the hero of an epic poem; but that, since his verses were disliked, he should content himself with only writing in prose the history of the war, for which he had contracted with a Leipsic bookseller, and in which nothing was to be left out, but himself and his proceedings.

Meanwhile apprehensions of a very different sort from those in which the Muses had any share, began to appal the stout heart of Mavroyeni. The northern frontier of his principality immediately bordering on the Austrian states, gave him little uneasiness. This nature had sufficiently fortified, by a barrier of mountains, only interrupted by a few narrow defiles scarcely less inexpugnable than the heights on either side. The vulnerable part of Valachia consisted in its Eastern boundary, which lay open to the neighbouring province of Moldavia, occupied by the Russians. Almost at the outset of the war, these barbarians had entered that principality, had taken Yassi its capital, and had made prisoner Ipsilanti its Hospodar; and, though they had been driven back upon Chotim, they threatened every day to recover the lost ground, and to advance to where only a small rivulet, running through a dead flat, separated the confines of Moldavia from those of Valachia.

To defend this line of frontier most immediately threatened, Mavroyeni had early fixed, for the rendezvous of his chief forces, upon the plain of Fockshan, which took its name from an open place on the borders of the two principalities, belonging half to the one and half to the other. Thither were ordered in April, from Bucharest, the arnaoots, of which I commanded the principal division, together with as many seïmen and provincial jenissaries as could be mustered. At the same time were marched thither from Sophia, where the Visier had now established his head quarters, several divisions of infantry and cavalry from the grand army – the stipendiary jenissaries under the command of their sangeaks or generals by promotion, and the feudal spahees under that of their agas by descent. When all were arrived, the collective force at Fockshan might amount to twelve or thirteen thousand men. Of these various troops, however, none were to be depended upon, save the Albanians, brave by nature, and only deficient in tactics and in discipline. Most of the jenissaries, or infantry, came from Anadoly.[5] They were men engaged in the professions of peace, forcibly torn from their wives and families, and who only marched on foot when they could not afford a horse. The spahees, or horse soldiers, on the contrary, often only holding their zeeameth or timar[6] from some grandee, as the wages of domestic service, or sent as substitutes by the real fieffee, a woman or a child, scarce knew for the most part how to sit on horseback, and would have looked better on foot. Obliged to furnish their own equipment and to find their own provisions, they were only occupied in calculating the length of their journey and the hour of their return; only stayed while the pillage of friends or foes afforded them a subsistence, and as soon as this mode of supply failed, considered themselves free to depart, and without asking leave, hurried back to their homes. The provisions supplied by government, and contracted for by the commanders, were, as usual, partly from neglect, and partly from fraud, at once so insufficient and so bad, that it was difficult to say which was calculated to produce the speediest mortality, their abundance, or their failure. Destitute of all regular magazines, the troops must have been if not poisoned at least famished, but for the immense train of volunteer tellals, or retailers, who always follow a Turkish camp, impede the progress of the army, and obstruct its retreat. When the pay of the soldiers runs short, these accommodating gentry take, in exchange for the necessaries with which they supply them, their arms, their accountrements, and their horses. Thence, on a sudden emergency, half the Turkish infantry appear disarmed, and half the cavalry dismounted.

These disorders Mavroyeni saw, but could not cure. Only part of the forces at Fockshan were furnished from his principality, and he durst not remind the remainder by unwelcome innovations, that the man who had been raised over the heads of so many Turks and Moslemen, was a yaoor and a Greek. When, however, on joining the camp, his own eyes were struck with the unwieldy and disjointed force brought together, he felt dismayed, and trembled for the issue. One day, going round with me to ascertain the observance of some new regulations, which he found wholly neglected, he could not help bursting out, – "You know, Selim," cried he, "I am not a coward; I have sometimes given proof of bravery, while prudence might still have seemed the virtue best suited to my station; and if at this juncture nothing but valour was required to insure victory, I should feel little fear of a defeat: but what can one look forward to with such a motley assemblage; and on what quality, preeminent on our side, can one found the least hope of advantage in the conflict?"

"On that," answered I, trying to cheer the prince, "which the hireling member of those admirably drilled corps of Christendom – fighting for a cause he understands not, and for interests to which he is a stranger, – wholly wants; on that which alone, in the undisciplined gatherings of the Turks, often compensates for every absence of order, of tactics, and of subordination; on that which has often made the bands, led on by its powerful stimulus, beat double their numbers – on fanaticism! on the enthusiastic intrepidity with which the Moslim soldier contemns, nay courts in battle a death which he regards as the surest passport to eternal bliss!"

Somewhat revived by this speech: "It is singular," replied Mavroyeni smiling, "that a Greek should be the person most desirous not to see Turkish fanaticism abate; most anxious not to let the fair-headed Northern hordes afresh plant the cross on the banks of the Bosphorus: – but so my strange fate ordains; and this blessing I can only pray Heaven in its goodness to grant!"

CHAPTER XIV.

For such a length of time had the supreme Visier remained stationary at Sophia, that Constantinople began loudly to murmur at his inactivity. To restore the capital to good humour, Youssoof resolved to sacrifice a part of his army. The Banat of Temeswar was the theatre chosen for this farce – or rather, tragedy. The attention of the few Austrian forces left in that province was however first to be diverted. For that purpose the commander in chief directed Mavroyeni to attack successively all the passes between Valachia and Transilvania, and sent him a reinforcement of about four thousand fresh troops, half foot and half cavalry. With these, and what other troops he could afford to draw from the camp at Fockshan, the Bey successively tried his strength against the passes of Terzburg, of Vulcan, and of Rothenturm; but the expeditions against these formidable defiles all ended alike in failures, and Mavroyeni now wished to give up the destructive and hopeless attempt. The Visier was more confident. Having crossed the Danube at Widdin, and skirted with his army the western borders of Valachia, he renewed his orders to the prince to make a more vigorous assault on the still untried passes in the vicinity of Cronstadt – a rich and commercial town, whither the fugitive Boyars had sent all their treasures for safety. The Bey hereupon formed at Valeni a fresh force, consisting of about three thousand Spahees, already broke into the business by the attack of the former passes, and of about two thousand five hundred arnaoots and jenissaries, drawn fresh from the camp of Fockshan, and consequently new in this species of warfare. Some German deserters from the different passes, well acquainted with their intricacies and defence, were to serve as guides; and the pass of Bozan was the first to be attacked.

To me had been confided the conduct of the expedition: mine was to be the glory or the disgrace of the result; and, accordingly, I determined that nothing should be wanting which skill or vigilance (I do not mention courage) could effect to ensure complete success.

On the ninth of August I sent on from Valeni six hundred spahees, who the same day reached the vicinity of the Austrians, and threw themselves into an abandoned entrenchment opposite their lines. On the tenth I led on the principal division, composed of eight hundred arnaoots and twelve hundred more spahees. We halted within three leagues of our advanced guard, and were joined a few hours later by the remainder of the cavalry, and by all the infantry. Early on the eleventh our whole collective force arrived under the heights of Poru-Ilke, the first object of contention.

To secure this commanding eminence was a point both essential and difficult: but, gently sloping towards the Austrian lines, it could not fail of being, on the slightest suspicion of such a design immediately occupied by a troop of horse stationed in observation on their right flank. For the purpose of deceiving this corps I made our spahees and jenissaries advance leisurely under the hill, as if with the intention only to pass round its base, and while they engaged the attention of the Austrians, our arnaoots attempted the most practicable part of the ascent, on the reverse of the eminence, and succeeded to drag our artillery up to its top; only halting within a few yards of the brow, and of the enemy's line of sight. This manœuvre at last happily achieved, I gave the signal for all the troops still advancing in the hollow to wheel to the right, and to scramble up the hill; and the moment the Austrian cavalry set forward in hopes to gain its summit the first, every inch of its level appeared, as if by magic, covered with our arnaoots, who, sending forth loud shoots of defiance, straightway opened their fire.

At this unexpected sight the Austrians, already in full gallop, again suddenly stopped; for a moment looked in unutterable consternation alternately at our Albanians above, whom they dared not approach, and at our spahees below, who already baffled their pursuit; and at last again wheeled about, and, in despair, resumed their original position.

It was a fine thing to behold the troops, first marching silently in the hollow defile, all at once, under the cheers of their comrades on the hill, rush at full speed up its steep and rugged sides, cut their way through copse and briar, scale heights that seemed inaccessible, leap like goats from crag to crag, stumble, fall, rise again, help or push each other on – the foremost serving as stepping stones to those behind, who in their turn, hauled up the clusters over whose backs they had vaulted – and amidst the thunder of the enemy's incessant fire, which our troops tried to drown in their wild and stunning shouts.

At last, with incredible labour, they overcame every obstacle, vaulted on the summit of the hill, and there joined and shook hands with their comrades already in full possession of the height.

In this eligible position, commanding the Austrian lines in front, and screened in the rear by a curtain of brushwood, which left the enemy equally unable to guess our numbers or to effect our dislodgment, we spent the night. While darkness lasted the atmosphere was clear, and the stars twinkled in the firmament with their brightest radiance; but with the sun rose so dense a fog, that it seemed to spread an impenetrable veil before every object, and things became less visible in the morning than they had been during the night. Determined to avail myself of this invisibility, I sent our foremost spahees – still watching as well as watched from their entrenchment, – to charge the Austrian horse, again immoveably fixed to the right of the hostile lines.

Attacked on a side on which they thought themselves secure, and prevented by the fog from discerning the number of their assailants, these heroes were seized with a sudden panic, took to flight at the first fire, and yielded up to my spahees their advantageous position.

Meantime I led the main body of my troops down the hill. The right side of its declivity was screened by the continuation of the copse through which my arnaoots had penetrated, the left side by that of the precipice which my jenissaries had scaled, and in front hung the mist, which equally prevented our seeing, or being seen, at ten yards distance.

A pretended Austrian deserter had engaged to point out to us the most practicable mode of turning the enemy's entrenchments. The fellow was riding by my side, but a something suspicious in his look and manner induced me closely to watch his motions. Suddenly I saw him waver, pull up his horse, pretend to turn aside for some frivolous purpose, and thinking the moment was his, dart forward, rush by me, and run away at full speed.

Our approach, our numbers and our disposition would, thanks to his agility, have been announced to the enemy just at the critical moment. I immediately pursued my fugitive, and fired both my pistols at him: but the fog prevented my taking aim, or even seeing where the traitor went. He soon vanished out of sight.

Little however did his deceit avail him. I scarce had proceeded fifty yards, ere I heard a something heavy tumble down the precipice, from which, as I advanced, arose dismal groans. They told me the fate of the double deserter. The fog had only saved him from being shot, to make him break his neck.

In pursuing the scoundrel, however, I had got on some way in front of my men; and on doubling a projecting crag, I all at once found myself in the midst of a cluster of Austrian huzzars. They had come out from their lines for the purpose of reconnoitering, they had been attracted towards us by the firing of my pistols, – the only warlike sound which broke the silence of our march; but had prudently stopped behind this screen of jutting rocks.

At this *rencontre* I gave myself up for lost. Still I determined to make some little attempt at an escape, ere I surrendered at discretion. "Friends," cried I therefore in Italian, "So you heard my signal! – Assist a Christian, rid me of my turban, and let me have a hat."

At this address all cheered me with loud huzzas. Every cap was waved in air; but while by that means every arm was engaged, I seized my time. Already the tramp of our horse shook the ground. Suddenly I wheeled about, and quick as lightning galloped back to my column. A volley of musketry, it is true, followed, to slacken my pace; but the balls only whizzed about my ears: none hit my person; and the huzzars, afraid to stay any longer, immediately sheered off.

We had scarcely advanced a hundred yards further, when the mist all at once cleared up, the hidden landscape became visible, and, within a pistol shot of our column, rose in full sight before us the Austrian lines. A tremendous fire from every battery immediately saluted me. I only answered by giving the signal for the assault; and while the body of spahees who had dislodged the enemy's cavalry fell upon their lines in flank, we stormed them in front.

Our arnaoots scrambled, with the help of their sabres, up the steep sides of the batteries, and our jenissaries extracted with their teeth the matches from the guns. The palisades were broken down, and the chevaux-de-frise* filled up with the slain: – for many were the brave that fell between the first assault and the forcing of the lines. At last the enemy's fire began to slacken, and their numbers diminished. A breach was made and from all sides our troops poured into the entrenchments like a resistless

* Editor's note to this edition: A defensive structure consisting of a movable obstacle composed of spikes attached to a wooden frame; used to obstruct cavalry.

torrent. But, though we beheld heaps of killed, we found nothing alive. The Austrians had fled with such precipitation, as not even to spike the guns which they could not carry off.

On advancing to the custom-house and other buildings which lay behind the now mastered fortifications, they too appeared abandoned. From high ground which these edifices occupied, the Austrians might distinctly be discerned, already at a considerable distance, trying to gain the narrow part of the defile which separated us from the frontier town of Cronstadt.

Harassed as we were, I still wished the pursuit to suffer no interruption. We therefore continued to press close upon the heels of the fugitives. It is true that in the ravine which we were entering, three hundred men in close order might with ease have arrested a whole army; but seized with a panic which grew as they advanced, every man among the Austrians was flying singly. One troop indeed of about thirty had kept together, and tried for a moment to check our progress. It only succeeded to encrease the bloodshed, and was soon entirely cut to pieces.

Presently, on turning some projecting ground, we beheld at a distance the outlet of the defile, and, at the now almost undoubted certainty of pushing on to Cronstadt without interruption, a general shout of joy arose among our men.

The only thing in the prospect which we did not much like, was a fancied appearance of some of the enemy, till now in full retreat, slackening their pace, soon after to halt and face about. At first indeed we doubted the accuracy of our optics, but presently we no longer could help yielding to the evidence of our senses.

On the first intelligence which had reached Cronstadt of the danger that threatened the pass of Bozan, three thousand men – nearly all the place contained – had been dispatched to strengthen this important outpost. Early on its march the first division of these troops met the foremost of the fugitives, and learning from them that the lines had been evacuated, pressed on, in hopes to stop our progress ere we had cleared the defile. All their comrades whom they fell in with were forced to turn back with them: only they were placed in the rear of the new comers, in order that our exhausted strength might have chiefly to contend with their own still undiminished vigour.

Little indeed were we in a condition to resist a charge of fresh cavalry, when, from the distant eminence on whose brow these new troops first rose in sight, they bore down upon us with all the advantage of a continued declivity. Still I resolved to make a stand, thinking the corps a small one; but when, just as we had engaged with this first division, a second, till then concealed in a hollow, appeared on the hill, I felt the game was up, and not a moment must be lost in making good our retreat.

On the first symptoms of the enemy's rallying, I had judged my harassed men in need of some extraordinary support. With this view I infused into them copious draughts of courage in a liquid shape. It did its office; speedily reached the heart, and mounted to the brain. A small party became so inflamed by its inspiration with the wish immediately to gain heaven the nearest way, that, not content to be quietly killed on the spot, they even climbed up a ledge of rocks overhanging the road, whence they contrived, by means of trees, stones &c. hurled down the precipice, to retard the progress of the Austrians while the rest of our troops effected in tolerable order their retrograde motion; and, after setting on fire the contumace,[1] and abandoning the dearly purchased entrenchments, we were enabled, with little additional loss, to regain the Valachian territory.

Seeing that the impending night prevented the enemy from pursuing us on our own ground, we now slackened our pace, and in a more leisurely manner proceeded back to Valeni.

One thing affected my troops very sensibly: it was the losing in the retreat most of the prisoners they had made in the pursuit. The stoutest and most active had found means to recover their liberty in the first confusion of our flight: the wounded and the disabled alone had remained in our hands; but these only impeded our march. Half of them, however, had the discretion soon to die of their own accord by the way; and those that seemed perversely determined to live on for no purpose but to give us trouble, found their proceeding of little advantage to themselves. They were mostly submitted to the operation of having their upper extremities severed from the remainder of their bodies, in order that the latter might encumber their captors no longer, and the former only be saved for the sake of the reward. I tried, indeed, to keep a few of the best looking heads fast on their shoulders; but it was a business in which my men felt extremely jealous of my interference. "They liked," they said, "to settle it their own way."

We were marching on pell-mell in the dark, when, come to a somewhat uneven pass, we found a saddle horse tied to a tree. My arnaoots recognized the animal as the steed of one of their comrades, who had gone on before with a Hungarian officer badly wounded, whom he wished to preserve – not so much from excess of humanity, as for the sake of his ransom. A few yards farther on, we stumbled upon a man lying in the road. Him I first supposed to be the Hungarian, who, unable to keep body and soul together on so rough a journey, had given up the ghost, and been left in that place, as unworthy of further conveyance. On examining more closely, it proved to our utter astonishment to be the arnaoot himself, quite dead, and with a deep gash in his side. As to the officer, no trace of him appeared.

The only idea which naturally suggested itself to my mind was that some of my Albanians had themselves dispatched their companion, for the sake of his envied prize: but this surmise I did not think it expedient to publish. The party around me all were, or pretended to be convinced, that Kara Mustapha must have been murdered by his own prisoner; and I was forced at last to grant that nothing seemed so likely to put a fellow of Kara Mustapha's size and strength off his guard, as a man half dead, bound hands and feet, and flung like a clothes bag across his horse's shoulders. – "Nay, so proud," added I, "does the culprit seem to have been of his achievement, that he has not even taken the murdered man's horse to assist him in his flight, but has walked away on foot, leaving the animal secured, on purpose to tell the tale of his prowess!"

My arnaoots paid little attention to this remark; but, hearing something stir among the bushes, all ran to the spot, and found the Hungarian, whom they had supposed far away, lying behind a tuft of trees, with his clothes half torn off; and what seemed more surprising, they found, not my suspicions but their own confirmed! – the officer himself, when accused of having killed his captor, scorning to deny the charge, and looking with a sort of complacency at the ensanguined blade of the knife with which he had done the deed, and which he still held firmly grasped in his hand.

"Wretch," now cried I, indignantly, in Italian, "what could induce you to murder the preserver of your life?"

"Its cold-blooded destroyer, rather call him," answered the officer, in a voice almost extinct. – "Finding that I encumbered his horse, and could not go on foot, the miscreant wanted to strip and then to kill me. A cutlass still lay concealed along my thigh. My hands being untied to take off my jacket, I drew out the knife unperceived, and, while the ruffian leaned over me to unclasp my belt, buried the trusty blade in his heart; then raised myself, and tried to mount his horse. The task exceeded my strength: feeling I could not accomplish it, I crept to these bushes, to die among them unperceived. Alas! even this, I find, is denied me!"

Fast as the officer's life seemed fleeting away, yet were the arnaoots, in their thirst to revenge one of their own body, still going to hasten its departure; when I interposed, and clasping their intended victim in my arms, tried to avert their sullen rage. During his narration, I had imagined I recognized in the dying man's disfigured countenance, that of an old acquaintance, – I may say: a sort of benefactor. I remembered in the days of my *cicerone-ship* at Pera, a young gentleman from Hermanstadt attached to the imperial mission, who had shown me much kindness. He was then, from his extraordinary beauty, called the Hungarian Apollo; and indeed was one of the finest youths I ever had beheld: nor less brave than handsome, or less amiable than brave. As a faithful biographer of other people's lives as well as my own, I am indeed forced to acknowledge that, where a fine eye shot forth its keenest darts, the heart of my Hungarian was a little too vulnerable; that too many of the premature fruits which happen to ripen on the Bosphorus was laid at his door; that the infant son of an embassadress of the highest rank, – a child beautiful as an angel, – bore to the son of Herman much too great a resemblance; that he was even supposed to have behaved in a way far from respectful to the venerable Pasha of Erzerum, one day that, suddenly seized in Boyook-deré[2] in the midst of all the diplomatic beaux and belles, by a troop of bostandjees – blindfolded, whipped into a close araba, and whirled away no one knew whither – he was in fact conveyed to the summer palace of this worthy Pasha's truant spouse; a lady of the imperial blood and less tender of her distant husband's feelings than she ought to have been: – but in many of these instances, Miazinsky, as it were, only yielded to positive violence; was often the first to deplore his personal attractions; went no further than was necessary to prevent a parcel of angels from exposing themselves in public; and, far from confining his charitable exertions to young and handsome females, showed much general benevolence, that scarce an act of humanity of any description came to light at Para which might not be brought home to the blushing Hungarian: – though, from equal solicitude to conceal his kind-hearted exertions of the latter as of the former species, his stolen marches often obtained the full praise of gallantry, when, in fact, they only deserved credit for vulgar goodness.

While, however, the youth's discretion continued unimpeached – insomuch as even to offend the vanity rather than excite the apprehensions of certain of his fair friends – his courage seemed on one occasion entirely to forsake him. It was at a gay supper with various foreigners. Another *jeune de langue*[3] – envious of his more favourable recaption in a quarter where both had been candidates for sweet smiles, – insulted him very grievously, and even went so far as to add to opprobrious language, contemptuous and threatening gestures. Every person looked aghast, expecting to see weapons of death drawn across the very supper table, and the yet untouched dainties all deluged in blood: but to the amazement of all beholders, the Hungarian, though reddening up to the eyes, continued otherwise unmoved, and made no signs of demanding satisfaction. I alone, who happened to be leaning over the back of a chair next to his own, knew what to think: for when a neighbour asked him in a whisper, how he could put up with such behaviour, I heard him answer under his breath, "Why disturb the short pleasure of so many cheerful guests? first let us finish this good supper, and then cut each others throats!"

And so in fact it was arranged. Never did Miazinsky's antagonist digest the good cheer of that night. Ere the dawn arose, Miazinsky most religiously killed him, begged his pardon for so doing, and then threw himself at his embassador's feet, to relate to him the necessity he had been under of removing his colleague. The Baron advised him *not* to wait for his answer, – a hint which he took: but as he was a favourite with all the family, the daughters included, and had the concurring testimony of the whole supper table to his unimpeachable behaviour, the single life he had shortened was excused in favour of the many in whose production he had been accessory; and his pardon was, through dint of great interest, at last obtained. Still was he obliged to relinquish the diplomatic career for which he seemed little qualified; but having shewn greater aptitude for the military profession, he failed not, in consequence of his high character and good conduct, as soon as the affair blew over, to obtain rapid promotion in the army.

Not only all these circumstances, but the person to whom they related, were still more distinctly impressed upon my memory. I still saw the young man at Pera, as he entered the Internuncio's drawing room – his fine athletic figure set off to the greatest advantage by his close Hungarian dress – striking every person present with the grace and elegance of his appearance, and causing every fan to flutter, and every female feature to glow. I even remembered that, little as I was apt to envy others for their looks, I had once run to a large mirror, in order to compare notes with the dazzling stranger; and though the poor creature now lying naked at my feet, encrusted with clotted blood and dust, – his eyes half closed, and his pallid sunken features all indented with scars, – differed most woefully in many respects from the brilliant image in my mind, yet did I discern in a few others such strong marks of identity, that I could only satisfy myself by asking point blank, whether I beheld the Count Miazinsky, formerly in the Austrian mission at Pera.

At these words the dying officer again opened his languid eyes, and looking at me earnestly, as if in his turn to find out who could thus recognize him in his present miserable condition, faintly answered, "I am he indeed: but you who ask the question, may I know who you are?"

"One," I replied, "whom, in the number of those you were eager to serve, you may not recollect; but one who cannot forget you, and would wish to do for your comfort what little this dreary place may leave in his power!"

Then turning to my arnaoots, who grinned with impatience at the constraint imposed upon their fury. "The Prophet," exclaimed I, "has given the faithful the choice of making their enemies captives, or of killing them on the spot; but he allows his followers not to begin with the one, and to end with the other. To this officer his poor remnant of life had been granted. It could not be retaken from him. In defending it against his aggressor, he has only made use of his undoubted right. He had therefore reconquered his freedom, when again I seized upon his person; and on that score, he now is mine – mine alone; and whoever shall at present dare to attempt his life, robs me of my property, and shall have me to account with for the deed!"

The assertion was true, and the tone made its truth be respected. Proceeding to do for the officer what little the untoward circumstances of the hour and place permitted, I made him swallow a few drops of the wine we had found in the house of Contumace. On its wetting his lips, he seemed for an instant to revive, and exclaimed: "Alas! It is my own Menesh you are giving me; that to which I used to treat my dearest friends. I may now drink it myself. Never more shall I see one to make welcome to this cordial of my own growth!" – and in truth, the transient spark of seeming amendment which enlivened the stranger's countenance was only a last gleam of the expiring lamp.

I wish to have tarried with him on the spot till daylight, or to have had him conveyed on in a litter to where we meant to halt; but the proposal to carry an infidel on Islamite shoulders, even though I offered to take my turn with the rest, was received by my proud Moslemen with such haughtiness that I durst not insist. All I could do for the poor Hungarian was to have him laid across a baggage mule, and to walk by his side; trying with one hand to steady his body, while with the other I supported his head.

In this position I saw him, as we marched on, by degrees grow fainter and fainter. At last, on some inward anxiety appearing to agitate his mind, I again stopped; and – in order that he might be relieved of what made his fleeting soul depart in such sadness, – conjured him to confide to me his utmost thoughts and wishes.

"Then would you," said he at last after some hesitation, and collecting all his remaining strength to speak more intelligibly, – "would you do a dying man one last great favour which God and your own heart alone can repay?"

"Any thing in my power;" I eagerly answered.

"God bless you!" replied he, – "Observe; my mother's address there is not time to give you. But knowing me, you will easily discover it. Send, oh! send her, – with a son's last duty, love, and gratitude – the account of my death, and a lock of my hair; and beg of her to divide that last token, – too well she knows where, and with whom!"

This request I pledged myself punctually to perform: then tried to administer the only consolation in my power – that of sympathy. Pressing the youth in my arms: "I feel," exclaimed I, "how hard it is to quit life in a strange land, far away from the endearments of parents and of friends!"

"Of these," answered the Hungarian, "I might have been deprived even dying nearer home; and it then would have been with greater bitterness. Here, at least, I can fancy all I miss – and the idea soothes my soul during the few yet remaining minutes, after which it no longer will signify where Miazinsky ceased to be!"

Tears started from my eyes: they fell on the officer's wan cheek. A slight pressure of his hand told me he felt their value, and thanked the giver for them. Soon however his breath almost became imperceptible. At last a sort of convulsive tremor ran through all his limbs, and again vanished. I examined his countenance. The moon, which had just risen in her full splendour, cast a bright gleam over his features. I saw him again open his eyes, and fix them upon me with an expression of gratitude which his palsied lips no longer could confirm. He however seized the hand I held clasped round his waist, made a sort of feeble effort to bring it to his mouth, once more uttered a faint sigh, stretched out his limbs, and died! – Eternal bliss attend his departed spirit!

His poor remains I wished to have preserved entire, in order to honour their funeral with decent rites; but on that subject my arnaoots were intractable. Forced, therefore, to content myself with the ample braids of the youth's raven hair, which I claimed for the purpose he had specified, I let my Albanians dispose as they chose of the remainder of his person.

After marching almost the whole night without interruption, we stopped just before day break to take a little rest. Having thus somewhat refreshed ourselves, we again proceeded, and towards the evening re-entered Valeni; – little thanked for laurels which, though we certainly reaped, we could not carry home; and only loaded with a few heads, which I would have felt little sure of not being those of my own slain Arnaoots, bagged by their companions, were it not that Moslemen warriors prudently shave their polls. Should my reader feel disposed to quarrel with my very minute account of this expedition, let him remember that I write principally for my own amusement; and to me, what event of the war could be so interesting as the affair of Bozan, of which I was the hero?

At Valeni, we soon received intelligence that not only that defile, but all the other passes into Transilvania were fortified in such a way as to preclude all further chance of retrieving our disappointment. The scheme of forcing them was therefore given up, and soon I received orders to march all the troops back to Fockshan, where from all quarters fresh clouds seemed to be gathering.

CHAPTER XV.

The Russians under Romanzow had early in the season retaken Yassi. The Austrians under Coburg had advanced to Adjoud. So far from heeding a Bimbashee[1] with about eighteen hundred men, whom Mavroyeni sent about the middle of October to dislodge from that place their out-posts, they still pushed on, and at last took possession of the town of Fockshan. Valachia now seemed in the utmost danger: the approaching winter alone suspended its fate. The combined armies, considering the entire occupation of Moldavia as progress sufficient for that year, went into quarters. Yassi became the resting-place of the Russians; Coburg stayed at Romane; while we remained, not entirely at ease, in our camp near Fockham.

On the other side of Valachia things wore not a more favourable aspect. Youssoof Visier had, by his irruption in the Banat of Temeswar, successively elated the Empire to the highest pitch of joy, and plunged it into the deepest affliction. So sudden had been the reduction of the province, and so great the terror spread by the Visier's success, that Buda, nay the Austrian capital itself, already fancied the Turks at its gates: – but a mightier hand than that of man marked Mehadieh as the utmost point of Youssoof's progress. Under the walls of that fortress the pestilential influence of a low marshy country, doubly envenomed by a season unusually wet, carried off his men in such numbers, that, in order to preserve a few, he was obliged abruptly to abandon his conquests. With the same speed with which he had led into the Banat a numerous and exulting army, he led out of it a handful of troops enfeebled by disease; and was compelled, at the close of the year, to conclude with the Austrians for the three first months of that ensuing, a mortifying armistice.

The confidence of the Turks in their naval commander had experienced an equally complete revulsion. When, early in the spring of 1788, Hassan Capitan-Pasha, with eighteen ships of the line, twenty frigates, and gunboats innumerable sailed up the Euxine to seek the Russian squadron near Kinburn, the whole empire augured from his valour and his force the most brilliant success. But when, as month succeeded month, defeat followed defeat; when first Hassan's gun-boats were destroyed by Nassau in the Liman; when, next, his fleet was repulsed with loss by Paul Jones at Gluboka; and when, lastly, his entire armament was annihilated by these two commanders united off Kinburn, – terror and dismay gradually filled each Moslemin heart, all clothed themselves in sackcloth and ashes, and all saw the hand of Providence raised against the breakers of the peace.

What then became the consternation of the faithful, when, on the seventeenth of December, Potemkin took the important fortress of Ockzakow! The shock produced by this event baffles all powers of description, – and, after a year marked by the imminent danger of Valachia, the loss of Moldavia, the destruction of the Turkish army, the annihilation of the Otthoman fleet, an inglorious armistice concluded with Austria, and a bulwark of the empire lost to the Russians, calamities seemed destined not to cease until the race of Othman should have been driven out of Europe. The populace of Constantinople, whose discontent at these distant defeats was still inflamed by the detachments from the Visier's army, which daily under their own eyes repassed the Bosphorus, in the most shattered condition, now with as loud a clamour demanded Youssoof's head, as before they had demanded his appointment.

Meanwhile, renouncing all further schemes of offensive warfare, the Visier determined to concentrate his forces as much as possible for the defence of the empire itself. He sent Mavroyeni five thousand additional men, which, distributed between Ardgis, Rimnik, Brankovano, Valeni and Kimpina, seemed to render secure the frontier of the principality; and himself, during the suspension of hostilities, marched into Bessarabia.

Already was he lifting his hand, to strike from this new point a blow in Moldavia, which promised us not only a return of security, but a renewal of success, when an event took place which damped all our hopes, and paralyzed all our strength.

This was the demise – unannounced by any previous warning – of the Sultan Abd-ool-Hameed, and the accession of his nephew Selim. Without the smallest preparation for so great a change, this prince suddenly passed, on the 7th of April 1789, from the confinement of the harem, to the throne of the Turkish despots.

Like all young men, Selim the Third was eager to undo all that his predecessor had done; and scarce had his beard attained a fortnight's growth,[2] when the two chief favourites of his uncle, Youssoof and Hassan, were suddenly removed from their exalted situations. Some difference, however, marked the manner. Hassan's age, his long services, and his former successes, still inspired for the veteran hero a sort of habitual veneration which the new monarch durst not wholly disregard. His disgrace was disguised under the semblance of a new favour. While the Capitana Bey,[3] Geretlu Hasseïn stepped into his place of High admiral, he rose to that of Beglier-bey of Roumili: but, not only was he removed from what seemed his proper element; he was commanded to march as Seraskier of the army of Bessarabia, and to recover the lost fortress of Ockzakow. Youssoof, less rooted in the affections of the nation, received a more unqualified dismissal. From the rank of supreme Visier he was degraded to that of Pasha of Widdin; while, the more to envenom the sting, the governor of that city, his inveterate enemy, was raised in his place to the supreme Visirate. This new commander in chief bore the surname of Djenazé, or the dead, from the state which his extreme ill health made him seem fast approaching.

As to Mavroyeni, he experienced not any immediate change in his situation. While danger was rife and energy required, he could not be spared; but the fall of his patron let loose all the forked tongues of envy, and a store of accusations was laid in, to be preferred against him at the first favourable opportunity. In fact, there was not a crime or an error which his enemies did not lay to his charge. He had mismanaged matters of which ministers never gave him the direction, embezzled sums which the treasury never sent, and cut off heads, not even for a moment absent from the shoulders of their legitimate owners. Indeed, if truth lies between the two extremes, he might be proved to have been a perfect character, from labouring at the same time under the most opposite and incompatible charges: for he was at once rapacious and profuse, timid and foolhardy, precipitate and dilatory, too lenient and too severe, a bigot and an infidel. But if, therefore, it seemed not so easy to determine in what precisely consisted his guilt, it was not the less evident that the punishment was quite decided upon, and would be inflicted as soon as the sentence, already pronounced *in petto*, could safely be executed. Of this circumstance Mavroyeni himself appeared fully sensible: and as in every Greek who departed from Bucharest he beheld an informer going to give fresh evidence against him, so, in every Turk who arrived in the place he saw only a messenger of his disgrace.

Thus situated; knowing that, the instant his principality was lost he too must fall; and yet hopeless of further supplies for its defence from the new Visier, rather anxious for his discomfiture than eager for his success, he exhausted all his private treasure in raising at his own expence a fresh body of troops, and, with what more men and ammunition he was able to withdraw from the force at Fockshan, marched to Rimnik, there to organise an attack to be made the same day on all the passes into Transilvania: hoping that distracted by the multiplicity of points to defend, the enemy might in some one or other prove vulnerable. He himself undertook to conduct the expedition against the pass of Temesch: but whether the Austrians were informed of his approach or only suspected his design, they met it by so vigorous a sally from their lines, that, before he could issue the final orders for a general attack, he was repulsed and forced back with considerable loss upon Gloyest. The scheme thus defeated ere it had had time to ripen, Mavroyeni recalled his troops from the Hungaria confines, and returned much dispirited to Rimnik, which henceforth he made his head quarters.

At the very outset of the affair of Temesch I had been wounded in the thigh by a ball nearly spent, which, grazing the bone, by degrees produced a painful exfoliation. Thus disabled for some time from serving, I left Rimnik, and returned to Bucharest, whither the Bey's own surgeon – the only one in the principality who knew a shin bone from a drum stick, – was sent once or twice to forward my cure.

In what way, soon after the minor events here described, Coburg and the Austrians, twice threatened by the Turks with annihilation, were twice saved by the unexampled diligence and bravery of Suwarrow, are events preserved from oblivion in the imperishable annals of general history, and which therefore I need not detail. Such at Rimnik was the rout of the Turks, notwithstanding Djenazé the commander – too ill to sit on horseback – held up the Koran from his carriage, and ordered the cannon to be fired on his own retreating troops, that the whole Otthoman camp fell into the hands of the enemy, while the very course of the Danube became obstructed by the number of wagons and corpses drowned in the Visier's flight across its crimsoned tide.

For a considerable time before this decisive event, Bucharest had been in that hopeless state – not devoid perhaps of its peculiar luxury – in which people, regardless of a future they may never witness, and unwilling any longer to make sacrifices of which they may never reap the distant fruits, yield without further restraint to every wildest suggestion of the present moment, and, induced by unavoidable ruin, rush with premeditated thoughtlessness into all the bold merriment of despair. Men and women, who never before had dared to stir disencumbered of the trammels of public opinion, and had measured every movement, studied every gesture, and prepared every look which might chance to have a witness, until it was become impossible any longer to tell how nature had moulded them, now resumed their original air, and carriage, and tone; and now for the first time cast away the irksome shackles of society, to display their genuine native character. No longer listening to prudential considerations, which no longer could repay the sacrifices they cost, the irascible now yielded to their temper, the coarse to their brutality, the malignant to their spite, the covetous to their love of rapine, nay even the prudes to their longing for open and unconstrained gallantry. I remember in particular one lady, besieged by a numerous troop of admirers, whose conjugal fidelity seemed proof, at the first opening of the campaign, against every form of blockade or of storm, but whose virtue exactly kept pace with the events of the war. At every check our forces met with, her severity relaxed: each battle lost removed some former scruple; and the bulletins from the army were the *billets-doux* in which her lovers might read their chance of success. Unapproachable while Youssoof's irruption in the Banat was the theme of every conversation: cold as ice during the attack upon the Transilvanian passes, she began to relent after the affair of Temesch: after the battle of Fockshan she bade her lovers hope; and the defeat of Rimnik became the signal for her unconditional surrender – "She had not the presumption," she said, "to think that, on the loss of a province, that of her poor virtue could be of any consequence!"

Equally modest were, on the score of their character, most of Mavroyeni's courtiers: they deemed their reputation full as little worth preserving as the lady. The most straightforward conduct in that respect was that of the Bey's own nephews, his Grammaticus and his Cameraz. These two youths agreed in conceiving that, on their employments leaving them, they might leave their employer. They only differed in their mode of doing it. When affairs began to look unpromising the Grammaticus begged to resign his office; the Cameraz, on the contrary, expressed great indignation at his brother's baseness, and swore that for his part he never would ask to quit his benefactor. Nor did he: for he afterwards went without leave. If, however, some public personages deserted the capital before the Prince thought of moving, others, to compensate, staid quietly when he went away. I mistake: as he went out at one gate of the city to retire to Turkey, his Boyars went out at the other, to meet and to welcome the Austrians, who immediately after the battle of Rimnik marched to his capital.

For my part, though I do not desire to boast of my fidelity, and might have pleaded, for staying, the bad grace with which – owing to my still festering wound – I must limp in his suite, I stupidly followed my patron. My great fear was that of seeing him miserably dejected on quitting that sovereignty which he had laboured so hard to obtain: but in this I was agreeably disappointed. After the depression produced by his defeats, the bustle and excitement of the journey rather caused in his spirits a sort of exhilaration. – "Who ever ascended a throne?" cried he, as we went out at the gates, "to sit at his ease? Who, that feared for his head, ever accepted a Sultan's favours? – come death when it may, I have lived to be a prince!"

This temper lasted until we reached the Danube. Arrived in sight of that noble stream, which a few years before he had crossed in the first bloom of his grandeur, and which now again he was to cross in the decline of his fortunes, stripped of all his dearly purchased honours, a fugitive and a presumptive criminal, Mavroyeni – prince as he had lived to be – paused, cast back a wistful look, and, unable to tear himself away at once from the object of his life's long cherished schemes, refused to proceed further, until informed that Coburg had actually entered his capital. This intelligence he had not long to wait for. He soon heard how the victors had been hailed by the nobles of the country, then bade his principality adieu for ever, and stepped into the boat.

Out of evil sometimes comes good. Djenazé, with the battle of Rimnik, also lost the Visirate: but being called the dead already, Selim probably thought it not worth while to take his life. Having, however, in consequence of his lieutenant's reverses and others, conceived a surfeit of the war, the Sultan now conferred the high office vacated on Hassan our old Capitan-Pasha, whose pacific dispositions suited his sovereign's change of sentiments. Immediately on his appointment the new commander proceeded to the head quarters now at Schumlah, whither, with reviving hopes and spirits, now likewise went Mavroyeni, to meet his ancient master.

It would have delighted a stoic to see these two old personages, who so well understood each other, greet, and wag their beards together. Such, it is said, was their emotion on first embracing, as absolutely to force from their features of brass a few iron tears. None however remain to confirm the assertion. In fact, the Prince and the Pasha were all in all to each other. To Hassan, the assistance of Mavroyeni seemed the pledge of diplomatic success; while to Mavroyeni, the support of Hassan seemed positively as essential as physical existence. But short, alas, was the joy! Hassan, like Moses, had been destined to view from afar only the object of all his wishes, the end of all his toils – the long sought and at last remotely glimmering peace. Fate had ordained he should not witness its consummation. After a whole winter spent in arduous and tiresome negotiations, an armistice was only just agreed upon, when, on the twentieth of March, 1790, Ghazi Hassan, after a few hours illness, ended as others do his long and brilliant career. His enemies were accused of having shortened his life; – but he was ninety when he died.

Of Hassan, nothing now remains save his memory. This however will endure in all its splendour while the Turkish empire lasts. The single cloud[4] which dims the setting sun cannot produce forgetfulness of the many hours during which it shed its undiminished radiance! As a youth, I witnessed Hassan's expedition to the Morea. More matured, I followed him in that to Egypt. His history, his achievements exerted over my destinies that remote but unceasing influence which the luminary of the world exerts alike over all the living things of the earth, whether he directly gladdens them with his aspect, or whether, lighting up other regions, he be hidden from their view. As I beheld the meridian glory, so I beheld the last refulgence of his dazzling career; and not only while Hassan lived did my fate remain indirectly linked to his fortunes, but even at his death did the mournful chill which pervaded the empire, extend its benumbing influence to my remote and narrow orbit. Of the brightness which he poured forth in his zenith, a few beams had been reflected upon my humble person, and the long shadow he left at his decline, involved my fate likewise in its wide extending darkness.

His demise again raised the hopes and views of the party inclined for the war. A simple Aga of Rustchook was appointed his successor, merely because, many years before, this turbulent Moslemin had contrived to raise a quarrel with Prince Repnin, when that nobleman passed through his town as messenger of peace. Private animosity was considered the pledge of military skill. I need scarcely add, that in proportion as Hassan had been a friend to Mavroyeni, Hassan's successor thought himself bound to be his rancorous enemy: but Mavroyeni had a secret enemy, not in the least distrusted by him, far more dangerous than all that stood confessed, – and this was himself.

The ever present foe in question – whose councils uniformly prevailed over those of all his friends – had contrived by degrees wholly to estrange him from his nephew Stephan, the then drogueman of the fleet: and not without reason; inasmuch as the said Stephanos – one of those anomalous beings, who prefer the lower niches of office where unassuming industry plods on unmolested, to its higher pinnacles where ambition sits rocking in the lap of danger – in order the better to watch the course and to counteract the consequences of the intrigues carried on against his uncle, had with unheard-of obstinacy himself wholly abstained from intriguing; and neither exhausted his strength in idle clamour, nor exasperated his enemies by useless invective. A behaviour so different from his own could not but appear suspicious to that sagacious uncle: – he determined that it should not avail his too moderate nephew: and the man who, never above nor ever below the duties of his office, had seen Ghazi Hassan succeeded in the command of the navy by Hassan of Crete, and Hassan of Crete by Husseïn the Georgian; and had still under the minion of the Sultan as under the idol of the people, preserved unimpaired and unimpeached his fidelity towards his principals as well as his devotion to his kindred, was by his infatuated relation, and in return for all his great services, devoted to feel the last effects of his now almost powerless animosity. What little wealth and influence Mavroyeni still possessed was destined by him to purchase his nephew disgrace – and, if necessary, his death.

Frightened at this resolution, the execution of which must render inevitable the ruin of the prince and of all his adherents, I went to him, and without much circumlocution, set forth all the certain consequences of his rash design. But, soured by disappointment, Mavroyeni was become incapable of dispassionate reasoning. He resembled one who, while ascending a precipice and only looking upwards, has proceeded on with a collected mind and a firm and steady pace, but who, when again descending he sees the whole abyss before him, grows giddy, and from the very apprehension of danger, plunges headlong into destruction. Offended at my boldness, but unable to refute my arguments, he only involved me in the ill-founded mistrust his faithful agent had incurred; and answered my remonstrances with abuse. "You are all villains alike," cried he, foaming with rage. – "All engaged in the same plot; all leagued against my life; all watching open mouthed for my expected spoil!"

My breath was not wasted in useless refutations of so unmerited a reproach. I only stated that if the prince persisted in obliging his enemies, by removing the last prop of his house, his friends must provide for their own safety; – and left him to profit by the warning.

But to no purpose! – for he persisted in demanding the dismissal of his nephew; and as the favour he solicited was precisely of that description which his bitterest enemies were the most anxious to see realised, he soon obtained his wish. Stephan, his relation and friend was dismissed, and in order that the change might be more sensibly felt, Handgerly, who had pursued him with the most inveterate hatred, was appointed in his nephew's place. I would now have been fully justified in retiring immediately: but two motives still operated to prolong my stay: – some silly remains of attachment for an old though unjust patron, and some reluctance to resign my commission, just as the cure of my wounds allowed me to resume my duty.

It is true my services seemed little likely to be wanted any longer. The pacific influence which for an instant was seen to hover over the Turkish councils, had winged its way northward, and had settled permanently on those of Austria. Joseph the Second, the author of the war, who, through his ill judged mode of enforcing designs salutary in themselves, had driven to open rebellion all his dominions from the Danube to the Scheld – Joseph the Second was no more! After quenching the flame he had raised, by cancelling at one stroke on his death-bed all the toilsome reforms of his whole life, he had resigned his breath under the pressure of every public calamity and private distress, which could embitter the last moments of a man replete at once with pride and feeling; and Leopold his brother and his successor, reluctantly transferred from the peaceful banks of the Arno to all the storms that raged round the Imperial throne, had already infused among the Austrian troops a spirit so different, that, during the whole of the summer they contented themselves with quietly looking at the Turks across the Danube; when, unluckily, the Pasha of Widdin, – the ever restless Youssoof – mistook this desire of tranquillity for a proof of weakness, and determined with his own forces and those of Mavroyeni, to dislodge the enemy from his neighbourhood. He summoned the Bey to join him with his remaining troops; and the Bey came at his call.

On the 14th of August Youssoof ordered Mavroyeni's division to pass the river; intending – as soon as the detachment should be sufficiently entrenched near the village of Kalafath, by which it was covered – to follow with the remainder of his army, higher up the stream, so as to put the enemy between two fires. But the uncourteous enemy suffered not this scheme to ripen; and advancing unperceived in the night, attacked us on the twenty-sixth of the month, at dawn of day, with very superior numbers. It is true that that, by availing myself of some high ground which we commanded to turn the flank of the Austrians and to fall upon their rear, I made them believe for a moment that our plan had succeeded, and that Youssoof himself was giving them chase: but this diversion came too late, and was too trifling to save us. Already were the Austrians in full possession of our lines.

Amid the scene of carnage which ensued, dare I introduce the fate of a flesh-pot, which, humble as seems the object, yet by the vicissitudes it experienced, forms a remarkable episode in the general picture? Time out of mind this capacious utensil had been the solace, the rallying point, the support of a most respectable oda[5] of jenissaries. The members of this division were trailing away the ample vessel with all the celerity which its unwieldy size and little pliant form permitted, when, as it majestically retreated in all its unbending sturdiness before the advancing enemy, surrounded by its whole troop of ministers and of satellites, from the Astshee-bashee or head cook of the orta down to the lowest regimental scullery-boy, and from the largest kettle to the smallest stew-pan, it happened to be spied by a knot of Austrian huzzars. With them to see was to covet. Immediately they determined to effect its conquest; while the regiment which boasted its property showed equal determination to defend to the last drop of its blood, what so often had sustained the life and renovated the vigour of its members. The conflict therefore was long and sanguinary. At one time the Austrians seemed victors, at another the Turks again recovered the highly prized utensil; and not until the unresisting victim of the fierce contest, now hauled one way, now pulled the other, had witnessed the fall of all its Moslemin defenders, did it pass from the hands of the faithful into those of the infidels; but with a face as round, and sleek, and smooth as ever; unmindful of the streams of blood spilt in its behalf, and little seeming to care itself who filled its ample belly, or lit the accustomed fire under its enormous base.

Ye who value words more than things, look not with contempt upon this scene of what may pass in your minds for misapplied heroism! Learn that the very fundamental organization of the jenissaries renders the vessel in which are cooked their daily rations the rallying point of each regiment – the token whose loss casts a lasting dishonour upon those to whom it belonged: and that, provided the common soldier has a something of which he connects the defence with his individual fame, it signifies little whether it be a copper vessel, or a piece of painted silk; an eagle or a flesh pot.

My division had suffered the least in our defeat. I therefore led it back round the village to protect their re-embarking of the other troops; but could not prevent a scene of indescribable confusion. Hundreds of wretches, unable to reach the craft collected at some distance on the river, plunged headlong into the stream, and there found the death they had escaped in the entrenchments. The number of the drowned exceeded that of the slain. Several boats full of soldiers were sunk on the passage: a cannon ball went right through the barge which conveyed the Prince; and, had it struck the frail skiff a second sooner, must have ended his fate in the Danube; but Mavroyeni was not born to be drowned!

Having with a handful of arnaoots remained the very last on the hostile side of the river, I expected to be completely cut off for want of conveyance, and to have drunk the sherbet of martyrdom, little as it was to my taste – when at some distance I perceived a raft moored among some rushes, which thus far had escaped all observation. I pointed it out to three or four of my best men, and with them jumped upon and pushed it off. Paddling towards the Turkish shore we soon became a conspicuous mark, and were treated accordingly. Luckily the current quickly carried us a good way down the stream, and though many balls whizzed over our heads, none entered very deep into our bodies. The most I brought back to Turkey was a couple of flesh wounds. Even these, it is true, I could willingly have dispensed with, in spite of the delicious odour which the Koran asserts to exhale from wounds produced by infidel weapons; and particularly as the Turks show themselves too resigned to the will of Providence to bring in the suite of their armies men so hostile to the awards of fate as surgeons.

Youssoof had set his heart on his long-planned *coup de main*. The failure of our preparatory movements did not prevent him from attempting it two days after; and the only use he made of our defeat was to excuse his own. The whole blame of Youssoof's discomfiture fell upon Mavroyeni, and a long list of complaints against the Prince reached the Porte from the frontier, just as Handgerly had been raking up in the capital the old story of the Seraff Petracki, and representing Mavroyeni as possessed of all the treasure lost to the Sultan by the execution of his cashier. Blows so dire, coming so fast upon each other, seemed to render the Prince's ruin inevitable. Each effort he had made to recover his lost ground, had only caused him to fall another step; and it appeared as if fate had been intent only to lead him from one misfortune to another so gradually, as, without breaking his proud spirit at once, to bend it by little and little completely to the ground.

Unequivocal signs of the utmost depression showed themselves more and more every day, amid all his unsuccessful attempts to keep up his lofty manner. The supernatural informer with whom, in more prosperous days, he used to threaten others he had himself began to believe in, nay, to dread; for from a good genius the familiar spirit seemed by degrees to have grown into an avenging demon, who pursued his own employer by day and by night. Fixing his haggard eyes on vacancy, the Prince would sometimes, as in a fit of raving, address the invisible fiend, beg a truce to his fancied persecutions, or enter into a regular defence of the conduct he had held in his government: and once, in the middle of a numerous circle as he was giving way to the transient somnolence which of late frequently overpowered his senses, and afforded a short respite from the goadings of his mind, I experienced the unspeakable horror of seeing him – after some time moving his lips like one engaged in secret converse – at last start up convulsively from his seat, wildly open his eyes, and exclaim in a voice of thunder: "Hellish spirit you lie! It is not I who did it: – it is not I who burnt the barn, feigned to have been full of corn: nor I who charged for the deserters, never estranged from their sovereign: nor I who buried in a bean field the military chest, captured in my dispatches by a troop of hulans: nor I who poisoned the cup . . . ."

Here my outstretched hand, laid on my patron's lips, at last succeeded to stop the frightful current of his words. I dragged him out of the room: and might perhaps have succeeded by degrees to quiet him, but for his ghostly director, who unfortunately determined this once to assert his office, and recommended the Prince to say his prayers. The moment was ill chosen: "Cursed priest," cried the Bey, "how can my words hope to rise, when you see the vampire wings flap to beat them down again!"

The day after this scene I was sent for to the Prince's closet: he seemed then quite composed. "Selim," said he, "my hour of fate approaches. It would be foolish to suppose that I could much longer avert the evil day. I therefore wish you to tell me your accustomed candour, which you think most for my glory: to take the business into my own hands, and by a death that may seem the result of my own choice, to balk my persecutors of their expected triumph; or, with a calmness and fortitude perhaps more difficult than a precipitate suicide, to await the executioner?"

"Sir," answered I gravely, "we all know that a king, a general, a statesman may, without the smallest scruple, sacrifice to a mistaken piece of policy, a foolish pique, or a silly point of honour, as many unwilling victims as the magnitude of the object shall require. In the like manner we are told that even a private gentleman may sacrifice a certain fraction of his own body, – an arm, a leg, or both, – provided it be to secure greater durability to the paltry parts preserved. We are even assured by grave divines, that both potentates and private individuals may make themselves defunct on earth to every social duty, by becoming monks or anchorets, – and be highly praised for the deed: but however troublesome a man's existence may be to himself and to others; however greatly his voluntary removal might oblige all the world; however much his death would be a private and a public benefit, none dare dispose of their sum total of life, or remove their entire being from a worse to a better world. This act, which might do the performer much good, and could injure no one else, is of all crimes the most heinous."

"Pshaw," cried Mavroyeni, "I did not call you in to retail to me the common place cant either of Christians or Mohammedans, which latter perhaps would have added that, as the hour of death is written on our foreheads, we are not able to hasten it, if so inclined. I sent to consult you, as a man, who encumbered with the prejudices of neither creed, would honestly tell me which of the two steps left for me to choose, was likely to figure most handsomely in history. Ancient heroes have been praised for dying without the least necessity; modern worthies for resigning themselves to live without the smallest hopes: and I cannot make up my mind to which will look best in the eyes of the world!"

"To live, beyond all doubt!" cried I, – "The living every where figure better than the dead! Besides, it is the fashion of the country, which no one should despise. People will only suspect some low born rascal, or some low bred disease of having envied you the honour of the Sultan's bow string; and the witnesses of your heroism may only be hanged as the authors of your death!"

Mavroyeni still preserved a lurking love for life. Not only he resigned himself to the remnant left him; but in order to render that remnant more secure, he even determined to remove it out of Youssoof's reach.

Again was I going to accompany my patron. He had indeed forfeited all claims upon the loyalty of his adherents, by his wanton perverseness in increasing their dangers: but still it went against my feelings to leave him in his fallen state. So far, however, from appearing thankful for this devotion, he now, to my utter astonishment, began to consider it as an importunity: "He had seen me," he said, "much distinguished by Youssoof: he knew I was the Pasha's spy; and the last and only service I still could render a once kind and indulgent master – to whom I still owed some obedience – was to withdraw for ever from his presence!"

The opportunity which I had wished for of distinguishing myself once more, and of earning among men an honourable name, ere I left the Prince and the army for ever, I had found at Kalafath. When, therefore, I found the reproaches for not departing according to my promise daily repeated, I resolved at last to go. Watching a moment of comparative serenity in Mavroyeni's temper, I entered his chamber, kissed his hand, and begged his commands for the capital.

At these words he turned pale; and looked as much aghast as if there never had been any question of my leaving him.

"Sir," said I, "did you not yourself, only yesterday, upbraid me for staying?"

"Ah," cried he, "could you then take at his word, a man maddened by the misfortunes heaped upon him!" Then, rising from his seat, and wildly pacing the room: – "My affairs must be desperate indeed," continued he, "since it is come to this!" but again sitting down, as if ashamed of betraying so much weakness, "No!" exclaimed he in a calmer tone; "the Sultan knows all that I have done for the empire; he cannot desire my annihilation!"

I tried to confirm the Bey in this more soothing idea, and fancied he had recovered some tranquillity, when again he broke out with more violence than before. "It is useless," he cried, "any longer to conceal from you my state. A dreadful gloom oppresses my soul. Spectres of all descriptions unceasingly hover around my steps: they assume every most frightful shape. At this very moment one – two – three – a whole host, whisper in my ear every dire and dreadful presage!"

"And is there among them no angel of light," cried I, "to tell your Highness that by speeding to the capital, I may perhaps retrieve your fortunes? You know, sir, my ancient intimacy with young Mavrocordato; his influence with his father; the relationship of that father with Handgerly; his connection, through his son, with the Souzzos; his riches, his sway, his ambition. Long has he aspired at the principality, and some compromise might be made by which his interest and his fortune should be employed to secure your life, on condition of your ceding to him, on the return of peace, all your still subsisting claims upon Valachia."

This expedient was but a straw: the falling prince caught at it greedily; and now pressed me himself to go, in order to put the scheme into execution. After sending for me but the week before, in order to discuss the propriety of seeking death by his own hands, he now conjured me to do all I could to save his life.

Yet when I came to bid him farewell, he hardly would permit me to depart. Laying on my hand his cold and clammy palm, "Selim, Selim," cried he, as if oppressed with anguish, "you, who have known me from your youth; who have ever found me indulgent and kind, save when you rejected my kindness; over whom I ever kept a watchful eye, even when you thought I had justly abandoned you; henceforth, make me the only return in your power: allow not those things to be imputed to my weakness, which were only the result of my necessities. When my conduct in my principality is canvassed, recall to mind my means. What I have done, say with what I did it: and when the rest of the world shall unite to condemn me, remember your ancient patron, and dare to defend his memory."

I felt moved, and was on the point of giving up the journey. But what good could my stay produce? I therefore gently disembarrassed my hand from the Bey's almost convulsive grasp, and said: "I was sure I still should see him triumph over all his enemies."

"It shall be," replied he, a little calmer, "as Heaven ordains. To myself my warning spirit whispers: my days draw to their close. Go thou and prosper!"

I went; – but prospered not!

Mavroyeni, though he immediately quitted the vicinity of Widdin, removed not to a great distance. His first station was Arvanito-Chori, a mean village: but, constantly shifting his quarters from one place to another as if to elude pursuit, he still kept hovering over the borders of his principality, like the moth, which with wings already singed still flies round the candle, but at every circle narrows more and more its orbit, until it pitches on the spot marked for its final exit.

To Mavroyeni this spot was Bella. There it was that suddenly appeared before the Bey, no longer a mere airy phantom, but the Capidgee of flesh and blood, commissioned to confer upon him the palm of martyrdom.[6] Mavroyeni had kept in reserve, when all other means should fail, an expedient on which he placed implicit reliance. "My firm conviction," said he to the Sultan's messenger, "has always been that a good Christian must be a bad subject. For how can he show zeal for his sovereign and his country, whose religion enjoins entire detachment from this nether world? I therefore have long inwardly bowed to the truth of Islamism; and now only wish publicly to embrace its holy law, and to be numbered among the faithful."

Upon this, the Prince took from his bosom a small Koran, which he carried on purpose, kissed it devoutly, and desired to make his profession of faith. Such a request even a capidjee durst not deny him: he was suffered to perform at his full leisure his orisons, his genuflections, and his ablutions. Only when all was concluded, the capidgee expressed his satisfaction that he now was enabled to send to Heaven so sincere a believer.

What could be done? No enthusiastic mob here pressed around to take under its protection a young and pitied neophyte. Before the hoary sinner stood no one but his cold-blooded executioner, intent only upon the performance of his office. Seeing all further subterfuge therefore useless, Mavroyeni at last armed himself with resolution, and determined quietly to submit to his fate. Yet he could not, as he knelt down, help exclaiming: "I deserve not this, at least from my sovereign! May he, in his wide extended realms, find a Greek more faithful!" He said no more, uncovered his neck, suffered the fatal bow-string to be fastened round his throat – and fell a corpse.

CHAPTER XVI.

If my destinies never enabled me to shine forth, like the rarer suns of the creation, with any inherent splendour of my own; if my vagrant disposition never allowed me even to reflect with steadiness the borrowed lustre of a regular satellite; if at all times I rather in my desultory rambles resembled the erratic comet, either so near some nobler orb as to be lost in its blaze, or so remote from every star in the firmament as to be abandoned to its own native obscurity, still had I thus far in my career at least at distant intervals shone with some little radiance derived from the reflection of loftier names: but this resource now ceases; this passport to public notice henceforth is denied me. Hassan and Mavroyeni already are no more; and if Youssoof, by concluding the war he kindled, still claims a page in history's weightier volume, he no longer comes within the compass of this desultory sketch. Nor will other luminaries arise to succeed these setting stars. Whatever instruments of great changes or workers of great mischief may still appear, will move in an orbit so distant from my reader's view, as scarcely to preserve in his eyes any impressive size. Henceforth I shall constantly have to thrust my own insignificant person foremost on the stage; and to draw from my own common place vicissitudes alone, all my means of interesting or attaching my readers.

Nor is the want of great names, in whose radiance to walk, the only growing disadvantage of these pages. The humbler person on whom henceforth exclusively devolves the task of occupying the reader's attention, must even be resigned to lose, as the work advances, the faint halo which might thus far have appertained to his own person. He no longer can expect to retain that power of exciting interest, or of obtaining the favour or the forgiveness of the world, which might have been hoped for at the commencement of this confession. In its earlier chapters the discourse was concerning a raw stripling, – a youth hurried away by the restlessness of his incipient being: and the immaturity of adolescence, as it enhances the merit of what is good, so it disposes to view with indulgence what is reprehensible. Of the faults of a boy, the greater number are ascribed to his newness in the world, to his not yet being initiated in its manifold mysteries, to his not yet distrusting its older and warier tenants. The graces of youth secure the forgiveness of more advanced age: but that happy era, that period of delightful dreams once gone by, no more mercy must be looked for. Every action is considered as the result of a character formed, of a deliberate will: – it is scanned with minuteness, and it is judged with severity. If it betray the smallest error, not only the deed is condemned, but the author is pursued by man's implacable hatred. "Of one so confirmed in evil, an example is all that can be made:" exclaims an unsympathetic world; and where the Anastasius of sixteen might have obtained a full and unqualified pardon for his transgressions, the Anastasius of twenty-eight must expect to meet with all the rigour of unmitigated justice.

If therefore I only wrote for others, here is the place where I would lay down my pen: but I write for myself – and I proceed! The very incidents which, more confined to my own individual self, may have less merit in the eyes of strangers, are those which my mind oftener recalls, and dwells upon with most complacency.

"The more haste, the less speed," says the proverb; and the proverb speaks true. So anxious was I, on leaving Widdin, to get to Stambool, that my hurry forced me to stop short in the middle of my race. Still weak on setting out, and unprovided with Mohammed's angel wings to screen me on the road from a scorching sun, I was overcome by heat and fatigue early on the journey, and fell ill at Boorgas. What I hated more than Jews do pork and gunpowder, – attendants and gallipots, – now again beset me. Wholly defenceless, I was assailed by half a dozen physicians and nurses at once. They took forcible possession of my apartment, and waged over my body as fierce a contest as ever did the Greeks and the Trojans over that of Patroclus, In truth, this was lucky; for my safety only lay in numbers. The sons of Esculapius and the daughters of Hygeïa neutralized each other's schemes; and I escaped, like a small district wedged in between greater powers, which owes its preservation to their unceasing rivalship. The first tranquil slumber which I had enjoyed since my malady was broken by the stray blows that fell from the hands of the two trusty persons hired to watch by my bed, as they were engaged across my pillow in a scuffle for my purse. Each tried to gloss over his own conduct, by accusing the other of having come to murder me.

Fresh from witnessing events of some importance, it was during my convalescence that I first bethought myself of relieving its tedium by writing my memoirs. "They must," – thought I, – "if consonant to truth, speak too ill of their author, not to be sure of finding readers;" and that idea encouraged me to begin the execution of the arduous design. I am not even certain whether, – though wishing never to deviate from the most scrupulous veracity, – I have not sometimes, out of respect for the public taste, made myself somewhat worse than the world gave me credit for being. If any of my readers should entertain a suspicion of that sort, I leave it to his own discretion to adopt or to reject it: – I shall quarrel with him for neither.

When sufficiently recovered, I proceeded to the capital and visited the Fanar; but no longer, as I had intended, to make interest for Mavroyeni. His cares in this world were over ere I quitted Boorgas; and I had no other object but to afford my friends and well-wishers an opportunity of realizing the warm professions lavished upon me at my departure for Valachia. It would be unfair to say they were wholly denied or forgotten. One person, whom I reminded of his promises, observed that he had pledged himself in much stronger terms than those I quoted: – but to whom? To one going to join Mavroyeni in the plentitude of his power. "Now, prove yourself at this present speaking to be that man:" he added, "and you shall find me staunch to my word." I applauded the frankness of this answer. There was a delicacy in not wishing to wheedle me by empty words out of an esteem, which there was a determination not to deserve by friendly actions.

The filth of the Fanar now displayed to me all its lustre: it was like the contents of a sewer, when, through a chink in the vault, the sun darts its beams full upon their unsightly stream; and much did the nauseous spectacle increase my veneration for the wisdom of the Turks! "Sensible, sagacious, profound people," thought I, "how much your judgement is to be admired, in simplifying, as you do, all your dealings with the Greeks! Powerful as you may fancy your grasp, still, if after catching those serpents, you only allowed them an instant to turn about in your hands, they would infallibly slip through your fingers, dart back into their native slime, and elude your sharpest search. Were you to employ with that deceitful race the slow and circumspect mode of judicial proceeding which the squeamishness of the Christendom thinks necessary in those matters, your indolence, your credulity – your *bonhomie*, if I may call it so – would never get the better of their artifice and subterfuges: you would never be able to follow and to lay hold of them in their endless turnings and windings; and with the moral certainty of being imposed upon by every individual of that wily nation, you must submit to be cheated out of every para of your property, and out of every inch of your estates. But, wise and judicious people! far more securely do you go to work. In your fiscal administration you scorn those innumerable offices, and checks, and verifications, which, in each empire in Christendom, for every ten individuals directly engaged in collecting the revenue, employ twenty others to watch those ten, and thus consume half the income of the state in the collecting of the other half. In the same way, in your judicial proceedings you wave those endless forms, and ministers, and tribunals; those interminable interrogatories, and scrutinies, and confrontations, which, in each state in Europe busy half the population about the rights and misdemeanours of the other half, let nine offenders out of ten escape, and often only inflict on the tenth a tardy and inadequate punishment. Sometimes, indeed, through your peremptory mode of proceeding, you mistake the innocent for the guilty; – but what of that! – You are always sure at least of attaining one great aim of penal justice, that of striking the mind with a salutary terror! Nor should *You*, in this my humble panegyric, lack your proper share of praise, wise and noble Sultan, holy vicar of the prophet, Imperial Manslayer[1]! entitled every day to cut off lawfully fourteen heads, without assigning any reason for their fall: – you, who, by making an implicit obedience to your will the express condition of every public employment throughout your vast empire, have secured yourself against losing the smallest part of your prerogative, through any delay, however great, in its exercise. Regarding each officer of the state only in the light of one of the smaller and more numerous reservoirs, distributed on more distant points of your domain to receive at first hand the produce of dews, and drip, and rills, ere the collective mass be poured into the single greater central basin of your all-absorbing treasury, you give yourself no trouble to check the dishonesty, or to prevent the peculations of your agents. You rather for a while connive at, and favour, and lend your own authority to his exactions, which will enable you, when afterwards you squeeze him out, to combine greater profit with a more signal shew of justice. In permitting a temporary defalcation from your treasury, you consider yourselves as only lending out your capital at more usurious interest. Nine long years, while your work is done for you gratuitously, you feign to sleep, and the tenth you awake from your deceitful trance; like the roused lion you look round where grazes the fattest prey, stretch your ample claw, crush your devoted victim, and make every drop of his blood, so long withheld from your appetite, at last flow into the capacious bowels of your insatiable hazné!"

But the more I admired the system, as a mere indifferent spectator, the les I felt inclined to illustrate its principles by my own example. Having already with such infinite toil and danger – at the cost of my repose and my health – devoted so great a portion of that life that fleets away so fast, to climbing the rugged and slippery path of distinction, in order every time I thought I had attained a certain height only again to slide back to the point from whence I first started, I determined no longer to sacrifice to the same thankless task what still might remain mine of health and of vigour. Instead of the vain sound of titles and the unsubstantial advantages of rank, I determined to seek the more lasting and more tangible prerogatives of a well-filled purse, and, by the laudable thirst for solid gold, to drive out of my mind the depraved appetite for mere unsubstantial fame. "The way to honours," cried I in my new species of enthusiasm, "is a steep and narrow path, where few can rise abreast, and those that follow only try to push down and to pass by the foremost. It is a path which can only be ascended by arduous and abrupt leaps; while at every higher step the risk of stumbling and being dashed to pieces increases in a tenfold ratio. It is a path where distances ever deceive; and what from below appeared the highest summit, when attained, only is found the base of still loftier crags, bearing fruits still more empty and bitter to the taste! "But the way to wealth," exclaimed I, "is a wide acclivity, accessible to all without danger or fatigue: it is a road along which you may to a nicety calculate the progress made and the chance of further advancement; where success depends not on the caprice and favour of patrons, but on the exertions of the wayfarer himself; where, as his way proceeds, he rests on a wider and more solid foundation, finds greater helps still to rise on, and yet needs them less; it is a road, in fine, along which such fruits only are gathered, as purchase or comprehend all the tangible blessings which man values here below!"

In this new view of things, I soon laid down my plan of future conduct. While in Valachia Mavroyeni made his harvest, I had been gleaning in his suite. Formerly, in my soberest moods, I would have hastened to get rid at least of half my ready cash, and contented myself with leaving the other half slowly to beget a puny progeny. But this suited not my present temper. Each of my thousands was in time to grow to a million; and with millions in question, the difference of one half seemed too great an object to trifle with.

Now therefore behold Selim – the gay, the extravagant, the dissipated Selim, all at once transformed into a plodding financier; as much on the watch to turn a para, as formerly he had been on the alert for every means to spend his purses; carefully calculating the interest of each incoming piastre, and deeply groaning after each outgoing aspre: no longer only seeking to dispose of his capital in the way which should give the least trouble, but racking his brains to place his funds in the mode best fitted to secure that grand desideratum – that sort of philosopher's stone – perfect security, combined with exorbitant interest: no longer enquiring, when introduced to a stranger, whether he was a pleasant companion, but whether he passed for a man of substance, orderly in his affairs and punctual in his payments; lamenting the insecurity of investments, the badness of the times, and the high price of provisions; voting servants a pest; looking with pity on the extravagant youths of the age, who preferred gold lace on their backs to gold pieces in their girdle; lending them money at fifty per-cent out of pure charity; wondering how any body could seek, in his attire and equipage, the short lived merits of novelty and fashion, rather than the lasting recommendations of costing little, and wearing well, and – strange to tell – as proud of a cautious demure look, a smug jacket without binding, and a single half starved waiting-boy, as ever he had been of a giddy hair brained manner, clothes stiff with embroidery, and insolent pampered servants, more supercilious than their master.

In a cool sedate reflective person, so entire a change of tastes and of behaviour, I suppose, could not have taken place so suddenly. It could only have been the work of time, and would have displayed a graduated progress. But I possessed not that even temperature of mind which steers clear of extremes: I never could do any thing in moderation. However different might become the object of pursuit, the ardour of the chase with me still remained the same; and the greater the impetus with which I had rushed on in any direction, the stronger, when I met with a check, became the recoil in the opposite direction. My soul fired at the recent instances I had witnessed in Mavrocordato and others, of immense fortunes made in trade; and, already in love with wealth on its own account, I doubly reverenced it in view of the power obtainable through its influence: for ambition would never leave me entirely quiet; but when it was turned out of doors, it stole in at the window, and mixed its persuasions with the other motives that determined me to become in spite of every obstacle a first-rate merchant. So fast galloped my imagination, that already I saw myself standing with one leg in Cashmere and with the other in St. Domingo, with the right hand loading hemp at St. Petersburg and with the left gold and negroes on the Guinea coast; and covering with my vessels at once the Atlantic and the Mediterranean, the Euxine and the South Sea. I had genius; I could, if I chose, force perseverance; and the only trifles wanted were capital, credit, and correspondents.

Providence had just kept in store for me the only person ready to hold all these at my disposal on the shortest notice. I found every thing needful in an old Moslemin, grown enormously rich through nothing but his undeviating perseverance to do all that, by common calculation, ought to have reduced him to beggary. In the true spirit of predestination, Welid maintained that no mode of conduct so infallibly begot ill-luck as caution. "It manifested mistrust," he said, "in the ways of Providence; and one single pious ejaculation at the outset of an enterprise, was worth all the calculations of worldly wisdom." Indeed, Welid might quote his whole life in proof of this doctrine.

But – to go no further back in the recapitulation than the instances of the last twelvemonth: – the Porte had sent away for riotous behaviour the Sclavonians who do the garden work about Constantinople, just at that period of the spring when the setting fruits require constant irrigation. All Welid's neighbours strained every nerve to supply the deficiency, while Welid alone saw his oranges, his citrons, his pumpkins, and his pasteques droop, wholly unmoved; and only exclaimed, "God is great!" – What was the consequence? The sky, usually of brass in that season, all at once opened its sluices and made Welid's *agrumi*, on the very brink of annihilation, yield a double crop.

Again: the unusual rains, in the hottest month of the year, had produced a dreadful plague. Most of Welid's friends took some precautions against the infection, while Welid alone seemed by preference to go where the malady was rifest, and only repeated, "God is great!" – What ensued? Not a finger of Welid's ached all the time, but he became heir to every one of his relations, who had evinced more prudence.

And again: the dampness of the summer was followed by an autumn so dry, that every night saw Constantinople disturbed by some dreadful conflagration. Several of Welid's acquaintance therefore watched their premises, while Welid heard the cry of yan-guen-var[2] in his very yard, without saying any thing but "God is great!" – How did the business end? Welid's house indeed was burnt to the ground; but the falling walls discovered a deposit of gold and jewels, sufficient to build a score of palaces.

What, therefore, could be more natural than for Welid to infer, that the more imprudences he committed, the less he could fail to prosper? Nor did he lack examples of the mischiefs arising from a more wary conduct; for – not to mention his own brother, who, with a sincere and heart-felt wish for wealth, had, from the mere apprehension of making a bad hit, never made a good one; nor his nephew, who, grudging a servant's wages, had, in his loneliness, been murdered by a band of robbers; nor his cousin, who, to save his old vessel a scouring, had sold his gold for brass – what but Emin's resorting to medicine in a malady from which he might have recovered, had made him take a deadly poison? What but Talib's fear of a pursuing foe had caused him to fall into a torrent, and be drowned? And what but Nasser's inventing a most ingenious trap for thieves, had kept him confined by the leg in his own fetters, until he died of hunger amidst all his dearly purchased treasure?

The vast fortune which Welid had, by his imprudence, acquired, I advised him to employ in some grand speculation, and to make me his partner in it. Others might not have thought me the fittest person for a commercial associate, but I repeated Allah-kierim[3] until Welid committed all his affairs to my management. We went, he, his son, and myself, to Smyrna, there freighted a vessel with cotton, and resolved to carry our merchandize to Marseilles, where we could not fail to find a good market. As I contributed but little toward the purchase, my portion was to be but small in the profits: this, however, remained a tacit clause between us, too well understood to be expressed. No regular account, no legal vouchers, no memorandum whatever in writing was drawn up of our respective shares. Welid was not a man to trouble himself about such formalities. "Each knew his own," he said, "and that was enough."

In one respect, however, he showed an invincible obstinacy. He had taken it into his head that it would be manifesting his trust in Providence to hire the first vessel he should meet with. This happened to be precisely the oldest and craziest concern in the harbour; a thing on the eve of being broken up, as unfit for service. The circumstance, however, so far from deterring, only confirmed Welid in his purpose. He thought it a most fortunate opportunity, of signalizing his reliance on heaven; and no entreaty or remonstrance could make him desist from freighting this miserable wreck, in preference to a dozen stout vessels disengaged. He would not even insure. It was flying in the face of Providence, and almost as bad as atheism or blasphemy; so that, unable to persuade my partner, I had insurance made in my own name on the whole cargo.

We now set sail. Hardly had we got into the latitude of Chios, when Welid's son – as hale a boy to all appearance as ever was seen -suddenly fell ill, and died. Our crew, chiefly Provençals, doubted not his being a victim to the plague, which had begun to spread in Smyrna; and they became almost petrified with terror. Welid himself, though he had appeared fond of his child while alive, shed not a tear on his death, bore his loss with his inherent apathy, and only as usual exclaimed, "God is great!" I felt so angry with him for his insensibility, that I longed to see him go to the shades after his boy!

There was nothing to hinder me from realizing that wish myself. The sailors only wondered that so infirm an old man as Welid – after having as it were sat open-mouthed to inhale a contagion, which had snatched away a robust youth – should still continue to breathe: and my putting an end to a thing so out of all rule as my partner's escaping on this occasion his almost inevitable fate, seemed but a just return for his having exposed all our lives in a rotten vessel. Indeed, it was a proceeding which, in my situation, few of my former acquaintances would have considered as any thing more than a fair retaliation, or would have hesitated to accomplish forthwith; even though it must have entailed upon them all the encumbrance of remaining sole possessors of the joint cargo. Yet, unaccountable as it may seem, and scarcely justifiable in the eyes of many, I did nothing to get rid of old Welid: but suffered him to live on unmolested. It is true, that scarcely had his son breathed his last, than there arose a storm, of which the very first blast shivered our frail bark to splinters. It made twelve fine young sailors and their captain go to the bottom, but kindly spared Welid and me; and as the cargo was now lost at all events, I determined to atone for whatever evil thought might, without my leave, have risen in my breast respecting it, by doing my best to save my partner. I lugged him after me on a floating hen-coup; and, as it had not required an out of the way rough sea to make an end of our crazy skiff, this vehicle supported its load, until the wind and current carried us ashore on the neighbouring coast of Samos.

Welid, who had only suffered himself to be saved, like one of his bales of cotton or bags of corn, without making a positive resistance, experienced on this rather trying occasion so little extraordinary wear and tear of body or mind, that, weak and old as he was, he still brought ashore strength enough to cry out with great satisfaction on the loss of his cargo, as he had done on that of his child: "God is great!" while I, on whom had fallen all the weight of exertion, could scarce articulate from exhaustion.

Our shipwreck close to the land, in broad day light, had collected round us a number of fishermen, all impressed with becoming gratitude towards Providence, not so much for having spared our lives, as for having destroyed our vessel on their shores. Too late, however, to push our persons back into the waves from which we had just emerged, they exerted themselves the other way; and helped us on, lest we should witness their proceedings in regard to the wreck. The little money we had in our pockets was employed in getting ourselves conveyed, as soon as the storm subsided, to Kooshadasi on the coast of Anadoly; but this short voyage completely exhausted our finances, and on our arrival we had not a para left.

Nor were we, for the present, in want of a para. The Turk, where bigotry interferes not with his better feelings, is as charitable as he is confiding. He neither attributes good fortune entirely to man's own sagacity, nor ill-luck solely to his imprudence; and neither is apt to listen with suspicion to the tale of the indigent, nor to cast blame on the conduct of the unfortunate. Looking upon adversity as proceeding from the same high source from whence flows prosperity – feeling as little degraded by the pressure of God's hand upon him, as elated by its support, he confers charity without pride, as he asks it without meanness. We, therefore, who came as supplicants, in need of every thing, found every thing we needed. Every inhabitant vied with the rest in supplying our necessities, and providing for our comforts. Hence Welid, who wanted repose, resolved to avail himself for a few days of the hospitality so handsomely tendered; while I only requested a horse and a guide, to take me on to Smyrna. The two animals soon were found, and I set off.

Our halting-place, the first night, was a mean-looking hamlet, situated in a narrow defile. The next day, after leaning a little more to the right than appeared our due course, we arrived early in the afternoon at a largish place in the plain. As we were to stop till the next morning, I established myself in a coffee-house, while Dimitracki the guide went to look after my horse. Scarce had I lighted my pipe and begun to sip my coffee, when a tchawoosh, followed by two or three peasants, walked in, and summoned me before the Soo-bashee.[4]

Where bullying seems to be the thing intended, the best way is to bully the first. Many a man continues troublesome only because he has begun to be so, and knows not how to leave off. "I have no business with your Soo-bashee," said I, therefore, to the messenger – "If he wants me, here I sit" – and immediately I squared myself a little more than I had done before. Accordingly the tchawoosh went away, and the Soo-bashee came, followed by a posse of blackguards of all colours and sizes. My own guide Dimitracki, the greatest of all, brought up the rear, and stood peeping between the elbows of those before him.

I gave the magistrate a nod between civil and familiar. He gave me nothing in return, but, gravely squatting himself down at the other end of the ragged sofa, bade my guide draw near. Dimitracki advanced, hanging his head, and afraid to meet my eyes. "So this man," cried the Soo-bashee, addressing him, but eying me, "is a Russian spy."

"Nothing can be more certain," answered my guide, clearing his windpipe, and trying to look resolute. "Let him speak, and you will know him to be a Greek by his accent. He is the very man who betrayed Ockzakow to the Russians. There was Stavros, and Mavros, and Kokinos, and Proto, and Psaro, and Georgio, and Mareacki, and Michaelacki, and Manolacki, and I don't know how many more of us, who witnessed the whole proceeding. I know him as I do my father."

A wag here observing that that was not saying much, Dimitracki grew angry, corroborated his assertion by the most violent oaths, and called upon another Greek of the name of Petracki to vouch for his veracity.

Petracki of course confirmed all that Dimitracki had asserted: he even went further. "Indeed your worship," cried he, "there is no end to this man's iniquities. For, besides betraying both Ockzakow and Bender, it is he – and I have it from the best authority – who assisted the enemy in intercepting, near Hissar, your worship's own boat-load of corn."

The affair of Ockzakow and Bender the Soo-bashee might perhaps have overlooked, as not within his province; but the corn was too much. Almost choaked with passion: "Ah wretch," cried he; "I could stab you with my own hands. But I respect the law: I shall therefore only send you bound hands and feet to Tireh; where the Moot-sellim, who is my friend, will be sure to see you hanged."

"No, no!" cried a parcel of fanatical Osmanlees, "we have stones enough for him here!"

I pledged myself to prove my innocence at Smyrna; but I scarce was listened to. "Any traitor," observed the party, "was sure of protection in that nest of infidelity, among the Frank Consuls;" and the Soo-bashee himself began to be abused for not seeing me disposed of on the spot. Either frightened or pretending to be so, he called Heaven to witness he had no hand in what might happen; and then bade me be handed over to the mob, whom he told to act as they thought proper.

So they seemed resolved to do; for all were drawing their cutlasses. A flourish was all I had left for it. Spiridion's pocket book still kept its place in my bosom. Solemnly pulling it out: "By the dread seal of our sovereign enclosed in this case," exclaimed I emphatically, "I command you, slaves, to disperse. Tremble to impede my progress! For each hair of my head a life shall answer."

The audience looked aghast, the rioters slunk away, and the Aga begged to provide me with a suitable escort. "I want none," I replied; "an invisible guardian watches over my safety. The wretch who brought me to this place, alone shall go onward with me."

That was exactly what Dimitracki felt least inclined to do. His little scheme had been to appropriate my horse; and to obviate any opposition on my part, he had hit upon the expedient of swearing away my life. He now became so frightened that he fell upon his knees, and confessed all his untruths. "He had told them out of sheer loyalty, and in reality, I ought to feel obliged to him; but all he asked for, was to go with me no further." I protested I could not give up his company, and had him closely watched, while I condescendingly accepted a lodging for the night under the Aga's roof.

At sunrise I again set off, ordering Dimitracki to take the lead. I destined him a remembrance that should benefit other travellers: but I soon found it easier to lodge a musket-ball in his side than to bestow a milder correction on his back. The fellow looked as strong as a Hercules; and, though pacing on before me in gloomy silence, with his head stuck in his stomach and his eyes cast on the ground, he seemed so constantly on the alert, that it was quite impossible to take him by surprise. Even when we halted to take a little rest, instead of lying down, as he had done on the first days, behind the bushes, he stationed himself with his back against a tree, and his face turned to me, so that I could not stir a step unperceived; and though he pretended to sleep, it was only with one eye. Every time I approached him, he jumped upon his legs, to ask me what I wanted.

At last we came to a pass in the mountains which looked propitious to my scheme. Here, having succeeded with some management to knock the fellow down, and to tie his hands and feet, I gave him the destined drubbing with unsparing liberality; which done, I fastened him to a tree, there to ruminate at his leisure upon the wholesome lesson. Ismir's gulph was in sight, and fortunately I wanted a guide no longer.

My first care on arriving was to recover the insurance on the shipwrecked cargo. After some delay, occasioned by legal enquiries, affidavits, &c., I got indemnified for every bale of cotton put on board. Welid, who in the mean time had also re-appeared, declined to share in the recovery, as he had refused to share in the insurance. It was only by stratagem I could make him accept a small part of the produce. No way cured, however, by his loss, of his blind confidence in his destiny, he continued to commit fresh imprudences, until from the condition of a wealthy merchant he became reduced to that of a poor basket-maker; but whenever we met, he still would lay aside his osier twigs to point to heaven and cry out: "God is great!"

While following up the recovery of my insurance, I fell in with a curious personage, – a Turk who had sought the protection of the French consulate at Smyrna. Descended from a Sultana, Isaac-Bey had in his boyhood been selected as playmate to the present Sultan. Soon, however, his fickle disposition made him quit the seclusion of the seraglio for the command of a galley. His jovial humour and his freedom from Turkish prejudices caused him to be much courted in the different sea-ports by the Frank merchants; and their conversation inspired him with a wish to behold Christendom. All at once Isaac-Bey disappeared from his station, and the next news of the truant came from Naples. Some said his escape had the sanction of his master, desirous through his old confidant to explore the arts of Europe, and to learn which of them might be transplanted with success to the Turkish dominions; nor was Isaac-Bey at any pains to contradict the report. Statesmen, therefore, courted in him the favourite of his future sovereign, as the fair did the favourite of nature. The genteel Turk became the fashion in Christendom, and every body wanted to see a Frenchified Moslemin, who ate an *omelette au lard*, drank champagne, and wore a miniature of his Circassian mistress.

It was entertaining enough to hear Isaac give an account of his journey. "Unaccustomed," said he, "as I was, to the shocking sight of men an women mixing in public, or posture-making exhibited otherwise than for hire, how did I stare, when, on my arrival in Christendom, I was taken to a ball at the house of a Bey. I thought little of the dancing. None of the females knew how to shake their hips; but their faces I liked, spite of their plastered heads. I went up to the one that led off, and watching my opportunity, slipped a purse into her hand. I thought she would have boxed my ears, and every body turned up their eyes in astonishment, the lady being wife to the first Visier. In my own mind the impropriety rested with herself: but the adventure made me cautious how I spoke. Before the unsuccessful overture, I had secretly destined three or four of the damsels present an apartment in my harem on the channel; unfortunately, one was the daughter of the Reïs-Effendi, the other the wife of the Cazi-Asker,[5] and the third the Spanish embassadress: so that all I durst offer them was a pinch of snuff."

"At Rome I went to see the grand Mufti of the Christians, who bears the same title with our Greek papases. He appeared a very modest, well behaved, quiet gentleman. His suit made more fuss about him than he did about himself. They dressed and undressed him a dozen times in the middle of the church, changed his caps, fed him, and sang to him. As I stood a good way from the table, which was richly decked out with gold cups and candlesticks, I took the leading performers in this show, with their sleek faces, their laced petticoats, and their long trains, for the pontiff's wives; they were only his cardinals. In fact, he is not allowed to marry, though – like our Sultan – he has his troop of medjboobs.[6] These, however, he keeps, not to guard his harem, but to sing in his chapel; and so dismally do they squall with their shrill pipes, that it is called a *Miserere*. Finding Rome a very ruinous place, I was glad to leave it."

"From Italy," continued the Bey, "where I saw nothing but priests and *cavalier-serventes*, I went to France, where I was pestered by *petit-maîtres* and philosophers: but they so often exchanged characters, that I never could tell which was which. Strangely was my poor Turkish brain puzzled on discovering the favourite pastime of a nation, reckoned the merriest in the world. It consisted in a thing called tragedies, whose only purpose is to rend the heart with grief. Should the performance raise a single smile, the author is undone. Much, however, as I was bidden to cry, I could not help roaring out with laughter, when I saw an old princess in a hoop three yards wide die for love of a prince with his cheeks painted all over: but my bad taste excited great contempt. One day they took me to a representation of Turks; as if I had not seen real ones enough. Luckily I did not find them out: for the fellow in the feathered night cap I certainly would have knocked down, for daring to travestie our holy Prophet. The place called the Opera, with its fine show of dancing girls, pleased me the most of any. The first time indeed of my going there, on seeing a superb palace crumble to pieces, I thought there was an earthquake, and ran out as fast as possible, expecting the whole house to come down about my ears: but by degrees I got used to those accidents, and though I could never think all the jaw before the scenes otherwise than very tiresome, I often thought the show behind them exceedingly pleasant."

"The French are all prodigious talkers; but those who never ceased were a sect called economists. They were for making the country produce nothing but what might be put into the stomach: forgetting that men have eyes as well as palates, and that if the former find nothing to feed upon, the latter will consume double quantities – were it only to kill time; and thus turn economy into waste. This I ventured to observe: but they shrugged up their shoulders, and said I was a Turk!"

"Being so near England I had a mind to visit London. My French friends – I mean of the female sex – strongly opposed the idea. 'It would ruin all my newly acquired French good breeding. Besides,' added Madame de Mirian, 'those islanders are so proud of the ditch which shuts them out from the world, that life is scarce long enough to thaw the icy coldness of their first reception. They will indeed tell you, as they did me, that if your lungs can but stand their smoke a dozen years, you may be admitted to the honour of stirring their fire, – that is to say, of finding yourself at home in their chimney corner; but, in the mean time, if you dress like themselves, you will be left to your own meditations; and if you vary from them, were it only in the width of your shoe-straps, you will be stifled with impertinent curiosity: to say nothing of their churlishness in not admitting strangers otherwise than by sea, and prohibiting all French articles!'

"These last instances of ill breeding persuaded me: and as I had a French article of which I was very fond, I stayed at Paris till the accession of my Imperial master made me return home, and console myself for the pleasures I quitted by the honours which awaited me."

"The first which I received was an order for my exile at Lemnos: but this was not the last. My enemies accused me of having, in my rambles, not only ridiculed the laws of the Prophet, but committed the dignity of the Sultan. So great a crime required the greatest punishment. Sitting mournfully in the boat in which I fancied myself going to the place of my banishment, my eye caught the looking glass at the prow, and in that mirror the reflection of my conductor, seated behind me, just as he was shewing the boatmen how in half an hour my head would be bouncing at my feet. Judge of my situation. A French tragedy was nothing to it. At Paris I had quite got out of such transactions.

"Arrived at the Dardanelles, I was stowed in the dungeon of the castle, while my guardians loaded the great gun that was to announce to the world my happy exit, by the inestimable honour of the Padishah's own commands. Just at that moment, Seïd-Aly, returned from blockading the Russians in the Black-Sea, was passing full sail with his squadron through the straights. He failed not to claim the ancient privilege of the fleet to liberate a prisoner in the castle. But what was his delight to find himself by that means – spite of every opposition – the preserver of his old friend! My sudden translation from a dark underground dungeon filled with fierce executioners, to a brilliant state cabin skimming the waves, in which each face showed a friend, had such an effect on my senses, that at first I thought the whole business a dream, and kept feeling myself all over – and especially my neck – before I could believe it a reality.

"Seïd was giving chase to the pirate Lambro. Ere he proceeded, he deposited me in this place, under the safeguard of the French flag. I have been here some time, but now no longer regret my disgrace, since it procures me the inestimable felicity of your acquaintance."

At this extravagant compliment I burst out laughing, – told Isaac-Bey I was glad to see how much he had profited by his travels, and made him laugh too. We, however, became friends in earnest; and while I remained at Smyrna, scarce a day passed without our drinking together – hidden behind the tri-coloured flag newly hoisted – a glass of muscadel to the health of the little French article, saved from the English custom-house.

NOTES

CHAPTER I

1 p.145. *Masr*: Cairo.
2 p.145. *Kalish*: Canal, or cut, communicating with the Nile. That which runs through Cairo and feeds its different birkets or lakes is opened every year with great solemnity, when the Nile has attained the requisite height.
3 p.145. *Birkets*: excavated ground in and about Cairo, transformed, after the rise of the Nile, into tanks, on which the inhabitants go in boats.
4 p.145. *Tried to spit in my own face*: see Vol. 1, Chapter 13, note 2.
5 p.147. *Franguestan*: land of the Franks; name given by the Mohammedans to Europe.
6 p.147. *As if it had been his own*: Anastasius can only allude to such trifles as the partition of Poland; nothing like the Congress of Vienna having yet been witnesses at that period.
7 p.148. *The felt*: which the mamlukes practise to cleave at a single stroke with their sabres.
8 p.149. *Seratches*: domestics of the Bey, who are not slaves.
9 p.149. *Tchibookdjee*: pipe-bearer; from thchibook, pipe.
10 p.149. *Maallim:* master; Arabic form of address to gentry of an inferior description.
11 p.149. *The lake Yusbekich*: one of the handsomest birkets or lakes in Cairo.
12 p.151. *El Azhar*: one of the great religious foundations at Cairo for the promotion of science; but where, of course, all science which is considered as any way militating against the interest of the foundation, is utterly discouraged.

CHAPTER II

1 p.155. *Caimakam*: lieutenant or official representative of a public personage. The Grand Visier, when he takes the command of the Turkish army, leaves his Caïmakam at Constantinople.
2 p.155. *Mokhadam:* servant who, in Egypt, precedes public officers with a staff called nabood, to drive away the mob.
3 p.155. *Bazirghian*: merchant or purveyor of a man in office, by whom he is paid in drafts on his estates or government.
4 p.156. *Samoor*: spotted fur much esteemed in the Levant.
5 p.156. *Fellahs*: peasants; who in Egypt are all of Arabic extraction, and hold the land according to different tenures; though considered in general as serfs.
6 p.156. *Kawasses*: servants who follow their masters on foot.
7 p.157. *Shehoods*: notables of a village or district.
8 p.157. *Khandgea*: boot for passengers, used on the Nile.
9 p.159. *Miri*: territorial imposition of Egypt.

CHAPTER III

1 p.165. *Hashish*: an intoxicating drug.
2 p.166. *Hazadar*: treasurer, - from hazné, treasury.
3 p.166. *Luxuriant crops*: among the Mohammedans slaves are not suffered to let their beards grow: this appendage therefore is always a sign of freedom; and generally marks official dignity, or at least gravity of deportment. Having been once suffered to grow, it is thought indecorous and almost profane again to shave it.
4 p.167. *Somebody's mother*: allusive to an exclamation of anger, much in use among the Turks.

5 p.168. *Kohl*: a black and almost impalpable powder, used to tinge the eyelids, and supposed to strengthen the sight.
6 p.168. *The Padi-shah*: the emperor: title given to the Sultan.
7 p.168. *Surmeh*: another name for kohl.
8 p.168. *Henna*: a red juice, extracted from a plant, with which the Egyptians dye their women, and the Persians their horses.
9 p.169. *Alme*: the singular of Awali or singers.
10 p.171. *Clapping her hands:* which in the East, where servants are always in waiting in the room, stands in lieu of ringing the bell.

CHAPTER IV

1 p.172. *Abbah:* Arab cloak.
2 p.174. *Bedawee:* or Bedoween.

CHAPTER V

1 p.181. *Koobbees*: sepulchral chapels.
2 p.183. *Zaims*: vessels which navigate the Red Sea.
3 p.183. *Nileh*: indigo.

CHAPTER VI

1 p.185. *Hadjee*: a pilgrim; from hadj, pilgrimage. All Mohammedans are enjoined by the Prophet to perform that to Mekkah in person, or at least by proxy.
2 p.185. *Kaaba*: the holy house of Mekkah, originally built by the angels of Paradise: in its wall is inserted the black stone, probably of atmospheric origin, already worshipped by the Arabs prior to Mohammed, who found the superstition in its favour too deeply rooted to contend with.
3 p.185. *Coorban Bayram*: festival which takes place forty days after that of the Bayram.
4 p.185. *Kishr*: a beverage much used in Arabia.
5 p.186. *Dives*: celebrated magicians.
6 p.186. *The bird Roc*: a fabulous bird of prodigious size.
7 p.186. *Simoom*: the poisonous wind of the desert.
8 p.187. It is customary with men of letters in Arabia to assume a number of surnames, borrowed from different circumstances.
9 p.188. *The balance Wézn*: in which, according to the Koran, are weighed man's good and evil actions.
10 p.188. *Afrite*: evil spirit; demon.
11 p.189. *Birket-el-hadj*: the lake near Cairo, on whose banks the pilgrims bound for Mekkah assemble.
12 p.190. *The Shereef of Mekkah*: the prince or sovereign of the country.
13 p.190. *Djezzar*: whom it fell to our lot to defend against Bonaparte.
14 p.190. *The Hadj*: or caravan of pilgrims.
15 p.190. *Bosniac guard*: some of the Turkish Pashas or governors of provinces have Bosniac soldiers for their body guards, as others have Albanians, and others Koords or Turkmen.
16 p.190. *Deli-bash*: or officer of Delis.
17 p.193. *Firmans*: passports from the Grand Signior.
18 p.193. *Crals*: petty sovereigns of Christendom.

CHAPTER VII

1 p.195. *Seraff*: cashier, banker.

CHAPTER VIII

1 p.207. *Before the holy doors*: According to the ritual of the Greek church the priest alone enters the sanctuary, which is divided from the nave by a screen, the doors of which are called the holy doors.

CHAPTER IX

1 p.212. *The infidel hill*: on which stands Pera, the quarter of the Franks.
2 p.214. *Capidjee*: a gentleman usher of the Grand Signior. The capidjees are wont to carry to the governors of the provinces the commands, favours, and bowstrings of the Sultan.
3 p.215. *Iskiudar*: Scutari; situated opposite Constantinople, on the Asiatic shore.

CHAPTER X

1 p.224. *Nea-Moni*: rich monastery on the island of Chios.
2 p.224. *Fior di Levante*: emphatic epithet of praise given by Greek islanders to Chios.
3 p.228. *Despots*: title given to Greek archbishops.

CHAPTER XI

1 p.242. *His Koordiah body-guard*: The Koors and Turkmen are mountaineers of Anadoly, who often carry their tents to a great distance from their native provinces, combine a predatory and a pastoral life, and form the body-guard of the Asiatic Pashas, as the mountaineers of Albania form that of the governors of Turkey in Europe.
2 p.242. *Dellis*: properly madmen: species of troops who in the Turkish army act as the forlorn hope.
3 p.243. *Baïrak:* company.
4 p.245. *Which in fact he had:* namely Alexander – or Iskandar – bey; commonly called by the Franks Scanderbeg.
5 p.246. *Tootoondjee:* officer who carries the tobacco-pouch of a great man.

CHAPTER XII

1 p.251. *The seven towers*: state prison of Constantinople, in which the Porte shuts up the ministers of hostile powers who are dilatory in taking their departure, under pretence of protecting them from the insults of the mob.
2 p.252. *Mohammed's vicar*: namely the Sultan – in his capacity as heir to the Kaliphate; and who, therefore, in his wars with the Christian powers, hoists the sacred standard of the Prophet, as if only going to war for the defence of Islamism.
3 p.254. *Mikmandars*: officer who in Turkey accompanies ambassadors and other distinguished travellers as purveyor.
4 p.256. *Ekatharina:* pronounced Yekatharina: equivalent among the Russians to Evkatharina: the great and the good Katharina.
5 p.257. *Boyars*: the indigenous nobles of Valachia and Moldavia.

CHAPTER XIII

1 p.259. *Roumooms*: name which the Valachians give themselves.
2 p.263. *Suleiman the Just*: whom we call *the magnificent.*
3 p.264. *Seraskier: - Hospodar*: the first means a Turkish general of division; the latter is the title given to the Greek governors of Valachia and Moldavia.
4 p.265. *Divan Effende*: Turkish secretary of the Hospodar's divan.
5 p.269. *Anadoly*: or Anatolia – as it is marked in our maps – is the name given by the Turks to Asia Minor.
6 p.269. *Zeeameth or timar*: feudal fiefs, which only differ in the number of men properly mounted, whom the holders are obliged to furnish in war.

CHAPTER XIV

1 p.275. *The Contumace*: name given by the Austrians to the custom-houses of the Hungarian passes.
2 p.276. *Boyookderé*: beautiful villages on the shores of the Bosphorus, chiefly inhabited by Frank ambassadors and their suite.
3 p.277. *Jeune de langue*: appellation given to young gentlemen admitted in the different diplomatic missions at Constantinople, for the purpose of learning the eastern languages.

CHAPTER XV

1 p.280. *Bimbashee:* Turkish colonel.
2 p.281. *A forthnight's growth*: a new Sultan only lets his beard grow from the day of his accession.
3 p.281. *Capitana-bey*: first in command in the Turkish navy after the Captain Pasha.
4 p.284. *The single cloud*: alluding, I suppose, to Hassan's defeat at Tobak.
5 p.286.*Oda or Orta*: Turkish regiment: those of the janissaries attach great importance to the preservation of the vessel in which they cook their pilau; and the officers of their kitchen possess from the head cook down to the lowest regimental scullery boy, their regular rank in the army.
6 p.291. *The palm of martyrdom:* according to the Mohammedan prejudice, the favour of the bowstring conferred by the Kaliph of the faithful, or his representative, ensures in the next world all the rewards of martyrdom.

CHAPTER XVI

1 p.294. *Imperial manslayer*: one of the titles assumed by his gracious Majesty the Grand Signior.
2 p.297. *Yan-guen-var*: the cry of fire in the city of Constantinople.
3 p.297. *Allah-kierim*: God is great! the usual exclamation of devotion, surprise, or resignation among the Mohammedans.
4 p.299. *The Soo-basdee*: inferior officer, commanding a village or small district.
5 p.301. *The Cazi-Asker*: title of the chief magistrate among the Turks, and therefore probably applied by Isaac-Bey to the Lord Chancellor; as the appellation of Rëis Effende seems to be a secretary of state; and that of grand Mufti of the Christians, to his holiness the Pope.
6 p.302. *Medjboobs*: persons qualified to act as guardians of the harem.

VOLUME III

CHAPTER I.

Had my fancy for trade continued in full force, Smyrna was the place to gratify that taste to the utmost of my faculties. In that trucking, trafficking city, peoples' ideas run upon nothing but merchandise: their discourse only varies between the exchanges and the markets: their heads are full of figs and raisins, and their whole hearts wrapped up in cotton and broad cloths: they suppose man created for nothing but to buy and sell; and whoever makes not these occupations the sole business of his life, seems to them to neglect the end of his existence. I verily believe they marry for no other purpose but to keep up the race of merchants.

But that unbounded indulgence in the luxuries of commerce was rather calculated to give a man of my variable appetite a surfeit of sweets. Full two months had now elapsed since I first launched into the commercial line – a circumstance sufficient in itself to diminish my enthusiasm for its charms; and in the course of those two months a single fortunate speculation had rendered me independent of its drudgery. I therefore slackened my ardour, began to lose the good opinion of the Smyrniotes, and, reciprocating their abated regard, resolved again to return to Stambool; there to become, if possible, a Pasha for my money. The plan indeed might not be quite consistent with my recent solemn renunciation of all ambitious schemes when yet fresh from seeing their dismal end in Valachia; but – when was I consistent; or when was not the wish to rise the ruling passion of my soul?

My last mercantile transaction at Smyrna consisted in buying of Isaac-Bey a pair of pistols, made for use in England, and rendered ornamental in Turkey. They were destined for Hadjee Bollad-Ogloo, chief of the mighty house of Kara-Osman, lords paramount of a great part of Anadoly. I had long purposed visiting this venerable old Aga (for notwithstanding his real power, his nominal rank rose no higher) at Magnesia his residence; and now, in my way to the capital, put the often abandoned scheme in execution.

When presented to the chief, in his thriving residence; "Accept these arms," and I, "as the homage of a grateful traveller, who has found them useless amid the security which you have established in your wide domain."

Hadjee-Bollad received my offering, not with the contemptuous indifference of a Constantinopolitan upstart, afraid lest the smallest symptom of admiration should be construed into an acknowledgment of inferiority; but with the courteousness of one, whose ancestors had for many generations back stood high in the public estimation, as well as himself. He praised the beauty of the present, and appeared anxious to make an immediate trial of its excellence. "Age," said he, "has somewhat impaired my strength: but between this sort of weapon and my hand there has subsisted so long an acquaintance, that they often still seem to understand each other, almost without my participation."

He then, from his very seat, took aim athwart the wooden trellice of the window at a magpie chattering on the top of a cypress-tree in the court. To this bird had been given the name of Tchapan-Ogloo. It was that of another great territorial proprietor in Anadoly, the rival of the house of Kara-Osman in wealth, in power, and in extent of domain. He fired exclaiming, "Fall, Tchapan-Ogloo!" and brought down the bird.

"I do not know," continued he, in great glee at his achievement, "whether you think your present thrown away, but I am quite sure that the one of which I am going to beg your acceptance, cannot be better bestowed." This was a handsome horse, richly caparisoned, which Hadjee Bollad desired me to keep, "in remembrance," he said, "of the patriarch of Magnesia."

Impatient to justify his compliment, I vaulted into the saddle, wrested a spear out of the hands of an attendant, and at full gallop hurled it deep into the trunk of the tree on which had sat the magpie.

"Well done!" cried the Aga. "Your race I perceive has been like my own: with this difference, that you are just starting in the career, and I am near its end. You may tell them so at Stambool: but lest their joy at hearing it be too extravagant, tell them too that the old stock leaves a few offsets – like yourself!"

I had intended to proceed on my journey the same day: but, without pressing me to stay, the Aga seemed to have taken it so fully for granted that I could not think of going, as to deprive me of all resolution to take leave. I had not even an opportunity of representing the prolongation of my visit as a deviation from my original plan. To the Aga's hospitable disposition it would have appeared like owning a nefarious design.

Seeing me in admiration of the activity and bustle which prevailed throughout his residence: – of the piles of cotton, the strings of camels, the goods loading and unloading, and the guides coming and going: "this," said the Aga, "is only our peace establishment: but we are equally well equipped for war. At a day's notice we can bring into the field twenty thousand sturdy horsemen, as well mounted as armed, for the defence of the Empire – or for our own!"

"And with so much wealth," cried I, "and so much power, you have been able to avoid the Sultan's dangerous honours?"

"It has cost us a little," hastily rejoined Hadjee. "We have paid greater sums to keep our head out of the noose, than others do to thrust theirs into it: but simple Agas we came into the world, and simple Agas we are determined, God granting, to go out of it. Independence, and the right of leaving our vast domain, inherited from a long line of ancestors, to a long line of descendants, would be ill exchanged for the empty name of Visier, with the certainty of servitude, and the probability of confiscation of the paternal estate!"[1]

At this moment a steward advanced to inform Hadjee that a troop of Albanians, fled from the oppression of some Roumiliote Pasha, were just come to crave his protection, and to beg some employment – or some waste land.

"Tell them," replied the Aga, "they shall have both." Then turning to me: "in granting such requests," he added, "the giver is the gainer." I praised him for his liberality.

"Praise me for my sense," answered he, "in having discovered, that my income bears more fruit in my tenant's hands, than in my own coffers. You complimented me on the security of my roads. It was obtained, not by watching my subjects, but by giving them work. When people toil in mind and in body to improve their own property, they have not leisure to covet that of others."

For three days my ears feasted on Hadjee's wisdom, and my palate on his good fare: on the fourth I took leave of my kind host. "I suppose," said he, "you only quit me to go and visit the younger branches of my family at Bergamo[2] and at Yayakeui." I answered that I had not time at present for so desirable a circuit; but begged permission on my return from Stambool again to visit the chief of so noble a house. "Then do not tarry long," answered Hadjee: "I myself have a journey to perform, in which, old as I am, ten to one but I out-run you, spite of all your activity." On this we took leave. I mounted my new horse, and departed.

But, though my person sped onward, my mind, as if wholly detached from its case of flesh and blood, continued stationary with Hadjee. It seemed riveted to the happy spot where the old Aga exercised his mild dominion; and all the way to Constantinople, my thoughts still dwelt at Magnesia. There was in its, to me, novel scene – in that tranquil enjoyment of life's present sweets, first truly witnessed under Hadjee's friendly roof – an inexpressible charm. It left insipid, it almost converted into positive pain, in the comparison, the pitiful half-tasted pleasures, snatched from fleeting time by the wretched victim to ambitious schemes: – schemes of which the labour is certain, the accomplishment doubtful, and the very success productive only of fruits too often insipid or bitter.

It was true, indeed, that many possessed not the means thus to saunter at leisure, like Hadjee-Aga, along paths strewn with roses. The greater number of mortals must first clear their way through tracts bristling with thorns and briars: they must toil to support life, ere they could afford leisure for its enjoyment. I myself had experienced that condition: I myself had been obliged to labour hard for a competency; nay, had found all my hard labour of no avail to obtain it; and only an event wholly unlooked-for amid all my schemes had at last given me that independence so long pursued in vain.

But I finally possessed it; and I might now purchase every luxury of life, calculated to exempt from ambition's maddening thirst: – I might now command every species of tangible gratification, save only that which consists in the power of diffusing extensive misery. Pleasant dwellings, a plenteous board, a handsome retinue of servants, a well-assorted harem, and whatever else was of a nature to delight the sense, were things now within my easy reach; and the only circumstance still wanting to set them off to the greatest advantage was the power of inflicting a certain quantity of starvation and torture, wherever the too bright sunshine of the picture might require the relief of deeper shadows; – the right to maintain a certain number of humbler instruments and witnesses of my pleasures, who should tremble at my frown, and turn pale when I spoke.

But, for the sake only of a few additional relishes, was it worth my while again to risk the fortune already acquired, and to sacrifice the comforts already brought within my compass, when a thousand were at present the additional chances against my success in new schemes of aggrandisement; and a thousand more the hazards against the possession of the objects sought, answering my expectations?

How often had I, in my various wanderings, from the mountain's highest apex espied from some distant valley, which, thus indistinctly perceived, seemed to promise as soon as entered an end to all fatigue, and to my wearisome journey a concluding stage on a velvet turf; but which, on a nearer approach, proved a sink of swamps and quagmires, a thousand times more irksome and vexatious than the steep and rugged path encountered at my outset!

Even thus it fared with every object of human pursuit. When considered from that distance which only left its leading features discernible, each alike promised a series of unalloyed enjoyments; and each, when its lesser details rose in sight, only showed itself the harbour of a thousand petty troubles, nameless inconveniences, and hourly cares and restraints, waiting to devour inch by inch the felicity of that possession which, viewed in the gross, seemed so attractive.

"Away, then," cried I, "for ever away all further chase after these visions, as lying as they are gaudy – after these fire-flies of the mind, which only flit over swamps, and, when caught, leave a sting! Who would wish for their unsubstantial glare, while rich fruits, ripe for gathering, grow by his way-side?" – and, hereupon, lest I should dearly purchase disappointment, I determined for ever to renounce distant schemes, of whatever sort or description they might be: – for, fool as I still was, I forgot that there may be great pleasure in the pursuit even of an object found worthless when attained; and that he manages his means of happiness but poorly, who, while his existence affords room for realities and dreams – while, in fact, dreams are wanted to fill up the unavoidable chasms intervening between the few pleasing realities – renounced all those airy but delightful phantoms of the imagination – last to exhaust or to cloy.

Indeed I made a mistake more woeful still than that of only renouncing whatever depended for its final attainment on future contingencies. Contemplating Hadjee-Aga, my new model, only in a small part of his conduct, and not considering that the charm which surrounded his tranquillity, derived, like that of the immovable sun, from the extensive diffusion of its beneficial influence, I contracted my plan of present enjoyment until it became wholly selfish and sensual. Wholly intent upon those pleasures which flourish only in youth, and health, and freedom, I overlooked the other better portion of those allotted to man, which do not fade even in age, in infirmity, and in durance.

The merit of the new design I had conceived; the wisdom of thus founding the whole fabric of my earthly on gratifications wholly tangible still continued the ruling theme of my self-applauding thoughts when I began to discover Scutari, the principal outpost of the capital on the Asiatic shore; and in the neighbourhood of that city, – harshly edging the horizon, – the black streak of cypress groves that mark its immense cemeteries, the last resting place of those who, dying in Constantinople, fear that their bones may some day be disturbed, if committed to the unhallowed ground of Europe.

A dense and motionless cloud of stagnant vapours ever shrouds these dreary realms. From afar a chilling sensation informs the traveller that he approaches their dark and dismal precincts; and as he approaches them, an icy blast, rising from their inmost bosom, rushes forth to meet his breath, suddenly strikes his chest, and seems to oppose his progress. His very horse snuffs up the deadly effluvia with signs of manifest terror, and exhaling a cold sweat, advances reluctantly over a hollow shaking ground, which loudly re-echoes his slow and fearful step. So long and so busily has time been at work to fill this spot with the sad relics of mortality, – so repeatedly has Constantinople poured into this ultimate receptacle almost its whole contents, that the capital of the living, spite of its immense population, scarce counts a single inhabitant for every ten silent inmates of this city of the dead. Already do its fields of mouldering bodies, and its gardens of blooming sepulchres in every direction stretch far away across the brow of the hills, and the hollow of the valleys: already are the avenues which cross each other on every side in this domain of death so lengthened, that the weary stranger, from whatever point he comes, has to travel many a mile between endless rows of marshalled tombs shaded by mournful cypresses, ere he reaches his journey's seemingly receding end; and yet every year does this common patrimony of all the heirs to decay still exhibit a rapidly increasing size, a fresh and wider line of boundary, and a new belt of young plantations, growing up between new flower beds of graves. [4]

As I hurried through this awful repository, the pale far-stretching monumental ranges rose in sight, and again receded rapidly from my view in such unceasing succession, that at last I fancied some spell possessed my soul, some fascination kept locked my senses; and I therefore still increased my speed, as if only on quitting these melancholy abodes I could hope to shake off my waking delusion. Nor was it until, near the verge of the funereal forest through which I had been pacing for a full hour, a brighter light again gleamed athwart the ghost-like trees, that I stopped to look round, and to take a more leisurely survey of the ground I had traversed.

"There," said I to myself, "lie, scarce one foot beneath the surface of a soil, swelling, and ready on every point to burst with its festering contents, more than half the generations whom death has continued to mow down for near four centuries in the vast capital of Islamism. There lie, side by side, on the same level, in cells the size of their bodies, and only distinguished by a marble turban somewhat longer or deeper, – somewhat rounder or squarer, – personages in life far as heaven and earth asunder, in birth, in station, in gifts of nature, and in long laboured acquirements. There lie, sunk alike in their last sleep, – alike food for the loathsome worm, – the conqueror who filled the universe with his name, and the peasant scarce known in his own hamlet: Sultan Mahmoud, and Sultan Mahmoud's perhaps more deserving horse[5]: elders bending under the weight of years, and infants of a single hour; men with intellects of angels, and men with understandings inferior to those of brutes, the beauty of Georgia, and the black of Sennaar; Visiers, beggars, heroes and women. There perhaps mingle their insensible dust the corrupt judge and the innocent he condemned, the murdered man and his murderer, the adulteress and her injured husband, the master and his meanest slave. There vile insects consume the hand of the artist, the brain of the philosopher, the eye which sparkled with celestial fire, and the lip from which flowed irresistible eloquence! All the soil pressed by me for the last two hours, once was animated like myself; all the mould which now clings to my feet, once formed limbs and features like my own! Like myself, all this black unseemly dust once thought, and willed, and moved! – And I, creature of clay like those here buried; I, who travel through life as I do on this road, with the remains of past generations strewed around me; I who, whether my journey last a few hours more or less, must still, like those here deposited, in a short time rejoin the silent tenants of some cluster of tombs, be stretched out by the side of some already sleeping corpse, and be left to rest, for the remainder of time, with all my hopes and fears – all my faculties and prospects, – on a cold couch of clammy earth: – shall I leave the rose to blush along my path unheeded, the purple grape to wither over my head? and in the idle pursuit of some dream of distant grandeur that may delude me while I live, spurn all the delights which invite my embrace? Far from my thoughts be such folly! Whatever tempts let me take: whatever bears the name of enjoyment, henceforth, let me, while I can, make my own!"

It was thus that scenes, which at other times, and with a mind differently predisposed, might have frightened away every scheme of enjoyment in which the sense had a share, now only made me hug my wholly sensual plan with greater paternal fondness.

On my arrival at Constantinople I proceeded to execute my sage intentions without loss of time. So constantly did I keep the fear of death before my eyes, that I suffered none of the pleasures of life to escape me: nor the least unseasonable reflection to break in upon my wiser employment of my hours. I wanted no attendant to remind me daily that I was mortal; but, wholly unadmonished, lived each day as if it was to be my last.

While scudding full sail down the stream of pleasure, a sudden side puff of the most extravagant ambition I ever yet had conceived, blew across the current, and drove me for a time wholly from my forward course. It was occasioned by a report, true or false, but sedulously spread at Pera, of the state of complete anarchy into which had fallen the autocratical boudoir of all the Russias, by the dismissal, or discomfiture, or death, of some reigning favourite. Two or three youngsters, it was added, gifted only with overweening presumption, had attempted to succeed him, but had died of mere fright previous to their installation. In this situation of affairs it struck me that I might have a chance, and need only be seen, to charm and win the prize.

The adventure seemed worth while trying every way. In the first place, a Greek of talent was always sure of promotion in the Russian service. It is true, I had been in that of the Turks: but *that* circumstance only rendered my posture the more promising. Friends, after all, were friends; while enemies must be won over. It is true, moreover, that there was a great disparity between the lady's age and mine: but I knew that if I could get over the objection, she would; and in order not to let it arrest me, determined only to see in every furrow of her face the fold of a well filled purse, and in every spot or freckle on her fair skin, the insignia of some brilliant order. Once, therefore, a smart tight laced colonel in Catherine's own Bréóbraïskî body guard, who doubted the rest? Not Anastasius for certain! "Chill of age nor of climate," cried I, "shall stop me; I shall grasp at all, become another Potemkin, rule an empire, have a court, alternate between arranging fetes and planning campaigns; pay my card-money in diamonds, make mosaïc-work of provinces, plant orange and citron groves on hanging terraces of icicles, and, when tired of illuminations on the Neva, set on fire the Bosphorus, – and transport the seat of empire from the vicinity of the White Sea, to the shores of the Black Sea!"

I had already put myself into regular training; and for the purpose of stimulating my ardour by the daily contemplation of the great Ekatharina's charms, had actually, Mohammedan as I was, bought a plaster bust of her Majesty, in more respects than one, as I was told, greatly resembling the original; when a little Greek baggage of Pera stepped in between, and audaciously seized upon the destined minister of the auto-cratrix of all the Russias.

The place where I sat by preference, while combining my plan. was my bow window; and this bow window happened to face a gaze-boo on the opposite side of the way, where usually sat, in the same manner musing on her projects, a fair Greek widow, who, it seems, was not reserving herself for any Northern potentate whatsoever. Somehow the fascinating Katello contrived – without the least intention – to shew me through the trellice work of her Shah-nishin[6], almost every item of her various attractions (and she possessed a good many,) in regular successsion.

First was beheld – by mere chance – a bright eye, very dark, full of fire, and not at all the worse for wear, notwithstanding all the service it had seen. It incautiously showed itself while in the innocent act of watching the state of the weather, and the aspect of the clouds. Next peeped out – lest I should think there was but one – its companion to the left, very much resembling the other in most particulars, and which went forth into the street very much upon the same guileless errand. In adjusting these said eyes to the small openings left by the laths, came in view somewhat lower than themselves, the tip of a little nose very prettily turned. Presently some acquaintance of the lady's on my side of the street, – but whom I never could descry, – gave cause for certain signs in dumb shew, chiefly performed by a pair of pouting lips of the true vermillion hue; and these signs were accompanied by certain looks, whose lightning glanced so close by me, as actually almost to singe off the end of my left mustachio. Nor did the reluctant display of attractions end here. Ever and anon the settling of the perverse blinds required the ministry of a certain number of rosy fingers, most gracefully tapered; but these ill trained attendants set about their task with such provoking awkwardness, that for the most part two round white arms were obliged in their turn to venture out as auxiliaries, for the purpose of reinstating what the hands had undone. In fine, one day, more than usual efforts to put to rights an entangled window curtain caused such dreadful confusion, that, through the double care of adjusting the drapery overhead, without deranging that situated lower, neither object was attained, and at last the upholstery of the room came down on that of its fair tenant. Civility now no longer permitted me to remain an inactive spectator of my neighbour's embarrassments. I ran down to my door and up to the opposite window, and tried to extricate the adorable widow from her manifold difficulties. Until that instant I had only had sight of her person in detached samples: and what I now saw in the piece, did not belie their promise. It seemed to defy criticism throughout. I, who could worship the cloven foot itself, *bien chaussé*, was fascinated with the one I beheld, and, like another Mark Anthony, gave up for love the empire of the world!

In order that the union might begin with speed, and yet be of a nature to terminate with decency, we agreed upon one of those short hand marriages, called upon by the Turks cabeen. – but, for the purpose of avoiding the obloquy to which nuptials of this sort are liable, notwithstanding their legality, ours were to be a secret; and, assuredly, if safety lies in numbers, no secret could be safer, for all the world was told of it: – yet did the wary widow furthermore insist, in order the better to cloak my good reception in private, upon my abusing her roundly in public; – a clause, from which the natural gallantry recoiled at first as from some atrocious crime.

But by degrees I gave into the scheme more readily. In fact – from what change in my optics I know not – I began after a time to think that some fault might be found here and there without doing great violence to truth. Some of the deceitful Katello's beauties seemed, in my eyes at least, much diminished, and others wholly vanished. Her eyebrows had lost their evenness, and her lips their colour: her very eyes, I could have sworn, had shrunk in their sockets: and though her mouth was become proportionably larger, this scarce made amends for the other abridgements. What I had before viewed as a beauty spot, I now saw as a huge mole; and a certain easy languor of gait, had grown into a positive lameness. The lady pretended to be little better pleased with the bargain herself; nay, when I boasted of my zeal in following her instructions, and, in particular, of the unfavourable description I had given of her ankles, so far from retracting her complaints and resuming her good humour, she fell into a most outrageous passion, and cried, "It was her conduct, not her person, she had bidden me abuse!"

I promised to do so yet, paid the forfeit money, and resumed my liberty. Enough had now been achieved in my opinion, in the way of marriage, for the acquittal of my Mohammedan conscience; to the peace of which I deemed four wives by no means necessary, either simultaneously or even successively, whatever may be thought on the subject in Christendom, – nay, whatever may be asserted even by the more strict and rigorous among my Islamite friends themselves, who ceased not to din in my ears that celibacy was a continual transgression of the law, and that every man as well as woman of a religious turn of mind made it a point of duty to live constantly married, in some way or other. Neither the charms of a young Halebeen[7] of sixteen, described to me by my female scouts as already weighing eighty okkas, nor even those of a young lady from Adrianople, a year or two older indeed, but weighing full half a kantar, could therefore conquer my obstinate resolution.

But I soon found that so entire an abandonment of the duties of matrimony was indulging overmuch in the delights of ease and quiet – was overshooting the purposed mark: that hard as may be the toil of too severe a task, equally heavy was the burden of idleness – equally irksome the lot of lacking all employment – equally oppressive the labour of having constantly to seek some new amusement; or, rather, of being constantly obliged to supply by some imaginary wants the absence of real substantial necessities. None of my contrivances struck at the root of the evil; and often, in the midst of the most boundless mirth and revelry, I caught myself regretting those times of toil and danger, when I used to have a meal one day and to go without the next; to lie down under a hedge one night and on that ensuing to remain like a stork upon my legs, and, always on the alert, alternately to smoke a pipe and to dispatch an enemy.

In the midst of this irksome ease, a letter came most opportunely from Smyrna to give a new impulse to my thoughts and wishes. It was written by a distant relation settled at Trieste, who, having employed his whole life in accumulating a considerable fortune, was now beginning to consider how to prevent its waste after his death. Grown old and infirm, he wished for some younger branch of the family stock, willing to bear him company during the remainder of his days, on condition of becoming his heir on his decease. Cassis Pharaoon, formerly collector of the customs at Cairo, but lately fled with all his treasure to the Emperor's dominions, had mentioned me as likely to acquit myself well in both offices; and my cousin, called to Smyrna on business, felt anxious to see me, and to sound my disposition. His invitation held out such flattering hopes, that I could not resist it, but again set out for the place of figs and raisins; determined to out-do them in sweetness, in my intercourse with my well-intentioned relation.

Before I could reach Broossa the night had come on. Its obscurity just allowed me to perceive, creeping among the tombs, a something which bore a suspicious look, and at first left me doubtful whether I should honour it with my notice, or continue my way. Curiosity at last got the better of discretion. I followed the vision; bidding it, whether man, demon, or jackal, to stop and to answer. But, as I advanced it silently retreated, and with so much speed, that I must have lost the scent, but for a gravestone, over which it had the ill-luck to stumble. It now, to my great amazement, divided in two. One part remained motionless where it had fallen, the other kept running on; and both, as it proved, with equal reason for their different behaviour, – the stationary half being nothing but a sack full of dead men's bones, the moving one the living thief who was conveying them away. Again I cried to this personage to stop, or I should shoot him: and he now faced about; but fell upon his knees and, in the shape of a caloyer, related his story to move me to compassion. Sub-deacon to one of the monasteries on the Agios Oros, he was with his Archimandrite on an eleemosynary tour. At the last place of halting the worthy pair had found their stock of holy ware run so low as to require replenishing. The nearest burying ground offered the readiest means: and the contents of the bag were nothing more than a few straggling bones of Turks, picked up in the said repository, to compose a fresh assortment of Christian relics.

On hearing this account, "Wretch," cried I, "who thus come to despoil our graves! What should prevent me from making a relic of yourself?"

"Only the circumstance," humbly replied the caloyer, "that it would not be worth the while – at least in the way of punishment. My halcyon days are over. The route marked out in our credentials draws to a close; and in less than a fortnight we must perforce return to our convent, to fast, and pray, and see nothing in a human form worth looking on, for the remainder of our lives!"

"Then to kill you would be a mercy!" said I, and let the fellow go – glad myself to reach a not too distant khan where I soon retired to rest. Unfortunately the caloyer's bag of bones, thus irregularly canonised, had reminded me of a favourite topic of Eugenius, namely, the gradual change that takes place in the component elements of each organic body, and the successive appropriation that may thence happen of the same organic particles by different bodies; and the idea of what must be the consequence of this ordination haunting me as I went to sleep, I dreamt that I saw a parcel of souls exceedingly distressed at the sound of the last summons, one half from finding themselves each pulled different ways by bodies of different ages which they had during their lives successively tenanted; and the other half, from finding no bodies at all left for their reception; – the materials of those which they had inhabited having since being purloined by later generations. So great an effect had the embarrassment of these poor souls upon me, that I rose in the utmost perturbation, and stumbling over some camel-drivers asleep in the passage, I mistook them for unoccupied carcasses, of which I was going to dispose in favour of the hapless destitutes, when a powerful resistance at once roused and rendered me sensible of my error. My humane endeavours had this good effect, however, that in an instant the whole khan was on foot, and I enabled thereby to set off at as early an hour as my anxiety to reach Smyrna had made me wish overnight.

Alas! on my arrival in that city, I found I needed not have made so much diligence. My loving cousin Delvinioti had returned to Trieste even before I set off from Stambool, and without so much as leaving a note or message to account for the abrupt proceeding. This was rather mortifying, and made me look foolish. I stormed, and raved, and blustered: I considered whether I should not go after my perfidious relation, and call him out in single combat; but at last, recollecting that the disclosure of one slight provokes others, I determined to look highly pleased; swore I only returned to Smyrna for the benefit of the climate, and, to make good my assertion, resolved to stay the winter, and to spend all my money, that I might seem very happy!

CHAPTER II.

In most heirs to humanity thirty seems to be an age at which those wilder passions, produced more by the heat of the blood than by the perversion of the reason, having exhaled their greatest fire, though they may still warm, no longer torture the frame: and that age I had now attained; – and I might now, according to the usual course of things, consider myself safe from all danger of being hurried headlong, by the madness of uncontrollable desires, into an abyss of misery and regret.

But if the different species of noxious principles, physical and moral, too liberally mixed up in our natures, are by most constitutions thrown off at a single crisis, which, mortal when most severe, renders life more secure where it has ended favourably, they find others incapable, either from the strength of the virus, to expel it entirely in the first conflict, however, great be the effort and complete appear the victory. In these, when all the poison is considered as exhaled and all the danger as past, there will – at the very moment when every agonized heart of friend or parent hails the deceitful vision of an infallible recovery – take place a relapse; – and this relapse ends in death!

Thus it happened to me. At the very period when, having for the first time magnanimously withstood some very powerful temptations, I deemed myself safe thenceforward from those fiercer tyrants of the heart which lie chiefly in ambush for their victim on the threshold of manhood; when I began foolishly to exult on my firmness; – as if I had only by this forbearance been collecting more copious materials for a more destructive conflagration, – a flame arose in my breast, which shook my whole being – body and soul – unto its very basis; and left the remainder of my worthless life a scene of ruin, remorse, and desolation!

Yet did the events commence in gaiety, which ended thus fatally!

In the course of my former mercantile transactions at Smyrna, I had made in that city a few sober acquaintances, whom I used occasionally to visit. The men with whom I habitually lived were a more jovial set: – amphibious beings, found in all sea-ports, who consider the land only as a place of passage, regard the sea as their proper element, and feel equally at home wherever its waves waft their restless existence: who, like the pebbles on the beach, which the tide alternately covers and leaves exposed, lose, through constant friction, all their original distinctness of shape, present one uniform similarity of rude, indiscriminate polish, and with a very complete assortment of the vices of every different region which they in turns frequent, seem to belong to no one race, or country, or religion in particular.

In order to exclude irrevocably from their society all such individuals as might feel the smallest natural tendency to a sober and sedate deportment, these giddy sons of joy had once upon a day devoted one entire forenoon to business, and had drawn up a long list of regulations, which every candidate proposed was held to subscribe ere he could obtain the high honour of admission. As for me, so anxious was I pay the noble fraternity every compliment in my power, that I put my name to the conditions blindfold.

On pursuing them afterwards, however, I found but little which every spirited young fellow does not think himself, even in the absence of a positive engagement, equally bound in mere honour to comply with: for who – to use the language of the place in which this noble association had sprung up – would become a principal in a connubial firm, and take a female partner at his own risk and peril, that could, by trading on another man's bottom, add to his other pleasures the inexpressible delight of making perhaps his most intimate friend a bankrupt both in honour and happiness? What youth of true refinement could brook in the object of his worship a conduct so indelicate as that of selling her person, in a mercantile way, for a definite jointure, while she might mark the difference of her feelings from those of the mere venal system, by disregarding every dictate of interest or of prudence? Where is the man of spirit who would be content with exerting purchased rights in an open, straightforward, legal manner, as long as he was enabled to add to his raptures all the zest of difficulties, and dangers, and mystery, and mischief? And what hero in gallantry would prize his mistress's devotion, unless it had been put to the test by breaking through every restraint of fear, shame, and pride? – And these were the whole of the conditions imposed by the rules of the society; but so tender-hearted were its members, that, while feeling the propriety of the restrictions which confined their choice, they nevertheless pitied most sincerely the number of poor females smitten with their charms, to whom they were prevented from extending the solace of their attentions.

Absolutely stunned by their jactitations, and obliged to assume the same tone in order to avoid contempt, I was, for the mere support of my character, in the act of engaging to find favour in a given time with whatever beauty might be considered as the most inaccessible in Smyrna, when, in the very midst of my boasting, I received the following note.

"You are a man of enterprise; you part with your money freely; you complain, I am told, of too much facility: but is not the game you pursue ignoble? You visit the house of Chrysopulo, and yet you overlook Euphrosyné!"

I made no doubt that this note had been indited by some of the party present – perhaps by the whole set, in council assembled. It seemed a sort of public defiance, a gauntlet thrown by all, which I must take up, or lose my reputation with my fellow rakes. I therefore read the epistle aloud, and pledged myself on the spot to gain the prize pointed out, or to forfeit the place I held in the society. Every head shook in doubt of my success, or rather every lip curled up in derision of my presumption. Flushed with wine, I felt my foolish pride alarmed, and offered to stake large and unequal sums all round the circle on what I imagined to be a certain conquest. They were eagerly accepted: I found myself engaged ere I scarcely knew to what; and when I looked round, I had the satisfaction to see all my friends chuckle inwardly, as if already in possession of my money.

The subject of the fatal wager was a young lady related to a wealthy Greek merchant, with whose wife she lived as a companion. Euphrosyné passed for a great beauty, and had recently been betrothed, it was said, to the son of another Greek merchant, likewise very opulent. Money, therefore, which on all other occasions I had found an useful weapon of attack, was in this instance turned against me, and converted into a powerful means of defence.

I used indeed, as stated in the insidious note, sometimes to call upon the family of which the fair Euphrosyné formed so great an ornament. Its experienced chief had assisted me in some of my mercantile purchases: but these meetings on mere business Euphrosyné's beauties were never allowed to illumine with their radiance. The destined husband himself could scarce ever get sight of his intended spouse. The moment that even his licensed footsteps were head to approach, the older females of the family used to conjure the nymph away, or at least to form round her person a fence so impenetrable, as so set at defiance her swain's hottest fire of sighs and glances. What wonder, therefore, that a stranger and a Mohammedan, whose visits were necessarily rare, and whose appearance put to flight the Aegis of age or ugliness, should never have beheld this paragon of perfection, or known aught of her charms but from common report?

This circumstance, however, no longer had power to influence my conduct. Such was the dilemma into which my thoughtlessness had betrayed me, that, even were Euphrosyné to offer to my eyes no charms whatsoever, I still must obtain her, or submit to ruin, – ruin of a reputation in truth sufficiently despicable; and ruin of a fortune which I wanted the courage to despise.

Upon the whole, therefore, I rather wished not to behold my destined victim sooner than was absolutely necessary for the execution of my nefarious purpose; lest a countenance so heavenly as hers was said to be, should disarm my villainy of the coolness requisite to crown its attempts. All that I wanted in the first instance was to gain some intelligence among the inferior inhabitants of the fortress menaced, as, not yet exalted to the angelic state, might favour from within whatever operations from without against the citadel might be deemed most expedient..

On this subject I began intensely to meditate very earnestly the moment the long protracted revels of the night permitted me to go home and lay down my weary limbs; and on this same subject I still continued meditating with equal intensity, as, after the late and lazy rising of the next morning, I trailed my torpid limbs to the door, in order to inhale, with fresh air, fresh ideas and fresh spirits.

Alas! Cupid, fond of mischief, saw what was hatching in my breast. In the midst of my uncertainty he sent tripping by my threshold, as if going on her mornings errands, one of the female attendants of the very family, selected by our society to writhe under the pangs of unmerited dishonour; and one of no less consequence than Euphrosyné's own waiting woman; the very person whom, in my unprincipled eagerness I could have implored my stars to throw in my way. The waiting woman's face, – I do not know why, seemed familiar to me; and equally familiar to her appeared to be my own features: for on catching my eye she curtsied so graciously as almost to assure me by her mere manner, of an unlimited devotion to my most unbounded wishes.

It would have been positively churlish toward the smiling nymph, as well as neglectful of my own interest, to let so fair an opportunity slip through my fingers. After some requisite ceremonial on my part, and a decent demur on hers, I induced the diligent

Sophia to enter my abode; and there! – but of what consequence is it that I should detail by what arguments she was won over to my purpose? Suffice it to state, that, on disclosing my situation and wishes, so poorly acted was the indispensable preliminary abhorrence of my proposal, as almost to make me conceive, from the facility of the waiting woman, a prejudice against the fair fame of the mistress herself. A well filled purse, given on the spot as an earnest, and a considerable sum of money, pledged as a more substantial final reward on the completion of the business, sufficed very soon to be obtain a promise of unrestricted cooperation in all my designs. It was only when so ready a compliance elicited the loud thanks it deserved, that the lady made some faint attempt at disclaiming a title to my somewhat distressing gratitude. "Had Euphrosyné been suspected of harbouring the smallest spark of affection for her future consort," she now thought it incumbent upon her to state, "not all the treasures in the universe would have obtained from her so much as a mere patient listening to my scheme: but the contrary being notorious, she in fact favoured my suit as much from anxiety for her mistresses happiness, as from compassion for my sufferings." This first intelligence, however, so kindly vouchsafed me of a circumstance so well known to all, was of no avail in saving the suivante's modesty from fresh blushes. I only praised her considerate motives the more, in doing for the sake of her mistress, what I had only supposed her to have undertaken for mine. Nor was the information of a nature to lessen the satisfaction I felt at the result of the *rencontre*. It rendered my design at once less heinous in the conception, and less difficult to execute. To erase old impressions ere new ones are substituted, is an arduous task, and of doubtful success; but on a blank sheet of paper, what penman, even of the most ordinary abilities, flourishes not away as he pleases?

Fully as Sophia understood the object to the achievement of which she had kindly pledged her good offices, to be independent of any very violent feelings of love on my part, she nevertheless could not help observing how much it might be forwarded by some such sort of sentiment on the part of Euphrosyné: and after sagaciously adding that nothing was so essential to falling in love with people as seeing them, she proposed to submit me for the approval of her mistress, in a walk with a large party of friends, planned for the next day in the fields outside the city. "It is absolutely necessary," cried she, "that you should be there by accident. Take no notice of us, but only give us an opportunity of noticing you. Mine shall be the care to improve the incident. A turn or two will suffice; – then, away again, on your life! – and wait patiently till the next morning disclose to you what conversation may have taken place at bed time."

The hint was not lost upon one so eager as Anastasius to embrace whatever could gratify his vanity. With more than usual attention, therefore, to my toilet, I began the next day. I attired myself, not richly, – for on some occasions I felt jealous of my own dress, and fearful lest my finery should eclipse my person, – but as becomingly as possible. No insignificant gew gaws were permitted to conceal the athletic structure of my frame, and the graceful knitting of my limbs. A mere tuft of jasmine, white as my own teeth, was made to relieve the brown polish of my skin, and the jetty black of my beard; and art and nature were, throughout my whole appearance, blended in such just proportions, as every where to contrast with and to relieve each other.

Thus attired for conquest, I sallied forth on a solitary ramble, and sought the verdant meadows with as much eagerness as does the fiery courser, when, liberated after long confinement from his gloomy stable, he rejoins in the fields with loud neighings his blithe and prancing companions.

Not long had I reached the happy valley when the youthful troop appeared, and by long peals of laughter proclaimed its deceitful security from danger. I first kept myself concealed at a distance; let the giggling girls duly begin their sports; and only, when from my ambush I saw them fairly entrapped in a small and secluded nook, of which I commanded the entrance, did I, like one attracted by the noise, leisurely step forward, to petrify the gay band by my sudden appearance. Every gambol immediately ceased; and long before I could come up with the outermost detachment, was every scarf and shawl at its office to conceal its fair owner under a treble envelope. The change from the brightest sunshine to a sky all clouded over, is less rapid even in the inconstant month of March. I therefore only once walked round the party, more to be seen than to see, and having cast a single furtive look on its soaring leader, or rather on the ample veils which completely dimmed her lustre, I immediately retired with the air of one who begs pardon for an unintentional intrusion, which he dares not exult in, but cannot regret.

It may be supposed that through all Euphrosyné's jealous fences of silk and wool and cotton – rendered doubly impenetrable by every addition of fringe, and trimmings, and tassels – not one single feature of her face had been revealed to my searching eye; and even her figure had been but indistinctly discerned: but what of that? Such is the force of imagination, that I felt as if I had been permitted to dwell unto satiety on all I could have wished to see. I went away completely smitten with her air, her grace, her bounding step, her playful manner. What I had not been permitted to behold I moulded after my own taste; and all the rest of the day, and all the ensuing night, I kept my fancy busied with the beautiful image, chiefly of my own creation.

Early the next morning walked in my friend Sophia. Her practice was not to waste time in forms. I eagerly inquired what symptoms my appearance had produced in Chrysopulo's fair charge. "Draw your own conclusions," said the waiting woman, "I shall simply relate facts."

"As soon as bed time with Euphrosyné's bodice her nimble tongue was let loose, and the nightly hour arrived for reviewing the occurrences of the day, you came on the *tapis*; – for to have left unnoticed so remarkable an incident as that which interrupted the morning's sports, would have been the most suspicious circumstance of any. "You know the person, by whom we were thus surprised," said I, significantly."

"No," replied Euphrosyné; and wondered I should be able to remove her ignorance.

"That is no fault of mine," rejoined I, "when our good or evil stars have made him a friend of your cousin's, and a visitor at our house. Had I however conceived the possibility of our meeting so dangerous a youth in so secluded a spot, we should have directed our walk elsewhere. They say it is impossible to behold this Muslim, and to refrain from loving him."

"Nonsense!" cried Euphrosyné, with a forced laugh, and an involuntary sigh.

"Nonsense it probably is," resumed I, in a careless manner – "though I might, if I pleased, add what certainly is not."

"How?" cried Chrysopulo's cousin precipitately; – but immediately again checking herself, "No," added she, "do not tell me: it is no business of mine!"

"Indeed I would not tell you, even though you should entreat me," replied I, "unless you made me a solemn promise that I never should have cause to regret my too ready frankness."

"Euphrosyné now began to apprehend that the silence she had exacted might look like want of confidence in her own steadiness. "I make the promise you required," said she, "but merely lest you should fancy I fear any danger from your indiscretion."

"I then told the blushing girl that you had seen her, and suffered for her all the pangs of unrequited love. Emboldened by the silence with which this disclosure was received, I even went so far as to enlarge on your merits; but soon I found that agitation alone stopped the trembling maiden's breath. My comment gave her time to recover. Having however suffered me to begin the encomium unimpeded, she allowed me to conclude my speech unchecked, in order that her not cutting it short from the first might seem done with design. It was only when I no longer knew what to say, and hemmed as for an answer, that I was asked with an affected composure, to what all this was to lead?"

"I felt disconcerted, and Euphrosyné, after waiting a few seconds, desired I might not trouble myself to seek a reply: 'she must,' she said, 'inform her relations of my improper conversation.' I could only make her desist from this intention by recalling her promise."

This detail of Sophia's, however, sufficed to convince me (perhaps without justification) that the shaft which I had aimed at Euphrosyné's heart had not recoiled wholly unfelt, – that it had made some slight impression; and if I was going to propose further measures founded on this supposition, when a tremendous noise at the door of my lodging announced the riotous entrance of all my bosom friends. I only had time to thrust Sophia into my back room, and went out to meet the jolly party. So loud were the enquiries from all quarters respecting the progress of my love affair, that, terrified lest Sophia should hear them, and feel deterred from her perilous purpose, I tried to entice the troop away, by running down stairs the first. The whole procession followed; to my great relief under my conduct again sallied forth into the street, and proposed to take a turn on the quay, in which expedition, – disposed or not – I was forced to join: it however gave Sophia an opportunity of slipping away unperceived.

During the remainder of the morning I could think of nothing but Euphrosyné. From not feeling any desire to behold my charmer's features, I now was unable, from what I already had seen and heard, to rest until I had obtained of them a full and unrestrained view. The day happened to be a Greek festival. In the evening, by calling at Chrysopulo's, and entering his habitation unannounced, I was sure to find the whole family collected. – I determined to risk the adventure.

The peals of merriment which resounded through the house, both guided my footsteps and drowned the noise of my approach. Unperceived, I stepped into the very place of entertainment. Euphrosyné, seated in her costliest attire at the further end of the hall, had just begun to recount – half in speech, half in still more expressive pantomime – a playful story. Every eye and ear, riveted on her performance, was turned away from the door, and I advanced a considerable way into the room before my visit was perceived. When indeed my presence became noticed, such was the sensation it created that a kite could scarce have made a greater, alighting among the timid tenants of the poultry yard. All the females set up a warning shout, rushed forward, threw a veil over Euphrosyné's still unconscious face, and formed round her person an impenetrable fence. The merry tale with which the thoughtless girl was entertaining the company, immediately ceased; the magician she was in the act of killing with her bodkin, remained alive to do his mischief, and, in the confusion which pervaded the assembly, her own form, as if conjured away by witchcraft – rapidly vanished from my searching sight!

But it was too late: I had seen and I had heard! One single glance of her languishing black eyes from between her silken eye lashes, unrecalled, had met my own inquiring look: while, at the same time, one last expiring note of her soft melodious voice had, from her ambrosial lip, gently dropped upon my outstretched ear; and if the former had sunk like liquid fire into my heart's inmost core, the other continued to vibrate like last dying note of the lyre, on my maddened brain.

All the powers of language of course were inadequate to express the pleasure diffused among the Greek party by my unexpected visit. While the only object of my intrusion was most studiously kept out of sight, I was with the most indefatigable industry made welcome to every thing else in the house that could be named or thought of; was introduced to every individual I did not care to know, and was offered every dainty I did not wish to taste.

A statue could not have shown less sense of these unbounded civilities. Fascinated, and fixed in that same spot which had so lately felt the pressure of Euphrosyné's lovely limbs, I seemed half to enjoy her presence, and did not retire until wished by every person present, where indeed of my own accord I was going fast enough.

Having with faltering step reached my house, I there yielded myself up, body and soul, to my newly conceived delirium. Only after musing over the dying embers of my mangal[1] until my lamp burnt dim, did I seek my lonely couch. I then undressed and went to bed, but went not to repose. Instead of blood unquenchable flames seemed to flow through my veins: and, racked in every joint by the rage of passion became more hopeless in proportion as it had become ardent, I tossed about all night, trying to grasp my fair one's unsubstantial image. At last, exhausted by my fruitless efforts to give body and colour to the delusive phantom, all power of thought forsook me, and I sunk into a state, not of sleep, but of half conscious, half insensible, torpor.

I rose with the lark, though not as blithe; and counted the slowly passing hours until Sophia was to come. I panted for the appearance of this new depositary of my thoughts and schemes, no longer as before, merely to settle my plan of operations, but to talk of, to expatiate upon, to rave about Euphrosyné!

In vain I waited and waited; and at every footstep in the street, and at every rap at the door, and at every noise on the stairs, flew out to meet my wingless Iris. The faithless messenger came not at the time appointed; she came not after; she came not at all! Nor did note or message come in her stead to account for her non-appearance.

I would have gone, if I durst, to the house blessed by my angel's residence. I did all I could: I walked all day long in sight of its froward door. I watched all that went in, and all that went out. I kept myself in readiness, the moment Sophia appeared, to pounce like a hawk upon the dilatory suivante; but no Sophia did appear!

Meanwhile, every possible mode of ingratiating myself with the heavenly Euphrosyné passed through my, alas, less heavenly mind. According as she might be more or less sensible of the charms of gold, or accessible to the lures of vanity, or charitable or devout, the mere glitter of St Mark's dazzling images[2], or the glory of beholding the haughty Selim at her feet, or the pride of making him promise a thorough reformation, or the hope of saving his falling soul from perdition, might be tried, I thought, as bribes to win her affections: but which of these motives for listening to my suit assimilated most with her character, and what were the virtues or the faults in her disposition which might be rendered propitious to my views, remained to me a secret; for while the sun continued to light up this hemisphere, (and in wonder at my behaviour he certainly more than once forgot to move), I saw not my traitress of a waiting-woman darken the door with her slender shadow.

At dusk, however, and just as I was returning home entirely hopeless, the well known form brushed by me. I followed it to a retired spot, where, precipitately turning round, as if afraid to waste time: "What have you done!" exclaimed the agitated suivante; "Why would you shew yourself in the only place from which you should have staid away?"

"Only," answered I, "to see the lady I was making love to."

"And so," rejoined Sophia, "to lose her for ever, as now you inevitably must: for our abrupt visit last night has had the effect of producing all that you could have wished to prevent. The period of the nuptials, uncertain before, is now fixed for to-morrow!"

A short struggle in my breast kept my answer, during a few seconds, suspended on my lips: at last, with one concluding but victorious effort: "Sophia," replied I, my resolution is fixed! While I knew not Euphrosyné, while I yet felt no preference for that angel of heaven, come to render earth worth staying on, I could regard her ruin as my sport; but I have beheld the lovely girl, and have fallen into my own thrice cursed snare. Her innocent looks have melted the hardness of my heart. I no longer can bear, like the simoom, the fair and lovely floweret. I am now ready to perform any sacrifice for her permanent possession, – for a possession that may make me happy, without making her miserable. I shall attach her to my fate through the holy ties of wedlock. It is but paying a few sums which I deserve to lose, and feeding afterwards – as I shall have to do – upon love alone!

Sophia here set up a hellish laugh. As soon as the burst was over, "And so you think," cried she, "that all is to be settled to your liking by this magnanimous resolution; – that you have nothing more to do but to announce your pleasure, and take away your bride! Allow me to undeceive you. Euphrosyné's relations are rich, they are proud, and they are bigoted. Under no circumstances whatever would they suffer a kinswoman of theirs to marry a Mohammedan. No! not if the Sultan himself were come in person to demand her. Then judge whether you have a chance; and that with the faith of the whole family pledged to a wealthy young Greek, ready to tie the nuptial knot! Believe me, if you should ever wish Hymen ultimately to crown your flame, you must begin by rendering your success independent of that squeamish deity."

"Sophia," resumed I, "once more I tell you that my resolution is fixed. Adoring Euphrosyné as I do, nothing shall induce me to rob her existence of its bloom, her life of its lasting pride. For once I shall subdue my lawless passions; I shall pay the forfeit of my idle boastings. If after making sacrifices to her virtue and her peace so weighty as those of all fortune's value gifts, and all love's unfettered raptures, she accept me for her husband, well and good. Luxuries she will not find, but affection in abundance. If on the contrary she reject me: patience! For once in my life I shall have done what was right, at the expense of my vanity, my fortune and my happiness."

Sophie, at these words, turned pale. She seemed to labour with a fearful secret; but seeing me determined: "Man," cried she at last, "let not woman deceive you any longer. Fear not to despoil what has ceased to exist. I hitherto have felt loth to disclose the dark mystery, but rather than that I should suffer you to become the sport of an arrogant family, and the subject of a solemn mockery, I shall reveal to you all – all that hitherto remains a secret from a prying world. Then, learn that you no longer are in time to make on too tender a heart the first unlawful impression! Hot kisses have already pressed her lips, for whom you resign yourself to an unavailing martyrdom. The plant still flourishes green and gay; but other hands have culled the blossom."

Here Sophia put her mouth to my ear. I felt as if a snake crept into its folds, and deep sunk into my heart the venom of her frightful story. "As, however," added my confidant, after her tale had worked its way, – "the unlucky occurrence has hitherto been successfully hushed up, they are in the greater hurry to conclude a match, ere it be suspected by the party concerned."

"And this," exclaimed I, "is the conclusion of all my love; and innocence and purity then exist not on earth! Even where one would wish to worship them as things sacred, they elude one's keenest search; and woman's licentiousness out-strips the thoughts of man! Oh that a bud so fair, so young, should already contain the foul worm of corruption in its bosom! That another should already have rioted unrestrained in what with such painful struggles Anastasius himself was going to give up from sheer virtue!" And in my wrath I resolved no longer to sacrifice both pleasure and fortune to the shadow of an undeserved reputation. I resolved to resume my before abandoned scheme, no longer from love but from sheer resentment; at the same time binding Sophia by all that was most awful, never to divulge the odious secret, lest by its publication I should be prevented from reaping my golden harvest, as I had already been outstripped in gathering a wreath far dearer and more valued.

When however – the first ebullition over – I reconsidered the matter, the thought struck me that Sophia had only disclosed her mistress's secret shame from a fiendlike greediness, and in order not to lose the promised reward; and carrying this reflection somewhat further, I now conceived it possible that a motive, so powerful in her breast, might have made her invent what she pretended to divulge. Hereupon all my waverings returned, and at last – determined to remain on the right side – I reverted to my prior resolutions of giving up the pursuit: nay, from fear of fresh relapses, when I saw my informer preparing with a sanctified air to call the whole host of heaven as witnesses to her veracity, I stopped both my ears, and bravely ran away. The moment my astonished informer found her endeavours unavailing to bring me back, her oaths, methought, changed to curses; but these – uttered when I was already in full flight – died away on the distant breeze.

Half pleased, half angry with myself for my forbearance, I walked about the town, shunning my friends, to whom I had nothing to impart but what must gladded them at my expense, and seriously considering whether, both for the sake of their morals and my purse, I should not, by a sudden evolution, quit them and Smyrna for ever: when, in the midst of my meditations, a messenger, – of those that ply about the streets in search of commissions – struck me on the breast with a small bunch of flowers.

Skilled in the meaning of these mute heralds of love, I snatched the nosegay out of the rude hands by which it seemed profaned; but when I came to consider its arrangement, I found that all I had to learn had not been left to the vague language of the pink and gilly flower: their fragrant leaves concealed a note, and this note contained a lock of hair and a ring.

Eagerly I perused the billet. It began with reproaches: but they were of a nature to be endured with composure: "not less painful to a lady was the talk of making the last advances than the first; and were not the morrow the day when what had not been might never more be, no consideration would have induced the writer to inform me that a narrow passage only separated from the chamber of the married couple the closet where slept their young cousin; that this closet looked out upon a garden; and that this garden was only divided from the street by a low wall. "Sometimes,"– added a wary post-script, "careless servants would leave shutters unbolted: but always a sober family was in bed by twelve!"

Euphrosyné's handwriting I was a stranger to: and this note probably had only been penned by deputy; though couched in better terms than those generally used by servants: but in how far the professions of the maid had the sanction of the mistress, it was easy to try, and by an unerring test; and the difference between two thousand sequins to pay, or that sum to receive, made it well worth the while. Nor was there any time to be lost. The very next day – as the note itself suggested – would be too late for the experiment. Should I find the passage barred, it was but returning as I went. Why however suspect Sophia of risking a falsehood, which, as such, could not command success, must soon be discovered, and must end in her disgrace? For as to the idea of her scheming to betray me to Chrysopulo, though it had entered my brain, I held it not worthy of a moment's thought. I therefore determined to obey the welcome summons.

Ten minutes before the hour appointed my pistols were loaded, and my person lightened of all useless encumbrance. Wrapped up in my capote I sallied forth, found all things disposed according to promise, easily scaled the wall, had only to push open the blinds, and leaped in to the chamber of love, where, half covered only by a light Barbary haïck[3], Euphrosyné lay apparently unconscious of aught but the dreams that might flit through her youthful fancy. So sweet indeed seemed her slumbers, that, but for every convincing circumstance, they might have been mistaken for those of innocence, and once more made me hesitate for a moment, ere I threw off my cloak, deposited my pistols, and extinguished the lamp.

If at first the real or pretended sleep of my mistress somewhat surprised me; if that surprise grew greater at its long continuance; what was my astonishment when Euphrosyné at last only awoke to start from my embrace, and to utter loud screams, which the pressure of my hand was hardly able to stifle!

Her outcry had been heard ere it could be stopped. Chrysopulo himself had quitted his consort's side, and with the carbine which he always kept loaded, had run to whence proceeded the sound. With one effort he burst open the door of the closet.

Already I was standing near its threshold bolt upright, with my capote on, and my pistol pointed. In the dark the merchant mistook me for a robber: he fired his piece, and missed.

I now put mind to his breast. "All I wish," cried I, "is to make you listen. If you value your cousin's honour, favour my escape, and pretend that you were dreaming."

Chrysopulo, thus enlightened, now trembled with rage. His eyes glistened amid surrounding darkness like those of a maddened tiger. Yet, uncertain how to act, he remained motionless where he stood, while Euphrosyné, mute with shame and despair, was only heard striving to suppress her bitter sobs.

Meanwhile the report of the musket had roused the whole family. Chrysopulo's wife was crying "Murder," in her bed, the servants starting up from their first sleep, and the people that passed by in the street knocking at the door until the house shook to its very foundations. Each instant the noise increased, and the uproar came nearer. Another minute, and the immediate scene of action must witness a general eruption.

Chrysopulo now became sensible of the wisdom of my suggestion: rousing himself from his trance and pointing to the window, "Away, away!" he cried, but cried too late. Already a number of voices in the garden sent forth a confused murmur from the very spot where I must have alighted. Chrysopulo looked whether I might slip under his cousin's couch: – it was too low; or upon the wardrobe opposite: – it was too high.

Aghast, we now stared at each other, until in his perplexity, the trembling banker – for want of a better expedient – pushed me down in a corner, and there – tearing from off Euphrosyné's own couch its light covering, turned it into a cloak to my person and my guilt.

Just at this moment rushed in the whole posse. A thousand questions succeeded each other without intermission, and, all circumstances considered, the story which Chrysopulo made out in answer was sufficiently plausible. Euphrosyné's terror and confusion, with the other apparent objects of the scene, might, without any great stretch of probability, be attributed to her cousin's mistake; and the whole terminated to the satisfaction or rather dissatisfaction of the curious, who, fully expecting a long list of dreadful murders, were seemingly somewhat wroth at being put off with a bad dream, and went away wishing the rich Chrysopulo worse suppers or a better digestion.

Meantime, seeing so many people rush by her door, Chrysopulo's wife herself had mustered courage to follow the crowd. Being the last to come, she was the last to depart; or rather, she had a mind not to go away at all, and insisted on staying, in order to tranquillize her cousin's agitation. She mistrusted her husband's dream, and wanted to sift his conduct to the bottom: wherefore, unable to confide in her discretion, the alarmed Chrysopulo at once resolved to conquer her resistance by force. He took her by the arm, dragged her out of the room, and, lest she should return to listen, locked her up in her own chamber.

If, fearless myself, I had only reluctantly acted the coward for the sake of others, and had more than once felt tempted, while the mob remained assembled, to start up, to show myself, and to carry away as a trophy of my victory the instrument of my concealment, I now, when the coast was clear, and the way open for my own retreat, felt equally desirous of staying, and that, with views similar to those of Chrysopulo's wife, – namely, to obtain an explanation of a few circumstances not quite intelligible even to the framer of the plot himself: but for an enquiry of this sort neither the time nor place were fitted; and fresh noises at the door made me run, without further delay, to the still open window. I thence leaped into the garden, overset or trampled down every flower and vegetable in my way, and, after climbing the wall, got safe into the street, and back to my lonely lodging. There I lay down, and began to reflect on the inconstancy of women, who send flattering invitations and then scream out on finding them attended to, – until at last all my bewildered thoughts were hushed in sleep. The next morning, on awakening in my own bed, with every object around me as orderly and tranquil as the day before, it seemed as if, during the whole of the eventful night, I never had quitted my solitary pillow!

The first circumstance which afforded me distinct evidence of having trespassed on premises not my own, was Chrysopulo suddenly standing before me, as, still undressed, I lay musing on my couch. Determined to brazen out what could not be denied, I thanked him for the honour of his early enquiries, and begged he would be seated. He took little notice of these insolent civilities, but immediately coming to the point, "You have offered my hitherto unsullied house," said he, "the cruellest of injuries! How far you have succeeded, I neither know nor can bear to enquire. Should your baseness have been disappointed, the fault is not yours: yet, much as I am bound to abhor you, I must stoop to a request."

"Speak," said I, "a petition so agreeably introduced can scarcely meet with a refusal."

"Your crime," answered Chrysopulo, "is thus far only known to ourselves, and to whatever vile abettor of your wickedness may reside under our roof. Even Euphrosyné's intended husband presumes not to cast upon his future consort the smallest shadow of blame, or wishes to defer the long concerted nuptials. Humbly, therefore, let me entreat, that out of compassion for the object – the unfortunate object of your lawless violence – you will not carry your cruelty any further, or be so devoid of mercy as to boast of your base attempts. Divulge not the foul stain which you destined our house! Thus may we still hold up our heads among our envious countrymen; and the unhappy Euphrosyné still preserve both her husband and her honour!"

Moved by an entreaty so earnest and so discreet, I wholly forgot that I had only conceived the crime for the very purpose of that boasting which Chrsyopulo deprecated, felt as anxious as himself to prevent the consequences of my outrage, and said all I could to quiet his fears. Greatly relieved by my assurances, the merchant almost thanked me for my goodness, and returned home with a mind more at ease.

But as soon as he was gone, it recurred to me that the engagement I had taken must defeat the whole object of my achievement, and must silence all those claims on my companions for which I had thus laboured: – nay that, unless I published my victory, I must not only renounce what I had won, but pay what I had not lost; – that I must part with my whole earthly fortune, – that in actual possession as well as that in expectancy; and part with both for a fair one, who, even prior to the commencement of my homage, had no longer kept in store any remnant of virtue, through the sacrifice of which to console me for the riches thus renounced on her account. Consistent with the terms of my precipitate promise, I could not even divulge my success, after the object of my silence had been fully attained.

Deeply regretting my imprudence, and loudly cursing my good nature, I paced up and down my room, half dressed, and expecting every moment to see Sophia come and claim her vile, her now bootless reward: until tired at last of waiting, and attributing her delay to the bustle of the day, I proceeded to achieve my often interrupted toilet. Once indeed a slight temptation came across me to honour the wedding with my presence – to blast it with my breath – but I still had some grace left, and contented myself with awaiting at home, in the utmost anxiety, the news of the nuptials being happily completed.

CHAPTER III

I had scarcely given the last twist to my turban, when a distant clamour in the street drew me to the window, and made me espy a veiled female, whose uncertain gait and faultering steps had attracted the notice of a troop of foolish boys, and made them follow her with loud hootings. It was impossible not to set down in my mind one so carefully wrapped up and so desirous not to be known, as the partner of my guilt, coming to demand the wages of her iniquity; and all that baffled my utmost power of conjecture, was the change from Sophia's wonted boldness of demeanour, to such apparent timidity and helplessness, as that which she seemed to manifest on this occasion. I could only attribute the phenomenon to the discovery of her nefarious conduct, and to her consequent dismissal from Chrysopulo's family with every circumstance of reprobation and disgrace; on which account I immediately sallied forth to my ally's assistance. My surprise still increased, when, tendering the bewildered suivante a protecting arm, I first saw her hesitate, then shuddering withdraw the hand which already I held firmly grasped in mind, and at last only suffer herself to be dragged into my habitation, after the terror produced by the insults of the gathering mob had as it were entirely deprived her of consciousness; but my astonishment only rose to its highest pitch, when, tearing off the cumbrous veils, in order to give the fainting maiden some air, I beheld, instead of the daring Sophia, the gentle, the reserved Euphrosyné herself, who scarcely, on recovering her senses, had opened her eyes and cast them around her, when, again sinking down to the ground, she struck her face against the floor, and began wringing her hands with every symptom of the bitterest anguish.

The cause of her having quitted her home I was at a loss to conjecture, but the effect it had of bringing her to mine I hailed at first as a highly fortunate circumstance. Thus would my triumph be blazoned forth without my word bring broken. When, however, I witnessed the excess of my fair one's grief, contrasted as it was with my own joy, I too felt moved, tried to assuage her sorrow by every expression of pity and concern, and as soon as she seemed able to speak, ventured to enquire what had caused her coming forth thus unattended and forlorn, at the very time when I supposed all Smyrna collected to witness her nuptials?

"My nuptials," cried she with a bitter accent, – now first suffering her voice to strike my ear, – "when my dishonour is the universal theme!"

"The universal theme!" re-echoed I, – in my turn truly dismayed. "Then may heaven's direst curse alight upon her who has divulged it!"

"That was myself," replied Euphrosyné, "and your curse has struck home!"

I remained mute with surprise.

"Could I," rejoined my mistress, "to dishonour add deceit? Could I bring a dower of infamy to the man so noble, so generous, that even after my frightful tale he spurned me not away from him: – to the man who deigned in pity to affirm that my avowal of my involuntary shame rendered me worthier in his eyes, and gave him a stronger assurance of my fidelity, than if I had come to his arms as spotless in body as in mind?"

"And who," added I, "after this sublime speech ended by rejecting you."

"Ah no!" cried Euphrosyné, "it was I who rejected him: it was I who refused to carry reproach into the house of a stranger; and who for that crime was threatened by my own friends with being cast off, and thrown upon the wide world, helpless and unprotected! – But," added she, covering her face with her hands, and sobbing more bitterly than before, "I suffered not the threat to grow into a reality; I waited not to be turned out of doors. I resolved at once upon the only step which was left me; I asked permission to go to our church, in order that, in my fervent prayers, heaven might inspire me how to act: and, when alone and in the street, tried to find out your abode, and to seek refuge where alone I had claims."

"What then!" exclaimed I, "you set out from home determined to come to me? – and it was not the shouts of the mob only – I fancied I saw you shrinking from my touch, when, in compassion, I seized hold of your hand!"

"And could I execute the resolve which I had owned, and not shudder at the thoughts of its baleful consequences?"

These now began to present themselves to my own mind also, in long and fearful array. At first, indeed, the surprise on beholding Euphrosyné thus unexpectedly, the consciousness of my own iniquities, the exultation at seeing its triumph sealed without the smallest violation of my promise, and the sympathy excited by my mistress's evident sufferings, together with a thousand other mixed and indescribable sensations, had induced a momentary forgetfulness of all those reports against Euphrosyné's character, which had encouraged me to prosecute my plan, had made that plan receive its fulfilment, and had in their turn been confirmed by my very success. But on hearing not only of an act so uncalled for as Euphrosyné's spontaneous disclosure of her shame, so wanton as her refusal of her still urging suitor, and so strange as her deliberately leaving her husband for her despoiler, the truth – dimmed for a moment – seemed again to burst upon me, and with double conviction. I now conceived that even my crime might only be the pretence, rather than the real reason of Euphrosyné's renouncing an advantageous match. Her former dishonour again rising to my mind, lent even her present conduct the colouring of artifice; and, if I thought it hard upon me that an assignation proposed by my mistress herself, and that as not only the first, but also the last I could hope for, should end in her inflicting upon me the burthen of her permanent support, I thought it harder still to be thus heavily visited in consequence of the sins of others. That shelter, therefore, which I had gladly granted Euophrosyné under my roof, while it only seemed accidental and transient, I now began to grudge her when it appeared purposely sought, as the beginning only of a sojourn which was to have no end; and the burden of this permanent society was what I determined to ward off to the utmost of my power.

To give my real reasons for so doing was impossible. On reviewing every past circumstance, I felt that, from the first wording of the assignation to the close of the interview, matters had been so conducted as to leave me, with every presumptive evidence, not one positive proof of Euphrosyné's having willingly shared in my stolen pleasures. No argument against complying with her wishes, founded upon her complying too readily with mine – however valid in itself – I therefore knew would be admitted: and, as to the report of her prior guilt – even my own vanity shrunk from suffering an imputation so odious to lessen the merit of my victory, or the value of my prize: besides, I read in the streaming eyes piteously fixed on mine, pangs too acute still to increase them by a reproach, which must inflict equal agony, whether just or unfounded. Appearing, therefore, to speak more from tenderness for her whom I addressed than for myself, "Euphrosyné," said I, "It was unwise, methinks, to divulge what, but for your own spontaneous avowal, might have remained an inscrutable secret; it was a thousand times more unwise still, when you found that by an unexampled privilege this deterred not your suitor, yourself to refuse him; but it seems to me the very height of folly willingly to court every form of disgrace where, as it appears, you still may enjoy every species of distinction. You cannot justify your conduct in casting, without necessity, such a stain upon your family. Hasten then to repair the mischief while you still are in time; return home immediately, as if you had only offered up an hurried prayer in church, and obviate by your ready acceptance of the worthy Argyropoli all the impending consequences of your thoughtless and precipitate step!"

Alas! I addressed one who, wholly bewildered by her own feelings, heeded not a single word I spoke. Euphrosyné, fixing upon me an eye at once vacant and supplicating, continued to preserve an unbroken, and, as I thought, stubborn silence, until at last I deemed it necessary to use terms more decisive and peremptory. Taking two or three hasty strides across the room, as if still to encrease the ferment of my already heated blood: "Euphrosyné," cried I, "it is impossible you can stay with me. I myself am a wanderer on the face of the globe: to day here, to morrow perhaps flying to the earth's furthest extremity. Your remaining under my uncertain roof, can only end in total ruin to us both. I must insist upon your quitting my abode, ere your own be no longer accessible to your tardy repentance."

"Ah no!" now cried Euphrosyné, convulsively clasping my knees: "be not so barbarous! Shut not your own door against her, against whom you have barred every other once friendly door. Do not deny her whom you have dishonoured, the only asylum she has left. If I cannot be your wife, let me be your slave, your drudge. No service, however mean, shall I recoil from when you command. At least before you I shall not have to blush. In your eyes I shall not be what I must seem in those of others. I shall not from you incur the contempt I must expect from my former companions; and my diligence to execute the lowest offices you may require, will ensure me not wholly unearned at your hands, that bread which elsewhere I can only receive as an unmerited indulgence. Since I did a few days please your eye, I may still please it a few days longer: perhaps a few days longer I may therefore still wish to live; and when that last blessing, your love, is gone by; when my cheek faded with grief has lost the last attraction that could arrest your favour, then speak; then tell me so, that, burdening you no longer, I may retire – and die!"

Spite of the tears with which I answered this speech, the conviction that all might still by diligence be hushed up, was going to make me urge more strenuously than before Euphrosyné's immediate return, – when a new incident took place, which wholly changed my inclinations and my feelings.

This was no less than a sudden and forcible irruption in my abode of the maiden's relations. It had soon been discovered by them, that, instead of going to church, she had come to my house; and her friends had hereupon walked forth in a body to claim the stray lamb, and to bring her back. Chrysopulo himself indeed was not of the party: it only consisted of half a dozen of his nephews and cousins: but this posse unceremoniously enough broke in upon me just as I was urging my mistress by every motive in heaven and on earth not to delay her departure another minute; and immediately proceeded to effect by force, what I was only trying to obtain by persuasion.

My readers already know how little I liked being interfered with, and how apt I was to act in opposition to those around me from no other motive but to assert my independence, or to show my daring: they will not, therefore, be much surprised to hear that this incident caused an entire and sudden revolution in my sentiments with regard to Euphrosyné, and that, from wishing her to go while she expressed a wish to stay, I now would have detained her by force, even if she had wished to go. Taking hold, therefore, of the maiden by one arm, while Chrysopulo's friends were pulling her away by the other, I swore that nothing short of death should make me give up the maiden who had sought shelter under my wing; and as Euphrosyné herself, when appealed to, seemed to sanction my proceedings, by drawing her veil over her blushing features, her friends were at last persuaded, by the threatening gestures with which I accompanied my assurances, to give up all further attempts at violent measures.

In truth, they rejoiced in their hearts at having it to say that an insurmountable resistance had baffled all their efforts. Euphrosyné had early been left an orphan: her nearest of kin were all dead; and though the more distant relations to whose lot it fell to protect her, would have upheld their fair cousin most sedulously while they had any chance of deriving an additional lustre from her establishment in life, they were willing enough to drop the connection as soon as her situation was likely to reflect discredit on their name. However loud and boisterous therefore might be the wish they expressed of restoring her to her family, there lurked not the less satisfaction at the bottom, when they found her resolved not to go: and while they pretended to feel exceedingly hurt at her refusal, they took her at her word with the utmost alacrity; or rather, suffered her mere silence to stand for a denial. Devoutly lifting up their eyes to heaven, and drawing discordant groans from their flinty bosoms, they turned away from one whom they saw so irreclaimably abandoned, and hurried out of the house, lest she should change her mind ere they were out of hearing. When, however, they found themselves safe as they thought in the street, they stopt to announce for the benefit of all who passed by, their determination to renounce so unworthy a namesake. Thenceforth, they were to regard the nameless profligate as among the departed, and, happen what might, never more to inquire after her fate; and to their credit be it spoken, they adhered in that instance most religiously to their humane and pious vow.

My undisturbed possession of Chrysopulo's fair cousin, therefore, was now a matter settled; and the lofty, the admired Euphrosyné, who that very morning might still have beheld all Smyrna at her feet, saw herself before mid-day installed in the lodging of a roving adventurer, as his avowed and public mistress!

Of her maid Sophia the lovely girl could give no account. While Chrysopulo continued in hopes of seeing the affair hushed up, he abstained from rousing the anger of this fiend by expressing his suspicions: but the moment Euphrosyné herself had made public her adventure, Sophia, no longer feeling safe in the family, had disappeared: nor had she since been heard of; but her louring fate was the least of my cares.

The foremost at present was the payment of the sums I had won. The addition to my establishment permitted me not to be unmindful of my interests. As soon therefore as I had said and done whatever seemed most calculated to dispel Euphrosyné's settled gloom, I immediately walked to the meeting place of our society, and found its members in council assembled.

My first salutation was a demand upon each: but, to my unutterable dismay, the first answer was aloud and universal burst of laughter at my presumption! As soon as this peal of merriment subsided a little, I was told that I might think myself well off in having nothing to pay instead of to receive; and, on demanding a further explanation, I learnt that the infernal Sophia had been before hand with me, and the instant she left the house of Chrysopulo, had gone round to all my companions, in the first place indeed to inform them of my success with Euphrosyné; but, in the next, to comfort them with the assurance that it had only been the consequence of those prior adventures of the same sort, which my confidant had sworn to me never to divulge. Every person present therefore immediately called out: "A drawn wager!" and I was deemed disqualified from claiming a single para!

What could I do with a bad cause, and a parcel of fellows each to the full as sturdy as myself? Only this – to renounce with a good grace what I clearly saw I never should obtain, and to join in the laugh at my own impudence; "of which," I observed, "it was worth while, at any rate, to try the effect."

But tolerably as I had contrived to preserve my good humour with my strapping companions within, the case became different when, on returning to Euphrosyné, I met Sophia, coming, as I guessed, to receive the reward from those who had just mocked me the reward of her treachery.

Great as was the disappointment experienced in my purse, it seemed nothing to the wound inflicted on my pride. The fate of a lovely female had been connected with mine by links even more indissoluble even than those of matrimony, since a divorce could not restore her to her home; and this partner of my life had been branded with infamy, – and by her in whom she had most confided. The insulting epithets still rung in my ear which had been showered on my mistress through the spite of the infernal Sophia!

So conscious, indeed, was this wicked girl of her iniquity, that, far from seeming to harbour any thoughts of enforcing her still unsettled claims on her first employer, the moment she saw me she tried to make her escape, – but it was too late!

"Wretch!" cried I, "thus, then, you have performed your promise. Now behold in what way I perform mine!" And hereupon I seized her by the wrist, and retorting upon her, in the midst of the gaping crowd with every disgraceful epithet which her malignancy had drawn down upon Euphrosyné, I terrified the vile woman unto fainting, and then left her to recover in the filth of Smyrna's kennel! Thanks to this immersion, she tarried not to revive; and no sooner did the fury think herself safe from my wrath, than setting up a hellish laugh, "Wipe clean your Euphrosyné," cried she, "ere you bespatter others with your dirt!" and then walked off with threatening gestures, – alternately wishing me joy of my prize, and auguring me every misfortune under heaven. Heated as I was with passion, her curses made my blood run cold, and in return I would have chilled for ever the noisome tide in her own viper veins – but with a home thrust of my dagger; had I not been prevented by the mob from annihilating the reptile!

But its venomed bite left a print in my heart which no power could efface! To fail in all my schemes both of profit and of pride; to be burdened with the whole weight of my mistress's existence, while bereft of all esteem for her character; to feel myself the victim of the deceit or the sport of the caprice of one whose tenderness had been prostituted to others, – and more than that; to find the shame which I had hoped to bury in the inmost recesses of my own bosom, divulged to all the world; to be pointed at with derision by those very companions over whom I had made sure to triumph, was beyond what I had strength of mind to bear, – at least, to bear alone; and the embers of affection for my new inmate, still glowing in my breast when I last left my home, seemed all extinguished by what took place ere I re-entered my abode. If, however, I only returned to it with the determination of making my hapless guest a partaker in all the sufferings which she had drawn down upon my head, it was also with the full intent to keep the cause of my behaviour locked for ever within my own swelling heart! Why, indeed, dwell without necessity upon the painful thoughts of an infamy, of which I was unable to bring the proof, and despaired of extorting the confession!

Under her former playfulness of manner Euphrosyné it seems had always concealed great decision of character. She had shrunk from going home to a husband or from staying with friends, whose reproach she must fear or whose forbearance endure. Me alone she had considered as accountable for whatever home and felicity my offence had deprived her of elsewhere; and to me she had come for refuge, as to the only person who still owed her protection: but she had come oppressed with the sense of her dishonour; she had come so heart-struck with anguish, that, had the innate fertility of her imagination still made it put forth, amid all the disgrace of her situation, the smallest bud of sprightliness or fancy, she would have thought it a duty to repress or to crush the tender blossoms, as weeds, whose rank luxuriance ill became her fallen state. Nothing but the most unremitting tenderness on my part could in some degree have revived her drooping spirits.

But when, after my excursion and the act of justice on Sophia in which it ended, I reappeared before the still trembling Euphrosyné, she saw too soon that that cordial of the heart must not be expected. One look she cast upon my countenance, as I sat in silence, sufficed to inform her of the total change of sentiments; and the responsive look by which it was met tore for ever from her breast the last seeds of hope and of confidence. Like the wounded snail she shrunk within herself, and from thenceforth, cloaked in unceasing sadness, never more expanded to the sunshine of joy. With her buoyancy of spirits she seemed even to lose all her quickness of intellect, nay all her readiness of speech: so that, fearing to embark with her in serious conversation, and finding no response in her mind to lighter topics, I at last began to nauseate her seeming torpor, and to roam abroad even more frequently than before I had secured a companion at home; while she – poor miserable creature – dreading the sneers of an unfeeling world, passed her time under my roof in dismal and heart-breaking solitude.

Had the most patient endurance of the most intemperate sallies been able to soothe my disappointment and to soften my hardness, Euphrosyné's angelic sweetness must at last have conquered: but in my jaundiced eye her resignation only tended to strengthen the conviction of her shame; and I saw in her forbearance nothing but the consequence of her debasement, and the consciousness of her guilt! "Did her heart," thought I, "bear witness to a purity on which I dared the first to cast a blemish, she could not remain thus tame, thus spiritless, under such an aggravation of my wrongs; and either she would be the first to quit my merciless roof, or at least she would not so fearfully avoid giving me even the most unfounded pretence for denying her its shelter. She must merit her sufferings, to bear them so meekly!

Hence, even when really touched by the gentleness of my mistress, I seldom relented in my apparent sternness. In order to conquer, or at least to conceal sentiments, which I considered as effects only of weakness, I even forced myself on these occasions to increased severity. Unable to go the length of parting from a friendless outcast, even though – conformable to her own terms – the continuance of my love the measure of her stay, I almost banished myself entirely from my own home; and plunged more headlong than ever into extravagance and dissipation. Unto this period I had quaffed my wine, to enjoy its flavour: I now drank to drive away my senses. Unto this period I had gamed to beguile an idle hour: I now played to produce a feverish excitement of my spirits. I stayed out while I was able to renew my stake, and only returned home when utterly exhausted by my losses. Nay, when Euphrosyné, after sitting up alone all night, saw me return – pale and feverish – in the broad glare of the next morning, it was often only to be pursued by all the spleen collected during my nocturnal excesses. Yet she tarried on: for to me she had sacrificed her all; and though in me she found nothing but a thorn, yet by that thorn alone now hung her whole existence!

Euphrosyné was wont to be in readiness with a hot cup of coffee when I came in from my nightly revels. After gambling it served as a restorative; but after drinking it was the only thing capable of allaying the sort of temporary madness with which wine always affected my irritable brain. One morning when alternate losses at dice and libations to Bacchus had sent me home half frantic, instead of finding my mistress as usual all alacrity to minister the reviving draft, to chafe my throbbing temples, and to perform what other soothing offices her awe of me permitted, I found her lying on the floor in a trance. I only thought her asleep; but on attempting to lift her up, her features were bruised, and her face all besmeared with blood. Unnerved by excess, and shaking with agitation, my arm however was wholly unable to support even her light weight, and I let her drop again. She thought I did so on purpose, for raising her head with great effort, she fixed on my countenance her haggard tearless eyes, and clasping her hands together, now for the first time vented her anguish in audible words. "I had been warned." she cried, with half stifled emotion.

"How?" said I.

"That morning," answered she, "when unexpectedly you appeared among us in the meadow, you were scarcely out of sight when the cause of your coming was discussed. We agreed – foolish girls as we were – that chance alone had not brought you to that place, and drew lots to find out where lurked the secret attraction. I got the prize; if prize it could be called! A friend some years older than myself, observing my emotion, "Euphrosyné," she whispered, "if you care not for that stranger, frolic with him as you like: but if ever he should gain your affections, O! avoid him like a pestilence. From the moment he knows himself master of your heart, he will treat it as wayward children do their toys; he will not rest until he has broken it."

"This was but the first warning, and only given by a human voice," continued my mistress: "a higher admonition came straight from heaven! You know the marble image found in our field, which now adorns our garden. Once, they say, it was flesh and blood, – a hapless maiden like myself: but alas, less susceptible, and therefore turned into stone! On the night of your outrage, as I rose from the prayer which once used over to precede my repose, a deep hollow moan issued from its snowy bosom! Another and a louder shriek was heard when I spoke to Argyropoli; and one still more dismal than the former rent the air, when I left my kinsman's roof to fly to your arms!"

"And warned even by an insensible stone," I cried, "you would not see the precipice?"

"Ah!" exclaimed Euphrosyné, "reproach me with any thing but my love. It was that which, in spite of every circumstance that should have opened my eyes, still kept me y blind."

"Your love," cried I, "neither merits my reproach, nor yet calls for my praise. It depends not on ourselves to withhold our affections, as it depends not on us to renew a worn-out passion."

"Is it then true," cried Euphrosyné, "that you love me no more?"

"Has not that question been answered already?" said I peevishly; "but you will not understand, unless all is spoken!"

At these words Euphrosyné put her hands to her ears, as if fearing to hear her formal dismission; and immediately ran to shut herself in her adjoining chamber. I left the wayward girl to the solitude she sought, and, unable to obtain any refreshment at home, immediately went out again. Exhausted with watching, sleep overcame me in the coffee-house whither I had gone for my breakfast, and as soon as I felt somewhat recruited by my short rest, a detachment of our party carried me away by force, to make me woo fickle fortune afresh at the gaming table. Within the irresistible influence of its magic circle I stayed, and played, and drank, and slept, – and played, and drank, land slept again, – until, reeling out in the dark to go home, I fell from the steps, sprained my ankle, cut my face, and lay awhile senseless on the pavement. Carried in again as soon as discovered in this plight, it became my fate to be tied by the leg in the very gambling room which had already kept me spell-bound so long.

I was so far an economist of time, as always to devote that of forced confinement to the irksome business of reflection: and I had a great deal of that sort of occupation, accumulating on my hands, to employ my present leisure. The unconcern of my pretended friends on seeing me suffer, very soon made me draw unfavourable comparisons of their sentiments with those of Euphrosyné. Granting that she had been too susceptible before she knew me; how patient, how penitent, how devoted had she shown herself ever since! Yet, how cruel the return I had made, and how deep the last wound I had inflicted!

The thought grew so irksome, that, not daring to send for my mistress among a set of scoffers, and yet impatient to make her amends, I crept as soon as the dawn again arose, off my couch, stole away, and limped home.

When I knocked at my door, no one answered from within. Louder I therefore knocked and louder; but with no better success. At last my heart sunk within me, and my knees began to totter. Euphrosyné never stirred out: – could she – I dreaded to know the truth, and yet I was near going mad with the delay. She might be ill, and unable to come down, though not yet beyond the reach of succour, or the comfort of kindness! It was possible she heard me, and had not strength to answer or to let me in. Timely assistance still perhaps might save her: even tardy tenderness, though shewn too late to arrest her fleeting soul, might still at least allay the bitterness of its departure. A word, a look of sympathy might solace her last moments, and waft her spirit on lighter wings to heaven!

Frantic with impatience, I endeavoured to break open the sullen door, but could only curse its perverse steadiness in doing its duty. In despair at the delay I was going for an axe to hew it from its hinges, when an old deaf neighbour, who began to suspect she heard a noise, came down half dressed to lend her assistance. She employed nearly as much time before she let herself out, as I had lost in trying to get in. At last, however, her feeble efforts were crowned with success. Forth she came, and put on her spectacles to scrutinise my person. A deliberate survey having satisfied her respecting my identity, she thrust her withered arm deep in her ample pocket, and drew out fifty things which neither of us wanted, before she ended by producing the key of my lodging, which she put into my hands with a low courtesy, as having been left in her care by the lady who was taken her departure.

"Thank God! – I have not killed her!" was my first exclamation. "That weight at least is off my mind!" And as soon as I had sufficiently recovered my breath, I inquired of the old woman the time and circumstances of Euphrosyné's departure; – what conveyance had taken her away; in what direction she went; and, above all, what message she had left?

These were useless queries, and a fruitless expenditure of breath. It took me half an hour to make my neighbour hear me; and when I succeeded at last, so near was she to dotage, that I could make nothing of her answers. On my asking, as the easiest question to understand, how long the key had been in her possession, she could only say, "ever since it had been given her."

Despairing of more explicit intelligence outside my threshold, I went in, and in three strides reached the top of the stairs, and my own empty room. From that I ran into the next, equally empty and desolate; looked upon every table and shelf, under every seat and cushion, in every box and drawer, and behind every chest and wardrobe. My hopes were to find some letter, some note, some scrap of paper, written, if not in kindness, at least in anger, to inform me which way my poor girl had fled: but I looked in vain; there was nothing!

I possessed no clue whatever to a probable surmise; I could form no opinion on the strange event; I sat down in mute amazement, trying to think, and yet finding no point on which to fix my thoughts. At last, as my eyes continued to wander in total vacancy round the room, they fell upon some writing, which assuredly had not been intended to court my sight: for it run along the skirting of the wainscot, and could only have been written by Euophrosyné with her pencil as she lay on the ground. I stooped down to read, and only found some broken sentences, probably traced by my mistress the last time she left me, to seek refuge in solitude. The sense seemed addressed to herself more than to her destroyer, and the words were mostly effaced: – thus ran the few legible lines.

"At last he has spoken plainly! – I shall go – no matter where! – Let him rejoice: when he boasts of his triumphs over unsuspecting innocence; he may now add to all his former vauntings: "I have ruined Euphrosyné!" – and be proud to think a greater fall from purity by his hands!" Then followed a string of half obliterated words, among which all I could make out was an invocation to the Almighty not to cease pouring its blessings on my head, for all poor Euphrosyné's wrongs! A thousand daggers seemed, on reading this sentence, to pierce my heart at once.

Every thing remained as I had left it, except Euphrosyné alone! She had taken nothing with her; for she had nothing to take: the last articles of her apparel, worth any money, had been sold to supply her necessities, or rather my extravagance.

CHAPTER IV.

The painful chapter is concluded; – that chapter to which I looked forward with dismay; and which I hurried over with shame and sorrow. Frequently, during the dreary course of the last pages, has my hand felt as if arrested, and my pen ready to drop from my fingers: but I wished to offer in the faithful narrative of my injustice, the only sacrifice in my power to the memory of my Euphrosyné; and having performed this severe but wholesome penance, I seem to breathe somewhat more freely, and to proceed on the sequel of my narrative with less reluctance. Too forcibly, however, do I feel that the film which obscured my judgment during the sad events of which I have made a full confession, will be admitted with the unimpassioned reader as a feeble palliation only of my offences, and that even my bitter repentance itself will scarcely prevent the power of averting so deep an abhorrence of my fault, as must cast a blasting influence over the whole sequel of my tale.

After learning the fate of my unfortunate mistress, there still remained one other task of fearful anxiety to be performed; namely, to ascertain that of my not less pitiable child. I knew not whether the babe had followed its mother to the grave, or was still alive to share its father's misery: but no Sophia any longer intervening between me and the object of my search, it was soon successful. I discovered the poor people under whose humble roof my Euphrosyné had breathed her last; I found in their arms a lovely infant, depending on charity for its support, and learnt that the smiling babe was my own. External proof was not requisite to confirm the assertions of its foster-father: too brightly shone in the cherub's eye the heaven of its mother's looks;-that heaven in which, but for my own waywardness, I might have lived for ever blessed. Alexis had her radiant brow, her putting playful lip, her dimpled chin. The very rag which enveloped the poor infant was a relic of Euphrosyné's last earthly vestment: once, in her days of splendour, a rich tissue of purple and gold; – now so tarnished, so stripped of its original lustre, that it seemed to have continued to the last the faithful emblem of her, whose graceful limbs it had encircled until they waxed cold in death.

I pressed my child to my bosom, to my lips, to my eyes. Hurt by the roughness of my face, perhaps annoyed by the copious flowing of my tears, the poor babe began to cry. So full of terror were its looks, one might have fancied it had recognized its father: I therefore reluctantly laid it down again and discontinued my endearments: but fearful lest gratuitous care might have less merit in the execution than it had in the design, I told the poor people I should rid them of the burden, and take my child away. They turned pale at the intelligence, and, though rewarded to the full extent of my scanty means, wept on resigning my Alexis into other hands. What little sum I was able to raise by the sale of my remaining trinkets, I deposited for his maintenance with the most trustworthy people I could find: and then began to consider how I should live myself. The Turkish law, it is true, grants not to the disappointed creditor the vindictive pleasure of shutting up for life his disabled debtor, nor punishes the man who has got into debt, by preventing him from ever getting out of his creditor's books again; but still in Turkey, as elsewhere, one may starve even out of gaol.

There were some who would have had me inform my friend Spiridion of my distress: but I could not bear to ask a favour of one to whom I could make no return. "Far better was it," thought I, "to be indebted for my subsistence to my own bravery, than to the reluctant compassion of others." Weary of life, and anxious only to banish reflection, I meditated joining some of those bold fellows who, having occupied an abandoned district, imitate greater states, and very fairly tax the traveller for trespassing on their domain. Theirs was the employment – doubtless noble in itself – of transferring to the needy the superfluities of the affluent; and who could plead more pinching wants than a father burdened with the necessities of a motherless babe, and forced to fight for subsistence, or to see his infant starve! Nor in Turkey did the profession of a bandit lack its respectability. A high minded man might embrace the career of the haïdoot without blushing; while most busily employed in reaping its benefits, he still recognized certain principles of honour; and when tired of its perils, he found no obstacle – if fortunate enough never to have been caught in the fact – to laying down his dangerous trade unmolested, boasting of his past exploits, and seeking some safer and less precarious employment, on a par with such among his fellow citizens as had, in the capacity of magistrates or rulers, pursued the same profession more unostentatiously. Sick at heart and ruined in purse, I saw in a robber's life the only remedy for both diseases. Besides, the scheme, if well managed, might be rendered preparatory to another, which I had secretly cherished ever since the commencement of my embarrassments. At Bagdad was seated on the throne of the ancient Kaliphs, a Pasha more resembling an independent sovereign than a Sultan's representative. Himself the disposer of sundry lesser Pashaliks, his wide domain and constant warfare with his manifold neighbours offered to the soldier of fortune a fertile field for promotion. I wished to try his service. Some of the principal troops of banditti that grace the Turkish empire, lined the various roads to his capital; and I might, in my way to that new theatre of my ambition, either occasionally join their numerous marauding parties, or sportsman-like, take my gun, and singly arrest the flight of some passing traveller, to solace the tediousness or supply the necessities of my journey.

Nobler game, however, was for a moment near attracting me to more distant realms, where rulers themselves were despoiled, and kings hunted down. An Italian had dropped as if from the clouds at Smyrna, who in appearance only wooed the Muses, but in reality belonged to the sect of political propagandists, about that time disseminated all the world over, to preach emancipation from every bondage, natural, civil, and religious. The disturbance of my mind and the distress of my situation could not remain long concealed from the keen-eyed improvisator, and he resolved to make them subservient to his secret purposes.

"Listen," would he say in a prophetic tone: "The time is at hand when all the tottering monuments of ignorance, credulity, and superstition, no longer protected by the foolish awe they formerly inspired, shall strew the earth with their wrecks. Every where the young shoots of reason and liberty, starting from between the rents and crevices of the worn-out fabrics of feudalism, are becoming too vigorous any longer to be checked: they soon will burst asunder the baseless edifices of self-interest and prejudice, which have so long impeded their growth. Religious inquisition, judicial torture, monastic seclusion, tyranny, oppression, fanaticism, and all the other relics of barbarism are to be driven from the globe. Total annihilation awaits the whole code of hereditary rights, exclusive privileges, and mortifying distinctions, only derived by men born equal, from mouldering ancestors and musty parchments. Soon shall armorial bearings, empty titles, and frivolous orders cease to insult man's understanding. Whatever appeared great only through the mist of error; whatever was magnified into importance only through the medium of prejudice, shall have its deceitful size detected by the torch of reason, and shall then be hurled back into its pristine insignificance. Sceptered imbecility, nodding on its crazy thrones, shall ere long be laid prostrate in the dust; and subjects, making sovereigns their footstools, shall assert man's primeval equality, by mounting upon their tyrants' necks into their tyrants' places. Already does in more than one realm the hallowed work of regeneration advance with rapid strides: already, throughout Gallia, streams day and night the blood of victims: already dungeons forced open, castles levelled with the ground, and feudal records committed to the flames, mark the approach of a happier era; while one monarch shot in the midst of his court, and another dragged to the scaffold by his own subjects, are but the first fruits offered up at the new-raised shrine of liberty, whose temple must some day encompass the whole universe. You then, who here pine in inglorious sloth, drive away the tedium which oppresses your spirits, by joining the noble cause. Enlist among the uprising liberators of mankind. Leave this worn out empire of despotism and slavery, this den of tigers doomed to speedy destruction, and seek on the yellow banks of the Seine the blessed dawn of a fast spreading revolution. Hasten to that busy capital of all nations, where, from all quarters of the globe flock the lovers of liberty, and the haters of kings; and meet with welcome and with denizenship all who, mastered by their liberal feelings, yearn to establish, sword in hand, universal philanthropy. Your part on this grand theatre already is marked out for you. All you have to do is to present yourself in the august assembly of the great nation, as the representative of oppressed and mourning Greece. Be the eloquent, the pathetic organ of its ardent wish to share in the benefits which France confers on the world. Tell of the myriads that to her lift their imploring hands. Your person is showy, your lungs are potent, your speech untrammelled by troublesome timidity, and with a dress designed by the painter David (I would advise a Grecian tunic) and a few attitudes of uncontrollable emotion, imitated from the sublime Talma, it will be your own fault if, in the convention, you are not hailed as the worthy descendant of Harmoodius and Aristogiton!"

This rhapsody made me laugh; but I thought the subject serious. In the midst of all my grief, it interested my vanity, and I enquired the shortest way to Paris. We agreed that as soon as arrived on European ground, Cirico (the poet) should in view of his superior local knowledge act as my *avant courier*. Unfortunately his impatience marred the project. Desirous of giving a specimen of his talent, he improvised himself away from Smyrna ere I had the least intimation of his departure. In his hurry, he left his bill unpaid, and took away his landlord's silver spoons. This mistake cast a shade upon his doctrine. I bade mourning Greece wipe away her tears without me, and, instead of journeying in behalf of universal liberty to Paris, resumed the plan of my predatory expedition to Bagdad.

In conformity to the nature of my views, I set out lightly provisioned but heavily armed, and the first stage of my journey witnessed the first trial of my skill. At a hamlet where travellers sometimes stop to refresh, a caravan of Franks was waiting for the cool of the evening to proceed in greater comfort. Only come from Sedi-Keui, and only intending to visit Ephesus – or rather the spot once adorned by that city – these dilettanti in ruins had provided no guard. I proposed to two or three loiterers whom I picked up by the way to teach them more prudence. Neither I nor they, we agreed, would commit a serious robbery, but this was only a frolic; and we swore to each other faithfully to restore what we took, unless we thought it very particularly worth keeping.

A little circuit and a quicker pace brought us first to a defile, which, very soon after, and just at dusk, our travellers also entered. Their attendants were suffered to pass on; but we could not help interrupting a very earnest discussion in which the two principal personages, lagging behind a few paces, were engaged: – it was only for the purpose of demanding their money. The request they readily enough complied with; and to his purse, the elder of the two, in the excess of his liberality, moreover added a very appropriate lecture.

But for this circumstance, the orator's somewhat singular travelling garb would eternally have kept concealed from my knowledge that I had the honour of stripping the Baron H—, Swedish Consul-general at Smyrna, and my own much respected acquainttance. Residing in the summer season at Sedi-Keui, he had insisted on accompanying his young friend – an eastern tourist – on this antiquarian excursion; and I was the first object, not quite two thousand years old, which had probably engaged their attention. It was impossible to keep the money of a man whose good fare I had more than once enjoyed; wherefore, falling at the Consul's feet: "Take back your purse!" cried I; "it would bring me ill fortune; and I have had enough already!"

At these words H—— stared on me in mute astonishment, until, convinced that his senses did not deceive him, he at last exclaimed with a loud groan, "Selim Aga, for heaven's sake is it you ?'"

"It is," answered I.

"And what," resumed the consul, "can have brought you to this?'"

I blushed; and seeing my companions had chosen to decamp during the parley, "We are alone," said I, "let me go on with you to your next halting-place, and there you shall hear all."

The proposal was accepted, and the stage achieved in five or six hours, – for my travellers never went out of a foot-pace. By a little brook, under the already acceptable shade of a plane tree, we sat down an hour after sun-rise, and I told a not very exhilarating story. At its conclusion the consul was again entreated by me to take back his purse; but to this request he turned a deaf ear. He had not much liked, he owned, to have his viaticum forcibly taken from him; but he now earnestly begged I might think it worthy my acceptance.

"To what purpose?" exclaimed I: – "my object was to try my hand at a highway robbery, more for the sake of the act than the plunder. The things which money may purchase I can no longer prize. Life to me has lost its sweets!"

"Subdue your passions, young man;" answered H——, "it is to them you owe all your misery."

"Alas!" was my reply, "what am I to believe? Do not philosophers maintain that the passions are the only road to knowledge, to power and to virtue? that the inert being who never has felt their influence on his own mind, knows not how to guide the will of others, sees man as a machine whose movements baffle his skill, constantly miscalculates the conduct of his fellow creatures, and, only attempting to move men like blocks, by force, must find a resistance which mocks his inadequate impulse. Without the passion of love would women encounter the pangs which preserve our species on the globe? Without that for ruling would man endure the toil of maintaining public order amongst it? Is it not the passion of avarice alone that brings in contact, for universal benefit, the industry and the produce of the most distant countries? And what but the passion for fame makes man risk health, fortune, nay life itself, for the advantages, perhaps the amusement, of generations yet unborn? Like the heat of the sun, that of the passions may strengthen a few poisons, but alone it brings forth all the sweets and healthful plants of the creation."

H— shook his head. "It is feeling," said he, "which, like the sun's genial warmth, ripens each fairest fruit. Passions, like a scorching blaze, only burn them to ashes. Would you behold the effects of the former; look at my young friend here. Calm, healthful and blooming, he is the bee that sucks the flowers of every clime, some day to bestow their honey upon their grateful countrymen. Would you know the consequence of the latter; look in the brook beside you."

I advanced my head over the glassy pool: but from its deep bosom up rose to meet my searching eye, a countenance so pale and ghastly – a cheek so wan and so feverish, that I started back with horror. I felt the reproof, bowed assent, and said no more,

To his purse, which H— positively refused to take back, but allowed me, if I liked, to keep only as a loan, his companion, rich as well as romantic, now insisted on adding his mite. He tore a leaf out of his pocket-book, and with the pen and ink which he carried in a case about him, wrote a draft on a banker at Haleb, to whom he was already known. This order he made me promise solemnly to present.

Greatly could I have wished to devote to the new friends thus strangely gained the time destined by them to the survey of Ephesus: but I feared lest my presence might be a restraint upon the freedom of their rambles, and when Ayasolook rose in sight, with its Moorish mosque and its citadel, I blessed them, kissed the hand of the elder, embraced the younger, and went my lonely way.

As nothing happened in the sequel of my journey to answer the promises of the beginning, – as I stopped no more travellers on the road, nor received no more purses, I shall be brief. Alternately pushing on by land or by sea, according as opportunities offered, I found the one irksome and the other tedious. A Turkish vessel conveyed me to Scanderoon. The cabin had been hired – for a wealthy merchant's harem. Nothing so little seen except thunder ever made so much noise. On the least motion of the ship, all the women used to abuse the captain. The only instrument capable of restoring them to order was the husband's pipe stick: indeed it was much oftener applied to his wives' backs than to his own lips; and the whole of this good gentleman's active life seemed to be divided between a puff and a blow.

The very day I landed at Scanderoon I proceeded on to Baïlan, there to wait in a purer air a caravan of Armenian merchants. On the arrival of the good folks I thought I beheld, instead of the most pacific people on earth, a troop of Tartars, only breathing war and blood-shed. Each man looked like a walking armoury, stuck all round with every species of offensive weapon. In confidence, however, they soon desired me not to be alarmed: "they made it a rule," they said, "never to use the arms they carried."

Of this circumstance a detachment of Koordish horsemen[1] which we met on the road seemed perfectly aware. Though not quite half our number, they no sooner saw us approach, than they drew their sabres, flung a sheep-skin across the path, and civilly desired each of us to drop into it as we passed the sum of five piastres. I took the liberty of expostulating: but my friends were so averse to acts of violence and so anxious for the honour of paying my share of the contribution, that I could not, either in conscience or good breeding, deny them that pleasure. Notwithstanding these little *rencontres* might lead to a contrary conclusion, there are guards stationed in the narrow passages of the mountains, to protect the travellers, and to awe the banditti; but they constantly make mistakes, and inform the Koords of the approaching traveller, instead of warning the traveller of the neighbouring Koords.

The fourth and last night of our journey we stopped at Martahwan; a village of Ansariehs[2] of pleasurable notoriety among the Halebines. The owner of the hovel marked out for my lodging, however, seemed ill provided: but the piteous manner in which he apologized for the poorness of the entertainment, by informing me that his wife was dead, his daughter an infant, and his mother a decrepit old woman, made me hasten to relieve his mind, by stating that a mouthful of rice, and a corner to lie down in, were all the comforts I aspired at. As to the conductor of our caravan, whose whole life was spent in travelling backward and forward between Haleb and. Scanderoon, he had wisely contrived that his conveniences should not depend, like those of its other ever changing members, on the chances of the road. Taking advantage of the utmost latitude of the Mohammedan law, he had not only provided himself with four wives, but had distributed these so judiciously between the four stations of the journey, that, though every night on the road, he every night slept at home.

At Haleb I failed not to go—lest I might seem forgetful of the kindness shown me—to the suburb of Djedaïdé, and there to present the draft, given me by the young traveller for my trouble in waylaying him. It was addressed to an old Provençal merchant: a sort of humorist, who always appeared in a rage, never agreed with any body, contradicted himself when he found no one else to contradict, and, if a stranger to his whims incautiously fell into his opinion, took it as an affront, and demanded explanation. On my handing him the check, he alternately looked at the bill and at me, and seemed to wonder how the two came together. I tried to explain this to his satisfaction by launching out into the praises of the young traveller, and calling him quite the child of nature; but here I found I had got on the wrong scent. "Child of nature!" cried the Provençal , "no more than you, or I, or pickled olives. If he were, I should expect to be devoured by him. The human beings that are nearest to nature eat their enemies, make love to their mistresses by felling them to the ground with a club, beat out their wives' brains when they get tired of their persons, and inter with the dead mothers their living babes. Except such monsters as these, all our fellow creatures are in different degrees the children of art; the Indian and the Arab, as well as the European and the Chinese: for with reason begins art; and the first man who made use of the reasoning faculty – if it were only to scoop out a drinking bowl, or the point of a fishing hook – for ever took leave of simple nature; and did very wisely!"

After this *tirade*, the worthy gentleman, inviting me to be seated, informed me that finding little of the resource of conversation at Aleppo, where the natives were, to use his own words, *naturellement bêtes*, and his own countrymen *passablement animaux*, he had addicted himself to philosophy *à corps perdu*: – an expression perhaps not wholly applicable, as I found him on the contrary to be of the sect who, only seeking the useful, never by any chance lose sight of the body, and only estimate things according as they can be eaten or drank. "In fact, fragrant odours, delicious music, beautiful gardens and such like," my friend observed, "lose all their merit the moment one becomes deaf, or blind, or afflicted with a cold in the head!" He therefore – only esteeming *le solide*, – held them in great contempt, as totally unphilosophical; and, whenever they were praised in his hearing, used shrewdly to ask: "*à quoi bon tout cela*?"

Meanwhile, dinner being announced, he jumped up, and cried out with exceeding glee: "*allons-y, car il est très philosophique de manger*:" a truth to which I so fully assented that I was invited to take my share, and for once had an opportunity of beholding a sage truly intent upon putting his doctrine in practice. Indeed he did this to such a degree as almost to overshoot the mark, and to exceed the limits of utility; for, though at every one of the good dishes which a well trained confidential servant successively enumerated in a loud voice, he emphatically exclaimed, "*Eh mon Dieu, qu'est-ce que cela me fait*?" Yet, being wholly absorbed in the eloquent invective this gave rise to against the pernicious art of cookery, he went on practically evincing its dangers, until I feared his philosophy might end fatally, and was going to impart my apprehension to his servant, – when luckily the same idea struck this faithful domestic. He whispered something in his master's ear; who, hereupon reddened, and turning round to me, said, "*Je fais si peu attention à ce que je mange, que je suis sujet à m'oublier, et à ne pas discontinuer jusqu'à ce qu'on m'avertisse*:" in order to ensure the performance of which necessary office, the prudent Provençal had with infinite forecast granted his trusty attendant a considerable annuity; – but upon his own more philosophic life.

Dinner, desert, coffee and liqueurs being over, I thanked my host for his entertainment and took my leave. "Ah!" exclaimed he, "why must I remain here to look after pistachios and tobacco, while you are going to behold the august site of ancient Babylon; that cradle of wisdom, that fountain head of gnosticism, which let man into all the secrets of the Divine emanation, and into all the mysteries of the universal soul! No doubt you will tread with veneration its hallowed soil, kiss with rapture its sacred dust, and make an ample store of its inestimable bricks. But, no – you only go to seek the filthy gold of a Pasha!" I laughed; owned I saw more of the *utile* in a few sequins than in a whole cart load of worn out brick bats, with inscriptions which no one could understand, even though they should have been manufactured in Babylon; begged the merchant's commands for that august place, and took my departure.

To an unphilosophical traveller Aleppo was not a disagreeable abode, though it had its inconveniences. The stranger risked being torn to pieces by the shereefs if he liked the jenissaries best, stoned by the jenissaries if he preferred the shereefs, and knocked down by both if he liked neither preeminently. Every day the city was disturbed by the feuds between these rival bodies. I left them to settle their differences without my assistance, and made my bargain with the Kerwan-bashi of a small kafflé[3] for my conveyance to Bagdad. The conductor of the caravan was to defray all expenses, – tolls to Turks, Arabs and Turkmen included; and to go, not by the great desert, where we expected nothing but pilfering Bedoweens, pestilential winds, and clouds of parching dust, but by the longer and more agreeable circuit of Moossool, described as an uninterrupted succession of populous villages and cultivated tracts.

On the appointed day we set out. Among the party was an inquisitive prying marmoset, who could not rest until he had sifted out the business and profession of every member of the caravan. When it came to my turn to be cross-questioned, I honestly told him, under promise of betraying me to nobody, that I was a physician, disguised as a military man, to avoid the annoyance of consultations. The secret was soon buzzed about, and immediately the whole party paid court to no one but me. Each individual contrived in turns some opportunity cunningly to introduce the topics of health and disease, and in a discreet way to consult me on all his complaints, past, present, and future. One Arab only of the suite was endowed with so perversely good a constitution as not to be able to discover in himself the symptom of a single lurking ailment; and feelingly lamented his ill-luck in being obliged to forego so fine an opportunity for a cure. The first medicines I distributed were mere balls of bread and soap; but I soon found the bowels of the company too *exigeant* for so gentle a prescription. I therefore made bold to purloin some portion of a bale of ipecacuanha, directed to the missionaries at Bagdad, which I knew by the smell, and mixing it with some gunpowder, found the means to move and satisfy my friends. They were not particular rather as to the mode in which the medicine acted. A man in a fever slily drank off the restorative I had prepared for one with an abscess; and one in the colic put into his stomach the lotion intended for the leg of another who had broken his shin: but these trifles affected not my reputation. It presently grew so splendid, that in our evening halts I no longer dared to stir out of the khan where we stopped, for fear of being forcibly dragged away to feel pulses. Fortunately, the crossing of the small desert, which we preferred to coasting the banks of the Tigris, enabled me to drop my assumed character, by interrupting for a while the affluence of patients. I declared I was not a physician; and immediately the complaints of my travelling companions, which they thought radically cured, all returned upon them with double force.

Making a halt between Nissabeen and Mossool, we came in contact with a party of travellers, whose route crossed our track, and who halted near our own resting-place. At first our guides and the strangers conversed together very amicably, but presently high words arose between them, and the quarrel at last became so loud and violent that I expected it to end in a pitched battle. We thought it wisest not interfere, and contented ourselves with listening attentively. For a long while, however, none of us could make any thing of the dispute, except that it was about some great personage, whom, it seems, our Arabs had not mentioned with due reverence. When the matter came to be explained, this personage turned out to be the devil. The strangers were Yezidees; a sect who maintain that, whether Satan be at present in or out of favour in heaven, he continues not the less to exert great sway upon earth, and therefore ought to be treated with proper respect; and, as they think it wise to make friends every where – not knowing where their destiny may ultimately place them – they judiciously divide their worship between the powers of light and darkness. The party in question was on a pilgrimage from Mount Sindjar their residence, to the tomb of Schaich Adi, their patron.

Hearing all these circumstances, I immediately walked over to these worthy people, and begged most earnestly to state to them that we were all in reality much more in his satanic majesty's interests than we pretended; requested, for my own share particularly, to have a good word spoken for me in their prayers to him, and, after mutual civilities on parting, very respectfully wished them at the devil.

This gentleman, variously treated, continued for several days after to engross our whole conversation: – some thinking it spoke well for themselves to abuse him without moderation; others observing, that after all he owed not only his existence, but his propensities, like every created being, to the Author of all good; and could only act under express authority. This position was chiefly maintained by a fat, sleek, ruddy-faced Armenian. His nominal residence, he told me, was Yulfa,[4] his real abode any part of the road between Turkey, Persian and India. Already had he spent, in carrying merchandise backward and forward between those countries, two good thirds of man's ordinary span of life; and still did he as little as ever meditate a more tranquil mode of existence for the remainder of his days. It is true, that though Maallim Moorsa's body was in constant motion, his mind seemed stationary, and neither to advance nor to retrograde an inch: and it was no doubt owning to the complete repose of his intellectual part, that the corporeal portion so well stood the fatigue he made it undergo. With him, the sword, so far from wearing out the scabbard, appeared of no use but to keep that scabbard properly poised, amid the jolting of his horse and camel.

"Tell me, Maallim Moorsa," said I one day, as we stopped to water our camels, "what can tempt you, at your age and with your fortune, to toil harder, and to allow yourself fewer indulgences than the meanest of your own domestics? And far from home and friends to spend your days jolting on a rough-paced dromedary, and your nights sweltering in a wretched berth? Are hunger, thirst, burning sands, nipping blasts, tormenting insects, venomous reptiles, extortionary guides, rapacious enemies, ruinous engagements, and unexpected losses so very indispensable to your happiness, that you must travel hundreds and hundreds of miles in search of these little adventitious enjoyments?"

"I will tell you;" answered the placid Armenian. "It is habit, all powerful habit that makes me live as I do; – habit, more persuasive than the suggestions of reason, and the remonstrances of friends. When first I commenced my wandering mode of life, I only intended to continue it during a limited period. The repose at home which followed each journey seemed short, the setting out afresh was irksome: I reluctantly quitted a young and handsome wife, a group of fond and playful children, and a set of jovial and hospitable friends, for new fatigues and dangers, and never did I start without saying to myself: –"well! Let me only possess a decent competency, and I shall sit down never more to move, until packed up like my own goods, to be carried to the grave!"

"But mark the sequel! As years rolled on, my wife grew old and cross, my children left me to set up separate establishments, my convivial friends became sedate and parsimonious, and I myself by degrees began to lose, in my lonely journeys, my former keen relish for society. As with my increasing wealth my ideas of a decent competency enlarged, my taste for the things it was intended to secure diminished. Instead of feeling a greater impatience to get home, and more pleasure in staying under my own roof, than I used to do, I now find precisely the reverse to be the case. I travel homewards more leisurely; I am able to sleep more soundly on the night which precedes my arrival; and the happiness of being with my family sooner loses its zest. My increasing torpor of mind and of body more speedily crave that excitement which only the bustle and shaking of the caravan can give: the desire of returning to my business and journeys revives more quickly: I am bent with greater force upon still achieving one last lucrative expedition ere I sit down for ever; and I can less bear the idea of already crossing myself up, like the worm in the web of its own weaving, for the whole of the time that is to precede my final change."

"Man, man!" cried I, "struggle against this increasing restlessness; or what good are your riches to do yourself and others?"

"Alas, I have struggled!" replied the Armenian. "It was but the very last time of my being at home that I said to myself: Maallim Moorsa, Maalim Moorsa, dost thou mean never to be quiet? Thy daughters are well married, thy sons in excellent business, thou possessest three times as much as with thy old Rachel thou canst spend in the most profuse living. Then wander not any longer about the world, like one bereft of house and home; but, by staying among thy friends, and giving up all further ventures, secure thyself from the risk of losses and sorrows, and thereupon I forced myself to try to enter into all the various enjoyments of a sedentary life. But alas! the thing would not do: I soon found a noisome evil steal upon me, penetrate my inmost marrow, and spoil the relish of all my pleasure. It was not loss; it was not sorrow: but it was far more intolerable than either; – it was ennui! An insuperable listlessness took possession of my being, a nausea past all enduring pursued me incessantly. In the midst of friends, of good cheer, and of comforts of every description, I cast a look of envy upon every human being who set out to encounter new fatigues and dangers. The recital of the speculations, the purchases, the sales, the commissions and the profits of other merchants, made my heart bound, and my mouth water with longing. My own existence, while unemployed in similar transactions, appeared to me a mere blank, – or rather, a gloomy expanse of entire darkness; and my melancholy and pining must at last have brought me prematurely to the grave, had not, on the urgent entreaties of my friends, a sensible physician been called in to consider my case: for my mental uneasiness had by this time degenerated into an actual disease of body, which seemed to threaten a fatal termination!"

"And what could he prescribe" cried I – "in a case of this nature? was it rhubarb or senna; emollients or tonics?"

"Neither the one or the other; but two hundred pieces of shawl, with the addition of as many bales of silk as I had room for, to be bought in Cashmeer and to be sold at Smyrna. The very prescription made me revive. The moment I set about taking the remedy I felt like a fish put back into the water; my decaying strength returned, and my fading cheek resumed its pristine hue."

"Your case," said I, shrugging up my shoulders, "I see, is hopeless."

"I fear it is," answered Moorsa. "I have lived a constant traveller, and a traveller, I suppose, I shall die. On these roads on which I spent my youth and manhood, I feel destined to end my days. But I do not much repine at this ordination: it affords me a pleasure which no other could give. I talk not of that of seeing different manners and customs. Those are things we Armenians care little about. But while abroad, I fancy that all the beings I possess at home are angels; and I never stay at home long enough to be undeceived."

This account of Maallim Moorsa struck me forcibly: it sounded like a warning. If a heavy Armenian with a comfortable home, had found roving habits take, through dint of constant indulgence, such root in his constitution, as to despair of ever throwing it off, how much more was a state of incurable restlessness likely to overcome the confirmed disease of one who, like me, was by nature averse to domestication, and had not been able to wrest from fortune the least little clod of earth, on which to sit down, when tired of rambling, as in a spot subject to my own rule, but, like the loose sands of the desert, ever remained liable to be blown about from place to place, by every slightest gust of wind. I felt so alarmed at the danger, that I determined to avoid it, by fixing myself on the first opportunity. Already I possessed in my little Alexis a polar star, to which began to point all my thoughts, all my wishes, – a magnet, whose attraction I felt even when steering in a contrary direction. Him I should some day have near me, him I should educate, him I should make the sole object of my care: but to execute that project I must have a home; I must have means; – and in search of that home, and of those means, I must for the present go on wandering as before.

CHAPTER V.

On the thirty-ninth day of our departure from Aleppo, at the sixth hour of the afternoon, parched, dusty and cross, we reached a vast suburb of mud, traversed a long bridge of boats, and found ourselves in the celebrated city of Bagdad. As we slowly advanced towards our resting place, I could not help exclaiming at every step: "Is this the capital of Haroon-al-raschid? this the residence of Zobeïdé; this the favourite scene of eastern romance? Alas! how fallen from its ancient splendour!"

Suleiman still governed the vast pashalik of Bagdad; the last and highest fruit of many successive vicissitudes and promotions. A Georgian by birth, and by condition a Mamluke, he had, in 1775, on the death of his predecessor and patron, been appointed to the Motsellimlik of Basra. Besieged in that city by Kherim-khan, the usurper of the Persian monarchy, he held out fifteen months ere he surrendered the place; was, in consequences of the capitulation, carried a captive to Sheeras, and, after a two years detention, had, on the death of Kerim, the good fortune to be again restored to his government. To this subordinate appointment the Porte, in consideration of his valour and his services, soon after added the pashalik of Bagdad, the most extensive and powerful of the Turkish empire.

Long did Suleiman sustain with unexampled dignity the weight of his manifold honours. His warlike talents kept in awe the fierce hordes of tributary Koords and Arabs at the two opposite extremities of his vast province, while his justice and moderation endeared him to the milder inhabitants of the intervening districts. But ere I beheld his dominions his glory had begun to fade, his resplendent sun to set. For some time past both the body and the mind of the mighty Suleiman seemed to have lapsed from their former energy into a state of imbecility and torpor. Achmet, once a groom in Suleiman's stable, now held in his stead the reins of empire. In the capacity of the Pasha's kehaya, he enjoyed both the direction of his councils and the command of his armies: but he was not content merely to represent; he totally superseded his master. Suleiman was forgotten by his favourite; and while the Pasha only resembled the inert idol concealed in the sanctuary, the kehaya was the high-priest, who holding the keys of the adytum, ruled with a high hand the worshippers, and swept all the offerings left upon the altar.

My former situation and services in Turkey procured me access to this all powerful personage. I was received at his levee with the utmost courtesy. Nothing, indeed, could be more fascinating than Achmet's exterior. His features were fine, his figure noble, his manners dignified yet mild, his wit playful without pungency: he seemed to promote unrestrained liberty of speech, even where it attacked most directly his opinion and interests; his own expressions often dropped as if from an unguarded lip and a guileless heart. He spoke with affability to all, and never ceased bewailing the pomp his situation required. No passion ever could be perceived to disturb the serenity of his countenance, or the placidity of his temper. He would occasionally perform acts of great liberality; always expressed his repugnance to harsh or cruel measures, and when compelled by reasons of state to sign the death warrant even of his bitterest enemy, shed tears of sympathy which he seemed afraid to show.

But most deceitful was this fair outside. If angry emotions never ruffled Achmet's countenance, or fierce resentment never found a vent at Achmet's lips, they only rankled more fiercely within his impenetrable bosom. Humble in his manner, his heart swelled with unbounded pride: for every piastre he gave in gifts, his agents doubled their exactions tenfold: his aversions, his hatreds, undiscoverable in the presence of their object, broke out with greater virulence in distant times and places. The more he expatiated on the pleasure of pardoning, the more certain it was that he meditated some act of signal revenge; and if he sighed at being obliged to represent his master, it was because he longed for Suleiman's death, to be master himself.

Achmet had for some time been waging war in the Pasha's name with a religious sect, considered by the Turks as new and heretical, which daily acquired greater extension in Arabia, under the name of Wahhabees. As I was destined soon to come into contact with its followers, a short sketch of its origin and progress may not be inapposite in this place.

Islamism had found in the arid but extensive province of Nedjd – the inmost kernel of the Arabian desert – not only its first cradle but its firmest subsequent bulwark. While among the stationary and close-pressed population of the surrounding districts the doctrine of the Koran had become speedily subject to fermentation and change, and had by degrees ramified into numberless diversities of belief and of practice, the more hostile to each other in proportion as they presented less difference, it continued among the children of Anahsse, of Kaïbar and of Taï – few in number, distant in abode, thinly diffused over an immense and sterile desert, and ever moving from one part of its surface to another – to be transmitted from father to son in all its primitive purity. The erratic life of these Bedoweens allowed them little time to exhaust their intellect in idle speculations, to perplex their conscience with imaginary difficulties, and to pervert their creed by absurd explanations; it withheld from them the means of burdening their communities with a cumbrous hierarchy, or to waste their leisure on a complicated ritual; and throughout their vast but indefinite domain, the text of the Prophet continued in every age the only rule of the individual, the desert his only temple, and the leader of the tribe his only imam or priest. That constant motion of which the stream owes it limpidity preserved the faith of the wandering Arab from alloy, and his practices from corruption. Precisely, however, because the more undeviating adherence of the raving Bedoween to the original revelation of Mohammed had never been superseded by later doctrines, nor had clashed with subtler and more complicated tenets, it was never embodied by those that professed it into a separate code, nor stamped with a separate name, intended to distinguish these more orthodox Mussulmen from the remainder of the followers of Mohammed. They therefore attracted attention and excited obloquy the less, as their dispersion and their weakness prevented them from attempting to extend their faith, or to gain converts to their doctrine, but on the contrary made them readily display a temporary assimilation of their external practices with whatever ramification of the Mohammedan religion they were led amongst, either in the pursuit of business or a pleasure – in the tending of their flocks, or in the conduct of their caravans; and this the more easily, as their own worship was divested of peculiar forms, and their feelings towards the followers of a different doctrine free from that hatred which only arises from daily contact.

But totally different became the case, when the primitive opinions here set forth, no longer confined to the roving children of the sterile Nedjd, began by degrees to insinuate themselves among the stationary population thickly crowded in the fertile districts of Ared; – when that creed, which had been cherished only in silence in the lonely tent, became the topic of daily converse in towns and in villages. It was then that the belief adopted from the neighbouring Bedoween, marking more forcibly by greater approximation its difference from the tenets to which a more civilized Islamism had by degrees degenerated, began to excite attention, to produce enmity, and to cause among its followers a closer union with each other, and a more entire separation from those that remained faithful to their paternal creed.

And this happened toward the close of the seventeenth Christian century. At that period the districts of Ared – and that of Ayani – was ruled by a schaich of the name of Suleiman, descended from the same noble family of the Koreïsch – now reduced to a few obscure individuals – whence sprung the last of the prophets. This schaich derived a considerable income from the numerous herds of camels which he let out on hire, according to the custom of his country, and which yielded him an immense profit, especially at that season of the year when the Indian Mohammedans, performing their pilgrimage to the holy house, disembarked at Katif, and traversed Ared in their way to Mekkah: but, loaded with riches, Suleiman remained long unblessed with progeny. In this old age, and when he no longer had any hopes of offspring, Heaven most unexpectedly bestowed on him a son.

Extraordinary deviations from the regular course of nature are always remembered to have taken place at the birth of extraordinary personages; – and when the son of Suleiman rose to be the founder of a new sect, the proselytes to his doctrine failed not to record the phenomena which their predecessors had witnessed. Be it known, therefore, that, at the birth of this high fated child, an universal tremour convulsed the air, shook the earth, and made every mosque that rests upon the ground totter unto its foundations, and every minaret that shoots up in air topple on its base; and while, during several successive nights, cities, villages, castles and fields shone with a preternatural and brilliant light, the lamps which burned in the sepulchral chambers of Mohammed and of the other saints of Islamism went out, as if in anticipation of the fate that awaited them, in spite of every effort of imams and snuffers.

Abd-ool-wahhab, or the slave of the Most High, was the name given to the infant thus peculiarly marked as the favourite of Heaven. He was sent at an early age to study the law in the most celebrated medressés of Damascus, and there learnt from the subtlest Mohammedan doctors the best methods of impugning the corruptions of their creed. Accordingly, he no sooner returned among his fellow-citizens, ripe for reform of their faith, than he began publicly to preach the necessity of an entire abandonment of the corrupt tenets and superstitious practices which had so long disgraced Islamism.

The doctrine of Abd-ool-wahhab has been represented as pure deism: but nothing can be less consonant with truth than this assertion. The son of Suleiman not only maintained most strenuously the divine origin of the Koran; he might even be said to have rendered it the chief object of his reform to restore to the sacred text all its primitive importance and weight, by rejecting every article of faith or rule of conduct subsequently derived even from the oral precepts of the Prophet himself; by disencumbering the book divinely revealed of all the commentaries with which, in the course of time, its pages had been burdened; and by loudly proclaiming that, without any adventitious aid, the words brought from heaven by the angel Gabriel were alone able to supply all the spiritual wants of the faithful: for while Abd-ool-wahhab regarded the Koran as received directly from the Most High, he considered Mohammed its first promulgator as only an ordinary man, endowed with no one super-human character, no gift of miracles, nay, no peculiar sanctity whatever, transferable to his own deeds or sayings, as distinct from the sacred rescripts showered leaf by leaf upon him; and, above all, he treated the stamp of holiness affixed on other individuals – imams, doctors, or expounders of the law – blazoned forth in the later ages of Islamism, together with the pilgrimages performed to peculiar tombs, and the virtues attributed to peculiar relics, as absolute idolatry: whence, like every other apostle of a new doctrine, who only bows his head submissively to older established worships, while his own totters in the weakness of infancy, but raises his hands against them the moment his innovation have acquired sufficient strength – the first pious performance Abd-ool-wahhab enjoined his new disciples (as soon as enabled to achieve it) the destruction of the chapels of Mekkah and Medina, of Iman-Aly and Iman-Hussien, where Sunnees of Scheyees yearly unite in devout orisons to the ashes of pretended saints. Their dust was, like that of the desert, to be scattered in the wind; and the treasures which adorned their monuments were to reward the piety of their despoilers.

When about the middle of the eighteenth century, Abd-ool-wahhab, – oppressed with years of renown and sanctity, was at last gathered unto his fathers, his son Mohammed, educated like himself in the study of the law, and consequently also distinguished by the title of Moolah, succeeded him as preacher of the new doctrine. Moolah Mohammed gave himself more wholly up to its internal light, since that from without cheered not his eyes, – struck from his birth with incurable blindness. This circumstance indeed prevented him from leading out his proselytes himself, in the wars for the defence or propagation of his new creed, but Moolah Mohammed's achievements in battle could not be dispensed with; the irrefragrable truth of Wahhabism had already found a champion famed for martial description in Ibn-Sehood, the supreme ruler of Ared, who resided at Derayeh, and who became the temporal chief of the Wahhabees, while Moolah-Mohammed remained their spiritual leader.

From the moments that the new doctrine, adopted by old established princes, became enabled to add the force of arms to that of arguments, it made rapid and extensive progress. Almost immediately on the promulgation, its more recent name had sanctioned the tenets already professed of old by the roving tribes of the desert; and soon after its establishments in the Ared, the stationary Schaichs of the province of Kherdj enlisted under its banners. It now rapidly approached the Hedjas; and the Shereef of Mekkah, the guardian of the Kaaba, began to tremble for his power and for his dominions. Loudly inveighing against the apathy with which other states saw the danger approach them, he determined to avert it from the realms he ruled, by promoting a powerful diversion.

To the eastward of the Nedjd extends the half desert, half cultivated province of Hadjar; the ancient domain of the mighty tribe of Beni-Haled. One part of the year, Ibn-Arar its chief roves with his tents over the boundless plain, the other part he resided in El-Hassa the capital. This city once recognized the authority of the Sultan; but has since been reclaimed by its Arab founders. Turkish fortifications, however, still surround its precincts, and Turkish families form a principal part of its population. Its ayals or primates bore the Wahhabees, both in their quality as Osmanlees and as Sunnees, a peculiar hatred. Thence the Shereef of Mekkah found little difficulty in exciting them to hostilities against the spreading heretics. Arar took up arms and marched to Derayeh.

Already had internal anarchy and dissensions began to shake to its foundations the new doctrine. Nothing, therefore, seems more probable than that, like many older heresies, that of the Wahhabees would have blazed an instant in the district where it arose, and then have sunk again for ever into oblivion, had not the unseasonable interference of strangers providently preserved it from so inglorious a fate. The danger which threatened the Wahhabees from without, forced them to stifle their internal feuds. They united for common defence and safety. Sehood, before harassed by continual murmurings and mutinies, now found his subjects all obedience and zeal. And after several years of warfare with Arar, instead of the children of Beni-Haled getting nearer Derayeh, the sons of Wahhab had sensibly approached El-Hassa.

As soon as Abd-ool-azeez, the son and successor of Ibn-Sehood, felt himself secure on the side of Hadjar, he turned his views toward Mekkah. Revenge as well as avarice animated him against the chief of this holy city. But where all lived upon the holy things which he came to destroy, he found very few within the city disposed to second his attempts from without. It was only at the close of the third campaign that he got sight of the fortress of Tayif, situated on a high mountain, at a small distance from Mekkah; and before he could lay siege to the place, the death of his spiritual partner, Moolah-Mohammed, – whose earthly career had extended to near a century, – forced him, by the confusion it caused among his sectaries, to return to Derayeh.

The Shereef of Mekkah thought this the time for changing his defensive into an offensive war, and pursued the Wahhabees into their own territory. There, however, rapidly facing about, these sectaries, with their strength now refreshed, so completely routed his harassed army, that he was hardly able, in his flight, to reach the gates of his capital.

The Porte now awoke from its trance, and began to feel some alarm at the progress of the new sect. The Sultan directed the Pasha of Bagdad to provide for the defence of the holy city; and the Pasha of Bagdad transmitted the Sultan's instructions to his vassals, the Arab schaichs of Montefih and of Beni-Haled. Both chiefs prepared immediately to obey: but the schaich of Montefih was murdered by a disguised Wahhabee, in his own tent; and the schaich of Beni-Haled, after an unsuccessful campaign, saw El-Hassa, his capital, sacked by the victorious enemy, who took Sobier by storm, made Basra tremble, and threatened Meschid-Aly with annihilation.

Suleiman's kehaya at last himself determined to advance. In 1793 – the year before my arrival at Bagdad, – he had succeeded in making Abd-ool-azeez evacuate his new conquests, and return, though with immense plunder, to Derayeh. Great consternation continued, nevertheless, to prevail at Bagdad: for the Wahhab doctrine had now extended its sway to almost every part of Arabia north of Yemen, and had gained the very core of the tribe of Montefih itself, hitherto considered as the chief bulwark of the Othoman Empire against the new sectaries. It is true, the Turkish mob tried to hush its fears by asking with a sneer what could be effected by an undisciplined rabble armed only with matchlocks, against regular armies and fortified places; but the shrewder part of the community felt that no temporary check could ensure a vast province vulnerable in every point, an empire tottering to its base, and a militia enervated by sloth and luxury, against a race of men with bodies of steel, with souls of fire, whose abode was the inaccessible heart of the desert; whose patience of fatigues, hardships, and privations exceeded all idea, as their rapidity of motion baffled all calculation; who, heeding neither heat nor hunger nor yet thirst, performed with a rapidity which no other troops could emulate marches of a length in which no other troops could follow them; who fell in the most sudden manner on the points most distant from those prepared for their reception; who, on the smallest reverse always had their sands open behind them to retire to, beyond the reach of pursuit; whose obedience to their chiefs in whatever concerned the interests of their new creed knew no bounds, while their bravery in battle and their contempt of death were fed by a fanaticism far exceeding the long worn-out zeal of the Turks; and who, in all their expeditions, were equally animated by the interests of religion, and by the hopes of plunder. Nay, timid men pretended that in the very midst of Bagdad, in the broad face of day, Wahhabees had been seen, scarcely disguised, taking note of the individuals, and marking the houses, which their vengeance or their avarice had devoted to destruction.

Meanwhile Achmet kehaya was preparing to employ the leisure which the temporary retreat of these sectaries had left him, in an expedition against the district of Kara-Djoolan, one of the fiefs of the pashalik of Bagdad. Its Koordish inhabitants had of their own authority appointed one of their countrymen as governor, and this new delegate was trying to obtain the Pasha's confirmation by force of arms.

I offered to raise a corps of Dellis for this expedition, and was accepted. Knowing dispatch to be the soul of war, I did not in my recruits stickle much for age or size, and when my bairak[1] was complete, had the satisfaction of seeing it offer a most agreeable variety of ages and statures: – but what of that? courage was not measured by the inch, nor bravery estimated according to the colour of the beard. With my raw recruits I was ready for the kehaya, long before he was ready for me.

Babel's ancient confusion of tongues still seems to prevail at Bagdad. Turks, Persians, Indians, Jews, Egyptians, Greeks, and Arabs were constantly vying, which, in their various dialects, should outbawl the other. Among the motley group collected in the market place, the fat paunch and ruddy face of Maallim Ibrahim often shone preeminent. Whenever he saw me, he failed not to hail his old travelling companion; and one day that his mercantile transaction left him at leisure, he introduced the captain of Dellis to some Ispahan merchants, who had left their country on the dissensions which followed the elevation of the eunuch Aga Mohammed. They were scheyees, and certainly, in the eyes of a true sunnee, a very abominable set of people; for not only did they maintain Aly to be first in rightful succession to Mohammed, and not Aboo-bekr; but they made no scruple of carrying little paintings of pretty faces in their books of poetry. It was shocking to behold!

Notwithstanding such extreme relaxation of morals, I could not help thinking my Persians agreeable companions enough. They were the first men whom I had found anxious to mix with drudgery of trade the refinements of literature. One of them in particular, Aboo-Reza by name, possessed a very pretty turn for poetry himself. His imagination, it is true, was not of that soaring order which, like the eagle, rises far above the surface of the earth, and embraces in its rapid glance the most distant similitudes only viewed from the high vault of the heavens. It rather resembled the playful butterfly which, hovering near the enamelled surface of the field, is content to sip, in gaudy attire, the honied cup of each humble daisy half concealed among the herbage. He was happy in the art of seizing the à-propos of the moment, the flitting shadow of the insect in its noon day flight; and his impromptu verses on the events of the day were, by his friends, extolled far above the productions of Hafeez and of Ferdousi, – poets, as it was thought, grown somewhat musty with age. The most felicitous fits of inspiration used to seize him, when half a dozen of us were assembled in a little backroom, over a large bowl of a certain ruby coloured liquor, whose fumes seem in all ages to have had the property of exciting the poetic fervour. It was then that his eyes began to sparkle, and his lips to pour forth almost as many involuntary effusions as they admitted voluntary draughts of the inspiring nectar.

One evening Aboo-Reza looked so much more solemn than usual, that all wondered what monstrous mouse the mountain was going to produce. It kept us not long in suspense. Striking – for the purpose of enforcing silence – against the sonorous vessel round which we were seated: "Mourn Persian, mourn!" roared the expanding merchant: – "when the ancient gem of the empire, the primeval seat of the sovereign, the once proud and populous Ispahan lost its charm in the eyes of its master; when the rude hand of the intruder Time was suffered to rob its golden domes of their rich enamelled zones, and to wrap its silver lakes in veils of nauseous slime; when its crystal fountains only continued to play to the hooting owl; and its shady arbours to shelter the howling fox; when the king of kings cast the radiance of his favour no longer on the stately matron robed in gold, but on the warmer concubine crowned with roses; when gay Sheeraz, flushed with sparkling wine, received him to her bosom, – then began trouble and confusion to spread throughout the land; then burst open on all sides the flood gates of purple blood! – But when the whirlwind of war again tore up the blazing throne of the Sofis, scarcely rooted in the south, and, on its iron wings carried the fringed canopy of state to the frozen tracts of the North; when the gemmed carpet of the Sovereign, erst sprinkled with fragrant flowers, was spread on ice; when the benumbing shadow of frowning Demawend obscured the very brow of the ruler, and darkened the serenity of his once smiling aspect, – then, indeed, did the genius of the chilling blast imprint on eternal snows that melt not the seal of Persia's doom: then rushed forth to the destruction of Djemshid's tottering empire every demon of darkness; then spread far and wide over its withered plains the baneful offspring of the polar lightning; then did streams of ensanguined flames, crimsoning heaven's vault itself, reflect the earth's surface, deluged by the reeking tide; then – hushed all other sounds – was heard among the sun's orphan children nought but the wail of sorrow and the cry of despair!"[2]

Here Aboo-Reza stopped, to enjoy our admiration, and to collect our applause: but our lips continued locked in silent wonder at the sublime thought of delivering the aurora borealis of an army of Russian soldiers, – until real sounds of war seemed gathering at the door. All now trembled, all turned pale; each guest fixed inquiring looks on his neighbour, and at last in rushed a grim detachment of actual tangible soldiers. They were only those of our own Pasha, however, and came for the mere purpose of lodging us in a place of security, as men who had attracted the attention of the police by their secret conventicles, and could only be conspirators against the state. The loudness of Aboo-Reza's voice, while reciting his effusion, had made this valiant troop-bent in quest of our party-stop at the door to listen; and the less its members had understood of the drift of the Aboo-Reza's rhapsody, the more they had considered it as an undeniable proof of the guilty purpose. Nothing, they all swore, could be so evident as that the peak of Demawend meant the Pasha's kehaya, and that we were the hurricane let loose for his destruction. This danger was averted by clapping us in prison, where we felt rather uncomfortable, notwithstanding Aboo-Reza's assurances that, die when we might, he had all our epitaphs ready written in his pocket.

A descendant of one of the tribes of Israel was the secret instigator of this attack upon our liberties. Formerly chief of the customs at Basra, the Jew Abd-allah had been removed from that situation on some complaint of the English factory. He was since become at Bagdad not only the cashier, but the chief counsellor of the kehaya, whose financial operations he managed entirely. Achmet would sooner have affronted many a great man in office than his little Jew. Abd-allah, leaving his ancient wife, with his old employment, at Basra, had entirely new furnished his harem at Bagdad; and it was said that, in honour of the young spouse with whom he adorned his new establishment, he abstained three whole days from usury, – the sabbath, however, included. Little had this proof of love availed him. The fascinating Sarah made but an inadequate return for such sacrifices; and while the husband passed his mornings with the kehaya, one or other of the kehaya's officers used to beguile the solitude of the wife. Anxious to get some money advanced me upon my bairak, I went several times to the seraff's. Sarah, from her grated balcony, espied my visits to her husband's serdar,[3] and seemed determined to console me for his backwardness. But as well might the fair Israelite have tried to communicate her new flame to a heap of ashes as to my worn-out heart. It was proof against all her attractions natural and acquired.

Among Jews and among gentiles, in Scripture and in fable, in ancient times and in modern, it has been in the invariable rule for ladies to accuse of too much warmth those in whom they found too little. Sarah departed not from the established rule. She represented me as having manifested a slight opinion of her virtue; and her husband was delighted to see its severity thus confirmed. He had heard of my nocturnal meetings with the Persian merchants. Forthwith he denounced us to the kehaya as guilty of treasonable practices; but, on an investigation, those of his wife alone came to light.

Our liberation followed speedily. The indignity of the imprisonment, however, rankled in my mind, and I swore to the kehaya an irreconcilable hatred. From different causes, many in Bagdad shared in this feeling; and a small knot of us, chiefly officers of the Jenissaries, never met without very freely expressing our resentment. One evening, in an armourer's shop where we used frequently to assemble, we by some chance began mimicking a Greek superstition. I knotted a handkerchief into a little puppet, christened it Achmet, and, after loading it with invectives, invited the party to plunge their swords into the little kehaya. Not until he was fairly demolished did we perceive-squatted in a dark corner of the shop – an Arab, who had been cheapening a lot of muskets. He seemed as little anxious to be noticed by us, as we were pleased to discover him: but our conversation had been in Turkish, and we gave ourselves little concern about the impression it might make on a Bedoween.

A few evenings after this meeting, as I passed through a back street far away from my lodging, I saw myself rather abruptly approached by a man enveloped in his abbah, who had been observing me for some time. I clapped my hand on my pistol: but the stranger, assuring me he came in peace, only begged a moment's audience, in some place where no one might overhear us. I made a sign to him to walk on before me, and when we got to an open area, bade him stop at some distance, and disclose his mysterious business.

He first disclosed his person: opening his cloak, he asked whether I remembered him.

"You are," replied I, "the Arab of Montefih, whom we met the other evening in Faristah's shop."

"Not of Montefih, thank God!" cried the stranger shaking his head; "not of that amphibious race, half Turk, half Arab, which pretends to respect the Bedoween, and yet pays tribute to the Pasha. Mine is a purer blood, and a less corrupt creed. I am a son of Anahsse, and a follower of Wahhab. Only to serve my faith do I stoop to wear the garb of my enemies: only to seek among my foes the weapons with which to slay them, do I breathe their foul atmosphere. You perhaps think my mission dangerous, – and so truly it may be in the sense of the world: – but know that, nevertheless, for one of us who falls in the performance of this task, fifty are found imploring to fill his place. We fear little on earth, whose wreath of glory is weaving in heaven! Your hatred to the kehaya is known to equal our own. Many a time have I stood unnoticed by your side, listening to your discourse and watching your actions, when you dared to paint him in his true colours. Then join, if not our belief, at least our measures. We want not bravery, nor zeal, but tactics and discipline. Such as bring among us military skill may expect the highest honours. Leisurely consult your feelings, and let me have your answer."

This answer I felt ready enough to give on the spot, provided I knew my friend commissioned to take it. I saw little prospect of advantage in staying at Bagdad, and I was inclined to try the Wahhabees. All I required on the part of the Arab was a sight of his credentials. In proof of his mission, he took off his turban and shewed me his poll:- it had not the lock of hair which other Mohammedans leave as a handle by which to be taken up to heaven. In further confirmation of his character, he pulled out of his bosom the signet of his leader; and as a third testimonial, he offered to introduce me to a conventicle of Arabs and others, friendly to his sect, who would vouch for his veracity. This party I saw, and was satisfied. Determining upon the journey, I received the seal of the fraternity, and settled the day on which I was to be furnished with the letters and other instruments, which the Arab purposed to commit to my care.

As I went home, I met one of those Tartar messengers of the Pasha, who, like Maallim Moorsa, spend their lives on the road; but only carrying words instead of wares, fly like lightning where the merchants creep like slugs. This man, Feiz-ullah by name, had served the Capitan-Pasha during his short visirate. I had done him some service on the banks of the Danube, which he now took the opportunity of repaying on those of the Tigris. "My friend Mehemet and myself were on the watch for you," cried he, as soon as he saw me. "What you may have done, I know not, nor care to know: but what will be done to you, if you stay, I can pretty well guess. In a long conference between the kehaya and the Jenissary-Aga, of which I caught a few words, your name was so frequently mentioned, and so angrily blended with the terms of conspiracy, secret meetings and Wahhabees, that I slipt out ere I got my message, in order to warn you not to stay till it is given me. As you value your life, leave Bagdad immediately.- Ishallah![4] you will be safe among the robbers of the desert.

On uttering these last words, my informer was already out of sight. I ran not after him for further particulars. A month's pay of my troop, just received, was still in my pocket; and purposing within the hour to review my noble dellis, I had ordered my horse round to a particular spot. Nothing remained for me to do but to hie me thither, and vault into my saddle. Bidding a mental adieu to my corps, which was actually waiting for me under arms, I borrowed its pay for my travelling expenses, clapped spurs to my steed, got out of the city by a circuitous route, overset a long file of barbers going in procession to the tomb of their patron the Prophet's barber, at Madaïn, crossed the bridge, traversed the suburbs, and reaching the outer gate, took the road to Hillah.

Divided in two by the Euphrates, and encompassed by delightful gardens, that city might, after a fatiguing journey, have tempted a less hurried traveller to repose; but I feared its constant intercourse with Bagdad, and pushed on to Kefil, where I stopped a few hours. Refreshed by my halt, I left the burying place of the prophet Ezechiel to go to that of the nephew of Mohammed. A wide desert intervenes between the two sanctuaries, and few were the thanks I gave the pious souls who, in the burning sands that lie between them, have built fifty houses of prayer, and not one place of rest. My lassitude at last grew so extreme as to throw me into utter despair: for my faithful courser, – till then wont to ride as on the wind, and scarce to leave the print of his hoof in the wavy sands – seemed still more worn-out than myself, was scarcely able to set one foot before the other and ready, at every step, to drop down from sheer fatigue. Yet I made him toil on – much as it grieved me – lest night should overtake us where we must both have perished from absolute want. At last, after several more hours of a slow and painful progress, during which I frequently was tempted to lie down, and breathe my last on the spot, I began to discern a luminous speck in the horizon, as if kindled all at once by some fairy torch. It looked from the boundless plain like a beacon descried at night on the wide ocean. Yet was it not a blazing fire, nor yet a twinkling star. It was the gilt cupola of the tomb of Aly, reflecting from its burnished surface the last rays of the setting sun. Its splendour, gleaming far in the desert, and marking amidst dreary solitudes the busy haunts of man, restored gladness to my drooping soul. I knew I saw the spot, however distant, which was to end my labours. Even my horse caught the influence. He shook his mane, pricked up his ears, snorted, and directing his wide expanded nostril to whence seemed to blow the fair promise of relief, made fresh efforts to reach the wished-for goal. I patted him on the neck in gratitude, and during the remainder of the journey kept my eye steadily riveted on the blazing dome as on my polar star. Anxiously I watched its increase, in order to judge of the lessening distance; but much time still elapsed, and many a wearisome step was still performed, and complete darkness overcast the lonely scene around me, ere I drew sensibly near the end of my journey. Nor did I quit the dismal mounds of barren sands which on all sides encompassed my scarce perceptible path, until at the very gates of the town. When indeed, in the uncertainty how much further I still might have to crawl, I saw the battlements over the pointed arch rise all at once before me, at the small distance of scarce fifty yards, I gave a scream of joy; and when I passed under the sounding vault, dark and gloomy as it looked, I felt as if entering the portals of paradise.

Arrived at the khan, my first care was directed to the faithful companion of my toil. I myself led my weary steed to the stall, and with one hand I stroked his panting loins in thanks for his services, while with the other I offered him his dearly earned repast. Alas! He would not touch his food, turned away from his drink, and lying down on the ground, thrust his head between his legs, cast on me his keen fully eye, and, seized with a convulsive shivering, fell on his side, and died.

"Oh my noble, my beloved steed! Who bore me through so many toils, and saved me from so many dangers; who with such gentleness combined such fire; whose mettle my voice ever could raise or could repress at will, – were then your unslackening efforts to save my life, to cost your own! Had I been Sultan Mahmoud, I would have raised a monument over your body; an Alexander, I would have built a city to your memory: Anastasius could only give you his tears!"

I looked about to replace my loss. An Arab brought me a horse, of whose high pedigree he exhibited the most splendid testimonials. I thought it prudent to enquire into the character of the seller himself. He had occasionally stopped travellers on the road, and he might, in ordinary matters, be a little addicted to lying, as well as to thieving; but in an affair in which his honour stood so materially committed as in the present, he was above suspicion. Sooner would he spill the blood of his father than falsely warrant that of his horse. All his certificates were authenticated: I made the purchase I could not avoid; ate my supper, and having bestowed on the kehaya a few hearty curses, lady down and soon fell asleep.

CHAPTER VI.

Earlier in the morning than a man might have preferred who had gone late to rest, I was awaked by a prodigious clamour. At first I thought Meschid-Aly on fire; then, invaded by the Wahhabees: but on rising found the noise only proceeded from a few sunnees and scheyees, assembled round the tomb of the saint to whom the place is consecrated, and engaged in a trial of lungs: – each sect endeavouring in its orisons to outbawl the other. Meschid-Aly belongs to the sunnee inhabitants, but derives its chief support from scheyee pilgrims. Within its precincts, therefore, neither persuasion dares to insult the other more grievously than by invoking with all its might its own peculiar patron: and the sunnees cry out Omar! And the scheyees bawl out Aly! until want of voice reduces both alike to silence.

Among the other strange faces, attracted like my own by the clamour, I espied some which I was quite sure I had left at Bagdad. This discovery made me resolve entirely to quit the jurisdiction of Suleiman, for the scarcely less extended though somewhat less definite domain of the powerful Arab Schaich of Montefih, whose authority extends far along the banks of the Phrat and of the Schat-el-Arab. I therefore crossed the city, and again plunged into the desert.

Winding round the western extremity of the dry basin of Nedgef, I insensibly advanced in the lonely waste, without precisely knowing whither I was in the first instance going, but intending by degrees to work my way from one lesser kabile[1] or tribe to another, until I should reach the domain of the Wahhabees, the final object of my journey. An old abbah covered my Turkish dress; a sack of rice on one side, and a cruise of water on the other, were suspended from my saddle; and thus carrying my bed and board, and at liberty to spread my table and couch wherever I pleased under the canopy of heaven, I trusted for the remainder to my pistols and to Providence, not doubting that I should soon reach some Bedoween camp, where I might claim hospitality and protection.

Meantime, beginning to feel entirely out of reach of my enemies, I experienced a lightness of heart and a freedom of breathing to which I had for some time been a stranger. It was rapture to me to roam at liberty through a plain without visible boundary, as over a vast trackless sea, where I might steer my course in any direction, or make for any point I choose, unchecked by fence, unimpeded by fence or hindrance, and only guided, while the day lasted, by the course of the sun, and when the dusk came on, by the glittering constellations which seemed to succeed to his glorious employment.

"Here," thought I, "ends the domain of civilized man; – of that man whose greater polish of surface only conceals greater hardness of heart; and who only receives a smoother edge to inflict deeper wounds. Here gilded daggers, silken bowstrings, and honied poisons no longer dance around my steps: here the name of a Sultan ceases to sanction measures which his mind never conceived, and the shadow of a Visier to smite men whom his own arm cannot reach: here no one obeys a sovereign he never saw, or is bound by laws he never heard of; here man will give, and woman will deny; here no walls are raised to keep travellers out, nor are tolls demanded for letting them in; no one here legally detains the property of the stranger, nor churlishly avoids his person. Here I may consider all things my eyes embrace as my own; and in a succession of short easy saunters, roam free as air unto my journey's end!"

At this period of my reverie, out started from behind a little knoll a fierce looking Bedoween, who, couching his lance against my breast, haughtily bade me stop. This was unexpected, and disagreeably interrupted my exultation at my newly acquired freedom of motion. The Arab pointed to a small group of goat-skin tents which I had taken for low mounds of earth, as to the place where I must go, whether I chose or not, and give an account of my views and proceedings. Seeing my opponent thus strongly backed, I thought it as well for the present to waive my privilege of unrestrained liberty, and to make a friend of him, ere he had leisure to treat me as an enemy. I therefore jumped off my horse, flung my pistols to the ground, and calling myself his guest, laid hold of his girdle. Disarmed by this act of submission, he changed his threatening tone into milder language, bade me welcome, and offered to conduct me to the schaich. So rapid indeed was in his breast the transition from hostile to hospitable feelings, that he insisted by the way on his right to entertain me himself, in consequences of having been the first of his troop to see me; and could only be diverted from his purpose, by my stating that I had special business with the chief.

At the entrance of the most roomy tent in the camp, sat on his wicker stool, surrounded by a number of naked children squatted on the ground before him, this eminent personage. Engaged in the homely occupation of teaching a favourite grandson to hurl the hollow reed in imitation of the heavier spear, – as yet too unwieldy for his infant arm, – the countenance of the sire seemed to radiate with rapturous delight at the feats of his anxious pupil; and his coal black eye, still sparkling with the fire of youth, shone the brighter from its contrast with the snow-white beard which marked his advanced age. On seeing me unexpectedly stand before him, he gave a start of surprise; but soon recovering his sedate, composed look, and seeming slightly to blush for its momentary confusion, he politely returned my salute; and when, having stated my wish to pass the night in his camp, I claimed his protection as a defenceless wanderer, my request was immediately granted with courteous readiness. The schaich's kindness stopped not here: calling out to a female occupied in the right-hand division of the tent, and whose exterior – as she peeped from under the carpet which concealed her employment – seemed the least of her merits: "Zeineb," cried he, "a stranger is come to us; make haste and bake some bread:" to which injunction the diligent Zeineb only replied by setting to work. "This beginning," said I to myself, "augurs well! Bread once broken with my host, I am safe under his roof."

A few minutes suffered for the diligent housewife to produce her handy work in the shape of large flat cakes, with the distinctive mark of her own industrious palm left impressed on the surface. These, with some sour camel's milk, and other equally primitive dainties, were set out before me, and I fell to. Soon seeing me sated: "Now go to repose," said the schaich: "when rested, I no longer shall hesitate to ask you who you are, whence come, and whither going?" This respite gave me pleasure. I made myself a bolster of a dromedary's pillion, and lying down, soon fell asleep.

On again awaking, I found the stars already twinkled in the firmament, as I did in their sockets the inquisitive eyes of a dozen of the notables of the tribe, ranged in a circle round the schaich to hear my story. I took my seat beside them, and expressed my readiness to attend to their questions. The answers remained in my own hands. What might be the politics of the party was as yet wholly unknown to me, and it seemed thus far equally unsafe to own whom I fled from, or whom I wished to join. "I am a Turkish officer;" said I, – "come from Bagdad, and journeying to El-Hassa.

This seemed to surprise the party. "Stranger," cried a little shrivelled old man, with a shrewd distrustful countenance and a harsh grating voice, "tell us, pray, what particular motive can induce you, thus alone as you are, to prefer the dangerous and difficult road of the desert, to the easy way by Basra, Sobier, Graïn, and Katif, which, in eighteen or twenty days at most, would be sure to bring you to your destination?"

The observation had a something so just and pertinent in it, as to be rather appalling. "I am a lover of difficulties," said I, laughing. "My soul contracts a rust in ease: a few rubs serve to keep it bright. Besides, I wished for an opportunity of paying homage to the virtues of Bedowees."

The party were too civil to tell me to my face they believed this whole flourish a lie: but I read it in their looks. They said, "they hoped my difficulties might not exceed my wishes, and that their virtues might answer my expectations;" whereupon, – the night advancing, – they took their leaves, and went to their respective homes.

As soon as I remained alone with my host: "Osmanlee," cried he in an earnest tone, "you conceal your true design. And yet, why should you disguise it? By giving us your confidence, you would secure our good offices. Believe me, it is not from frivolous curiosity I speak: Schiach Mansoor wants not topics for idle talk. Your own welfare makes me anxious that those just gone from this abode, if they had no real grounds for mistrusting you, should not be left to harbour unfounded suspicions; – above all, that those should not thwart your views from mere ignorance, who, if confided in, might assist them effectually. Should, however, the avowal of your object be distressing to your feelings, remain silent. I urge you no further."

There was in the tone as well as in the matter of this speech a something not only so earnest but so affectionate as half to unlock the secret cells in my heard. "Mansoor," said I, "a soldier in Roum, I fought the Sultan's battles in the name of the Prophet: I came to Bagdad's Pasha neither wholly destitute of rank, nor of renown; yet I was slighted, or, if noticed at all, it was by a proud kehaya, only to have snares laid against my life. From these I fly; from these I seek shelter in the depths of the desert."

"And of this," cried Mansoor; "you feared to apprise me? How unjustly! If the supreme chief, the Kbir of Montefih himself, the daring Hameed– vulnerable as he is on the side where his peasantry or his flocks penetrate within the pale of Turkestan, – yet only pays Suleiman an unwilling allegiance, can you suppose that the lesser schaichs of his house, roaming so much deeper in the desert, should feel desirous to espouse the resentment, just or unjust, of every creature of the Sultan? Ah! so far from this being the case, rest assured that, if as a mere stranger we greet you with good will, as a sufferer by Achmet you may command our utmost services. The only risk you might run would be that of our suspecting a better understanding to exist between you and the kehaya than you avow, and the grievance you talk of to be only a feint, through means of which to draw out and to discover our secret sentiments. I still remember too well how Achmet, by calumniating me and my neighbour Beni-Tamin to each other, was near making the friends, the brothers of early youth, offer each other in old age the cup of perdition! But even with this example imprinted on my mind, my heart rejects such a thought, and you shall witness that we pay Suleiman the tribute of our herds, not of our feelings."

"But why," said I, – interrupting the schaich's harangue, – "with such proofs of treachery on the part of the Sultan's delegates, not prefer the security of an open rupture to the dangers of a secret enmity? Why not renounce at once all allegiance to Suleiman?"

"Ah!" replied Mansoor, "fate forbids my numbering myself among those chiefs so entirely beyond the Pasha's grasp as to have nothing whatever to fear from his resentment. My subjects live not all yet in the portable tent; move not all yet from place to place free and unconstrained as the antelope. Many of my vassals, fixed by the attraction of a richer soil, have driven deep in the ground the stakes on which rest their stationary huts, and, like plants, adhere to the clod of earth which their habitations compass. I myself, permitted for nine months of the year to forget that Suleiman exists, am obliged annually, during the three moons employed in collecting the contributions on my more distant tenants allured within his jurisdiction, to refresh my remembrance of his being, and to pay him my tithe of the monies I collect, and of the homage I receive."

At the thoughts of these periodically returning burdens of vassalage, a cloud seemed to overcast the schaich's countenance. Its serenity, however, soon returned, as, resuming his discourse, he added with increased animation; – "But I too, with my liability to incur wounds, possess my power to sting. Not only for every injury done to my few stationary tenants, can I retaliate tenfold on the Pasha's wholly immoveable population: I can refuse the escorts and the beasts of burthen wanted for the conveyance of his goods and the safety of his pilgrims: I can, if his heavily armed troops should venture into the desert, leave my battles to be fought by thirst and famine, by the stifling sands and by the fearful simoom; I can commit to the power of the elements the protection of Mansoor. Therefore, O stranger, since I now know who you are, rest secure; and may soft slumbers keep locked your eyelids the remainder of this night! Tomorrow, in honour of your coming, shall fall the fatted sheep."

There was nothing in this conversation with Mansoor calculated to disturb the repose to which I most willingly retired: accordingly it lasted, as little interrupted by irksome waking thoughts as by troubled dreams, until broad day light. My first care on getting up was to edify my host by the unction of my morning prayer; my next business to renew the evening's talk. I wanted to bring him on the subject of the Wahhabees. At first, he rather hung back, – apprehensive, no doubt, of committing himself: but the respectful terms in which I at all hazards mentioned the new sect, induced him at last to become more unreserved.

"Removed," said he, "as I am from the Ared, and on the borders of Irak, any avowed union with the sons of Wahhab would, in the present stage of their progress, be of little advantage to them and of certain detriment to myself. It must draw upon my head the wrath of Suleiman, without ensuring the support of Abd-ool-Azeez. Besides, a man of my years wants repose during the few days God still grants him to live;-were it only to prepare for death; and when the domain of the Wahhabees shall have made nearer approaches to my resting-place, it will then be for my children to see in how far they may think it expedient to join the standard of the new sectaries more openly: but though a sunnee in name, my religious sentiments have, in reality, always differed little from those of Abd-ool-Wahhab. Bigotry, therefore, raises not its insuperable barrier between me and his followers, and when all other barriers shall fall, and the opposite floods come near, they must of their own accord run into each other."

The only thing which, after this candid confession of Mansoor's sentiments, still restrained me from disclosing all my own designs, was the presence of his youngest child, – a boy of ten or twelve years of age, who, standing by the side of his father, and alternately fixing his keen eye on whichever of us spoke, seemed with outstretched ears to catch our words almost ere they fell from our lips, and imbibed them as the thirsting plant drinks the summer dews. "Might it not be well," whispered I therefore, to the schaich, "to send to his sports this watchful lad, whose lips move not, but whose mind devours all we say?"

"Does it?" cried Mansoor; "ah! then by all means let him stay: let him attend to the converse of men; that by so doing he may learn to become one! Fear not his indiscretion: he has left the womens' chamber; like ourselves he has learnt to fetter his tongue." On such a commendation from his parent a Greek boy would have spoken to assure me of his silence; the young Arab only looked his delight, in the bright glow which suffused his downy cheek.

I now freely confessed to Mansoor that my destination was Derayeh. "My acquaintance with the plans and resources of the government of Bagdad," said I, "might be useful, and my wish to see them marred, must at all events be acceptable."

Hereupon Mansoor ruminated a little: – at last, "Since such is your design," cried he, "I think I may do a thing which will forward it, and be of advantage to both. For some time past I have been thinking of sending Abd-ool-Azeez a token of good-will. I shall avail myself of this opportunity. The bearers of my offerings may be your guides and escorts, and you the bearer of my assurance of peace and amity."

This mission I most gladly accepted; and the preparations were immediately begun. The difficulty lay not in mustering the gifts: – they had been long collected for the purpose. The most prominent consisted of two handsome blood mares, "able," – observed Mansoor – "though without wings to fly;" an abbah tissued with gold; some rich Damascus blades, and some choice Persian stuffs from the markets of Bagdad and Basra: but the spoke in the wheel seemed to be the letter which was to accompany these presents. Mansoor's secretary was become a recording angel in the regions above: Mansoor himself never had shone as penman; and as to his vassals at present in the camp, they were more remarkable for wielding the reed whose point is steeped in blood, than that whose end is dipped in ink. My whole embassy was on the point of falling to the ground for want of a scribe.

In this dilemma I bethought myself of my own *savoir-faire*. It is true it extended not, in Eastern characters, beyond the most ordinary Nesh-khi sort. For want, however, of a more skilful hand, I offered mine, such as it was; not indeed to write in Arabic; – that was out of all question: – but to indite an epistle in Turkish.

After a little hesitation, my services were accepted. I was told the substance of what I was to pen, and left to give it my own form. For this purpose I retired to the most secluded corner of the tent, and sat down to my work. Alas! I soon felt that neither materials for writing, nor leisure to meditate, could carry me through with the task I had so incautiously undertaken. I sat poring on my endless sheet of paper, like a school boy at his theme, biting my nails, and not knowing what to write. At last a bright thought came to my relief. "Why not, where my Turkish lore failed me, eke it out with Greek, and conceal the scantiness of the substance, under the exuberance of the ornament?"

By this expedient the manuscript was at last completed, and brought it to the schaich. He looked it over with an air of astonishment. "I do not," said he, – twirling his turban round and round on his head, and straining his eyes to make out a sentence, – "pretend to be conversant in Turkish writing; but I sometimes have seen the penmanship of the Divan, and certainly it never looked like this!"

"No more it could," I boldly answered. "People in the north are constantly changing their fashions. They now think it graceful in the Othoman chancery to combine the Greek characters with the Persian phraseology. But if this new mode displeases you, – give back the letter, and let me tear it!"

"No, no," earnestly cried the old schaich, holding my hand from executing the sentence. "The letter has already cost us trouble enough. If it should not be very intelligible, Allah-akbar: God is great! my presents will explain its meaning." So saying, he dipped his seal in the ink, and impressed it on the paper. It was then rolled up, enclosed in a case sewed by Zeineb's own henna-tipped fingers, and handed over to my care.

Meantime the fatted sheep was already smoking in the platter. Invited to the feast, all the chiefs of the camp flocked to the schaich's tent. An inferior sort of self invited guests followed. None were refused that came; and each sating his appetite in the order of his arrival, and then retiring to make room for others, the tide of comers and goers ceased when the carcase was stripped to the bone.

Now commenced the bustle of my departure. In order to elude the hawk's eye of the roving freebooter I enveloped my Greek features after the country fashion in a striped handkerchief, a gift of the fair Zeineb. The horses were led out, and the guides sallied forth.

"These trusty servants," cried Mansoor, "will take you the shortest and safest road to my neighbour the Schaich (I think he said) of Schoreifath. Coming as you do from me, he will receive you well, and, when you leave him, will give you a fresh escort. From camp to camp you thus finally will reach Derayeh. Here and there, however, you will find perilous passes. All the Kabile's are not equally friendly: some might be named with whom meeting is fighting; and lately the combats have been so sanguinary, that the private vengeance to be sated on both sides leaves little hopes of a reconciliation. Mind, therefore, every where to enquire, and always to be prepared both for defence and flight. But on this subject my friend Nasser, more advanced in the desert than your servant, will give you more pointed directions." – Then, taking me aside, and charging me to inform Abd-ool-Azeez how well disposed he was to his cause, but how ill situated to shew that disposition except by his backwardness in assisting Suleiman, the schaich held the stirrup for me to mount, and bade me farewell. I set forward just as the sun dropped behind the horizon, and followed by the Arabs, the led mares, and the camels which carried the presents, slowly proceeded on.

The month of March was just opening, and the heat, save only at mid-day, still easily borne. The verdant carpet of the desert, bruised by the horses hoofs, emitted at night its most aromatic exhalations; and the plants and shrubs in full bloom sent forth invisible clouds of the most powerful perfumes. So deep appeared in the morning the dye with which the scarlet anemonies and purple hyacinth enamelled the blushing plain unto the utmost verge of the horizon, that the rosy tint of the dawn only seemed their fainter reflection cast upon the blue sky. Every where our cattle found abundant pasture, and our own appetite feasted on milk of an ambrosial flavour.

Two short days' journey and a half, unclouded by any danger or molestation, took us to Nasser's camp. It is true that now and then, like a single fleece in the azure sky, appeared far off in the desert some solitary Bedoween, seeming to rove in quest of plunder: but none came within hearing distance, except one small party; and this, the moment it recognized the Arabs of schaich Mansoor, again quietly walked off, and vanished in space.

The same hospitality which had marked the reception of Mansoor, shone pre-eminent in that of Nasser. In him I even found, with less loquacity, a more ready frankness. All within and around him savoured stronger of the freedom of the desert. The wife of Mansoor had only suffered herself to be perceived: the consort of Nasser came forth, and met our gaze undaunted. Not only she permitted me to see her features unveiled, but she very minutely scrutinized my own. A native of the West was, I suppose, a novel sight to the lady: for my person and my attire seemed equally to attract her attention. Indeed her investigations became by degrees so close, that, to my great satisfaction, the husband thought fit at last to interfere. I must otherwise have been, by little and little, completely undressed. Even after she had been compelled reluctantly to retire, I heard the fair Farsané (or whatever was her name) loudly complain to her sympathizing maids of the check offered by her husband to her inquisitive spirit.

The attentions of the wife did not prevent the husband from pressing me to stay beyond the time I had limited; but it was done with that blended warmth and discretion, which left me an entire liberty to accept or to refuse. Indeed, combining with the energy of the desert all the politeness of the courtier, the schaich was like a rock covered with flowers. Seeing me determined to proceed, he gave me all the assistance in his power, and advised me by means of a little circuit to avoid his next neighbour, with whom he was on indifferent terms; then, having supplied me with a double provision of rice and dates and with an increased escort, he wished me a prosperous journey, and tarried at the entrance of his tent while I remained in sight.

For the purpose of eluding as much as possible all observation, I now travelled only at night. Before the dawn arose, the body of the caravan used to dive into one of those hollows which break the surface of the Arab plain; while only one of its members, lying down on the edge of the cavity, staid outside to keep watch. Thus we made way but slowly, and only at the end of five days' march reached the encampment of scaich Amroo, chief of the tribe bound by the strongest ties of reciprocal services to that of Nasser. With this schaich, therefore, I determined to tarry two whole nights; a resolution for which I had to pay somewhat more than the cost of my entertainment.

As the blood mare sent by Mansoor to Abd-ool-Azeez had been declared on all hands perfectly irresistible, nothing was omitted to assist human weakness in withstanding her charms. No beauty in a harem could be more strictly watched, both on the road and at halting-places; where her conductor never lay down to sleep until he had tied round his own waist one end of the chain of which the other end fastened the legs of his charge: but even that could not daunt the daring of an Arab – a stranger in Amroo's camp, and only attracted by the report of our arrival. Irresistibly smitten with the beauteous mare, he had actually succeeded in severing her fetters by means of a file, when, awakened by some accidental noise, her keeper started up, and caught the culprit in the fact.

The greater evil thus obviated, all that remained to do was to prevent a lesser one still impending, by extorting from the thief his right to shove the burden of the fine he had incurred on the shoulders of some innocent bystander, whom he might succeed to touch either with his person or his garment; and for this purpose the bastinado was without delay applied. Unfortunately, while every wary Arab kept carefully aloof during the operation, I alone, attracted by my curiosity, and not knowing my danger, must obtrude my person, on purpose to meet the robber's skull-cap, thrown at me in the midst of the infliction which he himself was suffering. Hit by the villainous garment, I became in honour bound to pay the weaver's ransom; but in return for this good office I had the pleasure of hearing him recount all his former achievements to an admiring audience – delighted that I should so providentially have prevented his brilliant career from receiving a check. In short, if I had paid it dearly, I had liberated a hero. In the desert a man's thefts are only called his gains.

On my next march we took such exceeding precautions to avoid a particular horde against which I had been cautioned, that we walked right into the midst of it. The encampment had moved from the spot which we were supposed to occupy to be most safe from its intrusion, and to arrive at which we had been tacking all the way. A considerable sum was accordingly demanded of us for leave to proceed. "You escort," said the spokesman, "strangers whom we distrust, and you carry goods which owe us a toll." This observation suggested to me the idea of trying the virtue of my cipher received at

Bagdad. "Let the chief himself," cried I, "come forward, and state his claims." This he presently did. Taking him by the wrist, I whispered in his ear the Wahhab watchword, and showed him the signet. At this sight he looked scared, for some time darted his eyes in silence on the instrument as on a talisman which kept his limbs and features spell bound, and then, waving his hand, "pass on," he cried in surly disappointment, – and immediately fell away behind his wondering attendants.

This incident greatly enhanced my importance among my own troop. Mansoor's Arabs now saw very clearly that I was some great personage, respected even in the heart of the desert; and they paid me additional deference. It went not, however, so far as to agree with me in an unqualified reprobation of the fines levied by the Bedoween on the passenger. "What the last schaich with whom we fell in had attempted was certainly very wrong, but what they themselves did was perfectly right. Because people allowed themselves the free range of their own premises, were they to lose the right of keeping out strangers? When the incautious traveller neglected to make his bargain, to be sure he was mulcted; sometimes even he was stripped to the skin: but what then? were not they the descendants of Ismail? Had not Ismail been unjustly disinherited by Ibrahim his father, and had not the posterity of Ismail an undoubted right to seize upon its lawful inheritance, in whatever hands it might have fallen?" – I attempted not to combat this argument. All I did was inwardly to pray that I might meet as few as possible of these disinherited children.

The remainder of the journey only offered a tiresome repetition of fatiguing marches and of tedious halts; of wells missed in one place and found filled up in another; of skirmishes and of flights. Our reception in the different camps varied throughout every intermediate degree between the most cordial friendship, and positive fighting: and so uninterrupted was the succession of expostulations, of threats and of protestation, that, ere we had achieved half the way, my voice became almost extinct, and I had to argue in complete dumb show. Every tribe in whose vicinity we came, supplied our caravan with some new member, glad of the opportunity to reach, under our protection, some neighbouring district; and as those who joined us constantly exceeded in number those that fell off, our troop at last grew formidable enough to awe an enemy of moderate strength. This was fortunate: for the further we advanced, the greater became the concupiscence excited by Mansoor's mares. Every Arab on the road would gladly have given for them wife, children, and friends.

Before the end of the journey, we had to encounter an enemy more formidable than any Arab tribe, not excepting the most savage of the desert. I mean the dread samiel. Our caravan was slowly pacing through the boundless plain, – the horses' steps sounding more hollow than usual on the earth, and a more awful stillness reigning in the atmosphere. Suddenly a lurid glare overspread the eastern extremity of the horizon, while a thick sulphureous mist arose from the ground, which – first revolving round and round in rapid eddies, – next mounted up to the sky, and finally overcast with threatening darkness the whole heavenly vault. At these terrific symptoms our Arabs turned pale, and goaded on our cattle with headlong hurry – in order, if possible, still to outrun the baleful blast. But in vain! Hoarsely murmuring, the hot stream swept the ground with frightful speed, and, much as we might quicken our pace, gained fast upon us. Perceiving themselves encompassed on all sides by its fiery breath our people shrieked with terror, our very cattle howled with instinctive anguish, and all that had life fell flat on the ground, burying nose and mouth deep in the shifting sands, – in hopes that the envenomed current, gliding over the prostrate limbs, might not penetrate into the vitals.

Near half an hour did the raging hurricane keep us thus riveted to the ground, without daring to move or to speak or scarce to draw breath, and soon entirely covered with a fine impalpable dust, which not only found its way into every fold of our garments, but, as we afterwards found, into every inmost recess of our boxes and luggage, – when at last our beasts of burthen, as if awaking out of a profound trance, began to shake themselves, and, by all again of one accord rising upon their legs, gave the signal that the danger was past. Every creature now stood up that was able, and thanked Providence for his escape. Only one member of the caravan, a foreign merchant, – too tardy perhaps in prostrating himself before an unknown enemy, – rose no more. On approaching, we already found him breathless, and weltering in the thick black blood that gushed in streams from his nose, mouth, and ears. My guides lost no time in committing his corrupt mass to the earth, ere the limbs should detach themselves from the swelling trunk: then heaped some stones over the spot, to protect it from the insults of the ounce and jackal; and, – these short rites and simple monuments completed, – again proceeded onwards.

This catastrophe closed the adventures of the desert. Soon after we began to descry before us, like a cloud of more benign and promising aspect, the distant mountains of the Nedjd and the domain of the Wahhabees; and with rapturous delight our long procession by degrees penetrated into verdant vallies filled with date and lemon trees, intermixed with towns and villages. After resting at Ramah, at Makren, and in other places equally inviting by their situation and their produce, we at last reached Derayeh, the capital.

CHAPTER VII.

No sooner had my person and Mansoor's presents been made fit to present themselves before Abd-ool-Azeez, than I requested an audience in all due diplomatic form. This was immediately granted. It took place in the open air, at the gates of what I must needs call – more from the dignity of its tenant than its own – a palace; and the schaich received me squatted on a rush mat. Notwithstanding his advanced age of seventy-five, he still displayed good features and a handsome though somewhat harsh and forbidding countenance, and through all the affected meanness of his dress, shone a lofty and commanding air. I felt a sensation of awkwardness at the richness of my own apparel, so much exceeding that of the high personage whose favour I came to seek. On this subject, however, I might have spared myself any uneasiness. The schaich seemed to contemplate my glitter – if noticed by him at all – with perfect indifference; and when I presented to him the gifts of Mansoor, he cast upon them the careless survey of a man who considers such things as beneath his attention. The letter certainly puzzled him: he seemed to feel as if it ought not, and he saved himself by his supercilious glance the embarrassment of owning that he knew not what to make of it. When at the conclusion of my harangue I repeated to him the sentence, and shewed the signet, imparted to me by his emissary at Bagdad, his brow unfurled and his features relaxed into a more affable expression. Still he remained, after I had done, a few moments musing and silent. At last: "Stranger," said he, in a slow and deliberate manner; "wonder not if an old warrior, accustomed to treachery and deceit, should not feel immediate confidence in Mansoor's protestations. If the light of truth has really penetrated his heart, the Lord be thanked, especially by himself, who must be the greatest gainer, – since the choicest blessings of heaven, both here and hereafter, never fail to reward sincere conversion: but I know the faith of Turks, and I distrust the very Arab whose breath mingles often with theirs. Mansoor's artful conduct may have deceived you, and it is only on trial that I shall think myself secure of his sincerity. The decisive hour," added he, suddenly starting up from his seat, "is perhaps not far off, when all who appear not for us shall be treated as if they had been against us. The spears already are pointing, and, at a distance which no other eye can reach, I already perceive the war dust rising. As to you, stay among us: in the midst of my own children no treachery can reach me, and I shall have pleasure in trying your talents."

I expressed my thanks; and fancying that the schaich, during our conversation, had eyed my pistols with peculiar complacency, resolved upon the sacrifice of these showy weapons, to conciliate his good will. Arabs of all ages, like children, always think most desirable the thing that is withheld from them. Thence Abd-ool-Azeez showed himself much more gratified with my pair of pistols, than with all the rich presents of Mansoor. He immediately directed that my expences should be defrayed, and, recommending his new guest to the care of his attendants, mounted his horse and rode off, followed by a numerous and motley suite.

Scarcely had he proceeded a dozen yards, when, just at the turning of the street, he was met by a young man also on horseback, arriving from the country, and like himself attended by a considerable retinue. The opinion which the air of the stranger made me conceive of his importance, was fully confirmed by the reception which he met with from the schaich of the Wahhabees. This chief – who seemed not in general to waste his courtesies – immediately turned back with the new comer, and when both were dismounted, there commenced between them a conflict of civilities partly in speech and partly in dumb show, which lasted several minutes. Each repeated the same inquiries and the same protestation a dozen times, and each a dozen times touched the hand of the other. In the midst, however, of this mutual assault of politeness I still thought I could discern in Abd-ool-Azeez's manner a sort of conscious superiority; and the imposing reserve which tempered his professions, formed a strong contrast with the visible eagerness of expression and gesture of the stranger. This latter, they told me, was the schaich of a smaller kabile, connected with the chief of the Wahhabees by the double tie of kindred and of vassalage.

Presently the two personages sat down in the court of the palace, and seemed preparing to discuss an affair of importance. The fear of appearing curious made me retire out of hearing; a ceremony which seemed entirely waived by the rest of the bystanders. The conference soon became animated. Gesticulation, which is never spared among the Arabs, rose higher and higher; opinions seemed more and more to clash; and such at last became the loudness of vociferation and the violence of gesture, that, from expecting to see the two chiefs devour each other with caresses, I now began to apprehend the same result from very different preliminaries. In the midst of my surmises, some words which reached me where I stood struck me as relating to myself. I now accused my stupidity in tarrying so long to guess the subject of the dispute. The chiefs had met in perfect amity; they had sat down to converse with the utmost good humour; and the only subject of difference which could have arisen must be *my* visit and *my* merits. Nothing seemed so clear as that one of the schaichs was my advocate, and the other my enemy. At this discovery all my former discretion forsook me, and, as the audience increased every instant in numbers and in boisterousness, I resolved to mix with the crowd, and to advance within hearing. The first words which distinctly struck my ear were – an unqualified sentence of death.

A thunder bolt falling at my feet could not have more astounded me. Had the measure been practicable, I would immediately have sought safety in flight. But fearful to betray my fear, and to draw upon me the eyes of the multitude by attempting to force my way through their closely wedged ranks, I was contented with making myself as small as possible, in order to elude observation. With a throbbing heart I continued to listen: – but my palpitation prevented me from hearing another word, and all I could do was to watch the looks of the disputants. After the hawk's eye of Abd-ood-Azeez had several times wandered round and round the crowd as if seeking its prey, I at last saw it pounce upon me, and remain from that moment remain steadfast. "It is all over with me now!" thought I; and indeed an Arab to my right made but too intelligible a sign to another on my left, that no mercy must be expected. The confirmation of my surmises had made me well nigh sink in the ground, when a third Arab who stood before me, shrugging up his shoulders, cried out: 'His fate is sealed;" and then with a deep sigh added: "Alas! poor Omar!"

Oh! how I felt relieved on hearing that death was to be Omar's portion, not mine. My heart dilated, my lungs expanded, and my blood again began to flow. Ashamed of my silly apprehensions, I stretched myself, resumed my erect posture, and felt as if I rose the whole height of my head above the surrounding multitude, over which I now cast all round a complacent look.

"Who is this Omar?" said I to my neighbour; "whose fate seems to excite such interest?"

"The boast of his tribe, the flower of his family, and the pride of his parents," answered the man, wiping the tears from his face.

"And for these offences," resumed I, "doomed to inevitable death?"

"Tis too certain," replied my informer. "His liberality excited the envy of the ferocious Mooktar, who, only intent upon tempting Providence by the daily recension of his growing riches, never admitted mortal man to partake of his goods. Wroth that Omar, less wealthy, should yet be more respected, he added outrage to jealousy, every where insulted the object of his hate, and even lifted his lance against him; until at last Omar, in defence of his own life, took the life of his foe. Hereupon, lest Mooktar's powerful relations should sacrifice justice to pride, he absconded, and his antagonist's friends swore to revenge their slaughtered kinsman on whatever friend of the homicide – within the reach of their spears. From this sanguinary resolve they now in part desist. They agree to accept a ransom for the lives of Omar's kindred; but from their mercy Omar himself, of course, remains excluded. If found, he still must fall. Ibn-Aly, the strange schaich, himself related to Omar, came in hopes of the youth's inclusion in this compromise. He has just been representing in the strongest terms to our chief – to whom Mooktar owed vassalage – the intolerable provocations on one side, and the long patience, and at last, the unpremeditated retort on the other: but in vain! Even Abd-ool-Azeez cannot compel Mooktar's friends to renounce the price of blood, – the right they have on Omar's life. Behold them all ranged in a row behind our schaich, hissing like scotched snakes: see the looks of rage they dart on Omar's kinsmen, ranged on the opposite side behind their own chief Aly. Does it not seem as if each troop were only waiting for the signal to fall on the other like beasts of prey, mad with the thirst for blood?"

This account of my neighbour's was confirmed by the words which Abd-ool-Azeez now uttered. "Omar," said he, "has incurred capital punishment, and while he remains concealed the sentence cannot be mitigated. If he have any thing to allege in his defence, let him come forward; let him plead his own cause: let him submit, should he fail in proving his innocence, to the wrath his crime deserves. In fine, let him seek the grant of his forfeited life in the generosity of his adversaries, and not in the impotence of their resentment."

"I understand," replied with a bitter smile the strange schaich, "Omar is to be, by a false hope of pardon, drawn out of his concealment, in order that his enemies, spurning his defence, may at their leisure riot in his destruction."

Abd-ool-Azeez gave the stranger a daunting look, but coolly proceeded. "I doubt not," rejoined he, "that the kinsmen of the deceased would pledge themselves for the safety of the murderer, not only while the pleading lasted, but until he were again conducted beyond the pale of this district. What say they?" exclaimed he, looking all round, as if to invite the party concerned to confirm his supposition.

"We would, we would;" answered several voices from among the cluster of Mooktar's relations; and this was the first symptom, on their part, of a return to feelings less implacable. But what became the universal astonishment when, upon this, a young man of the most prepossessing appearance, after struggling to break away from among the followers of Ibn-Aly, at last was seen to spring forward into the open space left between the two schaichs as an arena for combat, and to offer to the astonished eyes of the beholders the actually present Omar! Submitting only to concealment in compliance with his friends' desires, this noble minded youth had impatiently brooked the crouching attitude of fear and disguise. He thought the circumstances of his case needed only be known to make his most inveterate antagonists own the guiltlessness of his conduct; and the confused and tumultuous assent of some of Mooktar's kinsmen to the proposal of the supreme schaich he had considered a challenge which his character no longer allowed him to disregard. But Omar wholly trusted to the dictates of justice; he had left out of his reckoning the suggestions of passion. When the brothers of the deceased, – those who most reluctantly had yielded even to the partial compromise in favour of the innocent friends of the guilty Omar, – saw darkening the ground on which they stood, and defying their anger within reach of their poniards, the youth himself whom they had so long and so fruitlessly sought, they could not contain their fury. Drawing the already sharpened dagger out of his bosom, the eldest of the party sprung forward like a tiger upon his unsuspecting prey, and plunged the shining blade into Omar's side, ere the attendants of the schaich had leisure to watch or presence of mind to arrest his heavy arm: – the blood spouted from the wound upon its very author!

At this sight the prince sprang up; and, rending his vestment: "Friends of Mooktar," he cried, "what have you done? Under my own eyes, in my very court, thus to break the faith just pledged, to perjure yourselves, to set me at nought, and to disgrace our whole tribe! O Arab, Arab! time, while it lasts, never can wipe out this foul stain!" – and he beat his naked breast.

"Our assent," answered deeply blushing the almost breathless offender, "only rested on the solemn assurance that none of the murderer's friends knew what spot on earth was defiled by his presence: you see, he mocked our wrath from the midst of their troop."

"And what of that?" resumed the schaich. "To me you had committed the task of procuring you justice; and all know whether I fulfilled my trust. Speak, foes of Omar, as well as his friends, if I showed any undue partiality. But you have infringed your promise; you have trodden upon your engagement; and if Omar dies, murder has only been repaid by equal murder. Your own blood will have to atone for the blood which you spilt."

These words were heard by Omar. Weak as he was, and expecting his wound to prove mortal, yet could he not brook to rest the fairness of his own character merely on the foul deed of his adversaries. He insisted on making the defence which before had been granted him, and proving his entire innocence. The schaich gave the requisite permission; and in order that his almost extinct voice might be heard, immediately imposed on all the strictest silence.

Supported by two of his nearest relations Omar now advanced, and in words few and faint but most clear and impressive stated the manifold insults he had received, and the daily forbearance he had shown, until provocations baffling all human patience had extorted the chastisement, which even then had not been intended to end in Mooktar's death. Few were those among his hearers who, when he concluded his speech, pronounced him not in their hearts far more than merely acquitted: – worthy of applause, of reward, of every honour.

But among those was not the supreme schaich. Whether prompted by extreme love of justice, or by a latent bias toward his own tribe: "Omar," exclaimed he to the dismay of all, "you have chosen to rest your safety on the merits of your case, and have compelled me to sit in judgment on one I could have wished to save. I own you deserving of pity, but I cannot pronounce you entitled to pardon. That word may not pass my lips."

Then, turning to the kinsmen of Mooktar: "Friends of the slain," continued he, "I am going to deliver into your hands that which, though in part too hastily anticipated, yet in its whole is yours. I am going to give you full possession of your victim. If, not satisfied with having drawn blood for blood, you must have the full certainty of taking life for life, achieve your work of vengeance; plunge deeper your daggers onto the heart of Omar; and secure yourselves against any remaining possibility of his surviving his wound and boasting of his deed."

At these cruel words, Omar, exhausted with agitation and with loss of blood, fell senseless on the pavement; his friends uttered mournful groans, and the leader of his enemies, having whetted his knife on the steps of the palace, stooped to perform the last act of revenge, by plunging his poniard to the hilt in the heart of the already speechless youth: – when Abd-ool-Azeez, yet holding back his hand, in a louder voice continued.

"Having thus," said he, " performed my duty both as arbitrator and as judge, let me, however, add this one thing more, that the act I am forced to permit must perpetuate between two distinguished families the rancour just kindled, and doom their enmity only to end in the destruction of the tribes to which they belong. I therefore denounce, as ruler of these realms, as minister of the Most High, and as apostle of the only pure faith, on whoever shall draw down upon his country so heavy an evil as my eternal malediction. Cursed be the hand that shall advance to extinguish the embers of an already fleeting life; cursed the lip that shall from an already agonized enemy withhold a free and unqualified forgiveness!"

"Yes; cursed be that hand, and cursed be those lips!" now re-echoed in unison from all the beholders – save one, who himself, however, as if already struck by the anathema, and no longer daring to oppose the universal impulse, now with a ghastly look and quivering lip faintly uttered: "Take my pardon;" and, overwhelmed with disappointment and rage, fell back among his troop – and disappeared.

Shouts of joy now arose from every quarter. Of the dead Mooktar all further thoughts were dismissed, and the still breathing Omar alone continued the object of general solicitude. Abd-ool-Azeez assigned him a small abode near the palace; and thither the youth was carried on the shoulders of his friends, but with little hopes of saving his life. In honour of the reconciliation between the two families the supreme chief ordered a sumptuous feast. While the entertainment was preparing he presented me to his kinsman. "This stranger," said he, "is come to bend the knee with us to the Most High in the rightful worship. He abandons the luxuries of the Turks for the frugal life of Wahhabees, and brings the sciences taught in cities, that they may fructify in our camps." Then, turning to me: – "The Othomans" added he, "boast of once having conquered these regions. Their armies crossed them indeed – but as the arrow cleaves the air, without leaving a trace. The Wahhabees soon shall march through the land of the Turks: but they shall go as the plough goes through the ground – cutting up all it meets in its way, and leaving behind it an indelible track. In vain, to conceal his wrinkles, old Suleiman paints his careworn face: at the bare sound of our name the paleness of fear overcasts all his features, and proclaims the true feelings of his bosom through the lying crimson that glows on his cheek!"

The repast being ready, the various groups of guests sat down round the loaded platters, according to their rank. Mine, being that of a foreign ambassador, procured me the honour of a place near the schaichs. Scarce had I, according to the country fashion, thrust my fingers in the dish, when an Arab, so enveloped in his haïck that his figure was not more cognizable than his face, walked into the room, with great solemnity approached the place where I sat, put the hem of my garment to his lips, and his lips to my ear, and in a whisper interrupted by loud and frequent sobs invited me to leave my dinner, and to go where he should precede me. He most obstinately indeed refused to explain who he was, and for what purpose he desired my company, but there appeared something so earnest and impressive in his manner that I could not say nay; and though my neighbours pressed me to stay, and loudly inveighed against the unmannerly Arab who called a new comer away from the feast at its very beginning, I followed my mysterious herald, and bade him lead the way.

Contenting himself with thanking me for yielding to his entreaty by a silent but earnest pressure of the hand, he conducted me to a hovel at the bottom of a narrow lane. There, gently opening the door of a back room into which he preceded me on tip toes, he ushered me amongst a large assembly of persons of both sexes, so intent upon the object around which they were collected, that he was obliged to push them aside in order to show me where lay, on a species of litter, wan, pale, and seeming at the last gasp, the wounded Omar.

The party assembled round this poor youth were his parents and relations, who, when Ibn-Aly his cousin set out for Derayeh to negotiate his safety, had not been able to prevent him – impatient as he felt under the imputation of cowardice – from following, mixed among his kinsman's suite; and had, therefore, in their turn also followed, in order if possible to check his impetuosity, or at least to support his valour: – a circumstance which enabled them after the imprudence he committed immediately to come forward to his assistance, and to afford him all the care his situation required. Though his wound seemed not to have reached the vital parts, yet had Mooktar's dagger gone deep in his breast, and the fever and debility it had left rendered his state to all appearances so critical, that his friends felt the utmost apprehension for his life. Hearing that a stranger had arrived at Derayeh skilled in the knowledge of the West, they determined to request his advice; and it was the father –– the afflicted Beder himself – who came for me to the palace. The fear of marring the hilarity of the feast by his mournful looks had made him conceal his face, and the dread of incurring the reproaches of the host for taking away his guest, had induced him to keep closed his lips. Even now that, out of hearing of the mirthful board and arrived with me near the bed of sickness, he attempted to speak, he could only point in silence to his son, lying almost insensible on his couch, – and moved his lips in vain to request my assistance. No sound came, and the tears which mechanically trickled down his cheeks belied the look of composure forced upon his struggling features. As to his wife and daughters, they made not even an attempt to suppress their emotion. Casting away all Mussulman reserve, they convulsively grasped my hand, covered it with kisses, and bathed it in tears. "Cure, ah cure our loved Omar!" they cried with heart-rending moans; "for we know that it is in your power."

This supposition was rather appalling; and the first thing I did was to disclaim every pretension to infallibility.

After that protest, which, however seriously uttered, met with but little credence, I walked up to the patient, and, surrounded by an immoveable and breathless circle, endeavoured to ascertain Omar's condition. The chief medicine which on due investigation his case seemed to require, was bodily rest and mental composure.

"Sir," said I, therefore to the father, whose breath seemed suspended, while I spoke, but whose eyes devoured my words: "the character in which I come to this country is that of envoy of Schaich Mansoor, not of disciple of Ibn-Senna. What little skill in medicine I may possess was acquired as an object of curiosity, not as a means of profit. The gratuitousness of my assistance entitles me to stipulate beforehand for the most implicit obedience to all my prescriptions."

"Order us to wrest from Aly's tomb his plumed turban," hereupon cried the father. "Command us to crawl on our bare knees to the Kaaba," exclaimed the mother. "Bid us renounce all the honours of the married state," spoke, in faultering accents, the daughters.

"All these," I observed, "would be very difficult achievements; but of very little efficacy as a cure. A much easier proceeding might be of infinitely more advantage: namely, for the relations not to keep the patient in a constant fever by their alarms and their surmises; but to retire, to stay outside the room, and not to re-enter it, except with my permission."

This prescription, however, was in itself much too easily obeyed, to have a chance of being enforced without the utmost difficulty. Nothing but the absolute certainty of losing their son, with which they were threatened, could make the good people clear the chamber, and commit their dearest treasure to my sole unwatched care.

Left alone with my patient I in a careless way mixed up a draught, and with an air of important solemnity composed a charm; pledged myself only for the efficacy of the amulet, but took care to see the potion drunk off to the last drop. The confidence in the spell, the composing nature of the medicine, and the quiet of the room, procured the youth a refreshing sleep, and when he awoke he found his fever abated and his strength recruited. I now dressed his wound, gave him some liquid food, and, calling in his friends, showed them the improvement in his looks. But so loud were their exclamations of joy, and so boisterous the blessings they bestowed on my ancestors for three generations back, that I soon turned them all out again. My part of Cerberus was unremittingly supported, until long intervals of tranquillity and visits of an instant only had removed all danger. When, owing to his good constitution, the youth became visibly convalescent, I stepped modestly forward to receive the thanks due to nature for preserving the hopes of a powerful house; – and these were not withheld. Had I saved Omar only through dint of the most consummate skill and the most unwearied toil, the expressions of gratitude could not have been more ardent or more sincere.

CHAPTER VIII.

Abd-ool-Azeez had provided me at Derayeh with a lodging such as became a guest of my distinction. In fair weather it let in no rain, and in foul it stopped not the water from running out, My meals, which came ready dressed from the schaich's own kitchen, had at least one great merit; that of affording little excitement to intemperance. Now and then there arrived in single state, before or after my dinner, a plate of sweet-meats or a bowl of hoshab, as a more pointed mark of attention – on which occasions I failed not to be in all the requisite ecstasies. The strictness of the Wahhabee tenets forbade my being entertained with bands of singers and dancers; but one might have fancied that I was expected myself to perform for the amusement of the curious from the number that attended my levee every morning, ere I went out to pay my own court to the prince, or to visit my patient. With the schaich I used to talk of Suleiman, of his force, his policy, the intrigues of those who usurped his authority, and the cabals of those who coveted his succession. With Omar I used to handle a topic to me still more interesting: my own dear self. I related to him every extraordinary object I had seen, and every strange adventure I had experienced.

No one could help loving the young Bedoween. Combining gentleness with spirit, and modesty with noble pride, his mind displayed in the midst of the desert the cultivation of the college and the graces of a court. While lying on his bed of sickness, he would make me hour after hour continue my narrations, though they often drew a deep sigh from his bosom; and when my breath was exhausted, he would in his turn take up the discourse, and relate the history of his tribe and the vicissitudes of his family. What he loved most to expatiate upon was the purity of his blood and the virtues of his parents: his eyes glistened on telling me how his father – abhorring the frequent divorces in vogue among the Arabs, and the sacrifice they made of lasting affections to transient enjoyments, had never had any wife but his mother; and how he himself proposed to follow his sire's good example. So exalted were his sentiments and so pleasing his conversation, that, when I shut my eyes, I sometimes could fancy I heard my friend Spiridion. Externals only differed; their hearts wore the same hue. Indeed, what all the sublime moral precepts of the young Greek, urged expressly for my benefit, could not affect the simple expression of noble sentiments which dropped unintentionally from the artless Arab in great measure brought about: they operated a real and important change in my own disposition, – for my heart was now, softened by sorrow, and steadied by experience; and poets say that the clay must be moistened by the dews from heaven, ere it can imbibe the fragrance of the neighbouring rose.

What wonder, then, that the constant interchange between us, of varied information on my part, and of valuable principle on that of my patient, should by degrees have cemented between us a sincere and tender friendship. It acquired such intensity that, after the period had been fixed for Omar's return to El-Gaddeh, the place of his residence, he found means to linger at Derayeh some time longer on the score of debility, in order to put off the evil day of our separation; and when he no longer could urge any new excuse for staying, he made it his last solemn request, on taking leave of the great schaich, that I might be permitted to accompany him home, and to stay under his roof. This favour the prince was prevailed upon, after some demur, to grant: but only for a limited period, and on the express condition that I should hold myself in readiness to return to Derayeh the moment I was summoned.

At El-Gaddeh, and in Beder's abode, I need not say that I felt more at ease than I had done at Derayeh, fed from the prince's own kitchen My kind hosts treated me to every diversion which the country afforded. Sometimes we went out hunting, at others we witnessed sports of agility and strength; and on the days we passed at home, Omar used to collect all the poets and story tellers of the country to pay me compliments more graceful than merited. According to their accounts of these veracious gentlemen, I might trace my descent at my pleasure either from the Genii or the Peris; and as to my achievements, – the thousands which Antar slew every morning before breakfast, without a hair on his head being hurt, were child's play in comparison. Omar's relations and friends behaved to me as if all these fictions were fact: his father seemed to rejoice in our growing attachment, and Ibn-Aly himself, the head of the family as well as of the tribe, paid me every most flattering attention. Strange to tell, but true – the place where in the course of my chequered life I experienced most of that glowing kindness which springs from the heart, was that where I sat down the greatest stranger, and which, in point of geographical situation, lay furthest removed from the land of my birth.

I yet only reckoned the length of my stay at El-Gaddeh by single days, when one evening, returning with Omar from a camp pitched on the skirts of the desert, the youth suddenly stopped to contemplate the setting sun. After some time watching its decline with a pensive air; "Selim," said he, pointing to that part of the horizon where its broad disk was rapidly gliding behind the earthly globe, "your heart, I fear, still lingers there. Do what we may, some day we shall see you take up your staff, and bend back your steps to the regions of the West."

"Omar," answered I, "*there* certainly arose the first affections of my youth; In those regions were knit the strongest ties that bind my soul! It seems as if alone my autumn could enjoy its second spring." – And though this speech might seem only framed for the occasion, and intended to enhance the merit of my stay, it had begun to be the language of truth. When I thought of my no longer existing Euphrosyné, of my still – as I hoped – breathing Alexis, and of my ever faithful friend Spiridion, tears of tenderness started in my eye, and the longing to return to the soil which had been blessed by their shadow, really made my heart swell with ill suppressed emotion.

"Ah!" rejoined Omar, "why cannot we offer you, among us, ties strong as those that draw you away! I wished my Selim to marry one of my sisters, in order that our blood might be mixed; that you might strike root in our soil. O that my parents, who do dote upon the preserver of their son, would for once sacrifice the pride of their race to the promptings of their gratitude and the dictates of love!"

"Sir," replied I, somewhat nettled, "supposing you parents wished for the alliance, know you that I can accept it? I told you before that I once was married: I told you that

I had had for my wife the daughter of a Bey of Egypt: I since have sworn never to plight my vows again. Inform your parents of this engagement, in order that they may be troubled on my account neither with scruples or with fears. To free them from all restraint, and to rid them of all uneasiness, I soon shall return to Derayeh. Indeed I am to blame – in my situation – thus to stay away from the great schaich, to whom my employers sent me."

"Forgive the unintentional offence," resumed Omar, covering his eye with his hand. "I could mean no reflection on your birth. The genuine Arab thinks the purity of his pedigree sullied even by mixture with the Tartar blood of the Sultans, – who probably would with equal care shun the taint of the Arab race. These are man's follies in every quarter of the globe!"

An effort now was made to turn the conversation to other topics; but with little success. Constrained, it soon languished, and finally died away. Omar, so far from appearing relieved by the indifference I expressed to the prejudices of his friends, would rather have seen me anxious to overcome their objections. He regretted my lukewarm desire for a permanent connection with his house; and from the day of this excursion a despondency came over him, which, having its source in the mind, baffled every power of medicine.

Finding I could afford my friend little solace by my stay, and was wasting my time at El-Gaddeh, I seriously prepared to make good my words, and return to Derayeh. The hour was already fixed for my departure, when Ibn-Aly sent to speak with me.

"Selim," said he, as soon as we were alone, "you have now associated with us long enough to know our customs and our disposition. See whether you could like for ever to turn away from the West, and sit down among our tribes, so you were made a sharer in all their prerogatives, – so you were given a wife from that house in which you already have gained so many friends. I must not conceal from you that my kinsmen have brought their minds to this proposal only after a considerable struggle. Rarely we marry out of our district, more rarely still out of our country: but such is the love we bear Omar, and such the fear which his languor inspires us with of losing him, that for his sake we not only permit, we ardently desire the union, which may fix you for ever in the land of the Wahhabees. Nor need you fear that objections, wholly unconnected with your person, when once removed, will leave a root from which to spring up afresh. Once adopted as the son of my friends, you may to the end of your days rely on their support and affection."

Had an alliance with the children of Wahhab never been proposed to me, I should probably have regarded it as a thing from which my mind must, in its present state, have utterly recoiled. I had originally sought the Wahhabees only in order to fly from Suleiman, and I had since only prolonged my stay with them because I could nowhere else expect so hospitable a reception; but though resigned to live for a while in Arabia, it was not among Arabs I wished to die. Unfortunately, after people so proud as these lords of the desert had overcome their own overweening scruples, it became expedient for me to conquer my more reasonable reluctance, and to accept the connection, or to quit the abode of those by whom it was tendered. I could not tarry where I had refused what was offered with so great an effort, and was considered as so signal an honour. I therefore resolved upon the sacrifice of my feelings to my situation: but, still apprehensive of diminishing my importance by too ready an acceptance of an offer unwillingly made, I appeared yet a while to hang back, and again alleged my vow, as I had done before to Omar. *That* circumstance, however, was not admitted to have any weight but what my inclination gave it. No oath, taken during my state of darkness, could remain binding after my eyes were opened to the true light; and on Ibn-Aly assuring me very solemnly that the Wahhabee was only held to perform what the Wahhabee had promised, I yielded at last to so powerful an argument. The sanction of the grand schaich, however, was deemed necessary, before a marriage so greatly out of the common rule could be concluded: it was asked, and, after some little hesitation, obtained.

Among sisters all equally straight, of whose faces I had scarce had a glimpse of during their brother's danger at Derayeh, and whose voices I had seldom heard since their return to El-Gaddeh, I harboured no preference, and therefore submitted implicitly to the choice of my friends: it fell upon the eldest of the brood, who still remained unmarried; – a maiden no longer reckoned quite in her prime, as she had attained the mature age of fifteen. The reason of her continuing so unusual a time a barren plant in so prolific a soil, was not, however, the want either of inclination to take a husband, or of charms to attract one. It arose from the untimely death of two young men both of distinguished rank, to whom she had been successively betrothed. The one fell in battle, the other was cut off by a fever; and perhaps the idea of some fatality attached to her name had since kept off other suitors. I felt no superstition on that score, and was as well pleased with the fair one allotted me as I would have been with any other female of the family. No sooner had the union obtained Abd-ool-Azeez's consent, than, for fear I suppose lest the new suitor should again slip through the noose, the wedding day was fixed at a very early period.

All my remaining cash was employed in fitting out my future spouse with necklaces and bracelets, ear, nose, wrist, finger, ankle, and toe rings, – which, though a Wahhabee, I found that, as a woman, my bride could endure. The presents which in my turn I received from her parents and friends were of a more useful description: a fine horse completely equipped with mace, lance, and carbine; a commodious goat skin tent, with its apartment to the right and left; a Persian carpet; a handsome sofa case, and a variety of household articles. My friend Omar, anxious to see me in every respect on a par with the proudest of his house, supplied whatever others might omit. I except pipes and chaplets: Wahhabees neither smoke nor count their beads.

The very last items of the *ménage* of which I was permitted to make an inventory, were, as usual, the charms of my bride. When, however, after running from tent to tent – as is deemed absolutely indispensable among decorous females – in order to escape me, she at last suffered herself to be caught by her more nimble companions, and brought by force to her expectant bridegroom, I could not help thinking that others, more worth pursuing, had come more readily; and found nothing to drive from my mind the deep sunk image of my Euphrosyné. The circumstance was rather a relief to my feelings than a disappointment to my taste. Had Aïsché been so superlatively handsome as to fan into a fresh blaze the embers of my heart, I should have felt as if committing an infidelity to the memory of her whom I could now only honour by unavailing regrets. Not that the sister of Omar must positively be called plain. The sun indeed might have found little to spoil in her complexion, had it been allowed freely to shine upon her person: but with teeth as white as ivory and eyes and hair as black as jet, she had a countenance which, like Omar's, beamed with sweetness, and the Arabs all declared that her limbs resembled the branches of the date tree waving in the wind; which only meant, that she moved very gracefully. Her features, besides, were regular, and the least touch of those cosmetics, so plentifully used by our artful Chiotes, would have enabled her in a civilized country to pass for a positive beauty, or at least for a very captivating brunette, – had she not most perversely destroyed her chance for ever, by having every prominent part of her face, neck, and arms, indelibly sprigged over in marks of gunpowder, after the most approved pattern.

Her mind, like her person, resembled that of her brother. With every amiable quality, it retained all that diffidence of its own worth, which those are the oftenest unencumbered with who ought to feel it the most. It was fraught with every amiable quality; in its overflowings of love and of confidence, I learnt what even Omar had carefully kept from my knowledge; namely that, while employed at Derayeh in curing the wound of the brother, I had unconsciously transfixed with Cupid's dart the tender hearts of the sister. Her secret passion had, perhaps, contributed as much as the professed friendship of Omar to determine the parents in favour of the union. The solicitude of these worthy people in behalf of their children remained not unrewarded: – the son and the daughter, each obtaining what they so long had wished for, each seemed to acquire new health and new spirits.

But if the bud, which had pined for want of the refreshing dews from heaven, now revived, it revived only to become the sport of storms and whirlwinds: for where warm affections are considered as the homage due, cold esteem soon is construed into the crime of aversion, – and that crime tarried not to be laid to my charge. At first, indeed, Aïsché sought the cause only in herself. "Alas!" cried she, "how should a poor Bedoween girl be able to fix those affections on which have been lavished all the fascinations of the women of the cities! Nature has not given me their charms, nor education their art. I have only my poor simple love with which to retain love; and they say that the more of its ardours are bestowed, the fewer are obtained in return." But by degrees my restless spouse began to render my own imaginary fickleness responsible for her disappointments. In a country where the heart resembles a volcano whose eruptions never cease, the fires of my bosom could not be supposed so entirely to slumber, and superior attractions abroad were regarded as the cause of my insufficient warmth at home.

No protestation I made could remove this idea: no behaviour natural or assumed could quiet these tenderly cherished fears. My actions, my gestures, my very look, – ever watched, ever weighed, and ever found wanting – were ever considered as confirming my treason. The most opposite conduct incurred the same sinister interpretations. Aïsché was always ready to believe without proofs what she dreaded without reason. Her ingenuity had no employment but to establish my imaginary crimes, and to build upon them her real unhappiness. Did her unfounded jealousies complete the depression of my spirits "she saw how matters stood: her person, no longer possessed the smallest power to please; her love could not afford me the least solace; her very company was become to me a burthen!" Did, on the contrary, in spite of her unceasing anxiety, a momentary glimpse of cheerfulness unfurrow my brow, "she wondered at the sudden change, she tried to find out what success abroad could extend its influence to my very home!" The most insidious scrutiny was my constant welcome; and after succeeding to perplex me completely by questions, the answers to which, however differently framed, ever led to the same predetermined conclusions, Aïsché was always sure to found upon the very embarrassment which caused by her unjust surmises their undeniable confirmation – until at last I no longer knew how to act or to look, ever had in her presence had an air of constraint, concealed from her my most innocent actions as if disgraceful or culpable, and, thanks to her own unremitting labour, with a clear conscience always wore a face of guilt.

The brother, with whom I spent every hour of my absence from the sister, at last succeeded by his representations to remove in a certain degree my consort's suspicions of my unimpeachable fidelity. Who would not have thought every point of repose and of comfort carried by this change? Not at all! Tender minds must have their grievances: – they are to them food and raiment. It was a worse symptom that nothing could attach me: it showed a total disgust of the country; it increased the danger of losing me altogether. From only fearing I might withdraw from her arms, Aïsché now began to tremble lest some day I should entirely abandon her home, her country, and her friends. The moment she saw me at all thoughtful, she was sure I meditated nothing less than to make my escape, and to return to the land of my fathers. It was useless to deny the charge: the stronger the protestations I made, the closer Aïsché seemed to cling to her chimera. "Speak not; utter not a syllable, give me no assurance," she would cry in her agitation; "I know you Osmanlees abhor truth. If you pledge not your word, if you waste not your faith in empty vows, you may perhaps continue to love me, to stay with me, to press me to your bosom a little while longer; but if you make a promise, if you take an oath, I am undone at once. The promise only made to be broken, the oath only taken for the sake of perjury, will goad you on the faster to my destruction; and you will have no rest till I am become a deserted, forsaken, widowed wretch!" And hereupon she would sometimes clasp her hands round my neck, imploring that before I abandoned her I would plunge my dagger to her heart, lest she should survive my loss. At other times she would throw herself on the ground, and with loud wailings tear her hair and beat her breast, as if my desertion had already come to pass.

Earlier in life I should only have felt the impatience produced by these unfounded apprehensions. I now also considered the principle when they arose, and forgave the effect in view of the cause. By degrees gratitude for that cause even grew into sincere affection; and, could I for a moment have forgotten Euphrosyné, it might have ended in a return of still more ardent feelings; but love – such as woman delights in – was no longer to be felt by Anastasius for the living!

Stern war itself had lost in my eyes much of its wonted charms; and very fortunately, as matters stood. Somewhat more singed than usual by its ardour in returning their last addresses, the Wahhabees, though not sufficiently scorched to stay quietly at home, yet felt not disposed this season to seek its chances at an inconvenient distance. While some of the yet unsubdued kabiles of Montefih and Beni-Haled were making nearer approaches than they had done of late years to the domain of Abd-ool-Azeez, that portion of the Schaich's own subjects, whose chief residence was in towns and villages, shewed greater dilatoriness than in preceding seasons to lead their flocks into the desert for pasture. It was even doubted awhile whether Ibn-Sehood, Abd-ool-Azeez's eldest son, to whom his father had for some years past on account of his great age intrusted the conduct of his warlike expeditions, would go into camp at all; and there seemed at one moment no chance whatever of my beholding the stopping of the least caravan, or the plundering of the smallest sanctuary, in honour of God; when all at once the whole nation, men, women, and children, sallied forth from their stationary habitations, to pitch their tents in the wilderness.

Each tribe had its separate camp, at the distance of a league or two from its nearest neighbours. In each camp the tent of the chief occupied the most elevated and central spot; round him the members of his own family formed the innermost circle; and round these again his remoter vassals and subjects ranged themselves in circles still concentric but of wider circumstance whose relative distance marked their respective ranks and possessions.

Ibn-Sehood's encampment of course was the most considerable. To that as to head quarters was sent from all the smaller and remoter camps, constant intelligence of every interesting occurrence in their immediate vicinity. *There* also the Schaichs of the minor divisions met, to hold council with the commander on the general plan of the campaign, and to receive their several instructions respecting its conduct. Ibn-Sehood's camp was the capital for actions, as Derayeh was that for repose.

The assemblage of tents among which stood my own, professedly bore a warlike form and had a warlike destination; yet it must be owned that slight were the shades of difference between the Bedoween's most martial array, and their most peaceful establishment. Even in times of profoundest peace the Arab of the desert lives in camps, constantly moving from place to place, and ready alike for attack and for defence; and during the periods of the briskest warfare the combatants still only advance and retreat surrounded by their families, and as solicitous to feed their flocks as to fight their enemies. On ordinary occasions each subordinate schaich at the head of his immediate subjects, halts, moves on, attacks or flies as his individual fancy or judgment prompts him; dreams not of acting in concert with his brother schaichs; and evinces no sort of attention to the movements of the chief ruler. It is only when the commander of the whole nation purposes some definite expedition or coup-de-main of great importance and short duration, that all the lesser schaichs and their vassals close in round his standard. Nor do they even consider themselves as engaged to assist him longer than suits their own convenience. As soon as they become tired of the service, or find the plunder short of their expectations, – without asking leave of the commander, or waiting the end of the campaign – they quietly secede, and return to their own peculiar district. The voice of fanaticism, the interests of religion may at times excite to the most daring and perilous enterprises; but they fail to enforce a patient and persevering discipline; and nothing do the Wahhab tribes so much resemble in their mode of warfare as those swarms of devouring locusts, offspring of the same country, who often when least expected invade a district, according as the wind sets one way or another fall on this field or on that, and when all is devoured, again rise, fly elsewhere, and nowhere leave the marks of a permanent possession.

Some of the Wahhab divisions more to the westward had, very soon after encamping, the happiness to be engaged in skirmishes with the children of Beni-Haled. Our camp was left in a state of inactivity somewhat longer. Once or twice, indeed, we received intelligence from our scouts of hostile detachments hovering at a distance. Ibn-Aly immediately gave the signal for the alert, and sallied forth with all that were able to bear arms; but the first time we could not even, spite of all our diligence, get sight of the retreating enemy. In our second rally, indeed, we descried him, and in such superior force, that we had our tents taken down and our harems packed up in baskets, in order to be ready for retreat if necessary; but on this occasion as on the former the foe at our approach fell back and disappeared in the desert, without giving us any other trouble than that of again unpacking our families, and unfolding our tents. My regrets were not outrageous. The age was past of my disinterested passion for blows; and I saw a chance of little else, where Arab met Arab.

Nothing thus materially accelerating or retarding the swiftness of our march, except the greater or less abundance of provender for our horses and pasture for our sheep, we advanced till within three or four conacks[1] of El-hassa. Unfortunately the facility of our progress had lulled us into a fatal security. Every evening the whole camp used at an early hour to yield to the sweets of repose, trusting almost entirely for safety to the vigilance of the watch dogs that guarded its approaches. One night a most tremendous barking of our four-footed sentinels spread on a sudden a general alarm. Those among us already sunk in the arms of sleep started up, and those still watchful ran to their weapons. Busy with some preparations for the next day's march, I had continued up, and already had incurred reproaches for my restlessness, when this appalling concert drove away for the moment all thoughts save of combat. I took a hasty farewell of Aïsché, ran to untie my horse's legs,[2] vaulted into my saddle, and rode in the direction whence the noise proceeded. The whole camp was already stirring. Every one issued forth in the greatest confusion from his tent to inquire of the other what had happened; but this no one could tell. Presently a distant clash of lances gave to our apprehensions a more definite form and a greater intensity. A hostile detachment, which the whole day before was perceived to keep us in sight, had contrived, under favour of the night, to approach us in such complete silence as to leave every one of our vedettes on two legs unaware of its proximity, until our more watchful four-footed outposts raised their warning howl. Not knowing the number of our assailants, darkness with its magnifying powers reported it to be so great that retreat was judged the only means of escaping discomfiture. Even this, however, could not be effected except under cover of a partial resistance; and as soon as Ibn-Aly had collected a sufficient number of men, he went out in quest of the enemy. I joined him on his way, as did my friend Omar. Never was disorder equal to that which our camp now presented. The group of watch dogs first alarmed, had, by their howlings, gradually set barking all the remainder in the most opposite quarters; whence, with the certainty of being attacked on some point, we knew not in the least where to direct our defence, ran like blind people to the sound, and left the guidance of our motions entirely to chance. Sometimes thinking ourselves in contact with the enemy when farthest from the point of his attack, and at others fancying our assailants a mile off when in the midst of their troop, our offensive and our defensive operations were equally ill timed: half the night we fought with empty space, and the other half pursued our own comrades. The watch dogs themselves, bewildered by the engagement, and no longer distinguishing in the fray between friends and foes, fell on both alike, and not only by their incessant yells so increased the horrors of the fight, but by their savage fury so augmented the bloodshed, that we were obliged to kill several of our old guardians, now unwittingly become our destroyers. As, however, every instant brought from the interior of the camp fresh supplies to the scene of action, we contrived to make a stout defence, without sensibly losing ground.

Meantime the portion of the tribe not engaged in its protection, was no less busily employed in its removal. Some were taking down the tents, others putting up the utensils and baggage, others again loading the beasts of burthen – while here and there a party stole out, and, unseen by the hostile troop, drove the cattle into the part of the desert most out of reach of danger. Thus, in less than two hours, the whole camp was broken up, and on the move. The combatants on our side hereupon began to slacken their exertions, and to keep up a more retreating skirmish. This was the easier as the enemy himself, finding an unlooked for resistance, seemed more anxious to secure the booty made, than to incur fresh blows in trying to make further prizes, and testified a great desire to slink quietly away, ere the dawn should discover his weakness, and to increase our strength by reinforcements from the neighbouring camp. Thus, while we fell back in one direction, our assailants did the same in the other; and several times we were greatly tempted to wheel about, and to attempt the recovery of our captured equipages: but the fear of a surprise overcame this desire. Continuing our retrograde movement unslackened while darkness lasted, we compassed a distance of near six leagues from the place of combat before the incipient dawn threw any light upon our condition. The first rays of the sun shewed the whole plain, as far as the eye could reach, covered with camels and other beasts of burthen, pacing singly or in small groups, loaded with tents, luggage, women and children, and intermixed with droves of oxen and flocks of sheep, who were every moment endeavouring to stop and to graze, unconscious of danger. The horsemen, who thus far had kept together in tolerably close order, now fell asunder like a bundle of sticks untied, and eagerly set off, each for some different point of the compass; so that presently nothing was seen in every direction but warriors crossing each other at full speed like shooting stars: each seeking, among the widely dispersed apparatus of the camp, his own family, furniture, and equipages.

For my part, I soon had the satisfaction of descrying my Aïsché, exalted in the midst of her retinue on a dromedary as tall as a house, towering above all her surrounding women, and, bating the uneasiness she had felt on my account, in perfect health as well as safety. On seeing me, after much anxious search, suddenly reappear before her eyes alive and unhurt, her joy was indescribable: she gave a scream of delight; and at the same moment her whole suite welcomed me with shouts of pleasure.

It is dreadful at all times to lose what we love; but far more dreadful is the shock, when, after a period of intense alarm, the loss takes place just as all danger seems to be gone by, and nothing apparently remains but to exult in a renewed term of safety and bliss; – when the fresh blow of sorrow is struck just as the heart begins anew to dilate with all the fullest exuberance of frantic joy; and above all, when that blow arises, not from the evil dreaded, but precisely from its being overcome.

Such was my fate. Forgetting her exalted situation or unable to check her impatience, Aïsché tried, unassisted, to meet my embrace. In the hurry of the break up, her camel had been loosely girt. The sudden pressure made the pillion turn; she fell to the ground, received a hurt which her conditions rendered mortal, and in a few hours expired in my arms.

Assuredly at no time had my love for the living Aïsché equalled the passion kindled in my breast for Euphrosyné, conceived since I lost her. But without being a headlong passion, my regard for my Bedoween wife was a sincere attachment. It rested on esteem and on gratitude, on endearing recollections and on fond and flattering hopes; and I had begun to feel the value even of a love, for which I could only make a less ardent return. All was dashed to the ground in an instant, – and long I dwelt on the first of my sorrows inflicted by Providence alone, and free from all mixture of self reproach.

CHAPTER IX.

The first anguish of my feelings had scarcely begun to subside, when the schaichs of the different Wahhab tribes received a summons to meet Ibn-Sehood with their followers near a particular well in the desert, whence they were to start on a distant expedition. The name of the enemy, or the point of attack, we were, according to the custom of the Wahhab commanders, only to learn on setting out from the place of rendezvous. Ample room was left, mean while, for conjecture, and every instant new surmises arose, and were abandoned for others of still later birth. Some expected a coup-de-main on Mekkah, others an attempt upon Imam-Aly. From all quarters the schaichs of every rank hastened with their vassals to the spot where the secret was to be disclosed, some on dromedaries swifter than the wind, others, on steeds not less fleet; one half armed with pistols and match-locks, the other accoutred only with sabres and lances; and none encumbered with more provision than two skins could hold – the one filled with flour, and the other with water. When collected, we might muster about fifteen thousand men; though our enemies, deceived by the rapidity of our motions, and the distant points on which we often appeared almost at the same instant, gave us credit for far superior numbers. No army could be better appointed than ours both for offensive and defensive warfare, or could combine more active courage with more passive hardihood. Every where the wariest caution accompanied the most undaunted fanaticism, and whatever the supreme schaich of the nation might command for the advancement of the faith, his followers expressed themselves determined to achieve, or to die. In short, we seemed to hold in our hands the fate of the Turkish empire.

But here let me for a moment interrupt my narration: warned by aches which had only relented for a while to return with double fury, let me enquire for what purpose my memoirs were begun, and in what guise I must pursue them to insure its attainment. The interruption will not be long, and the story proceed the more rapidly afterwards.

Unprincipled as my conduct must have appeared throughout, I might perhaps propitiate my reader, by representing this unqualified disclosure of its errors as a sort of voluntary penance, intended to atone for my manifold offences. That I regret them is most true; that I wish I could wipe them away – were it with tears of blood – I conceal not: but far from Anastasius even the show of believing, that where bitter tears and better deeds have not purified the sinner in the fullness of life, an idle disclosure of his errors, only extorted by fear on the brink of eternity, could still intercept his downfall, and closing in his face the yawning furnaces of hell, waft him triumphantly to the portals of heaven; – and as to the very design of daring the opinion of the world, of defying its vengeance, and of masking my misdeeds a subject of contemptuous boasting, – on the eve of escaping from all human pursuit in the protecting arms of death, – fast approaching that cell where the shafts of man's resentment no longer can hurt my insensible remains, – it would too soon for my credit be recognized as the vain vaunting only of secure cowardice.

Anastasius has not, in thrusting his foolish life upon the world, been actuated by motive either so distant as the first, or so daring as the second.

In a strange country, uncheered by a single voice not wholly new to my years, and on a bed of sickness, – only to be exchanged for the cold pillow of death, but retaining in a body worn out by suffering a mind still reckless, still struggling with its fetters, – how can I beguile the heavily creeping hours, how obtain a moment's forgetfulness of my prostration, how divert my thoughts from the future which no longer can be mine, but by directing all the remaining strength of my faculties to the contemplation of that past of which I had my share. Thus only, though the sun of my days is set to rise no more, and though the voice of my friends can reach me no longer, – though the gay are far off, and the good are gone by, – may I still, in the twilight which precedes my last sleep, conjure up round my couch both the dead and the distant, and in my silence and solitude converse with the world.

This indeed must, throughout every page of these memoirs, have been recognized as the only aim of their writer; for every where my views have been directed to my external condition rather than to my internal emotions. Every where I have sought the amusement of describing scenes beheld, rather than the occupation of analysing sentiments experienced; every where I have exhibited myself rather as an unconcerned spectator in the world's motley drama, than as an actor very deeply concerned in the plot; every where I have tried to force myself to gaiety, even with a heart filled with anguish. Intent only on finding for each new passing day its fresh chapter, I have strung together characters as I met them, and incidents as they revolved before my too aching eyes; and lest my employment should fail me ere I became reckless of my occupation, I have sought rather to spin out my materials in a good long prosing journal, than to compose them in a round and compact tale.

And in this way I would have gone on to the end of my narration, had not during its course a new object sprung up, a new interest arisen, a new wish invaded my unresisting mind.

And so it has happened: for that passion which, once admitted into the human breast, never again quits its hold; that passion which, when the more volatile desires of youth and vigour yield to age and infirmity, only founds on their ruins its more exclusive empire; that passion which enables the decaying elder to survive its own existence by living on the past and the future, when the present eludes his feeble grasp; that passion which, daunted by nothing but obscurity and silence, represents the oblivion of the world as the direst of calamities, and prefers the fellest persecution to peaceful insignificance; that passion, by men called vanity, but the best gift of the gods, could not see me thus carefully collecting the materials of my life, without prompting me to combine them into a monument fitted to last after my death, and to inform after-ages that I too, like millions of others, had strutted my short hour on the stage of this globe: and, lest a circumstance so momentous to the world should be left unrecorded or should only be partially told, I now feel a wish to bring to its regular conclusion, what before I had not had time to finish; I now should regret being torn away from my narrative, before I had carried it down to that decisive day, which saw me placed in a situation no longer liable to changes worth recording: – for, though I too well know that in my present situation I can only have for my readers those strangers of the West, who from their distant corner of the globe watch the inhabitants of its more genial zones, as children do a worm, to wonder at its motions, and to thank God that they are formed of other mould, yet even a small niche in their remembrance seems so much preferable to entire oblivion, that, lest I might not otherwise have appeared to possess monstrosities sufficient to find favour in their eyes, I have, perhaps, even exaggerated my infirmities and kept back my better qualities, as of no value except to the owner.

Every succeeding hour, however, now begins to warn me in a more audible voice, that, unless my pen makes greater speed, my illness – gaining ground too fast upon it – must defeat this new object, and bring my life to a conclusion ere my tale is achieved. To be able still to attain the goal, I must henceforth loiter less on the road; I must make shorter halts in those insulated spots, neither connected with what precedes nor with what follows; and, since my sojourn among the Wahhabees proved to be of that description, except in as far as, by breaking through my old habits and suggesting new thoughts, it enables me to return to civilised regions with a mind more matured, and feelings greatly chastened, I shall dispatch the account of its remainder as concisely as possible.

Suffice it, therefore, to say with regard to the great schemes mediated by the Wahhabees, that, whatever might be their purport, I beheld not their execution. Suleïman's crafty kehaya, informed of my stay among these sectaries, and aware of the advantage they might derive from my counsels, hastened to effect the greatest injury his enmity could do me – that of making me appear his friend. So ingeniously was the bearer of a letter from the miscreant, fraught with whatever might give my conduct the appearance of treachery towards my employers, made to fall into their hands, that Abd-ool-Azeez could not refrain from summoning me before him to vindicate my innocence, or to suffer for my crime. My punishment was to consist in utter expulsion from the tribe whose countenance I had forfeited. Former hospitality forbade severer penalties.

Had my Aïsché – permitted to preserve her innocent existence – promised to cheer with tender care the evening of my restless life, even simple banishment might have seemed an infliction sufficiently severe. Reconciled by habit to the manners of the Wahhabees, I could gladly have ended my days where, only seeking refuge from an enemy, I had most unexpectedly found friends, a family and a home. One object had indeed by degrees so strongly entwined itself with all my future schemes, as to have become an indispensable condition of my felicity in whatever abode I might choose; and this was my darling child, my Alexis: but him I had purposed soon to send for; and then – forgetting and forgotten in the land of my birth, – I might, without repining, resign my breath among strangers, and leave my worthless bones to whiten in the desert.

But far differently now stood the case. Aïsché was no more, and I again become the lone mortal whom a single Arab stopped on his first entering the desert. Since the loss of that which had endeared to me its sands, the secret wish to press the hallowed ground which bore my Alexis had revived with such intensity, that other schemes lost their relish in my eyes. To return to the only being in this world whom I could call my own, to bestow upon him that paternal care which he thus far had never known, to cherish him in my long estranged bosom, and to render him the sole and permanent solace of my remaining days, was henceforth the only happiness after which I thirsted; and, under the influence of this all-subduing feeling, I almost hailed Achmet's fraud as a fortunate event, – as a circumstance which, by causing me to be banished from the desert for hostile intentions harboured against the Wahhabees long ere I had experienced their kindness, might spare me the pain of appearing, in contempt of all gratitude, to leave them from choice, after all their best gifts had again brightened my existence.

When, therefore, the charge of treachery was preferred against me, when the kehaya's letter was read, and when my expected defence kept every breath suspended, every eye intently gazing and every neck on the stretch, – I only answered the accusation with sullen and haughty silence: but, if that very strangeness of my behaviour made Abd-ool-Azeez doubt my guilt, and Omar loudly assert my innocence-it left the one without power to absolve, and the other without means of detaining me. They suffered the wayward stranger to depart from among them, and I disdainfully went on my way: taking with me only – a few endearing recollections excepted – the little I had brought. My course, lying westward, I bent my steps at once towards the setting sun, and…

[*In this place the manuscript leaves us to regret the loss a few pages, which have been either cancelled by the author himself, or torn out by strange hands after his death. The interruption, however, seems to be of little consequence; the text, where it recommences, shews Anastasius moving on a new but not very distant stage, and describing only a different Arab tribe from that among which, – as he himself says –he found, and again lost, a friend, a wife, and a home.*]

It is – he resumes – the most numerous and powerful of those which reside in the interior of the Hedjas. Its principle schaich can singly bring into the field an army of upwards of three thousand horse, well armed and well equipped: nearly twenty inferior schaichs acknowledge him as their supreme lord; and the great schaich of the tribe of Anahssé, who resides in Keïbar in the Nedjd, never fails, in any expedition worthy of their joint powers, to assist him with a numerous division of his choicest troops.

By means of this union of strength, the Arabs of the Harb find themselves enabled to mock the Sultan, whenever he still tries to revive his obsolete claims to the sovereignty of that province; and for the permission to lead the pilgrims through its trackless sands on their journey to Mekkah, they exact from his representative the Pasha of Damascus a yearly fine, which this visier fails not in his turn to charge to the account of the Porte.

Djezzar, who in the year 1794 still reigned at Damascus as well as at Acre, persuaded himself that a double escort would carry him across the Hedjas more usefully and more agreeably than the payment of this impost; and when the schaichs of the desert presented themselves on his passage to claim the customary toll, they only received an insulting refusal. Unprepared for compulsory measures, they were for the moment obliged to abide the indignity, but early the next season the schaichs of the Harb and of Anahssé quitted their abodes of Keïbar and of Khaff, to watch in their camps the opportunity for joint and just revenge.

The annual march of the Hadj is so regular, the different stations where it halts are so exactly determined, the day and hour of its passing through every district on its route vary so little, that whatever Bedoween may have any suits to settle with any of its divisions, need only consult their own convenience as to the time and place. They may stop the caravan according to their pleasure either in its coming or its return, and of the far stretching string of pilgrims they may select for their respondents just whatever part they think most likely to afford them both easy and ample satisfaction.

On this present occasion the caravan was suffered in its outward march to reach Mekkah unmolested, in order that, on its return, a presumptuous security might render it an easier prey. The vicinity of Khedieh, a town situated two days' journey from Medineh, was fixed upon as the spot most favourable for the mediated surprise; and as the pilgrims always make a three days halt at Medineh, in order to pay their devotions at the Prophet's tomb, the day on which they were to arrive in that city was that of our departure from our different stations, to meet near the walls of Khedieh.

The Emir's own division was the foremost to arrive at the place of rendezvous. It took post behind a small hill, whose summit afforded every convenience for watching the approaching Hadj, and whose reverse was equally well adopted for concealing our own force. Emissaries were immediately dispatched to reconnoitre, and to report at what distance the pilgrims might still be.

Meantime the Emir went about giving his last instructions to his troops. "Remember!" said he; "we only wish to obtain our dues from an unjust vizier; not to injure a set of unoffending hadjees. Therefore, attack property – but spare lives. Direct your chief efforts where you see the most merchandise, and the fewest soldiers. Useless shedding of blood should be avoided. If we kill the Osmanlees, who will hereafter want our camels?"

This excellent advice seemed for once fated to be thrown away. The scouts sent out had advanced but a very little way before they returned utterly dismayed, and already from a distance making signs of bad news. As soon as within hearing: "All is lost," they cried. "The miscreant Djezzar, pushing on from Medineh the very day of his arrival, is already gone. Perhaps from some eminence the rear of his force may still appear in sight!"

At these provoking words, the Emir immediately galloped off at full speed to a commanding height, about half a mile off, to ascertain whether he had indeed been twice deceived by the wily Bosniaque. Most of us followed. Arrived within a few yards of the summit we dismounted, and, crouching down, advanced among the bushes.

In an instant all conjecture was at an end. Along the furthermost outskirts of the boundless plain still remained clearly discernible the long dark line of close wedged pilgrims, winding their weary way through the white sands, like a black and slender millipede whose anterior extremity already has entered some crevice, while the thousand legs of the body and tail still move in sight. Ere, however, the other still wanting detachments had joined our force, it would have been foolhardiness to pursue the enemy, and after we were all collected, it would be too late to overtake his flying troops. So adieu all our brilliant hopes! A bird's eye view of the fleeting caravan was the reward of our mighty preparations.

At this sight a deep gloom overspread the Emir's countenance. He struck his spear with fury into the ground, convulsively grasped the long braid of black hair which hung over his shoulders, and, after musing awhile, – his eyes all the time fiercely rolling in his head – "Let us return," he cried, "to our homes: and after having sounded the trump of war through the desert, hush, if we can, the irksome echo!"

Down the hill he now again rushed, and after him all his followers, heaping every variety of malediction upon that vile Djezzar, who, against all rule and precedent, had hurried on where no Pasha had ever hurried on before, – and that, too, for no purpose but to give us the slip.

Just as we got to the bottom of the hill, came scrambling up to meet us the last of our scouts. We cared so little for a fresh confirmation of our disappointment, that ere the man had time to unclose his lips we desired him not take the trouble of delivering his message, and this the more, as he seemed to carry a face of joy which we thought exceedingly ill timed, and for which the Emir gave him a sharp and proper rebuke. Long therefore did he struggle, and many fruitless attempts did he make, before he could convey to our understandings that he really brought good news; – and this was its purport.

The Pasha of Damascus, goaded by his evil conscience, had indeed escaped our vengeful clutches; but the Bey of Egypt still remained at Medineh, and was to escort back part of the way, in addition to his Cairo caravan, a great portion of that of Syria, which, wholly unprepared for Djezzar's diligence, had been left in the care of trusty El-Ashkar. The number of pilgrims would thus be nearly the same as before, and that of troops alone sensibly diminished: but this reduction, though it might leave the Emir fewer laurels to gather, he could contemplate with becoming philosophy. Out therefore he poured his whole weight of anxiety in one single long protracted sigh of relief and of joy; and scarce was it brought to a conclusion, when all the different divisions of our allies, still wanting, arrived in sight at once. We now spent the night in delightful expectations, and the next morning stationed ourselves in ambush behind a range of low hills, a few hundred yards from the track of the looked-for caravan.

According to immemorial custom, the Magarbis or men from the West – in other words the Barbaresques, – in going form the rear, and in returning the van of the Cairo Hadj. Loaded with arms, and light of baggage, they were deemed unworthy the honour of our notice. So far from attempting to stop these honest gentlemen, apt to deal in no weighty article save blows, we, on the contrary, wished Heaven might speed them on their way. Even the lofty Osman himself, who came next with his kehayas, his body guard, and his remaining troops, we permitted to pass unmolested; though I longed to break one more lance with some of my old Cairo cronies: but when the great fat merchants, who kept aloof even from their own escort, – as much feared by them as any

Arabs, – in their turn were seen to approach, panting with heat, and in a cluster formed for the very purpose that we might lay hands upon it and seize it at one grasp, the eyes of our men glistened with joy, and my fingers began to itch like those of a physician at sight of his fee. In the interval between the passing on of the worthless fry which preceded and the approach of these men of substance, we sprang forward, and posting ourselves in the middle of the way, cut off the rear completely from the body of the caravan, and called to our friends to stop and be rifled.

At the shouts of terror occasioned by this little compliment, it is said that the great Ashkar himself disdained not to turn round his head, in order to inquire the cause: of which being duly informed, he valiantly clapped his stirrups to his horse, and set off at full speed; – all his veterans gallantly followed the example of their chief.

Thus abandoned by their defenders, the pilgrims only sought to save their persons, and left their property to its fate. In less than five minutes the whole field of battle was strewed with camels, horses, and mules, laden with every sort of goods. We had nothing to do but to gather the manna showered around by Providence. Every man seized upon what was nearest to him, and when two or three happened to pull at the same parcel, they drew their sabres and divided the bundle.

Where predatory expeditions like the present were considered as praiseworthy, not only in the leaders of tribes but in their humblest followers; where each successful robbery only conferred fresh distinction on it authors; where every wayfaring man resigned himself before hand to the chance of being despoiled, and the sufferer regretted his loss without blaming his assailant, I carried not my scruples of honesty so far as alone to deny myself a share in the common privilege: but it was my folly on this occasion to be fastidious in its exercise. I would not strip a poor pedlar or a hadjee in humble trim. All the ordinary pickings I haughtily passed by, and abandoned with a look of contempt to the greedier Arabs. Indeed I did worse. To my eternal shame be it spoken, I assisted two or three wretches in making their escape, after helping them to lift up their bundles. At the same time I felt no very insurmountable objection to some single rich equipage falling in my way, rather than in that of a parcel of vagabonds who would not know its value or feel obliged to its owner. Unfortunately I proceeded on so far in my desultory ramble, – disdaining every unimportant gift of fortune which I met, – that at last I met nothing more, got clean out of the track of the plunder, and fell in with no further booty either great or small.

I now began to repent me of my squeamishness. Small prizes after all were better than blanks; and it happened not unfrequently that a pilgrim's tattered garments concealed a perfectly whole purse. This reflection would have urged me to retrace my steps backward, but that I was sure of no longer finding even what I had left untouched. While my time had been spent in idle promenading, there was little doubt that the field must have been gleaned by my more industrious companions unto the last ear.

Precisely, however, when I thought all chance of doing any good entirely gone by, fortune was pleased to reward my forbearance. In an interstice between two small hillocks which suddenly opened upon my view, appeared at the head of a string of camels heavily laden a well mounted merchant, only intent upon rejoining the hindmost troop of the Bey's soldiers, just diving into a hollow before him.

I cried to the diligent hadjee to stop, and to deliver up his property, – and thus addressed he thought fit to look round; but seeing me quite alone, he only answered: "I was welcome to whatever I could take," – and spurred on his horse the faster. He judged rightly enough, that unsupported as I was, I could scarce be deemed a match for six or eight sturdy and well armed fellows, who, while he spoke, sprung forth from behind his towering camels, and, grinning from ear to ear at their master's ready wit, showed me with their white teeth the black muzzles of their guns. This sight somewhat cooled the ardour of my pursuit: from a full gallop I fell into a canter, and from that into a trot, until at last I pulled up entirely, and, puzzled how to act, stood awhile stock still, not liking to advance, and not less averse to retiring empty-handed.

Fortunately at that moment came up from the eastward a troop of ten or twelve Arabs, belonging to a tribe usually buried in the deepest sands of the desert. These gentlemen had not originally participated in our plan of attacking the Hadj, but hearing of the scheme by accident, had advanced beyond their usual beat, on the mere chance of what they might pick up. Most readily they consented – on seeing my dilemma – to lend me their assistance; while the merchant's escort, perceiving this reinforcement, at once passed from a show of the utmost resolution to that of the most dastardly fear. In their confusion these brave guardians of the property committed to their care, fired from behind their four footed battery one single volley, – just to exasperate their pursuers, – and then scampered off with all their might, leaving me in undisturbed possession of the goods and chattels which their master had before most formally made over to me, in the presence of reputable witnesses.

Luckily I had to divide the richest prize of the caravan with the most ignorant Arabs of the desert. My associates in this excellent affair only valued goods according to their bulk and weight. The refuse articles, the outside envelopes – coarse cottons, clumsy shaloons, stuffs like packing cloth, and trinkets like horse trappings, – were what they chiefly coveted. The shawls fine as cobwebs, the muslins thin as gossamer, the silks like summer clouds, they held in utter contempt. A bag of pearls from the Ormus bank, of the size of full-grown filberts, they tasted; but finding them hard and insipid, they flung the good-for-nothing vetches away, and left them for me to cram into my girdle. In like manner, when,-searching about for the pearls which had dropped out, – I picked up a little casket which lay by itself on the ground, and seemed to have been lost only from a special anxiety to save it, my tasteful friends, who saw nothing in the oriental rubies and diamonds – none in the truth much larger than myrtleberries –of which it was brimful, but a parcel of glass beads fit only for children, let me keep them in exchange for a huge bale of calicoes. In consequence of these two lucky hits, I became so generous in the division of the remainder of the spoil, that, grave as the party seemed by nature, they could not help smiling at my folly; and I have no doubt that some facetiousness on the subject would have come out in the due time, but for the fear which haunted my companions of being observed, treated by the Emir's followers as interlopers, and made to give an account of their capture. This rather serious consideration now rendered them anxious to be gone, and with good wishes to me and significant glances at each other, they sped away.

I myself was not sorry to find a secluded nook, safe from intrusion, in which to take the first inventory of my new riches. When I opened them out, and viewed in its full blaze the treasure I possessed, I fell upon my knees, and devoutly thanked Providence for having made the merchant to whom I owed it a wag, and for inspiring him with a witticism which, without being particularly good in itself, was nevertheless a most happy one for his despoiler whom it enabled to keep the property acquired, with a safe conscience. This act of devout gratitude performed, I neatly inserted my baubles between the folds of my belt and the pleats of my turban, and thus safe from the danger of exciting envy, went back to our party, trailing after me – with great apparent exertion – an enormous bundle of very ordinary goods, fully resigned to the raillery which I met with from the Arabs for bringing home, among such much valuable plunder so contemptible a capture.

My present opulence would alone have sufficed to renew my yearnings after more polished regions, had I felt none before. Undoubtedly poverty was easiest to be borne among the poor: but with a pocket full of pearls and diamonds, who could live upon dry locusts? Especially when possessing in the West, as I did, a little treasure far more precious than diamonds and pearls, which the gems I had gained would enable me to adorn like the little jewel of my heart. The longing to return to Smyrna, already powerfully felt among the Wahhabees, now increased in Nadder's camp to such a degree that the soil of the desert seemed to burn under my feet. An impression began to haunt me that, unless I quitted it immediately, some insurmountable obstacle would inevitably keep me spell-bound for the remainder of my life.

My companions, however, were not people to intrust with these feelings. They dealt not much in sentimentality, but had a notion of keeping in the desert things earned in the desert. With a proper respect for this prejudice I equipped myself as if only going to visit a neighbouring camp, and set out at a slow pace, in a careless and indolent manner: but, like a school boy who designs to play truant I by degrees quickened my step, got into an easy trot, from that into a canter, and finally, – as soon as I had turned the last corner from which I thought I could be watched, – clapped my stirrups to my horse, and darted through the plain.

I had scarce performed three leagues, when a little way before me appeared a personage whose accoutrement belonged not to the desert, and who in fact proved to be a hadjee separated from his companions by the discomfiture of the morning. I spurred on to join the stranger, as he did with all his might and main to avoid me. At last, finding his pursuer gain ground fast upon him, he looked back, and without stopping or taking the least aim, fired at me both his pistols. Neither of them fortunately bore within thirty yards of the mark: but I took the will for the deed, and ran at the uncourteous pilgrim with my spear couched. He escaped the shock by his alacrity in ducking. Not choosing to waste my powder or to alarm the desert, I hereupon drew my dagger. My hadjee now assumed a most piteous and supplicating posture. "Crush not," he cried, "the insect that crawls in the dust. It was fright alone made me fire. I never show the least symptom of bravery except when terrified out of my senses!" – The defence made me laugh.

"Take your life;" said I, "but give up your money."

"Alas!" replied the hadjee, "what money would you have me possess? – I who am contracted for; and visit the holy places as proxy only for a rich man, who takes care not to pay me, until he receives at my own hands the vouchers for my performance of the pilgrimage!" The excuse was ingenious; but my friend proved to have a purse of gold notwithstanding, and I doubted a while whether I should not take the money which, by his own account, he did not want, and the pistols which he knew not how to use: but the ample fortune which I had just acquired enabled me to distain the paltry prize. So I wished the *insect* well through the deep sands – and resumed my former pace.

Unwilling to travel close on the heels of the caravan which I had helped to lighten of its burthen, I determined to lean rather more to the left, and to steer towards Acre, in preference to Damascus. Long, therefore, was the journey, and many were the perils, and much was I beholden to the swiftness of my horse, even though I only travelled in the night-time. Sometimes I had a guide; but mostly the stars alone directed my course. Equally tired of listening to the one and looking at the other, I built innumerable castles in the air, and formed endless schemes for my future conduct; but, first and foremost, – laugh not, reader – was that of becoming inflexibly honest!

When arrived within half a days journey of Acre, I considered in what shape I might best meet the gaze of cities. Constant alarms and fatigues had so altered my appearance that it was impossible to know me. My eyes were sunk in their sockets, and my bones starting through the skin. By contriving on the road to run my lance through my foot I had produced a wound, and this wound was become so envenomed an ulcer, that it made a halt an indispensable condition to the cure. At the same time, in the residence of Djezzar, whose displeasure I had once before incurred by cropping a friar's beard, and had now deserved afresh by curtailing a pilgrim's equipage, some disguise seemed advisable. The character of a Bedoween agreeing ill with my long features and unguttural accent, I determined upon the less difficult part of a Turkish Santon.[1] Its sacred garb would enable me at once to avoid the inconveniences of poverty, and the suspicion of wealth. The transformation was speedily effected. I pushed on again, and soon reached Acre, – just two years from the day on which I left Bagdad.

The first face I met in the city appeared short of its nose; – I had witnessed that deficiency elsewhere. The next was minus an eye; – that, too, is sometimes seen in other countries: – but the third had no ears, the fourth no lips; and there seemed to be walking about as many people possessed of one hand only as of two. At last, meeting a man whom I was not afraid to question on this local singularity, in as much as – by some singular piece of good luck apparently – he still retained the possession of his full set of limbs and features, I civilly accosted him, expressed my joy at seeing his eyes, ears, nose, mouth, &c. all complete; and finally begged to ask how it had happened that this occurrence was so rare at Acre?

"You are a stranger, it seems" answered the man, "and have not yet been taught, the mark of our master: it is by these peculiarities our shepherd knows his flock. Every sinner here receives it; – but, remember, some saints are not exempted."

I thanked my informer for this friendly caution, and little enamoured of Djezzar's ugly mark, gave, in the abode which I reluctantly sought, as little éclat to my sanctity as possible. Unambitious of extending my fame, I only made the few pious grimaces, and performed the few miraculous cures, which I could not possibly avoid in support of my character. My healing powers, however, – like those of most sainted personages, – proved very little convertible to my own use. Amidst all the bedevilled whom I exorcised, and all the epileptics whom I *unfitted*, my own wound healed very slowly. In the meant time my host – a man of some intelligence – gave me a short history of Djezzar, which I shall insert here, as only to get rid, during a few pages, of that eternal *I* which haunts all the rest of my narrative.

CHAPTER X.

Bosnia brought forth the monster, since most appropriately surnamed el-Djezzar or the Butcher. Born a Christian, and bred a carpenter, young Dimitri first signalized himself by slaying his brother with his axe. This feat compelled him to fly from his country: but as gratitude is the characteristic of noble minds, and as one of the implements of Dimitri's trade had been the instrument of his fratricide, he in after times remembered the instrument which had opened his way to greatness, and to his other titles added that of Aboo-balta, or father of the axe. The place in which he first sought refuge, was that sink of every vice and asylum of every miscreant, the capital. On the road he had subsisted by begging, on his arrival he sold himself as a slave. His flaxen hair and fair complexion suited the Cairo market. Aly-bey became his purchaser. Converted to Islamism, and called by the name of Achmet, our hero soon distinguished himself by his proficiency in magic[1]; – and under the guidance of Egypt's ambitious ruler, this art remained not in Achmet's hands an idle pursuit: it afforded him the means of conjuring away with more adroitness such as had either disobliged, or had obliged the Bey too much. Many heavy debts of gratitude were thus cancelled in a way which left the conferrers no possibility of complaining. For these services Aly-bey first created Achmet a kiachef, and next, governor of the Bahaïré. It was in this province that one single year's exploits were sufficient to acquire for him the title of Djezzar: but his patron, conceiving some suspicions of his fidelity, ended not the less that year by destining for the Butcher himself that reward which, through his means, he had conferred on so many others. Informed of his danger, Achmet now a second time fled for his life. He found an hospitable reception at the court of Osman, Pasha of Damascus. This Visier was waging war at the time against the Arab Daher, by inheritance prince of the small territory of Saphad, and, by conquest, ruler of the larger district of Acre – dismembered from the pashalik of Seïde. He sent Djezzar against the successful enemy at the head of a troop of his own countrymen – of Bosniaques: but spite of their valour and achievements, the Butcher could not prevent Daher from at last rendering Seïde itself an appendage to Acre, as Acre had formerly been to Seïde.

A singular race, inserted between the sea on one side and Mount Lebanon on the other, it owes allegiance to the government of Seïde. Its name is Deroozi, its capital Dair-el-Khammar or the city of the Moon, and its religion a remnant of the theology of the ancient Magi. In their schools the initiated, as I am told, were taught that all things sensible and intellectual emanated from a single first essence; that the souls of particular individuals – brute or human – were only so many different lesser portions detached from this primal essence through an act of its own volition; that, deprived on their first separation of their former consciousness, these lesser divisions of the great Whole were only awakened to different degrees of partial knowledge, through means of the different species of bodily envelopes which it pleased the supreme Essence, their parent, successively to weave around them; that the apparent removal and transmigration of these distinct souls only arose from the formation and decay of the various bodies by which they were in turns occupied; and finally that, as all things sensible and intellectual first from a single primary Essence, so all things emanated were ultimately again, after a vast circle of vicissitudes and developments – each rising in perfection beyond every former one – to be reabsorbed into that primary Essence, and made partakers of its unbounded knowledge, and power, and glory. It must however be owned, that, if the knowing ones among the other sects prevailing in Syria, pretend to trace in the belief of the Deroozi the wrecks of this high and ancient doctrine, the vulgar herd of the Mohammedans and Christians of that province, loth to burthen their intellects with such subtleties, cut the matter short by asserting the creed of the Deroozi to be the exact reverse of that of every other nation, and averring that whatever others abominate these pagans hold in reverence, and whatever others regard as sacred they treat as execrable; – and strange to tell, the Deroozi themselves, who might be expected to know best of any the truth, and to possess, though no one else did, the secret of their own doctrine, live in utter and contented ignorance on the subject. Among this singular nation not only religious practices, but religious creed, – not only rites, worship, offerings, fasts and prayers, but doctrine and faith – remain exclusively confined to a peculiar cast, named Akkhals or Sanctified; in whose society none can be admitted that have not previously given up all worldly concerns, and completely renounced the interest, the occupations, and the converse of the seculars. It is these who exclusively take upon themselves the faith, and hold themselves responsible for the salvation of the whole community; and while they are so jealous of their knowledge that they suffer no secular even of own their nation to be initiated in their dogmas, they are so intolerant in their dogmas themselves, that they admit no individual of any other race to the salvation exclusively reserved for their own nation. In vain would a stranger wish to subscribe to their doctrine, or desire to be received into their community. The gates of eternal bliss remain not the less shut against him for ever. He might during the whole of his life profess the religion of the Deroozi with unremitting zeal: still must he at his death, like the infidel he was born, be forbidden their higher heaven; and only go to whatever less enviable place is reserved for the remainder of his unenlightened race.

As to the seculars, called by the priests Djahels or simples, they are all, from the prince down to the peasant, held alike exempt from the performance of religious practices, and from the profession of religious tenets. The Emir or sovereign of the nation is not more than the meanest of his subjects, admitted by the Akkhals to the mysteries of their belief or to the secrets of their worship; but, having no rites or doctrine of their own, the Deroozi laymen are the more ready to adopt in respect to externals, those of whatever more powerful nation it is their policy to court; – whence their town and villages are filled with mosques, which the inhabitants never enter except when visited by a Turk.

Among the Deroozi as among the Arabs, every subject is a citizen, and every lay-citizen a soldier. Military exercises are reckoned by this warlike nation the highest of pleasures, and contempt of death the first of virtues. Each district of their country obeys the commands, or rather enjoys the protection, of an hereditary Schaich, who with the utmost simplicity of manners usually combines the loftiest pride of birth, and while he excludes no one from his table, deems very few worthy of his alliance. Among these families that of Schebab enjoys the privilege of supplying the general ruler of the nation, who, chosen by his brother chiefs, takes the title of Emir and resides at Dair-el-Khammar. His authority is limited, and on every affair of consequence he consults the other chiefs.

To the north of the land of the Deroozi lies the country of the Mawarnee or Maronites, called Kesrowan, and divided, like the former, into lesser districts governed by hereditary schaichs. This province pays allegiance to the Emir of the Deroozi, who holds it of the Pasha of Trabloos, as he does his own district of the Pasha of Seïde. The character and mode of living of the Maronites only differ from those of the Deroozi in a very few particulars, such as must naturally arise from the Christian religion they profess, and the communication they have with the sea, through the port of Bayroot. The inhabitants of the Kesrowan display greater industry, and possess more skill in business than their neighbours the Deroozi; and thence the Deroozi Schaichs generally chose Maronites as stewards to their estates, and preceptors to their children: the difference of creed forming a less weighty objection, where the tutor is only called upon to abstain from inculcating in his pupil any religious belief whatsoever.

Emir Melhem, one of their rulers of whom the Deroozi speak with the most veneration, was among the few men who wish to leave an interval between the pride of sovereignty and the nothingness of the grave. He abdicated his worldly power, left the society of the djahels, and among the Akkhals commenced preparing his soul for its higher flight, about four years previous to its release from its earthly shackles. His brother Mansoor was, by the schaichs of Dair-el-Khammar, named regent of the Deroozi until his son Youssoof should come of age; but Youssoof saw himself, through the interest of Sad-el-Koori his guardian, – a Maronite of the noble family of the Awâkri, – immediately recognized as ruler of the Kesrowan. Of this honour the young Prince appeared fully worthy. In the course of a single campaign he conquered and re-annexed to his province the district of Djebaīl, long dismembered from it by a horde of Scheyee Moslemen, called Mootaweelis, living on the reverse of Mount Lebanon in the fertile plain of Baalbeït.

Military renown thus adding its support to his hereditary rights, Youssoof early claimed the sovereignty of the Deroozi, with such means of enforcing his pretensions as Mansoor, his uncle, thought it prudent not to disregard. Clothing necessity in the garb of virtue, this chief professed only to have held the supreme authority in trust for his nephew, and in 1770 solemnly placed on Youssoof's finger the seal of the reigning sovereign.

This event took place while Daher, prince of Acre, was pursuing his conquests in Syria. Not satisfied with taking Seïde, he at last laid siege to Bayroot, the seaport of the Kesrowan, to which Djezzar had retreated before him. The Butcher succeeded in driving back the Arab, but instead of restoring Bayroot to Youssoof its rightful prince, for whom he had undertaken to defend the place, he now declared he only held it in trust for the Sultan; and with Youssoof's treasures, deposited in it for safety, bought the investiture for himself. When, soon after, Hassan Capitan-Pasha drove Daher out of Acre and Seïde, he was prevailed upon to confer the whole of these Pashaliks on Djezzar, in recompense for his loyalty.

Following the example of his Arab predecessor, Djezzar made Acre his residence in preference to Seïde. The place was capable of an easier defence, both on the sea and the land side. Nor did he only give it strength: he also added beauty. The splendid relics of Tyre and Caesarea were employed to adorn its new erections; and soon arose within Acre's turreted walls, a palace, a mosque, a bazaar, and a bath, whose architecture, achieved as if by magic, seemed worthy of the Devas.

But joy was banished from these gorgeous edifices. Djezzar's rapacity suffered it to enter neither the hovels of the little nor the conacks of the great. By converting every source of wealth into an article of monopoly, he kept his subjects poor, while he measured out his taxes as if he suffered them to grow rich, and, when his cupidity by its excess defeated its own purpose, it was in acts of refined cruelty that he sought his consolation. Every rising sun saw the torture applied; every day that passed was marked by fresh executions. The tyrant's glittering galleries re-echoed only with moans, his polished pavements were moistened with tears, and his marble terraces seemed adorned with chrystal rills, only in order that their pure waters might wash away the streams of blood with which they daily were crimsoned. The wailings of the tortured mixed themselves with the murmur of the fountains; and from behind the porphyry and jasper panels of Djezzar's wide extending porticoes, were heard the groans of wretches, expiring immured within their unrelenting walls.

According to the immemorial custom of all Eastern despots, their treasure and their wives are kept in the same enclosure, under the same ponderous bolts. The sacredness of the gynecoeum is rendered subservient to the security of the hazné. In Djezzar's intended palace and citadel, however, a greater excess of distrust had chosen a still more mysterious spot for Plutus's sanctuary: the most internal recesses of the Butcher's harem only formed the outermost entrance of the receptacle where lay concealed his gold. Strength without and secrecy within guarded this holy of holies. High ramparts, deep fosses, and bulwarks bristling with cannon surrounded the sacred cells, and dark subterraneous passages only led to them by the most intricate windings. Of these Djezzar alone possessed both the design and the key: – never had their hapless artificers been permitted to return to the day light which they quitted to build them; and their knowledge and their bodies still reposed within their fatal works. While none of the officers of the palace durst follow Djezzar into his harem, none of the tenants of the harem itself were suffered to cast after him the slightest look of enquiry, when, like a threatening meteor he rushed by his women, darted through their numerous chambers, and vanished at last in the mysterious labyrinth that led to his treasure.

Djezzar was a barbarous husband as well as a merciless master. His Mamlukes, therefore, succeeded in opening a correspondence with his wives, for the purpose of procuring his death and dividing his spoil. No one knows what foe to humanity betrayed the well concerted plot: all saw too soon that Djezzar knew his danger. Infuriate he rushed into his harem, and for awhile stabbed indiscriminately all he met in his way.

But soon he regretted the too easy death vouchsafed to the first victims of his rage, and caused the remainder to envy, by the tortures he made them endure, the milder fate of their predecessors. His own hands – it is said – submitted to the rack those charms in which he had rioted by preference, and the greatness of the raptures he had tasted, became the measure of the pangs he inflicted.[2]

Even the seclusion and the thick walls of the women's chambers, could not stifle the cries of so many suffering wretches. The Mamlukes heard, and guessed their own impending fate. Immediately they rose, stormed the batteries which surrounded the sanctuary, and, mastering their crested summits, pointed its own cannon against the fortress, and against the relentless tyrant wading in blood within its precincts.

Unable to make his escape without falling into the hands of his enemies, Djezzar now plunged into the deepest recesses of his treasury. There he shut himself in with his hoards; and there, alone, and without the smallest chance of any other mortal following to assist or to defend him, – to bring him intelligence or take his orders, – he remained stretched on his heaps of gold, in expectation of every instant being discovered, and dragged out at once to light and to death.

An hour was thus spent, by the Mamlukes in incessant firing, and by Djezzar in indescribable anguish. That period elapsed, the fire of the assailants began to slacken and to leave longer pauses, until by degrees the report of musketry entirely ceased, and even the roar of cannon only was heard at distant periods. At last all din of arms subsided in a dead and awful silence. Djezzar no longer doubted that the harem was forced, and the Mamlukes only employed in seeking the hidden entrance of his last retreat. Every instant their approaching footsteps seemed to vibrate nearer on his ear; – and thus he spent another hour is still greater agony than the first.

The continued tranquillity however now began to cast upon his mind a gleam of hope. With watchful ear and cautious tread he crept forth: – but first only a few paces beyond the inmost vault; – by degrees a little further into the winding galleries; – and at last unto the very verge of the forbidden precincts. There, having again listened awhile at the grated door, without being able to perceive any sound, he ventured to open the ponderous jaws of the iron gate, and finally, with breath suspended and faltering steps, he again issued forth into the realms of light.

Here, the various chambers of the harem were the first he re-entered: but in them he only beheld – still exposed to all the garish glare of day – the mangled carcases he had left. All was silent; and, but for the pale corpses lying about, all was solitary. No living being – neither foe nor domestic, – presented himself on the Butcher's way in these his will-stocked shambles, until, bursting forth from their enclosure,, he all at once beheld, marshalled in two long rows at its entrance and hailing him with loud acclamations, his faithful Bosniaques. This chosen band was the tyrant's bulwark against the just wrath of his remaining subjects. Having fallen on the Mamlukes and forced them to retire, its chiefs were waiting for their master's appearance, to acquaint him with his safety, and the flight of the rebels: – the greatest part of these ill-fated men were afterwards slain in a pitched battle near Seïde.

Meanwhile Osman, pasha of Damascus, had died, and Mehemed, Osman's eldest son and successor, had been poisoned by Derwish, his younger brother Djezzar, – possessed of more troops and more money than Derwish, – now bullied the Sultan and bribed the ministers into giving him the investiture of that important government. Still, however, only considering Damascus as a precarious possession, and Acre as a sort of patrimony, the Butcher continued to make the place of his creation that of his habitual residence. His accession of power only enabled him to pursue more steadily his plan of weakening the Deroozi into gradual and complete subjection. The allegiance which the Emir owed him as Pasha of Seïde, he made a pretence for interfering in all the affairs of the country; and whatever Schaichs of Youssoof's family formed a cabal against their chief, were always sure of support from Djezzar. Long, however, did Youssoof, in spite of this insidious conduct, forbear from open hostilities against the lord to whom he owed allegiance; but at last he found the only means to avoid ruin was to embrace rebellion. He rose up in arms against Djezzar, gave him battle, was defeated, and with the remnant of his army fled into the fastness of the Kesrowan, which had always preserved unimpaired their loyalty to Melhem's son.

Djezzar offered the Prince a free pardon, on condition of suing for it at Acre. Youssoof left his two sons Sad-el-din and Selim under the care of his trusty Maronites, and with his old preceptor Sad-el-koori, who still continued his adviser, went to the Bucher's court. He was admitted, was caressed at first, was soon found fault with, was lured into a fresh semblance of mutiny, and with his faithful tutor was condemned to death. In vain the whole Kesrowan interceded for a beloved prince and for a respected countryman. Djezzar never forgave; and the prince and the tutor were led out to meet their doom.

It is reported that on their way to the place of execution, Youssoof, seeing all his fair prospects end in a gibbet, could not refrain from reproaching his aged counsellor with having made him the victim of his own ambitious views. "But for you," he exclaimed, "I might have died of old age!"

"Your father," answered the firmer Sad-el-koori, "charged me to make you live a sovereign. I may have erred in the means, but I too pay the penalty. I asked nothing from you when in power; I followed you when ruined; I accompany you in death. What more could I do?"

The Prince burst into tears; embraced, and begged his tutor's pardon. They were hung side by side from the part of Acre's wall which faces Mount Lebanon; – and Youssoof's last dying look fell on the blue mountains of his distant dominion.

During his persecution of Youssoof, Djezzar had annexed to the pashalik of Acre the district of Saphad by the assassination of Daher's sons, the valley of Baalbeït by the destruction of the Mootawelis, and the territories of Tabarieh and Caesarea by the expulsion of the Arabs of Sakr. One place alone, in the very heart of Djezzar's new acquisitions, – the poor and smallest district of Nabloos, – derided all his efforts. Aboo-Djerrar its Schaich – nestled aloft in his inexpugnable castle of Sannoor – preserved his independence amid his subdued neighbours; and it is said that his sturdy resistance gave Djezzar more pain than all his other successes could afford him pleasure.

Djezzar had, however, now attained that degree of power of independence, which induced the Porte to send him alternately avowed favours and concealed daggers. The former were all duly acknowledged, and, by some unlucky chance, the latter never reached their destination. Their bearers disappeared, and, as usual, were no more inquired after. At last a new device was struck out. According to one of those ancient customs held more sacred in Turkey than positive laws, the Pasha of Trabloos, who, on the pilgrims' return from Mekkah brings them at a fixed place a supply of fresh provisions, only enjoys the honours of the two horse-tails, in order that his lesser rank may not clash with the pre-eminence of the Emir-Hadj. The year 1794 beheld the first exception to this rule. Geretly Husseïn, ex-Capitan Pasha, and governor of Trabloos, went to meet the caravan, preceded by three tails. The circumstance looked suspicious. Djezzar saw in Geretly a personage qualified to step into his place. He determined to be before hand with his entertainer, and sent him a jar, properly sealed, of the holy water from the well Zemzem. Geretly drank – and died.

It was for the fifth time that Djezzar, in his quality of Pasha of Damascus, conducted the holy caravan to Mekkah, when, as related, he chose to defraud of their dues the children of Anahssé. I have already shewn how they resented the injury, and how the offending leader escaped the avenging blow, contrived to make it miss his guilty head, and let it fall upon the innocent hadjees, by gliding from under the hand already lifted to strike. Djezzar arrived safe and sound at Damascus about the time I reached Acre; but he made so short a stay in the place, that, ere any one yet thought him near, he entered his own sea-girt capital.

A bomb, bursting in the middle of its assembled population, could not have spread at Acre a greater dismay than did Djezzar's arrival. Immediately every eye became fixed, every tongue tied, and every limb motionless and paralyzed, as if by the force of a fascination. None durst speak, or look, or even listen: for the fate of all Djezzar's enemies, cut off one after the other, made the vulgar believe in the supernatural powers he affected; while the wise dreaded what supplied the place of magic, – spies who informed him of every thing, and agents who stopped at nothing.

For my own part, I no sooner heard in the evening that the Butcher had come in at one gate, than I prepared, a cripple as I still was, to take my departure the next morning at the other. But even this proved too great a delay. Just as I was slipping my last parcel of diamonds into my belt, in stepped a messenger of the Pasha, to summon me before his master. I ran for my santon's cloak. "Spare yourself that trouble!" said the fellow; "We know you well enough; wary eyes watched your proceedings when at Khedieh you murdered the wealthy Djiaffar, and plundered his rich equipage!"

The most heinous part of this accusation certainty laboured under the defect of falsehood. Still it came too near the truth to leave me any hopes of escaping through the difference between the fact and fiction; especially with Djezzar for my arbitrator. The point therefore was, not to constitute him judge of the matter. With this view: "Your name, pray?" said I to the messenger. – "What can it signify?" cried he in answer. "I ask it as a favour;" replied I. – "Well then: Mustapha Sakal;" surlily rejoined the messenger.

"Mustapha Sakal!" I now exclaimed; "You are the very man I have been seeking. Know that, before I approached the poor dear dying Djiaffer, – who never was killed in his life, – in order to afford him in his misfortune what assistance I could render, he said to me in an unintelligible voice: 'generous stranger, you look so honest that I must trust you with my last bequest. Seek, among the servants of the Emir-Hadj, for a youth of rare merit, named Mustapha, for whom I always entertained, unknown to himself, a particular regard; and give him in my name this valuable jewel.' I cannot doubt, O Mustapha Sakal! but you are the person. So take the gem. But as the Emir-Hadj is unreasonable enough to constitute himself universal legatee to all who die under his special protection, assist me to make my escape, lest in my dreams I should blab out your good luck."

The tchawoosh entered into the spirit of my tale, even beyond my intention. "It can only be," said he, taking the jewel without any ceremony "from the total failure of his memory, that the worthy Djiaffer asserted my ignorance of his regard for my person, since, besides the bauble you give me, he promised me at his demise a hundred sequins, which no doubt you will pay me with equal readiness." "Truly;" answered I – fearful there might be no end to the codicils – "he never mentioned the sequins; nor have I them to give."

The tchawoosh hereupon grew insolent. "Look in your belt," he cried, "and you will find them;" at the same time laying his broad fist upon me, and beginning to use violence. The question now seemed whether it might not be expedient to do by Mustapha, what I had *not* done by Djiaffer; and while debating the thing in my mind, I at all events grasped the dagger concealed under my saint's cloak, – when all at once a loud noise was heard at the door. It boded Mustapha as little good as myself. Fearing that a second messenger might come to supersede him in his office, he turned as pale as ashes, and with a haggard look and wild gesture: "Off," he cried; "off to the mountains this instant!" I waited not a second bidding. Rushing by some person in the passage whom I stopped not to look at, I was in a trice out of Acre, and in less than an hour out of sight of its loftiest towers; – having left my horse behind me as my hostage.

All the remainder of the day was spent in making the most of my way. Toward dusk I lay down among some bushes, slept a few hours, and, while yet the stars twinkled in the firmament, rose again, and performed several leagues, ere the sun opened to my right the purple gates of the morning. I made such speed that its setting saw me clear of Djezzar's dread dominions; for in recompense of his last frolic, the Porte had just taken from him the Pashalik of Damascus, toward which I was travelling.

The next day, two leagues only from its capital, while pacing pretty smartly and quite wrapt up in thought, I felt myself suddenly slapped on the back by an arm of lead. Djezzar and his myrmidons still haunted my imagination; and without looking round, I set off at full speed, until a cry of: "Comrade, whither scampering so fast?" made me stop and face the enemy. He was not the most terrific in the world; and only appeared in the shape of a derwish with his sugar loaf cap, who laughed at my panic most outrageously.

I laughed in my turn, and in this merry mood we approached. "As one of the godly like myself," cried the derwish," I was going to offer you hospitality in our convent at Damascus." I readily accepted an invitation which would prevent my being seen in public, and we proceeded on together.

Entering a small village on the road, my companion made a sudden stop. "Hark ye, comrade," said he; "a bright thought this minute strikes me. We are so near our journey's end, that without a little management, we must stumble upon home before we are aware of it. Let us therefore make the most of what little time remains ours; particularly as the sun is hot, and we have not, like the prophet, a canopy of angels to shelter us from its rays."

Upon this he lugged me, without waiting my answer, into the house of a Syriac Christian, where it seems he was well known. After saluting the party within, he boldly called for an okka of the best wine. I must have looked surprised, for he added, "It is to rub my limbs with, and bad stuff gives the cramp." The wine was brought, and set before us in a little back room safe from unwelcome intrusion.

As soon as seated; "I have little faith," observed our derwish, "in external applications: therefore, O my soul!" added he in an emphatic tone, "bend all your thoughts upon Heaven, lest you share in the defilement which, much against my will, I am going to inflict upon my body." And hereupon, carefully stroking up his whiskers, in order that they too should avoid partaking in the sin of his lips, he applied the vessel to his mouth, and most devoutly began his internal ablution. For some minutes he continued in this employment, with uplifted eyes and an appearance of entire abstraction; until I at last began to think that he and the jug would part no more. This, however, finally happened, but with a long protracted sigh; after which he handed the half empty vessel to me. The santon therefore easily finished what the derwish had begun; and setting down the jar, I took up my staff to march out.

This movement was still premature. Making the most of time had, with my derwish, a more extensive signification than I apprehended. "Not so fast," brother, said he, "This place affords other gifts of Providence besides the juice of the grape, which man should not in his presumption contemn;" and forthwith he went and whispered significantly to our host, who upon the hint stepped out.

Faithful to his rule of making the most of time, our derwish meanwhile fell mumbling his evening orisons, in order that matters of business might all be dispatched ere our landlord returned; but this diligence proved fruitless. The personage came back empty handed, throwing the fault on the vast demands of the last caravan of pilgrims. The holy satyr, therefore, had no further motive for delay, and we proceeded on our way.

I could not help expressing some wonder, as we went along, at his very open indulgence in prophane pleasures, marked as he was by his religious habit: but the observation seemed only to excite his raillery. "How you mistake my drift!" answered he, with a pious sigh. "If I mix with sinners, it is but to mend them; and how could this be done, if I were to scare them by a premature severity of manners?"

My companion's whole system of ethics seemed of a piece with this small specimen. "It is your half sinners only," he cried soon after, "who risk most to find the gates of Paradise shut against them. Carry the thing to its proper length, and the danger subsides: – you then are sure of salvation."

This doctrine sounding new in my ears, I begged an explanation. "Why," exclaimed he, "is it not acting against one's conscience, that alone constitutes what is wrong, and leads to damnation?" – I agreed.

"Then," replied he, "if you only sin on, until habit has silenced that officious monitor, and prevents your thinking any more about its qualms, is it not as clear as day light, that you revert to a state of perfect innocence?"

All I had to do was to regret that so incontrovertible a truth should be so little understood: only I took care – as my companion night possibly have attained that degree of perfection – to keep him in my eye during the remainder of the journey: nor was I sorry to arrive at the convent, where he introduced me in form to his brethren.

Whatever met my eyes in the monastery, seemed at first sight to breathe the very essence of holiness. None of the derwishes walked otherwise than with downcast eyes. Their domestics kept time in their work with pious ejaculations; and the very cats of the convent looked as if, like Mohammed's tabby, they were constantly meditating on the perfections of the Koran. A word whispered by my travelling companion in the ears of the superior, speedily produced an entire change of scene, and procured me ocular demonstration of what small boundaries divide saint and sinner. The minor gaieties of the evening ended in a grand burlesque on the pious ecstasies with which the order edified the public.

The sort of gravity which I could not help preserving among scenes of grossness no longer to my taste, was noticed, and appeared to give umbrage. One of the derwishes, taking me aside: "What ails you, brother?" said he, "I thought we had been sticks of the same bundle; but I know not what to make of you. As we let ourselves out, you draw in. Have we mistaken our man?"

I felt the danger of encouraging this idea. "By no means;" answered I, rousing myself to looks sprightly. "My foot just now pains me a little. But for that circumstance you would be astonished at my mirth;" and immediately I poured out a volley of bad jokes to prove my assertion. Still did I most joyfully hail the dawn, which saw me safe out of the tekkieh,[3] and again on the road. As I paced along, I smiled to think I should have lived to feel myself in danger from being too demure.

CHAPTER XI.

A little kafflé[1] of Mussulmen happened to be, like myself, bound for Hems. I joined it, and, in my quality of santon, acted as Imam[2] to the party. It was I who settled the whole business of the common worship, took the lead in the prayers of my companions, and chid those who appeared inattentive in their devotions.

The city of Hems tempted me to take a few days rest. Caravans from the most distant parts of the empire, by making that place their thoroughfare; give it an appearance of uncommon bustle. In the bazaar my santon's habit and practices collected round me such a crowd, that the Motsellim thought fit to inquire into my vocation. Little disposed to answer his questions, I pushed him aside, and darting forward, as if I saw something strange which no one else beheld, prostrated myself two or three times, and began to hold discourse with vacant space. It was evident to all present that I had visions; and the Motsellim began to be looked upon by the mob with an eye of wrath, for wishing to interrupt my converse with the world of spirits. He therefore prudently ceased to interpose his word, lest his voice should be silenced altogether, and slunk away, muttering a few curses on all the saints and santons that infested his district.

With the Motsellim had come the Moolah of the place. This latter looked significantly during the interrogatory, but abstained from speaking. I felt obliged to him for his discretion; and as soon as I was rid of the importunities of the governor, went and sat by the divine. "The fearful," said I to him, in a gracious manner, "build aloof on the inaccessible rock, but the secure mix with their brethren in the valley." My meaning was understood, and the Moolah, to show that he felt his place to be among the secure, began to let himself out. "How I envy you!" he exclaimed with a deep sigh.

I pointed to his costly fur, and to my ragged cloak. "No matter!" rejoined he, – "sackcloth is a bait for consideration full as much as silks: but by being offered to the mob only, has procured you what you sought."

This speech made me wish to raise my character in the Moolah's estimation. I gave him a few traits of my history, and he grew disposed in my favour. His mind was stored with much information, and hence it thirsted for more; while few of those he lived with had a single idea to add to his stock. The tenets and the views of the Wahhabees interested him particularly. I employed the greatest portion of my stay at Hems in giving him a description of these sectaries. In return he favoured me with a sketch of his own life.

"My father's humble roof," he said, "accidentally afforded shelter from a storm to a magistrate of high degree. On going away the cazi-asker[3], in order to save a present, gave his host a counsel. It was to send me to school, and to rely on his patronage. Till then my worthy parent had never boasted but of manufacturing good pipe-heads; he now fancied himself destined to be the author of a head of the law. His fortune was spent in placing me in a medressé[4], and my health ruined to do credit to the situation. My examination took place the same day with that of a dunce, descended from so long a line of distinguished dunces, that he received his degrees with unbounded applause for having answered right a single question, while I was near losing mine for answering one wrong. I was however qualified for promotion: but, to render it the more acceptable, my generous patron kept it back as long as possible; or rather did nothing for me till his son wanted a tutor. He then proposed the place to my necessities, and soon they saw me the reluctant khodgea[5] to the young bey-Moolah; – for he had been aggregated to the college of muderrees[6] before he knew his letters. It certainly was unnecessary for him to learn them after. Yet somehow my stupidity was several years in finding out the exceeding bad compliment I paid the father, by requiring diligence of the son. The mistake became evident, when, in recompense for devoting to his service the best years of my life, I was made cadee of a miserable country town. Since that first step my promotion has proceeded at the slowest rate our rules would admit of: and, too old now for new advancement here below, I only look for further promotion, where I wish my caziasker no worse punishment than himself becoming a preceptor, – were it an angel's family."

"Long may the sun still revolve!" said I to the Moolah as he finished his story, "ere you witness the accomplishment of your wish! Long may your wisdom still shine on Hems!"

With these I tarried two days only, and then pursued my way northward, through a smiling well watered plain, – thinking as I went along how dissatisfied the wealthy and the great always were with their lot. "Not so," added I, "the poor and the lowly;" – and to confirm myself in my assumption, I stopped to felicitate a passing peasant on the beauty and richness of his country.

"Reserve your congratulations," answered the clown surlily, "for the Mahwali Arabs; we sow, but they reap. El-Korfan, their Emir, lays upon us what contributions he pleases. The monopoly of camels for all the caravans that cross Syria has made him so rich and powerful, that he fears neither governor of Haleb nor Pasha of Damascus: and why should he; who can at his pleasure bring into the field his ten thousand well appointed horse!" – Having growled out this speech, my informer went on.

I had scarcely travelled two leagues farther, when my good fortune made me stumble upon this formidable schaich himself, just at that moment encamped in the middle of the road. He, too. was out of humour as well as the peasant. Numbers of his camels had perished in the desert. But his frowns made not the pilau in his tent look the less inviting. "Let the Pasha of Damascus dread his ill temper," thought I; "his ten thousand horse dare not hurt a hair of a houseless santon's head;" – and resolutely I walked in, made my salam, and sat down to the seasonable repast. Having refreshed myself, I thanked the Prince for his good cheer, and wishing him and his remaining camels good health, marched on to Hamah.

At Haleb, where I stopped next to purchase a new steed, I inquired for the French *philosophe*, – the worshipper of *l'utile*. Alas! the very annuity granted to the director of his health, on his own precious life, had been the unfortunate cause of his death. A becca-fico, swallowed too greedily, bone and all – lest the watchful servant should interpose his veto – had in an evil hour stuck in the philosopher's gullet, and choked him before the removal of his first course.

Descending into the plain which leads to Antakieh[7], some Turkmen invited me to their camp. As they were come all the way from Diarbek, their country, to dispose of their cattle in the Syrian markets, I thought I could not be far from the mark in saluting them as shepherds. But I mistook the thing completely: they were noblemen. The head of the troop had himself addressed by his followers as Aga; and, on introducing me to the lady his wife, who was churning her milk, and to the other ladies his daughters, who were, the one kneading a barley cake, the other working a sheep's wool carpet, and the third darning her own camel's hair trousers, he took an opportunity of informing me in his bad Turkish dialect, of the antiquity of his race and the pure nobility of his blood: "– a boast which he would not have thought it necessary to make, but that lately so many Christian peasants, fled from the oppression of their pashas, had assumed the name of Turkmen, and brought it into disrepute, by taking their revenge of their tyrannic governors on the innocent traveller." I professed myself highly delighted with the intelligence, and, after eating some cream cheese and drinking some buttermilk, in the most respectful manner bade the exalted circle adieu, and went on. Every step I performed I grew more impatient to cast off my rags – but the time was not yet come.

At Antakieh I made a party with three merchants, a jenissary, and some domestics, to go together to Scanderoon; there to embark for Smyrna, the final limit of my pilgrimage. The man of war was of course to be our defender. I had nothing to do but to pray, in my quality as santon, for Mahmood's success: – and what could seem less doubtful than that it must be entire in whatever he undertook. It did one's heart good, only to hear from his own lips – ere the journey was well begun – the whole list of feats of bravery he had at various times performed. When, indeed, a little further on the road, a discussion arose with a few wandering Koords who shewed a wish to fleece us, our protector's generous disposition got a little the better of his martial ardour: – "Was it worth while squabbling," he asked, "about a few piastres, especially with wretches whom if it came to fighting we could not help annihilating?"– but though, on this occasion, he deplored nothing so much as the valuable time we lost in these debates, yet, when a mile further on a countryman informed us of a more considerable detachment of the same tribe, stationed in a defile between us and our intended resting place, he was most strenuous for stopping altogether, and lying down where we were – only for the sake of coolness! However, seeing the merchants determined to push on, in spite of his raptures with the place, he took me aside, and sagaciously observing that in charging the enemy too vigorously, his belt, in which he had all his money, might burst, – begged of me in a whisper, as one protected by my holiness, to take charge of his purse. Unfortunately in attempting to slip it unseen by the merchants into my hand, the excessive courage which vibrated in his own, caused the bag to drop, and with such prodigious clatter as to attract every eye. Mahmood looked ready to faint, and only revived a little on my winking at him to leave the explanation of the affair to me. "The deuce," cried I, "is in these leaden images[8], which the Damascus derwishes have given me for their Smyrna brethren – people will fancy I am made up of gold!" – a speech which amused the merchants who thought the money mine, but positively enraptured Mahmood who thus escaped its being known as his.

I do not know what it was that – almost immediately after this transaction – got wrong about my saddle, and made me lag behind a little; but I do remember that, when I called to my companions to wait for me, the merchants thought it a clever joke to spur on their horses, and to leave the good santon, with his great bag of money, alone the road. I did not think it a very bad joke myself, and – determining to leave those that left me – while they turned to the left, I turned to the right. I even had the malice, when a little afterwards I caught a distant glimpse of their procession, just as they were entering the obnoxious defile mentioned above, to fire a pistol; at which they set off as if possessed, fancying all the Koords of Koordestan at their heels, – and very soon entirely disappeared.

Night coming on apace, I naturally missed my way, and the next morning I found I had considerably overshot Scanderoon, which could now be distinctly descried from the mountains. It would have been madness to turn back – with Mahmood's purse in my pocket. So I went on, refreshed myself at the first little village I reached, and there, having made inquiries respecting the road, resolved to give up all immediate thoughts of Smyrna, and to strike into the courier's track to Constantinople, from which I was not far distant. The capital, after all, must be the place for converting my jewels into gold. That weighty matter once accomplished, I should take up my Alexis at Smyrna in my way to Christendom, where I intended finally to settle, and to commence my new profession of an honest man.

I might have been travelling about five leagues in my new direction, and had just got into the track of the Tartar messengers, when, in fact, a personage of that description passed by me with the customary salute of peace. This I duly returned. Upon which, – the sound of my voice striking the courier as familiar to him – he looked round to survey me. "Heavens!" cried he presently, "is it the lord Selim I see in this strange attire?" "It is, Feiz-ullah," answered I, – who by this time had likewise recognized my friend. He was not other than the honest fellow who, at Bagdad, had cautioned me against staying in that city, and whom, for all the thanks I owed him, I now wished at the devil for his quicksightedness. "You see," continued I, "what it is to have a timorous conscience. I felt so oppressed with the weight of my sins – particularly that of having fought among those vile Wahhabees – that I begged of all the Saints in paradise to assist me in wiping out the stain. None heeded my prayer, save Hadjee-Becktash[9], who one night visited me in my sleep, and bade me take his habit. As you may perceive, it has extracted almost every impurity out of my heart, and I shall soon come forth as spotless as the new born babe. Meanwhile, tell me what is the news from Bagdad."

"Great," cried Feiz-ullah; "great indeed! I do not ask whether you remember your friend the kehaya. Suleiman had toiled so many years to give this faulty diamond a sort of false lustre, that he felt loth to throw away his labour, and to own his choice a bad one. Determined to leave a monument of his might, he was too old to begin a new creation. All the insinuations against Achmet therefore were treated as sheer envy; until a day when there came to hand a something passing hints; – a packet from the Reïs-Effendee, inclosing a letter to the Porte in the kehaya's own hand writing. It represented Suleiman as wholly superannuated; and the child of his favour only modestly proposed to set him aside, and to step into his place. On the receipt of this document, a divan was immediately convened of all the individuals hostile to the kehaya, and the business laid before them. Suleiman wished only to dismiss his old favourite; but being with much difficulty rendered sensible of the danger of this lenity, he at last reluctantly signed the kehaya's doom. Scarce was the order issued, when Achmet himself appeared. He suspected some plot against his authority, and came to daunt his enemies. Suleiman gave him the wonted reception, while the kehaya, casting a look of rage round the astonished circle, only seemed to count the new victims he intended immolating to his safety. No time was to be lost. Aly-khasnadar boldly rushes forward, and strikes the first blow: – all the rest follow. Dropping down on his knees Achmet now raises towards the Pasha his supplicating hands: but the Pasha had thrown his shawl over his face in order not too see the execution, and in an instant the favourite was dispatched. His mangled body, thrown out on the steps of the divan, remained exposed during the whole day to glut the greedy eyes of the populace, and his head," – added the Tartar, pointing to a little bundle tied behind him, – "I have here. As it has been carefully pickled, I entertain no doubt of carrying it safe to the Sultan, according to my instructions."

Feiz-ullah here stopping, I gave a deep sigh, not so much in compassion for Achmet, as from regret that all this had not happened sooner. It, however, brought me some real advantage, in addition to the pleasure one finds in the fall of an enemy. Feiz-ullah, as a public messenger, every where found horses ready at his command. It was more than santons did. He proposed to me to go in his company; and for the sake of sharing his privilege, I determined to keep up with his pace.

The Tartar rate of travelling leaves little leisure for a journal. The curiosities of the different cities I was scarce allowed time to investigate; but I had the best of every thing on the road. As to my companion he would not, even after the daintiest meal in the world forgo the douceur he expected for what he used to call the wear and tear of his teeth. Once indeed his demand was resisted, in a malkyané of the Sultana Validé, whose waywode swore he would not part with a single aspre of his mistress's slipper money for all the booted Tartars in the universe. Feiz-ullah had nothing to do but to curse the sovereign's mother for an old toothless jade as she was, without bowels of compassion. Except on this single occasion, the Tartar's whip, which never quitted his hand, was more than a sceptre to him, – it was an enchanter's wand: for, if kings themselves lose their right where there is nothing, this little instrument never failed to produce something; – fat fowls, for instance, where a hen had never cackled; sheep in good case, where there was not a blade of grass; and nice fruit where not a vegetable could be made to grow. Alternately applied with the same spirit to man and beast, its persuasive powers made the most jaded horse go on, and the most reluctant host supply an ample meal.

At Isnik I took leave of my companion, and, with all due respect for Hadjee-Becktash, of his shabby uniform. As we travelled along I had gradually collected all the articles of apparel necessary for my transformation. Here, a rich stuff for a turban; there, a handsome vest and cloak, further on, fine French cloth trousers; elsewhere, papooshes bright as burnished brass. With my parcel under my arm I entered a house of entertainment, engaged a snug back chamber, shut myself up, slipped off at a single shake all my uncouth rags, with impious hands shaved close my shaggy hair[10]; nay, without giving them the smallest warning, disturbed all the angels in my beard[11], and maimed the Lord knows how many tiny sprites, deemed its tenants for life; made a bonfire of my santon's cloak and staff; submitted my person to all sorts of ablution; and, thus purified by fire and water – after standing sometime gazing in a state of nature on the various articles of new apparel, methodically laid out in a circle around me, – proceeded leisurely to put on one by one the items of my new garb.

Stepping out of my cell after this refreshing process, so completely metamorphosed as not to be recognized even by the people in the shop through which I had to pass, I truly felt like the insect, which only casts off the unsightly slough of the butterfly, to come forth when older, a gayer, gaudier, nay younger butterfly. The species of ease and delight derived form my transformation, positively baffles all my powers of description. My chest seemed to dilate, my breathing to acquire a freedom before unknown, and my limbs and gait to have gained a fresh vigour and buoyancy. Though now advanced to the wrong side of thirty, and already beginning before to think myself grown old and faded, I might fancy I had dipped afresh in the fountain of youth. Like the revolving year, after passing through the decay of autumn and winter, I had recovered anew all the smiling attributes of spring.

The new companion with whom I engaged in the coffeehouse was suited to my new character, – a young Algerine captain of a man of war, come from Constantinople on business, and glad to have me as a fellow traveller to return with to the capital. We talked all the way; I, like all men already somewhat advanced in life, praising times past; while my companion would only laud in the present tense. "Hold your tongue," cried he, "about your great Hassan. Our little Husseïn" (Kootchook was the new Grand admiral's by-name) "is worth a dozen of him. We make more improvements in the navy in a day now, than you used to do in a twelvemonth. Husseïn sets about every thing at once, has every new invention before it comes out, never loses time in examining, and regularly every year new models the arsenal from end to end. It almost confuses one to see the builders he has collected from every country: France, Sweden, and whence not! – each speaking a different language; each following a different method, and each pointing out the faults of what all the others do. He would sooner build in the Chinese fashion, than copy any one who went before him; and his designs; when executed, will prove the finest in the world! Every dock yard in the empire, – Mytilene, Rhodes, Boodroon, the Dardanelles, Sinope and Galatsch, – is vying with the rest which shall knock up a ship of the line with the greatest speed; and the capital prepares to launch a three-decker so prodigious, that none of our seas will have room enough to work her." I laughed at the eulogium; wished my friend the command of this wonder, and stepped into the boat which landed me at Constantinople.

My first care was to enquire after the merchant who, at Khedieh, had so obligingly made me welcome to his travelling equipage, for the mere trouble of taking it. At Damascus I had understood him to be gone to the capital: in the capital I found that he had commenced the longer journey to heaven. For not only he was departed this world, but, in order to ensure a good reception in the next, he had piously bequeathed all his property to an hospital of cats and dogs, to the utter exclusion of his nearer relations, expressly disinherited, and in fact well able, as I heard, to spare his bequests. My finances being by nature somewhat less brilliant than those of the personages in question, I determined, upon this information, fairly to keep what I before thought I had fairly acquired, and on Djiaffer's own express terms: assured that I did not even do his four footed legatees – only named by a disposition subsequent to our meeting – an injury of which they could complain. There were donanmas[11] going forward in the capital; and the Porte, very busy purchasing at all hands diamonds for presents, afforded me an opportunity of selling part of mine to a very great advantage, and still to reserve the stones of the first water, for what I deemed the better markets of Vienna and Petersburg. Meantime, informed that some of Djiaffer's relations, less fortunate than the remainder, had fallen into want, I took upon myself to correct in their behalf their kinsman's omissions, and by paying them, like a good Moslemin, the tithe of my profit, restored them to ease and comfort. After this I felt quite at peace with my conscience, for retaining what certainly no other man breathing had any legal claims upon; – nor even, in truth, the cats themselves.

On each occasion of my passing through Constantinople since my separation from Spiridion at Chios, something or other had occurred to prevent our meeting: – either my own reluctance to intrude upon him; or his impending marriage which made it desirable to himself not to see me; or his absence from the Capital. I now made a fresh attempt to embrace my old friend, and called upon the father, but could not see the son. To the indescribable horror of all his friends and relations, he was actually gone on a voyage to the Venetian islands and to the other parts of Christendom; and that, from motives of mere curiosity, and without any views of advantage, save instruction! – The best chance I had to finding him was at Paris or in London.

Mavrocordato had a friend: – a man of weight and respectability, who, throughout all my different vicissitudes had constantly shewn me a more steady and uninterrupted interest than even Mavrocordato himself, and, while he never, it must be confessed, had risen quite so high in his admiration of my worth as the latter, never either fell quite so low in his estimation of my qualities, as Signor Mavrocordato had since chosen to do. I had particularly noticed Costandino Caridi for one circumstance in his conduct, in which he stood single among his countrymen: namely, that, though far from wealthy himself, he used to keep most aloof from me, whenever I seemed to have the greatest command of cash: – giving as his reason for this singularity, that I never became bearable until I was half starved. This old friend now met me with a totally new face; for, though he knew me to possess the amplest means, he yet paid me a degree of attention which I had never before been able to extort from him, even when I was absolutely in want of bread. In fact, he seemed so very determined to obtain complete possession of my mind by every species of address and flattery, that at last I grew distrustful of him whom I never had distrusted before, and conceived that, through daily society with men of a selfish and intriguing disposition, he had at last totally changed his own character. One day, indeed, I could not help telling him so in direct terms. Sick of his obsequiousness, and quite out of patience with his over-strained compliments on my wit, my figure and my taste, I ironically begged of him not to waste his breath in flattering one, who himself felt so impressed with his utter perfection in every particular, as to consider all attempts at praise as inadequate, and to loathe every compliment paid him to his face, except that addressed to his good sense, in sound and well timed abuse.

At this speech signor Caridi, instead of looking somewhat confused as I expected, began to laugh most immoderately; and forcibly taking me by the hand: "Bravo!" he cried, "this is at last as I wished it. I now have hopes, and shall report accordingly. My commission need no longer be deferred."

"Your commission?" I echoed.

"You remember," resumed Costandino; "your kinsman of Trieste, who so cruelly left you in the lurch at Smyrna?"

"I do," was my reply – "and as an egregious rogue."

"That is precisely," answered Caridi, "the thing he understood you to be; and the attribute which made him transfer his views from the son of his relative Sotiri, to another youth – an entire stranger to his blood; but who had been a clerk in his counting house, and seemed to bear himself as a lad of unexceptionable morals. Unfortunately, poor Elevtheri was not as sound in constitution as in principles; and when your cousin, adopting him as his son, thought it necessary to coax him into being his intended heir, the hapless youth had to undergo such excessive petting, and care, and exclusion from those fresh gales which he used formerly to inhale unrestrained, that the first draft of air he sat in, after he had become disaccustomed from its contact, he died of. Delvinioti, now again adrift, wrote to me to make fresh enquiries after his worthy cousin Anastasius, in order that, should age, or disappointment, or other desirable circumstances have produced wholesome fruits in his bosom, new proposals might be made him, on the old conditions. The letter which I received to this purpose is dated six months back; and I confess I had so little hopes of ever seeing you again, that I was going to answer it as relating to a desperate business, – when suddenly you reappeared. Since that period I have neglected no opportunity of watching your conduct, and trying your temper: and you yourself must do me the justice to own that I have laid every trap in your way which my imagination could suggest. I therefore now begin to think mere time has done enough, to warrant my expecting from motives so powerful as a respectable situation and a rich inheritance, all that still remains to be achieved: and I hesitate no longer to stamp your improvement with the mark of your cousin's splendid offer."

"Or rather," cried I, "to submit my prudence to some fresh and arduous trial in order to ascertain whether I am weak enough to be taken in a second time by the same wily relation, and can be made to perform another longer journey than the first, only to look at the conclusion like a more egregious fool."

"Right!" exclaimed Caridi, "you are fully warranted to form such a surmise, and therefore, as a security against its being realized, I see nothing for you to do, but to take this letter of credit to defray your expenses. It includes, as you see, every place on your way up the Adriatic, and ends with Trieste. Thus, after all, should you and your cousin not suit each other, you will have been franked during a pleasant voyage, and treated with a peep at Christendom, which, at any rate, I understand you meant to visit."

I had indeed occasionally thrown out some idea of the kind, as a thing which might be of advantage to my child's education: but when directly called upon to decide whether I chose to sit down for life in distant realms, to whose habits and manners I was a perfect stranger, I recoiled from the thought, and for a while kept turning a deaf ear to Caridi's remonstrances. At last he set in so strong a light the expedience, in my situation, of retiring to Franguestan, both for the purpose of securing my fortune to my son, and for that of providing him with the best instruction, that I suffered myself to be persuaded, and resolved, after taking up my Alexis at Smyrna, gradually to work my way out of the precincts of Islamism, and into those where soars the Cross. I deposited the letter of credit in my pocket-book, converted my cash into bills, and prepared for my journey. Unfortunately an illness which awaited me the moment I had leisure to attend to my health, and a stab I received one night in a mistake when convalescent, detained me about eight months longer, ere I was able finally to set out.

All things being ready at last for my departure from Stambool, I ascended the hill crowned by Noor-Osmany, and seeking the loftiest galleries of this superb building, took a last parting view of the proud capital which I had made the first scene of my youthful revels, which, during the fairest portion of my life I had considered as my home, and which I was now probably going to quit for ever. For the last time my eye, moistened with tears, wandered over the dimpled hills, glided along the winding waters, and dived into the deep and delicious dells, in which branch out its jagged shores. Reverting from these smiling outlets of its sea-beat suburbs to its busy centre, I surveyed in slow succession every chaplet of swelling cupolas, every grove of slender minarets, and every avenue of glittering porticoes, whose pinnacles dart their golden shafts from between the dark cypress trees into the azure sky. I dwelt on them as on things I never was to behold more; and not until the evening had deepened the veil it cast over the varied scene from orange to purple, and from purple to the sable hue of the night, did I tear myself away from the impressive spot. I then bade the city of Constantine farewell for ever, descended the high-crested hill, stepped into the heaving boat, turned my back upon the shore, and sunk my regrets in the sparkling wave, across which the moon had already flung a trembling bar of silvery light, pointing my way as it were to other regions yet unknown.

During the whole of my voyage to Smyrna, one only thought kept possession of my soul. It was the rapture which awaited me on landing, in pressing to my bosom my darling child. Four years and an half had now elapsed since his joyless birth: – he must be grown full of grace, loveliness and artless prattle; heir to all the charms of his mother, and ready to return all the endearments of his father: and such became, on stepping on shore, my impatience to behold the fond object of these daily dreams, that it scarcely left me patience to go with composure through the tedious forms and functions, from which none are exempt who transfer their persons finally from the watery element to a firmer footing on land.

When indeed, after traversing the busier parts of the city around the quay, I arrived at that remote and lonely suburb where I expected to find my affections crowned, and which, but for my melancholy search after my lost Euphrosyné, I might never had visited, or at least, have remembered: – when I passed by the obscure hovel which I entered while my lovely victim lay in all the agonies of child birth, praying for a last farewell look from her frantic destroyer; which I left without seeing her, and where she resigned her spotless soul to heaven, fresh clouds of despair seemed for a moment to overcast the sunshine of my hopes, and the solace of the son was forgotten in woes of the mother: or rather, I felt that after losing the parent as I did, I deserved not to find the child; – but this gloom again subsided when I beheld the abode where I had left my Alexis.

It was only on their threshold that my delightful vision at last vanished entirely. There I first heard, and from strangers, not only that the merchant entrusted with the small pittance for my child's support, had become a bankrupt, and had disappeared – but that even the woman, in whose care I had left my darling babe, had absconded. Nobody could give me the least information respecting herself or her charge; nor – what seemed the strangest part of the story – did distress or failure of the promised supplies appear to have been her motive; for so far from leaving a chance to any succour of reaching her, she had evidently taken pains to baffle all enquiry respecting the place of her concealment. Had Sophia still enjoyed the breath of life, I should . . . But she was gone to her doom! Yet might her evil spirit still haunt the scene of her infernal wickedness.

Once, on my homeward journey from the eternal desert – oppressed with heat, and in vain soliciting my cruise for a drop of water to wet my parched lips – I had, when on the point of fainting with exhaustion, beheld in a valley before me the semblance of limpid lake, ready to slake my raging thirst and to lave my wearied limbs, – had collected my last strength to reach its winding banks – and, when near the delusive spot, had found the visions a mere mockery, and nothing real around me save sands more dry and burning than those I had left behind: but what was this disappointment of the sense, – even with life at stake, – compared with that which struck my inmost mind at this dreadful moment? – for the anguish of the actual shock was still exceeded by the gloom of my forebodings, since it seemed that no other motive could have made the person I sought take pains to evade my enquiry, but having made away with, or abandoned my child. Probably it had long ceased to exist; long probably had my Alexis followed his hapless mother to the grave; and, while I was conjuring up in my fertile fancy every brightest image of his beauty and his sprightliness, his lifeless form was already mouldering in its grave: or if he still was permitted to breathe, in common with the meanest of insects, on this vile inhospitable earth, it could only be to experience sufferings worse than death: – every pang of illness, of desertion and of want. The least untoward feat I dared fancy for the relic of my adored Euphrosyné, was begging his bread like a wretched orphan from door to door. Even his father might have met him without knowing whom he met;-might have bestowed on his own babe the scanty boon of common and churlish charity!

Impressed with this idea, I examined with anxious solicitude every child on which fell my searching eye: stopped to enquire into its parentage and birth place; and suffered no little creature under five or six years of age to escape, until it had passed through the regular ordeal of my questions: but no child I beheld resembled my Alexis; none made my heart bound on meeting its first glance. "Ah!" was now my constant cry: "why had I ever lost sight even for an instant of that heart's only remaining treasure? Why had I roamed far from the humble abode in which centred all my joys? Would it not have been better a thousand times to possess my child without bread to eat, than all the riches of the universe without my darling child!"

At last a faint ray of hope broke in, and threw a gleam of light upon my dark despondency. It dimly shewed my mind a track to pursue, though it marked not its issue. Indeed so vague, so faint, so flitting remained the forms it here and there pointed out, that I feared to trust to them as to realities. A Smyrniote lady, who had witnessed my distress, and had even assisted me in my enquiries, send to inform me of a circumstance which she had heard by accident. The wife of a foreign Consul at Alexandria, on a visit the year before with a friend at Smyrna, was said on her return to Egypt to have taken with her in the capacity of waiting woman, a person intrusted by a stranger with a child of such singular beauty, that the consuless, unblessed with a family of her own, rather considered the unprotected babe as a prize than as an encumbrance. Further particulars to identify the child could not be collected at Smyrna, and rather than engage in a tedious and ineffectual correspondence with Alexandria, I resolved immediately to embark for that well known place.

Walking impatiently backward and forward on the quay, while the boat was getting ready, I spied a large circle of towns-people gathered round a janissary employed in telling a tale of wonder. It was no other than that of the innumerable Koords killed by the valiant Mahmood, in defending a certain purse which I pocketed on the road to Scanderoon, and still happened to have in my possession. Nor need I add, that Mahmood himself was the relater of his own achievements. At this instance of shameless bragging I could not resist slipping behind the fellow, and whispering in his ear: "Coward, you lie; here is the object of your vauntings, and claim it if you dare!" upon which, throwing the purse down before him, I folded my arms in each other, and waited some little time to see what step he would take; – but he only stood still, speechless and pale as a ghost, looking alternately at the money and at me, until, giving up all hopes of his uttering a syllable, I flung the purse to a beggar, and stepped into the boat.

CHAPTER XII.

Behold me now for the third and last time on my passage to Egypt; a country, after having been visited successively by famine, plague, and the Capitan-Pasha had, to crown its misfortunes, been at last divided between Ismaïl-bey, Schaich-el-belled at Cairo, and Ibrahim and Mourad, masters of the Saïd: an arrangement which increased the expenses of the chief in the same proportion in which it diminished his income; since it fixed on his very boundary an enemy, against whom it was necessary always to keep his province prepared. Fortunately Ismaïl's abilities were equal to his task. By his firmness he awed the open hostility of the party in Upper Egypt, and by his vigilance he defeated the treachery in his own councils: he made the heavier burthens which he was forced to impose, seem lighter by causing them to bear more equally on all classes; he applied himself with equal skill to curing wounds inflicted, and to obviate impending evils; and, finally, he carried from the mountains of Lybia to the city of Cairo, a line of walls, which frowned defiance on the undisciplined troops of the Beys in the Saïd.

After these labours Ismaïl seemed, in 1790, to have nothing further left to do but to sit down and enjoy the fruits of his toil, when that scourge of the East, the plague, imperfectly subdued, broke out afresh with a virulence far exceeding its former fury. From the close-wedged hovels of the poor it soon reached – more ravenous in proportion as it found richer food – to the spacious palaces of the great, and spread dismay and death among the haughty Mamlukes, as it had done among the humble natives. At last it penetrated into the abode of the Schaich-el-belled himself, and struck his dart at the chief, while in the very act of concerting measures to stem its devastations. In the midst of all his glory Ismaïl fell a prey to its vengeance, – and a few hours saw him dragged from the pinnacle of power to the brink of the grave.

But the disease which conquered his body could boast no conquest over his mighty soul. To the last his mind continued intent upon the welfare of Egypt. Finding his end draw near he cast his eyes around, to seek among his followers some one fit to become his successor, and to support, at his fall, the fabric which he had raised. Summoning all his friends into his presence, he offered the reversion of his dignity successively to Hassan-bey Djeddawee, to Aly-bey Defterdar, and to all his other veterans who seemed in any degree equal to the arduous task.

But no one dared to face it. Deprived, by the same scourge under which their chief was sinking, of the most faithful of their adherents, these ambitious leaders who at other times would have disputed sword in hand for Ismaïl's rich succession, now wholly unnerved, were compelled one by one to decline the tempting honours, when spread out before their eyes, these coveted grandeurs only waited their acceptance. The supreme rank, therefore, devolved on the very last of those to whom the offer was made – on Ismaïl's own creature, Osman, surnamed Toobbal; a youth as crooked in mind as he was distorted in body: but who alone with alacrity accepted what all the others, with deep regret, refused.

Wishing to give a last instance of his power, or, rather, to render manifest to all men breathing the last act of his authority, Ismaïl commanded the proclamation of Toobbal to take place while he himself still had life. From his death-bed he heard his successor announced; and gave up the ghost.

Toobbal had accepted the dignity of Schaich-el-belled, which he was conscious he could not maintain, only to sell it to the beys in the Saïd. He sent them speedy advice of the death of Ismaïl, and of the utter debility of his party. On this welcome intelligence they immediately descended along the Western bank of the Nile: but, startled by the unlooked for and new fortifications which they found at Dgizé, they retraced their steps backward until they could collect craft enough to cross the river; and, on the reverse of the chain of Arabic mountains, again redescended with such rapidity, that scarce had the Beys of Cairo received intelligence of their retreat from before Dgizé, when they rushed from behind the Mokhadem, and summoned the capital to surrender.

At this appalling intelligence the Beys marched out with what force they could muster, headed by the treacherous Toobbal. He seized the first opportunity of passing over to the enemy, whom he led triumphant into the capital, while his former party fled to the Saïd. There the remnant of Aly-bey's creations, and of Hassan's tools, reluctantly fixed his quarters; and there its now oldest leader, Djeddawee – suffered to resume his ancient government of Es-souan – had since been left undisturbed to reflect on his singular fate; a fate ever intent upon rendering the bravest of a fearless race celebrated only through his flights. Toobbal, who immediately abdicated his recent honours in favour of his new competitors, soon attained the oblivion he deserved; while the country to the south of Cairo was allotted to Ibrahim, and the regions lying northward of the capital fell to the share of Mourad.

The person who gave me the substance of this account was a middle-aged man, speaking Greek, of singular appearance, whom I met on my way at Cos. Fresh arrived from the country whither I was bound, he had excited my curiosity more still by his own consequential manner, than by the information he had to impart. On some slight offence given him in one of the coffee-houses under the gigantic plane-tree in the market place: – "Is this a treatment," he cried trembling with rage, "for a Capitan-Pasha!" at which words I started, and, after considering the personage for some time with encreased wonder: –"Capitan-Pasha! To whom I beseech!" was the question I could not help proposing.

"To Mourad-bey, to be sure," was the unexpected answer. "In order to maintain a Lord High Admiral,"– I ventured to observe, – "one should have the shadow of a navy."

"And who has its showiest substance," rejoined my informer, "if Mourad has not? His fleet rides at anchor under his very windows at Dgizé; is the best appointed within an hundred miles of the sea, and, when the Nile has attained its full height, sails up as high as Boolak, and down as low as Fostat. At other times indeed it remains properly moored along the quay of the palace, for fear of running aground in the river."

"Equal to its own merits, no doubt, were the naval achievements which raised you to the honour of commanding this fleet?"

"As you may suppose. – When Osman-bey Tamboodgee grew tired of the banishment which Hassan procured him to Stambool, I, Nicola-Hadjee of Tchesmé, was the man who conveyed him to Derneh, whence he easily regained his home. This signal service recommended me to his party, and made Mourad give me the command of his naval force, as soon as he learned my transcendent abilities. Unfortunately I was tenacious of the privileges attached to my high office. I one day battered a kiachef's windows for protecting a runaway sailor. This spirited act brought me into disgrace, and like other great people I now travel for a change of air."

"It gives me pleasure," replied I, "to find that the rage for novelties is not confined to Constantinople." I however condoled with the Ex-Capitan Pasha on his dismissal, and, having filled a bag with the fine bergamots of the island, miscalled Stanchio, reimbarked for my destination.

On the coast of Syria the reïs took on board, much against my advice, two Latin friars, – the one an Italian from the convent of Jerusalem, and the other a Spaniard from the hospice at Ramleh.

If they had been Greeks they could not have quarrelled more unceasingly. Under the delusion that no one understood their idiom, they were constantly refreshing each other's memory with all the little peccadilloes of their respective establishments. "The convent at Jerusalem had suffered the schismatics to invade all the sanctuaries; the hospice at Ramleh had bribed the Arabs to plunder the pilgrims: the monks of the former place had set their blood on fire with drams; those of the latter with pimento and quarrels."

That – whatever might be the cause – the humours of these representatives of their respective communities were actually in a state of high fermentation, no one could deny. More than once I expected an explosion, which would end fatally for both. Luckily breath only – not blood – was wasted; and we had the satisfaction to land both fra. Diego and fra. Giacomo, sound in body, though very sore in mind, on the quay of Alexandria.

My feet had not yet pressed the long looked-for shore, when I began to enquire for the consular mansion on which centred all my hopes. With trembling steps and throbbing heart I hied me to its threshold. A vague report, an idle story might have deceived me: I might have gone away from the child I came to seek; and when near the door, I was on the point of turning back, in order yet awhile to defer the inquiry, and to gather more fortitude for an answer, which must bring with it inexpressible happiness or bitter disappointment.

Apprehensive lest the sight of a stranger in the Turkish garb might alarm the family, I first gave a gentle knock. No one answered: – I then repeated the summons. A domestic at last appeared. "Both his master and mistress were out," he said, "and it was uncertain when they would return."

"Had they a child with them?" I asked.

"There was a child in the house."

"Found at Smyrna, – and belonging to a stranger?"

"Oh no! Brought up in the family by its own mother."

This seemed to dash all my hopes to the ground! However; "Might I see the little boy?" I asked.

He too had been taken out to walk.

"Where?"

"It was impossible to tell."

Perplexed, I now left word I would call again, and withdrew from the door in deep despondency. Yet when I reflected that the servants might be strangers to the concerns of their masters, and these latter not desirous to own their little favourite a foundling, I did not entirely despair. I paced up and down the road in sight of the mansion, to watch the coming home of the boy.

Nor was I long without descrying at a distance a child approaching, whose dress belonged not to the country. A female held it by the hand; but from *her* my very first glance recoiled as from a total stranger, – one who bore not the least resemblance to the nurse of my Alexis.

"It cannot be he!" sighed I to myself; – and yet, so playfully did the little fellow trip along, so erect was his gait, and so noble his mien; with so lively and inquisitive a manner did he stop to survey each new object on his way, that I envied his too happy parents, and could immediately have given up all paternal claims elsewhere, for a good title in the treasure before me. "Ah!" thought I, "had this angel been my own! But as he drew nearer, as by degrees I discerned more of his countenance and his features, as I became enabled more distinctly to trace the outline of his serene and radiant front, of his dimpled downy cheek and of his wavy coral lip, as above all he himself, with a look at once arch and innocent, fixed upon me his full bright eye – that eye which so eloquently spoke the heaven of his heart, – O God! O God! All Euphrosyné at once burst upon my sense; entire conviction in an instant filled my mind. I felt it must be, it *was* my own Alexis, my own babe, I beheld!

Unable to repress my emotion, I darted forward, and was going to clasp my child to my bosom, when the woman, who already from a distance had noticed my eager look, and had made a circuit to avoid me, frightened at my frantic manner, snatched up the infant, and ran screaming to the house.

Fearful of increasing her alarm, I purposely slackened my pace, and gave her time to gain admittance ere I followed her lovely charge to the door: but when I did, I found it immovably closed against me. No entreaty, however earnest, could obtain its being re-opened. "Strangers", was the plea, "never were admitted when the Consul was abroad." I was not even allowed, hard as I begged for it, another view of my Alexis from without. "What business could I have with the child? An evil eye, or an evil intent must with reason be apprehended;" and lest I should by my urgency confirm the growing distrust, I at last retired. But I had beheld my boy; and the tumult in my breast, though extreme, was a tumult of bliss!

As soon as, by my calculation, the Consular pair must be come home, I called again. After a little parleying within, of which I could not guess the drift, I was told I might see the lady.

This promised well. – "For the wife to encounter my visit" – thought I, – "she must know my business, and have made up her mind to acquiesce in my right." I was ushered into a back chamber, where, however, so many attendants crowded in after me, that it looked as if they either intended or expected some violence.

Presently walked in a stately matron, who, disdaining to be seated, and of course keeping me standing, asked with a sort of lofty civility in what she could oblige me, but, when informed of the purport of my visit, affected the utmost amazement at my demand. "She was wholly ignorant of the circumstances alluded to, – had no stranger's child under her roof. The little boy I met was the son of her own servant: – the mother, marrying again, had left him in her care; and she had no knowledge of any other child. As to the Smyrna transaction upon which I founded my claim, it must be the invention of some idle person, or the report of some enemy." In a word, my Alexis was refused me, and all my entreaties could not even obtain me the permission to give him a single embrace. It was feared I might cast some spell upon the child. "In fact" – it was observed – "I might have done so already:" and presently the lady, affecting apprehensions for herself, hastily withdrew, while her servants peremptorily urged me not to protract my intrusion.

Even I, at the moment, saw no advantage in staying; for, whether the consuless believed her own story or not, it was plain that she had framed it with deliberation, and meant to support it with boldness. Any remonstrance on my part could therefore only redouble her caution, and perhaps give me the appearance of temerity; – nay, be construed into an act of violence. It was wiser that I should appear to submit, until I had acquired a little more local information of the personages and circumstances, and had armed myself with such proof not only of my right to a child I had lost, but of its identity with the child I had found, as could not be resisted, either with justice, with reason, or with safety. Mean time I retired for the present; but full of dismay, doubt, and disappointment.

Invited by a stone that lay on the road-side, I sat down to ruminate upon what had occurred. "After all," was the first reflection which passed through my mind – "may not my excessive wish to find my child have deceived me? May I not have cause to distrust my own imagination rather that the veracity of others? So vague were the reports on which I came to Alexandria, so perfectly did my fears always balance my hopes, so little could I at any time have been justified in laying the least stress on my expectations, that, with an indifferent person addressed as I had been, the account of the consuless would have found implicit credence: and only because I was not sufficiently unconcerned in the business impartially to weigh the evidence on both sides; because I could only bear to dwell upon such circumstances as seemed to favour my own hopes; because the child I had met offered to the image impressed upon my mind a resemblance which I had been every where sighing to find, did I persevere thus to consider myself certain of what others would have long begun to doubt, – or rather – would have ceased to believe."

"Yet, was that resemblance itself on which I thus boldly built my conviction, so great as it appeared to my eagerness? Beauty alone surely could not make it so. However heavenly a child of Euphrosyné ought to be, it still was not the only child on this globe entitled to bear the countenance of a cherub! – and, as to any other more definite conditions of similitude, they could hardly yet be said to exist in a very striking degree in the still vague and uncertain lineaments of childhood, particularly where their very symmetry was such as to prevent any decisive peculiarity. However, supposing even the likeness to have been as great as it was possible to conceive, how often is such resemblance found to be the mere effect of chance!"

"Should then," continued I, "this single circumstance be allowed to outweigh the solemn assertions of people holding a respectable rank in society, and a conspicuous situation in the place: of people not seemingly interested to support a disgraceful tale of fraud, and, though taken wholly by surprise, yet agreeing perfectly in their account with that which their servants had given before them? – especially when the female I found about the child, instead of being the nurse I left with my babe, and whom an idle report had placed about the consuless as her own attendant, was a totally different person."

Here my reason, having urged all it could think of to check my imagination, ceased its remonstrances: but spite of its arguments, my feelings would not be convinced. When with the report spread at Smyrna, and with the consuless's own acknowledgement that a woman no longer in the family was mother to the child, I combined an indescribable something in the look and manner of all concerned, which bespoke them to be acting parts rehearsed before; – and, above all, when I reflected upon those internal yearnings first and only felt, among all the children I had seen, in favour of this angel now so near me, could only be considered as the cry of blood, I still persisted in my former belief, and resolved to set on foot, as soon as I had got a covering over my head, the most minute and circumstantial perquisitions.

My inquiries were chiefly carried out among the neighbours and tradesmen who, from their situation and concerns, must be best acquainted with the Consul's family and domestics – and this was the result:–

Neither the child, nor its pretended mother, had been known in Egypt previous to the lady's return form Smyrna. The person who called herself, but had never obtained belief for being the mother, had very soon after her arrival again quitted the consular mansion, to marry and to follow to his native island a Taooshan; and the little boy, left behind, had yet continued to experience in the consular family such truly parental tenderness, as to render evil tongues busy with the name of the Consul, and even with the fair fame of the consuless herself.

Mine was a totally different conclusion. When, in addition to the circumstances here mentioned, I moreover found the description of the pretended mother tally in every respect most accurately with the features and figure of the woman to whom I had entrusted my Alexis, I became confirmed in my original belief, and no longer retained the smallest doubt of two things: firstly, that the child was my own, and secondly, that the consul and his wife fully intended that I never should recover it. Determined in some way to obtain a treasure which nature had denied them, they had stooped to steal the offspring of another; and having already set at defiance both the tongues of slander and the voice of truth, it could not be doubted but that they were fully resolved to go any lengths in support of their imposition and their theft.

Nor did their's appear a scheme of danger or of difficulty. The testimony of a respectable family, fixed at Alexandria in a public situation, must intrinsically offer so much more weight than the bare assertion of a stranger, – of a roving individual, – on whom the very mode of his appearance cast the air of an adventurer, that, so far from the consul having to fear any blame for not admitting my unsupported claim, the only conduct for which he must unavoidably incur censure, would be giving easy credence to my statement, and committing to my suspicious care, upon my bare word, the fate of a lovely unprotected babe. Until I could back my pretensions by the most irrefragable proofs, the consul must be justified to every indifferent beholder in treating my claims, my complaints, and my threats as those of an impostor, only come with extortionary or vindictive views.

Yet how was I to obtain those proofs, the want of which must leave me patiently resigned to my wrongs, and quiet spectator of my Alexis remaining the undisputed property of strangers? My right to my own progeny had always appeared to me so notorious and so incontestable – I so fully expected to find its depositaries only sighing for a release from their trust, and alarmed at my protracted silence; I had so little idea that there existed on the face of the globe a being disposed to rear at his expence a stranger's child, the deserted offspring of an unknown stranger; and I so much less conceived the possibility of there being an individual anxious to claim my poor foundling as his own legitimate progeny, that not only I had never thought of bringing the legal vouchers for my paternity to Egypt, but had not even had its proofs duly established in the place where it commenced. How difficult, therefore, must it be, after so much time elapsed, to obtain on that subject any sufficient evidence! Euphrosyné, when she became a mother, was a deserted female; she died a lonely outcast; and Alexis, left from the moment he saw the light of day, in the obscurity of entire abandonment, had passed the first period of his wretched existence, unclaimed by a father, unowned by a relation, and in such entire concealment from all who could feel the least interest in substantiating his parentage, that I myself, the first time I beheld him, had to recur to testimonials on which no one else durst have relied, ere I pressed him to my bosom as my own flesh and blood. Even after that meeting, I had never come forward in the world as his parent: – on the contrary, – without on any occasion ostensibly affording him the care becoming that sacred character, I had only one instant – and as it were by stealth – beheld my babe, from that moment again to leave it wholly unenquired after, and to roam to the regions most distant from its abode. Two individuals indeed, possessed my secret, were apprised of my sentiments; the nurse entrusted with the person of my child, and the merchant depositary of the poor pittance left for its education: but the man was become a bankrupt, the woman had betrayed her trust. The one could nowhere be found to give evidence in my behalf; and the other was no doubt amply paid to back the untrue tale of my adversaries.

All these circumstances however only rendered my task more difficult, without in the least altering the line of conduct I was bound to pursue. Ere unavailing remonstrances could be safely changed into more peremptory measures, I must try to collect what judicial proofs – scanty though they might be – Providence had still left within my reach.

In order to proceed on this arduous business with all the advantages of local knowledge and all the diligence of a direct interest, I first thought of going back to Smyrna myself; thence, if necessary, to proceed on to Scyra, and to bribe the nurse in the cause of truth more richly than she had been in that of falsehood: but considerations which I durst not disregard prevented me from pursuing this plan. Common report represented the Consul and his family as intending early in spring to return to Europe. In that case my child would again be removed, and that to realms wholly beyond my confined sphere of action; – and whether the journey really was in agitation or not, to absent myself from Alexandria, or even in that place to lose sight a single instant of my boy, seemed to me highly dangerous, lest, availing themselves of the opportunity, his unjust detainers should drag him to some spot where they might baffle all my attempts to discover his abode, or at least deride all my efforts to enforce my right.

I therefore determined not to stir from where I was, and to employ the best and most intelligent of the friends I still possessed at Smyrna, to act for me in that city and in the Archipelago. Informing him of all the particulars of my case, I begged he would collect all the testimonials attainable in my favour. The letter was sent by a messenger, who promised to use the greatest possible speed; and, until I should receive the answer, I prayed to God to grant me patience.

The paltry lodging where meanwhile I fixed my residence obliquely faced the consular mansion. No important occurrence within its wall, productive of external symptoms, could well escape my observation; and while I hired three or four lynx-eyed emissaries to prowl about, and to report on every event at the outposts, I myself remained immovably stationed under my roof, where I commanded all the accessible parts of the corps-de-logis. Determined not to stir from my observatory while my Alexis remained in the opposite house, I continued day after day in the same unalterable posture, concealed behind the lattice work of my window, waiting an answer to my letter, and watching the abode of my child.

Sometimes, indeed, the tediousness of my situation was relieved by the inexpressible pleasure of seeing my Alexis himself, when taken out to enjoy his little exercise before the door; and beyond all conception was the rapture with which my eager eye pursued my darling infant, in the various little gambols and frolics, suggested by his delight at his short and rare emancipation from an irksome confinement: for even to him an excursion of the sort was now become a rare occurrence. It seems that the dread of my secret designs constantly haunted my adversaries, and never, after my visit, as before, did they suffer my child to be taken to any distance or even out of sight of the threshold, on which moreover – besides the woman who attended him – always stood waiting three or four male domestics, with eyes riveted on the boy during the whole of the time he remained out.

All this, however, proved how highly he was prized, with what tenderness he was treated, and how much his infantine happiness must be consulted, by those who detained him from his father; and amidst all my impatience I still blessed God, and sometimes almost my opponents themselves – miserable as they made me – for their love of my child.

For fear of unnecessarily exciting a premature alarm, which must still increase the distrust of the consular family and diminish the liberty of my boy, I took care never to show myself out of doors in the day time; and only at night, and when all else in Alexandria went to repose, ventured out to seek the little air and exercise which my health indispensably required.

The detached cluster of habitations of which mine was the humblest, stood nearly midway between the busy haunts of the modern town and the deserted site of the ancient city; and it was among the gloomy ruins of the latter that I by preference went at dusk to take my lonely walk. The few straggling pillars – some nodding on their bases and others deprived of their capitals – which, though dismal trunks at best, still stood erect among the prostrate remains around, as the lonely and deserted memorials of the splendid and busy scene of which they once formed a part, presented to my imagination a fate so like my own, that I often thought I read in the looks of these impassible monuments, the soothing sympathy withheld from me by man.

One evening, after a few hasty turns round that wide deserted area, which once contained the finest library, the most celebrated school, and the busiest population of antiquity, I sat down to rest myself in the most dreary part of the dreary solitude, on the margin of a yawning catacomb, whose sloping gallery seemed to penetrate unto the inmost bowels of the earth. Suddenly, in the midst of my melancholy musings, sprang up from the dark recesses of the subterraneous vault almost underneath my feet, a phantom of preternatural appearance, which, after taking two or three strides, stopped to look round; but no sooner caught the first glimpse of my person, than it again darted forward, and disappeared among the mouldering masses. Except two large glaring eyes, I had been able to distinguish no one feature intervening between the monstrous turban and enormous beard, which encircled the face of this strange figure. Its height seemed to exceed the ordinary stature of man. Wrapped up in an ample robe which trailed on the ground, it glided along rather than walked; and I thought that if it belonged to the world above ground, and not to that of the Gouls from which it came last, it could scarcely be regarded as any thing but a lineal descendant of Pharaoh's own body sorcerers.

To whatever class of beings the apparition might belong, this seemed equally certain, that it felt little wish to be better known: – but it was precisely that very circumstance which made me resolve to pursue it and find out its real nature; heedless of dangers which caution might not be able to see, or courage to overcome. The motion of my shadow, cast forward by the moon, officiously announcing my intention, the mysterious personage, who seemed to have stopped behind some wall or pier to reconnoitre his observer, again rushed forward from his ambush, and went on. It is true he lengthened his steps in such a way only as to avoid the appearance of positively running away from my pursuit: but his knowledge of the intricacies and windings of the place nevertheless gave him so great an advantage, that in spite of my superior agility I hardly gained ground upon him, except when I was expressly allowed to overshoot the mark, by his sliding behind some friendly wall or hillock, whence he no sooner saw me on a wrong scent, than away he again dived in an opposite directions.

Thus did the chase last full half an hour, when, to my utter astonishment, I found myself again brought back, by an immense circuit, to the mouth of the very cave from whose dark entrails the phantom fist had darted forth, and into whose unfathomable abyss it would now again irrecoverably have plunged, but for the circumstance most pointedly intended to avoid detection; – I mean the ample flow of its garment, which, just at the entrance of the vault, caught in a projecting stone, and in defiance of all the pulling and tearing of its wearer, would not be disentangled, and brought the mysterious fugitive to a dead stop.

I now grasped him tight round the waist, forced up his head which he was trying to hold down, and by the light of the moon beheld – with wonder beheld, spite of his enormous turban,– the Italian improvisatore who at Smyrna, after promising me promotion in the empire of reason, had cruelly left me to languish in that of despotism. "Heavens;" cried I, "Cirico, is it you?"

"It is," answered the detected poet; after he had stood a while considering whether he should say yes or no: "and would you had been in Erebus, ere you found me out!"

"And what business, may I ask, can a man, accustomed to preach Jacobinism along the highways, have to dress like a bearded Magus, and take up his abode under ground in the catacombs of Egypt?"

"Do you promise secrecy," said Cirico – looking at me earnestly.

"While I live," cried I; – "provided, for once, you choose to abstain from fiction."

"Then, listen," replied the son of Apollo; "and be content with plain prose," – upon which, offering me a seat beside him on the prostrate obelisk to which we now had advanced, he began as follows.

"You remember my sudden disappearance from Smyrna. Prompted however to my departure rather by an abstract wish to leave that city, than by a distinct preference for any other particular place, I had myself rowed to the first vessel in the harbour ready to set sail; and, when under weigh, asked whither I was going? To Alexandria was the answer, – and it pleased me. I remembered hearing a certain Embassador at Constantinople talk of his Consul in Egypt as a man entirely absorbed, not in trade or politics, but in magnetism; and it was on the never-sufficiently-to-be-praised virtues of that mysterious fluid that I built my little scheme. The chain of evidence as to my identity, between the sea ports of the Levant more to the westward, and Alexandria, was easily broken by my landing at Damiat, assuming the garb of the country, and only appearing at Alexandria some months after my departure from Smyrna, so completely smoke dried, and with such a beard, and such a benish, that, but for pulling off my turban as you did, you yourself would never have found me out. I therefore burst upon this new world like one of those torrents which, from an unknown source in the snow-Alps, plunge down all at once into the vale below. It must however be confessed that, when first introduced to the Consul on whom I intended to operate, in the character of an Italian nobleman on his way to the Pyramids, the colossal figure of the uncouth

Scythian, his shaksheer hanging about his heels, his turban awry on his head, and still more than all that, his face resembling that of an old leopard, with a pair of whiskers diverging from under his broad flat nose like the bristles of a clothes brush, so disconcerted me, as at first to put my whole story out of my head: nor was the little tale I had prepared of much use when recalled to my remembrance, as I found by the Consul's account that he himself was filled with so vast a supply of the magnetic virtue, as only to want a person as void of intellect as full of faith, for the purpose of being made the passive recipient of his all powerful influence. Nothing therefore was required of me in this affair, but to seem a chef-d'oeuvre of natural dullness – a vacuum that should contain no single thought of its own to clash with the brilliant coruscations of which I was to become the unconscious vehicle.

"And could an improvisatore of the first water," cried I, interrupting Cirico, "submit thus to conceal his talents; to hide his light under a bushel; to stem the tide of his poetic *estro*, by which I have been more than once nearly overwhelmed?"

"Friend!" resumed Cirico, "no difficulties could for an instant arrest a genius like mine. A plan immediately presented itself to my mind, which might combine in any proportion I wished the imbecility demanded of me by my magnetizer, and the uninterrupted worship I had vowed the Muses: – the Consul's offers were accepted; I left the Pyramids to their fate, and staid to be magnetized."

"But! – when thrown into the customary coma, in what shape do you think that the emanations of the Consul's intellect, with which his dumpy claws had been cramming me until the perspiration trickled like dew drops down his whiskers, flowed from my poetic lips? Can a bell – whatever substance may strike it – give any sound but that of metal? Can a harp, – touched by whom it may – be mistaken for a drum? Then let who might magnetize Giacinto Cirico, I still could only spout Italian operas. Availing myself of the leisure which my apparent idiocy gave me, to spend the whole day in compositions intended some time or other to eclipse those of Metastasio himself, I recited these high wrought productions of my own Muse, on the magnetic evenings as the spontaneous explosion of the Consul's prompting genius: and though this gentleman felt a little startled at first at the strange form his emanations assumed, and wondered he should have inspired me with the *scenas* of a pastoral or a ballet; he soon discovered in my recitativos and arias a mystic sense, as I soon derived from them a solid support: – for I affected to feel much exhausted by the operation, and took special care that the sittings should not be gratuitous."

"Even this, however, could hardly make me amends for the mortification I constantly experienced, since the consul felt so fearful lest the world might not give his magnetic virtue the credit of my effusions, that to my own face he used to tell every new comer what an idiot I was; until, to avoid this daily disgust, as well as the danger of being detected while at my work, I took the habit of retiring during the greater part of the day to these ruins, where I write undisturbed, and whence I only issue forth in the evening at the magnetic hour. I was just going to my task, when, by squatting yourself down over the mouth of my cavern, you kept me entrapped, until, fearing to be late I made a bold push, which ended in my discovery. But you are too honourable to betray one who reposes in you such unbounded confidence."

The poet here stopped, and left me to ruminate. After a few moments of equal silence on both sides, "Cirico," said I, "tell me one thing. I have a *pet* consul as well as yourself. I know they frequently visit. Is Signor R—— likewise bitten?"

"He is," replied the improvisatore.

"Then Heaven relents!" cried I, – and once again felt hope and joy revive: then told Cirico my story, and having concluded it; "now," added I "you must do me a favour. In your comas you must impress my consul – whether in song or in recitativo, no matter! – with the heinousness of keeping other people's children, and the inconvenience which may arise from such proceedings; and if by so doing you get mine restored to me, depend upon my eternal gratitude and services." Cirico promised to compose an interlude on purpose; and departed to join his expectant circle: – so did I to return to my lonely lodging.

And more lonely, more sad still was it fated to become: for presently even the transient gleams of happiness reflected upon its walls from the opposite mansion – the occasional glimpses I had of my child – were destined to cease; and this through my own fault too!

It happened the day after the interview with the poet. As usual my eyes were riveted upon the door of the consular mansion: as usual it began to vibrate slowly to turn upon its hinges, and, cautiously half opened, to let out as if by stealth my Alexis and his nurse, to take a little air within its immediate reach: but while the woman settles some part of her garment, the little fellow – moved by a sudden impulse – slily slips his hand through her negligent fingers, and feeling himself at liberty, darts forward like an arrow, and in play runs and hides behind my projecting wall. From my own window my eye plunging right upon him, beheld his sweet face peeping out now and then to enjoy his nurse's search; and down I rushed to embrace my heart's darling: – but already it was too late! Already had Alexis, unwilling to distress his favourite, run back to her arms; and when I came out, he seemed, by the warmth of his caresses, to be craving her pardon.

Could a father witness such endearments, and abstain from claiming his share! Great as was the imprudence of the act, I ran after my child, and in its nurse's own resisting arms, imprinted on its lovely face a thousand hurried kisses.

From the moment my person had appeared in sight, the woman had set up such a yell of frantic imprecations, as soon brought out into the road all the other too remiss attendants. Immediately they strove to tear the child away from me, – and fearful lest it should suffer in the struggle, I relinquished my hold; but going home I kissed as I went along each print of its dear little feet.

From that hour the sight of my darling boy was vouchsafed me no longer. One, two, three whole subsequent days – spent in the most anxious expectation and watching – were slowly brought to their conclusion, without my being able to perceive the least glimpse even of those to whose care my child seemed especially committed: and while in the day time I was thus disappointed of my former solace, I could as little at night obtain sight at Cirico. As if actuated by some new impulse, he had ceased frequenting his former haunts; he answered not even my notes of enquiry into the progress of the business entrusted to him; and at last it struck me that the traitor, aware how much I had to say to his disadvantage, so far from labouring in my cause, might rather be trying to avoid me altogether, and secure himself a firmer support by services elsewhere to my disadvantage. From his unaccountable silence as well as disappearance, I concluded that not only he had imparted to my adversaries all my designs, but had assisted them in eluding my vigilance and conveying my Alexis away. At this idea, which every thing I perceived only tended to confirm, I no longer felt able to set bounds to my paternal anguish; ran out on the road, into the street, and on the quay; and wherever I went, denounced the detainers of my child, loaded them with imprecations, and tried to stir up on the populace to demolish their abode. Of this sally too I had to pay the penalty.

Mourad, against whom I had joined the insurgents – Mourad, whom I since had fought with Hassan – Mourad, whose blood my hand had drawn, and whose face it had disfigured, now ruled the Bahairé, and consequently was master at Alexandria. How ill I must stand in the favour of this implacable Bey, could not fail to be found out to my detriment, by those interested in baffling my exertions, and marring my project. They represented me as a spy of the Porte upon the rulers of Egypt, and gave to the real object of my journey the colour of a mere pretence. Accordingly, a few days only after I had seen my Alexis for the last time, I received a formal injunction from the governor of the place, in the name of the authorities of Cairo, to quit the land of Egypt within twenty-four hours, under pain of instant forfeiture of life.

At this blow I almost lost my senses. "They triumph then!" I cried, "my inhuman oppressors. They part me for ever from the only object capable of throwing a charm over my remaining days! Then why seek to preserve an odious existence: why not take away my child by force, or perish in the attempt!" And hereupon I determined, unless my Alexis was restored to me immediately, to deal death around, and to end with myself; – and, drawing out my handjar, sallied forth into the street to execute my purpose.

At the very first turn I met a messenger sent by Cirico in search of my lodging. He slipped into my hands a pencil note, only containing these short words, "To the catacombs without delay!"

Without delay I went. I had always, it is true, believed Cirico to be a rogue; but not an ill natured rogue. Though he would most gladly have seen all the crowned heads of Europe struck like pumpkins upon poles, I was convinced that he would rather of the two help to keep that of a private friend upon its own shoulders. Already had he been waiting some time, when I reached the place appointed.

"Hush!" cried he in a solemn tone, seeing me more my lips to speak, "waste not uselessly your breath: it may be wanted hereafter. Magnetism; – that mystery which reveals all other mysteries – has informed me of all that you are burning to relate. I might have predicted it; but why announce evils which we cannot prevent!"

"Is this all you have to say?" exclaimed I, disappointed.

"Not at all;" answered Cirico. "The consul has by my magnetic speeches been made to feel compunction for his unjust proceedings: he is certain now your brat will bring him ill luck."

"Then why does he not restore the angel to its parent?"

"Because he is prevented by superior fears."

"Of what?"

"Of the thing to him most awful, – of his wife; whose attraction I always found to be of the negative sort. After my magnetic sleep I took R—— into a corner, and spoke to him broad awake. He then ventured to acknowledge his dread of his rib; and owned he would give the world to see justice done you, provided he had no hand in the doing. In short, you have his leave to recover your child in whatever way you please – by stratagem or by force."

"Little thanks to any man for that privilege;" cried I: – "such a sort of leave I might have taken without asking it."

"R—— means," rejoined the poet, "that if you should devise a clever method of smuggling the urchin out of his mansion, or even of entering it by storm, – if no measure less daring will do, he will not stand in the breach to repel you, nor yet struggle very hard to wrest the prize out of his hands."

"But if I fail, I must take all the consequences."

"Just so. He will then enforce in all its rigour the decree of the Beys, in order to clear himself to his loving wife from all suspicion of connivance."

I paused a while: – at last, "Cirico," cried I, "fires are frequent evils in these realms. Tell the Consul – the instant he smells the least smoke – not to fail turning his whole gynecaeum into the street." And thus having given a hint of my scheme, we discussed the best mode of execution,-having settled which, not without a good deal of argumentation, we parted for the present: but soon to meet again in a different spot.

CHAPTER XIII.

Beginning with the purpose in which my plan was to end, I first went to the harbour, to see what vessels were ready for sailing. Besides a felucca, brimful of fresh-made hadjees, going to be dropped at the different Barbary ports, I only found a small polacre laden with grain for Ancona, already in the roads, and only waiting the evening land-breeze to set sail. In consideration of the liberal price to be paid for the passage, the captain agreed to weigh anchor the instant I should come on board.

Thus provided on one element, I began to consider how to manage the opposite element on which my scheme depended: but I own I saw much greater difficulty in making an useful ally of fire than of water; and it puzzled me not a little how to raise a flame round the consular mansion and yet not to pass for an incendiary. The gynecaeum besides, which I was most anxious to smoke, lay at the back of the house, and stood screened from external approach by a high and impervious wall. To kindle combustibles under its well screened windows in such a way as to occasion a great fright and very little real mischief, might have baffled the skill of an abler engineer. My expedient was to suspend bundles of wool, straw, and other stuff, by means of wires to long slender poles.

The hour being arrived which was wont to witness the first consular slumbers, our hostile operations commenced. Part of my myrmidons hid themselves with their fire apparatus behind some rubbish near the quarter which I meant to alarm, and there waited my signal, while the remainder, with myself, lay perdu behind a low shed near the entrance door. The shrill whistle which was to set all in motion soon was sounded, and presently we saw slowly rise from behind the beleaguered building a thick column of smoke, which not only over-canopied the spreading roof, but circulated in a wavy stream round the various apartments. Loud cries of "Fire" hailed its appearance from without: the alarm was given to the inhabitants by repeated knocking at all the apertures; and, in a few minutes, it was evident that every soul in the mansion was on foot.

Yet did not a creature venture out. The door on which my eyes were riveted remained as immovably fast as before, and while the neighbours began to flock from all quarters to the spot, the inert inmates of the house seemed to make no attempt to escape.

My mind now again misgave me, and suspicions of every sort rushed into my imagination. Perhaps after all Cirico had played me false; perhaps the consul had found his courage or his cowardice fail him; perhaps my enemies were actually watching to surprise me in the commission of a seemingly heinous crime. Meanwhile minute after minute was elapsing: the night watch of the Franks would soon go its rounds; nay my combustibles, almost burnt out, threatened to put a speedy end to the siege, even independent of a sally or a rescue; – when no other fate could befall Alexis's miserable father but being driven out of Egypt, and forced to bid his child – his darling child – an everlasting farewell.

In this situation I had already begun to consider whether it might not be better to take myself off at once, than to await the issue of my desperate scheme, when at last the house door, – suddenly bursting open with a tremendous crash, – poured forth in one single rapid stream into the street a far longer string of females than I had fancied the whole mansion could contain.

The consuless herself led the van, enveloped in a loose wrapper. Immediately after came my Alexis, still flushed with rosy sleep, and in the arms of his nurse. A set of pale and ghastly attendants, screaming to attract notice, brought up the rear.

No time was to be lost: – while my trusty attendants darted across the way to break the line of the procession, and to insulate the nurse, I sprung forward to snatch away the child: but already had my figure caught the eye of his ever watchful guardian. She gave her usual warning scream, and instinctively all the other women echoed the yell. The concert brought around us all the bystanders who had gradually collected, and who, seeing a tall fellow lay hold of an infant and carry it off, stopped not to inquire his right, but immediately set up after me a general cry and pursuit.

For rendering it ineffectual I relied on my agility, assisted by the deep shadows of the night: but the pursuing troop was too near, and at every step I advanced, its numbers were encreased by all those who, running to the fire, met us on the way, and turned back to join the chase. The only thing I could do was to draw my yatagan, and, while with one arm I shielded my babe from the incessant shower of stones, with the other to brandish my weapon, and to beat off the pelting mob. Sometimes, in order to prevent being closed in upon, I was obliged to face about and to make a few passes, calculated to teach those who came too near their proper distance: but in so doing a sharp pebble hit my lovely infant's face, and made the blood gush in streams from his cheek. At this sight I grew desperate: my strength seemed to increase tenfold; and at every stroke of my sabre some miscreant was maimed, or bit the dust.

What power could resist a father fighting for his child! Terror gradually seized all the nearest rabble: the rest slackened their pace; and a certain space intervened between the pursuers and their intended prey. I was about a dozen yards ahead of the foremost, when the lanthorn, agreed upon as the signal of the boat, began to glimmer on the shore. I now mustered all my remaining strength, and, with only such few windings as were necessary to throw the bloodhounds off the scent, made for the beacon. Many, tired of the chase, had already given in; and a small portion only of the pack still kept yelping at a distance.

I therefore thought myself safe: – when all at once between me and the goal flashed like forked lightning two sabres, whose wearers, guessing my intention, had by a shorter cut got before me, and were now waiting to cut off my retreat.

What was to be done? – An instant I stopped and hesitated: but with a dozen rascals at my heels, and only two in front, I had no choice, and went forward. At the critical moment I suddenly waved my hand, and, as if addressing some friends stationed near, cried out to fire. The expectant pair on this started back, and looked round, while I seized my opportunity, and darted by them like a thunderbolt. They soon, however, rallied again, and one actually had his hand on my shoulder, and was at last going to stop my career, when, wheeling half round, I released my person at the expense of his fingers. The low reef now lay before me under which was moored the boat, and, having scrambled on the platform, I was going to leap in, when, just at that moment a loose stone made me slip, and I plunged into the waves between the rock and the barge. My child escaped all injury. Caught by Cirico, who stood on the projecting ledge waiting my arrival, he was handed safe to the sailors: but his father had less luck. The zeal of the boatmen to disentangle me, making them all press upon the side of the boat under which I lay wedged, their collective weight almost crushed me to death; and I was only extricated with a couple of ribs broken, my chest miserably bruised, and my loins almost pierced through by the sharpness of the rocks.

Having fainted the instant I was dragged into the boat, I continued in that state until conveyed on board the ship. There, when various applications had at last brought me to life again, I found that we were under weigh, and already far out at sea. Still could my first sensations scarcely be called very pleasant. With consciousness had come pain: my inward bruises now tortured me, and occasioned constant expectorations of blood. As soon, however, as I recovered my speech I enquired after my child, and he was pointed out to me by the captain, lying in a little crib, and just lapsed – after a world of woe – into a profound and tranquil sleep. When first put on board, the blood mixed with dust which entirely covered his face, had rendered him a frightful spectacle: but on the unsightly crust being washed off, there only remained a small cut under his eye, of little importance. His chief distresses had been those of his susceptible mind. Torn in the middle of the night from an elegant mansion, a troop of tender females, and an affectionate nurse, and that, to be the object of a sanguinary contest, to receive a smarting wound, and to be put on board a miserable vessel, where nothing met his eye but strange and hard featured sailors, whose very offices of kindness looked more like acts of violence, no wonder that the sensitive child should at first have shrunk with terror from the novel and appalling scene; – and it was only when exhausted with fruitless entreaties and crying, that he fell into the quiet slumber in which, on recovering my senses, I found the little angel deeply sunk.

Notwithstanding my aches and my weakness, when, after so many difficulties and dangers, I thus saw the object of all my hopes and fears at last safe in my possession, I could not be restrained from giving full scope to my raptures, crawled to the crib entrusted with my treasure, and there – afraid to disturb its soft slumbers – knelt and gazed upon it in an ecstasy of joy. Scarce could I believe so much loveliness to be my own, and in my transport – as I was afterwards told – I laughed and cried in turn, until the whole crew thought me positively crazed. By degrees, however, I became somewhat more composed: but as the ferment of my joy abated, my pains put in their claims afresh, until at last – unable to bear an upright posture –, I lay down by my babe, awaiting the moment when, breaking form his sleep, he should leave me at liberty to press him to my bosom.

Far different from mine however, were, on first awaking, my boy's own emotions. The moment he unclosed his eyes a look of terror overcast his sweet countenance. He stared fearfully around, seemed awhile wholly lost in amazement at things so new and strange, and then, recollecting the change he had experienced, burst into a flood of tears, and loudly called his paramana. In vain I addressed him in the most soothing language, – saying I was his father, and my care for my child should exceed all other care. His only answer was to entreat I would restore him to the friends from whom I had stolen him; and on my stating the impossibility of granting his petition, he loaded me with all the innocent invectives which his gall-less imagination could suggest. No peace offering of which I could think was accepted, whether addressed to the eye or the plate; all my gifts were spurned, and only a fast, protracted long beyond the usual period, could for an instant make hunger impose silence on grief. Reluctantly my Alexis then consented to take some food at my hands;-and at this was the first paternal office I ministered to my child. For several days I myself continued to want the nursing I bestowed. Only when I lay motionless on my back did the pain in my loins become bearable. The smallest exertion renewed all my agonies, and called forth fresh streams of blood from my chest. Insensibly, however, the symptoms of an internal injury became less alarming; the broken ribs seemed to knot again, and the external bruises healed apace: but I remained languid, incapable of enduring the least fatigue, totally bereft of appetite, and seldom visited by refreshing slumbers.

Those of my child were my only cordial. Determined not to be disheartened by his first repulses, which only showed the steadiness of his infant mind, I continued my endearments with unwearied perseverance, until at last I gained his good-will and his confidence. Many, it is true, were the days ere I could drive from his memory the constant thoughts of his regretted home, and even after he seemed in general reconciled to the change, he would still at particular hours, and sometimes in the very midst of his mirth and laughter, display a sudden revulsion of features, and break into fresh and poignant paroxysms of grief: but in the yet soft and pliant organs of his infant brain the impression of things and persons wholly gone by were gradually effaced, and the later objects which replaced these, stamped on it their fresher and more recent forms with at least equal force: he accustomed himself to his situation, and recovered his serenity. His anxious mind became susceptible of a new species of uneasiness, – that of losing sight of me: and at last, won over entirely by my love, he transferred to his father all the warm affections of his susceptible heart.

He even gave me more than he had given yet: for, to the singularly early development of his reason and moral feeling, his former guardians had not yet thought of addressing themselves; and by appealing the first to these new expanding faculties, I obtained over him a stronger hold, while I paid him a more flattering homage, than he had yet experienced. Mine had been the first consolatory speeches: – it was he now who studied to soothe my sufferings in his care; who unceasingly watched my countenance, and studied to alleviate every symptom of my complaint; amused me with his prattle when I felt in good spirits, and lay down in silence by my side, when I looked dejected and sorrowful. How, therefore, – in the absence of all other feelings, and on the cessation of every other tie, – I began to dote on this sole object of all my thoughts and projects, no words can express. Hour after hour I hung over his cherub face, contemplating as in a mirror that of his lovely and unhappy mother; and many a time, when his heavenly smile beamed upon me, when his little arms hung round my neck, and when his lips imprinted soft kisses on my cheek, I thought: "Anastasius, Anastasius, what has thou done to deserve such a blessing? Tremble lest it should prove an honied cup, offered to thy lips by an avenging Providence, only for an instant to be tasted, – then dashed to the ground!"

Our voyage was prosperous enough, until we got into the latitude of Cerigo. There a perverse tramontana seemed to lie in wait with no other object than to shut against us the narrow entrance of the Adriatic. If now and then the wind did come about for a moment, we no sooner began to make a little way than, as if on purpose to mock us, it immediately again shifted back to its old quarter. It afforded a Malthese privateer every convenience for making us bring to; and the ship's papers being deemed somewhat suspicious, and the cargo Turkish property outright, the vessel was compelled to change its course to Maltha; there to undergo legal investigation. That island wanted corn, and the captain himself seemed to have no objection to a shorter voyage and a better market. Useless, under such circumstances, would have been the opposition of a passenger. What is he by the side of the cargo, – by that of a single bale of goods? And I comforted myself with the thought, that I should sooner be on land, and more speedily obtain medical advice.

A lazaretto is a sort of purgatory, intervening between the regions of infidelity and the realms of true belief; and quarantine may be termed an ordeal through which all must pass, who, coming from the one, seek admittance into the other. Arrived in my place of temporary confinement at Maltha, I employed the period required to prove my freedom from one species of disease, in taking remedies for another, less violent – but, alas! more tenacious. The inward soreness continued unabated, spite of all the emollients and drugs liberally supplied me from the medicine chest of a traveller, who had been encaged, on his return from a voyage to the Levant, about the same time with myself.

Designing, I suppose, to write a book, Signor Lauri (that was the gentleman's name) seemed as anxious to settle his estimate of his nations which he had just quitted, as I felt desirous of forming an opinion of those whose precincts I was on the point of entering; whence our conversation turned chiefly turned upon the difference between the natives of the East and those of the West. The predestinarian principles of the former found in my friend a doughty opponent – which he was particularly fond of handling. "What" – used he to exclaim, sagaciously knitting his brow – "can be more absurd in theory, and prejudicial in practice – more destructive of all prudence, and more inimical to all exertion – than to maintain that, whatever be the nature of intervening occurrences, certain peculiar leading events, widely distant from each other – such as the choice of a wife, the birth of a child, the accession to an estate, the hour of death, or our state in the life hereafter, – must still take the same course? It is totally denying all connection between cause and effect."

"You are right," I answered: "that connection appears to preserve, from the very first origins of things unto their last perceptible development, a continuity so entire, so unbroken, that instead of this partial, disjointed, incomplete predestination, only existing by halves, only ruling a few detached incidents of our lives, only presenting insulated phenomena, arising from no previous cause, and producing no subsequent effects, we can admit nothing short of an universal pre-ordination, embracing alike every minutest occurrence and every most important event of our existence."

Here my friend's disturbance increased: he asked what was to become, with such an universal predestination, of our free-agency, our free-will?

"Whatever can or may," was my answer. "Even he would think himself possessed of free-agency in its utmost fullness, from his hand being ever left to execute uncontrolled every wildest wish of his mind, (and how few there are that labour under so dire a misfortune!) is still not a free-agent in the smallest degree, since the will from which his actions proceed is not free."

"The will itself not free!" cried Lauri, quite aghast; – "and that, even where, instead of being the immediate result of some headlong, over-ruling passion, it should be the slow and deliberate offspring of the longest suspense, and the most mature consideration?"

"Not even then," I resumed. "The first desire of modifying the will according to such mature consideration, of submitting it to such protracted suspense (conditions witnessed but seldom) can only have arisen from such a mass of knowledge unintentionally acquired, and such a concurrence of impressions unintentionally experienced, as must render the later results more obviously than ever the effect only of circumstances wholly incompatible with the inherent freedom of that will."

"Then let us at least," cried Lauri in complete despair, "– thus tied hands and feet – derive from our indestructible fetters another species of comfort: let us no longer struggle to obtain what we may wish for; but lie still, and suffer ourselves to be quietly swept down the stream of our uncontrollable destiny. Our efforts to mend it must be all in vain."

"And are you so blind," replied I rather bluntly, "as not to perceive that whatever faculty of commanding future events we lose by a partial and disjointed predestination – according to which, as certain occurrences happen without regular causes, others must remain unproductive of regular consequences – is more than restored to us by a pre-ordination so universal, that nothing can arise except from an uninterrupted series of prior modifications; that, consequently, when we employ the means uniformly appropriated by Providence to peculiar ends, we have no failure to fear except from the opposition of other modifications, as yet unknown perhaps, but equally subjected by that Providence to definite rules; and finally, that, though our will and our knowledge must ever proceed from some of the prior phenomena of that pre-ordination, that very knowledge and will may themselves in their turn produce some of its later yet undeveloped ramifications? Name a single instance of the power in man to command, to calculate, to foresee future events, founded on his experience of past occurrences, which can originate in any thing but the necessary pre-ordained connection between them."

"Still," muttered Lauri, – "whatever left our will invariably depending on our knowledge, and our knowledge on extraneous circumstances, must annihilate our claim to eternal rewards, and our liability to everlasting punishment."

"Why then," was my reply, "let us give up altogether those sufferings without end, which, of use neither to deter nor to correct, seem after all a little reconcilable with the justice or the goodness of a Creator, who, having made his creatures fallible, would hardly, at any period of time, shut the gates of mercy for ever against the repentant sinner. Indeed, it may be questioned, in my opinion, whether even a penal retribution limited in its duration is, logically speaking, consistent with the relation between a creature in a retrospective view entirely passive, and his omnipotent Creator; or admissible otherwise than between man and man."

"Take away the legality of punishments," cried Lauri with a victorious smile, "and you take away the existence of deserts!"

"To insist on the smallest deserts with respect to his Maker," I answered, "seems to me in man the height of presumption. Man had no right to be born: he owes his existence, his very virtues, to the bounty of his Creator, and to that bounty I am content to owe all my happiness, here and hereafter, even if I were to be raised to the perfection of an angel; and as to punishments, or, in other words, sufferings not arising immediately from the nature of the deeds, or from the desire of producing amendment in the author – I myself, wretched creature, prone to passion, and often inflamed by an irresistible thirst for vengeance as I am, could inflict chastisement on my own sweet babe, and for faults for which I scarce can blame him, otherwise than in order to render him ultimately both better and happier!"

"Adieu, then," resumed Lauri piteously, "if not to all motives for exertion, at least to all exertions in the cause of virtue! Your preordination, and the utter absence of accountability it implies, cannot fail to afford to those that desire it a free licence for every vice!"

"A licence so injurious, so depreciable," I observed, "could only derive from a doctrine – if such there be – which should destroy the natural, the inherent, the eternal connection between good deeds and happiness; and should admit a chance of obtaining bliss eternal, without renouncing evil."

"But mine, " added I, "is not a doctrine. However much preordination may seem to cancel man's accountability, and to take from his sufferings the character of direct punishment, it is not the less true (and too well I feel it!) that, according to that very preordination, misery is on this side of the grave or on the other the unavoidable consequence of evil, and real permanent happiness only attainable through corresponding goodness; and is so the more, from the very strictness of that preordination."

"But what boots," Lauri asked, "even a preordination thus directed, without that free agency, that free will, which alone can enable us to turn its laws to our advantage?"

"As soon," was my answer, "as the knowledge of an indispensable connection between virtue and happiness reaches our heart, our will must, from its very want of freedom, its very subservience to our knowledge, become unavoidably abhorrent from evil; and until a knowledge of such a connection is attained, the utmost freedom of will could still not induce a preference for good. Who, therefore, has – no matter how – himself attained that knowledge, will rather endeavour to lead others, through its diffusion and empire over their will, irresistibly to good, than risk tempting them, by insisting on the freedom of their volition, to try its independence in resisting virtue's voice; and since I have (not without paying dearly for it) at last obtained a glimpse of this valuable knowledge, with you, my Alexis!" added I, embracing my child, "let me begin the pleasing task of rendering it fruitful!"

For the sake of this darling child, I gave up a project, to the performance of which I had long pertinaciously clung: – it was that of a solemn and public abjuration of Islamism. This scheme, it is true, had already been forcibly combated by Caridi, the chief promoter of my voyage to Trieste "Why," used he to say, "make your return to the faith of your fathers, which in reality can only be an act of the mind, a spectacle for the multitude? It is a thing more likely to scandalize than to edify: to remind people that the church suffered an infidelity, than that it recovered a stray sheep:' – but though my reason gave assent to the remark, my heart still recoiled from the counsel. I always seemed to be composed of two wholly distinct persons: the one argumentative, sophistical; the other entirely under the influence of my imagination; and these different beings never became sufficiently amalgamated into one single uninterrupted identity. Now, of those two persons the latter was the one which exerted most sway on this occasion. I felt as if it wanting all the outward shew of penitence, all the external demonstration of sorrow, effectually to atone for my errors, and to hush my remorse. To lie in the dead of night, on the cold pavement of the church, before the cross of our Saviour or the shrine of my patron saint; to wash the steps of the sanctuary with my tears, or to make its walls re-echo with my moanings, seemed to be that which could alone restore to my mind its composure, and to my heart its tranquillity; but my Alexis had attained that age at which the spectacle of my penance must convey to him the suspicion of my shame – the knowledge of my guilt; – and what tender parent can give up the esteem of his child! Nay, even if the acknowledgements of my transgressions were not to lower me in his estimation, the memory of my debasement might lower his own value in the eyes of the world. Whatever conditions, therefore, my more scrupulous cousin might exact from me at a later period, on my arrival in Trieste, I determined for the present only to slide back into the bosom of the church unperceived, and to avail myself of the high walls and deep solitude of my prison, to resume in silence the solemn rites of my ancestors, and the old, often regretted, Christian name of Anastasius, given me by my parents.

Determined to shake off as much as possible all that marked the native of the East, and to adopt all that might assist me to assimilate with the children of the West, I proceeded from the inward to the outward man; but though my person was no longer as erst the dearest idol of my heart, I yet continued sufficiently impressed with the advantage of good looks, to feel a very different sensation on quitting the Osmanlee attire from that which I had experienced on doffing the Santon's rags. It seemed to me a sort of degradation to exchange the rich and graceful garb of the East, which either shews the limbs as nature moulded them, or makes amends for their concealment by ample and majestic drapery, for a dress which confines without covering, disfigures without protecting, gives the gravest man the air of a mountebank, and, from the uncouth shape of the shreds sowed together, only looks like the invention of penury for the use of beggars: – and when I came to mutilating my very person, to cutting into its quick; – when, without being able to give my face a feminine softness, I was only going to deprive it of the signs of manhood; to sever from my lips my long cherished mustachios, I own it required all the philosophical reflections I could muster upon the nothingness of a few hairs, to persuade me to lay the fearful steel to their roots.

But what was the difficulty of changing the outward trappings of the body, to that of dismissing the habits rooted in the inmost recesses of the mind? What was that of adopting the dress which the tailor could model, to that of assuming manners which must be the result of the nicest observation and the longest practice? In the East a different age, and sex, and nation, and rank and profession, however closely intermixed with the others, still retains its peculiar garb and formulas, its stated place and boundaries, as distinctly marked as they are immutably fixed. In the East centuries succeed centuries; new generations step on those which have gone before them, and empires themselves are founded and are destroyed, without the limits that circumscribe the different races of men and orders of society being confounded or transgressed. In the East nothing in point of forms, of address, and of manners is indefinite, or arbitrary, or mutable, or left to the impulse of the moment or the taste of the individual. In the East therefore it is easy to learn by rote the unchangeable exigencies of society; and every individual, whatever situation he may obtain – whether from a slave he become a master, from a civilian a soldier, or from a subject a sovereign – immediately knows how to fit himself to his new place, and how to act his new part, void of embarrassment and awkwardness; nay – of vulgarity.

Far different appeared the system of the West! There, on the contrary, whatever the eye could view or the mind comprehend – from the most fundamental organization of states to the most superficial gloss of social intercourse, seemed unfixed, discretional, subject to constant revolution, and like the coat of the cameleon, borrowing a different hue from every passing cloud. There each different sex, age, nation, rank and profession, instead of the strongly marked outlines and forcibly contrasted colours of the East, on all sides only shewed blending shades, evanescent forms, prominences rubbed away, and features confounded – tones, looks, and language, distinguished only by gradations so imperceptible, by shades so delicate, that a long study alone could disclose the theory, and long habit alone teach the performance of their ultimate refinements. There the prejudices of the individual, constantly at variance with the laws of the land, and the duties imposed by religion, uniformly clashing with the latitude required by custom, were each to be in turns distinguished and yet blended, obeyed and yet disregarded, without the act appearing an effort, or the effect producing a discordance; nay, there, the mind, always kept on the stretch, was not even allowed to unbend in repose after business was ended, but must still, in the hours of leisure – not hours of relaxation – encounter the new toil of constantly supplying matter for discourse, suited at once to the peculiar character of the speaker, and to those of the diversified listeners.

Yet did it now become my task – alone, untutored and uncounselled – to embody with my original substance, ideas and habits, these intangible new forms and these indefinable new shades, which many of the natives themselves but awkwardly wear; – and that at an age too when the cast of my own character was fixed and stiffened into irremediable permanence by the cold hand of time: on pain of exciting the sneers of the cold, fastidious, unsympathizing spectators of the new stage which I was going, uncheered and unsupported, to tread. – Arduous was the task; small the hope of success!

In fact, whether from the loss of health and the prostration of spirits I had laboured under, ever since the accident which marked the last pressure of my feet on the shores of the East, or whether from the more appalling form assumed by the new objects before me as I approached them nearer, I every day began to contemplate with encreasing awe the idea of encountering a new world with which I had nothing in common. Every day that new world presented itself to my imagination more as a gloomy desert, to me without interest, without friends, and without happiness. The people of Europe seemed heartless, the virtues of the Franks frigid, the very crimes of the West dull and prosaïc; and I was like a plant which, reared in all the warmth of a hothouse, is going all at once to be launched into all the inclemency of an atmosphere, ripe with chilling blasts and nipping frosts.

Far, therefore, from waiting with impatience for the period that was to dismiss me from the narrow cell of my quarantine into the unlimited space of this new scene, I could not help looking forward to it with trepidation. As long as I remained within the pale of the establishment devoted to purification from my eastern stains, I felt as if only standing on the extremest verge of my native realms; as if not yet entirely removed from all contact with the parental soil, and not yet entirely beyond the influence of the paternal atmosphere; as if still able to fall back at will upon the fostering bosom on which I had been reared, and to regain by a timely retreat all my native rights and privileges: – but the threshold of the Lazaretto once crossed; the barred doors of the quarantine ground once closed behind me, it seemed as if a barrier deep as the centre of the earth, high as the heavenly vault, was to rise between the scenes of my youth and the remainder of my dreary existence; as if nothing that had been, could preserve the last connection with what was still to be.

When, therefore, the hour of my liberation struck; when I was bidden to walk forth, – ready to take my flight, and, like the bird driven from its downy nest, to plunge into boundless space, – I shrunk back, and for a few moments still doubted whether I should not after all forego my rash design, and, instead of walking forth among strangers, rather stay, and seek the first vessel in which I might return to the genial shores of the East.

But one great, one mighty thought superseded all others, and determined me to proceed. It was not for myself I went, – it was for my child: it was to perfect his education, to secure his future welfare, to render him in all respects a man different from his father. This idea gave resolution to my mind. I saw my luggage removed, took my Alexis by the hand, and hastily walked out.

Yet when, – arrived in the midst of the space that separates the precincts of the Lazaretto from the remainder of the Malthese territory, – I heard the fatal gates, only opened to let me out, again close with hollow clang, the awful sound sent through my inmost marrow; my heart seemed to sink within me, and, turning round, for the last time to contemplate the porch whence I had reluctantly gone forth, I could not help once more bidding all I left farewell. "Glorious sun of the East!" cried I with faltering tongue, "balmy breath of the Levant – warm affections of my beloved Greece, – adieu for ever! The season of flowers is gone by: that of storms and whirlwinds howls before me. Among the frosts of the North I must seek my future fortunes: a cradle of ice must rock my future hopes. For the bleak wastes and black firs of Gothic climes I am going to exchange the myrtle groves of Grecian valleys; and perhaps on the further borders of the chilly Neva it may be my fate to cherish the last remembrance of Ionia and of Chios!"

Thus saying, I took my cherub in my arms, pressed him against my panting bosom, inclined my face against his downy cheek – and went on.

CHAPTER XIV.

Anxious to gain the place of my destination, I hired a speronara to convey me to Sicily. As I passed under the galleys in Valetta harbour, and contemplated the batteries bristling on its shore: "See;" said to me one of my boatmen, "those engines of war employed to diffuse a religion of peace, by men who take the vows of priests and lead the lives of soldiers. One would suppose man short-lived and perishable enough by nature to have no need of so many contrivances of art, still to abridge his brief existence, and that not piece meal but wholesale: but so it is notwithstanding; and you who come from Turkey may perhaps smile to find in Christendom the trade of inflicting death a favourite livelihood!"

Etna fumed as I passed by: Charybdis shook, and Scylla growled: yet I land unimpeded at Messina, and there soon re-imbarked straight for Naples.

The inhabitants of this capital built upon a volcano seemed to me completely gone out of their senses. From the lowest lazzaroni up to their fishing, fowling, lazzaroni king, they were all rejoicing in a peace just concluded with revolutionary France, as madly as if war could thenceforth be no more. I carried letters from Maltha to two personages of the *nobiltà*: a gentleman and a lady; and had the extreme satisfaction of finding myself precisely recommended to the two people in all Naples who hated each other most cordially. M. de Silva was a wit: – on my first visit to him he took particular pains to warn me against the least attempt at consistency in my words or my actions. "Like our bodies," he observed, "our minds – and consequently our opinions and our feelings – must necessarily change every day; and he who, for the sake of that chimera consistency, is determined ever to adhere to what in some luckless moment he uttered, must sooner or later renounce all pretensions to truth." – To Silva's honour be it spoken; the doctrine which he preached he likewise practiced.

Me. de B——, being no wit, on the contrary made that consistency, which Silva regarded as the mark of a servile spirit, her principal boast. It had not prevented her – it is true – from changing her lovers very frequently: but that she accounted for. Finding her speak philosophically of her own proceedings – I begged of her one day to explain to me how, with so much freedom of manner, she had contrived to incur so little censure? "By leaving my reputation," answered she, "as all good Christians should do all their concerns, entirely to the care of Providence; showing others the indulgence I wanted for myself, and not imaging that to whitening my own conduct by blackening that of others." This was not wit, assuredly, nor even a happy choice of metaphor; but, to my mind, a sound, well-wearing sentiment.

Wishing to cultivate the society of both my friends with equal care, I took it into my head to patch up a peace between them. This treaty presented greater difficulties than had done that with France; for while Silva maintained that many things might be better, and was even supposed secretly to work at their improvement. Me. de B—— was for leaving every thing – her complexion excepted – as she found it. "Were we to live for ever on this globe," she used to say, "there would be ample time for every experiment, political as well as other; but, as matters stand, how are those to be indemnified who lose their lives in the process before the end is obtained? What can posterity do for them, that they should be happy to die for posterity?"

Upon the principle of not doing too much for posterity, Me. de B—— persevered in her *eloignement* from Silva; who, in revenge, undertook to estrange me from her parties; and for this purpose proposed to take me to a dinner of literary friends, – "with whom," he added, "it was absolutely necessary I should be acquainted."

I always bowed to necessity, which on this occasion, however, seemed synonymous with impossibility: for what chance had a stranger of slipping in a word, or of obtaining an answer, with men who all fancied to have rehearsed their parts beforehand. Accordingly I hardly opened my lips: but Silva, who fancied he had shone, returned home in raptures with his day. "Had you sufficient quickness," cried he, – "barbarian as you are – to observe the incessant circulation of the most ethereal wit? How at first a few light sparks began to flash at random from different points of the electric circle; each in turns eliciting fresh scintillations from the opposite quarter, until at last the whole table fired up into one single uninterrupted blaze of the most brilliant eloquence, repartee, and bon mot. What preparations, what vigilance, what readiness such conversation requires! What triumphs and what mortifications it causes! – Depend upon it, the repose of half the party has been disturbed for a fortnight, by the good things the other half said this evening."

"Charming effects," cried I, "of a convivial meeting!"

"And yet," resumed Silva, "you have not seen the genius of the party: he likes to make himself in request. To morrow we go and rouse him in his own den!"

A part of this den consisted of a handsome library, into which visitors were shewn while the genius prepared for his impromptu effusions. The levee had already begun. Three or four personages occupied the farthest recess of the room. One was humming a bravura air as he walked backwards and forwards, another trying steps and attitudes, a third poring upon a huge folio of prints, and the fourth, the moment we walked in, turned from us so abruptly to contemplate a small picture hung up in a niche, that I never saw his face.

My own attention was wholly engaged by the books. Those I had seen at Pera seemed to me a school-boy's bundle compared with this abyss of knowledge. Besides the shelves against the wall, absolutely bending under the weight of authors already marshalled in regular battle array against every denomination of ignorance – some heavy armed, others as light troops, others again as voltigeurs, belonging to no division in particular, but hovering in turns over the outskirts of each, – the very floor was covered with piles of still unsorted science, lying stewed about in a confused mass. I was amazed at the sight. "How many square feet of reading," cried I, "are here collected in one single apartment! How many ideas, good, bad, indifferent, true, erroneous and contradictory are jumbled together – some lying, some standing, some on end, and some, I apprehend, head over heels: – and will my poor Alexis have to cram all this lumber into his brain, ere he can pass among Franks for a man of understanding!"

"If he did," replied Silva, "I am afraid he would scarcely have a spare corner left for his own ideas: but the thing is wholly out of the question. Formerly, no dust equalled that of books for blinding people's eyes; modern wits wipe it clean away: – they write indeed, but no one reads. Even philosophers have ceased to prize knowledge the more for being at second hand. Men of talent now buy libraries only to say: 'they never read!'"

A clatter of doors, and a shuffle of slippers, now announced the approach of the genius. He appeared with locks dishevelled and a wild stare, intended for a look of inspiration; ran up to us in an ecstasy! embraced Silva, then me; then asked who I was; then congratulated himself upon beholding a Greek, and me upon beholding him; then dragged us by main force into what he called his sanctum; then told us the quartetto we had left in his anti-room consisted of a poet, a scene painter, a musical composer and a ballet master, all waiting his directions for the new opera; then complained of the endless labours his taste entailed upon him; then shewed us the list of the virtuosi and virtuose he patronized; then ran out as if bitten by the tarantula; then came in again making a thousand apologies; then informed us that Horace had no energy and Virgil no pathos; then recited an ode, three sonnets, and half the first canto of an epic poem of his own composing; then stopped to receive our applause, and to contemplate his person in the looking glass; then took a few lozenges to ease his chest; then asked me whether I did not infinitely prefer the misty sublime – that of Ossian – to that of Homer; then threw out a witticism or two, which he laughed at most heartily, and we also out of complaisance; then entreated to see me every day, except six of the week on which he was engaged; then made an appointment with us at the masked ball at San Carlo, and then dismissed us to return to the sons of Apollo whom he had left in his library.

Forced to join the party to the masquerade, I found but little pleasure in this to me novel entertainment. At first indeed the sight dazzled, but it soon tired, and at last annoyed me. I could not get rid of a soothsayer, who had singled me out as the object of his pursuit. Succeeding at last to take hold of my arm, and putting his mouth to my ear: "You think this form a borrowed one:" he whispered, – "undeceived yourself. People put on masks to exhibit their characters undisguised. I see, in reality, all that is hidden from others."

"Then who is it you are speaking to?" was the first question.

"A stranger:" was the answer.

"Doubtless! but from what country?"

"One to which you have sworn not to return."

"My name?"

"A Christian badge cast away among the Turks."

"You have seen me unmasked."

"For that, I must see have seen you undressed: – your present ordinary garb is itself but a mask assumed very recently; and I know that which lies deeper than even your inmost garment."

"What?"

"An asses skin!"

Here I began to wax wroth. "How so! Are you ashamed of a friend's last remembrance? Do your Spiridon's tablets begin to lie heavy on your bosom?" – was the query occasioned by my anger.

At these words my surprise increased. The sacred momento was indeed composed of the substance which bears the vulgar name[1] by which it was specified: but to no mortal in Christendom had I yet imparted its existence: – "Who can you be?" cried I, more eagerly than before.

"*That* I came not here to tell: but to morrow night at the same hour meet me here again; and when you see me retire, dare to follow me."

I promised, and came: we withdrew together; and, after going the length of three or four streets, the wizard entered a mean looking house, where I was ushered by him into a room dimly lighted, up four pair of stairs.

Here my entertainer unmasked, and to my surprise shewed features of which I had not the smallest remembrance. Still it was something to see a real face of any sort in so suspicious a place.

"Now tell me" – said I . . . .

"Questions," interrupted the stranger, "are here only answered by the dead: – evoke whom you please."

In faltering accents I named Euphrosyné. The wizard shook his head. Then Helena: – he frowned. – Anagnosti then! "What demon," he now cried, "makes you enumerate all those whom you have injured?"

"You cannot raise spirits;" answered I sneeringly.

"Ere you judge, name some being you have served," replied the wizard: – "Cirico for instance."

"Cirico is alive."

"He is dead: last night, at Alexandria, he fell into a coma, and never woke again."

"Then be it Cirico." – And Cirico appeared.

The poet so evidently showed as much of the flesh and blood as ever had entered into his spare composition, that I ran to embrace him: but I grasped only unsubstantial air! Startled at the circumstance, I stepped back: – again the spectre advanced, and probably by this time I looked a little scared; for on the phantom opening its mouth to begin a solemn speech, it fixed its eyes upon me, and burst out into a loud peal of laughter.

"Where ghosts laugh," cried I, "there needs must be a joke:" – and I again sprang forward. Again the figure vanished; this time no longer dismayed, I rushed on, overset every thing in my way, and groped about until I hawled forth from behind a table the real Cirico, whose image only I had thus far seen, reflected by some optical contrivance.

"And so I catch you again," I cried; "and at your old tricks too!"

"You do," was the poet's reply, "but no longer unwillingly: however, – as this is but an uncomfortable place, – we shall leave my Gaëtano to settle matters here, and adjourn to a coffeehouse, where I will tell you all."

Seated in the *bottega*, over our *rinfreschi*: "When you quitted Egypt," – began the improvisatore, – "I had just killed the last princess of my tragedy, and secured the last sequin of my patron. It therefore became expedient to return to Italy, – were it only to claim that diamond on your finger there, which you promised me for my services, but in your fainting fit on the beach at Alexandria, forgot to bestow. A plausible pretence for leaving the consul was the least of my difficulties. I asserted that the operas which I had spouted were mine: he claimed them as his: we quarrelled, and we parted. I soon found a passage straight for this place, and in this place a patron in that transcendent genius under whose roof . . ."

"I yesterday," – cried I, finishing the sentence: "met you, afraid of being recognized, and in company with a dancer, a fiddler, and a scene shifter. But take your stone, and . . ."

"Receive in return an unpromised billet-doux," – resumed Cirico, handing me a letter, of which the very form and superscription bespoke a female writer.

"What," exclaimed I; "Apollo turned Mercury!" – But my suspicions for once did the poet injustice: the letter was dated from Alexandria, and the signature, that of the consuless, my defeated adversary.

"You know," – she wrote, – "how at Smyrna I found in a miserable hovel an infant unblessed by a parent's care. Both nurse and child were pining for want; both revived under my roof: but soon the affections of the servant wandered from her charge to a young taooshan, while mine became wholly centred in the lovely boy. Seeing him hourly grow in all that is excellent, I became so wrapped up in the feelings and duties of a mother, as to forget that there still existed a father, – when in an evil hour you appeared!"

"Parental rights over the offspring of unwedded love are unacknowledged in law, and by you could not even be maintained in equity. Your child must have perished but for the care of strangers: and, after strangers alone had cultivated its young mind, as well as supplied all its wants, – alone had rescued it from ignorance and from vice, as well as from misery and death, – it belonged not to you to reap what you had not sowed. To have yielded up into your unhallowed hands the angel, whose keen sensibilities I had pledged myself by the very pains taken to cherish them, never to expose to the risk of being wounded; to have tamely suffered that angel to pass, – as it was likely to do under your guidance, – not only from consequence to contempt, and from care to neglect, but from purity to corruption, and from happiness to misery, I must have been bereft of common humanity: and had you possessed the feelings of a father, you yourself must have wished the tried and tender guardian of your offspring to have ever remained, as she was become, its mother."

"You did not: you recovered your boy, and rendered me anew childless. Yet such is the love I still bear your Alexis, that for his sake I even humble myself before you, and stoop to prefer a prayer to him whom otherwise I must have cursed; and it is this: – that you will duly weigh in your mind the situation and prospects of which your rashness has robbed your child, by wresting him from my arms; and that you will thence deduce how heavy is become in his behalf your own responsibility, and how much it behoves you to do, in order to make him amends for all he has lost. Perform this with pious intentness; be as tender a father as you have been a thoughtless one; and you may still at her last hour obtain the blessings of the once happy

ATHENAIS."

This letter leaving me little in a mood to enjoy Cirico's humour, I went home immediately, and over the very pillow of my child, already hushed in sweet repose, vowed rigidly to perform its contents. Many years before I had received a similar appeal to my parental feelings, in behalf of another offspring of my lawless passions, by another hapless mother, like Euphrosyné deserted and dead. The two epistles seemed intended for companions. "If I live," thought I, "they shall be hung up in my chamber, be ever under my eyes; – and by deserving the blessings promised in the one, I may perhaps still avert the curses threatened in the other!"

Meanwhile I determined to hasten to my destination: for so far from the pharmacopeia of Italy re-establishing my Greek constitution, I had fresh and frequent returns of aggravated illness, and felt anxious at least to leave my boy an orphan only among such as were able to supply a father's care. On mentioning to Silva my intention of quitting Naples: "Good!" said he, "I too want to change its air, in order to absent myself from a lady who has made love to me so long that she now persuades herself it was I who made love to her, and resents her own mistake as my infidelity. We will travel together."

And so we did. For the first time in my life I journeyed in a square box on wheels: two servants having their backs and the two gentlemen their faces turned towards the way we went; while my little Alexis, the most delighted and the most amusing of the party, sat between us like a gem surrounded by its inferior accompaniments.

As I approached the ancient mistress of the world, the eternal city, the destroyer of Greece, my heart beat high. But, alas! If he who names Rome names energy, names strength, he who beholds her in her present fallen state, beholds nothing but feebleness and imbecility: – he beholds the prostrate members of a giant, and corruption at work among their mouldering remains. Sheep graze round the altar where captive monarchs were slaughtered in the name of Jove the great and the good, and silence reigns in that arena where eighty thousand spectators could at once count the pangs of wretches, tortured in frightful reality to represent some ancient fable. The very monuments of a more recent date only arise, like fresher weeds, out of the ashes of former decay: – they are only the fungus, starting forth from the creviced based of some nobler pile, and which, by feeding on that fabric's substance, achieves its destruction.

Silva seemed to enjoy my disappointment; satire was his profession. "These people," said he, "cannot prevent the sun of their fine climate from shining at its stated hours, but they make their streets impervious to its cheering light: – a deep gloom meets the eye wherever towers man's abode. They cannot prohibit the rich vegetation of their fertile soil from diffusing its fragrance, but they collect every villainous odour to subdue nature's sweets, and convert one sense at least into means of torture. They cannot cancel the spring's ancient privilege of enamelling alike with flowers the hill and the valley, the garden and desert, but they tarry in their fetid town till the magic has vanished, and autumn sears the leaf, and embrowns the parched meadow: – no one thinks of country rambles before the summer's close. They cannot stop the crystal rills while gushing down the mountain's slope, but they suffer their acqueducts to ooze out the captive stream, and to convert the healthy plain into a pestilential marsh. They cannot dive into the inmost recesses of the human brain, to nip its very first germs every brightest faculty, but, conducting its developments as the Chinese do that of their peach and plum trees, they encompass each tender shoot of the intellect with so many minute fetters, religious, political and social, that dwarfs are produced where giants were intended. Their manuscripts are not suffered to be inspected; their pictures are left to rot; their very city has been allowed to slip from its seven hills into the sink between. They clip their trees into men, and their men into singers. In their vaunted Last Judgment heaven appears far more dismal than hell. Their law deems infamous not the thief, but the magistrate – the bargello. Their tribunals sell justice to the highest bidder; their churches protect from it the criminal; and the huge temple on which we now stand (for from St. Peter's proud dome went forth this bitter diatribe) – built at the expense of all Christendom on a foundation which stands awry, and with a cupola which yawns with rents, – contains absolutions for every sin as well as confessionals appropriated to every language. A priest, habituated only to the duties of humility and obedience during the greatest portion of his life, near its close becomes the sovereign, and assumes the supreme power when his failing faculties fit him to think only of death: and as each inferior member of the imbecile government like its tottering chief must forego a lawful lineage, so are of each statesmen the views oblique, and the ways devious and crooked. The word virtue indeed exists in the language, but is applied to skill in singing; and as to valour, the former signification of the same word, it is a quality which during so many ages has been let out for hire, first in the gross by the condottiere, and next more in detail by the professed bravo, that it is become discreditable, and cowardice, under the name of caution, forms not only the privilege of the priest, but the pride of the cavalier. Visit a friend in the day time and he surveys you through a grated hole in his entrance door, ere he dares to let you in: venture out at night, and from a distance you are bidden to avert your eyes, lest one murder witnessed should necessitate a second. The very head of the church, when in the holy of the holies, dares not take the consecrated wine except through a gilded reed, lest his lips should suck in poison; and in the heart of his capital the Pontiff of Rome keeps in his pay – for the safety of his person – the rude mountaineer of Swisserland, as your Turkish pasha does the barbarian from Epirus and from Koordestan. Thank God, however, this map of imbecility and vice hies fast to its fate: for if by a late submission which the Romans call a treaty, the rotten grant of St. Peter's rich domain is yet saved a while from utter ruin, its seals are all torn off, and its ornaments effaced.[2] Nature herself conspires with man in the work of just destruction. In that sky so transparent lurks a permanent poison, which, formerly only creeping like the adder along the hollow valley, now soars like the eagle above the steepest hill, and invades the last abodes once safe from its intrusion. Thus shall soon the world's ancient mistress again return to nought; and as the herdsman erst wandered in solitude where Rome in later days arose, so shall the herdsman again wander in solitude where Rome has ceased to be."

Silva here ending his effusion, we again began to descend the thousand and one steps which we had, to my great fatigue, ascended. In the midst of our downward progress my companion abruptly stopped short, as if struck with a sudden thought. "So near the abode of your ancient Gods," he cried, "they might feel offended if we did not pay them a farewell visit, previous to their forced departure for the banks of the Seine. This is their second grand removal since the days of Praxiteles. – Let us go to the Vatican, and see them packing up."

Already tired, and somewhat peevish with encreasing weakness: "am I not sick enough" – cried I, – "of real man, that I must run after his image in stone and brass?" but after some ineffectual resistance at last suffered myself to be over-ruled. When indeed I beheld what was called the Apollo, the Mercury, the Jupiter, the Venus, and the other gods and goddesses of my forefathers, I cannot deny that I felt pleasure. "And can these fair forms," – thought I to myself – "have been the production of demons and of witchcraft? Can it be Satan that smiles on those lovely lips? If so, ah, what could withstand his wiles!" – and with one deep sigh my heart absolved all paganism. I almost wished to have lived in those ages and amid that worship whose wrecks still looked so attractive; and I repined at the gloom of a religion whose temples, adorned like charnel-houses, display even in the freshness of the finest marbles, the features of death and the forms of corruption.

Scarcely had we reached our lodging when Silva was called upon by a friend, who advised him to leave Rome immediately, lest he should be entombed alive in the mausoleum which emperor Adrian only destined for his repose after death.

"What have I done," cried Silva, astonished, "to be thus treated to the honours of a state criminal? – Assassination, blasphemy, profanation would have been overlooked in this indulgent place: but can I have said that the Pope starved his subjects to enrich his nephew Braschi, or that the nephew sold the state to buy the Pontine marshes? – can I have maintained that prince Borghese's gems were modern, or princess Lanti's charms antique? – In fine, can I have admired Pasquino's wit, or abused Pius's leg?"

"You once returned a bow from the arch-fiend Cagliostro," answered my friend, "– and asserted that free masonry and treason were not always synonymous."

"If so," exclaimed Silva, "let us depart this instant! From real offences I might, at Rome at least, have escaped. With imaginary crimes there is no contending."

Accordingly we set off the same evening, in the very teeth of the still white and threatening Apennines. I left a hundred plans unexecuted and performances unfinished, connected with my Alexis. On contemplating from the last hill which allowed a view of Rome – as if painted on the bar of gold left by its setting sun – that long range of purple domes so beautiful in its appearance, and yet destined to so speedy a decline, I felt amid my own accelerating steps towards dissolution, some comfort in the thought that, like the lowliest individuals, the proudest empires of the present day were hastening towards a certain and a proximate end.

The ascent of the mountains seemed to last an eternity. At Narni we found every horse in the place engaged for Arezzo: at Terni the same; and the same at Spoleto. Nor was it otherwise at Foligno. I began to complain, but excited little sympathy. "When saints perform miracles," was the answer, "sinners should stay at home." A person enclined to cavil might have replied that three drunken cobblers reeling in a wine vault, could see the madonna roll her eyes about any where as well as at Arezzo: but the prodigy was become a mine of wealth to its before distressed church, and I held my tongue. "Truth," as Silva observed, "is a bad travelling companion."

After passing through several cities which looked like the deserted habitations of the Titans, in which had crept a race of pigmies, we arrived at Loretto, where, pulled one way by a guardian of the holy house, anxious that I should wipe away my old sins, and the other by a fair vender of crucifixes, desirous that I should commence a new score, I was only saved from leaving my cloak in the hands of the syren, by a pilgrim who had stolen it before.

At Ancona Silva pressed me to go on with him to Venice. "The sun of St. Mark indeed is set:" he cried, – "its proud Aristocrats were so long considering to whom they should sell themselves, that the bargain was struck at last without their participation: but, though, Austria has finally swallowed up the fat and torpid oyster of the lagunas, the empty shell still glitters, and is worth beholding."

"Silva," – was my answer, "were I still the man I was, I might perhaps (whether right or wrong) wish to become something more than a mere spectator of European changes. At a moment when all the old monarchies of Europe are ploughing up to receive the seeds of a more promising system, I might myself like to assist in somewhere planting that tree without roots of which the fruits are yet worth gathering: but you need only look at me to see that the gods no longer permit my health the exertion, or my spirits the hazard." "Here," added I, – laying my hand on my Alexis curly head, – "is the sole remaining object of all my solicitude. Him I wish to place in a safe harbour. Do you then jolt on to Venice. As to me I must be carried, as it shall please the winds and waves, to Trieste."

And ill it pleased these capricious, these democratic powers, to smooth my journey in the small felucca in which I embarked, the day after I had celebrated the accomplishment of my boy's fifth year. Scarce had we been six hours at sea when there arose from the north-west a most tremendous storm. We closed our hatches, took in as much sail as possible, and prepared to meet the hurricane. Every instant it encreased, and at last the sea ran so high that our deck was completely under water. The vessel soon sprung a leak, and the hold filled so fast that every man who could be spared from the deck, ran to the pumps: – I among the rest, as soon as I had lashed my poor boy to his crib; – though small was my strength, and trifling my assistance.

Contrary to every suggestion of common sense the reïs resolved to run in between the nearest islets on the coast of Dalmatia. It was in vain to represent the danger of striking against some hidden reef, or stranding upon a lee-shore; and we only wondered which of the two would be our fate, when providentially the storm abated as suddenly as it had arisen, and enabled us with our ship full of water, and our rigging all in tatters to put into a little creek on the island of Melada. Here we found a Ragusan vessel, driven in by the same storm, but with a miserably foul bill of health; in so much that the crews unguardedly missing, we learnt to our great dismay what we must make up our minds, on our arrival at Trieste, to a fresh quarantine.

I now recollected that just at midnight, and when the storm raged most furiously, a tremendous flash of lightning, which seemed to set the heavens on fire, had for a moment brought before my dazzled eyes the frightful vision of the spectre-ship, doomed, as I was told, ever to sail with unstayed speed round the globe, announcing destruction to the crews which beheld it. The vision appeared as if advancing full sail to run our vessel down; then vanished as if by magic, and left no trace behind. Immediately the storm was hushed, the wind dropped, and all the danger of shipwreck ceased. The plague seemed, therefore, the foe by which – I concluded – we were to fall: but on enquiry, none save myself had seen the phantom.

CHAPTER XV.

As soon as the damage was repaired, we again hurried on board, and put to sea. All now looked most propitious. Nothing could exceed the serenity of the weather: we skudded right before the wind – now become a steady breeze; and though my health had not greatly benefited by my late severe labour, yet the sea-air seemed a balm destined to heal the injuries of the sea-water. My aches were less acute, and my spirits more buoyant than for some time past; and as I lay on the deck basking in the April sun, with the purple dolphins sporting around the ship, and my own little cherub playing by my side, more visions of delights unutterable danced in my imagination, than there sparkled liquid diamonds upon the azure wave. With that yet untasted repose which I should now soon enjoy, my ailments, I thought, might still slowly subside: or, if I was doomed never more to recover my former vigour, what then? It was neither in the palaestra nor on the race ground that I purposed to shine. I should only be the fitter for that tranquil life, henceforth the only object of my tempered wishes. My cousin's letter had promised me a brilliant lot, and – what was better – my own pockets ensured me a decent competence. The refinements of an European education should add every external elegance to my boy's innate excellence, and, having myself moderately enjoyed the good things of this world, while striving to deserve the better promised in the next, I should, ere my friends became tired of my dotage, resign my last breath in the arms of my child.

The blue sky seemed to smile upon my cheerful thoughts, and the green wave to murmur approbation of my plan. Almighty God! What was there in it so heinous, to deserve that an inexorable fate should cast it to the winds?

In the midst of my dream of happiness, my eye fell upon the darling object which could alone render that dream a reality. Insensibly my child's prattle had diminished – the cheerful sound of his voice had subsided in an unusual silence. I thought he looked pale: – his eyes seemed heavy, and his lips felt parched. The rose, that every morning still so fresh, so erect on its stalk, at mid-day hung its heavy head, discoloured, wan, and fading: – but so frequently had the billows, during the fury of the storm, drenched my boy's little crib, that I could not wonder he should have felt their effects of their protracted fury, at least in the shape of a severe cold. I put him to bed, and tried to hush him to sleep. Soon, however, his face grew flushed, and his pulse became feverish. I failed alike in my endeavours to procure him repose and to afford him amusement: – but though play things were repulsed, and tales no longer attended to, still he could not bear me an instant out of his sight; nor would he take any thing except at my hands. Even when – as too soon it did – his reason began to wander, his filial affection retained its pristine hold of his heart. It had grown into an adoration of his equally doting father; and the mere consciousness of my presence seemed to relieve his uneasiness.

Had not joy, just before, possessed me so entirely, alarm would not so soon have mastered my whole being: but I had throughout life found every transport of happiness, much exceeding the ordinary measure, followed by some unforeseen calamity; and my exultation had just risen to so unusual a pitch, that at once my dismay became proportionably deep. A sense of dreadful apprehension soon completely chilled my blood: I felt convinced that I had only been carried to so high a pinnacle of joy, in order to be hurled with greater ruin into an abyss of woe. Such became my anxiety to reach Trieste, and to obtain the best medical assistance, that even while the ship continued to cleave the waves like an arrow, I fancied it lay like a log upon the main. How then did my pangs increase when, as if in resentment of my unjust complaints, the breeze, dying away, really left our keel motionless on the waters. My anguish baffled all expression.

In truth I do not know how I preserved my senses, except from the need I stood in of their aid: – for while we lay cursed with absolute immobility, and the sun ever found us on rising in the same place where it had left us at setting, my child – my darling child – was every instant growing worse, and sinking apace under the pressure of illness. To the deep and flushing glow of a complexion far exceeding in its transient brilliancy even the brightest hues of health, had succeeded a settled, unchanging, deadly paleness. His eye, whose round full orb was wont to beam upon me with mild but fervent radiance, now dim and wandering, for the most part remained half closed; and, when-roused by my address – my angel child strove to raise his languid look, and to meet my fearful glance, it was to show all the mild radiance of his countenance extinguished. In the more violent bursts indeed of his unceasing delirium, his wasting features sometimes acquired a fresh but sad expression. He would then start up, and with his feeble hands clasped together, and big tears rolling down his faded cheeks, beg in the most moving terms to be restored to his home: but mostly he seemed absorbed in inward musings, and – no longer taking note of the passing hour – he frequently during the course of the day moved his pallid lips, as if repeating to himself the little prayer which he had been wont to say at bed time and at rising, and the blessings I had taught him to add, addressed to his mother in behalf of his father. If, – wretched to see him thus, and doubly agonized to think that I alone had been the cause – I burst out into tears which I strove to hide, his perception of outward objects seemed all at once for a moment to return. He asked me whether I was hurt, and would lament that, young and feeble as he was, he could not yet nurse me as he wished; – but promised me better care when he should grow stronger.

In this way hour after hour and day after day rolled on, without any progress in our voyage, while all I had left to do was to sit doubled over my child's couch, watching all his wants, and studying all his looks, – trying, but in vain, to discover some amendment. "O for those days!" – I now thought, – "when a calm at sea appeared an intolerable evil, only because it stopped some tide of folly, or delayed some scheme of vice!"

At last one afternoon, when, totally exhausted with want of sleep, I sat down by my child in all the composure of torpid despair, the sailors rushed in one and all: – for even they had felt my agony, and doted on my boy. They came to cheer me with better tidings. A breeze had just sprung up! The waves had again begun to ripple, and the lazy keel to stir. As minute pressed on minute the motion of the ship became swifter; and presently, – as if nothing had been wanting but a first impulse, – we again dashed through the waves with all our former speed.

Every hour now brought us visibly nearer the inmost recess of the deep Adriatic, and the end of our journey. Pola seemed to glide by like a vision: presently we passed Fiume: we saw Capo d'Istria but a few minutes: – at last we descried Trieste itself! Another half hour, and every separate house became visible; and not long after we ran full sail into the harbour. The sails were taken in, the anchor was dropped, and a boat instantly came along side.

All the necessary preparations had been made for immediately conveying my patient on shore. Wrapped up in a shawl, he was lifted out of his crib, laid on a pillow, and lowered into the boat, where I held him in my lap, protected to the best of my power from the roughness of the blast and the dashing of the spray, until we reached the quay.

In my distress I had totally forgotten the taint contracted at Melada, and had purposed, the instant we stepped on shore, to carry my child straight to a physician. New anguish pierced my soul when two bayonets crossed upon my breast forced me, in spite of my alternate supplication and rage, to remain on the jettee, there to wait his coming and his previous scrutiny of all our healthy crew. All I could obtain as a special favour was a messenger to hurry his approach, while, panting for his arrival, I sat down with my Alexis in my arms under a low shed which kept off a pelting shower. I scarce know how long this situation lasted. My mind was so wrapped up in the danger of my boy as to remain wholly unconscious of the bustle around, except when the removal of some cask or barrel forced me to shift my station. Yet, while wholly deaf to the unceasing din of the place, I could discern the faintest rumour that seemed to announce the approaching physician. O how I cursed his unfeeling delay: how I would have paved his way with gold, to have hastened his coming! – and yet a something whispered continually in my ear that the utmost speed of man no longer could avail.

Ah! that at least, confirmed in this sad persuasion, I might have tasted the heart-rending pleasure of bestowing upon my departing child the last earthly endearments! – but, tranquil, composed and softly slumbering as he looked, I feared to disturb a repose, on which I founded my only remaining hopes. All at once, in the midst of my despair, I saw a sort of smile light up my darling's features, and, hard as I strove to guard against all vain illusions, I could not at this sight stop a ray of gladness from gliding unchecked into my trembling heart. Short, however, was the joy: soon vanished the deceitful symptom! On a closer view it only appeared to have been a slight convulsion which had hurried over my child's now tranquil countenance, as will sometimes dart over the smooth mirror of a dormant lake the image of a bird in the air. It looked like the response of a departing angel, to those already on high, that hailed his speedy coming. The soul of my Alexis was fast preparing for its flight.

Lest he might feel ill at ease in my lap, I laid him down upon my cloak, and kneeled by his side to watch the growing change in his features. The present now was all to me: the future I knew I no longer should reck. Feeling my breath close to his cheek, he half opened his eye, looked as if after a long absence again suddenly recognized his father, and – putting out his little mouth – seemed to crave one last token of love. The temptation was too powerful: I gently pressed my lip upon that of my babe, and gathered from it the proffered kiss. Life's last faint spark was just going forth, and I caught it on the threshold. Scarce had I drawn back my face, when all respiration ceased. His eye-strings broke, his features fell, and his limbs stiffened for ever. All was over: Alexis was no more – Euphrosyné avenged, – and Anastasius the wretch he had long deserved to be!

I shed no tears; I moaned not; I made myself not a spectacle for the gaping multitude: but, ordered to the lazaretto, I threw my cloak over what had been my heart's best treasure, and, with the sacred burden in my arms, silently proceeded to where I was shewn my temporary prison. There, in the lonely cell allotted for my more favoured confinement, I found leisure to make myself acquainted with my grief, and to contemplate in its altered – its new condition, that countenance, that form and those features, once all the company I coveted upon this globe, and now leaving me in solitude, though placed by my side.

At the outset of my voyage from the East, when, on recovering my scattered senses, the first object which met my eyes was my adored child, after infinite toil and misgivings at last safe in my possession, I had in all the ecstasy of unutterable joy, fallen on my knees beside the sweet babe, wrapt in soft slumbers before me. Now, at the close of the same voyage, and arrived at the place of my long looked-for destination, but with my hopes entirely blasted, my happiness destroyed, and the being for whom all was undertaken and achieved no more, I knelt a second time in all the agony of grief beyond utterance beside that same beloved boy, again lying before me, but – a breathless corpse! At first, indeed, I gazed as if insensible of the awful change. My mind was so confused, so bewildered, that – perhaps from excess of grief – I seemed not to feel at all, and could only upbraid myself for my strange insensibility. My imagination refused to conceive that lovely frame, so lately still the seat of the warmest affection and the tenderest piety, as nothing now but a clod of icy clay, unconscious of my anguish, insensible to my embrace. Steadfastly as I contemplated my wretchedness, it was so great that neither eye nor intellect could compass its extent, – and for a while I thought I must be labouring under some dreadful dream, whose illusion would vanish, and whose end would be my waking.

But when, from the object immediately before me I carried my eye to more distant points, to wider circles of time and space: – when I reflected that on my child alone I had built all my remaining prospects of earthly comfort and joy; that for my child alone I had left country, home, and friends – and had come to encounter strange regions, climes, and people; that to my child's converse alone I looked for all the solace of what few days might still be vouchsafed me, as well as to his piety for the few flowers that at my death might deck my bier; that in his beloved arms I had hoped to breathe my last; nay, that a thousand times in the idle fancies of my entranced brain I had flattered myself with leaving him such a blessing to the world as by the virtues of the son to atone for the sins of the father, and to cause the sire himself to be blessed in his offspring; and when from these excursions of my distracted mind I reverted to what was left me of these fond and foolish visions, – then it was that my grief at last forced its way through the weight of bodily stupor by which it seemed compressed, and that the floodgates of my tears, long locked, at last burst open. Then did my increased agony find vent, and no longer wear the semblance of a stone-like apathy.

It was not my child whose change demanded pity. He had indeed, by my ill-fated fondness, been torn from a scene of every bliss which could surround his tender years. From a nursery of comforts he had been taken by force on a journey of privations and perils, and his series of youthful sufferings had ended in a painful illness and a premature death: – but what of that? Heaven, it has long been acknowledged, marks its favourites by an early removal from this abode of sorrow. My child's short cares were over; and his irksome career closed at its very outset. He had quitted a world of bitterness and corruption, ere yet his susceptible heart had felt its cruel thorns, or his pure mind had been sullied by its foulness. Called away, while in the gay spring of his existence tears only soft as April showers had yet bedewed his rosy cheeks, he had been wafted on high, still robed in all the brightness of his native innocence, and, ere his guileless mind could yet have lost aught of its holiness, he had joined his brother angels in the realms of bliss eternal. There, – while his father was still struggling on the stormy sea of life, – he, already safe from ill, dwelt in endless glory in the bosom of his Maker.

But I – I alone – remained oppressed by a weight of woe unutterable! Partly by chance, partly from my own fault, every relation, every friend, every common acquaintance with which I had commenced life – estranged by degrees through my own wayward conduct – had left me a being wholly insulated, precisely at that age when, weaned from a deceitful world, man beings to want comfort at home. Frightened at my increasing loneliness, I had in my turn looked out for a something on which to bestow those affections, doomed to run to waste just as they began to rise. Long I sought, often fancied I held; and often again either rejected or lost the prize. At last Heaven seemed to pity my loneliness, and to favour my search – to smile upon a feeling so blameless. After much anxiety and sore disappointment, I found the wished-for solace – and found it in my own child, long severed from my arms.

Him I beheld where I could least have expected it: him, after much fear and doubt, I regained; and him I thenceforth destined to become my only solace, – the support and the joy of my remaining life. That, with regard to this last and dearest treasure of my soul I had, for once, acted up to my fair intentions and fulfilled all my duties, my heart bore me witness. From the moment I obtained possession of my Alexis he became the sole object of my unceasing solicitude, the sole theme of my constant contemplation. Casting off all other thoughts, spurning far away from me all other vain pursuits; no longer caring for aught of which he was not the sole end and motive, nor engaging in aught which promoted not his benefit, I devoted to him all the strength of my body, and all the powers of my mind: I watched over his development by day and by night.

Heaven seemed for a while determined to reward with its utmost liberality so irreproachable a sentiment. Almost from the first hour of my possessing him I reaped every day some fresh fruit of my care, and received earnests every day of far richer fruits still ripening. My Alexis possessed exquisite faculties; and the slightest culture sufficed to elicit them. At first indeed he had looked upon me as any enemy; as one who had torn him forcibly from his friends: but at last, – and when convinced by my tenderness of the excess of my affection – he had realized all my long trembling hopes; had fulfilled in every way all my most ardent wishes; had begun to return my undivided fondness with all the fervour of his own affectionate disposition. No child ever doted on a mother as he did on his father: – and, if our love even becomes rivetted to an object by the mere unrequited care and pains bestowed upon it, how unbounded became, with the return which I experienced, my adoration of my angel child, need or can I describe! He alone was the joy of my eyes, and the pride of my vain glorious heart; and, as I walked forth with him in public; as I saw every stranger gazing at his lovely countenance, smiling at his playful prattle, and almost spellbound by the charm that seemed to hover around his person, parental exultation swelled that foolish heart within me, and made my eyes overflow with rapturous delight. I seemed only to move along for the purpose of enjoying a constant triumph.

Nay, – that parental fondness which, bearing in all its parts on one single point, and in that single point finding the firmest support, must under any circumstances have acquired an unexampled intensity, had still had its growth accelerated beyond the ordinary measure by the peculiarities of my anomalous condition.

That very same instant which had, on Egypt's barren shore, brought my labours for the possession of my child to a happy conclusion, had also witnessed the beginning of my incessantly continued journey toward the distant point which was to be my final goal, and where I hoped to sit down at last in peaceful enjoyment of the treasures I had won. From the momentous period which had seen my Alexis first pressed to my still panting bosom, every later successive day – nay, almost every successive hour – had beheld me wafted to some new point under the heavens, to some new latitude on the earth, wholly distinct and different from the preceding ones. No region, no city, no abode had, since my departure from Alexandria, afforded me a permanent sojourn, or fixed me long enough to excite in my breast the smallest local attachment, the least fondness of which I had not brought the seeds in my own bosom: – or should even in any place some slight interest have arisen, not unlawful in itself, and which might in a more stationary condition have been allowed to take some hold of my heart, have covered with some fair exotic the spots left bare by the native attachments eradicated, and have in some degree divided my affections with my soul's chief treasure, – bereft, from the ever changing scene through which I had hurried, of all leisure for its cultivation, I had sedulously crushed its first shoots, as those of an intruding and troublesome stranger.

But the more my state of incessant locomotion had thus made all else pass by unregarded, or unable to leave any permanent impression, the more had it caused my own child, my only never failing companion, to entwine himself with double force round every fibre of the paternal heart: – for, at the same time that that constant impulse forward which both sire and son obeyed, had suffered no other object to enter into the smallest competition with my boy for my genuine affections, it had occasioned an uninterrupted closeness in our daily intercourse, had demanded on my part a minuteness of parental offices with respect to my child's little person, had given me a habit of unremittingly hearing his sweet voice, nay had, amid all this seeming sameness of sentiments and impressions, thrown a variety in the places, the modes, and the circumstances of our relative existence and endearments, infinitely exceeding what any stationary condition, even with my Alexis – and no one else but him – ever clinging to my side, could have afforded. The short, the happy period of my life, marked by the recovery of my Euphrosyné's last bequest, had offered the treasure, not merely – as does in most cases so transient a possession – in one place, one pursuit, one form: it had offered my Alexis, while constantly placed in view, yet constantly in a different form, and action, and mode of being: it had offered him successively in Egypt, at Maltha, in Sicily, at Naples, at Rome, at Ancona, and in every place either of repose or thoroughfare intervening between these distant points: it had offered him in capitals and on the road, at rest and in action; now gliding in a light skiff on the waves, now whirled on smoking wheels over hill and dale; now wondering at the sights of cities, now enjoying rural amusements and scenery; now in the simple garb of the infant traveller, now gorgeously attired for the admiration of crowds; now all alertness, and rousing by his arch and playful caresses even his listless father, now himself oppressed with the fatigues of the journey and asleep in my arms; and thus I had gone on from place to place, collecting and compressing in a small space a variety of pictures of his infantine person, pursuits and adventures – all lovely and yet all different – far beyond what the longest period of years could have accumulated in the slow changes of a stationary existence; and which, carefully treasured up in my memory, and always present to my imagination, had furnished by their multitude materials for an affection and a worship far exceeding what even tender parents, when distracted by a variety of ties, can find to divide among their numerous offspring, – and, at the eve of accomplishing my labours, and reaching my destination, this all absorbing adoration of a child in appearance not less full of bodily health than replete with moral excellence, was already ushering me into a scene of rapturous and yet lawful felicity only expected to end with my own life, when all at once a Providence – mindful of my sins when I had forgotten them, – had even reversed the course of nature to cut short that existence on which my own depended, to destroy at one blow my new and hard earned happiness, and to leave me, from one possessed of all his heart desired, a forlorn wretch, in a strange country, and among a stranger race; – with not one object to cling to on this side an obscure and lonely grave.

Yet with such dismal thoughts rending my mind, and the more dreary object laid out before my eyes, did the benumbing powers of affliction itself – of an affliction perfect in all its parts, and, by no longer leaving room for hope or fear, not longer affording an excitement or permitting a struggle – at last procure me a short respite from its sting. Yielding to the torpor which by degrees came over my senses, I fell into a profound sleep; and the trance lasted unbroken until the dawn of the following day: but the moment of waking was dreadful beyond all former moments. I had dreamed of my child; I had, in the lying vision, seen him convalescent: my heart's treasure had again seemed to revive and to thank me for a care no longer wanted, when – awaking with a burst of joy, and turning round, – I saw – O God of heavens!

I now afresh gave way to my despair; with frantic violence hugged to my bosom the cold corpse of my boy, and swore no earthly power should tear it from my arms. – until by degrees the mild entreaties of my fellow prisoners made my grief assume a less insensate form.

After frequent relapses I prepared to perform to my child's sad remains the last duties of a man, a Christian, and a father. In the gloomy precincts of the lazaretto I saw the narrow cell dug, which henceforth was to hold all I cared for on earth. Then, kissing for the last time those faded eyes which never more were to beam upon me, and those livid lips which no longer felt the pressure of mine, I suffered the dreary winding-sheet of death to shroud from my further view my angel's altered features; and carried him weeping to his last home: but when the moment came – after the priest had concluded his office – to lower into the foul jaws of the grave, and to resign to corruption that lovely body – that last relic of my short lived felicity, I scarce felt courage for the dismal task: I clung to what I was going to lose, until fresh violence became necessary; and when over the idol of my boastful heart I again beheld the ground made like all other ground: "Now come," cried I, "whenever it list, my own final hour! I shall hail it as the healer of sorrows; as the friend who springs forward to receive suffering man, when all other friends depart."

Sad indeed was the void which I found from those days, when I could not go out even for a few minutes, without paying the tribute of a farewell embrace, and could never come home without finding a sweet welcome awaiting me on the very threshold: when every look of sorrow I betrayed was met by filial sympathy, and every glance of satisfaction I gave filled my child's heart with gladness. Ah! While these raptures had been mine, the very confinement of a lazaretto had been a scene of joy: now that they were to be no more, the liberation from my prison only promised fresh grief.

Soon, however, the period of enlargement came: – for the quarantine had only been incurred by an untoward accident; and in a very few days I received a formal notice that its term had expired. Once more I went to the hallowed spot where lay buried all my hopes, and once more bedewed its turf with bitter tears: – then, retiring with slow and lingering steps, I left the sad enclosure, and launched forth again into the haunts of men.

But I re-entered them without joy, as I did without anxiety. Things gone by no longer gave a value to things to come. The golden link by which the past had been connected with the future, had been broken – been snapped asunder. The Anastasius of the morrow was no longer the Anastasius of the eve. The wide new world I was going to tread was a world devoid of interest; and the vast new prospects unfolding to my view, were prospects without life, animation or sunshine. Struck by heaven's vengeful lightning, my soul saw nothing in the dark surrounding waste to cheer its deathlike sadness, and shrunk from every slightest exertion as from an Herculean labour. On every stone I met in my way, I could have laid me down to die.

My only consolation consisted in the multiplicity of my sufferings, and in the sage speculations of the medical professors whom I consulted on my health, in order to get rid of the gratuitous prescriptions of the multitude: for though the members of the faculty seemed to think it likely that the effects of the storm at Melada, the anxious watching during my child's illness, and more than all, the grief for his loss, might have very much aggravated the symptoms of the original complaint, yet they agreed unanimously that even without these additional circumstances, the internal injury received on the beach at Alexandria – whether in the lungs, or the liver, or the spleen, no matter – must still alike have ended in my not very distant demise: – and, what cruel regret, what dire forebodings must have disturbed my death bed, had I been obliged to leave my Alexis in a strange land, a helpless unprotected orphan, exposed not only to all the violence of the rapacious, but all the wiles of the profligate; and perhaps, in the weakness of unsuspecting childhood, not only stripped of his property, but despoiled – for ever despoiled – of his more precious innocence, I even now shuddered to think of. The dread of such consequences must have rendered the last hour of my life the most painful of my existence. Instead of that, my child's short account on earth was closed for ever, ere the least alloy of evil could dim his spotless purity. – His bliss eternal was sealed beyond repeal. Of his endless happiness no doubt could be harboured any longer. Self; worthless self was all I henceforth had to think of; and the pangs of that self alone to lessen – if I could.

And even of these too well deserved sufferings the sting was greatly blunted – the edge was removed – by the consciousness that their period was limited. My loneliness upon earth could not be of long duration; my punishment here below must soon end: nay, the very torments that might, in the severity of eternal justice, await me hereafter, would be soothed by knowing that my child shared not in them, but, while his father paid the penalty of his manifold offences, enjoyed in other realms the reward of his piety: – and I sometimes even presumed to think that perhaps, after so dire an affliction, so severe a trial as that which concluded my earthly career, some portion even of my own heavy debt might be remitted: – when the last moment of my stay here below, which the parting from my still earth-bound child must have rendered the most irksome of my life, would, by reuniting me for ever to my angel above, become the most blessed of my unwished-for existence.

Meantime, – a stranger in the place to which my destiny had brought me, and not ranking among those privileged children of the globe, licensed to indulge to the utmost of their wish in every luxury, even unto that of grief, – I felt I must bestir myself, under pain of being, like a bruised reed, crushed and flung on the dunghill. Accordingly I resolved, if dead to pleasure, at least to rouse myself to business, and, hushing in my heart those deep sorrows which no one around me could share in or alleviate, to look, to speak, and to act, in public, like other men.

My first exertion was to enquire after the kindly intentioned kinsman, whose invitation had brought me to Trieste, but whose existence I had for a time wholly forgotten. On waking from my trance, and remembering my relation, I rather wondered that he should not, in my distress, have been the first to seek me out. Alas! he too had, since I last heard from him, paid the debt of nature, and disabled me from paying that of gratitude. I say of gratitude, – for though his will had been left in the main as it stood before my journey; it has been burthened with a handsome legacy in my favour, to soften my disappointment, in case I should be found to have complied with his summons. The bequest put me at once in possession of a considerable sum of ready money, when I would have wanted spirits to convert into cash my now loathed jewels.

Trieste, which I had before intended to make my permanent residence, was become since my misfortune the place least fitted for my abode. Not only the living multitudes of a commercial city has not leisure to sympathize with my situation, but the very inanimate objects it presented, were of the sort most discordant with my present frame of mind. Those rocks which, left in their native ruggedness, would have harmonized with my gloomy feelings, here were only beheld shaped in bustling quays and busy wharfs: those forests which, abandoned to silence and solitude, might have favoured my melancholy musings, here were only to be viewed, transformed into noisy hulks and naked masts. Gold was the only substance worshipped on this altar of Mammon, in its pure primitive shape; but gold was precisely the only one which I would rather have seen by a later transformation converted into whatever could have given my mind a wholesome abstraction from its sorrows. I therefore thought that, if I returned at all among my fellow creatures, it should only be where I found them collected in such myriads, as to recover amidst their overflowing crowd all the privileges of solitude. Upon this principle Vienna became destined in my mind for my ultimate abode.

While I staid at Trieste however, people would insist upon diverting me. It was a difficult undertaking, with my mind full of sorrow and an abscess forming in my side. Once only, finding myself somewhat easier than usual, I abruptly left my couch, and indulged my curiosity by going to a party.

I own that, when launched into its vortex, and beholding a number of figures towards whom I felt no attraction either of kindred, country, or even common interests, amusements or language, whirl around me in idle hurry, nay, sometimes stop in the midst of their inane bustle to look at myself, to point me out to each other, and to see how my adventures sat upon me; – reflecting moreover how soon even this mere spectacle must to me cease altogether, – I felt a sort of pleasure. But it was the pleasure of one who wanders in the delusion of a morning dream, through imaginary meads and gardens, among phantoms flitting about him in their twilight revels; and who feels all the while that they only wait, to glide off and disappear, for that approaching dawn which must break his sleep, and cause his final waking among scenes and beings of a different nature.

Loth to leave the place where slept my Alexis, and for ever to quit the last shore to which my child had been wafted, – finding my only solace in listening day after day on the quay facing the lazaretto, to the surf beating against its piers in slow and solemn pulses, I do not know how long I might still have remained at Trieste, taking no account of time, but, while ever intending to go, ever putting off my journey, had not the fear of travelling late in the season made me resolve before the summer should wholly pass by, to secure my winter quarters.

Not long therefore after the memorable treaty of Campo Formio, which filled Trieste with joy, by sacrificing Venice, a brilliant autumn eve saw brought to their conclusion the short preparations for my departure the next morning.

My bills paid, my passports signed, my post horses ordered; – having nothing further to think of or to settle in the place I was leaving, – I went to take my last turn on my favourite quay.

The sun was just dropping behind the purple expanse of the Adriatic, and I, indulging my favourite dream, that perhaps the glorious luminary, which not only through its constant emanations supports the inferior surrounding planets, but by its central situation is itself exempted from all the vicissitudes they suffer, might be the first halting place of the blessed that depart from other orbs, and in its bright bosom might harbour my own Alexis, – when I was diverted from this object of vague and distant contemplation by one less remote – namely two persons, apparently just released from quarantine, who were advancing towards the city, and consequently towards me. They wore the Greek dress, and, common as the sight was at Trieste, it yet engaged my attention as one which would become rare on my impending removal. Of the two strangers the shortest particularly attracted my notice. As he approached, a crowd of confused images rushed upon my mind. I almost fancied I saw – but the thing seemed improbable; – and yet at every successive step which brought him nearer, the impression, so far from lessening acquired greater strength, until at last I grew quite convinced of its truth. The person I gazed upon must be – it was Spiridion! Spite of his darker complexion and his more manly forms, I no longer could doubt I beheld the friend of former days. As to himself, – intent upon the surrounding scenery, he would have passed me by unheeded, but for my stopping directly in his way, in order to take one more silent survey of his person, ere I ventured to hail my long estranged companion.

Thus pointedly approached, he looked at me in his turn, first indeed with an expression only of surprise, at being thus scrutinized, apparently by a Frank, but, by degrees, with a more fixed stare – as of one under a delusion which he strives in vain to shake off. He gazed alternately on my features, which proclaimed an old friend, and on my dress, which bespoke an entire stranger.

Human patience could hold out no longer: "Am I then so changed," cried I, "that even my Spiridion cannot recognize his – I would have said once beloved – Anastasius?"

My voice was still the same. At its once familiar sounds the son of Mavrocordato seemed seized with a sudden thrilling, and again stepped back: but this time in wonder – in amazement.

"And is it then really," cried he at last, "Anastasius I behold?"

Nothing but the diffidence, tardy offspring of misfortune, had prevented me, the moment I recognize my friend, from clasping him in my arms. Could I have suspected that, without the same cause on his part, he would have evinced a similar hesitation to press me to his bosom, no temptation would have induced me to make myself known. I would have let him pass by unstayed; and never – no! never would I again, with my consent, have thrown myself in his way. His cold reception chilled me to the heart, and paralyzed my tongue. Spiridion saw me appalled, and Spiridion enjoyed the sight! Without one single word to relieve my embarrassment, he waited in solemn silence my tardy and faultering speech. His looks seemed to say: "each his turn: your's came first." And yet no cold and calculating motive could have found access to his breast – to that breast pure and generous as the sun. But he had witnessed all my errors, and he knew not my repentance.

For this, however, I made not at the time the allowance which was due: – "Spiridion," cried I, as soon as I felt able to speak, "your searching eye need not tell me what I already know too well. I no longer am he who looked defiance at all on earth; and at Heaven itself. Sickness and sorrow have bent me to the ground:" – and, overcome by my recollections, I burst into tears.

A slight blush of shame now tinged Spiridion's features. In a faltering voice, he attempted an excuse – probably as little understood by himself as it was by me; and, labouring to repress a rising emotion, told me where he meant to lodge, and begged I would call upon him.

Thus constrained in his very apologies, he only, in trying to withdraw the dagger thrust into my bosom, gave me fresh pangs. I inclined my head to thank him, but raised it with a glance of conscious independence, and leaving to the friend of my youth, as my last legacy, a faint smile of reproof, darted away.

As soon as Spiridion was out of sight I turned back, and went home. All my business at Trieste was concluded. I determined to set off immediately. My chaise was brought round: the horses put to it, and my trunks fastened on.

Among the stones reserved from Khedieh was a singularly beautiful ruby. Often pressed to sell the precious gem, I had always refused to part with my carbuncle. It had been set apart to please my own eye, – perhaps, some day, to purchase a powerful patron. But to pleasure I was become indifferent, and I no longer needed an earthly patron. I slipped the sparkling stone, wrapped up in paper, between the folds of Spiridion's pocket book, which till now had never been out of my bosom, and, putting the whole under cover, sent it to him with the following superscription:

"To one who for his friend once gave up all, and whose devotion is best remembered when it no longer can avail, Anastasius, rich in worthless jewels, poor in all beside, sends this last token of ancient affections, and of endless gratitude."

No sooner was the parcel out of my sight, than I too departed.

CHAPTER XVI.

It was my intention to have travelled all night: but at the second stage want of horses stopped my progress. I therefore desired some refreshment; a fire, and a bed. The stove was lighted, a slice of cold meat set before me between a bottle of wine and a flask of more potent spirits; and, in answer to the last of my requests, the female who acted as waiter, pointed to a huge mountain of eiderdown in a corner of the room.

Having finished my supper, and hanging over the slowly warming stove, I insensibly fell into a review of all the various and motley vicessitudes which had marked my portion of that changeful dream called human life. First I went back to its remotest periods, to those spent in the place of my nativity; played over all the gambols of my infancy, and all the frolics of my boy-hood; viewed in its minutest details the paternal abode, remembered the most trivial incidents of the family circle, and heard the peculiar sound of voice of each of its members – their gossip, their scolding, and their loud peals of laughter – with a distinctness and a proximity which left the memory of the more important events of later years comparatively vague, dark, indistinct reminiscences. With the rekindling of my youngest flame, and with the retracing of my earliest flight, – that disgraceful flight which cut me off from all connection with the land of my birth, and entirely divided the first stage of my life from all its later periods, – I closed the first chapter of my history.

Scarce could my heart even now refrain from bounding, as I recalled the rapturous intoxication of my spirits, when, in the morning of my days, – like the young pilgrim with locks flowing in the wind, and wallet carelessly flung across the shoulder, – I set out upon the second stage of my journey through life: when, simply but smartly attired, the soft down just budding on my lips, and the infant hopes expanding in my mind, I went forth with erect crest and buoyant step, in quest of pleasure and of fame; and finally when in the Morea, reaping an ample harvest of both, I achieved my first prowess and heard my first praises. Hassan's lip had long been silenced by death: but the music of his applause still rung in my ears.

Launched next into the maddening vortex of the capital, I still smiled at the recollection of the Jew doctor, shuddered at that of the Bagnio, and, though quite alone, averted my eyes as from a spectre, on remembering Anagnosti, pale, bloody, and with my murderous dagger buried in his breast! To fly the ghastly image I crossed the main, roamed in the plains of Egypt, and, after seeing myself successively a kiachef rioting in luxury and an outcast fleeing for his life, I in turns became a humble hadjee crawling on his knees at Mekkah, and a conceited coxcomb sporting his saucy wit at Stambool.

Now rose predominant the figure of my friend Spiridion! I mean the Spiridion all heart, all affection, of former days, – between whom and his namesake of yesterday the connecting link seemed wanting. Parted, by my own fault, from my only real friend, I again roved, successively a soldier of fortune at Cairo, a warrior in Wallachia, and a merchant on the Bosphorus.

But Ismir! But Euphrosyné! – The thought harrowed up my soul. To pluck the gnawing worm from my bosom, I plunged into the deepest desert, and joined the most daring of sectaries. At last, become a tender husband, I suffered for my sins in my amendment, and soon consigned to earth a fond and virtuous wife, when – spurned by one friend as I had spurned another – I fled to Arabs less godly but less faithless than the Wahhabees, and, under their new banners, founded my worldly fortune in plains of Khedieh. Growing a coward as I grew rich, I pursued – loaded with rubies and clothed in rags – my solitary course towards the setting sun, until casting off my slough in the concealment of the capital, I flew on the wings of parental love to the coast of Egypt; – and at Alexandria sought, saw, and won my child!

Oh! That I could here end my last chapter: that, to so many friends and relations, protectors and protected, one after the other swept away from the earth, I had not to add . . . . but so it was! – and now, with all that I looked forward to of joy, of pride, and of stay, laid prostrate for ever, I had nothing left me but to sink irretrievably under one of those sorrows the more corroding, because they are unshared, unnoticed, unimagined by the surrounding throng; – and to waste away my small remains of life in tears resembling the rain drops that fall into the sea, untold, unheeded, and without leaving a trace.

Such was the feeling of sad, of entire abandonment in which my reflections terminated, that, to drive them away and to warm my withered heart, I rapidly drank off several draughts of the spirits placed beside me: after which, without undressing, I crept under the swelling featherbed, desiring I might be called the instant the horses – expected home in the night – were ready to take me on.

In bed I found sleep, but not repose. A feverish restlessness insensibly grew as it were into a continuation of the last adventures of my life. I fancied myself dead, and lying in my coffin. The dim tapers already cast around the funereal glare which was to light my stiffened body to the darkness of the grave. Yet had I a faint perception of what was going forward. My limbs indeed were immoveable; but my eyes beheld, and my ears retained the power of hearing.

First appeared, as in a twilight, the persons most closely linked to my existence: my parents, Helena, Mavroyeni, and others. Their busts – for nothing more of them was perceptible – seemed floating in air. Sometimes they advanced, as if to take a nearer look at my countenance, gazed some time on me in silence, and then again retired, making room for others, who in their turn performed the same evolutions, and, after sating their curiosity, equally vanished in space. Two persons only of the mute assemblage remained, after all the rest had disappeared. At first they presented no features which I recognized, but insensibly they assumed the resemblance, the one of Euphrosyné, the other of a venerable priest with a long snow-white beard, whom I had seen at Pera. Euphrosyné began by contemplating me awhile, like all the phantoms that had preceded her, in total silence, and, though seeming to smile sweet forgiveness on her unfeeling ravisher, wore a funereal look which thrilled me to the soul. She repeatedly beckoned to me with emphatic gesture to join her: but each time my leaden limbs refused to do their office. At last the old man spoke. "In vain," he cried, "you try to meet. Your paths in life ever lay too far asunder."

"Ah!" now exclaimed in her turn the weeping maiden – whose voice, till then unheard, thrilled me to the soul: – "if he cannot come to me, I can at least go to him!"- and with outstretched arms she sprung forward to share my darker destiny; but her lifeless form only fell like a mill stone on my chest. Gasping for breath, struggled to disengage myself from the intolerable load, – when, suddenly, what I held in close embrace no longer was Euphrosyné, but – the fiend Sophia!

Rage now welled my breast, as fury flashed from the eyes of my antagonist. The lion and the serpent grappled. Each fixed his fangs in the others quivering flesh: each strove to pluck the heart from the other's bleeding bosom: – until at last the baseless ledge on which we fought in air, gave way with a tremendous crash.

Twined in each others arms down we now sank together; and I continued falling, until I woke at last in inexpressible horror, and found myself lying on the floor of the room, weltering in a stream of real blood, drawn forth from my vitals by my unconscious exertions. The confusion of my ideas just left me time enough to rejoice that I had only been dreaming, ere returning perception brought to my remembrance how much there was in my dream of sad reality.

Scarce inferior to the fancied music of the spheres themselves, sounded at that moment in my stunned ear the hoarse note of the horn, which informed me that the driver was seated on his horse. Ill as I felt I thought I cold not get away too fast. The post-master indeed had informed me of a novelty, only witnessed since these before peaceful regions had become the seat of war: namely robbers prowling in the neighbourhood. But who durst lay unhallowed hands on the already sentenced criminal! My death warrant, long signed, kept my life charmed, until the fatal hour of its lawful execution; and evil glances fall not more innocuous on spirits broken with sorrow, than would the deadliest dagger on my heavy heart, already turned to stone by grief.

Disregarding therefore every entreaty and sinister foreboding of the landlord and his crew, I wrapped myself in my cloak, stepped into my calesh, and spite of the still undiminished darkness, rolled on again with renovated speed.

All that day, and all the ensuing night, I continued travelling without interruption: for, greatly as I wanted rest, I could no where bring myself to stop. It was only in proportion as I felt my body whirled along with greater speed, that my mind seemed to find somewhat more repose. A mysterious impulse, as it were, goaded me on without ceasing.

The sun of the third day was already lengthening the partial shadows that precede its disappearance, when I entered an extended heath, to whose beautiful and varied weeds heaven's declining luminary at that instant lent to the glowing transparency which announces its proximate setting. With singular force did the gaudy scene revive all the deep-felt impressions which one of a similar description had once made on my younger mind in the plains of Ak-hissar: or rather; it produced one of those moments in my life, when my sensations became so exactly the counterpart of what they once had been, at some definite prior period perhaps long gone by, as to suggest the idea of my having, in a new point of space, reverted to an already experienced point of time; and of my going over afresh some former portion of my existence, already elapsed.

And, in fact, may not things created perform circles in time as they do in space? May not the limited scope of our present perceptions be alone the cause that prevents our embracing the vast revolutions produced by duration, as we compass the smaller circuits performed within the equally inconceivable boundaries of extensions? – and may not one of the brightest prerogatives of that more perfect promised state, when time is said to cease, consist in that removal of its partial barriers, through means of which we shall be permitted equally to see the past in the future, and the future in the past?

Be that as it may: – no scene could, in the splendour of its detail, exceed the one which my mind thus irresistibly retraced. Every where a carpet of anemones, hyacinths, and narcissuses covered the undulating ground. The oleander, the cistus and the rhododendrons, blushing with crimson blossoms, marked the wide margins of the diminished torrents: glowing heaths, odoriferous genistas, thyme, lavender and jasmine, started from every fissure of the marble-streaked rock; while its surface was clothed in a moss of emerald green, through which trickled diamond drops of never failing water. Alternate tufts of arbutus, and mimosa, and bay, intermixed with the wild rose and myrtle, canopied the beetling brow of the crag; but from the deep bosom of the dell between, shot up out of the richer soil, likely stately pillars supporting a ceiling of fretwork, the ilex, the poplar, and the wide spreading plane. Here and there a presumptuous creeper – wily sychophant, raised by his very pliancy – overwhelmed with parasitic blossoms the topmost boughs of the tree on which it fastened; and from its supporter's mighty limbs, again fell in gay festoons to the ground. The air was loaded with fragrance: birds of every hue balanced their light forms on the bending twigs, and myriads of gilded insects emulated in brilliancy the flowers round whose honied cup they hovered.

Yet, while other artists prize their meanest productions, nature often seems to set so little value upon her choicest works, that this paradise lay in a secluded nook, far not only from the more beaten track of the traveller, but even from the haunts of the thinly scattered natives. No path ran through it is any direction: its very outskirts were scarce ever pressed by the foot of man, and its inmost recesses had not perhaps for centuries been darkened by his shadow. Every where the most lovely plants sprung up and again faded every year, without a single instant meeting the human eye: – but the concealment of these wonders produced not the least slackening in their progress: the activity of nature was not checked or diminished by the ignorance of man! Still did each later season see each varied form of vegetation, reckless of human blindness, expand at its due period, blow its full time in all its wonted splendour, and perform every successive function of its maturation and seeding, as it had done each former year.

Had I thence only inferred how little that self assumed lord of the creation, man, goes for in the eyes of Providence, even on that very globe of which he calls himself the supreme master, and which he considers as created for his sole use and purposes, the induction would probably have been just, though thus far little consoling: – but I went further. Since it seemed incompatible with all perfect wisdom that wonders capable of affording exquisite delight, should be endlessly renewed only to be endlessly unenjoyed – endlessly wasted, I inferred that even our own humble globe might be visited, unknown to us its ostensible tenants, by higher beings than ourselves, hovering in purer forms over their primitive haunts, and mixing unperceived with their still mortal kindred. Who could tell that the spirit of my own Alexis – wafted on the sun's untiring beams from its higher abode – might not at times flit among them; might not have sat on yon fair tulip which I so fondly gazed upon, and which bent its graceful head as I slowly passed by.

But time runs short! I may not dwell on such rambling reflections, – I must hasten on to the goal.

Some little perverse incidents, indeed, seemed now and then to start up on very purpose to keep it longer in prospect. My carriage broke down at one place: in another I myself was stunned by a fall: – but these incidental rubs affected me no longer. The single deep affliction which encompassed my heart, served as an impenetrable Ægis against all lesser ills. It rendered me impervious to their superficial punctures. Never emerging from that twilight in which there are no partial shades, since there are no partial lights, my mind, no longer accessible to hope, no longer felt the pressure of disappointment.

A little before the dawn of the fourth day however, there arose a somewhat singular circumstance, which affected me sufficiently to give a new direction to my movements. A pretty sharp ascent had made me alight among the Carinthian hills, to walk a few yards, and shake off the morning chill, by which I felt quite benumbed. The road lay across a dark forest of firs, whose outline already was marked by the pale light of the morning against the cold grey sky, but whose deep bosom still presented unbroken all the black and mysterious indistinctness of night. The trees in their funereal hues seemed sable mourners, gliding in long procession down the hills, to range themselves on my passage: the bleak winds breathed through their waving boughs deep and mournful sighs, and the torrent, dashed from rock to rock, roared with hollow murmur in the chasm below.

All at once I heard – or thought I heard – in the wood a dismal moan, as from one in pain. I stopped, held my breath, turned my ear the way whence proceeded the sound, and, from within a close thicket not thirty yards distant, fancied some one addressed me the following words: "Speed on Anastasius; thou hast not far to go."

My blood curdled in my veins: a chill of terror, thus far unknown, crept all over my person; I felt an inward shudder, – yet I determined to look bold. But, though I dashed like one delirious among the rustling bushes, I found no trace of mortal man!

My first attempt was to laugh off the incident. No one joined in my uninfectious mirth; and soon the forced smile died away on my own lips.

Whether however the ominous words had actually vibrated on my ears, or had only rung in my heated brain, what did it signify? There needed not an express message from the shades below to inform me that my company was waited for: that, with a frame rent at every joint, I was at best but a vampire, only permitted to walk among the living until the last awful summons should fix it for ever among the vaster myriads already under ground. After a long period of very little change in my bodily state, I had felt my sufferings encrease so rapidly, since the fatal dream at the first stage from Trieste, that I could almost, by the regular and distinct progress of my declension, compute the utmost term I might reach, and the hour at which my last sand must run out, and make me bid this world farewell.

And little – in truth – did I reck my hastened fate. Even in my fullest vigour both of body and of mind, I had often prayed that I might not grow old, – had endeavoured only to crowd events so thickly within the span of my existence, that its varied recollections might make my career, however short, appear longer on retrospect than the longest life of dull undistinguished uniformity. – "Rather," – had I often exclaimed – "let me even be felled to the ground, while an ample store of verdant boughs, waving in the breeze, may yet grace my sudden fall, than be permitted to wither on my stalk, unable to offer any attraction or to resent any injury, and indebted as for an obligations to those who merely suffer my presence. Let me not outlive all those from whom I might have obtained a passing tear, only to excite derision in those destined to outlive me!"

And now that health and spirits were already drained to the last drop; – now that, cankered by an inward worm, each bough already withered hung drooping to the ground, and not even a shoot remained to cheer by its later spring my own untimely autumn; – now that both what I loved best and what I hated most had already attained the final goal before me, – could I still wish to live – to live alone in the universe, without a spark of affection, or even of animosity, left, to light with its fire my last lingering steps: Could I brook to stand, like the scathed oak in the wilderness, a conspicuous monument of Heaven's fiercest wrath? – God forbid!

Then, what was the use of torturing my worn-out frame, only to seek far away what I might find so near? I could die any where.

Immediately I formed my resolution. Two stages back I remembered being struck by the appearance of a fir-clothed cottage, close to a country town, whose few inhabitants – kept up somewhat later than usual by some holiday festivity – had attracted my notice by their cheerful clusters. "Might not" – thought I – "that gold, now become so indifferent to its weary possessor, obtain me the loan of this coveted habitation, for the short time my body wanted one above ground?"

This I determined to try; but found obstacles to my scheme even sooner than I had expected. My driver was of the true German breed – an automaton who, throughout the whole length of his stage, could only move according to the impulse received on setting out. The advantage of receiving full payment for a task only half performed, was what his brain refused to conceive: only, he never had heard of people stopping half way on their journey, to turn back to whence they came; and he never should – God helping – lend his assistance to such an innovation. The cane was shaken in vain at this imperturbable idiot, – even the pistol's threatening muzzle made to exert its dumb oratory close to his ear, without the smallest effect. The immoveable *schwager* would rather be shot dead on the spot than submit to become instrumental in the nefarious deed of turning his horses heads: so that my servant had to pull him at last off his brother brute, and to usurp his lawful place, ere I could effect my retrograde movement: – nor did I consider this as one of the least achievements of my life.

Equally arduous did I, on my return to L——, find the main business which brought me back. The owners of the cottage – dull plodding people like the postboy – wanted time to consider of my singular proposal. They could not resolve on such a measure in a hurry: and the first determination they were able – after much hesitation – to come to, only consisted in a promise of the habitation at a period so remote, that I must have taken possession of a more lasting mansion long ere it arrived. Even when afterwards the wary couple agreed – on the strength of my ill looks, and hollow cough – to let me have the hovel immediately for the whole term of my life, they still evinced some desire of inserting as a clause in the lease, *when* I was to die. At last, however, through dint of constantly enhancing my offers, all difficulties were overcome. I took possession of my cot, and my tenacious landlord went away, half grumbling at his good bargain, half grinning at my strange whim, and wondering at the stranger price I paid for its indulgence.

The last stage of my terrestrial journey thus achieved, the last place of halting on this side the house to be changed no more thus occupied, I immediately made the few arrangements necessary for the comfort of my transient abode, and sent for a physician from the neighbouring town, to render my bargain as little losing as possible. On examining my symptoms the sage shook his head, and judiciously observed that I might linger a good while yet, or might die very soon: but would do well at all events, to take his medicine. This I received, but took care not to waste on my incurable ailments: notwithstanding which cautious conduct my weakness soon encreased to such a degree, that a walk round my garden became an exertion.

Near me lived a young couple, whom my other neighbours made the constant theme of their praise: – and most disinterested it seemed; for the husband had only gained, by serving his country as a soldier, some severe and painful wounds, while the wife had lost, by preferring the wounded soldier to a hale peasant with a heavy purse, the countenance of all her kindred. In return she had secured the smiles of a large family of her own; and her only embarrassment was how to give her children bread. Of love alone there remained a most plentiful store: but even of this ingredient it was difficult to say whether, by rendering each consort an object of constant anxiety to the other, it alleviated their sufferings or encreased their solicitude.

To get sight of these worthy people was not so easy as it might seem. They were proud; they liked not a stranger to witness their honourable indigence, and they dreaded the importunate offer of his superfluity. Even when at last – through dint of unabating perseverance – I obtained leave to visit them, they shewed the greatest ingenuity in eluding the drift of my visits. With respect to the state of their finances they were downright hypocrites. One would have supposed they wanted for nothing. Fate however ordained me to collect from their own mouths – without any thanks to their candour – the most practicable mode of relieving their necessities.

Once, on a Sunday evening, as the husband, at rest from the week's labour, and with only the weight of his own little wife hanging on his arm, had sat listening across the fence which divided our properties, to the narrative of some of my adventures, and had heard with equal awe and concern how the soundest parts of my life had been full of death spots; how pride, passion, love and hatred – every feeling, every lure, and every stimulus – had in turns swayed my existence with such ill-poised force, that each during its reign wholly silenced all the rest, until, exhausted by indulgence, each again left its rivals to take a dire revenge; how by my own ingenuity I had contrived ever to render useless all the gifts profusely showered upon me; and how finally my whole life had been a struggle with a bounteous Providence, which should do and which undo the most, – the little woman at the conclusion of the story fetched a deep sigh, and the husband hereupon giving her a sharpish look, she with a blush observed, what a pity it was, a tale so eventful and so strange should remain unrecorded: – Conrad was so good a penman!

At first I spurned the idea. I had indeed learnt a little of the world, and at my cost; but of composition I knew nothing; and though, in my days of buoyancy and conceit, I might frequently have planned to gratify the world with my motley memoirs, in my days of humiliation and weakness I recoiled from the arduous task. That very weakness, however, at last persuaded me. I was no longer able to take any exercise, and I wanted some occupation sufficiently interesting to prevent a still restless mind from preying upon a feeble and failing body. Besides – I own that I felt a faint wish not to let oblivion wholly blot out of man's remembrance the name of Anastasius. Nor could the scheme encounter great difficulty on the score of the difference of idiom between me and my destined secretary: for Conrad, educated as a gentleman, had moreover acquired in his campaigns a sufficient knowledge of the French language – our thus far ordinary medium of communication – to write in it correctly what I should dictate.

If, therefore, I still only caught at the proposal slowly; if I still a while made a shew of outward reluctance survive my inward assent, it was only to obtain on my own terms the assistance proffered – and to extort a right to estimate, at least in a limited degree, my obligations to my scribe, as merchants do the services rendered by their correspondents, – a proceeding, however, so haughtily rejected at first, that I must have despaired of success, but for the soft whisperings of pity in the bosom of my new friends. They saw my frame waste away so fast, that at last they blushed to let an unseasonable – I may say an unsympathising – delicacy, any longer deprive my few remaining days of their only solace; and permitted me to name them in my will. This I eagerly did, and then committed to their care my person and my frame. No sooner was the bargain thus struck, that we sat down. I dictated, – more or less at a time, according to my strength and spirits – Conrad wrote: and this is the fruit.

Upon the whole the task has afforded me a salutary relief from the tedium of my constrained situation. Only when I have happened, while ruminating upon my own affairs, to cast my eyes upon my honoured scribe – who sits there smiling to be thus himself unexpectedly brought forward, while waiting with uplifted pen the sequel of my meditations – and chanced to catch the stolen glances of affection exchanged between him and his amiable helpmate, working by his side, some drops of bitterness would mix even with this last pleasure. "such," thought I, "might have been my own fate with my Euphrosyné; and such also......" but already Conrad's incipient frown checks my digressing any further.

Once or twice, indeed, encreasing weakness has been near putting a stop to my work, in the midst of its progress. Each time, however, the performance was, after a short interruption, again duly resumed: – and Heaven has at last permitted its completion.

At thirty five I here complete its last page and sentence. At thirty five I take leave of all further earthly concerns: at thirty five I close, – never more to re-open it – the crowded volume of my toilsome life. In a few weeks, days – perhaps hours – will for ever drop over my person, my actions, and my errors, the dark curtain of death; – when nothing will remain of the once vain and haughty Anastasius, but an empty name, and a heap of noisome ashes.

O ye who tread their scattered remnants! – ere you execrate that name, the theme of so much obloquy, remember my sufferings: be merciful to my memory, – and may Heaven's mercy rest upon yourselves!

Here ends the author's own narrative: what follows has been added from the account of the gentleman he names Conrad.

Anastasius, having completed the last pages of his memoirs with great effort only, fell almost immediately after into an irremediable languor. Every day that dawned now threatened – or rather promised – to be his last: for his existence was become so full of misery, that his end seemed desirable. Yet could not his sufferings – intense as they were – for a moment subdue his fortitude. Never was he heard to utter a syllable of impatience or complaint. Whenever his debility permitted him to converse, the theme was his adored child. "Were my heart opened" – said he one day – "you would find his name inscribed in its core. In the winning of my Alexis I lost health and strength, but it was the losing of him which gave me the death blow. Now that nothing more remains for me to do but to prepare for my exit, I could have wished – had I been a great man, enabled to indulge all his fancies – to be carried to the spot where he lies, there to breathe my last by his beloved side: but such luxuries an outcast, a homeless wanderer must not think of. Enough for me, when my hour is at hand, to have in his gentle spirit an angel on high, to intercede with his Father in Heaven, for his expiring earthly parent."

The third morning after this speech, Conrad, coming in at an early hour, found not his patient, as usual, on his pillow. Anastasius has made shift to creep out of bed, and was kneeling before a chair on which rested his face. At first he seemed in a swoon: – but, discerning the approach of his friend, he held out his trembling hand to him, and, trying to raise his head, faintly cried out: "Heaven takes pity at last. Thanks, O thanks for all your goodness!" – and immediately relapsed. After a second interval of apparent absence, a second fit of momentary consciousness followed, when Conrad, stooping, heard the poor sufferer utter, but in a voice almost extinct: "O my Alexis, I come!" and immediately saw his head fall forward again. Conrad now tried to lift him into bed, in order that he might be more at ease. There was no occasion: Anastasius was no more.

His body, laid out – by those who owed to him their restoration to comfort and affluence – in a sort of state, was by them committed to its last mansion with somewhat more solemnity than he had desired. They inherited half his property: the other half had been bequeathed to the poor of the place; and, though staunch Roman Catholics, its inhabitants – it is said – still bless the memory of the young Greek.

NOTES.

CHAPTER I

1 p.310. *Confiscation of the paternal estate*: Those who accept offices and titles from the Sultan are considered as submitting to become his slaves, and to give him an arbitrary right over their lives and inheritance.
2 p.311. *Bergamo*: the ancient Pergamus.
3 p.312. *Its immense cemeteries*: Among the Turks, in proportion as death extends his conquests, cemeteries are enlarged; and the cypress-trees planted round the tombs often give them the appearance of a forest. The burying-places near Scutari are immense; from the predilection which even the Turks of Europe preserve for being buried in Asia.
4 p.313. *New flower-beds of graves*: The Turks frequently plant flowers on their tombs, which are open at the top for that purpose.
5 p.313. *Sultan Mahmoud's horse*: actually interred in the cemetery of Scutari, under a dome supported by eight pillars.
6 p.315. *Shah-nishin*: name given to the projecting windows or gazebos in use at Constantinople.
7 p.316. *Halabeen*: from Halch or Aleppo.

CHAPTER II

1 p.325. *Mangal*: Turkish brasier.
2 p.326. *St. Mark's dazzling images*: Venetian sequins, stamped with the figure of that saint, and the most current gold coin in the Levant.
3 p.329. *Haïck*: cotton cloak, worn by the Barbaresques.

CHAPTER IV

1 p.347. *Koordish horsemen*: the Koords, or inhabitants of Koordistan, lead, like the Tartars, a pastoral and and predatory life; and roam all over Asia Minor, for the purposes of pasture and plunder.
2 p.347. *Ansariehs*: a tribe supposed to worship the evil spirit, and, unlike the Mohammedans, by no means tenacious of the chastity of their wives and daughters.
3 p.349. *Kafflé*: small caravan.
4 p.350. *Yulfa*: a suburb of Isaphan.

CHAPTER V

1 p.358. *Baïrak*: Tukish standard, or regiment.
2 p.360. This rhapsody seems to allude to the seat of the Persian empire having being successively transferred from Ispahan to Sheeraz, and from Sheeraz to Teheran.
3 p.360. *Serdar*: reception room.
4 p.362. *Ishallah*: please God!

CHAPTER VI

1 p.365. *Kabilé*: small Arab tribe, subordinate to a larger.

CHAPTER VIII

1 p.390. *Within three or four Conacks*: or days journey.
2 p.390. *To untie my horse's legs*: The Arab mode of securing horses during the night consists in tying their legs to a stake driven in the ground.

CHAPTER IX

1 p.402. *Turkish santon*: or itinerant saint; of the sort that travel about, living upon the credulity and superstition of the lower orders.

CHAPTER X

1 p.404. *He soon distinguished himself by his proficiency in magic*: an art believed in by all the mamlukes, and cultivated by many.
2 p.408. Sir Sydney Smith, in his dispatches to government, calls Djezzar Pasha (whom we had the honour of supporting at the expense of British blood and treasure as well was the Beys of Egypt), the *energetic* old man.
3 p.413. *Tekkieh*: a monastery or building in which the dervishes perform their devout exercises.

CHAPTER XI

1 p.414. *Kafflé*: vide supra, p.349.
2 p.414. *Iman*: priest.
3 p.414. *Cazi-asker*: chief of the order o Turkish magistrates, of which there are two; one for Roumili, and one for Anadoly.
4 p.414. *Medressé*: Mohammedan endowed college.
5 p.415. *Khodgea*: teacher, preceptor.
6 p.415. *Muderrees*: members of the higher departments of law.
7 p.416. *Antakieh*: the ancient Antioch.
8 p.416.*Leaden images*: of their saints, which some of the orders of derwishes distribute.
9 p.417. *Hadjee-Becktash*: the patron saint of one of the principal orders of derwishes.
10 p.419. *My shaggy hair*: some derwishes deviate from the custom of the Turks, in wearing their hair very long.
11 p.419. *Disturbed all the angels in my beard*: the Mohammedans, from some such prejudice, deem it a sin, after once they have suffered their beards to grow, to cut them off again.
12 p.420. *Donanmas*: Fêtes given by the Turkish government on the occasion of public rejoicings, &c.

CHAPTER XIV

1 p.453. *Vulgar name*: prepared skin, called in French *peau d'âne*.
2 p.456. *Its seals are all torn off, and its ornaments effaced*: by the treaty of Tolentino, concluded by the Pope and Bonaparte, the fairest provinces of the Patrimony of St.Peter, and the finest statues of the Vatican, had been ceded to the French.

APPENDIX I.

A Visual Study of Thomas Hope

John Rodenbeck

In addition to the triumph and decline of neo-classicism and Egyptomania, Thomas Hope lived through other cultural changes. One was a shift of fashion in England from Turcomania to Philhellenism, two attitudes that may now seem incompatible, though both are reflected in *Anastasius.* Hope was indeed a neo-Classicist and a fervent admirer of the arts and culture of ancient Greece, but he was no Philhellene and found much to love in Ottoman Turkey.

The Ottoman Empire had been a powerful European presence for centuries. Its territories included what are now Greece, Macedonia, Bulgaria, Rumania, Moldova, Albania, Croatia, Bosnia, Serbia, Montenegro, Slovenia, most of Hungary and Slovakia, and parts of southern Poland and Ukraine, where things as basic as everyday language, cuisine, music, and multitudinous place-names still testify to Ottoman influence and authority. Abutting the empires of Austria and Russia, the Empire frequently acted in alliance with France to curb the challenge of Habsburgs or Romanovs.

This Franco-Ottoman partnership was the reason for the ten-month visit to France of Lala Süleyman Ağa, Chief Eunuch, former Governor of the Abode of Felicity, special envoy to the young Louis XIV (1638-1715) from the even younger Sultan Mehmet IV (1642-1693). Lasting from August 1669 to May 1670, his sojourn inspired at least one permanent monument. Heading an entourage of twenty, Süleyman remained visibly unimpressed by the Sun King's displays of luxury and pomp. To one clueless French courtier who asked him if he had observed the quality and number of Louis's diamonds, Süleyman remarked that in both respects the Sun King was worse bedizened than the Ottoman Sultan's horse.

Almost immediately after Süleyman's departure, Louis requested Molière (1622-1673) and Lully (1632-1687) to compose a comic ballet with Turkish themes, for which a famous adventurer attached to the court, the Chevalier d'Arvieux (1635-1702), would supply technical advice. The result was a theatrical masterpiece, *Le Bourgeois Gentilhomme* (1670), in which both Molière and Lully performed rôles and which includes a hilarious Turkish episode, accompanied by Lully's pseudo-Turkish music.

During the same era a multi-volumed work called *The Turkish Spy*, published first in France in 1684, inaugurated the vogue for "Oriental" letters that would come to include Montesqieu's *Lettres persanes* (1721, 1754) and Goldsmith's "Chinese Letters" (*The Citizen of the World,* 1762). The beginning of real Turcomania in Western Europe could probably be assigned, however, to 1721, when the Grand Vezir Nevflehirli Damat Ibrahim Pasha sent Yirmisekiz Çelebi zâde Mehmet Effendi at the head of another major embassy, this time to the court of Philippe d'Orléans (1673-1723). For the next six decades or so the polite and cultivated classes throughout Europe delectated in the Turkish Novel and Turkish Tale – let us recall that the garden where the hero of

Voltaire's *Candide* (1759) finally does his cultivating is in fact in Turkey – the Turkish Comedy, the Turkish Opera, interior decoration and even architecture *à la turc,* not to mention Turkish picnics and masquerade balls. The notion that Turcomania in Europe arose from the *Turkish Embassy Letters* of Lady Mary Wortley Montagu is obvious nonsense: their posthumous publication in 1763, some 45 years after her return from a 14-month stay in Constantinople, was clearly not a cause of Turcomania, but rather one of its effects.

One of the more lasting influences during this period came from Turkish military bands, which were acquired by the courts of Saxony, Poland, Russia, Austria, France, and several other countries. Playing Turkish music, they demonstrated the use of cymbals, the triangle, and the bass drum to composers like Mozart (1756-1791). The disguises worn by Ferrando and Guglielmo as "Albanians" in *Così fan tutte* are, of course, Turkish military uniforms; and Mozart created Turkish effects in the finale of the piano sonata in A major, K. 331, in *Entführung aus dem Serail*, and in his Six German Dances, K. 571. So did Haydn (1732-1809) (*e.g.*, in the second movement of the "Military" Symphony, no. 100 in G major) and Beethoven (1770-1827) (*e.g.*, in his incidental music for *The Ruins of Athens,* in the march preceding the tenor solo – "Froh, wie seine Sonne fliegen" – in the last movement of the Ninth Symphony, and in several of his Twelve German Dances). And so did many other contemporary and subsequent makers of Western music, where Turkish effects have remained a permanent and recognizable feature. A superb Archiv recording by Concerto Köln and Sarband, *The Waltz: Ecstasy and Mysticism*, released in 2005, explores the mutual influences between Germanic and Turkish music during the late-eighteenth and early-nineteenth centuries.

At the height of eighteenth-century Turcomania, even untravelled artists like Lancret (1690-1743), Étienne Jeaurat (1699-1789), Jacques de Lajouë 1686-1761), Jacques Aved (1702-1766), Boucher (1703-1770), and Jean-Baptiste Leprince (1734-1781) made portraits of such models as the marquise de Sainte-Maure, the marquise de Pleumartin, the marquise de Bonne, and the comtesse de Magnac in authentic Turkish dress, while Fragonard (1732-1806) would paint a series of erotically idealized sultans and sultanas. For his patroness, Mme. de Pompadour, who became the Louis XV's *maîtresse en titre* in 1745, Carle van Loo (1705-1765) painted three decorative works in which Turkish costumes clothe ideal figures in neo-classic settings.

The great Swiss-born artist Jean-Étienne Liotard (1702-1789), who had actually lived in Constantinople and himself customarily wore Turkish clothes, now made portraits in Turkish garb of such highly placed subjects as Princess Marie-Adelaïde (1732-1800), fourth daughter of Louis XV and the only one actually reared at Court. In England likewise, which he visited in 1754-55 and again in 1772-1774, Liotard painted ladies of the nobility and gentry in Turkish dress. His local rivals and imitators in the same costume portrait genre included major painters like Joshua Reynolds (1724-1792), George Romney (1734-1802), and John Singleton Copley (1738-1815), as well as minor ones like Joseph Highmore (1692-1780) and Francis Cotes (1724-1770). George Willison (1741-1797), who specialized in demi-mondaines, based his portrait of the fashionable prostitute Nancy Parsons on a picture of Liotard's presumed to be of Maria

Gunning, Duchess of Coventry. Even after the rise of neo-Classical styles, in the early years of the following century, the *shawl* and the *turban* – both words are Persian in origin, the latter entering English by way of Turkish – remained essential to the costume repertoire of well-dressed European or American women.

Meanwhile in 1762 Antoine de Favray (1706-1798) followed Liotard's example and went to Constantinople itself, where he stayed nine years, painting genre scenes and official records of another generation of foreign dignitaries. Notable are two portraits: the first, painted in 1766, of Charles Gravier, comte de Vergennes (1717-1787), French ambassador to Constantinople (1754-1768); and the second, painted two years later, of the ambassador's freshly acquired native-born wife, Annette Duvivier de Testa (1730-1798). The comtesse had previously been married to one of the Testa, a prominent Genoese family already settled in Pera for several centuries. Widowed at the age of 24, she had become the ambassador's mistress and bore him two children before their marriage. Vergennes went on under Louis XVI to become Foreign Minister and win fame as the central figure in promoting official and vigorous French support for the American Revolution. Favray portrayed both in Turkish dress. Favray's own self-portrait, painted in 1778, after his return to France, shows him also in Turkish dress, with a Rousseauistic *qalpaq* on his head, but wearing the cross of the Knights of Malta and a quizzical expression, posed as if drawing back a curtain to disclose a tourist's distant view of Ayasofya/Hagia Sophia and the Theodosian wall.

Equally significant with such works of art were more ephemeral appearances of Turkish clothing, for both men and women, at such occasions as masked balls, routs, and receptions. The famous Turkish reception given at Fonthill during Christmastide of 1781 by the 22-year-old William Beckford (1759-1844) lasted three days and was an occasion so inimitable that it may have marked the apogee of Turcomania which, like all fashions, was to have its day. Dressing authentically *à la turc* could hardly have survived in any case the clothing reforms instituted in 1826 and 1829 under Mahmut II (1808-1839) in the Empire itself, when a standard and style of clothing began to be adapted from the Western dress that was so uniform, drab, joyless, and prosaic as to discourage imitation. Men surrendered early to this change, but it took nearly a century for Kemal Atatürk (1881-1938) to complete Mahmut's revolution by extending it to women. The portraits of men and women dressed in traditional pre-reform Ottoman clothes continued to be painted, of course, but with an additional element of affected antiquarianism.

In 1798, nearing 30, and recently returned from Constantinople, Hope had himself painted in Turkish dress. Such a gesture, as we have just seen, had been customary among Eastern travellers for at least a century earlier and would remain a fanciful indulgence, even among ordinary citizens, for three or four decades afterwards. The famous portrait that ensued, by Sir William Beechey, RA (1753-1839) acquired by the National Portrait Gallery in 1967, shows Hope wearing an outfit that has been mistakenly identified as the uniform of a low-ranking Greek sailor, thus missing the point of the picture. The costume is in fact mentioned early in the novel itself (Volume I. Chapter III):

> I swore I would some day, cost what it might, doff my uncouth headdress for one of these smart turbans of gilt brocade, worn with such a saucy air over one ear by the Pasha's Tshawooshes – gentlemen who were seen everywhere, lounging about as if they had nothing to do but display their handsome legs, their vests stiff with gold lace, and their impudent bullying faces.

Tshawoosh or *tchawoosh* – Hope uses both spellings – is equivalent to the modern Turkish *çavufl* and, according to context, means "officer, sergeant, usher, or *huissier.*" In Volume I, Chapter XIV the costume is described at length and in detail:

> In the refinements of his toilet . . . Aly tchawoosh [Aly is an officer in the entourage of the Kapudan-Pasha, the Grand Admiral, precisely one of "the Pasha's Tshawooshes" whose clothing Anastasius had envied earlier] might be considered as a finished Osmanlee. Nothing could excel the exquisite taste of his apparel. His turban attracted the eye less even by the costliness of texture than by its elegance of form. A band of green and gold tissue, diagonally crossing the forehead, was made completely to conceal one ear, and as completely to display the other . . . . His dress of the finest broadcloth and velvet, made after the most dashing Barbary cut, was covered all over with gold embroidery, so thickly embossed as to appear almost massive. His chest, uncovered down to the girdle, and his arms bared up to the shoulder, displayed all the bright polish of his skin. His capote was draped so as with infinite grace to break the too formal symmetry of his costume. In short, his *handjar* [dagger] with its gilt handle, his watch with its concealed miniature, his tobacco pouch of knitted gold, his pipe mounted in opaque amber, and with his pistols with diamond-cut hilt, were all in the style of the most consummate *petit maître*; and if, spite of all his pains, my friend Aly was not without exception the handsomest man in the Ottoman empire, none could deny his being one of the best dressed, His air and manner harmonized with his attire. A confident look, an insolent and sneering tone, and an indolent yet swaggering gait, bespoke him to be, what indeed it was his utmost ambition to appear, a thorough rake.

Hope obviously saw Aly's costume as a work of art, as Lord Byron (1788-1824) did the Albanian costume he bought a decade later in Ottoman Greece. Such clothes, Byron wrote to his mother, on 12 November 1809, were "magnifiques" and "the only expensive items in this country." Five years later Byron had himself painted in his Albanian costume by Thomas Philips, who also made two copies, one of which is now in the National Portrait Gallery, the other in the office of John Murray, publisher of both Byron and Hope. The original hangs in the British Embassy in Athens; and Byron's costume itself, given by the poet to Lady Elphinstone for use in masquerades, is now on display in Bowood House, Wiltshire.

Similar costumes to Hope's are shown on one plate in the classic work on the subject, Field Marshal Mahmud Salih ᶜArif Pasha's *Les anciens costumes de l'Empire Ottomane depuis l'origine de la Monarchie jusqu'à la Réforme du Sultan Mahmoud*

[*Majmu^{c}at tesavir ^{c}uthmani*] (Paris: Lemercier, n.d. [*ca.* 1863-]: Plate 5, the only plate devoted to the pre-reform Ottoman navy, shows the Grand Admiral with his *chef des pages* and five other representative members of his entourage, all dressed rather like Hope's Aly, none displaying any obvious insignia. One of them, who is shirtless and turbanless, is identified in the Field Marshal's commentary (pp. 16-17 of the accompanying text) as merely an able seaman, but the others are all styled *çavufl.* The two most senior (figures 18 and 19) sport *yatagans,* rather than *khanjars.* The figure that most nearly resembles the description from *Anastasius* is number 20, an officer in the marine detachment called "The Naked Sailors."

The figure that most obviously resembles the portrait itself, however, is number 22, an officer of the Galata Detachment. Field Marshal ^{c}Arif Pasha notes that they are all wearing the slippers peculiar to the Terskhane (= modern Turkish *tersane*), the Shipyard, headquarters of the Admiralty, often translated as the "Arsenal/Arsénal/ Arsenale." (Both the Turkish word and the English/French/Italian words come from the Arabic *dar flinâ^{c}ah,* "place of manufacture," but the Western meanings have wandered much further from their Eastern source.) ^{c}Arif Pasha confesses that as a youngster in the early 1820s he "developed a taste for this curious and brilliant costume" and won the authorization of his grandfather to have a complete ensemble made, which he wore on outings with friends.

Hope not only shared, but anticipated the Field Marshal's taste. In his portrait the turban is more gold than green, he has not bared his chest, and the pistols have been laid aside, but all the other elements in the description of Aly's appearance are present, the watch and tobacco pouch being suggested by the gold chains to which they are attached. The presence of the latter is additionally confirmed by the lighted and burning *çibuq*, the long pipe held in Hope's left hand, its smoking head at rest on the ground, one of the necessary accoutrements of an Ottoman gentleman. Hope's figure has been described as wearing two cloaks draped over a shoulder, but it may well be just one, of red broadcloth lined with green silk.

He seems also not to be bare-legged, as has been suggested, but to be wearing plain rose-colored hose, like figures 20 and 22 in the Field Marshal's Plate 5 and in contrast with figures 18 and 19, the two senior officers, whose hose are elaborately embroidered. Other details are even more interesting. The large gold-encrusted oval visible in the lower corner of the right-hand side of the outermost of Hope's two sleeveless jackets frames a *tuğra* – a calligraphic device that is normally a monogrammed full name – embroidered in gold thread. An edge of its mate shows on the other side from beneath the model's left hand.

The two *yeleks* or sleeveless jackets worn by Hope in the portrait are in fact now in the possession of the National Portrait Gallery, a gift of Mrs. H. W. Law, Hope's great-granddaughter, in 1968. Thanks to Erika Ingham and the staff of the Heinz Archive and Library, National Portrait Gallery, I had the privilege of examining them personally in early April 2007 and found some interesting details.

The only *tuğra* visible in the portrait, for example, has been depicted backwards and is therefore more or less illegible, but this state of things is not due to any mistake by the artist, who has shown the clothes exactly as they looked to him and still are: the reversed and illegible *tuğra* on the left-hand side of Hope's outer *yelek* is in fact a mirrored version of another *tuğra* concealed on the right lapel, which is legible, but nevertheless enigmatic. Two *tuğras,* one the mirror-image of the other, are also embroidered on the scarlet under-*yelek*, but are concealed in the portrait by Hope's cummerbund. They are in reversed positions from those on the outer *yelek*, with the legible one on Hope's left and its mirrored opposite this time on his right. As a comparison of it with the original portrait and with these garments indicates, the photographic version of the portrait printed both on the cover of *Cornucopia,* Volume I, Issue 5, 1993/1994, and with the text of the cover article, which shows the one visible *tuğra* running in the right direction and thus theoretically legible, has in fact been reversed, no doubt in the interest of good cover design.

Hope deliberately had himself portrayed as a Turkish Muslim: the richness of his apparel alone indicates that no Christian is depicted here and certainly no low-ranking Greek sailor. Under the empire's sumptuary laws even red slippers of the kind he wears in this portrait were specifically allowed only to Muslims. John Cam Hobhouse (1786-1869), Byron's travelling companion in the Ottoman Empire, noted in his diary entry for Wednesday, 30 May 1810, that Selim's first act as sultan, more than two decades earlier, had been to oversee the beheading of a Greek whom he had informally encountered and who had been imprudently shod in slippers of a colour forbidden within the Empire to his nation and religion.

Behind Hope in the portrait is not just a generic mosque or a tourist's view of Ayasofya, moreover, but a specific view of the fifteenth-century mosque of Abu Ayyub al-Ansari, Standard-Bearer of the Prophet, at Eyüp Sultan on the Golden Horn, which Beechey copied from a rendering of the same view that was recorded and preserved by Hope himself. It still exists among the drawings Hope assembled in Athens and Constantinople, five volumes of which are now owned by the Benaki Museum.

Hope's watercolour and sepia version of this view already had special historical value: it depicted the Abu Ayyub mosque as he saw it during his lengthy sojourn in Constantinople, *i.e.*, as it was before it was demolished (in 1798, having been damaged by an earthquake in 1766) and rebuilt (in 1800). Its two minarets, which had survived the earthquake intact, were retained; and reconstruction followed the original plan, but a band of fenestration was added to the dome to create a clerestory. Hope and Beechey thus show us the architecture as it looked originally, before this innovative addition.

The most sacrosanct spot in Constantinople, the mosque of Abu Ayyub at Eyüp Sultan, remains a Muslim pilgrimage site and is surrounded by the cemeteries that supplied Hope with a wealth of fountains, tombs, and monuments from which to copy the Ottoman design-motifs that are recorded in the same albums. Executed either by Hope himself or by an artist he commissioned, this particular view was coincidentally published in the cover article on Hope in *Cornucopia,* Volume I, Issue 5, which also shows examples of these design-motifs, one of which actually appears in the portrait, as the uppermost of the two decorative elements in the wall on Hope's left. Probably under Hope's exacting instructions, Beechey thus almost certainly made use of these albums for the background of the portrait. A footman would have been sent with them to the artist's house and studio in Harley Street, which were a mere three-minute walk from Hope's house in Duchess Street.

Beechey went on to paint many other portraits, but none as brilliant. At least two, one of which is now in the superb collection of British portraits at Compton Verney in Warwickshire, likewise depicted a sitter in Oriental dress. The sitter for both was Mirza Abu'l-Hassan Khan, Ambassador Plenipotentiary of Persia in London from 1809 to 1811, who recorded in his diaries his delight at encountering the artist's children during sessions in Harley Street.

Hope's portrait was displayed in the Royal Academy for several months in 1799, then hung prominently in the staircase-hall of the house in Duchess Street, where an enamel copy by Henry Bone (1755-1832?) was displayed nearby. A pencil drawing by Bone for this enamel is also in the National Portrait Gallery. Two watercolour copies by G. P. Harding (1780-1853) are in the British Museum. The portrait was then, it seems, eventually moved to the dining room at the Deepdene, Hope's country residence in Surrey. A variant painted by Adam Buck (1759-1833) dating from 1805, showing Hope in a different costume with a felucca in the background, is in the collection of the Society of Dilettanti. Hope also commissioned another portrait of himself in Turkish dress in 1805 from Sir Thomas Lawrence (1769-1830), but the commission was never fulfilled.

APPENDIX II.

Sándor Baumgarten, Hope's Forgotten Champion

Jerry Nolan

Le Crepuscule neo-classique. Thomas Hope (Paris: Didier, 1958), 272pp.

It was probably after reading *Anastasius* that Sándor Baumgarten (1893-1970), the independent Hungarian scholar, wanted to write the life of its author. At the beginning of his research, Baumgarten read in the *Literary Gazette* (1831) that the paper hoped that 'some competent person will prepare and lay before the public an ample account of the life, travels and writings of Mr. Hope, convinced as we are that it would be peculiarly interesting to the literary, scientific and higher circles of society.' Quite early on in his researches, Baumgarten began to feel that he had given himself a task which had been utterly neglected over four or five generations. The challenge was not only to find some original Hope documents but to develop his own skills to match the many interests of such a widely travelled and knowledgeable man. The very extensive bibliography in Baumgarten's book displayed just how far and wide into primary and secondary sources he ranged in search of Hope. There was much use made of published correspondence, memoirs and contemporary criticism. One of the most notable successes of the enterprise was the tracking down of Hope unpublished letters in the British Museum, the Bodleian Library, the Bibliothèque of Geneva, the Bibliothèque Municipale of Bassano del Grappa, the Bibliothèque Nationale in Paris and the Bibliothèque Royale in Copenhagen. The sheer paucity of primary sources led Baumgarten to think that many things which could have facilitated his research must have been either stupidly or wickedly destroyed. Baumgarten's suspicion fell on members of Hope's family, probably his grandson, who might well have suppressed the evidence for their father's dissenting voice in order to protect their own exalted ambitious plans to rise high in British society, and this suspicion turned into full scale conviction as the researcher began to piece together his own portrait of Hope by means of the study of the published writings and of reactions from his contemporaries. Baumgarten's stroke of genius was that he structured his book in such a way that the attentive reader is put into pole position to observe Hope in a series of double-roles which reveal the dialectical rhythms of his experiences.

Banker and Aesthete

Baumgarten studies Hope's self-understanding as a member of one of the great banking families at the time by highlighting Hope's published account of his childhood love of architectural drawing when other children were concentrating on more or less correct reproductions of familiar images such as flowers and landscapes. Later in life Hope copied engravings of many places including the ruined sites in Asia Minor and went on to draw much of what he saw on his Grand Tour of the Orient. Baumgarten discusses dilettantism as an element in his character but shifts the emphasis onto Hope's efforts to admit the wider public to his house in Duchess Street, London where they could admire and learn from the display there of great art from many cultures. In Baumgarten's view, Hope believed that works of art belong also to the community and should never be 'at home in churlish cabinets concealed'. Baumgarten tells the story of how Hope's wealth was used as a patron and draws special attention to the case of the Danish sculptor Bertel Thorvaldsen whom he rescued during a visit to Rome in March 1803 on the very day the sculptor, who had run out of money, was about to be expelled by the police of the Vatican State. Hope was to play Maecenas to the ever grateful sculptor.

Neo-Classicist and Transculturalist

In his view of Hope as neo-classicist, Bamgarten reveals his own considerable hostility to the tendency of associating Hope too closely with the spread of neo-classical taste in design during the Regency period. Baumgarten's opposition to neo-classicism is implied in the book's title. For him, neo-classicism was the new intolerant religion favoured by those Enlightenment enthusiasts who, in order to become Greek and Roman again, seemed determined if necessary to disenfranchise themselves from everything else. Hope is criticized for his involvement in some of the ephemeral reviews of the neo-classical movement which, according to Baumgarten, were read by the devotees with as much fervour as diocesan bulletins were consumed by the Christian party faithful. These devotees went on rather quickly to imitate the Christian religion further by exposing heretics and turncoats among the themselves and by opposing Christianity itself when each Doric column erected in Edinburgh or on the lands of the Northern Semiramis was seen as a challenge to the Kirk or Orthodoxy. Unfortunately Baumgarten does not pause in this tirade long enough to seek the explanation of *how* Hope managed to be *simultaneously* neo-classicist in some areas and cross-culturalist overall. More attention to details included in Hope long review of world cultures in his *Essay on Man* would have helped on this point. However what Baumgarten does manage to do is to rescue Hope from being captured as their prisoner, then or afterwards, by the neo-classical aesthetes.

Christian and World Philosopher

Baumgarten refers to *Essay on Man* when he quotes the opinion on the book by Thomas Carlyle who had praised and recommended *Anastasius*. Carlyle dismissed the book as 'this monstrous anomaly, where all sciences are heaped and huddled together and the principles of all are, with a childlike innocence, plied hither and tither…a general agglomerate of all facts, notions, whims and observations as they lie in the brain of an English gentleman.' Baumgarten confesses to feeling attracted to Hope's sense of wonder before the universe which surely must stretch far beyond the stretch of Christian thought when the realization dawns that human beings on this globe are running around on a miniscule part of the prodigious universe – so prodigious that no human should pretend to be certain about its curvature. For Baumgarten, Hope seemed to be on a path which was to lead to the development of scientific knowledge – ahead of Einstein, in fact! Baumgarten lacked the philosophical knowledge to examine in depth Hope's suggestions for the way forward in science, but he was determined to encourage his readers to begin to think like Hope and move beyond the limits set by Carlyle.

Family Man and Angry Rebel

One of Baumgarten's most striking conclusions is that Thomas Hope was so little understood and appreciated by his wife and sons. Samuel Rogers's opinion is quoted on the trials and tribulations of the 'poet-banker' whom Baumgarten readily identifies as Hope: 'He has a wife who inflicts on him each season two or three immense evening parties. During one of them, totally lost, with his elbows on the mantelpiece, he was accosted by a gentleman who said to him, "Sire, as neither you nor I know anyone here, the best would be, I believe, to go home.' Baumgarten argues that one of the reasons why Hope remained a social outsider was that English society never forgot and forgave him for his non-English origins. Baumgarten is highly sceptical about the role of Hope's eldest son Henry Thomas in the posthumous publication of *Essay on the History of Architecture* posthumously in 1835, when only part of the work was ever published and believes that the most interesting and revelatory pages, those which best characterized their author, never saw the light of day and must have been disposed of by somebody nearby. Commenting on the final Hope sale at Christie's in 1917 of the heirlooms inherited down the family line from Hope's eldest son Henry Thomas, Baumgarten's scorn is obvious: 'One can understand: why force a great grandson to lug after himself all this bric-a-brac, all this past? Over there the war was pushing up the prices of works of art; we forgive…' Baumgarten viewed with scepticism the testimony of Irene Law in *The Book of the Beresford Hopes* (1928) where her great admiration for her grandfather Alexander J. B. Beresford Hope led her towards the belittlement of the achievements of her great-grandfather Thomas. Baumgarten warms to one of Hope's cries of social rebellion in *Essay on Man* – now at last the man can talk freely! - by quoting from a passage about the unjust leisure class who consume their fortune in 'an empty, sterile and hollow ostentation, keeping up a stupid pomp.'

The Bombshell of *Anastasius*

Chapter XI 'Un Don Juan en Prose' (pp. 164-206) is the *tour de force* of the book. Marshalling a vast range of sources, Baumgarten quite brilliantly recreates the sensational drama which happened in Regency society among the Whigs and the Tories when this bombshell of a novel was lobbed into the public domain. Baumgarten gives a remarkably balanced account of supporters and opponents, many of them strident, by quoting chapter and verse across the vigorously expressed divisions. The ongoing editions, translations and sales of the book at the time confirmed the enormous impact on the many who read the account of Anastasius, the world traveller. The chapter's title has misled some critics to jump to the conclusion that Baumgarten is taking the story of Anastasius to be a variation on the legend of Don Juan. Actually Baumgarten is drawing attention to the original nature and instant fame of Byron's Don Juan because Byron was giving to the old legend a highly original angle by using the adventures of a *vulnerable* Don Juan as a vehicle for a biting satirical view of the unquestioned orthodoxies of contemporary society, so, like Byron, Hope was confronting the public with unpalatable truths about the drift of civilization. Baumgarten concludes by deeply regretting the fact that while Byron's unfinished work continued to challenge generations of readers, Hope's completed work with its perennial message for humanity too quickly became one of yesterday's irrelevant works.

Two Reviews of Baumgarten's Hope

There were two significant reviews of Baumgarten's book about Hope published in England. David Irwin in *The Burlington Magazine*, December 1959 complained about Baumgarten's inadequate analysis of Hope's attitude to Greek antiquity in general and to Hope's own acquisition of Greek art in Italy. Irwin went on to regret that Baumgarten failed to discuss thoroughly Hope's eclecticism especially as Hope, in his book about furniture in 1807, used illustrations based on classical, Egyptian and Oriental sources to show his aesthetic preferences. Another question left unanswered by Baumgarten, in Irwin's view, was the nature of the eclecticism as shown in the portrait by Beechey when Hope had himself painted in Turkish dress. Douglas Dakin, in *The Modern Language Review* January 1960, described the book as a scholarly monograph. Dakin sympathized with Baumgarten's problems caused by the chronic unavailability of primary sources and expressed deep regret that Hope had never found a Boswell. Dakin's response to Hope's *Essay on Man* was positive: 'Hope, the former dilettante whose classicism had been a religion and perhaps an escape, endeavoured to come to grips with life in all its aspects and to understand nature.' What Dakin liked most in Baumgarten's book was the way in which he 'skilfully builds up the picture of Hope growing older in the changing environment'. Dakin concluded by recommending that the book would be extremely valuable in an English translation. Irwin's concerns were addressed by David Watkin in his 1968 book *Thomas Hope and the Neo-Classical Idea*. Dakin's concerns have never really been addressed – most significantly, an English translation of his book has never appeared. Neither Irwin nor Dakin showed much enthusiasm for a re-launch of *Anastasius* but Dakin referred to the work – in passing – as 'brilliant'.

Hope for Baumgarten

This publication of The Long Riders' Guild *Anastasius* fulfils Baumgarten's dream of the long awaited resurrection from the dead of the work by Hope which he championed most passionately. Already the LRG is planning to republish Baumgarten's book about Hope in that long awaited English translation because – for all its hectic pace of researching, strong personal opinions, inevitable gaps, minor inaccuracies, inaccurate details, hasty final proof-reading – *Le Crépuscule néo-classique:.Thomas Hope* is a work to treasure not only for its many insights into a complex Regency figure, whose *range* of achievements tends to elude cultural historians, but also as a prime example of a scholar's romantic travelling across countries in person and in imagination to find out more about a kindred spirit!

APPENDIX III.

'Racial' Politics and Personal Ethics in Thomas Hope's *Anastasius*

Ludmilla Kostova

Published anonymously in 1819, *Anastasius, or Memoirs of a Greek Written at the Close of the Eighteenth Century* turned into one of the literary sensations of the 1820s. It was read by Walter Scott and Mary Shelley, and even Byron, the age's greatest celebrity or 'star', claimed to have 'wept bitterly over many pages of it [because] *he* had not written it'.[1] However, interest in the novel subsequently waned and it fell into oblivion, only occasionally punctuated by brief complimentary or derogatory references.[2] This state of affairs still persists, despite the enduring critical favour for historicism, which has considerably broadened the traditional literary canon by stimulating the rediscovery and reinterpretation of long-forgotten texts.

Significantly, even when interest in *Anastasius* was at its height, the prevalent attitude to the novel's author Thomas Hope was rather dismissive. That wealthy dilettante of Dutch-Scottish descent had acquired a sorry reputation for eccentric pranks and displays of conspicuous consumption which all but obscured his valuable contributions to architecture, painting, costume- and furniture-design. Moreover, a society that was resolutely moving away from the sporadic cosmopolitanism of the Enlightenment and embracing the ideological premises of insular nationalism found it difficult to tolerate Hope's ineffaceable *foreignness*: gibes at his 'effeminate face and manner' and 'broken English'[3] were frequent, as were sneers at the triviality of his aesthetic pursuits. That he could possess a literary talent comparable to Byron's appeared incredible to a lot of *Anastasius*'s early readers. When the fact of the dilettante's authorship became known, the serious press reacted with disbelief. Thus Sydney Smith, one of the founders of the *Edinburgh Review*, exclaimed:

> Is this Mr. Thomas Hope? Is this the man of chairs and tables – the gentleman of sphinxes – the Oedipus of coal-boxes – he who meditated on muffineers and planned pokers? – Where has he hidden all this eloquence and poetry up to this hour? – how is it that he has, all of a sudden, burst out into descriptions which would not disgrace the pen of Tacitus – and displayed a depth of feeling, and a vigour of imagination, which Lord Byron could not excel![4]

His colleague of *Blackwood's Magazine* seemed to entertain even stronger doubts on Hope's capacity to produce such an ambitious text. Apart from suggesting that 'the man of chairs and tables' 'had been beguiled to stand godfather to the abandoned progeny of the noble poet [i.e. Byron]',[5] the journalist claimed that Hope lacked 'an intimate knowledge' of the novel's setting which comprised practically the whole of the borderless, ethnically and culturally hybrid region known as the Levant.[6] Such a remark was eminently unfair to Hope, who had provided positive proof of his extensive travelling by, *inter alia*, including his own 'exotic' drawings in his book *The Costumes of the Ancients* (1809) and its 1812 sequel *Designs of Modern Costumes*. He therefore responded by writing a letter to the Editor of *Blackwood's Magazine* mentioning his early journeys through different parts of the Ottoman Empire and asserting his familiarity with local history, customs and languages. His novel, he averred, was a vehicle for his own observations on the East and had been completed long before 'Lord Byron's admirable productions appeared'.[7]

As David Watkin has suggested, the published text of *Anastasius* may have been based on notes written in French in the course of Hope's tour of Turkey, Egypt, Syria and Greece.[8] However, it seems reasonable to assume that the original version was revised as it was translated into English[9] and might thus have imbibed certain Byronic elements in the process. This might explain the reactions to the novel which were noted above. Overall, what may be termed the *Anastasian* controversy is instructive insofar as it provides insights into early nineteenth-century British social and cultural life. Hope's impressive career as a writer, collector, patron of eminent artists, and practitioner of the 'applied arts' (a term he himself coined) could not dispel prejudice and gain him the recognition he so well deserved. While we should in principle resist the sentimental impulse of commiserating with 'the Oedipus of coal-boxes' on account of his position as 'a displaced Dutchman with Scottish background [sic]', as Reşat Kasaba has recently done,[10] we should nevertheless acknowledge the difficulties Hope must have experienced in a society with a rising predilection for ethnic and cultural purity and corresponding distrust of figures that appeared in any way hybrid or 'impure'.[11]

Anastasius was made available to the reading public at a time when the political destiny of Greece was an important topic of public debate: in 1819 the Greek War of Independence was only two years away. It therefore seems reasonable to inquire whether Hope's ideological stance was close to that of late eighteenth- and early nineteenth-century supporters of Greek liberation or whether he espoused the more conservative, pro-Ottoman position.[12] The novel does contain passages that flout Western European attempts to portray the modern Greeks as the long-suffering heirs of classical Hellas. In spite of this, claiming that *Anastasius* presents 'the real Greeks of eastern Mediterranean [sic]' as 'too poor, too religious, and too well integrated into the Ottoman Empire to respond to the call' of European Philhellenes for 'the rescue of Greek civilisation from the Turkish rule',[13] as Kasaba has tried to do, appears simplistic. My own contention is that the novel fruitfully engages with the late eighteenth- and early nineteenth-century Western European controversy over the character and historical destiny of the modern Greeks. The problem of continuity between them and the ancient Hellenes is the object of speculation and debate in the text itself and, as will be shown further on, may be linked to Hope's understanding of the newly established analytical category of '*race*'. The novel considers the possibility of forging a Greek identity which is free from the tinge of servility and crass ambition, usually imputed to the modern Greeks by Philhellenes and Hellenophobes alike, and is based on personal integrity and mutually beneficial relations with others. Significantly, the text eschews closure and reading it in monological terms, either as an expression of *unadulterated* Philhellenic feeling or of pro-Ottoman bias, detracts from the wealth of ideas and richness of human experience that it aims at conveying.

The emergence of '*race*' as a classificatory category and the gradual establishment of a new 'racial science' at the close of the eighteenth and the beginning of the nineteenth centuries added a new dimension to controversies over ethnic identity such as the one concerning the Greeks.[14] Insights from the new area of inquiry combined with earlier reflections on different forms of government in order to explain historical change and cultural difference. Hope's own position on the rise and fall of 'races' and the government of 'nations'[15] is abundantly illustrated by his voluminous *Essay on the Origins and Prospects of Man* (1831). Although he mostly worked on it after the publication of *Anastasius,* we may nevertheless assume that the ideas expressed in the *Essay* were not characteristic of the final years of his life only but were accumulated gradually from his youth onwards. This is borne out by the text's wide conceptual scope and diverse examples from ancient and modern history. A reading of relevant passages from the *Essay* should shed light on Hope's representation of different ethnic ('racial') groups in *Anastasius* and prepare us for the encounters of the novel's narrator with them.

I. Hope's 'Racial' Politics: Greeks, Egyptians, Arabs and Others

An Essay on the Origin and Prospect of Man (1831) is long, repetitive and occasionally incoherent but nevertheless provides first-hand knowledge of Hope's views on history and the 'progress' or decline of 'races'. The text comprises a series of critical engagements with eighteenth- and early nineteenth-century ideas on the 'racial' diversity of 'the family of Man', different forms of political government and their affinity with 'racial' essences, the relationship between freedom and happiness, aesthetic taste and the development of the arts.

As already stated above, the emergence of the new classificatory term was among the ideological and anthropological highlights of Hope's time. Since the author of *Anastasius* was a cosmopolitan figure with numerous contacts with continental savants, he must have been familiar with some of the specialised German writing on the subject. While he does not mention Johann Friedrich Blumenbach's key texts, he expresses views that are to a certain extent similar to those of the founder of racial anthropology. Thus, like Blumenbach, Hope supports the monogenist conception of human origins and refers to the Caucasus as 'the first cradle of the first scriptural pair'.[16] Moreover, he repeatedly identifies that region as the depository of superior 'racial' stock. While Hope does not use the adjective 'Caucasian', which Blumenbach coined, he claims that the modern population of the Caucasus is still distinguished by the finest physical qualities:

> To this day, the Circassians and Georgians boast the features, in most regular proportion [...] and these fascinations they still retain in their genial regions at so much later an age than elsewhere, as not to render incredible the period to which Homer extended the beauty of Helen. (E, III, 308-9)

The Caucasus is also described as 'the first birthplace of the [ancient] Greeks' whom Hope regards as the highest of known human 'races' (E, III, 308). The ancient Greeks migrated out of it and were subsequently 'degraded' through the 'remixture' of their blood with that of 'inferior', non-Hellenic blood into the original pure "Caucasian' stock. Nevertheless, the 'partial remains' of the 'pre-eminent forms of which their art offered the imitation' are still discernible even among 'their degenerate descendants'. Physically at least, the modern Greeks are not all that far removed from their ancient ancestors. However, rather than attributing their 'degeneracy' to Ottoman despotism, as a number of his contemporaries in Western Europe had done,[17] Hope claims a *'racial'* cause for it: the admixture of inferior, non-Hellenic blood into the original pure 'Caucasian' stock.

For Hope 'race' is decidedly 'a category of physical classification' but it also functions as 'an analytic category of culture'[18] and intellectual achievement. For instance, we are told about the ancient Greeks that they possessed 'the highest capabilities of mind' as well as 'the highest organisation of body' (E, II, 412). Their intellectual superiority was borne out by the fact that they 'made in art and science the furthest strides in the most opposite directions' with 'the least assistance from foreign example and tuition'. Besides, their achievements in those spheres still provide an example for 'later nations'.

As the above quotations indicate, Hope's use of 'race' is inconsistent. On the one hand, 'race' functions as a *transnational* or, as we might say today, *transethnic,* category (as it did with Blumenbach),[19] while, on the other, it designates separate groups within the larger entities that Blumenbach singled out as the '*Hauptrassen im Menschengeschlechte*'.[20] In the second case it seems to be synonymous with 'nation' or 'tribe'. Thus Chapter XXXVI, Volume III, which is entitled 'Characteristics Natural and Acquired of Some of the Higher Human Races', looks in turn at the ancient Egyptians, the Arabs of the Middle Ages and the modern period, and the ancient and modern Greeks. Rather than defining these groups as *branches* of Blumenbach's *Hauptrassen*, Hope identifies them as *'races'* in their own right. Occasionally he also terms them 'nations' and 'tribes' (E, III, 308 ff).

Apart from denoting physical, mental and cultural characteristics, 'race' also functions as an aesthetic category in Hope's discourse. This was already partially illustrated by the above references to the Greeks and other 'Caucasians'. Hope's admiration for the Greeks betrays the influence of Johann Joachim Winckelmann. There can be very little doubt that he was familiar with the work of the leader of European neoclassicism. David Watkin remarks on the close links between Winckelmann and the Hope family.[21] As with Winckelmann, Hope's comments on the physical superiority of the ancient Greeks reflect his familiarity with examples of ancient sculpture. In his Introduction to his *Costumes of the Ancients* (1809) he remarks that 'in former days [he] had had the good fortune to visit most of the celebrated Musea abroad'.[22] Unlike Winckelmann, however, Hope also travelled through the Ottoman Empire and familiarised himself with the life of the modern Greeks and some of the other inhabitants of the Levant.

As David Roessel has shown, apart from being associated with superior physical beauty and credited with the establishment of ineffable standards of artistic taste, the ancient Greeks were likewise celebrated for their democratic traditions.[23] Opposition to Oriental despotism in the wars against the Persian Empire was considered to be the highest manifestation of the Greek civic spirit and love of liberty. Such motifs were stressed in typological readings of ancient Greek history by representatives of Western European romanticism. However, one could also find traces of them in earlier texts and statements by key figures of the Enlightenment. Oriental despotism was believed to curb the workings of reason and thus stunt the development of learning. [24] Hope certainly follows this Enlightenment tradition when he problematises accounts of the superior knowledge of the East from which the ancient Greeks were believed to have benefited. He agrees that the 'tenets' of the philosophy and religious beliefs that the Greeks borrowed from the East were 'most sublime' but asserts that they were 'intermixed', among the Orientals, with 'absurdities the most glaring' (E, III, 327). Moreover, Eastern societies were priest-ridden and the clerical hierarchy concealed 'the sublime truths they chance[d] to possess from the knowledge of the vulgar' (E, III, 328). This was a sure sign, in Hope's opinion, that 'these truths' had not been discovered by 'the vigour of native intellect' but had been passed down to them by 'some race earlier and higher' (E, III, 328). Hope hints several times that the 'race' in question was that of the Atlantes, who must have been 'almost entirely overwhelmed' by 'some of the dire deluges that afflicted this globe' (E, III, 328).

The perfect 'race' thus belongs to the immemorial past. There is no direct evidence of its existence. Its superior qualities can only be inferred from 'the sublime truths' that Eastern 'nations chance[d] to posses' but made a point of concealing from 'the vulgar' and accounts of the exceptional traits and achievements of the ancient Greeks. Hope remarks that even the latter 'reserved some record of a nation still more highly gifted than [themselves]' and 'retraced its existence in those Titans afterwards subdued by their gods" (E, II, 414). For the author of *Anastasius* the 'racial' history of humanity appears to have been marked by a general tendency to decline rather than progress. Individuals or specific groups could preserve and, if circumstances permitted, perpetuate elements of what (given Hope's advocacy of the monogenist doctrine) constituted humanity's original stock of exceptional mental and physical characteristics.

The Eurocentric (or should we say, *pro-Caucasian*?) element in Hope's thought is most apparent in his pronouncements on the ancient Egyptians and the Arabs of the Middle Ages and modern times. He represents Ancient Egypt as the quintessential repressive society: wily priests 'carefully concealed [....] the sounder doctrine they had borrowed from the east' while the common people 'were abandoned to the grossest superstition' (E, III, 279). Moreover, 'the nation was divided into castes' lest 'each man should adopt the calling for which nature and his situation fitted him best' (E, III, 279). Such a society could not prosper, and, in Hope's view, the Egyptians' 'horror of the sea' likewise contributed to that end (E, III, 279). This 'horror' and 'the deserts that surrounded the land of Egypt' doomed them to isolation. As a result, 'while other nations advanced, Egypt only experienced a corresponding decline' (E, III, 279). Hope further maintains that ancient Egypt was the embodiment of *vis inertiae* (the force of inertia). He identifies the country's 'indestructible monuments and incorruptible mummies' as the outward signs of that principle (E, III, 280). There is an opposition in the *Essay* between the active spirit of the 'Caucasian' Greeks and the essential passivity of the Egyptians who were predominantly confined to their own country. Significantly, a latter-day version of this opposition is incorporated into the Egyptian chapters of Hope's novel: as active 'Caucasian' migrants, Anastasius and the Mamelukes, who govern Egypt, are contrasted with the passive indigenes.

Arabs are similarly portrayed as restricted to their 'native deserts' (E, III, 282). However, this is also presented as an advantage: because of this lack of mobility 'their race remains [...] pure and unadulterated' (E, III, 282). Their hospitality, which 'only finds bounds in their means' (E, III, 282), is the chief manifestation of that 'purity'. While underscoring the pastoral virtue of hospitality, Hope disavows the 'credit [Arabs] have been given for intellectual powers beyond their deserts' (E, III, 283):

> When their later descendants filled the thrones of Bagdad [sic] and Cairo, and founded the schools of Damascus and Grenada, it was under the tuition of the Greeks of Constantinople. *These people of a higher race* remained to the last their teachers in mathematics, in medicine, in astronomy, in philosophy, and in whatever abstract sciences the Arabs had the credit of cultivating… In the fine arts they never attained any eminence [my emphasis]. (E, III, 283)

Greek (and by implication, Caucasian-European) superiority is thus asserted once again. In the novel Anastasius is represented as decidedly more 'civilised' than the Arabs he comes into contact with (the primitive Wahhabees [sic] of the desert), but is also shown as deficient in their pastoral virtues. His friendly relationship with them, however, points to another Greek characteristic which Hope notes in his *Essay*: their 'urbanity' to fellow citizens and strangers alike and the 'flexibility of organisation' that enabled them to 'adopt the manners [...] of those among whom they resided' (E, III, 320).

The latter quality is morally ambiguous insofar as it turned some Greeks into 'obsequious courtiers in the palaces of the Persian satraps' and, later, in 'the courts of the Mohameddan kaliphs' (E, III, 320). In *Anastasius* this particular feature is emphasised by the Phanariot Mavroyeni,[25] himself an obsequious servant of the Ottoman establishment, who also claims that there is no fundamental difference between the ancient and modern Greeks. For Mavroyeni, 'credulity, versatility, and thirst of distinctions, from the earliest periods, formed, still form, and ever will continue to form, the basis of the Greek character'[26]. This line of argument indicates that despite certain affinity with the Philhellenic interpretations of the Greek condition, Hope did not subscribe to the view of 'the pure essence of [ancient] Greece'.[27] For him cultural mediation, albeit through collaboration with foreign masters, was a distinctive Greek trait manifesting itself in antiquity as well as 'at the close of the eighteenth century'. His novel explores the ethico-political implications of the trait.

Eventually Hope accounts for what he perceives as the 'degradation' of the modern Greeks in the following way:

> As entities raised highest, when their tide turns, fall lowest – as the very volubility of the Greeks, which made them advance more rapidly, when the impelling force failed, allowed them to retrograde faster – of that very nation once so great, so glorious, the remains, when subdued by, when remixed with, when corrupted by other nations of an inferior caste, lapsed into a state of degradation more complete than other nations, displaying a greater *vis inertiae*, would have done. All the elements of good, blended in them, decomposed more rapidly, and emitted a stronger taint. (E, III, 327)

The passage indicates that the force of inertia (*vis inertiae*) has a preservationist function and is thus not totally negative. Hope attributes the 'degradation' of the modern Greeks to its absence from their ancestors' psychological and cultural makeup. The principle of *vis inertiae*, to which he evidently assigns a role in world history, could have counterbalanced the negative effects of 'racial' 'remixing' and foreign conquest. Hope represents the disintegration of ancient Greek civilisation in strikingly physical terms as is evidenced by the reference to the 'strong taint' of 'decomposition'. The *Essay* (unlike the novel) says nothing about the reversibility of the process of civilisational 'debasement'. That Hope refrained from commenting on the future 'prospects' of the modern Greeks appears strange insofar as this particular text was produced after the Greek War of Independence and the establishment of an autonomous Greek state. Curiously, the *Essay* does not comment on the 'racial' status of the Turks either. No attempt is made to determine their place within 'the family of Man'.

Instead, the concluding chapters of the third volume consider the relationship between human happiness and such factors as independence, free agency, liberty, and education for the lower classes. Hope specifically considers the nature of despotism, generally recognised as a distinctive trait of the Ottoman government at the time. He indirectly engages Charles de Secondat Montesquieu, the most important Enlightenment theorist of state organisation, in a debate over it. For Montesquieu the despot (unlike the monarch who rules 'by fixed and established laws') 'draws everything along by will and caprices'.[28] The distinctive characteristic of a despotic government therefore is the absolute mastery of one man over the rest of the population irrespective of social rank or merit. Writing earlier than Hope, but documenting a later tour of the Levant than his, Byron's friend John Cam Hobhouse declared:

> It is remarked by Montesquieu, that in a despotic government power is deputed and descends entire. This transmission of absolute authority displays itself in Turkey by the total annihilation of every lower dignity in the presence of superior rank. Commanding amongst the Turks is sole and individual...[29]

Significantly, Hope opposes this conventionally liberal line of reasoning in his *Essay*. He begins by admitting the despotic character of Ottoman government but claims that 'even in Turkey the mass of the population is contented and happy' (E, III, 338). This is above all due to the restricted influence that ruling despots are in a position to exercise:

> [I]n a despotic government, even if the despot swerves from the best dispositions respecting his subjects – if he becomes an oppressor, a tyrant – his single weight can only press hard on a few individuals immediately surrounding him. It requires infinite study before oppression can be so organised as to descend in regular gradation from the highest orders to the lowest; and this very study leaves a constant chance of events by which its effects may be counteracted. (E, III, 338-9)

Ottoman despotism is thus 'underdeveloped' but this, in Hope's view, is preferable to the kind of government in which 'there is, in a great many individuals, a great deal of freedom, [...], a great deal of power over a great many others'. The control exercised by the latter form of government would be much greater and the outcome for the governed would be 'great suffering, great unhappiness, great misery'. According to Hope, the ancient Greek 'commonwealths' and 'those of Italy' in the Middle Ages provided instances of high political organisation that led to individual unhappiness. It is difficult to reconcile this inference with his earlier admiration of the ancient Greeks and his castigation of caste restrictions in ancient Egypt.

Such contradictions underscore the hybrid character of Hope's thought and his apparent unwillingness to opt for ideological closure of any kind. For me the concluding emphasis on *individual* happiness is indicative of the writer's reluctance to generalise or to move beyond lived experience. Needless to say, the *particularist* approach, which he opted for, was eventually bound to lead to confusion. This may explain why his *Essay* was neglected by commentators. I hope to show that Hope's novel *Anastasius* is characterised by the same emphasis on the particular.

II. *Anastasius:* Chronicling History's Manifold Games

In a recent article on interpreting Philip Meadows Taylor's 1839 novel *Confessions of a Thug*, Mary Poovey remarks on 'the nature and purpose of fictional narratives' in the following terms:

> [They] constitute a complex, sometimes self-contradictory, tissue of rhetorical engagements with social and literary issues, all of which leave traces in the text that require theoretically informed interpretive paradigms and that benefit from historical research.[30]

Studying the 'traces' of Hope's novel's 'engagements with literary issues' poses some problems. As was shown earlier, nineteenth-century readers underscored the text's affinity with Byron's *oeuvres*, especially with *Don Juan*. In a recent article about

James Morier's *Hajji Baba*, James Watt follows this line of interpretation by representing Hope's novel as an example of 'the Oriental picaresque'.[31] In his view, this subgenre 'employed the device of the wandering hero or *pícaro*, already popularised in the period by Byron, as a means of surveying… [Oriental] society and staging contacts between [Orientals] and Europeans'.[32] Hope himself describes *Anastasius* as 'a historic novel' (E, III, 357), thus aligning it with a different set of literary conventions. The two views are not incompatible. Insofar as the text portrays the Ottoman Empire as the site of 'an all pervasive,… [occasionally] comic corruption',[33] it is close to the Oriental picaresque as defined by Watt. On the other hand, Hope *historicises* Anastasius' story by placing it 'at the close of the eighteenth century' and by envisaging the possibility of change, if not for the (anti-)hero himself, then for some of the novel's other Greek characters. Such elements contrast with the representation of the immutability of Eastern life in the Oriental picaresque.[34] In addition, Hope's novel bears some resemblance to the Enlightenment romance of ideas, of which Voltaire's *Candide* is the best known example, in the sense that certain characters in it represent specific ideological positions that Anastasius either embraces or rejects. The text thus 'writes across' genres,[35] and its generic indeterminacy corresponds to its ideological relativism.

Irony is the novel's dominant trope, the only exceptions being the sentimental episodes dealing with Anagnosti, Euphrosyné and Alexis, and the 'polemical' chapters recounting Spiridion's attempts to recall Anastasius from his 'career of vice'. The protagonist is a modern Greek living in the conditions of Ottoman despotism. The liberal trend in eighteenth- and nineteenth-century Western European thought, which was briefly considered above, stressed the preoccupation of the subjects of Oriental despots with 'personal advancement, to the exclusion of any larger [moral or social] concerns'.[36] Despite his contestation of some of Montesquieu's *dicta*, Hope had no illusions about the demoralising effects of Ottoman despotism. As a result, in the context of the novel, most characters 'ha[ve] to shape their moral stature in a highly ambivalent fashion'[37] because 'survival [often] depends on a partial, studied reversal of normal virtue and vice'.[38]

In the course of the narrative, Hope's protagonist emerges as a *border* figure, repeatedly making and unmaking the divide between self and other, as he switches from a Christian to a Muslim identity and plays a variety of morally dubious roles in his quasi-Byronic thirst for new experiences. The author underscores Anastasius' liminal status by drawing attention to his '*droguemanic* blood [my emphasis] (A, I, 64)[39], his own activities as an interpreter and guide in Istanbul and his close association with the Phanariot 'aristocracy' through a considerable part of the novel. To understand the full impact of these aspects of *Anastasius*, we need to consider the part that Levantine dragomans played in the Western cultural imaginary in the late eighteenth and early nineteenth centuries.

(i) The Spook of Dragomanism

In his authoritative book about Western fantasies of the East, Alain Grosrichard claims that 'from the end of the seventeenth century through all the eighteenth, a spectre haunted Europe: the spectre of despotism'.[40] To my mind, his statement could be modified as follows: apart from being haunted by the grand spectre of despotism, Western Europeans were occasionally amused and irritated by *the minor spook of dragomanism*. The dragoman, who could play the part of an interpreter, tourist guide, political adviser, and/or spy was a key figure in the Ottoman Empire. Michael Cronin has drawn attention to a recurrent emphasis in culture on the ambivalence of the interpreter's trade.[41] While on rare occasions, 'the monopoly of the scarce resources of language can confer on [the profession] a prestige and authority normally reserved for myth and majesty',[42] it has far more often been perceived as a necessary evil in the post-Babelian world of uncontrollable linguistic diversity. As a result the individuals practising it have systematically been exposed to distrust and denigration. The old adage of '*traduttore, tradittore*' suggesting that the language mediator is an unwitting or fully conscious traitor is one of the signs of this attitude.

Interpreting played an important role in the Ottoman Empire, particularly in big commercial centres such as Istanbul where the mixture of ethnicities and languages was indeed Babelian. An old Levantine folk song identifies dragomans (*dragomanni)* as one of the three evils of the capital's 'Western' district of Pera alongside with the 'plague and fires (*peste, fuoco*).'[43] However, unlike the plague and fires, dragomans were indispensable to both Westerners visiting the Empire and to their eminent hosts in it. This is borne out by, among other things, the ubiquity of the word *dragoman,* or versions of it, in European languages.

Historically speaking, there were two categories of dragomans. On the one hand, there were the interpreters of 'Frankish' descent, i.e. descendants of Italian and French settlers in/invaders of the Levant, who mostly worked for Western embassies and missions and were based in Pera. Eventually, this group also came to include well-educated Catholic Armenians and uniate Greeks. On the other hand, there were the dragomans of the Phanar, the part of Istanbul where the Patriarch of the Eastern Orthodox Church resided together with other dignitaries, who traced their descent back to the Byzantine aristocracy. Predictably, they were Eastern Orthodox in creed and were predominantly – but not exclusively – Greek by ethnic extraction.[44] The Phanariot dragomans established themselves as interpreters working for the Sublime Porte and key Ottoman functionaries such as the Capitan (*Kapudan)* Pasha, the Admiral of the Ottoman navy. Dragomans occupying such positions of trust could become temporary rulers of the two trans-Danubian principalities of Wallachia and Moldavia. That was the main attraction of the profession for educated Greeks and other Eastern Orthodox Christians plying the dragoman's trade in the Ottoman Empire.

Late eighteenth- and early nineteenth-century British travel writing and fiction about the Levant exhibit a preoccupation with the Phanariot group, despite the fact that the dragomans working for the British Embassy belonged to the 'Frankish' one.[45] Thus Lady Elizabeth Craven ironically speaks of her encounter with the Prince of Wallachia and his family, who went so far as to claim her as an acquaintance from the Phanar.[46] Hobhouse describes a visit to the Caimacam or Vice-Vizier of Istanbul in the suite of the British Ambassador in the course of which he was able to observe a Phanariot dragoman in action. He claims that the dragoman presented 'a mournful picture of the wretchedness of dignified slavery'.[47] Further on Hobhouse wonders at the persistence with which Greek Phanariots sought 'the perpetual humiliation attendant upon the office of Dragoman' and 'the very uncertain tenure by which the mimic sceptres of [Wallachia and Moldavia] are held'.[48] For him this persistence is a sign of the overall degeneracy of upper-crust modern Greek society in which the heroic virtues of the ancient Greeks have been replaced by 'a love of pomp'[49] and cheap vanity. Hobhouse does not spare the dragomans' womenfolk either: he pronounces the wives and daughters of the Phanariot 'nobles' to be no better than their menfolk. They 'are fostered in every luxury and all the soft pomp of the Asiatics', and, predictably, this 'improves neither their tempers nor their manners'.[50]

Hobhouse's representation of the dragomans probably influenced Mary Shelley's portrayal of Evadne, the disruptive *femme fatale* of her 1826 grim futuristic fantasy *The Last Man*. Burdened with the 'bad blood' of many generations of unworthy pseudo-aristocratic ancestors (for Mary Shelley's novel is set in the late twenty-first century, and 'the first Dragoman of the Porte of Greek extraction' lived in the 1600s[51]), Evadne 'naturally' subverts order and wreaks havoc in every sphere of life. It has been suggested that she functions as Pandora in the context of the novel and that 'the misery she unleashes into the world is the plague - which literally enters the world with her death, replacing her as a destructive female agent'. [52]

Given the bad press that dragomans and their families received from travellers and fiction writers alike, Hope's choice of a protagonist is indeed striking but, as must have become clear by now, quite logical. The author himself apparently thought Phanariot dragomans central to his plot because he provided an appendix to the book containing 'Details respecting the Fanariotes [sic] of Constantinople'.[53]

(ii) 'Great Causes' Versus 'Minute Circumstances'

Commenting on his own conversion to Islam, Anastasius declares that 'historians often err in attributing to a single *great cause* the effect of many *minute circumstances* combined [my emphasis]'. (A, I, 77) The narrator evidently advocates a *particularist* approach to history and disavows the unequivocal privileging of 'single great causes'. The statement provides an insight into the way in which his own story is constructed as well as guidance to prospective readers. One of the distinctive traits of Hope's text is tension between ideologically prominent Western interpretations of the modern Greek condition and the author's own observations filtered through the fictive consciousness of his narrator. To trace the complex process of interaction between these two strands of representation, we need to consider some of the twists and turns of the novel's plot and their political-symbolic implications.

As was indicated above, the alienation of modern Greeks from the great achievements of their ancestors was a recurrent motif in late eighteenth- and early nineteenth-century Philhellenic thought. Their degenerate state was signalled by, among other things, the state of child-like barbarism into which they were supposed to have lapsed, thus reversing the Enlightenment paradigm of human progress from savagery to civilisation. Western European travelogues and historiographic commentaries abound in disparaging descriptions of seemingly irrational social customs and instances of primitive superstition.[54] In Hope's novel this reversal to a child-like state is 'diagnosed' by Anastasius himself, who describes his predicament in the following terms:

> [I was] a being of mere instinct; a child over which the cravings of the sense still reigned uncontrolled; and which, like all children, still acknowledged no subjection save to superior strength; still could be made to obey the voice of reason, or even the dictates of caution, by no other means but those of physical compulsion. (A, II, 203)

This self-diagnosis is the (anti-)hero's judgement on his own early life. Among the factors shaping it is his family background. Anastasius is the youngest son of Signor Sotiri, a petty Greek dragoman working for the French consul on the island of Chios. Sotiri's interpreting is typically represented in an ironic light: 'being very deaf, he never heard what was his business to translate' (A, I, 1) but, then, 'the necessity of a drogueman reporting speeches as he received them' (A, I, 4) is pronounced to be an utter impossibility anyway. An emphasis is further laid on Sotiri's love of profit: he turns a conflict between Russia and Turkey into a source of income and is absolutely unmoved by Russian attempts to foment a Greek rebellion against Ottoman rule. Generally speaking, opportunism, greed and petty vanity characterise the behaviour of Anastasius' parents and siblings. Religion cannot counterbalance those tendencies as it has been reduced to a set of irrational, superstitious practices: Signor Sotiri, for instance, gets his silkworms 'carefully exorcised' every year before their spinning time. (A, I, 1)

Anastasius early learns the value of compromise. Finding a congenial occupation that would suit his active disposition turns out to be impossible: he is 'prohibited by the Turks from the trade of a soldier, and by my parents from that of a sailor'. (A, I, 4) His parents suggest a career in the church and he eventually has to accept this because 'I ... saw nothing better'. (A, I, 4) Despite his willingness to settle for this compromise, Anastasius still differs from his parents. Thus, he appears to be inspired by the example of Achilles:

> I affected great admiration for Achilles ... and regretted that I was not born two thousand years ago to be his Patroclus. In my fits of heroism I swore to treat the Turks as he had done the Trojans, and for a time dreamt of nothing but putting to the sword the whole Seraglio – dwarfs, eunuchs, and all. (A, I, 4)

This instance of rudimentary nationalism evokes an archetypal conflict between East and West: the war of the Achaens against 'oriental' Troy. Significantly, Anastasius dislikes reading even Homer and is not directly influenced by the *Iliad*, which is the classic statement of the conflict. His identification with Achilles is through later stories that he has been told about him. This indicates Anastasius's alienation from what should be his cultural legacy. However, his adolescent admiration for Achilles is nevertheless an expression of elementary hatred of oppression. His parents are wary of such feelings and admonish him not to disclose them in public: 'just rancour, they said, gathers strength by being repressed – [u]pon this principle they cringed to the ground to every Moslemin they met'. (A, I, 4)

The parents' bad example makes Anastasius irresponsible and insensitive to the sufferings of others. His early selfishness is illustrated by his relationship with Helena, the French consul's daughter, whom he seduces and abandons. Further on in the text he is to treat a string of other female characters in a similar way. Within the early nineteenth-century British cultural context, literary conventions had established a sharp contrast between heartless seducers and caring, protective males who were prepared to become good husbands and loving fathers. Even Byron had to take that distinction into account when he constructed the character of Don Juan: his Spaniard does not seduce and abandon his teenage mistress Haidée but the young woman's piratical father steps in and separates the lovers. In presenting a literary figure that emphatically flouts the convention Hope apparently aimed at illustrating the degradation of the Greek moral character.

Anastasius leaves Chios because he fears the consequences of Helena's seduction and is literally thrown upon a world of violent action, political intrigue and flagrant dishonesty to which, however, he manages to adjust fairly easily. His 'droguemanic blood' does not predispose him to any form of idealism. The Phanariot Mavroyeni, dragoman to the Capitan Pasha, takes Anastasius under his wing because he senses an inner kinship with him. Mavroyeni has apparently inherited 'the flexibility of organisation' which Hope saw as a typically Greek characteristic. His 'dexterity' and the patronage of the Capitan Pasha have enabled him to supplant 'the old and long-respected drogueman of the navy' (A, I, 15) and to become the admiral's adviser and friend as well as his interpreter. Significantly, he hails Anastasius as a 'little Greek rascal', (A, I, 16) makes him his coffee bearer and eventually takes him to Istanbul.

Anastasius familiarises himself with his master's circle but is not taken in by the pretentious behaviour of the Phanariot 'aristocracy'. His parents' lessons in opportunism and moral relativism, it turns out, have also instilled a fair amount of healthy scepticism in him. Anastasius is eventually expelled from Mavroyeni's household because of his compromising love affair with an upper-class Phanariot woman. His next master is a Jewish quack doctor whose fraudulent practices result in both of them being imprisoned in the dreaded prison of the Bagnio. In the prison Anastasius is thrown together with Agnosti, a young Greek of his own age, to whom he swears eternal friendship but does not scruple to betray later on.

For some time the narrator plies the dragoman's trade and this brings him into contact with Western European travellers whose weaknesses he exploits. In his new capacity he even considers acquiring a *berat*, a special licence which placed its holder under the protection of a particular foreign nation and 'exempted him from Ottoman taxes, justice and – not least – clothing restrictions'.[55] While at first such licences were only issued to dragomans and business agents working for foreign merchants, ambassadors and consuls, the practice soon turned into a lucrative business with *berats* changing hands for money. Anastasius describes the prospective advantages of becoming a *beratli* (*berat* holder) thus:

> [A]t once [I] would find [myself] transformed into a reputed Italian, or German, or Frenchman, wear the gaudiest colours in competition with the Turks themselves, and strut about the streets in that *summum bonum*, a pair of yellow papooshes. (A, I, 70)

The passage denotes the instability of identity in Anastasius' world. It constantly changes insofar as there is no system of solid religious or moral values that can produce a sense of continuity between past and present and guarantee permanence. The narrator gets yet another opportunity to change his identity as he attracts the attention of Padre Ambroggio, 'an Italian missionary of the Propaganda', who attempts to convert him to Roman Catholicism (A, I, 70). However, the spiritual act of religious conversion is brought down to the level of commercial exchange as 'for every Greek variation from the Latin creed I yielded up, he used to find me a new situation' (A, I, 70). Western Europeans, it turns out, are no less opportunistic than 'degenerate' Greeks.

Thus, Padre Ambroggio introduces Anastasius to Eugenius, a Western European traveller, who appears to be the priest's own 'antipode' insofar as he preaches 'reason, philosophy, and universal toleration'. (A, I, 77) The narrator accepts Eugenius as a mentor because 'some of his tenets ... had in them something plausible to my mind, and, if not true, seemed to my inexperience *ben trovati*'. (A, I, 77) The traveller is apparently a Deist who rejects 'revealed religion' and is convinced that differences between systems of religious beliefs are immaterial. The relativism that he justifies through Western rationalist philosophy is in tune with the utilitarian lessons of Anastasius' parents. Ironically, like them, he favours a social conduct based on hypocrisy:

> [H]e only contended for the appeal to reason on points of internal faith, and urged, in external practices, the propriety of conforming to the established worship; - and, not from selfish but philanthropic motives[...] (A, I, 78)

For Anastasius this line of reasoning provides justification for his right to convert to Islam: since 'the Koran [is] the supreme law' in the Empire he should support it and thus be admitted to 'places and preferments from which I otherwise must remain shut out'. (A, I, 78) The immediate cause of his conversion is the discovery of his relationship with an upper-class Turkish woman but, as he himself points out, 'the seemingly bold measure had long been preparing *in petto*; and the unexpected dilemma [...] may only be said to have fixed the period for its execution'. (A, I, 77)

Through all vicissitudes of fortune Anastasius succeeds in preserving his remarkable vitality. He is motivated by a strong desire to experience life to the full. Together with his native intelligence and scepticism these qualities make him superior to both the Turks as 'native' Orientals and to other converts, such as the Mamelukes of Egypt. This superiority also recalls Hope's opinion of the Greeks expressed in his *Essay.* Anastasius' journeys through Egypt, Nubia and Syria link his fictional life to the civilisational clashes outlined in the later text but also emphasise the disorganised state of the vast Ottoman Empire and hence, the 'underdeveloped' state of the Oriental despotism specific to it. The authorities in Istanbul are evidently not in a position to maintain effective control over the far-flung provinces and local chiefs fight for power to the detriment of ordinary people.

The Egyptian chapters also convey an impression of the Ottoman Empire as a site inhabited by displaced persons. The Mamelukes, who rule the country, are for the most part Georgians and Circassians from the Caucasus and, since they themselves are converts to Islam, tend to look down on cradle Muslims. Tartar princes ruled Egypt before them (A, I, 127). As Anastasius travels down the Nile into the interior of the country, he encounters an Ethiopian woman, who was married to a black eunuch in Istanbul and subsequently returned to Africa to find 'some proper husband' who would 'make [her] amends for [her] empty honours' (A, I, 123). Identities are modified or forged anew as individuals move, or are transported, from place to place. Most of the novel's episodic characters seem to be intent upon survival, economic prosperity and personal happiness. Like Anastasius himself, they are full of irrepressible vitality which is expressed in the manifest lack of physical stasis. The latter quality correlates with the novel's ideological openness.

Predictably, Anastasius leaves Egypt. Rather than being engulfed by the Mameluke culture of the land, he is provided with yet another opportunity to change his ways and restore his Greek Christian identity. The character, who attempts to help Anastasius gain maturity, is Spiridion Mavrocordato. Despite the fact that he is a Phanariot, Spiridion embodies the best aspects of modern Greek culture. The Mavrocordatos are said to trace their descent 'to a younger branch' of the Byzantine imperial family but Anastasius is sceptical of this claim and avers that they had 'the latter and more certain honour of being related to several of the princes of Valachia'. (A, II, 195) Consequently, Spiridion is not free from the taint of 'droguemanic blood' either. However, in his case its bad effects are counterbalanced by the 'expansive mind' which he has 'received from nature' and which has 'resisted even the contracting powers of Greek education'. (A, II, 200) Spiridion is the only Greek 'with whom morality weigh[s] more than dogma'. (A, II, 201) He thus embodies a new type of enlightened Greek identity. Spiridion aims at awakening Anastasius's dormant moral sense and helping him perform a civilisational leap out of the state of child-like primitivism up to a higher stage of intellectual development. In his attempts to influence the narrator he is motivated by friendship but also by the recognition of his potential for great deeds:

> [H]e often would say he observed in me a singular and romantic turn of mind, capable of becoming as enthusiastic in the cause of virtue as it had been unrestrained in the career of vice. He believed that the same energy and boldness … might render me pre-eminent in all that was exalted and noble[…](A, II, 201).

Spiridion may have been modelled on Prince Alexander Mavrocordatos (1791–1865), who was famous all over Europe as a champion of the cause of Greek independence and numbered Byron, Percy and Mary Shelley among his acquaintances. Later on he was to fill a number of government posts in independent Greece. However, one should not press the parallel too much because the story of Anastasius deals with a time predating both the prince's maturity and what Hope (rather than his narrator) describes as modern Greece's 'miraculous emancipation from the bondage of error and superstition'. (A, II, 200). Moreover, unlike the historical Prince Mavrocordatos, whose chequered career included a number of decisive political victories, Spiridion's scheme of reforming Anastasius fails. The failure is partially due to events over which he has no control and which involve members of the narrator's opportunistic family. Their greed for material possessions, it turns out, has completely silenced the claims of blood and kinship. However, another reason for Spiridion's lack of success is Anastasius' rejection of his conception of 'the social compact' (A, II, 222) as the fundamental principle of state organisation in Ottoman Turkey.

The protagonist's speech on the subject prefigures some of the arguments of later Balkan revolutionaries who similarly found Ottoman rule incompatible with European ideas of civil government.[56] Besides, like the nationalists of the future, Anastasius is exasperated by the passivity and submission of the Greeks in the face of oppression:

> Am I alive… and do I hear a Greek, and under the yoke of the Turks, talk of a social compact – of an agreement intended for mutual benefit, support and protection, as of a thing actually subsisting; as of a thing that should regulate his conduct to his masters? Ah! Had I only discovered the faintest trace of any such agreement between Christianity and Islamism, and had I found, in those for whose security it was framed, the least disposition to enforce its terms and to resist its infraction, who would have been more proud than myself of remaining a Greek, of standing by my oppressed countrymen, and of maintaining the glorious struggle to the last drop of my blood! But … in these realms the contract, if ever it existed, had been perverted, or rather had been torn, rent asunder, cast away! (A, II, 222).

What distinguishes Anastasius from the future leaders of national revolutions in South Eastern Europe, however, is his determination to 'resume [his] rights of nature, and the primeval state of warfare against all worth attacking'. (A, II, 222). Most members of the region's national elites were to follow Spiridion in trying to raise the consciousness of the oppressed rather than opting for Anastasius' individualist vision of a Hobbesian state of nature marked by 'the war of all against all'. That Hope should have anticipated the drift of future political controversies about the character and destiny of the Ottoman Empire appears remarkable especially when measured against his British contemporaries' dismissive attitude to his abilities and stock of knowledge. What is likewise noteworthy is the presence of the serious chapters dealing with Spiridion and his scheme of moral regeneration in a text otherwise dominated by irony and ethical relativism. This poses the question of the novel's coherence. The answer is that as readers we are denied the comfort and facility that this narrative strategy bestows. The novel is concerned with so many issues and presents such a wealth of scenes and episodes that fitting them all into neat ideological or ethical categories is out of the question. On the other hand, certain narrative strands appear to be more amenable to classification than others.

Anastasius' relationship with Spiridion belongs to the latter category. The two friends eventually part company. While Anastasius returns to his old way of life, Spiridion appears to have benefited from their discussion and to have learned a lesson in personal ethics and humility. He gives up 'the perilous race of ambition' for which his father has been preparing him, i.e. the dragoman's dream of a 'mimic sceptre' in Wallachia or Moldavia, and finds happiness in the morally beneficial private sphere of family and close friends. (A, II, 238).

The rest of the novel explores the failure of Anastasius' own scheme of waging war against 'all worth attacking'. The twists and turns of the plot demonstrate the futility of individualism and ambition. Anastasius returns to Egypt to find that his old patron is dead and the country's turbulent state is, if anything, changed for the worse. He then departs for Europe and joins Mavroyeni, who has become Prince of Wallachia. His old master's fate illustrates the uselessness of serving a despotic government. Mavroyeni is mortally afraid of displeasing the Sultan and being suspected of treachery at a difficult time when the Ottoman Empire has to deal with Russian military aspirations, on the one hand, and Austrian attacks, on the other. Despite his determination to remain loyal to the Ottoman side, he is found guilty of treason and duly executed.

In the course of his later travels Anastasius encounters a number of characters whom he likes and respects such as the Frenchified Isaac Bey, who tells him about his adventures in Western Europe, (A, II, 301-303) Hadgee Bollad-Ogloo of Anatolia, (A, III, 309-310) and the primitive Wahhabees of the desert. (A, III, 383-395) They are free of ambition and greed and extend kindness and hospitality to him. Isaac Bey, Hadgee Bollad and the Wahhabbees have achieved a certain level of personal contentment because they do not compete in 'the perilous race of ambition'.

The (anti-)hero loses his own chance of personal happiness because of his inability to return Euphrosyné's love and to take care of her and the child she has given birth to. After her tragic death and the discovery that he has fathered a son, Anastasius decides to change. The change, however, is postponed: he wishes to amass sufficient wealth by following his old course of violence so that he will be able to ensure his son's future. In this he also fails: the child dies as Anastasius reaches Trieste to which he intends to re-settle and to provide his son Alexis with a Western education. The novel ends with the dying Anastasius dictating his memoir to Conrad, an Austrian, who has been wounded in the wars and needs money to support his family.

III. Conclusion

We are thus left with Anastasius' memoir as the only material trace of his existence. This book, which records his moral flaws and acts of irresponsibility and downright cruelty, is to serve a practical and morally beneficial purpose. The money that Conrad has earned from writing down the memoir is to be spent on food and clothing for his wife and children and is thus to contribute to the preservation of a nuclear family. Most late eighteenth- and virtually all nineteenth-century novelists never tired of stressing the importance of the nuclear family. That was a key element within the social structure, the element that ensured the survival of national/ethnic groups. Anastasius did not succeed in creating a nuclear family of his own but posthumously provides for Conrad's.

Such an ending might at first glance appear completely inappropriate for a novel that discusses, among other things, the chances that modern Greeks might have of acquiring self-respect and forging an identity that is based on contractual and mutually advantageous interpersonal relations. Why is it then that Hope's text concerns itself with the fate of an *Austrian* family? Attention could have focused instead on Spiridion's wife and offspring. Could Hope's final choice reflect the culturally and politically superior position that Western Europe had acquired during the Enlightenment[57] and thus hint that a text could only acquire significance when made available to a Western public?

The latter view is definitely out of tune with the relativist atmosphere of the novel and Anastasius' (and Hope's) refusal to privilege Western Europe over the Levant in an absolute and unequivocal way. In fact one of the striking features of Hope's text is that it represents the world as *shared* space in which people cross and re-cross borders and objects change hands. An amusing episode in the Egyptian section of the novel presents a Muslim 'factor', who gives a Franciscan friar a small bag of coffee beans from Santo Domingo and instructs him to send the beans to his friends in Christendom. 'When well roasted… they will drink them for pure Mokka and admire how superior they are in flavour to the vile West-India coffee'. (A, I, 121) The beans were brought from America by Europeans, made their way to an Egyptian market and are about to re-enter Europe as 'pure Mokka' from the East. The episode clearly problematises concepts of originality and authenticity. Nothing is unique in the relativist and particularist universe of the novel.

The fate of the memoir is not all that different from that of the coffee beans. The Greek 'rascal' Anastasius tells the story of his life in French and it is written down by the Austrian Conrad, who may have been wounded in the war against Ottoman Turkey in which Anastasius also fought but on the opposite side. Banal though it may sound, the text's 'hero' is *life* perceived as a series of journeys from one place to another. The journeys lead to unexpected configurations of 'minute circumstances' that problematise the effects of 'Great Causes'. The moral parameters of the Greek 'race' or of any other kind of identity that emerge in the process cannot be defined through the simplistic opposition of good and evil. While the resultant 'impurity' and 'bending' of ethical categories should not be celebrated for their own sake, it should nevertheless be acknowledged that fundamentally ironic fictional narratives such as Hope's provide an antidote to 'pure', monological, hero-centred accounts of national growth and individual development, thus inviting us to rethink the terrains of literature and history.

Professor Ludmilla Kostova
University of Veliko Turnovo, Bulgaria

Ludmilla K. Kostova is Associate Professor of British literature and cultural studies at St. Cyril and St. Methodius University of Veliko Turnovo, Bulgaria. She has published widely on eighteenth-century, romantic and modern British literature and has repeatedly organised seminars and chaired panels on travel writing and cultural encounters. Her book Tales of the Periphery: the Balkans in Nineteenth-Century British Writing *(1997) has been frequently cited by specialists in the field. Kostova 'discovered' Thomas Hope's Anastasius three years ago and has since been trying to attract attention to this unjustly neglected text. Her article 'Degeneration, Regeneration and the Moral Parameters of Greekness in Thomas Hope's Anastasius, Or Memoirs of a Greek' recently came out in a special issue of Comparative Critical Studies 4. 2 (2007).*

---

[1] Quoted in *Memoirs of the Life of Thomas Hope* by V.R. in *Anastasius, or Memoirs of a Greek Written at the Close of the Eighteenth Century*, 2 vols. (Paris: Baudry's Foreign Library, 1831), I, p.v.

[2] For a more detailed commentary on the novel's reception, see John Rodenbeck's essay on *Anastasius* in this volume.

[3] Lord Glenbervie wrote about Hope in 1801: 'He is a little ill-looking man about thirty, with a sort of effeminate face and manner, and speaking a kind of language which you are in doubt whether to think merely affected or what is called broken English', quoted in David Watkin, *Thomas Hope 1769 – 1831 and the Neoclassical Idea* (London: John Murray, 1968), p. 8

[4] Sydney Smith, *Edinburgh Review* XXXV (1821), pp. 92 ff.

[5] Quoted in 'Memoirs of the Life of Thomas Hope' by V. R., in *Anastasius, or Memoirs of a Greek Written at the Close of the Eighteenth Century*, 2 vols. (Paris: Baudry's Foreign Library, 1831), I, p. v.

[6] The Levant has recently been defined by Desanka Schwara as an essentially *borderless* region. She maintains that the term was originally applied to the Eastern Adriatic and Eastern Mediterranean coasts but eventually came to include other sites such as the Black Sea port of Odessa, for instance. See her article 'Rediscovering the Levant: A Heterogeneous Structure as a Homogeneous Historical Region', *European Review of History—Revue Europeenne d'Histoire*10 (2003), 2, pp. 233 – 251. In eighteenth- and nineteenth-century British travel writing and fiction, however, the name appears to be largely synonymous with the Ottoman 'Orient'. Thus Alexander Pope refers to Lady Mary Wortley Montagu's sojourn *in the Levant*, although her journey through the Ottoman Empire included the interior of the Balkan Peninsula as well as 'properly' Levantine localities such as Istanbul and Eastern Mediterranean port cities. Byron and Hobhouse also spoke about having been to the Levant, despite the fact that they mostly travelled through the interior of Albania and Greece and briefly visited Istanbul and the coast of Asia Minor.

[7] 'Memoirs of the Life of Thomas Hope', I, p. viii.

[8] David Watkin, *Thomas Hope*, p. 5.

[9] According to Philip Mansel, '*Anastasius* was revised with the help of [Hope's] sons' tutor Rev. J. Hitchens, later Vicar of Sunninghill near Hope's house in Surrey'. He bases his opinion on 'a book by Hope's descendants'. See his article 'Thomas Hope and the Neoclassical Revolution', http://www.philipmansel.com/index.asp?page=5, downloaded on 23. 03. 2007.

[10] Reşat Kasaba, 'The Enlightenment, Greek Civilization and the Ottoman Empire: Reflections on Thomas Hope's *Anastasius*', *Journal of Historical Sociology* 16 (2003), 1, p. 17.

[11] On the symbolic significance of (im)purity in social contexts, see Mary Douglas, *Purity and Danger* (London and New York: Routledge, 1966, reprinted 2002), esp. pp. 1 – 23.

[12] For William St. Clair early nineteenth-century Philhellenism represented 'the extreme left of the political spectrum within which British politics was then conducted'. See his *That Greece Might Still Be Free: The Philhellenes in the War of Independence* (Oxford: Oxford University Press, 1972), p. 146. I follow him in regarding the pro-Ottoman political stance as an expression of right-wing politics. Such a view is supported by later political developments during the Victorian period. On Victorian attitudes to the Ottoman Empire, see Ludmilla Kostova, *Tales of the Periphery: the Balkans in Nineteenth-Century British Writing* (Veliko Turnovo: St. Cyril and St. Methodius Press, 1997), pp. 116-127 and pp. 161-192.

[13] Kasaba, 'The Enlightenment', p. 1.

[14] Apart from Martin Bernal's 'classic' *Black Athena. The Afroasiatic Roots of Classical Civilization* (London: Free Association Books, 1987), more recent publications on race as a classificatory category include Thomas Junker, 'Blumenbach's Racial Geometry', *Isis* 89 (1998), 498 – 501, Robert Bernasconi, 'With What Must the Philosophy of World History Begin? On the Racial Basis of Hegel's Eurocentrism', *Nineteenth-Century Contexts* 22 (2000), 171 – 201, Anne K. Mellor, 'Frankenstein, Racial Science, and the Yellow Peril', *Nineteenth-Century Contexts* 23 (2001), 1 – 28, and Sara Eigen, 'Self, Race and Species: J. S. Blumenbach's Atlas Experiment', *The German Quarterly* 277 (Summer 2005), 277 – 298.

[15] On the multiple meanings and uses of 'race' and 'nation' in late eighteenth- and nineteenth-century British contexts, see Ludmilla Kostova, *Tales of the Periphery*, pp. 17 – 18.

[16] Thomas Hope, *An Essay on the Origin and Prospect of Man*, 3 vols. (London: John Murray, 1831), II, p. 410. All subsequent references will be given in the text.

[17] See David Roessel, *In Byron's Shadow. Modern Greece in the English and American Imagination* (Oxford and New York: Oxford University Press, 2002), pp. 21 – 25.

[18] Eigen, 'Self, Race, and Species', p. 278.

[19] Mellor credits Blumenbach with the establishment of the concept of race as 'a stable, *transnational*, biological or genetic category [my emphasis]' of classification. See her 'Frankenstein', p. 4.

[20] Quoted in Eigen, 'Self', p. 277.

[21] A member of the Hope family offered to accompany Winckelmann to Istanbul. See Watkin, *Thomas Hope,* p. 5.

[22] Thomas Hope, *Costumes of the Greeks and Romans* (New York: Dover Publications Inc., 1962), p. xvii.

[23] Roessel, *In Byron's Shadow*, p. 26.

[24] Roessel, *In Byron's Shadow*, p. 15.

[25] This character was based on Nikolaos Mavroyenis (1738 – 90), initially a Phanariot dragoman, who was appointed Prince of Wallachia by the Porte in 1786, and faithfully supported the Ottoman side in the war with Russia and Austria. Despite his loyalty, Sultan Selim III sentenced him to death in 1790 and he was executed at Byala in present-day Bulgaria. The Romanian version of his name is Nicolae Mavrogheni. A street in central Bucharest is called after him. For a brief commentary on Mavrogheni's activities as Prince of Wallachia and Romanian responses to the Wallachian section of *Anastasius*, see Evgenia Gavriliu, *English Culture in the Romanian Countries (1790 – 1850)* (Braila: Editura EVRIKA, 1996), pp. 146-49.

[26] Thomas Hope, *Anastasius* (Glasgow, KY: The Long Riders' Guild Press, 2008), I. p. 32. All subsequent references are to this edition and will be given in the text.

[27] Bernal, *Black Athena*, p. 292.

[28] Charles de Secondat Montesquieu, *The Spirit of the Laws*, translated by Anne M. Cohler, Basia Carolyn Miller, and Harold Samuel Stone (Cambridge: Cambridge University Press, 1989), II. 1.

[29] John Cam Hobhouse, *Travels in Albania and Other Provinces of Turkey in 1809 & 1810*, 2 vols. (London: John Murray, 1813), II, pp. 986-7.

[30] Mary Poovey, 'Ambiguity and Historicism: Interpreting *Confessions of a Thug*', *Narrative* 12 (January 2004), 1, p. 15.

[31] James Watt, 'James Morier and the Oriental Picaresque', in *Comedy, Fantasy and Colonialism*, edited by Graeme Harper (London and New York: Continuum, 2002), p. 59.
[32] Watt, 'James Morier', p. 58.
[33] Watt, 'James Morier', p. 63.
[34] Watt, 'James Morier', p. 67.
[35] Debbie Lisle, *The Global Politics of Contemporary Travel Writing* (Cambridge: Cambridge University Press, 2006), p. 31.
[36] Watt, 'James Morier', p. 62.
[37] Svetozar Koljevic, *The Epic in the Making* (Oxford: Clarendon, 1980), p. 192.
[38] Anne Pennington and Peter Levi, *Marko the Prince* (New York: Putnam, 1984), p. ix.
[39] For different versions of the word 'dragoman/drogueman' and a detailed etymology, see Bernard Lewis, *From Babel to Dragomans. Interpreting the Middle East* (London: Phoenix, 2004), p. 22. The word's variant '*tergiuman*' is also used in Hope's text.
[40] Alain Grosrichard, *The Sultan's Court. European Fantasies of the East*, translated by Liz Heron (London: Verso, 1998), p. 3.
[41] Michael Cronin, 'The Empire Talks Back: Orality, Heteronomy and the Cultural Turn in Interpreting Studies, in *The Interpreting Studies Reader*, edited by F. Poechhacker and Miriam Schlesinger (London: Routledge, 2002), pp. 386 – 395. See also Cronin's recent book *Translation and Identity* (London and New York: Routledge, 2006), pp. 75-119.
[42] Cronin, *Translation and Identity*, p. 79.
[43] '*A Pera ci sono tre malanni: peste, fuoco e dragomanni',* quoted in Alexander H. de Groot, '*Die Levantinischen Dragomanen. Einheimische und Fremde im Eigenene Land. Kultur- und Sprachgrenzen zwischen Ost und West (1453 – 1914)',*
www.let.leidenuniv.nl/tcimo/tulp/Research/ahdg1.pdf, downloaded on 30. 10. 2006.
[44] On the Bulgarian origin of Prince Stefan Bogoridi (born Stoyko Tsonkov Stoykov), see *Knyaz Stefan Bogoridi* [*Prince Stefan Bogoridi*], edited by Ivan Radev (Veliko Turnovo: St. Cyril and St. Methodius Press, 1994), pp. 5 – 28. Bogoridi was Dragoman of the Ottoman Navy, Governor of Galati (1812 – 1819), Caimacam of Moldavia (1821 – 1822), and Governor of Samos.
[45] According to Hobhouse, '[t]here are four dragomans attached to the English embassy… Mr. Pisani, descended, I believe, from an ancient Venetian family of Galata, is the chief interpreter: he speaks the English language with the utmost purity…', *Travels,* II, p. 828.
[46] For a commentary on Craven, see Ludmilla Kostova, 'Constructing Oriental Interiors: Two Eighteenth-Century Women Travellers and Their Easts', in *Travel Writing and the Female Imaginary*, edited by Vita Fortunati, Rita Monticelli and Maurizio Ascari (Bologna: Patron Editore, 2001), pp. 17 – 33.
[47] Hobhouse, *Travels*, I, p. 515.
[48] Hobhouse, *Travels*, I, p. 515.
[49] Hobhouse, *Travels*, I, p. 517.
[50] Hobhouse, *Travels*, I, p. 517.
[51] Hobhouse, *Travels*, I, p. 516.
[52] Anne McWhir, 'Introduction', Mary Wollstonecraft Shelley, *The Last Man*. (Peterborough, Ontario: Broadview Literary Texts, 1996), p. xxiii.
[53] See the 1831 Paris edition, II, 413 – 434.
[54] Dom Augustin Calmet's 1749 *Traite sur les Apparitions des esprits et sur les vampires* provides a number of examples of modern Greek religious rites as well as instances of the belief in vampirism in Hungary, Moravia and other parts of Eastern Europe. For a commentary, see Marie-Helene Huet, 'Deadly Fears: Dom Augustin Calmet's Vampires and the Rule Over Death', *Eighteenth-Century Life* 21 (May 1997), 222 – 232.

[55] Mark Mazower, *Salonica. City of Ghosts. Christians, Muslims, and Jews, 1430 – 1950* (London: Harper Collins Publishers, 2004), p. 126.

[56] There are numerous examples of this attitude in Greek, Bulgarian, and Serbian historiography and fiction. By way of a specific example I can cite Bulgarian writer Ivan Vazov's 1893 novel *Pod igoto* (*Under the Yoke)*, anonymous English translation, London: Heinemann, 1894, esp. p. 121.

[57] For a commentary on the emergence of a new conceptual division in Europe, see Larry Wolff, *Inventing Eastern Europe: the Map of Civilization on the Mind of the Enlightenment* (Stanford: Stanford University Press, 1994), p. 7.

APPENDIX IV.

A Geographical and Chronological Study of Anastasius

Jerry Nolan

This section of the new edition of Hope's novel has been compiled by the Anastasius expert, Jerry Nolan, with the places visited for the first time by the central character in the novel marked in block capitals and bold.

Volume I

Chapter 1

On the island of **CHIOS**, Anastasius, the youngest and most rebellious of the seven children of the well-off Greek official interpreter of the French Consul, rejects the idea of becoming a Greek Orthodox priest and impetuously runs away to sea as a cabin boy on a Venetian brig, after the disappointment of an ardent love affair with a fellow musician, the Consul's young daughter Helena. Caught up soon afterwards in the war being waged in the region, Anastasius is captured and taken to Hassan's prison camp on **ARGOS**.

Chapter II

Anastasius sketches in the background history of the Turkish civil war. The confidences of Panayoti, a fellow prisoner, stimulates Anastasius to develop a lifelong empathy with the stories of fellow travellers. A little later, he finds himself in the fortunate position of being favourably spotted and later employed as a servant by Mavroyeni, a wealthy Greek adviser of the Hassan Capitan-pasha, who begins to take a fatherly interest in the young and promising fellow Greek.

Chapter III

On Mavroyeni's advice, Anastasius bears arms in one of Hassan's battles at **TRIPOLITZZA** against the Arnoots and greatly enhances his reputation by beheading and despoiling a retreating Albanian whose head he presents to the Pasha. After a severe attack of homesickness and an accident on his sea journey with Mavroyeni, he arrives at his new master's splendid house in **CONSTANTINOPLE** which has a deceptively modest facade.

Chapter IV

After a brief period of social success as Mavroyeni's favoured secretary, Anastasius begins a somewhat tortuous affair with a domineering older woman, Theophania, the wife of an important official, during which Anastasius refuses to be brow-beaten. When the grand affair inevitably ends, events lead to the dismissal of Anastasius from Mavroyeni's service, a development unexpectedly welcomed by Anastasius because he needs to travel on.

Chapter V

Now totally adrift in Constantinople, Anastasius discusses his grim prospects in life with another sudden older friend, Vasili, who has worked out how the poor survive in the supremely beautiful city. Suddenly Anastasius finds himself working under a new master – a Jewish physician, Yacoob – but their business of curing the city's sick ends quickly when a jealous rival has them both sent to prison for law-breaking.

Chapter VI

Anastasius observes and records life within the Baglio prison in the beautiful city: the atrocious conditions; the vile torturer Achmet; the inspiring heroism of Mackari; the unfilled dream of rescue by Mavroyeni; his rising contempt for Yacoob; precarious survival during the awful plague; above all the stirrings of a very emotional friendship with another young Greek prisoner, Anagnositi, who agrees to tell Anastasius his family story which began near Corinth.

Chapter VII

The friendship between Anastasius and Agagnositi begins to grow under the harsh conditions of the Baglio. Agagnosti is the stage dancer who combines moral rectitude, effeminacy, devotion and bigotry, and a capacity for affection; and whose relationships with his parents, in particular his religious mother, helps to explain his curious mixture of attitudes. The two young Greeks have their union of friendship blessed by an Orthodox priest. Inexplicably Anastasius is suddenly released, and most reluctantly parted from his dear friend.

Chapter VIII

Again a pauper on the streets of Constantinople, a very ill Anastasius is taken to the filthy St. Demetrius hospital. After being cured of the plague, he begins to use his talents variously: as a guide for foreign travellers in the city, an advisor to various individuals, a go-between bearing illicit love letters. Profits earned from these activities turn Anastasius into a person of some financial substance.

Chapter IX

After rejecting Padre Ambrogio's attempts to convert him to Roman Catholicism, Anastasius next becomes a rich dissatisfied wife's lover. His tempting intrigue vanquishes an infatuated Esmé. The affair ends when the husband exposes his wife but fails to capture his wife's lover. Chased by Esmé's slaves, a desperate Anastasius finds refuge in a mosque.

Chapter X

Anastasius sees the end of the affair with Esmé as the occasion rather than the cause of his conversion to the great aristocracy of Islam among the Turks. He makes light of the significance of his conversion to Father Ambrogio. As the neophyte Selim, he views the prospect of the long preparatory instruction from a Sunnee moolah, with something of what has now become a characteristically satirical eye.

Chapter XI

While celebrating St. George's Festival with new Muslim companions, Anastasius/ Selim [A/S] becomes angry when his finery is bespattered. Feelings of dismay overwhelm him when he encounters an accusing Agagnosti who feels truly appalled by his friend's apostasy and neglect, before committing suicide on A/S's drawn dagger. A/S escapes from the law with the help of his new friends and remorse by resorting to horse-riding sport and by taking opium, before the irresistible urge to travel on reasserts itself.

Chapter XII

After a brief friendship with star-gazing Derwish who insists on entertaining wild dreams of uncovering valuable ancient ruins, A/S plans, on hearing the news of his wealthy mother's death, to lay claim to what has been left to his sister, Roxana for whom he feels no respect. After a very stormy boat journey, A/S visits his father at home in Chios, only to be rejected for his betrayal of the family's traditions in becoming a Muslim.

Chapter XIII

A/S visits the nun Sister Agnes who was entrusted with a final letter from his first abandoned mistress Helena who lost both her own life and that of her child. A/S is angered by the nun's relentless hostility and rushes off to **SAMOS** to mourn at Helena's tomb. On reaching **NAXOS**, A/S claims his mother's estate and after a savage battle of wits with cousin Marco, the estate's manager, he departs with a big bag of money.

Chapter XIV

On his way to **RHODES**, A/S becomes friendly with the Cretan Aly whose costume much impresses him, but whose subsequent fear of the stormy sea and disinterest in historical ruins on Rhodes leaves A/S, who takes all in his stride, very unimpressed. The ruthless commander of the ship, the Bey, recommends A/S to go to Egypt to enlist in the Mamlukes, a prospect which mightily appeals to the young adventurer.

Chapter XV

A/S records calling at **CASTEL-ROSSO** after a false alarm, and then at a perversely witty **ALEXANDRIA**. At **RASCHID**, A/S meets up with a group of female slaves sold into Egypt, listens to the life story of the defiant slave girl Hamida and is fascinated by the brazen advances of an Abyssinian negress. In a boat on the Nile, A/S is excited by a spectacular religious festival at **MEKTOOBES**, and then asks a friend for a brief historical introduction to the politics of Egypt.

Chapter XVI

A/S records his friend's survey of the line of Egypt's political history since its conquest by the Arabs. The account highlights the rise of the military slaves, or the Mamlukes, to eminent positions. What most fascinates A/S is the account of the heroic survival of the Bey Hassan, whom he well remembers meeting after his own capture from the Venetian brig. During the voyage, A/S hears about other beys, Ibrahim and Mourad, who are sworn enemies of the great Hassan.

Volume II

Chapter I

Once in **CAIRO**, A/S visits the palace of the Bey Suleiman who is much impressed by his friend's letter of recommendation of the young Greek to a court mainly peopled with Mamlukes. A/S's friendship with Rashooan is short lived when the young Georgian, Suleiman's favourite, is given away as a gift to his uncle. A/S develops quite a playful relationship with his new master who tests him and favours him, and whose sudden illness A/S helps to cure, to the dismay of the jealous Mamlukes.

Chapter II

Suleiman appoints A/S to be his lieutenant in the district of **SAMANHOOD**. A/S celebrates in Cairo and attracts a thief's attention. He travels with an entourage for four weeks tending to various duties before arriving at his bleak residence where the prospect of future duties seems off-putting. Suddenly recalled to Cairo, a somewhat alarmed A/S feels that he may have lost his patron's favour, but then is pleasantly surprised by the Bey's fulsome welcome.

Chapter III

Suleiman warns A/S of the likelihood of Cairo soon becoming a battlefield, without immediately clarifying future plans for his protégé. Then the Georgian Ayoob offers A/S patronage, including marriage to his pretty sister Zelidah. In turn Suleiman appoints A/S as kiaschef and offers marriage to his daughter Khadidge. After frantic moments of indecision, A/S accepts Suleiman's offer. The marriage of A/S and Khadidge is followed by a period during which the couple indulge in a life style of mutual languor.

Chapter IV

A/S prowls about his district, often in disguise, to observe the lives of the peasants. Soon news of Khadidge's sudden death in Cairo reaches him. The threat to Cairo from the Beys in Northern Egypt becomes more immediate. His father-in-law Suleiman supports A/S's demand for a vigorous response but the majority opinion decides in favour of Ayoob's more measured manoeuvres. A/S is given command of a small troop for the defence of the city.

Chapter V

When the Beys in Cairo decide to quit the city, they are attacked by the enemy. During fierce engagements, an enraged A/S suffers minor injuries. During negotiations, A/S is betrayed by the expedient Suleiman and subsequently escapes northwards where he manages to survive and to escape across the Red sea to the port of **DJEDDA** where he hears the news that famine and plague began ravaging Egypt after his flight.

Chapter VI

In Djedda A/S makes a friend of Sidi Malek who introduces him to his pet astrologer with whom A/S has a serious quarrel. When A/S observes suffering Egyptian friends on their way to **MEKKAH**, he joins them and practices his Muslim devotions. A/S accompanies the pilgrims to **MEDINAH** during which he makes a friend of Mahmood, a Cypriote, and then goes on to **DAMASCUS** where he eventually boards a vessel bound for Constantinople, alongside a cargo of black slaves.

Chapter VII

Once more in Constantinople, A/S learns that his old patron Mavroyeni has been appointed governor of Valachia, the highest position for a Greek in the Turkish empire. A/S meets his childhood friend Spiridion, the son of one of his father's best friends Mavrocordato, whom A/S now hires to manage his financial affairs. With increasing alarm, A/S concludes that Spiridion is harbouring the ambition of changing Selim of the Kaaba back to being Anastasius of the Cross.

Chapter VIII

While A/S venerates Spiridion's character for the calm and dignity of his life and occupation, he feels averse towards his old friend's desire to stop his taking pride in the turban. A/S reflects on the significance of the contrast between how as Anastasius he saved his friend's young life and how as Selim he now very much resents Spiridion's threat to his liberty. When Spiridion's disapproving father stops being his banker, A/S turns for advice to Mavrocordato's neighbour and enemy, the Armenian Aiden

Chapter IX

When the Armenian absconds with A/S's money, Spiridion turns up to offer sympathy and gold. After killing a threatening enemy on a road near Spiridion's home, A/S retreats to Constantinople. Again Spiridion seeks him out and spontaneously offers to take responsibility for the killing. Voyaging on a boat away from the city, Spiridion tries desperately to convert his friend from his life of vice, an attempt which gives rise to a spirited argument between them about the nature of human life and of Turkish society.

Chapter X

A/S learns of his father's death, and hears of the island rumours about himself – bey, beggar, or dead? On arrival on Chios, still accompanied by Spiridion, to claim his inheritance, Anastasius tries hard to deal fairly with his brothers, which much impresses Spiridon who ignores his father's order to return home to respectability. Anastasius's suppressed anger produces violent delirium. While recovering, he shoots at his brothers, causing minor injuries to both. A despairing Spiridion obeys his father and a hurt A/S, treasuring his friend's abandoned pocket-book, renounces Chios, and resolves to join the Turks on Cyprus.

Chapter XI

A/S reaches **CYPRUS** to see Hassan's war fleet on the sea for Egypt. Hassan's army defeats the army of the Cairo beys near **MANTOOBES** and marches onto Cairo. A/S joins the reinforcements being organised by Abdi to march from Gaza to Cairo across the desert. On arrival at Cairo, now a Turkish camp, A/S is appointed by Hassan as a lieutenant in his campaign. A/S proceeds to capture and ransom one of Suleiman's officers before surveying with pity the losses on the battlefield at **SIOOT.**

Chapter XII

After Hassan has signed a treaty with the rebel beys, he offers A/S the opportunity to accompany his troops back to Constantinople. Back in the city, A/S makes an unsuccessful attempt to meet Spiridion. Once Russia and Austria declare war on the empire, A/S decides to go to the main theatre of war in Valachia where he will link up again with Mavroyeni. On the way to Bucharest, he meets Father Kyrillos, an admirer of Catherine the Great, and Georgacki Condilly, who has just been dismissed as Mavroyeni's cup-bearer.

Chapter XIII

A/S finds **BUCHAREST** preparing for war. Mayroyeni remembers Anastasius as a clever lad given to pranks. A/S talks about his time in Egypt in discreet terms. Maroyeni complains about his many enemies in Valachia. After indecision about offering him a post, Mayroyeni gives A/S a military posting, and a place in his circle of close advisers. Maroyeni often thinks about his posthumous fame and legacy, most of all savouring the irony that he was a Greek who defended the Turkish empire against Christendom.

Chapter XIV

A/S is ordered to attack **BOZAN**, one of the mountain passes controlled by the Austrians near the prosperous town of **CRONSTADT**. The dangerous campaign produces low treachery, numerous casualties, and atrocities. A/S recognises one of the wounded prisoners, Count Miazinsky, whom he had met as a fine athletic Hungarian youth, and whom he now tries to protect from hostile Muslim troops. When the count dies, A/S takes some of his braided hair for remembrance, as all the Turkish troops are ordered to retreat in good order.

Chapter XV

Austrian and Russian successes continue in the region. The rout of Hassan's fleet strikes terror into Turkish hearts. Following the succession of Sultan Selim III to power in 1789, Mayroyeni, in unstable Bucharest, becomes the object of many accusations. When Selim III confers high office on Hassan, Mavroyeni and Hassan meet to converse amiably with each other. After Hassan's death in 1790, Mavroyeni's fortune declines quickly. A/S remains by the side of an old master, until ordered to leave by the master himself. By order of the Sultan, Mavroyeni, by then ready to become a Muslim convert, is mercilessly executed.

Chapter XVI

A/S reflects on the line of his life so far: how he has climbed a slippery road as Selim to a certain distinction and fame in the empire, only to find himself now sliding back to the starting point as Anastasius. Suddenly he wants to succeed financially in world trade. Back in Constantinople, he chooses a new master, Welid a very wealthy and pious Muslim. As they begin pursuing their plans, both A/S and Welid are shipwrecked on Anadoly. Skipping quickly onto **SMYRNA**, A/S meets Isaac-Bey in the French consulate who talks endlessly about widespread European admiration of his fashionable Muslim Clothes.

Volume III

Chapter 1

A/S concludes successful mercantile transactions in Smyrna with the sale of ornamented pistols to the venerable Hadjee-Aga. Grim reflection about the dead in the vast cemetery near **SCUTARI** only reinforces his plan of enjoying life as it comes. Once more in Constantinople. A/S thinks about serving Catherine the Great, and feels much attracted to the Greek widow Ketello with whom he contracts a very short term marriage according to Muslim custom. When A/S returns to Smyrna to take up an expected post, he angrily discovers that he has been deceived by his sponsor.

Chapter II

In Smyrna A/S is wagered by others to conquer the young, beautiful and wealthy Greek lady Euphrosyné, about to be married. A/S enlists her maid Sophia to help him in the conquest of Euphrosyné. A/S's distant adoration of Euphrosyné quickly grows. Sophia warns him of the disadvantage of being a Muslim in such a quest. A fully armed A/S arrives in the family household causing much panic. A/S reluctantly withdraws, but secretly plans to disrupt Euphrosyné's forthcoming wedding.

Chapter III

A distraught Euphrosyné comes to A/S seeking refuge from the plans for her wedding and pleads with him to protect her. Unready to take another wife, A/S decides to let her stay only when her cousins arrive demanding her return. After bitter arguments with A/S, Euphrosyné suddenly leaves. Then A/S discovers that he has been used in the whole affair by the scheming Sophia whom he mercilessly punishes. Later when A/S discovers that Euphrosyné has given birth to his child and died among strangers, he feels thoroughly ashamed of his treatment of one who he comes to acknowledge as his one true love.

Chapter IV

A/S tracks down his infant son Alexis and makes financial provision for his care. A/S meets in Smyrna an Italian poet Cirico who encourages him to go to Paris to join the revolutionary forces of liberty. When Cirico goes off without warning, A/S decides to seek a new line in the service of the Pasha in Bagdad: towards which he begins to travel by boat and caravan, meeting various fellow travellers on the way. Gradually Anastasius begins to imagine his little son Alexis as the future polar star in his life.

Chapter V

In **BAGDAD** A/S appears before the ageing warlike Pasha Suleiman, a Georgian and a Mamluke, and of his favourite Achmet who has been given the task of rooting out the Wahhabees, an Islamic sect characterised by adherence to the strict teaching of the Koran and by opposition to the more lax Muslim sects such as the sunnees and schyees. Bagdad itself has a mixture of races – Turks, Persians, Indians, Jews, Egyptians, Greeks and Arabs. A/S meets the Persian poet Aboo-Reza, the Jewish financier Abd-allah and a Wahhab. After observing Achmet's devious methods in action, A/S decides to join the Wahhabees in the desert. During a long journey a distraught A/S replaces his beloved steed who dies of sheer exhaustion.

Chapter VI

Relieved to have escaped from the domain of civilised man, A/S encounters the camp of Schaich Menssor on his route. Very opposed to the activities of the Pasha and Achmet in Bagdad, Mensoor appoints A/S as his envoy to the Wahhabee court of Abd-ool-Azeez in Derrayeh. On his way there with a troop, A/S has a tedious journey with occasional skirmishes and meetings with tribes who cannot but admire Mensoor's Arab mares. A crisis occurs when the party is engulfed in a sulphurous desert hurricane. Shortly afterwards, the domain of the Wahhabees comes into glorious view.

Chapter VII

In **DERAYEH**, A/S delivers Mensoor's presents and letter to Abd-ool-Azeez, schaich of the Wahhabees. A/S witnesses the case of Omar who killed an enemy Mooktar and went into hiding. When Omar suddenly appears before Abd-ool-Azeez, he is stabbed by Mooktar's kinsmen. A wounded Omar explains how he was much provoked by Mooktar. After hesitation, Abd-ool-Azeez reconciles the warring families. At a great feast, Abd-ool-Azeez praises A/S for supporting the Wahhabee opposition to the Turks. Omar's father begs A/S to save the life of his wounded son, which he somehow manages to accomplish.

Chapter VIII

A deep friendship develops between A/S and Omar whose noble sentiments remind Anastasius strongly of Spiridion. A/S accompanies Omar to his very hospitable home in **EL-GADDEH**. Omar begs the reluctant A/S to marry one of his sisters. Only when the family head Ibn-Aly flatters him, does A/S finally agree. A/S marries Aische who much resembles Omar. After the wedding, A/S feels restless and haunted by the memory of Euphrosyné. Being a Wahhabee means being ever ready for attack or defence and on the move. When welcoming her husband home, Aische falls off her dromedary, and dies in his arms.

Chapter IX

As an aside on the wavering line of his own life story, an ailing Anastasius expresses the need to bring his memoir to a quick conclusion. Achmet's lying tactics lead to A/S being banished from the Wahhabee sect by Abd-ool-Azeez. Finding himself again without a wife, a friend and a home, A/S seeks consolation in the image of his Alexis. A/S gets entangled in disputes about the collection of taxes from Hadj pilgrims in the vicinity of Medinah and is then involved in seizing goods from the rich merchant pilgrims. After amassing some treasure, A/S sets out for Acre on a swift horse, in the disguise of a Turkish itinerant saint.

Chapter X

In **ACRE**, A/S encounters the regime of the tyrant el-Djezzar (the Butcher), a former Bosnian Christian who murdered his brother before fleeing into the Arab world where, on becoming a convert to Islam, he is rewarded by his new masters when he is given command of Acre. Conducting a regime of terror, especially in dealings with harems and rivals, el-Djezzar still commissions many buildings in the city, including walls, a palace and a mosque. When A/S flees from Acre rather quickly, he meets a derwish who takes him to a monastery where pious ecstasies appear as burlesques, from which A/S quickly flees.

Chapter XI

A/S acts as a prayer-leading iman in a group bound for **HEMS** where he meets the loquacious Moolah Hadjee-Becktash. A/S arrives in Constantinople in a new set of fashionable clothing. Spiridian is rumoured to be either Paris or London. An old friend, Costandio Cariri, offers to finance a trip to Trieste, a good city to do business in. A/S dreams of taking his Alexis far away from the eternal desert. After his failure to find Alexis in Smyrna, A/S decides to revisit Egypt.

Chapter XII

A/S proceeds along the coast of Syria and lands at Alexandria. On the basis of some intelligence about the whereabouts of Alexis, A/S visits a consulate where he sees a young boy whom he instantly identifies as Alexis. A/S is denied access to this boy because it is claimed that the boy is the son of a former member of the household. The explanation fails to convince A/S who again meets Cirico, by chance, near the catacombs. The Bey Mourad confronts and banishes A/S from Egypt as a dangerous spy. Cirico explains his plan in which the consul might well be willing to arrange for the A/S's seizure of the boy.

Chapter XIII

A/S snatches the little boy from the nurse but has to fight off a crowd of hostile bystanders, before escaping with the child whom he believes to be his only son onto a waiting boat bound for the Adriatic. The boy quite reluctantly accepts A/S as his doting father. While in quarantine at the Lazaretto on **MALTHA**, A/S ponders if he should publicly reject Islamism on his return to Christendom. He contrasts the changing West and the unchanging East. The prospect of living in a heartless Europe seems daunting for A/S, but he persists in thinking that Alexis ought to be educated in the West.

Chapter XIV

Father and son journey onto **NAPLES** where A/S delivers letters to two of the nobility who seem pleased about the recent peace treaty with revolutionary France. A/S is impressed by M. de Silva's extensive library, left unmoved by a masquerade, and surprised by yet another meeting with Cirico. A/S and Alexis go onto **ROME** with Silva in a horse-drawn carriage. Silva provides a biting commentary on Rome in cultural decline as an European capital. There are attempts at **LORETTO** to convert him to Christ which A/S utterly dismisses. Travelling on a dirty Regusan vessel means quarantine for father and son in Trieste.

Chapter XV

On the final approach to Trieste, Alexis falls ill. A calm following a storm agonisingly slows down the sea approach to Trieste. At last disembarking at **TRIESTE**, A/S lies in a frantic state of mind beside the dying Alexis awaiting the arrival of a physician. Alexis dies in his arms. A/S buries his son within the gloomy precincts of the lazaretto. On emerging into the city where he had hoped to raise his son, A/S is deeply depressed. Unexpectedly, he meets Spiridion on a quay, but his childhood friend responds coldly, whereupon A/S posts to Spiridion the long treasured pocket-book with a gem inside, and leaves Trieste.

Chapter XVI

Anastasius recalls being revisited by persons and events closely linked with his traveller's life. He conjures up a beautiful landscape with a carpet of splendid flowers and trees where he imagines the spirit of Alexis living on. Anastasius, aged about thirty five, longs for journey's end. In the company of his future literary editor, the German Conrad, Anastasius travels northwards to settle in an **AUSTRIAN VILLAGE**. After Anastasius's death, Conrad preserves his memoirs and notes that his generous bequests to the local Roman Catholic villagers caused them to remember and revere him as 'the young Greek'.

Our Current List of Titles

Abdullah, Morag Mary, *My Khyber Marriage* - Morag Murray departed on a lifetime of adventure when she met and fell in love with Sirdar Ikbal Ali Shah, the son of an Afghan warlord. Leaving the comforts of her middle-class home in Scotland, Morag followed her husband into a Central Asia still largely unchanged since the 19th century.

Abernathy, Miles, *Ride the Wind* – the amazing true story of the little Abernathy Boys, who made a series of astonishing journeys in the United States, starting in 1909 when they were aged five and nine!

Beard, John, *Saddles East* – John Beard determined as a child that he wanted to see the Wild West from the back of a horse after a visit to Cody's legendary Wild West show. Yet it was only in 1948 – more than sixty years after seeing the flamboyant American showman – that Beard and his wife Lulu finally set off to follow their dreams.

Beker, Ana, *The Courage to Ride* – Determined to out-do Tschiffely, Beker made a 17,000 mile mounted odyssey across the Americas in the late 1940s that would fix her place in the annals of equestrian travel history.

Bird, Isabella, *Among the Tibetans* – A rousing 1889 adventure, an enchanting travelogue, a forgotten peek at a mountain kingdom swept away by the waves of time.

Bird, Isabella, *On Horseback* in *Hawaii* – The Victorian explorer's first horseback journey, in which she learns to ride astride, in early 1873.

Bird, Isabella, *Journeys in Persia and Kurdistan, Volumes 1 and 2* – The intrepid Englishwoman undertakes another gruelling journey in 1890.

Bird, Isabella, *A Lady's Life in the Rocky Mountains* – The story of Isabella Bird's adventures during the winter of 1873 when she explored the magnificent unspoiled wilderness of Colorado. Truly a classic.

Bird, Isabella, *Unbeaten Tracks in Japan, Volumes One and Two* – A 600-mile solo ride through Japan undertaken by the intrepid British traveller in 1878.

Blackmore, Charles, *In the Footsteps of Lawrence of Arabia* - In February 1985, fifty years after T. E. Lawrence was killed in a motor bicycle accident in Dorset, Captain Charles Blackmore and three others of the Royal Green Jackets Regiment set out to retrace Lawrence's exploits in the Arab Revolt during the First World War. They spent twenty-nine days with meagre supplies and under extreme conditions, riding and walking to the source of the Lawrence legend.

Boniface, Lieutenant Jonathan, *The Cavalry Horse and his Pack* – Quite simply the most important book ever written in the English language by a military man on the subject of equestrian travel.

Borrow, George, *The Bible in Spain* – Once upon a time, this book was as famous as *The Da Vinci Code* is today. Within weeks of its publication, it became one of the greatest bestsellers of the 19th century. It was read avidly by men like William Thackeray, Theodore Roosevelt, Winston Churchill, Charles Darwin and everybody who was anybody in that age of taste and sophistication. It is a tale of pure adventure. It tells the exploits of the brilliant polyglot George Borrow, who was sent to Madrid in 1835 to sell Spanish language Bibles. The country was at civil war; the Church objected strongly to translated scripture and the roads were infested by bandits, beggars and outcasts. He was nearly killed, by accident, assault or execution, as he rode on horseback all over the Peninsula to peddle his forbidden books. He hid with peasants, travelled with smugglers, found a hospitable shelter in the caves of Spanish Gypsies.

Borrow, George, *Lavengro* - This remarkable book describes the coming of age of an authentic genius, George Borrow himself, who by the end of his life mastered 60 languages, the mythology of a dozen nations and the literature of two thousand years. Step by step it guides us through the enchanted landscapes of his childhood in the early 19th century.

Borrow, George, *The Romany Rye* – Sequel to *Lavengro, The Romany Rye* tells the story of Borrow's vagabond years in the 1820s, when he trekked along with the free spirits of Britain's open roads. These were the pristine days before the railroads wiped out the travelling habits of ages; before harsher laws and constables put a stop to all vagrancy; before the repeal of the Corn Laws, the advent of the Empire and the machinery of the Industrial Revolution turned England into a wealthier but much bleaker place.

Borrow, George, *Wild Wales* – This is much more than a straightforward travel account. It is a book rich with characters, complete with princes, heroes, villains and rogues. In its pages we meet the delightful John Jones and the comical Tom Jenkins, we are introduced to Owain Glyndwr and his struggles against the English Crown. Great poets like Dafydd ap Gwilym share space with robbers like the Plant de Bat and the Robin Hood like Twm Shone Catti.

Bosanquet, Mary, *Saddlebags for Suitcases* – In 1939 Bosanquet set out to ride from Vancouver, Canada, to New York. Along the way she was wooed by love-struck cowboys, chased by a grizzly bear and even suspected of being a Nazi spy, scouting out Canada in preparation for a German invasion. A truly delightful book.

de Bourboulon, Catherine, *Shanghai à Moscou (French)* – the story of how a young Scottish woman and her aristocratic French husband travelled overland from Shanghai to Moscow in the late 19th Century.

Brown, Donald; *Journey from the Arctic* – A truly remarkable account of how Brown, his Danish companion and their two trusty horses attempt the impossible, to cross the silent Arctic plateaus, thread their way through the giant Swedish forests, and finally discover a passage around the treacherous Norwegian marshes.

Bruce, Clarence Dalrymple, *In the Hoofprints of Marco Polo* – The author made a dangerous journey from Srinagar to Peking in 1905, mounted on a trusty 13-hand Kashmiri pony, then wrote this wonderful book.

Burnaby, Frederick*; A Ride to Khiva* – Burnaby fills every page with a memorable cast of characters, including hard-riding Cossacks, nomadic Tartars, vodka-guzzling sleigh-drivers and a legion of peasant ruffians.

Burnaby, Frederick, *On Horseback through Asia Minor* – Armed with a rifle, a small stock of medicines, and a single faithful servant, the equestrian traveler rode through a hotbed of intrigue and high adventure in wild inhospitable country, encountering Kurds, Circassians, Armenians, and Persian pashas.

Carter, General William, *Horses, Saddles and Bridles* – This book covers a wide range of topics including basic training of the horse and care of its equipment. It also provides a fascinating look back into equestrian travel history.

Cayley, George, *Bridle Roads of Spain* – Truly one of the greatest equestrian travel accounts of the 19th Century.

Chase, J. Smeaton, *California Coast Trails* – This classic book describes the author's journey from Mexico to Oregon along the coast of California in the 1890s.

Chase, J. Smeaton, *California Desert Trails* – Famous British naturalist J. Smeaton Chase mounted up and rode into the Mojave Desert to undertake the longest equestrian study of its kind in modern history.

Chitty, Susan, and Hinde, Thomas, *The Great Donkey Walk* - When biographer Susan Chitty and her novelist husband, Thomas Hinde, decided it was time to embark on a family adventure, they did it in style. In Santiago they bought two donkeys whom they named Hannibal and Hamilcar. Their two small daughters, Miranda (7) and Jessica (3) were to ride Hamilcar. Hannibal, meanwhile, carried the baggage. The walk they planned to undertake was nothing short of the breadth of southern Europe.

Christian, Glynn, *Fragile Paradise: The discovery of Fletcher Christian, "Bounty" Mutineer* – the great-great-great-great-grandson of the *Bounty* mutineer brings to life a fascinating and complex character history has portrayed as both hero and villain, and the real story behind a mutiny that continues to divide opinion more than 200 years later. The result is a brilliant and compelling historical detective story, full of intrigue, jealousy, revenge and adventure on the high seas.

Clark, Leonard, *Marching Wind, The* – The panoramic story of a mounted exploration in the remote and savage heart of Asia, a place where adventure, danger, and intrigue were the daily backdrop to wild tribesman and equestrian exploits.

Clark, Leonard, *A Wanderer Till I Die* – In a world with lax passport control, no airlines, and few rules, the young man from San Francisco floats effortlessly from one adventure to the next. When he's not drinking whisky at the Raffles Hotel or listening to the "St. Louis Blues" on the phonograph in the jungle, he's searching for Malaysian treasure, being captured by Toradja head-hunters, interrogated by Japanese intelligence officers and lured into shady deals by European gun-runners.

Cobbett, William, *Rural Rides, Volumes 1 and 2* – In the early 1820s Cobbett set out on horseback to make a series of personal tours through the English countryside. These books contain what many believe to be the best accounts of rural England ever written, and remain enduring classics.

Codman, John, *Winter Sketches from the Saddle* – This classic book was first published in 1888. It recommends riding for your health and describes the septuagenarian author's many equestrian journeys through New England during the winter of 1887 on his faithful mare, Fanny.

Cunninghame Graham, Jean, *Gaucho Laird* – A superbly readable biography of the author's famous great-uncle, Robert "Don Roberto" Cunninghame Graham.

Cunninghame Graham, Robert, *Horses of the Conquest* – The author uncovered manuscripts which had lain forgotten for centuries, and wrote this book, as he said, out of gratitude to the horses of Columbus and the Conquistadors who shaped history.

Cunninghame Graham, Robert, *Magreb-el-Acksa* – The thrilling tale of how "Don Roberto" was kidnapped in Morocco!

Cunninghame Graham, Robert, *Rodeo* – An omnibus of the finest work of the man they called "the uncrowned King of Scotland," edited by his friend Aimé Tschiffely.
Cunninghame Graham, Robert, *Tales of Horsemen* – Ten of the most beautifully-written equestrian stories ever set to paper.
Cunninghame Graham, Robert, *Vanished Arcadia* – This haunting story about the Jesuit missions in South America from 1550 to 1767 was the inspiration behind the best-selling film *The Mission.*
Daly, H.W., *Manual of Pack Transportation* – This book is the author's masterpiece. It contains a wealth of information on various pack saddles, ropes and equipment, how to secure every type of load imaginable and instructions on how to organize a pack train.
Dixie, Lady Florence, *Riding Across Patagonia* – When asked in 1879 why she wanted to travel to such an outlandish place as Patagonia, the author replied without hesitation that she was taking to the saddle in order to flee from the strict confines of polite Victorian society. This is the story of how the aristocrat successfully traded the perils of a London parlor for the wind-borne freedom of a wild Patagonian bronco.
Dodwell, Christina, *Beyond Siberia* – The intrepid author goes to Russia's Far East to join the reindeer-herding people in winter.
Dodwell, Christina, *An Explorer's Handbook* – The author tells you everything you want to know about travelling: how to find suitable pack animals, how to feed and shelter yourself. She also has sensible and entertaining advice about dealing with unwanted visitors and the inevitable bureaucrats.
Dodwell, Christina, *Madagascar Travels* – Christina explores the hidden corners of this amazing island and, as usual, makes friends with its people.
Dodwell, Christina, *A Traveller in China* – The author sets off alone across China, starting with a horse and then transferring to an inflatable canoe.
Dodwell, Christina, *A Traveller on Horseback* – Christina Dodwell rides through Eastern Turkey and Iran in the late 1980s. The Sunday Telegraph wrote of the author's "courage and insatiable wanderlust," and in this book she demonstrates her gift for communicating her zest for adventure.
Dodwell, Christina, *Travels in Papua New Guinea* – Christina Dodwell spends two years exploring an island little known to the outside world. She travelled by foot, horse and dugout canoe among the Stone-Age tribes.
Dodwell, Christina, *Travels with Fortune* – the truly amazing account of the courageous author's first journey – a three-year odyssey around Africa by Landrover, bus, lorry, horse, camel, and dugout canoe!
Dodwell, Christina, *Travels with Pegasus* – This time Christina takes to the air! This is the story of her unconventional journey across North Africa in a micro-light!
Duncan, John, *Travels in Western Africa in 1845 and 1846* – The author, a Lifeguardsman from Scotland, tells the hair-raising tale of his two journeys to what is now Benin. Sadly, Duncan has been forgotten until today, and we are proud to get this book back into print.
Ehlers, Otto, *Im Sattel durch die Fürstenhöfe Indiens* – In June 1890 the young German adventurer, Ehlers, lay very ill. His doctor gave him a choice: either go home to Germany or travel to Kashmir. So of course the Long Rider chose the latter. This is a thrilling yet humorous book about the author's adventures.
Farson, Negley, *Caucasian Journey* – A thrilling account of a dangerous equestrian journey made in 1929, this is an amply illustrated adventure classic.
Fox, Ernest, *Travels in Afghanistan* – The thrilling tale of a 1937 journey through the mountains, valleys, and deserts of this forbidden realm, including visits to such fabled places as the medieval city of Heart, the towering Hindu Kush mountains, and the legendary Khyber Pass.
Gall, Sandy, *Afghanistan – Agony of a Nation* - Sandy Gall has made three trips to Afghanistan to report the war there: in 1982, 1984 and again in 1986. This book is an account of his last journey and what he found. He chose to revisit the man he believes is the outstanding commander in Afghanistan: Ahmed Shah Masud, a dashing Tajik who is trying to organise resistance to the Russians on a regional, and eventually national scale.
Gall, Sandy, *Behind Russian Lines* – In the summer of 1982, Sandy Gall set off for Afghanistan on what turned out to be the hardest assignment of his life. During his career as a reporter he had covered plenty of wars and revolutions before, but this was the first time he had been required to walk all the way to an assignment and all the way back again, dodging Russian bombs *en route*.
Gall, Sandy, *Salang* – As the Western world waits for the announcement that Russia will withdraw her troops from Afghanistan, an undercover operation is mounted in Whitehall which is designed to increase the difficulties of Russia's occupying force in the bitter war against Afghan guerrilla bands. The author has set the plot of this gripping novel against the upheaval of the final Russian withdrawal.
Gallard, Babette, *Riding the Milky Way* – An essential guide to anyone planning to ride the ancient pilgrimage route to Santiago di Compostella, and a highly readable story for armchair travellers.

Galton, Francis, *The Art of Travel* – Originally published in 1855, this book became an instant classic and was used by a host of now-famous explorers, including Sir Richard Francis Burton of Mecca fame. Readers can learn how to ride horses, handle elephants, avoid cobras, pull teeth, find water in a desert, and construct a sleeping bag out of fur.
Glazier, Willard, *Ocean to Ocean on Horseback* – This book about the author's journey from New York to the Pacific in 1875 contains every kind of mounted adventure imaginable. Amply illustrated with pen and ink drawings of the time, the book remains a timeless equestrian adventure classic.
Goodwin, Joseph, *Through Mexico on Horseback* – The author and his companion, Robert Horiguichi, the sophisticated, multi-lingual son of an imperial Japanese diplomat, set out in 1931 to cross Mexico. They were totally unprepared for the deserts, quicksand and brigands they were to encounter during their adventure.
Grant, David, *The Wagon Travel Handbook* - David Grant is the legendary Scottish wagon-master who journeyed around the world with his family in a horse-drawn wagon. Grant has filled *The Wagon Travel Handbook* with all the practical information a first time-wagon traveller will need before setting out, including sections on interior and exterior wagon design, choice of draught animals, veterinary requirements and frontier formalities.
Gray, David and Lukas Novotny, ***Mounted Archery in the Americas*** – This fascinating and amply illustrated book charts the history of mounted archery from its ancient roots on the steppes of Eurasia thousands of years ago to its current resurgence in popularity in the Americas. It also provides the reader with up-to-the-minute practical information gleaned from a unique team of the world's leading experts.
Hanbury-Tenison, Marika, *For Better, For Worse* – The author, an excellent story-teller, writes about her adventures visiting and living among the Indians of Central Brazil.
Hanbury-Tenison, Marika, *A Slice of Spice* – The fresh and vivid account of the author's hazardous journey to the Indonesian Islands with her husband, Robin.
Hanbury-Tenison, Robin, *Chinese Adventure* – The story of a unique journey in which the explorer Robin Hanbury-Tenison and his wife Louella rode on horseback alongside the Great Wall of China in 1986.
Hanbury-Tenison, Robin, *Fragile Eden* – The wonderful story of Robin and Louella Hanbury-Tenison's exploration of New Zealand on horseback in 1988. They rode alone together through what they describe as 'some of the most dramatic and exciting country we have ever seen.'
Hanbury-Tenison, Robin, *Mulu: The Rainforest* – This was the first popular book to bring to the world's attention the significance of the rain forests to our fragile ecosystem. It is a timely reminder of our need to preserve them for the future.
Hanbury-Tenison, Robin, *A Pattern of Peoples* – The author and his wife, Marika, spent three months travelling through Indonesia's outer islands and writes with his usual flair and sensitivity about the tribes he found there.
Hanbury-Tenison, Robin, *A Question of Survival* – This superb book played a hugely significant role in bringing the plight of Brazil's Indians to the world's attention.
Hanbury-Tenison, Robin, *The Rough and the Smooth* – The incredible story of two journeys in South America. Neither had been attempted before, and both were considered impossible!
Hanbury-Tenison, Robin, *Spanish Pilgrimage* – Robin and Louella Hanbury-Tenison went to Santiago de Compostela in a traditional way – riding on white horses over long-forgotten tracks. In the process they discovered more about the people and the country than any conventional traveller would learn. Their adventures are vividly and entertainingly recounted in this delightful and highly readable book.
Hanbury-Tenison, Robin, *White Horses over France* – This enchanting book tells the story of a magical journey and how, in fulfilment of a personal dream, the first Camargue horses set foot on British soil in the late summer of 1984.
Hanbury-Tenison, Robin, *Worlds Apart – an Explorer's Life* – The author's battle to preserve the quality of life under threat from developers and machines infuses this autobiography with a passion and conviction which makes it impossible to put down.
Hanbury-Tenison, Robin, *Worlds Within – Reflections in the Sand* – This book is full of the adventure you would expect from a man of action like Robin Hanbury-Tenison. However, it is also filled with the type of rare knowledge that was revealed to other desert travellers like Lawrence, Doughty and Thesiger.
Haslund, Henning, *Mongolian Adventure* – An epic tale inhabited by a cast of characters no longer present in this lackluster world, shamans who set themselves on fire, rebel leaders who sacked towns, and wild horsemen whose ancestors conquered the world.
Hassanein, A. M. Hassanein, *The Lost Oases* - At the dawning of the 20th century the vast desert of Libya remained one of last unexplored places on Earth. Sir Hassanein, the dashing Egyptian diplomat turned explorer, befriended the Muslim leaders of the elusive Senussi Brotherhood who controlled the deserts

further on, and became aware of rumours of a "lost oasis" which lay even deeper in the desert. In 1923 the explorer led a small caravan on a remarkable seven month journey across the centre of Libya.

Heath, Frank, *Forty Million Hoofbeats* – Heath set out in 1925 to follow his dream of riding to all 48 of the Continental United States. The journey lasted more than two years, during which time Heath and his mare, Gypsy Queen, became inseparable companions.

Higginbotham, Mary, *In Genuine Cowgirl Fashion* - The life story of Two Gun Nan Aspinwall, the first woman to ride across the United States alone. Riding from San Francisco to New York City in 1910-11, Nan covered 4,496 miles during 180 days in the saddle.

Hinde, Thomas, *The Great Donkey Walk* – Biographer Susan Chitty and her novelist husband, Thomas Hinde, travelled from Spain's Santiago to Salonica in faraway Greece. Their two small daughters, Miranda (7) and Jessica (3) were rode one donkey, while the other donkey carried the baggage. Reading this delightful book is leisurely and continuing pleasure.

Holt, William, *Ride a White Horse* – After rescuing a cart horse, Trigger, from slaughter and nursing him back to health, the 67-year-old Holt and his horse set out in 1964 on an incredible 9,000 mile, non-stop journey through western Europe.

Hopkins, Frank T., *Hidalgo and Other Stories* – For the first time in history, here are the collected writings of Frank T. Hopkins, the counterfeit cowboy whose endurance racing claims and Old West fantasies have polarized the equestrian world.

James, Jeremy, *Saddletramp* – The classic story of Jeremy James' journey from Turkey to Wales, on an unplanned route with an inaccurate compass, unreadable map and the unfailing aid of villagers who seemed to have as little sense of direction as he had.

James, Jeremy, *Vagabond* – The wonderful tale of the author's journey from Bulgaria to Berlin offers a refreshing, witty and often surprising view of Eastern Europe and the collapse of communism.

Jankovich, Miklós, *They Rode into Europe* (Translated by Anthony Dent) – Together, Jankovich and Dent created an equestrian study of unparalleled importance. The history of the world was shaped to a large extent by men on horseback who, because of the animals under them, were able to travel great distances, thus bringing about that exchange of ideas and inventions which is a fundamental requisite of human progress.

Jebb, Louisa, *By Desert Ways to Baghdad and Damascus* – From the pen of a gifted writer and intrepid traveller, this is one of the greatest equestrian travel books of all time.

Kluckhohn, Clyde, *To the Foot of the Rainbow* – This is not just a exciting true tale of equestrian adventure. It is a moving account of a young man's search for physical perfection in a desert world still untouched by the recently-born twentieth century.

Lambie, Thomas, *Boots and Saddles in Africa* – Lambie's story of his equestrian journeys is told with the grit and realism that marks a true classic.

Landor, Henry Savage, *In the Forbidden Land* – Illustrated with hundreds of photographs and drawings, this blood-chilling account of equestrian adventure makes for page-turning excitement.

Langlet, Valdemar, *Till Häst Genom Ryssland (Swedish)* – Denna reseskildring rymmer många ögonblicksbilder av möten med människor, från morgonbad med Lev Tolstoi till samtal med Tartarer och fotografering av fagra skördeflickor. Rikt illustrerad med foto och teckningar.

Leigh, Margaret, *My Kingdom for a Horse* – In the autumn of 1939 the author rode from Cornwall to Scotland, resulting in one of the most delightful equestrian journeys of the early twentieth century. This book is full of keen observations of a rural England that no longer exists.

Lester, Mary, *A Lady's Ride across Spanish Honduras in 1881* – This is a gem of a book, with a very entertaining account of Mary's vivid, day-to-day life in the saddle.

Littauer, Vladimir, *Horseman's Progress* - This book presents the story of educated riding since its inception four centuries ago. Vladimir Littauer relates in a most entertaining way how dressage was improved; how forward riding was developed by an Italian cavalry officer and how the new natural method for field riding and jumping swept dressage into the background. It is a gold mine of accurate, intelligent, and authoritative instruction – much more than mere history.

Littauer, Vladimir, *Russian Hussar* – Vladimir Littauer served in the Russian Imperial Cavalry from 1911 to 1920. This book recounts, with humour and modesty, his experiences as a cadet at the Nicholas Cavalry School in St. Petersburg, through the hair-raising struggles of the First World War and the trauma of the Russian Revolution, to his escape in 1920. By the time you turn the last page, you will feel as if you have galloped beside the author through the early years of his amazing life.

MacDermot, Brian, *Cult of the Sacred Spear* – here is that rarest of travel books, an exploration not only of a distant land but of a man's own heart. A confederation of pastoral people located in Southern Sudan and western Ethiopia, the Nuer warriors were famous for staging cattle raids against larger tribes and successfully resisted European colonization. Brian MacDermot, London stockbroker, entered into Nuer society as a stranger and emerged as Rial Nyang, an adopted member of the tribe. This book recounts this extraordinary emotional journey, regaling the reader with tales of pagan gods, warriors on mysterious missions, and finally the approach of warfare that continues to swirl across this part of Africa today.

Maillart, Ella, *Turkestan Solo* – A vivid account of a 1930s journey through this wonderful, mysterious and dangerous portion of the world, complete with its Kirghiz eagle hunters, lurking Soviet secret police, and the timeless nomads that still inhabited the desolate steppes of Central Asia.

Marcy, Randolph, *The Prairie Traveler* – There were a lot of things you packed into your saddlebags or the wagon before setting off to cross the North American wilderness in the 1850s. A gun and an axe were obvious necessities. Yet many pioneers were just as adamant about placing a copy of Captain Randolph Marcy's classic book close at hand.

Marsden, Kate, *Riding through Siberia: A Mounted Medical Mission in 1891* – This immensely readable book is a mixture of adventure, extreme hardship and compassion as the author travels the Great Siberian Post Road.

Marsh, Hippisley Cunliffe, *A Ride Through Islam* – A British officer rides through Persia and Afghanistan to India in 1873. Full of adventures, and with observant remarks on the local Turkoman equestrian traditions.

Theodore Mason, *The South Pole Ponies,* – The touching and totally forgotten story of the little horses who gave their all to both Scott and Shackleton in their attempts to reach the South Pole.

MacCann, William, *Viaje a Caballo* – Spanish-language edition of the British author's equestrian journey around Argentina in 1848.

Meline, James, *Two Thousand Miles on Horseback: Kansas to Santa Fé in 1866* – A beautifully written, eye witness account of a United States that is no more.

Muir Watson, Sharon, *The Colour of Courage* – The remarkable true story of the epic horse trip made by the first people to travel Australia's then-unmarked Bicentennial National Trail. There are enough adventures here to satisfy even the most jaded reader.

Naysmith, Gordon, *The Will to Win* – This book recounts the only equestrian journey of its kind undertaken during the 20th century - a mounted trip stretching across 16 countries. Gordon Naysmith, a Scottish pentathlete and former military man, set out in 1970 to ride from the tip of the African continent to the 1972 Olympic Games in distant Germany.

Ondaatje, Christopher, *Leopard in the Afternoon* – The captivating story of a journey through some of Africa's most spectacular haunts. It is also touched with poignancy and regret for a vanishing wilderness – a world threatened with extinction.

Ondaatje, Christopher, *The Man-Eater of Punanai* – a fascinating story of a past rediscovered through a remarkable journey to one of the most exotic countries in the world — Sri Lanka. Full of drama and history, it not only relives the incredible story of a man-eating leopard that terrorized the tiny village of Punanai in the early part of the century, but also allows the author to come to terms with the ghost of his charismatic but tyrannical father.

Ondaatje, Christopher, *Sindh Revisited* – This is the extraordinarily sensitive account of the author's quest to uncover the secrets of the seven years Richard Burton spent in India in the army of the East India Company from 1842 to 1849. "If I wanted to fill the gap in my understanding of Richard Burton, I would have to do something that had never been done before: follow in his footsteps in India…" The journey covered thousands of miles—trekking across deserts where ancient tribes meet modern civilization in the valley of the mighty Indus River.

O'Connor, Derek, *The King's Stranger* – a superb biography of the forgotten Scottish explorer, John Duncan.

O'Reilly, Basha, *Count Pompeii – Stallion of the Steppes* – the story of Basha's journey from Russia with her stallion, Count Pompeii, told for children. This is the first book in the *Little Long Rider* series.

O'Reilly, CuChullaine, (Editor) *The Horse Travel Handbook* – this accumulated knowledge of a million miles in the saddle tells you everything you need to know about travelling with your horse!

O'Reilly, CuChullaine, (Editor) *The Horse Travel Journal* – a unique book to take on your ride and record your experiences. Includes the world's first equestrian travel "pictionary" to help you in foreign countries.

O'Reilly, CuChullaine, *Khyber Knights* – Told with grit and realism by one of the world's foremost equestrian explorers, "Khyber Knights" has been penned the way lives are lived, not how books are written.

O'Reilly, CuChullaine, (Editor) *The Long Riders, Volume One* – The first of five unforgettable volumes of exhilarating travel tales.

Östrup, J, (*Swedish), Växlande Horisont* – The thrilling account of the author's journey to Central Asia from 1891 to 1893.

Patterson, George, *Gods and Guerrillas* – The true and gripping story of how the author went secretly into Tibet to film the Chinese invaders of his adopted country. Will make your heart pound with excitement!

Patterson, George, *Journey with Loshay: A Tibetan Odyssey* – This is an amazing book written by a truly remarkable man! Relying both on his companionship with God and on his own strength, he undertook a life few can have known, and a journey of emergency across the wildest parts of Tibet.

Patterson, George, *Patterson of Tibet* – Patterson was a Scottish medical missionary who went to Tibet shortly after the second World War. There he became Tibetan in all but name, adapting to the culture and learning the language fluently. This intense autobiography reveals how Patterson crossed swords with India's Prime Minister Nehru, helped with the rescue of the Dalai Lama and befriended a host of unique world figures ranging from Yehudi Menhuin to Eric Clapton. This is a vividly-written account of a life of high adventure and spiritual odyssey.

Pocock, Roger, *Following the Frontier* – Pocock was one of the nineteenth century's most influential equestrian travelers. Within the covers of this book is the detailed account of Pocock's horse ride along the infamous Outlaw Trail, a 3,000 mile solo journey that took the adventurer from Canada to Mexico City.

Pocock, Roger, *Horses* – Pocock set out to document the wisdom of the late 19th and early 20th Centuries into a book unique for its time. His concerns for attempting to preserve equestrian knowledge were based on cruel reality. More than 300,000 horses had been destroyed during the recent Boer War. Though Pocock enjoyed a reputation for dangerous living, his observations on horses were praised by the leading thinkers of his day.

Post, Charles Johnson, *Horse Packing* – Originally published in 1914, this book was an instant success, incorporating as it did the very essence of the science of packing horses and mules. It makes fascinating reading for students of the horse or history.

Ray, G. W., *Through Five Republics on Horseback* – In 1889 a British explorer – part-time missionary and full-time adventure junky – set out to find a lost tribe of sun-worshipping natives in the unexplored forests of Paraguay. The journey was so brutal that it defies belief.

Rink, Bjarke, *The Centaur Legacy* – This immensely entertaining and historically important book provides the first ever in-depth study into how man's partnership with his equine companion changed the course of history and accelerated human development.

Ross, Julian, *Travels in an Unknown Country* – A delightful book about modern horseback travel in an enchanting country, which once marked the eastern borders of the Roman Empire – Romania.

Ross, Martin and Somerville, E, *Beggars on Horseback* – The hilarious adventures of two aristocratic Irish cousins on an 1894 riding tour of Wales.

Ruxton, George, *Adventures in Mexico* – The story of a young British army officer who rode from Vera Cruz to Santa Fe, Mexico in 1847. At times the author exhibits a fearlessness which borders on insanity. He ignores dire warnings, rides through deadly deserts, and dares murderers to attack him. It is a delightful and invigorating tale of a time and place now long gone.

von Salzman, Erich, *Im Sattel durch Zentralasien* – The astonishing tale of the author's journey through China, Turkistan and back to his home in Germany – 6000 kilometres in 176 days!

Schwarz, Hans *(German), Vier Pferde, Ein Hund und Drei Soldaten* – In the early 1930s the author and his two companions rode through Liechtenstein, Austria, Romania, Albania, Yugoslavia, to Turkey, then rode back again!

Schwarz, Otto (*German), Reisen mit dem Pferd* – the Swiss Long Rider with more miles in the saddle than anyone else tells his wonderful story, and a long appendix tells the reader how to follow in his footsteps.

Scott, Robert, *Scott's Last Expedition* – Many people are unaware that Scott recruited Yakut ponies from Siberia for his doomed expedition to the South Pole in 1909. Here is the remarkable story of men and horses who all paid the ultimate sacrifice.

Shackleton, Ernest, *Aurora Australis* - The members of the British Antarctic Expedition of 1907-1908 wrote this delightful and surprisingly funny book. It was printed on the spot "at the sign of the Penguin"!

Skrede, Wilfred, *Across the Roof of the World* – This epic equestrian travel tale of a wartime journey across Russia, China, Turkestan and India is laced with unforgettable excitement.

Stevens, Thomas, *Through Russia on a Mustang* – Mounted on his faithful horse, Texas, Stevens crossed the Steppes in search of adventure. Cantering across the pages of this classic tale is a cast of nineteenth century Russian misfits, peasants, aristocrats—and even famed Cossack Long Rider Dmitri Peshkov.

Stevenson, Robert L., *Travels with a Donkey* – In 1878, the author set out to explore the remote Cevennes mountains of France. He travelled alone, unless you count his stubborn and manipulative pack-donkey, Modestine. This book is a true classic.

Strong, Anna Louise, *Road to the Grey Pamir* – With Stalin's encouragement, Strong rode into the seldom-seen Pamir mountains of faraway Tadjikistan. The political renegade turned equestrian explorer soon discovered more adventure than she had anticipated.

Sykes, Ella, *Through Persia on a Sidesaddle* – Ella Sykes rode side-saddle 2,000 miles across Persia, a country few European woman had ever visited. Mind you, she traveled in style, accompanied by her Swiss maid and 50 camels loaded with china, crystal, linens and fine wine.

Trevelyan, Raleigh, *The Golden Oriole* – The author was born in the world of the Raj. Drawing on journeys in search of his family's long Anglo-Indian past and on the sparkling reminiscences and diaries of the family and their friends (such as E. M. Forster), the author brilliantly evokes the entire sweep of the vanished British empire in India in all its sadness and glory, its grief and triumph.

Trinkler, Emile, *Through the Heart of Afghanistan* – In the early 1920s the author made a legendary trip across a country now recalled only in legends.

Tschiffely, Aimé, *Bohemia Junction* – "Forty years of adventurous living condensed into one book."

Tschiffely, Aimé, *Bridle Paths* – a final poetic look at a now-vanished Britain.

Tschiffely, Aimé, *Mancha y Gato Cuentan sus Aventuras* – The Spanish-language version of *The Tale of Two Horses* – the story of the author's famous journey as told by the horses.

Tschiffely, Aimé, *The Tale of Two Horses* – The story of Tschiffely's famous journey from Buenos Aires to Washington, DC, narrated by his two equine heroes, Mancha and Gato. Their unique point of view is guaranteed to delight children and adults alike.

Tschiffely, Aimé, *This Way Southward* – the most famous equestrian explorer of the twentieth century decides to make a perilous journey across the U-boat infested Atlantic.

Tschiffely, Aimé, *Tschiffely's Ride* – The true story of the most famous equestrian journey of the twentieth century – 10,000 miles with two Criollo geldings from Argentina to Washington, DC. A new edition is coming soon with a Foreword by his literary heir!

Tschiffely, Aimé, *Tschiffely's Ritt* – The German-language translation of *Tschiffely's Ride* – the most famous equestrian journey of its day.

Ure, John, *Cucumber Sandwiches in the Andes* – No-one who wasn't mad as a hatter would try to take a horse across the Andes by one of the highest passes between Chile and the Argentine. That was what John Ure was told on his way to the British Embassy in Santiago – so he set out to find a few certifiable kindred spirits. Fans of equestrian travel and of Latin America will be enchanted by this delightful book.

Warner, Charles Dudley, *On Horseback in Virginia* – A prolific author, and a great friend of Mark Twain, Warner made witty and perceptive contributions to the world of nineteenth century American literature. This book about the author's equestrian adventures is full of fascinating descriptions of nineteenth century America.

Weale, Magdalene, *Through the Highlands of Shropshire* – It was 1933 and Magdalene Weale was faced with a dilemma: how to best explore her beloved English countryside? By horse, of course! This enchanting book invokes a gentle, softer world inhabited by gracious country lairds, wise farmers, and jolly inn keepers.

Weeks, Edwin Lord, *Artist Explorer* – A young American artist and superb writer travels through Persia to India in 1892.

Wentworth Day, J., *Wartime Ride* – In 1939 the author decided the time was right for an extended horseback ride through England! While parts of his country were being ravaged by war, Wentworth Day discovered an inland oasis of mellow harvest fields, moated Tudor farmhouses, peaceful country halls, and fishing villages.

Von Westarp, Eberhard, *Unter Halbmond und Sonne* – (German) – Im Sattel durch die asiatische Türkei und Persien.

Wilkins, Messanie, *Last of the Saddle Tramps* – Told she had little time left to live, the author decided to ride from her native Maine to the Pacific. Accompanied by her faithful horse, Tarzan, Wilkins suffered through any number of obstacles, including blistering deserts and freezing snow storms – and defied the doctors by living for another 20 years!

Wilson, Andrew, *The Abode of Snow* – One of the best accounts of overland equestrian travel ever written about the wild lands that lie between Tibet and Afghanistan.

de Windt, Harry, *A Ride to India* – Part science, all adventure, this book takes the reader for a thrilling canter across the Persian Empire of the 1890s.

Winthrop, Theodore, *Saddle and Canoe* – This book paints a vibrant picture of 1850s life in the Pacific Northwest and covers the author's travels along the Straits of Juan De Fuca, on Vancouver Island, across the Naches Pass, and on to The Dalles, in Oregon Territory. This is truly an historic travel account.

Woolf, Leonard, *Stories of the East* – Three short stories which are of vital importance in understanding the author's mistrust of and dislike for colonialism, which provide disturbing commentaries about the disintegration of the colonial process.
Woolf, Leonard, *Village in the Jungle* – Despite being virtually unknown this is an important classic, rare among English novels of the Edwardian era. While most take the viewpoint of the *coloniser*, Woolf tells his tale of native life in a colonial outpost from the point of view of the *colonised.* It is also a tale of superstition and murder set against a backdrop of the jungle that threatens to swallow everything up in its path. Widely regarded as one of the best books in English about Ceylon, *The Village in the Jungle* is regarded in Sri Lanka today as a national treasure.
Younghusband, George, *Eighteen Hundred Miles on a Burmese Pony* – One of the funniest and most enchanting books about equestrian travel of the nineteenth century, featuring "Joe" the naughty Burmese pony!

We are constantly adding new titles to our collections, so please check our websites for Horse Travel Books, Classic Travel Books, and The Long Riders' Guild Academic Foundation:

www.horsetravelbooks.com - www.classictravelbooks.com – www.lrgaf.org

www.ingramcontent.com/pod-product-compliance
Lightning Source LLC
Chambersburg PA
CBHW081131300726
48982CB00005B/923

* 9 7 8 1 5 9 0 4 8 2 8 2 7 *